A SCIENCE FICTION ARGOSY

EDITED BY
Damon Knight

SIMON AND SCHUSTER
NEW YORK

PUBLISHED BY SIMON AND SCHUSTER
ROCKEFELLER CENTER, 630 FIFTH AVENUE
NEW YORK, NEW YORK 10020

DESIGNED BY IRVING PERKINS
MANUFACTURED IN THE UNITED STATES OF AMERICA

Introduction

SOME FEW years ago, when I was the only teen-aged science fiction addict in Hood River, Oregon, I prowled the stacks of the local library for books like *Etidorhpa,* by John Uri Lloyd,[1] and *The Mysterious Island,* by Jules Verne.[2] I ordered novels by H. G. Wells from the state library. I sent away to England for secondhand volumes by Olaf Stapledon and Thorne Smith. Like a pornographer looking for pornography, I ferreted out science fiction in *The American Magazine, The Saturday Evening Post, The American Boy,* but I never got enough. There were three American s.f. magazines, and a scattering of hardcover books published over the last half-century, and that was all.

Nowadays—well, you know what it's like nowadays. Twenty years ago anthologists felt they had to justify themselves when they added another s.f. anthology to the fifty then in existence. What am I to say now about the five hundredth?

My idea in compiling this book was simply to put together the biggest and most comprehensive collection of good science fiction that I possibly could. It includes two complete novels, two novellas, and more than twenty shorter pieces by old and new masters. The novels are the two most famous s.f. books of the fifties, Theodore Sturgeon's *More Than Human* and Alfred Bester's *The Demolished Man.* Both were originally published in hardcover, but in small editions, now long out of print and rarely seen. By deliberately discarding all limitations of theme and length, I was able to use not only these two books, but also many excellent stories that just would not

[1] What I chiefly remember about this muddled book is the statement that when you shine a light obliquely into your eye, the veined pattern you see is the image of your brain.

[2] But not *20,000 Leagues Under the Sea*—the library did not have it, and I never even heard of it until years later, except as part of the parodic title of a book by Robert Benchley.

fit into other collections. In the process, I think I have achieved a more faithful portrait of the field than ever before.

This book reflects the changes that magazine science fiction underwent beginning in 1937, under three remarkable editors: John W. Campbell (*Astounding,* later renamed *Analog*), Anthony Boucher (*The Magazine of Fantasy and Science Fiction,* which he founded with J. Francis McComas), and H. L. Gold (*Galaxy*). As a result of their work, the commercial s.f. field began groping its way back to the literary standards it had abandoned in the nineteen-twenties under Hugo Gernsback and others. It's interesting to note that for years s.f. anthologies drew very largely on material published outside the magazines; now such material is becoming popular again. As evidence that the two streams of science fiction are merging, I offer the stories in this book. Unless you happen to know their publishing history, I think you will find it hard to tell which stories were originally published in the s.f. magazines and which elsewhere.

The oldest story in the book, John Collier's "Green Thoughts," gives us a convenient bridge to still earlier work—it is a parody of H. G. Wells's "The Flowering of the Strange Orchid"—and the newest story, Robert Sheckley's "Can You Feel Anything When I Do This?," is a parody of all sorts of things, including Karel Čapek's *R.U.R.* and Lester del Rey's "Helen O'Loy." In between are twenty-four stories, most of which date from the fifties and sixties. Nine stories come from *The Magazine of Fantasy and Science Fiction,* seven from *Astounding/Analog,* only three from *Galaxy* (but that includes both novels), and five from other sources. There are seven stories about time travel (every one based on a different idea). There are three stories of space travel, three of marvelous inventions (no two remotely alike), three of life in the future (three different futures), three about psi powers, two about ghosts (counting Kate Wilhelm's "Somerset Dreams," which may be about something else —but see for yourself), one about witchcraft (but it is science fiction), and three marvelously unclassifiable stories—"One Ordinary Day, With Peanuts," by Shirley Jackson, "Built Up Logically," by Howard Schoenfeld, and "Rump-Titty-Titty-Tum-*Tah*-Tee," by Fritz Leiber. Some of these stories have never been anthologized before; some have been anthologized more than once, in volumes now out of print and hard to find. In my belief they are all stories that will be anthologized again—and again—because they have the qualities that make for lasting pleasure.

This is the kind of big meaty selection I wish someone had given me when I was a teen-aged science fiction addict in Hood River, Oregon.

DAMON KNIGHT

Madeira Beach, Fla.
November 22, 1971

Contents

Book 1

Book 2

Book 1

GREEN THOUGHTS

by John Collier

THE ORCHID had been sent among the effects of his friend, who had come by a lonely and mysterious death on the expedition. Or he had bought it among a miscellaneous lot, "unclassified," at the close of the auction. I forget which, but one or the other it certainly was; moreover, even in its dry, brown, dormant root state, this orchid had a certain sinister quality. It looked, with its bunched and ragged projections, like a huge dead insect, or a rigid yet a gripping hand, hideously gnarled, or a grotesquely whiskered, threatening face. Would you not have known what sort of an orchid it was?

Mr. Mannering did not know. He read nothing but catalogues and books on fertilisers. He unpacked the new acquisition with a solicitude absurd enough in any case, towards any orchid, or primrose either, in the twentieth century, but idiotic, foolhardy, doom-eager, when extended to an orchid thus come by, in appearance thus. And in his traditional obtuseness he at once planted it in what he called "the Observation Ward," facetious fellow! a hothouse built against the south wall of his dumpy red dwelling. Here he set always the most interesting additions to his collection, and especially weak and sickly plants, for there was a glass door in his study wall, through which he could see into this hothouse, so that the weak and sickly plants could encounter no crisis without his immediate knowledge and his tender care.

This plant, however, proved hardy enough. At the ends of thick and stringy stalks, it opened out bunches of darkly shining leaves, and soon it spread in every direction, usurping so much space that first one, then another, then all its neighbours had to be removed to a hothouse at the end of the garden. It was, Cousin Jane said, a regular hop-vine. The comparison was little to the point. At the ends of the stalks, just before the leaves began, were set groups of tendrils, which hung idly, serving no apparent purpose. Mr. Mannering thought that very probably these were vestigial organs, a heritage from some period when the plant had been a climber. But when were the vestigial tendrils of an ex-climber half or quarter so thick and strong?

After a long time, sets of tiny buds appeared here and there among the extravagant foliage. Soon they opened into small flowers, miserable little things; they looked like flies' heads. How disappointed I should have been, and you would too, I hope, or Doyle and Wells have lived and writ in vain. One naturally expects a large, garish, sinister bloom, like a sea anemone, or a Chinese lantern, or a hippopotamus yawning, on any important orchid; and should it be an unclassified one as well, I think one has every right to insist on a sickly and overpowering scent into the bargain.

Mr. Mannering did not mind at all. Indeed, apart from his joy and happiness in being the discoverer and godfather of a new sort of orchid, he felt only a mild and scientific interest in the fact that the paltry blossoms were so very much like flies' heads. Could it be to attract other flies for food, or as fertilisers? But then, why like their heads?

It was a few days later that Cousin Jane's cat disappeared. This was a great blow to Cousin Jane, but Mr. Mannering was not, in his heart of hearts, greatly sorry. He was not fond of the cat, for he could not open the smallest chink in a glass roof, for ventilation, but that creature would squeeze through somehow, to enjoy the warmth, and in this way it had broken many a tender shoot. But before poor Cousin Jane had lamented two days, something happened that so engrossed Mr. Mannering that he had no mind left at all with which to sympathise with her affliction, nor to make at breakfast kind and hypocritical enquiries after the lost cat. A strange new bud appeared on the orchid. It was clearly evident that there would be two quite different sorts of bloom on this one plant, as sometimes happens in such fantastic corners of the vegetable world, and that the new flower would be very different in size and structure from the earlier ones. It grew bigger and bigger, till it was as big as one's fist.

And just then, it could never have been more inopportune, an affair of the most unpleasant, the most distressing nature summoned Mr. Mannering to town. It was his wretched nephew, in trouble again; and this time so deeply and so very disgracefully that it took all Mr. Mannering's generosity, and all his influence too, to extricate the worthless young man. Indeed as soon as he saw the state of affairs, he told the prodigal that this was the very last time he might expect assistance, that his vices and his ingratitude had long cancelled all affection between them, and that for this last helping hand he was indebted only to his mother's memory, and to no faith on the part of his uncle either in his repentance or his reformation. He wrote, moreover, to Cousin Jane, to relieve his feelings, telling her of the whole business, and adding that the only thing to do was to cut the young man off entirely. He begged her, also, to send immediate news of any development on the part of his orchid.

When he got back to Torquay, Cousin Jane had disappeared. The situation was extremely annoying. Their only servant was a cook, who was very old, and very stupid, and very deaf. She suffered, besides, from an obsession, due to the fact that for many years Mr. Mannering had had no conversation with her in which he had not included an impressive reminder that she must always, no matter what might happen, keep the big kitchen stove up to a certain pitch of activity. For this stove, besides supplying the house with hot water, heated the pipes in the "Observation Ward," to which the daily gardener who had charge of the other hothouses had no access. By this time she had come to regard her duties as stoker as her chief *raison d'être,* and it was difficult to penetrate her deafness with any question which her stupidity and her obsession did not somehow transmute into an enquiry after the stove, and this, of course, was especially the case when Mr. Mannering spoke to her. All he could disentangle was what she had volunteered on first seeing him, that his cousin had not been seen for three days, that she had left without saying a word. Mr. Mannering was perplexed and annoyed, but, being a man of method, secretary, indeed, of his County's Lodge of the Royal Antediluvian Order of Orchid Growers, he thought it best to postpone further enquiries until he had refreshed himself a little after his long and tiring journey. A full supply of energy was necessary to extract any information from the old cook; besides, there was probably a note somewhere. It was only natural that before he went to his room, Mr. Mannering should peep into the hothouse, just to make sure that the wonderful orchid had come to no harm during the inconsiderate absence of Cousin Jane. As soon as he opened the door, his eyes fell upon the bud; it had changed in shape very considerably, and had increased in size to the bigness of a human head. It is no exaggeration to state that Mr. Mannering remained rooted to the spot, with his eyes fixed upon this wonderful bud, for fully five minutes.

But, you will ask, why did he not see her clothes on the floor? Well, as a matter of fact, to be perfectly plain and straightforward (it is a delicate point), there were no clothes on the floor. To avoid all shilly-shallying, I must tell you that Cousin Jane, though of course she was thoroughly, entirely estimable in every respect, though she was well over forty, too, was given to the study, and in fact to the practice, of certain of the very latest ideas on the dual culture of the soul and body. Swedish, and German, neo-Greek and all that. You will understand, no doubt. And the orchid-house was the warmest place available. I must proceed with the order of events.

Mr. Mannering at length withdrew his eyes from this stupendous bud, and (disciplined in his pleasures as all great souls are) decided that he must temporarily abandon this . . . this positive Peak in Darien, and devote his attention to the grey exigencies of everyday life. But although his body dutifully ascended the stairs, heart, mind and soul all remained, like the three kings of old, in adoration of the plant. Here we see another side to Mr. Mannering's character. Although he was philosophical to the point of insensibility over the miserable smallness of the earlier flowers, yet he was now as much gratified by the magnitude of the great new bud as you or I might be. Is not the orchid-grower a man with a heart–like you? Hence, it was not unnatural that Mr. Mannering, while in his bath, should be full of the most exalted visions of the blossoming of his heart's darling, his vegetable god-child. It would be the largest known, by far: complex as a dream, or dazzlingly simple. It would open like a dancer, or like the sun rising. Why, it might be opening at this very moment! At this thought Mr. Mannering could restrain himself no longer; he rose from the steamy water, and, wrapping his bath-towel robe about him, hurried down to the hothouse, scarcely staying to dry himself, though he was subject to colds.

The bud had not yet opened; it still reared its unbroken head among the glossy, fleshy foliage, and he now saw, what he had had no eyes for previously, how very exuberant that foliage had grown. Suddenly he realised with astonishment that this huge bud was not that which had appeared before he went away. That one had been lower down on the plant. Where was it now, then? Why, this new thrust and spread of foliage concealed it from him. He walked across, and discovered it. It had opened into a bloom. And as he looked at this bloom, his astonishment grew to stupefaction, one might say to petrification, for it is a fact that Mr. Mannering remained rooted to the spot, with his eyes fixed on the flower, for fully fifteen minutes. The flower was an exact replica of the head of Cousin Jane's lost cat. The similitude was so exact, so lifelike, that Mr. Mannering's first movement, after the fifteen minutes, was to seize his bath-towel robe, to draw it about him, for he was a modest man, and the cat, though bought for a Tom, had proved to be quite the reverse. I relate this to show how much character, spirit, *presence,* call it what you will, there was upon this floral cat's face. But although he made to seize his bath-towel robe, it was too late: he could not move; the new lusty foliage had closed in unperceived, the too lightly dismissed tendrils were everywhere upon him. He gave a few weak cries and sank to the ground, and there, as the Mr. Mannering of ordinary life, he passes out of this story. Just fancy!

Mr. Mannering sank into a coma, into an insensibility so deep that a black eternity passed before the first faint elements of his consciousness reassembled themselves in his brain. For of his brain was the centre of a new bud being made. Indeed, it was two or three days before this at first almost shapeless and quite primitive lump of organic matter had become sufficiently mature to be called Mr. Mannering at all. These days, which passed quickly enough, in a certain mild, not unpleasant excitement, in the outer world, seemed to the dimly working mind within the bud to resume the whole history of the development of our species, in a great many epochal parts.

A process analogous to the mutations of the embryo was being enacted here. At last the entity which was thus being rushed down an absurdly foreshortened vista of the ages arrived, slowing up, into the foreground. It became recognisable. The Seven Ages of Mr. Mannering were presented, as it were, in a series of close-ups, as in an educational film; his consciousness settled and cleared; the bud was mature, ready to open. At this point, I believe, Mr. Mannering's state of mind was exactly that of a patient, who, struggling up from vague dreams, wakening from under an anæsthetic, asks plaintively, "Where am I?" Then the bud opened, and he knew.

There was the hothouse, but seen from an unfamiliar angle; there, through the glass door, was his study, and there below him was the cat's head (Oh! *now* he knew) and there, and there beside him was Cousin Jane. He could not say a word, but then, neither could she. Perhaps it was as well. At the very least, he would have been forced to own that she had been in the right in an argument of long standing; she had always maintained that in the end no good would come of his preoccupation with "those unnatural flowers."

Yet it must be admitted that Mr. Mannering was not at first greatly put about by this extraordinary upheaval in his daily life. This, I think, was because he was interested, not only in private and personal matters, but in the wider and more general, one might say the biological, aspects of his metamorphosis: to the rest, simply because he was now a vegetable, he responded with a vegetable reaction. The impossibility of locomotion, for example, did not trouble him in the least, nor even the absence of body and limbs, any more than the cessation of that stream of rashers and tea, biscuits and glasses of milk, luncheon cutlets and so forth that had flowed in at his mouth for over fifty years, but which had now been reversed to a gentle, continuous, scarcely noticeable feeding from below. All the powerful influence of the physical upon the mental, therefore, inclined him towards tranquillity. But the physical is not all. Although no longer a man, he was still Mr. Mannering. Dear me! And from this anomaly, as soon as his scientific interest had subsided, issued a host of woes, mainly subjective in origin.

He was fretted, for instance, by the thought that he would now have no opportunity to name his orchid, nor to write a paper upon it, and, still worse, there grew up in his mind the abominable conviction that, as soon as his plight was discovered, it was he who would be named and classified, and that he himself would be the subject of a paper; possibly, even, of comment and criticism in the lay press. Like all orchid collectors, he was excessively shy and sensitive, and in his present situation these qualities brought him to the verge of wilting. Worse yet was the fear of being transplanted, thrust into some unfamiliar, draughty, probably public place. Being dug up! Ugh! A violent shudder pulsated through all the heavy foliage that sprang from Mr. Mannering's division of the plant. He awoke to consciousness of ghostly and remote sensations in the stem below, and in certain tufts of leaves that sprouted from it; they were somehow reminiscent of spine and heart and limbs. He felt quite a dryad.

In spite of all, however, the sunshine was very pleasant. The rich odour of hot spicy earth filled the hothouse. From a special fixture on the hot-water pipes a little warm steam oozed into the air. Mr. Mannering began to abandon himself to a feeling of *laissez-aller*. Just then, up in the corner of the glass roof, at the ventilator, he heard a persistent buzzing. Soon the note changed from one of irritation to a more complacent sound; a bee had managed to find his way, after some difficulty, through one of the tiny chinks in the metal work. The visitor came drifting down and down through the still, green air, as if into some subaqueous world, and he came to rest on one of those petals which were Mr. Mannering's eyebrows. Thence he commenced to explore one feature after another, and at last he settled heavily on the lower lip, which drooped under his weight and allowed him to crawl right into Mr. Mannering's mouth. This was quite a considerable shock, of course, but on the whole the sensation was neither as alarming nor as unpleasant as might have been expected; indeed, strange as it may sound, the appropriate word seemed to be something like . . . refreshing. Perhaps the little tongue had been coated.

But Mr. Mannering soon ceased his drowsy toying with the *mot juste,* when he saw the departed bee, after one or two lazy circlings, settle directly upon the maiden lip of Cousin Jane. Ominous as lightning, a simple botanical principle flashed across the mind of her wretched relative. Which principle? It is only too well known. Even the very babes and sucklings are familiar with it. Is it not drummed into their jaded ears by parents and governesses, curates and the family doctor; is it not Exercise One in the principal subject on the kindergarten curriculum? Cousin Jane was aware of it also, although, being the product of an earlier age, she might have remained still blessedly ignorant had not her cousin, vain, garrulous, proselytising fool, attempted for years past to interest her in the rudiments of botany. How the miserable man upbraided himself now!

He saw two bunches of leaves just below the flower tremble and flutter, and rear themselves painfully upward into the very likeness of two shocked and protesting hands. He saw the soft and orderly petals of his cousin's face ruffle and incarnadine with rage and embarrassment, then turn sickly as a gardenia with horror and dismay. He thought, absurdly enough, of York and Lancaster. But what was he to do? All the rectitude implanted by his careful training, all the chivalry proper to an orchid-collector, boiled and surged beneath a paralytically calm exterior. He positively travailed in the effort to activate the muscles of his face, to assume an expression of grief, manly contrition, helplessness in the face of fate, willingness to make all honourable amends, all suffused with the light of a vague but solacing optimism; but it was all in vain. When he had strained till his nerves seemed likely to tear under the tension, the only movement he could achieve was a trivial flutter of the left eyelid—worse than nothing.

This incident completely aroused Mr. Mannering from his vegetable lethargy. He rebelled against the limitations of the form into which he had thus been cast while subjectively he remained all too human. Was he not still at heart a man, with a man's hopes, ideals, aspirations? And capacity for suffering.

When dusk came, and the opulent and sinister shapes of the great plant dimmed to a suggestiveness more powerfully impressive than had been its bright noonday luxuriance, and the atmosphere of a tropical forest filled the orchid house like an exile's dream, or the nostalgia of the saxophone; when the cat's whiskers drooped and even Cousin Jane's eyes slowly closed, the unhappy man remained awake, staring into the gathering darkness. Suddenly the light in the study was switched on. Two men entered the room. One of them was his lawyer, the other was his nephew.

"This is his study, as you know, of course," said the wicked nephew. "There's nothing here. I looked round when I came over on Wednesday."

"Ah, well!" said the lawyer. "It's a very queer business, an absolute mystery." He had evidently said so more than once before; they must have been discussing matters in another room. "Well, we must hope for the best. In the meantime, in all the circumstances, it's perhaps as well that you, as next of kin, should take charge of things here. We must hope for the best."

Saying this, the lawyer turned, about to go, and Mr. Mannering saw a malicious smile overspread the young man's face. The uneasiness which had overcome him at first sight of his nephew was intensified to fear and trembling at the sight of this smile.

When he had shown the lawyer out, the nephew returned to the study and looked around with a lively and sinister satisfaction. Then he cut a caper on the hearthrug. Mr. Mannering thought he had never seen anything so diabolical as this solitary expression of the glee of a venomous nature, at the prospect of unchecked sway here whence he had been outcast, license where he had been condemned. How vulgar petty triumph appeared, beheld thus; how disgusting petty spite, how appalling revengefulness and hardness of heart! He remembered suddenly that his nephew had been notable, in his repulsive childhood, for his cruelty to flies, tearing their wings off, and for his barbarity towards cats. A sort of dew might have been noticed upon the good man's forehead. It seemed to him that his nephew had only to glance that way and all would be discovered, although he might have remembered that it was impossible to see from the lighted room into the darkness in the hothouse. His own vision of events inside the room was, of course, only too clear.

On the mantelpiece stood a large unframed photograph of Mr. Mannering. His nephew soon caught sight of this, and strode across to confront it with a triumphant and insolent sneer. "What? You old Pharisee," said he, "taken her off for a trip to Brighton, have you? My God! How I hope you'll never come back! How I hope you've fallen over the cliffs, or got swept off by the tide or something! Anyway . . . I'll make hay while the sun shines. Ugh, you old skinflint, you!" And he reached forward his hand, on which the thumb held the middle finger bent and in check, and that finger, then released, rapped viciously upon the nose in the photograph. Then the usurping rascal left the room, and left all the lights on, presumably preferring the dining room with its tantalus and cellarette to the scholarly austerities of the study.

All night long the glare of electric light from the study fell full upon Mr. Mannering and his Cousin Jane, like the glare of a cheap and artificial sun. You, who have seen at midnight, in the park, a few insomniac asters standing stiff and startled under an arc light, all their weak colour bleached out of them by the drenching chemical radiance, neither asleep nor awake, but held fast in a tense, a neurasthenic trance, you can form an idea of how the night passed with this unhappy pair.

And towards morning an incident occurred, trivial in itself, no doubt, but sufficient then and there to add the last drop to poor Cousin Jane's discomfiture, and to her relative's embarrassment and remorse. Along the edge of the great earth-box in which the orchid was planted ran a small black mouse. It had wicked red eyes, a naked, evil snout and huge repellent ears, queer as a bat's. This creature ran straight over the lower leaves of Cousin Jane's part of the plant. It was simply appalling: the stringy main stem writhed like a hair on a coal fire, the leaves contracted in an agonised spasm, like seared mimosa; the terrified lady nearly uprooted herself in her convulsive horror. I think she would actually have done so had not the mouse hurried on past her.

But it had not gone more than a foot or so when it looked up and saw, bending over it, and seeming positively to bristle with life, that flower which had once been called Tib. There was a breathless pause. The mouse was obviously paralysed with terror, the cat could only look and long. Suddenly the more human watchers saw a sly frond of foliage curve softly outward and close in behind the hypnotised creature. Cousin Jane, who had been thinking exultantly, "Well now it'll go away and never, never, never come back," suddenly became aware of hideous possibilities. Summoning all her energy, and you must remember that she had been "out" some days longer than her cousin, and so had much more control of her leaves, she achieved a spasmodic flutter, enough to break the trance that held the mouse, so that, like a clockwork toy, it swung round and fled. But already the fell arm of the orchid had cut off its retreat, the mouse leapt straight at it, like a flash five tendrils at the end caught the fugitive and held it fast, and soon its body dwindled and was gone. Now the heart of Cousin Jane was troubled with horrid fears, and slowly and painfully she turned her weary face first to one side, then to the other, in a fever of anxiety as to where the new bud would appear. A sort of sucker, green and sappy, which twisted lightly about her main stem, and reared a blunt head, much like a tip of asparagus, close to her own, suddenly began to swell in the most suspicious manner. She squinted at it, fascinated and appalled. Could it be her imagination? It was not. . . . But, after all, what are these trifles?

Next evening the door opened again, and again the nephew entered the study. This time he was alone, and it was evident that he had come straight from table. He carried in his hand a decanter of whiskey capped by an inverted glass. Under his arm was a syphon. His face was distinctly flushed, and such a smile as is often seen in saloon bars played about his lips. These lips he occasionally pursed, while simultaneously his cheeks became a little distended; then they would suddenly collapse. He put down his burdens, and, turning to Mr. Mannering's cigar cabinet, produced a bunch of keys which he proceeded to try upon the lock, muttering vindictively at each abortive attempt, until it opened, when he helped himself from the best of its contents. Annoying as it was to witness this insolent appropriation of his property, and mortifying to see the contempt with which the cigar was smoked, the good gentleman found deeper cause for uneasiness in the thought that, with the possession of the keys, his abominable nephew had access to every private corner that was his.

At present, however, the usurper seemed indisposed to carry on investigations; he splashed a great deal of whiskey into the tumbler, and, relaxing into an attitude of extravagant comfort, proceeded to revolt his unseen audience by an exhibition of those animal grossnesses in which a certain type of man is wont to indulge when he fancies himself alone with his Maker. I mean wide, shameless yawning, sucking the teeth, or picking them with a fingernail, eructations, hawking, spitting even. But after a while, the young man began to tire of his own company; he had not yet had time to gather any of his pot-house companions into his uncle's home, and repeated recourse to the whiskey bottle only increased his longing for something to relieve the monotony. His eye fell upon the door of the orchid house. Sooner or later it was bound to have come to pass. Does this thought greatly console the condemned man when the fatal knock sounds upon the door of his cell? No. Nor were the hearts of the trembling pair in the hothouse at all succoured by the reflection.

As the nephew fumbled with the handle of the glass door, Cousin Jane slowly raised two fronds of leaves that grew on each side, high up on her stem, and sank her troubled head behind them. Mr. Mannering observed, in a sudden rapture of hope, that by this device she was fairly well concealed from any casual glance. Hastily he strove to follow her example. Unfortunately, he had not yet gained sufficient control of his—his limbs?—and all his tortured efforts could not raise them beyond an agonised horizontal. The door had opened, the nephew was feeling for the electric light switch just inside. It was a moment for one of the superlative achievements of panic. Mr. Mannering was well equipped for the occasion. Suddenly, at the cost of indescribable effort, he succeeded in raising the right frond, not straight upwards, it is true, but in a series of painful jerks along a curve outward and backward, and ascending by slow degrees till it attained the position of an arm held over the possessor's head from behind. Then, as the light flashed on, a spray of leaves at the very end of this frond spread out into a fan, rather like a very fleshy horse-chestnut leaf in structure, and covered the anxious face below. What a relief! And now the nephew advanced into the orchid house, and now the hidden pair simultaneously remembered the fatal presence of the cat. Simultaneously also, their very sap stood still in their veins. The nephew was walking along by the plant. The cat, a sagacious beast, "knew" with the infallible intuition of its kind that this was an idler, a parasite, a sensualist, gross and brutal, disrespectful to age, insolent to weakness, barbarous to cats. Therefore it remained very still, trusting to its low and somewhat retired position on the plant, and to protective mimicry and such things, and to the half-drunken condition of the nephew, to avoid his notice. But all in vain.

"What?" said the nephew. "What, a cat?" And he raised his hand to offer a blow at the harmless creature. Something in the dignified and unflinching demeanour of his victim must have penetrated into even his besotted mind, for the blow never fell, and the bully, a coward at heart as bullies invariably are, shifted his gaze from side to side to escape the steady, contemptuous stare of the courageous cat. Alas, his eye fell on something glimmering whitely behind the dark foliage. He brushed aside the intervening leaves that he might see what it was. It was Cousin Jane.

"Oh! Ah!" said the young man, in great confusion. "*You're* back. But what are you hiding there for?"

His sheepish stare became fixed, his mouth opened in bewilderment; then the true condition of things dawned upon his mind. Most of us would have at once instituted some attempts at communication, or at assistance of some kind, or at least have knelt down to thank our Creator that we had, by His grace, been spared such a fate, or perhaps have made haste from the orchid house to ensure against accidents. But alcohol had so inflamed the young man's hardened nature that he felt neither fear nor awe nor gratitude, and as for any spirit of helpfulness, that was as far as ever from his hard revengeful heart. As he grasped the situation a devilish smile overspread his face.

"Ha! Ha! Ha!" said he. "But where's the old man?"

He peered about the plant, looking eagerly for his uncle. In a moment he had located him, and raising the inadequate vizor of leaves, discovered beneath it the face of our hero, troubled with a hundred bitter emotions.

"Hullo, Narcissus!" said the nephew.

A long silence ensued. The nephew was so pleased that he could not say a word. He rubbed his hands together, and licked his lips, and stared and stared as a child might at a new toy.

"You're properly up a tree now," he said. "Yes, the tables are turned now all right, aren't they? Ha! Ha! Do you remember last time we met?"

A flicker of emotion passed over the face of the suffering blossom, betraying consciousness.

"Yes, you can hear what I say," added the tormentor. "Feel too, I expect. What about that?"

As he spoke, he stretched out his hand, and, seizing a delicate frill of fine, silvery filaments that grew as whiskers grow round the lower half of the flower, he administered a sharp tug. The result would have interested that ingenious experimenter, Sir J. C. Bose. Without pausing to note, however, even in the interests of science, the subtler shades of his uncle's reaction, content with the general effect of that devastating wince, the wretch chuckled with satisfaction, and, taking a long pull from the reeking butt of the stolen cigar, puffed the vile fumes straight into his victim's centre. The brute!

"How do you like that, John the Baptist?" he asked with a leer. "Good for the blight, you know. Just what you want!"

Something rustled upon his coat sleeve. Looking down, he saw a long stalk, well adorned with the fatal tendrils, groping its way over the arid and unsatisfactory surface. In a moment it had reached his wrist, he felt it fasten, but knocked it off as one would a leech, before it had time to establish its hold.

"Ugh!" said he. "So that's how it happens, is it? I think I'll keep outside till I get the hang of things a bit. *I* don't want to be made an Aunt Sally of. Though I shouldn't think they could get you with your clothes on." Struck by a sudden thought, he looked from his uncle to Cousin Jane, and from Cousin Jane back to his uncle again. He scanned the floor, and saw a single crumpled bath-towel robe lying in the shadow.

"Why," he said, "*well!* . . . Haw! Haw! Haw!" And with an odious backward leer, he made his way out of the orchid house.

Mr. Mannering felt that his suffering was capable of no increase. Yet he dreaded the morrow. His fevered imagination patterned the long night with waking nightmares, utterly fantastic visions of humiliation and torture. Torture! It was absurd, of course, for him to fear cold-blooded atrocities on the part of his nephew, but how he dreaded some outrageous whim that might tickle the youth's sense of humour, and lead him to *any* wanton freak, especially if he were drunk at the time. He thought of slugs and snails, espaliers and topiary. Oh! Oh! Oh! If only the monster would rest content with insults and mockery, with wasting his substance, ravaging his cherished possessions before his eyes, with occasional pulling at the whiskers, even! Then it might be possible to turn gradually from all that still remained in him of man, to subdue the passions, no longer to admire or desire, to go native, as it were, relapsing into the Nirvana of a vegetable dream. But in the morning he found this was not so easy.

In came the nephew, and, pausing only to utter the most perfunctory of jeers at his relatives in the glass house, he sat at the desk and unlocked the top drawer. He was evidently in search of money, his eagerness betrayed that; no doubt he had run through all he had filched from his uncle's pockets, and had not yet worked out a scheme for getting direct control of his bank account. However, the drawer held enough to cause the scoundrel to rub his hands with satisfaction, and, summoning the housekeeper, to bellow into her ear a reckless order upon the wine and spirit merchant.

"Get along with you," he shouted, when he had at last made her understand. "I shall have to get someone a bit more on the spot to wait on me! I can tell you that. Yes," he added to himself as the poor old woman hobbled away, deeply hurt by his bullying manner, "yes, a nice little parlour maid . . . . a nice little parlour maid."

He hunted in the Buff Book for the number of the local registry office. That afternoon he interviewed a succession of maidservants in his uncle's study. Those that happened to be plain, or too obviously respectable, he treated curtly and coldly; they soon made way for others. It was only when a girl was attractive (according to the young man's depraved tastes, that is), and also bore herself in a fast or brazen manner, that the interviews were at all prolonged. In these cases the nephew would conclude in a fashion that left no doubt at all in the minds of any of his auditors as to his real intentions. Once, for example, leaning forward, he took the girl by the chin, saying with an odious smirk, "There's no one else but me, and so you'd be treated just like one of the family; d'you see, my dear?" To another he would say, slipping his arm round her waist, "Do you think we shall get on well together? Will you make me nice and cosy and comfortable, eh?" He addressed one as "Baby," another as "Chicken." I can't imagine what poor Cousin Jane must have thought.

After this conduct had sent two or three in confusion from the room, there entered a young person of the most regrettable description, one whose character, betrayed as it was in her meretricious finery, her crude cosmetics and her tinted hair, showed yet more clearly in florid gesture and too facile smile. The nephew lost no time in coming to an arrangement with this creature. Indeed, her true nature was so obvious that the depraved young man only went through the farce of an ordinary interview as a sauce to his anticipations, enjoying the contrast between conventional dialogue and unbridled glances. She was to come next day. Mr. Mannering feared more for his unhappy cousin than for himself. "What scenes may she not have to witness," he thought, "that yellow cheek of hers to incarnadine?" If he only could have said a few words!

But that evening, when the nephew came to take his ease in the study, it was obvious that he was far more under the influence of liquor than had been the case before. His face, flushed patchily by the action of the spirits, wore a sullen sneer, an ominous light burned in that bleared eye, he muttered savagely under his breath. Clearly this fiend in human shape was what is known as "fighting drunk," clearly some trifle had set his vile temper in a blaze.

It is interesting to note, even at this stage, a sudden change in Mr. Mannering's reactions. They now seemed entirely egotistical, and were to be elicited only by stimuli directly associated with physical matters. The nephew kicked a hole in a screen in his drunken fury, he flung a burning cigar end down on the carpet, he scratched matches on the polished table. His uncle witnessed this with the calm of one whose sense of property and of dignity has become numbed and paralysed; he felt neither fury nor mortification. Had he, by one of those sudden strides by which all such development takes place, approached much nearer to his goal, complete vegetation? His concern for the threatened modesty of Cousin Jane, which had moved him so strongly only a few hours earlier, must have been the last dying flicker of exhausted altruism; that most human characteristic had faded from him. He felt that relief which certain sick people feel when they first notice the influence of a drug as an irregular blur on their consciousness of pain, or which unhappy lovers enjoy when they first rub their hands and skip about the room in a morning ecstasy of (probably illusory) indifference. But instead of running to the glass and rapturously greeting himself as a long-lost friend, as this latter class generally do, Mr. Mannering soberly prepared to bid his personality farewell. The change, however, in its present stage, was not an unmixed blessing. Narrowing in from the wider and more expressly human regions of his being, his consciousness now felt outside its focus not only pride and altruism, which had been responsible for much of his woe, but fortitude and detachment also, which, with quotation from the Greeks, had been his support before the whole battery of his distresses. Moreover, within its constricted circle, his ego was not reduced but concentrated; his serene, flowerlike indifference towards the ill-usage of his furniture was balanced by the absorbed, flowerlike single-mindedness of his terror at the thought of similar ill-usage directed towards himself. It is important now to appreciate this white, intense light of Mr. Mannering's apprehensions.

What a strange shock it would be, if, shall we say, in the third act of *Hamlet,* the mind, dispread in contemplation of diverse forces converging harmoniously on some still-distant consummation, was suddenly *jabbed* (as a sea anemone by a stick) by the spectacle of the King treading by chance upon Hamlet's toe, and causing him such annoyance, that, in a flash . . .

Inside the study the nephew still fumed and swore. On the mantelpiece stood an envelope, addressed in Mr. Mannering's handwriting to Cousin Jane. In it was the letter he had written from Town, describing his nephew's disgraceful conduct. The young man's eye fell upon this, and, unscrupulous, impelled by idle curiosity, he took it up and drew out the letter. As he read, his face grew a hundred times blacker than before.

"What?" he muttered. "'. . . a mere race course cad . . . a worthless vulgarian . . . a scoundrel of the sneaking sort' . . . and what's this? . . . '. . . cut him off absolutely' . . . What?" said he, with a horrifying oath. "*Would* you cut me off absolutely? Two can play at that game, you old devil!"

And he snatched up a large pair of scissors that lay on the desk, and burst into the hothouse.

Among fish, the dory, they say, screams when it is seized upon by man; among insects, the caterpillar of the death's-head moth is capable of a still, small shriek of terror; in the vegetable world, only the mandrake could voice its agony–till now.

THE RED QUEEN'S RACE

by Isaac Asimov

HERE'S A puzzle for you, if you like. Is it a crime to translate a chemistry textbook into Greek?

Or let's put it another way. If one of the country's largest atomic power plants is completely ruined in an unauthorized experiment, is an admitted accessory to that act a criminal?

These problems only developed with time, of course. We started with the atomic power plant—drained. I really mean *drained.* I don't know exactly how large the fissionable power source was—but in two flashing microseconds, it had all fissioned.

No explosion. No undue gamma-ray density. It was merely that every moving part in the entire structure was fused. The entire main building was mildly hot. The atmosphere for two miles in every direction was gently warm. Just a dead, useless building which later on took a hundred million dollars to replace.

It happened about three in the morning, and they found Elmer Tywood alone in the central source chamber. The findings of twenty-four close-packed hours can be summarized quickly.

1. Elmer Tywood—Ph.D., Sc.D., Fellow of This and Honorary That, onetime youthful participant of the original Manhattan Project, and now full Professor of Nuclear Physics—was no interloper. He had a Class-A Pass—Unlimited. But no record could be found as to his purpose in being there just then. A table on casters contained equipment which had not been made on any recorded requisition. It, too, was a single fused mass—not quite too hot to touch.

2. Elmer Tywood was dead. He lay next to the table, his face congested, nearly black. No radiation effect. No external force of any sort. The doctor said apoplexy.

3. In Elmer Tywood's office safe were found two puzzling items: i.e, twenty foolscap sheets of apparent mathematics, and a bound folio in a foreign language which turned out to be Greek, the subject matter, on translation, turning out to be chemistry.

The secrecy which poured over the whole mess was something so terrific as to make everything that touched it *dead.* It's the only word that can describe it. Twenty-seven men and women, all told, including the Secretary of Defense, the Secretary of Science, and two or three others so top-notch that they were completely unknown to the public entered the power plant during the period of investigation. Any man who had been in the plant that night, the physicist who had identified Tywood, the doctor who had examined him, were retired into virtual home arrest.

No newspaper ever got the story. No inside dopester got it. A few members of Congress got part of it.

And naturally so! Anyone or any group or any country that could suck all the available energy out of the equivalent of perhaps fifty to a hundred pounds of plutonium without exploding it had America's industry and America's defense so snugly in the palm of the hand that the light and life of over two hundred million people could be turned off between yawns.

Was it Tywood? Or Tywood and others? Or just others, through Tywood?

And my job? I was decoy–or front man, if you like. Someone had to hang around the university and ask questions about Tywood. After all, he was missing. It could be amnesia, a hold-up, a kidnapping, a killing, a runaway, insanity, accident–I could busy myself with that for five years and collect black looks, and maybe divert attention. To be sure, it didn't work out that way.

But don't think I was in on the whole case at the start. I wasn't one of the twenty-seven men I mentioned a while back, though my boss was. But I knew a little–enough to get started.

Professor John Keyser was also in Physics. I didn't get to him right away. There was a good deal of routine to cover first in as conscientious a way as I could. Quite meaningless. Quite necessary. But I was in Keyser's office now.

Professors' offices are distinctive. Nobody dusts them except some tired cleaning woman who hobbles in and out at eight in the morning, and the professor never notices the dust anyway. Lots of books without much arrangement. The ones close to the desk are used a lot–lectures are copied out of them. The ones out of reach are wherever a student put them back after borrowing them. Then there are professional journals that look cheap and are darned expensive, which are waiting about and which may some day be read. And plenty of paper on the desk, some of it scribbled on.

Keyser was an elderly man—one of Tywood's generation. His nose was big and rather red, and he smoked a pipe. He had that easy-going and nonpredatory look in his eyes that goes with an academic job—either because that kind of job attracts that kind of man or because that kind of job makes that kind of man.

I said: "What kind of work is Professor Tywood doing?"

"Research physics."

Answers like that bounce off me. Some years ago they used to get me mad. Now, I just said: "We know that, Professor. It's the details I'm after."

And he twinkled at me tolerantly. "Surely the details can't help much unless you're a research physicist yourself. Does it matter—under the circumstances?"

"Maybe not. But he's gone. If anything's happened to him in the way of"—I gestured, and deliberately clichéd—"foul play, his work may have something to do with it—unless he's rich and the motive is money."

Keyser chuckled dryly. "College professors are never rich. The commodity we peddle is but lightly considered, seeing how large the supply is."

I ignored that, too, because I know my looks are against me. Actually, I finished college with a "very good" translated into Latin so that the college president could understand it, and never played in a football game in my life. But I look rather the reverse.

I said: "Then we're left with his work to consider."

"You mean spies? International intrigue?"

"Why not? It's happened before! After all, he's a nuclear physicist, isn't he?"

"He is. But so are others. So am I."

"Ah, but perhaps he knows something you don't."

There was a stiffening to the jaw. When caught off guard, professors can act just like people. He said stiffly: "As I recall offhand, Tywood has published papers on the effect of liquid viscosity on the wings of the Rayleigh line, on higher-orbit field equation, and on spin-orbit coupling of two nucleons, but his main work is on quadrupole moments. I am quite competent in these matters."

"Is he working on quadrupole moments now?" I tried not to bat an eye, and I think I succeeded.

"Yes—in a way." He almost sneered. "He may be getting to the experimental stage finally. He's spent most of his life, it seems, working out the mathematical consequences of a special theory of his own."

"Like this," and I tossed a sheet of foolscap at him.

That sheet was one of those in the safe in Tywood's office. The chances, of course, were that the bundle meant nothing, if only because it was a professor's safe. That is, things are sometimes put in at the spur of the moment because the logical drawer was filled with unmarked exam papers. And, of course, nothing is ever taken out. We had found in that safe dusty little vials of yellowish crystals with scarcely legible labels, some mimeographed booklets dating back to World War II and marked "Restricted," a copy of an old college yearbook, and some correspondence concerning a possible position as Director of Research for American Electric, dated ten years back, and, of course, chemistry in Greek.

The foolscap was there, too. It was rolled up like a college diploma with a rubber band about it and had no label or descriptive title. Some twenty sheets were covered with ink marks, meticulous and small—

I had one sheet of that foolscap. I don't think any one man in the world had more than one sheet. And I'm sure that no man in the world but one knew that the loss of his particular sheet and of his particular life would be as nearly simultaneous as the government could make it.

So I tossed the sheet at Keyser, as if it were something I'd found blowing about the campus.

He stared at it and then looked at the back side, which was blank. His eyes moved down from the top to the bottom, then jumped back to the top.

"I don't know what this is about," he said, and the words seemed sour to his own taste.

I didn't say anything. Just folded the paper and shoved it back into the inside jacket pocket.

Keyser added petulantly: "It's a fallacy you laymen have that scientists can look at an equation and say, 'Ah, yes—' and go on to write a book about it. Mathematics has no existence of its own. It is merely an arbitrary code devised to describe physical observations or philosophical concepts. Every man can adapt it to his own particular needs. For instance no one can look at a symbol and be sure of what it means. So far, science has used every letter in the alphabet, large, small and italic, each symbolizing many different things. They have used bold-face letters, Gothic-type letters, Greek letters, both capital and small, subscripts, superscripts, asterisks, even Hebrew letters.

Different scientists use different symbols for the same concept and the same symbol for different concepts. So if you show a disconnected page like this to any man, without information as to the subject being investigated or the particular symbology used, he could absolutely not make sense out of it."

I interrupted: "But you said he was working on quadrupole moments. Does that make this sensible?" and I tapped the spot on my chest where the foolscap had been slowly scorching a hole in my jacket for two days.

"I can't tell. I saw none of the standard relationships that I'd expect to be involved. At least I recognized none. But I obviously can't commit myself."

There was a short silence, then he said: "I'll tell you. Why don't you check with his students?"

I lifted my eyebrows. "You mean in his classes?"

He seemed annoyed. "No, for heaven's sake. His research students! His doctoral candidates! They've been working with him. They'll know the details of that work better than I, or anyone in the faculty, could possibly know it."

"It's an idea," I said, casually. It was, too. I don't know why, but I wouldn't have thought of it myself. I guess it's because it's only natural to think that any professor knows more than any student.

Keyser latched on to a lapel as I rose to leave. "And, besides," he said, "I think you're on the wrong track. This is in confidence, you understand, and I wouldn't say it except for the unusual circumstances, but Tywood is not thought of too highly in the profession. Oh, he's an adequate teacher, I'll admit, but his research papers have never commanded respect. There has always been a tendency towards vague theorizing, unsupported by experimental evidence. That paper of yours is probably more of it. No one could possibly want to . . . er, kidnap him because of it."

"Is that so? I see. Any ideas, yourself, as to why he's gone, or where he's gone?"

"Nothing concrete," he said, pursing his lips, "but everyone knows he is a sick man. He had a stroke two years ago that kept him out of classes for a semester. He never did get well. His left side was paralyzed for a while and he still limps. Another stroke would kill him. It could come any time."

"You think he's dead, then?"

"It's not impossible."

"But where's the body, then?"

"Well, really– That is *your* job, I think."

It was, and I left.

I interviewed each one of Tywood's four research students in a volume of chaos called a research laboratory. These student research laboratories usually have two hopefuls working therein, said two constituting a floating population, since every year or so they are alternately replaced.

Consequently, the laboratory has its equipment stack in tiers. On the laboratory benches is the equipment immediately being used, and in three or four of the handiest drawers are replacements or supplements which are likely to be used. In the farther drawers, in the shelves reaching up to the ceiling, in odd corners, are fading remnants of the past student generations–oddments never used and never discarded. It is claimed, in fact, that no research student ever knew all the contents of his laboratory.

All four of Tywood's students were worried. But three were worried mainly by their own status. That is, by the possible effect the absence of Tywood might have on the status of their "problem." I dismissed those three–who all have their degrees now, I hope–and called back the fourth.

He had the most haggard look of all, and had been least communicative–which I considered a hopeful sign.

He now sat stiffly in the straight-backed chair at the right of the desk, while I leaned back in a creaky old swivel chair and pushed my hat off my forehead. His name was Edwin Howe and *he* did get his degree later on. I know that for sure, because he's a big wheel in the Department of Science now.

I said: "You do the same work the other boys do, I suppose?"

"It's all nuclear work in a way."

"But it's not all exactly the same?"

He shook his head slowly. "We take different angles. You have to have something clear-cut, you know, or you won't be able to publish. We've got to get our degrees."

He said it exactly the way you or I might say, "We've got to make a living." At that, maybe it's the same thing for them.

I said: "All right. What's *your* angle?"

He said: "I do the math. I mean, with Professor Tywood."

"What kind of math?"

And he smiled a little, getting the same sort of atmosphere about him that I had noticed in Professor Keyser's case that morning. A sort of "Do-you-really-think-I-can-explain-all-my-profound-thoughts-to-stupid-little-you?" sort of atmosphere.

All he said aloud, however, was: "That would be rather complicated to explain."

"I'll help you," I said. "Is that anything like it?" And I tossed the foolscap sheet at him.

He didn't give it any once over. He just snatched it up and let out a thin wail: "Where'd you get this?"

"From Tywood's safe."

"Do you have the rest of it, too?"

"It's safe," I hedged.

He relaxed a little—just a little. "You didn't show it to anybody, did you?"

"I showed it to Professor Keyser."

Howe made an impolite sound with his lower lip and front teeth. "*That* jackass. What did he say?"

I turned the palms of my hands upward and Howe laughed. Then he said, in an offhand manner: "Well, that's the sort of stuff I do."

"And what's it all about? Put it so I can understand it."

There was distinct hesitation. He said: "Now look. This is confidential stuff. Even Pop's other students don't know anything about it. I don't even think *I* know *all* about it. This isn't just a degree I'm after, you know. It's Pop Tywood's Nobel Prize, and it's going to be an Assistant Professorship for me at Cal Tech. This has got to be published before it's talked about."

And I shook my head slowly and made my words very soft: "No, son. You have it twisted. You'll have to talk about it before it's published, because Tywood's gone and maybe he's dead, and maybe he isn't. And if he's dead, maybe he's murdered. And when the department has a suspicion of murder, everybody talks. Now it will look bad for you, kid, if you try to keep some secrets."

It worked. I knew it would, because everyone reads murder mysteries and knows all the clichés. He jumped out of his chair and rattled the words off as if he had a script in front of him.

"Surely," he said, "you can't suspect *me* of . . . of anything like that. Why . . . why, my career—"

I shoved him back into his chair with the beginnings of a sweat on his forehead. I went into the next line: "I don't suspect anybody of anything *yet*. And you won't be in any trouble, if you talk, chum."

He was ready to talk. "Now this is all in strict confidence."

Poor guy. He didn't know the meaning of the word "strict." He was never out of eyeshot of an operator from that moment till the government decided to bury the whole case with one final comment of "?" Quote. Unquote. (I'm not kidding. To this day, the case is neither opened nor closed. It's just "?")

He said, dubiously; "You know what time travel is, I suppose?"

Sure I knew what time travel was. My oldest kid is twelve and he listens to the afternoon video programs till he swells up visibly with the junk he absorbs at the ears and eyes.

"What about time travel?" I said.

"In a sense, we can do it. Actually, it's only what you might call micro-temporal-translation–"

I almost lost my temper. In fact, I think I did. It seemed obvious that the squirt was trying to diddle me; and without subtlety. I'm used to having people think I look dumb; but not *that* dumb.

I said through the back of my throat: "Are you going to tell me that Tywood is out somewhere in time–like Ace Rogers, the Lone Time Ranger?" (That was Junior's favorite program–Ace Rogers was stopping Genghis Khan single-handed that week.)

But he looked as disgusted as I must have. "No," he yelled. "I don't know where Pop is. If you'd *listen* to me–I said micro-temporal-translation. Now this isn't a video show and it isn't magic; this happens to be science. For instance, you know about matter-energy equivalence, I suppose."

I nodded sourly. Everyone knows about that since Hiroshima in the last war but one.

"All right, then," he went on, "that's good for a start. Now if you take a known mass of matter and apply temporal translation to it–you know, send it back in time–you are, in effect, creating matter at the point in time to which you are sending it. To do that, you must use an amount of energy equivalent to the amount of matter you have created. In other words, to send a gram–or, say, an ounce–of anything back in time, you have to disintegrate an ounce of matter completely, to furnish the energy required."

"Hm-m-m," I said, "that's to create the ounce of matter in the past. But aren't you destroying an ounce of matter by removing it from the present? Doesn't that *create* the equivalent amount of energy?"

And he looked just about as annoyed as a fellow sitting on a bumblebee that wasn't quite dead. Apparently laymen are never supposed to question scientists.

He said: "I was trying to simplify it so you would understand it. Actually, it's more complicated. It would be very nice if we could use the energy of disappearance to cause it to disappear but that would be working in a circle, believe me. The requirements of entropy would forbid it. To put it more rigorously, the energy is required to overcome temporal inertia and it just works out so that the energy in ergs required to send back a mass, in grams, is equal to that mass times the square of the speed of light in centimeters per second. Which just happens to be the Einstein Mass-Energy Equivalence Equation. I can give you the mathematics, you know."

"I know," I waved some of that misplaced eagerness back. "But was all this worked out experimentally? Or is it just on paper?"

Obviously, the thing was to keep him talking.

He had that queer light in his eye that every research student gets, I am told, when he is asked to discuss his problem. He'll discuss it with anyone, even with a "dumb flatfoot"—which was convenient at the moment.

"You see," he said like a man slipping you the inside dope on a shady business deal, "what started the whole thing was this neutrino business. They've been trying to find that neutrino since the late thirties and they haven't succeeded. It's a subatomic particle which has no charge and has a mass much less than even an electron. Naturally, it's next to impossible to spot, and hasn't been spotted yet. But they keep looking because without assuming that a neutrino exists, the energetics of some nuclear reactions can't be balanced. So Pop Tywood got the idea about twenty years ago that some energy was disappearing, in the form of matter, back into time. We got working on that—or he did—and I'm the first student he's ever had tackle it along with him.

"Obviously, we had to work with tiny amounts of material and . . . well, it was just a stroke of genius on Pop's part to think of using traces of artificial radioactive isotopes. You could work with just a few micrograms of it, you know, by following its activity with counters. The variation of activity with time should follow a very definite and simple law which has never been altered by any laboratory condition known.

"Well, we'd send a speck back fifteen minutes, say, and fifteen minutes before we did that—everything was arranged automatically, you see—the count jumped to nearly double what it should be, fell off normally, and then dropped sharply at the moment it was sent back below where it would have been normally. The material overlapped itself in time, you see, and for fifteen minutes we counted the doubled material–"

I interrupted: "You mean you had the same atoms existing in two places at the same time."

"Yes," he said, with mild surprise, "why not? That's why we use so much energy–the equivalent of creating those atoms." And then he rushed on, "Now I'll tell you what my particular job is. If you send back the material fifteen minutes, it is apparently sent back to the same spot relative to the Earth despite the fact that in fifteen minutes, the Earth moved sixteen thousand miles around the Sun, and the Sun itself moved more thousand miles and so on. But there are certain tiny discrepancies which I've analyzed and which turn out to be due possibly to two causes.

"First, there is a frictional effect–if you can use such a term–so that matter does drift a little with respect to the Earth, depending on how far back in time it is sent, and on the nature of the material. Then, too, some of the discrepancy can only be explained by the assumption that passage through time itself takes time."

"How's that?" I said.

"What I mean is that some of the radioactivity is evenly spread throughout the time of translation as if the material tested had been reacting during backward passage through time by a constant amount. My figures show that–well, if you were to be moved backward in time, you would age one day for every hundred years. Or, to put it another way, if you could watch a time dial which recorded the time outside a 'time machine,' your watch would move forward twenty-four hours while the time dial moved back a hundred years. That's a universal constant, I think, because the speed of light is a universal constant. Anyway, that's my work."

After a few minutes, in which I chewed all this, I asked: "Where did you get the energy needed for your experiments?"

"They ran out a special line from the power plant. Pop's a big shot there, and swung the deal."

"Hm-m-m. What was the heaviest amount of material you sent into the past?"

"Oh"–he sent his eyes upward–"I think we shot back one hundredth of a milligram once. That's ten micrograms."

"Ever try sending anything into the future?"

"That won't work," he put in quickly. "Impossible. You can't change signs like that because the energy required becomes more than infinite. It's a one-way proposition."

I looked hard at my fingernails. "How much material could you send back in time if you fissioned about . . . oh, say, one hundred pounds of plutonium?" Things, I thought, were becoming, if anything, too obvious.

The answer came quickly: "In plutonium fission," he said, "not more than one or two percent of the mass is converted into energy. Therefore, one hundred pounds of plutonium when completely used up would send a pound or two back into time."

"Is that all? But could you handle all that energy? I mean a hundred pounds of plutonium can make quite an explosion."

"All relative," he said, a bit pompously. "If you took all that energy and let it loose a little at a time, you could handle it. If you released it all at once, but used it just as fast as you released it, you could still handle it. In sending back material through time, energy can be used much faster than it can possibly be released even through fission. Theoretically, anyway."

"But how do you get rid of it?"

"It's spread through time, naturally. Of course, the minimum time through which material could be transferred would, therefore, depend on the mass of the material. Otherwise, you're liable to have the energy density with time too high."

"All right, kid," I said. "I'm calling up headquarters, and they'll send a man here to take you home. You'll stay there awhile."

"But– What for?"

"It won't be for long."

It wasn't–and it was made up to him afterward.

I spent the evening at headquarters. We had a library there–a very special kind of library. The very morning after the fusion two or three operators had drifted quietly into the chemistry and physics libraries of the university. Experts in their way. They located every article Tywood had ever published in any scientific journal and had snapped each page. Nothing was disturbed otherwise.

Other men went through magazine files and through book lists. It ended with a room at headquarters that represented a complete Tywoodiana. Nor was there a definite purpose in doing this. It merely represented part of the thoroughness with which a problem of this sort is met.

I went through that library. Not the scientific papers. I knew there'd be nothing there that I wanted. But he had written a series of articles for a magazine twenty years back, and I read those. And I grabbed at every piece of private correspondence they had available.

After that I just sat and thought—and got scared.

I got to bed about four in the morning and had nightmares.

But I was in the Boss' private office at nine in the morning just the same.

He's a big man, the Boss, with iron-gray hair slicked down tight. He doesn't smoke, but he keeps a box of cigars on his desk and when he doesn't want to say anything for a few seconds, he picks one up, rolls it about a little, smells it, then sticks it right into the middle of his mouth and lights it in a very careful way. By that time, he either has something to say or doesn't have to say anything at all. Then he puts the cigar down and lets it burn to death.

He used up a box in about three weeks, and every Christmas half his gift-wraps held boxes of cigars.

He wasn't reaching for any cigars now, though. He just folded his big fists together on the desk and looked up at me from under a creased forehead. "What's boiling?"

I told him. Slowly, because micro-temporal-translation doesn't sit well with anybody, especially when you call it time travel, which I did. It's a sign of how serious things were that he only asked me once if I were crazy.

Then I was finished and we stared at each other.

He said: "And you think he tried to send something back in time —something weighing a pound or two—and blew an entire plant doing it?"

"It fits in," I said.

I let him go for a while. He was thinking and I wanted him to keep on thinking. I wanted him, if possible, to think of the same thing I was thinking, so that I wouldn't have to tell him—

Because I hated to *have* to tell him—

Because it was nuts, for one thing. And too horrible, for another.

So I kept quiet and he kept on thinking and every once in a while some of his thoughts came to the surface.

After a while, he said: "Assuming the student, Howe, to have told the truth—and you'd better check his notebooks, by the way, which I hope you've impounded—"

"The entire wing of that floor is out of bounds, sir. Edwards has the notebooks."

He went on: "All right. Assuming he told us all the truth he knows, why did Tywood jump from less than a milligram to a pound?"

His eyes came down and they were hard: "Now you're concentrating on the time-travel angle. To you, I gather, that is the crucial point, with the energy involved as incidental—purely incidental."

"Yes, sir," I said grimly. "I think exactly that."

"Have you considered that you might be wrong? That you might have matters inverted?"

"I don't quite get that."

"Well, look. You say you've read up on Tywood. All right. He was one of that bunch of scientists after World War II that fought the atom bomb; wanted a world state— You know about that, don't you?"

I nodded.

"He had a guilt complex," the Boss said with energy. "He'd helped work out the bomb, and he couldn't sleep nights thinking of what he'd done. He lived with that fear for years. And even though the bomb wasn't used in World War III, can you imagine what every day of uncertainty must have meant to him? Can you imagine the shriveling horror in his soul as he waited for others to make the decision at every crucial moment till the final Compromise of Sixty-five?

"We have a complete psychiatric analysis of Tywood and several others just like him, taken during the last war. Did you know that?"

"No, sir."

"It's true. We let up after Sixty-five, of course, because with the establishment of world control of atomic power, the scrapping of the atomic bomb stockpile in all countries, and the establishment of research liaison among the various spheres of influence on the planet, most of the ethical conflict in the scientific mind was removed.

"But the findings at the time were serious. In 1964, Tywood had a morbid subconscious hatred for the very concept of atomic power. He began to make mistakes, serious ones. Eventually, we were forced to take him off research of any kind. And several others as well, even though things were pretty bad at the time. We had just lost India, if you remember."

Considering that I was in India at the time, I remembered. But I still wasn't seeing his point.

"Now what," he continued, "if dregs of that attitude remained buried in Tywood to the very end. Don't you see that this time travel is a double-edged sword? Why throw a pound of anything into the past, anyway? For the sake of proving a point? He had proved his case just as much when he sent back a fraction of a milligram. That was good enough for the Nobel Prize, I suppose.

"But there was *one* thing he could do with a pound of matter that he couldn't do with a milligram, and that was *to drain a power plant.* So that was what he must have been after. He had discovered a way of consuming inconceivable quantities of energy. By sending back eighty pounds of dirt, he could remove all the existing plutonium in the world. End atomic power for an indefinite period."

I was completely unimpressed, but I tried not to make that too plain. I just said: "Do you think he could possibly have thought he could get away with it more than once?"

"This is all based on the fact that he wasn't a normal man. How do I know what he could imagine he could do? Besides, there may be men behind him—with less science and more brains—who are quite ready to continue onwards from this point."

"Have any of these men been found yet? Any evidence of such men?"

A little wait, and his hand reached for the cigar box. He stared at the cigar and turned it end for end. Just a little wait more. I was patient.

Then he put it down decisively without lighting it.

"No," he said.

He looked at me, and clear through me, and said: "Then you still don't go for that?"

I shrugged. "Well— It doesn't sound right."

"Do you have a notion of your own?"

"Yes. But I can't bring myself to talk about it. If I'm wrong, I'm the wrongest man that ever was; but if I'm right, I'm the rightest."

"I'll listen," he said, and he put his hand under the desk.

That was the pay-off. The room was armored, sound-proof, and radiation-proof to anything short of a nuclear explosion. And with that little signal showing on his secretary's desk, the President of the United States couldn't have interrupted us.

I leaned back and said: "Chief, do you happen to remember how you met your wife? Was it a little thing?"

He must have thought it a non sequitur. What else could he have thought? But he was giving me my head now; having his own reasons, I suppose.

He just smiled and said: "I sneezed and she turned around. It was at a street corner."

"What made you be on that street corner just then? What made her be? Do you remember just why you sneezed? Where you caught the cold? Or where the speck of dust came from? Imagine how many factors had to intersect in just the right place at just the right time for you to meet your wife."

"I suppose we would have met some other time, if not then?"

"But you can't *know* that. How do you know whom you *didn't* meet, because once when you might have turned around, you didn't; because once when you might have been late, you weren't. Your life forks at every instant, and you go down one of the forks, almost at random, and so does everyone else. Start twenty years ago, and the forks diverge further and further with time.

"You sneezed, and met a girl, and not another. As a consequence, you made certain decisions, and so did the girl, and so did the girl you didn't meet, and the man who did meet her, and the people you all met thereafter. And your family, her family, their family–and your children.

"Because you sneezed twenty years ago, five people, or fifty, or five hundred, might be dead now who would have been alive or might be alive, who would have been dead. Move it two hundred years ago: two thousand years ago, and a sneeze–even by someone no history ever heard of–might have meant that no one now alive would have been alive."

The boss rubbed the back of his head. "Widening ripples. I read a story once–"

"So did I. It's not a new idea–but I want you to think about it for a while, because I want to read to you from an article by Professor Elmer Tywood in a magazine twenty years old. It was just before the last war."

I had copies of the film in my pocket and the white wall made a beautiful screen, which was what it was meant to do. The Boss made a motion to turn about, but I waved him back.

"No, sir," I said. "I want to read this to you. And I want you to listen to it."

He leaned back.

"The article," I went on, "is entitled: 'Man's First Great Failure!' Remember, this was just before the war, when the bitter disappointment at the final failure of the United Nations was at its height. What I will read are some excerpts from the first part of the article. It goes like this:

"'. . . That Man, with his technical perfection, has failed to solve the great sociological problems of today is only the second immense tragedy that has come to the race. The first, and perhaps the greater, was that once these same great sociological problems *were* solved;

and yet these solutions were not permanent because the technical perfection we have today did not then exist.

"'It was a case of having bread without butter, or butter without bread. Never both together . . .

"'Consider the Hellenic world from which our philosophy, our mathematics, our ethics, our art, our literature—our entire culture, in fact—stem . . . In the days of Pericles, Greece, like our own world in microcosm, was a surprisingly modern potpourri of conflicting ideologies and ways of life. But then Rome came, adopting the culture, but bestowing, and enforcing, peace. To be sure, the Pax Romana lasted only two hundred years, but no like period has existed since. . . .

"'War was abolished. Nationalism did not exist. The Roman citizen was empire-wide. Paul of Tarsus and Flavius Josephus were Roman citizens. Spaniards, North Africans, Illyrians assumed the purple. Slavery existed, but it was an indiscriminate slavery, imposed as a punishment, incurred as the price of economic failure, brought on by the fortunes of war. No man was a *natural* slave, because of the color of his skin, or the place of his birth.

"'Religious toleration was complete. If an exception was made early in the case of the Christians, it was because they refused to accept the principle of toleration; because they insisted that only they themselves knew truth—a principle abhorrent to the civilized Roman. . . .

"'With all of Western culture under a single *polis*, with the cancer of religious and national particularism and exclusivism absent; with a high civilization in existence—why could not Man hold his gains?

"'It was because technologically, ancient Hellenism remained backward. It was because without a machine civilization, the price of leisure—and hence civilization and culture—for the few was slavery for the many. Because the civilization could not find the means to bring comfort and ease to *all* the population.

"'Therefore, the depressed classes turned to the other world, and to religions which spurned the material benefits of this world—so that science was made impossible in any true sense for over a millennium. And further, as the initial impetus of Hellenism waned, the empire lacked the technological powers to beat back the barbarians. In fact, it was not till after 1500 A.D. that war became sufficiently a function of the industrial resources of a nation to enable the settled people to defeat invading tribesmen and nomads with ease. . . .

" 'Imagine then, if somehow the ancient Greeks had learned just a hint of modern chemistry and physics. Imagine if the growth of the empire had been accompanied by the growth of science, technology and industry. Imagine an empire in which machinery replaced slaves; in which all men had a decent share of the world's goods; in which the legion became the armored column, against which no barbarians could stand. Imagine an empire which would therefore spread all over the world, *without* religious or national prejudices.

" 'An Empire of all men—all brothers—eventually all free. . . .

" 'If history could be changed. If that first great failure could have been prevented—' "

And I stopped at that point.

"Well?" said the Boss.

"Well," I said, "I think it isn't difficult to connect all that with the fact that Tywood blew an entire power plant in his anxiety to send something back to the past, while in his office safe we found sections of a chemistry textbook translated into Greek."

His face changed, while he considered.

Then, he said heavily: "But nothing's happened."

"I know. But then I've been told by Tywood's student that it takes a day to move back a century in time. Assuming that ancient Greece was the target area, we have twenty centuries, hence twenty days."

"But can it be stopped?"

"*I* wouldn't know. Tywood might, but he's dead."

The enormity of it all hit me at once, deeper than it had the night before—

All humanity was virtually under sentence of death. And while that was merely a horrible abstraction, the fact that reduced it to a thoroughly unbearable reality was that I was, too. And my wife, and my kid.

Further, it was a death without precedence. A ceasing to exist, and no more. The passing of a breath. The vanishing of a dream. The drift into eternal non-space and non-time of a shadow. I would not be dead at all, in fact. I would merely never have been born.

Or would I? Would I exist—my individuality—my ego—my soul, if you like? Another life? Other circumstances?

I thought none of that in words, then. But if a cold knot in the stomach could ever speak under the circumstances it would sound like that, I think.

The Boss moved in on my thoughts—hard.

"Then we have about two and a half weeks. No time to lose. Come on."

I grinned with one side of my mouth: "What do we do? Chase the book?"

"No," he replied coldly, "but there are two courses of action we must follow. First, you may be wrong—altogether. All of this circumstantial reasoning may still represent a false lead, perhaps deliberately thrown before us, to cover up the real truth. That must be checked.

"Secondly, you may be right—but there may be some way of stopping the book—other than chasing it in a time machine, I mean. If so, we must find out how."

"I would just like to say, sir, if this is a false lead, only a madman would consider it a believable one. So suppose I'm right, and suppose there's no way of stopping it?"

"Then, young fellow, I'm going to keep pretty busy for two and a half weeks, and I'd advise you to do the same. The time will pass more quickly that way."

Of course he was right.

"Where do we start?" I asked.

"The first thing we need is a list of all men and women on the government payroll under Tywood."

"Why?"

"Reasoning. Your specialty, you know. Tywood doesn't know Greek, I think we can assume with fair safety, so someone else must have done the translating. It isn't likely that anyone would do a job like that for nothing, and it isn't likely that Tywood would pay out of his personal funds—not on a professor's salary."

"He might," I pointed out, "have been interested in more secrecy than a government payroll affords."

"Why? Where was the danger? Is it a crime to translate a chemistry textbook into Greek? Who would ever deduce from that a plot such as you've described?"

It took us half an hour to turn up the name of Mycroft James Boulder, listed as "Consultant," and to find out that he was mentioned in the University Catalogue as Assistant Professor of Philosophy and to check by telephone that among his many accomplishments was a thorough knowledge of Attic Greek.

Which was a coincidence—because with the Boss reaching for his hat, the interoffice teletype clicked away and it turned out that Mycroft James Boulder was in the anteroom, at the end of a two-hour continuing insistence that he see the Boss.

The Boss put his hat back and opened his office door.

Professor Mycroft James Boulder was a gray man. His hair was gray and his eyes were gray. His suit was gray, too.

But most of all, his expression was gray; gray with a tension that seemed to twist at the lines in his thin face.

Boulder said softly: "I've been trying for three days to get a hearing, sir, with a responsible man. I can get no higher than yourself."

"I may be high enough," said the Boss. "What's on your mind?"

"It is quite important that I be granted an interview with Professor Tywood."

"Do you know where he is?"

"I am quite certain that he is in government custody."

"Why?"

"Because I know that he was planning an experiment which would entail the breaking of security regulations. Events since, as nearly as I can make them out, flow naturally from the supposition that security regulations have indeed been broken. I can presume then that the experiment has at least been attempted. I must discover whether it has been successfully concluded."

"Professor Boulder," said the Boss, "I believe you can read Greek."

"Yes, I can." Coolly.

"And have translated chemical texts for Professor Tywood on government money."

"Yes—as a legally employed consultant."

"Yet such translation, under the circumstances, constitutes a crime, since it makes you an accessory to Tywood's crime."

"You can establish a connection?"

"Can't you? Or haven't you heard of Tywood's notions on time travel, or . . . what do you call it . . . micro-temporal-translation?"

"Ah?" and Boulder smiled a little. "He's told you, then."

"No he hasn't," said the Boss harshly. "Professor Tywood is dead."

"What?" Then: "I don't believe you."

"He died of apoplexy. Look at this."

He had one of the photographs taken that first night in his wall safe. Tywood's face was distorted but recognizable—sprawled and dead.

Boulder's breath went in and out as if the gears were clogged.

He stared at the picture for three full minutes by the electric clock on the wall. "Where is this place?" he asked.

"The atomic power plant."

"Had he finished his experiment?"

The Boss shrugged. "There's no way of telling. He was dead when we found him."

Boulder's lips were pinched and colorless. "That must be determined somehow. A commission of scientists must be established, and, if necessary, the experiment must be repeated–"

But the Boss just looked at him, and reached for a cigar–I've never seen him take longer–and when he put it down, curled in its unused smoke, he said: "Tywood wrote an article for a magazine, twenty years ago–"

"Oh," and the professor's lips twisted, "is *that* what gave you your clue. You may ignore that. The man is only a physical scientist and knows nothing of either history or sociology. A schoolboy's dreams and nothing more."

"Then you don't think sending your translation back will inaugurate a Golden Age, do you?"

"Of course not. Do you think you can graft the developments of two thousand years of slow labor onto a child society not ready for it? Do you think a great invention or a great scientific principle is born full-grown in the mind of a genius divorced from his cultural milieu? Newton's enunciation of the Law of Gravity was delayed for twenty years because the then current figure for the Earth's diameter was wrong by ten percent. Archimedes almost discovered calculus, but failed because Arabic numerals, invented by some nameless Hindu or group of Hindus, were unknown to him.

"For that matter, the mere existence of a slave society in ancient Greece and Rome meant that machines could scarcely attract much attention–slaves being so much cheaper and more adaptable. And men of true intellect could scarcely be expected to spend their energies on devices intended for manual labor. Even Archimedes, the greatest engineer of antiquity, refused to publish any of his practical inventions–only mathematic abstractions. And when a young man asked Plato of what use geometry was, he was forthwith expelled from the academy as a man with a mean, unphilosophic soul.

"Science does not plunge forward–it inches along in the directions permitted by the greater forces that mold society and which are in turn molded by society. And no great man advances but on the shoulders of the society that surrounds him–"

The Boss interrupted him at that point. "Suppose you tell us what your part in Tywood's work was, then. We'll take your word for it that history cannot be changed."

"Oh it can, but not purposefully. You see, when Tywood first requested my services in the matter of translating certain textbook passages into Greek, I agreed for the money involved. But he wanted the translation on parchment; he insisted on the use of ancient Greek terminology—the language of Plato, to use his words—regardless of how I had to twist the literal significance of passages, and he wanted it handwritten in rolls.

"I was curious. I, too, found his magazine article. It was difficult for me to jump to the obvious conclusion since the achievements of modern science transcend the imaginings of philosophy in so many ways. But I learned the truth eventually, and it was at once obvious that Tywood's theory of changing history was infantile. There are twenty million variables for every instant of time, and no system of mathematics—no mathematic psychohistory, to coin a phrase—has yet been developed to handle that ocean of varying functions.

"In short, any variation of events two thousand years ago would change all subsequent history but in *no predictable way.*"

The Boss suggested, with a false quietness: "Like the pebble that starts the avalanche, right?"

"Exactly. You have some understanding of the situation, I see. I thought deeply for weeks before I proceeded, and then I realized how I must act—*must* act."

There was a low roar. The Boss stood up and his chair went over backward. He swung around his desk, and he had a hand on Boulder's throat. I was stepping out to stop him, but he waved me back.

He was only tightening the necktie a little. Boulder could still breathe. He had gone very white, and for all the time that the Boss talked, he restricted himself to just that—breathing.

And the Boss said: "Sure, I can see how you decided you must act. I know that some of you brain-sick philosophers think the world needs fixing. You want to throw the dice again and see what turns up. Maybe you don't even care if you're alive in the new setup—or that no one can possibly know what you've done. But you're going to create just the same. You're going to give God another chance so to speak.

"Maybe I just want to live—but the world could be worse. In twenty million different ways, it could be worse. A fellow named Wilder once wrote a play called *The Skin of Our Teeth.* Maybe you've read it. Its thesis was that mankind survived by just that skin of their teeth. No, I'm not going to give you a speech about the Ice Age nearly wiping us out. I don't know enough. I'm not even going to talk about the Greeks winning at Marathon; the Arabs being defeated at Tours; the Mongols turning back at the last minute without even being defeated—because I'm no historian.

"But take the twentieth century. The Germans were stopped at the Marne twice in World War I. Dunkirk happened in World War II, and somehow the Germans were stopped at Moscow and Stalingrad. We could have used the atom bomb in the last war and we didn't, and just when it looked as if both sides would have to, the Great Compromise happened—just because General Bruce was delayed in taking off from the Ceylon airfield long enough to receive the message directly. One after the other, just like that, all through history—lucky breaks. For every 'if' that didn't come true, that would have made wonder-men of all of us, if it had, there were twenty 'ifs' that didn't come true, that would have brought disaster to all of us, if they had.

"You're gambling on that one-in-twenty chance—gambling every life on Earth. And you've succeeded, too, because Tywood *did* send that text back."

He ground out that last sentence, and opened his fist, so that Boulder could fall out and back into his chair.

And Boulder laughed.

"You fool," he gasped bitterly, "how close you can be and yet how widely you can miss the mark. Tywood *did* send his book back then? You are sure of that?"

"No chemical textbook in Greek was found on the scene," said the Boss grimly, "and millions of calories of energy had disappeared. Which doesn't change the fact, however, that we have two and a half weeks in which to—make things interesting for you."

"Oh, nonsense. No foolish dramatics, please. Just listen to me, and try to understand. There were Greek philosophers once, named Leucippus and Democritus, who evolved an atomic theory. All matter, they said, was composed of atoms. Varieties of atoms were distinct and changeless and by their different combinations with each other formed the various substances found in nature. That theory was not the result of experiment or observation. It came into being, somehow, full-grown.

"The didactic Roman poet Lucretius, in his *'De Rerum Natura'*—

'On the Nature of Things'—elaborated on that theory and throughout manages to sound startlingly modern.

"In Hellenistic times, Hero built a steam engine and weapons of war became almost mechanized. The period has been referred to as an abortive mechanical age, which came to nothing because, somehow, it neither grew out of nor fitted into its social and economic milieu. Alexandrian science was a queer and rather inexplicable phenomenon.

"Then one might mention the old Roman legend about the books of the Sibyl that contained mysterious information direct from the gods—

"In other words, gentlemen, while you are right that any change in the course of past events, however trifling, would have incalculable consequences, and while I also believe that you are right in supposing that any random change is much more likely to be for the worse than for the better, I must point out that you are nevertheless wrong in your final conclusion.

"Because this *is the world in which the Greek chemistry text* was *sent back.*

"This has been a Red Queen's race, if you remember your *Through the Looking Glass.* In the Red Queen's country, one had to run as fast as one could merely to stay in the same place. And so it was in this case! Tywood may have thought he was creating a new world, but it was *I* who prepared the translations, and I took care that only such passages as would account for the queer scraps of knowledge the ancients apparently got from nowhere would be included.

"And my only intention, for all my racing, was to stay in the same place."

Three weeks passed; three months; three years. Nothing happened. When nothing happens, you have no proof. We gave up trying to explain, and we ended, the Boss and I, by doubting it ourselves.

The case never ended. Boulder could not be considered a criminal without being considered a world savior as well, and vice versa. He was ignored. And in the end, the case was neither solved, nor closed out; merely put in a file all by itself, under the designation "?" and buried in the deepest vault in Washington.

The Boss is in Washington now, a big wheel. And I'm Regional Head of the Bureau.

Boulder is still assistant professor, though. Promotions are slow at the University.

THE CURE

by Henry Kuttner and C. L. Moore

WHEN DAWSON got back from his vacation in Florida, he was feeling no better. He hadn't expected a miraculous cure. In fact, he hadn't expected anything. Now he sat morosely at his desk, staring out at the tower of the Empire State and vaguely hoping it would topple.

Carruthers, his partner in the law firm, came in and bummed a cigarette. "You look lousy, Fred," he remarked. "Why not go out and have a drink?"

"I don't want a drink," Dawson said. "Besides, it's too early. I had enough liquor in Florida."

"Maybe too much."

"No. What griped me was—I dunno."

"Great psychoses from little acorns grow," Carruthers said, his plump, pale face almost too casual.

"So now I'm nuts?"

"You could be. You could be. Give yourself time. Why this abnormal fear of psychiatrists, anyway? I got psychoanalyzed once."

"What happened?"

"I'm going to marry a tall, dark woman," Carruthers said. "Just the same, psychiatry isn't in the same class with astrology. Maybe you bit your grandmother when you were a child. Drag it out in the open. As long as you keep thinking, 'What big teeth you have,' you'll dwell in a morass of mental misery."

"I'm not in a morass," Dawson said. "It's just—"

"Yeah. Just— Listen, didn't you go to college with a guy named Hendricks?"

"I did."

"I met him in the elevator last week. He's moved here from Chicago. Got offices upstairs, on the twenty-fifth floor. He's supposed to be one of the best psychiatrists in this country. Why not go see him?"

"What could I say?" Dawson asked. "I'm not followed by little green men."

"Lucky man," Carruthers said. "I am. Day and night. They drink my liquor, too. Just tell Hendricks you smell dead flies. You probably pulled the wings off an anopheles when you were a tot. It's as simple as that, see?" He rose from his chair, put his hand on Dawson's shoulder, and added quietly, "Do it, Fred. As a favor to me."

"Um. Well–O.K."

"Good," Carruthers said, brightening. He looked at his wristwatch. "You're due at his office in five minutes. I made the appointment yesterday." He fled, ignoring the curse Dawson flung at his head. "Room twenty-five-forty," he called, and slammed the door.

Scowling, Dawson located his hat, left word with the receptionist as to his whereabouts, and rode the elevator up. He met a short, fat, cherubic man in tweeds emerging from twenty-five-forty. Mild blue eyes considered him through glistening contact lenses.

"Hello, Fred," the man said. "Don't you know me now, eh?"

"Raoul?" Dawson's voice was doubtful.

"Right. Raoul Hendricks, somewhat fatter after twenty-five years, I'm afraid. You look the same, though. Look, I was just going down to your office. I didn't have a chance to eat breakfast this morning. What about a bite downstairs?"

"Didn't Carruthers tell you–"

"We can kick that around better over food." Hendricks steered Dawson back to the elevator. "There's a lot I want to ask you about. The college chaps. I didn't keep in touch. I was in Europe most of the time."

"I kept in touch," Dawson said. "Remember Willard? He's just been indicted in an oil mix-up–"

They talked over onion soup and through the entrée. Hendricks listened, mostly. Sometimes he watched Dawson, though not pointedly. They were in an isolated booth, and, after coffee had been served, Hendricks lighted a cigarette and blew a smoke ring.

"You want a snap diagnosis?" he asked.

"O.K."

"You're worried about something. Do you know what it is?"

"Certainly I know," Dawson said. "It's a sort of daydream. But Carruthers told you that."

"He said you smelled dead flies."

Dawson laughed. "On a windowpane. A dusty windowpane. Probably it isn't that at all. I just got the impression, no more than that.

I never see anything. It's a sort of extension of sensory consciousness."

"It never occurs in your sleeping dreams?"

"If it does, I don't remember. It's always a flash. The worst part is that I *know* at the time that it's the windowpane that's real. Usually it happens when I'm doing some routine stuff. Suddenly I get this flash. It's instantaneous. I feel, very certainly, that whatever I happen to be doing at the time is a dream. And that really I'm somewhere smelling dead flies on a dusty windowpane."

"Like the Red King? You think somebody's dreaming you?"

"No. I'm dreaming–this." Dawson looked around the restaurant.

"Well," Hendricks said, "possibly you are." He stubbed out his cigarette. "We get into metaphysics at that point, and I'm lost. It doesn't matter which *is* the dream. The main thing is to believe in the dream while you're having it. Unless it's a nightmare."

"It isn't," Dawson said. "I've had a pretty good life so far."

"Then where are we? You don't know what's worrying you. The dream's merely a symbol. Once you realize what the symbol represents, the whole structure collapses, and any neuroses you may have are gone. As a general rule, anyway."

"Ghosts can't stand light, is that it?"

"That's it, exactly. Don't misunderstand me. Neuroses can build up eventually to true psychoses. You've got something like an olfactory hallucination. But there's no accompanying delusion. You know the windowpane isn't there."

"Yeah," Dawson said, "but there's something under my hand."

"Tactile hallucination? What does it feel like?"

"Cold and hard. I don't know what it is. If I move it, something will happen."

"Do you move it?"

After a long moment Dawson said, "No," very softly.

"Then move it," Hendricks advised. He took out pencil and paper and adjusted his watch. "Let's have a jury-rigged word-association test. O.K.?"

"Well–why?"

"To find out the causation of your windowpane. If there's a mental block, if the censor's working, it'll show up. Spring cleaning. If you clean a house regularly, you save a lot of work later. No chance for cobwebs to accumulate. Whereas if you let the stuff pile up, you're apt to get a real psychosis, with all the trimmings. As I just said, it's a question of finding the cause. Once you locate that, you know it's a straw dummy, and it doesn't bother you any more."

"What if it isn't a straw dummy?"

"Then, at least, you've recognized it, and can take steps to get rid of the incubus."

"I see," Dawson said slowly. "If I'd been responsible for a man's death years ago, I could buy peace of mind by taking care of his orphaned children."

"Read Dickens," Hendricks said. "Scrooge is a beautiful case history. Hallucinations, persecution complex, guilt complex–and atonement." He glanced at his watch. "Ready?"

"Ready."

When they had finished, Hendricks blinked at the results. "Normal," he said. "Too normal. A few odd quirks–but it takes more than one test to get any definite result. We don't want to be empirical –though it's sometimes necessary. Next time you have that daydream, move the gadget under your hand."

"I don't know if I can," Dawson said.

But Hendricks only laughed. "Neural paralysis of the astral," he suggested. "I'm relieved, Fred. I'd rather gathered you were slightly off your rocker. But the layman always overestimates mental quirks. Your friend Carruthers has probably got you a bit worried."

"Maybe."

"So you've got a hallucinatory daydream. That isn't uncommon. Once we find the cause, you'll have nothing left to worry about. Come in tomorrow, any time–give me a call first–and we'll give you a physical checkup. More coffee?"

"No," Dawson said, and presently left Hendricks at the elevator. He was feeling irrationally relieved. Though he discounted a good deal of the psychiatrist's professional optimism, he felt that the man's argument held water. There was logic in it. And certainly it was illogical to let a daydream influence his moods so strongly.

Back in his office, Dawson stood at the window, staring out over the serrated skyline. The low, hushed roar of traffic mounted from the canyons below. In forty-two years he had come a long way, partner in a law firm, member of a dozen clubs, taking an active interest in a variety of matters–a long way for a boy who had begun his career in an orphan asylum. He had married once, but there had been a divorce, amicable on both sides. Now it was more convenient to maintain a bachelor apartment near Central Park. He had money, prestige, power—none of which would help him if the hallucination developed.

On impulse he left the office and visited a medical library. What he found only confirmed Hendricks' remarks. Apparently, as long as he didn't believe in the real existence of the dusty windowpane, he was fairly safe. When he did, dissociation stepped in, and all but subjective, false logic would fail. Men have a vital need to believe they are acting rationally—and, since so many basic motives are too hidden and complicated to unscramble, they assign arbitrary meanings to their actions. But why a dusty windowpane?

"Yeah," Dawson thought, thumbing through pages. "If I believed in this dream, I'd—uh—erect secondary delusions. I'd think of a good reason why there *was* a windowpane. Only there isn't any reason, luckily."

As he walked out of the library, and saw the stream of street traffic before him, he suddenly felt that he was dreaming. And the windowpane was back again.

He knew he was lying close against it, his nose almost touching the glass, inhaling dust with every breath, and the smothering, dreary, somehow brownish odor of dead flies. It was singularly horrid—that feeling of suffocation and dead despair. He could feel the hard something under his hand, and he knew with a sudden sense of urgency that unless he moved it—*now*—he was more than likely to smother there with his nose against the glass, smother from sheer inertia, inability to move. He knew he *must* not slip back into the dream of being Dawson. This was reality. There was nothing tangible about Dawson and his fool's paradise and his dream city of New York. Yet he could lie here and die with the smell of dead flies in his nostrils, and Dawson would never suspect until that dreadful last moment between waking and death, when it was too late to move the—the hard object beneath his hand.

Traffic roared at him. He stood at the curb, white and sweating. The unreality of the scene before him was briefly shocking. He stood motionless, waiting until the hollow world had resumed its tangibility. Then, his lips tight, he hailed a taxi.

Two stiff shots of whiskey were comforting. He was able to contemplate working on the current brief, a liability case which presented no difficulties. Carruthers had gone to court, and he didn't see his partner that afternoon. Nor did the—hallucination—recur.

But, after dinner, Dawson telephoned his ex-wife, and spent the evening with her at a roof garden. He didn't drink much. He was trying to recapture something of the vital reality that had existed during the early part of their marriage. But he wasn't too successful.

The next morning Carruthers came in, perched on Dawson's desk, and cadged a cigarette. "What's the verdict?" he wanted to know. "Do you hear voices?"

"Often," Dawson said. "I'm hearing one now. Yours."

"But is Hendricks any good, really?"

Dawson felt unreasonably irritated. "Do you expect him to wave a magic wand? All therapy takes time."

"Therapy, huh? What did he say was wrong?"

"Nothing much." Dawson didn't want to discuss it. He opened a law book pointedly. Carruthers lit his cigarette, dropped the match into the wastebasket, and shrugged.

"Sorry. I'd thought–"

"Oh, I'm all right. Hendricks is pretty good, really. My nerves are a bit shot."

Comforted, Carruthers said something and went back to his office. Dawson turned a page, read a few words, and felt things close in. The morning sunlight, slanting through the window, faded abruptly. Under his hand was a cold, hard object, and strong in his nostrils was the dusty smell of despair. And this time he knew it was reality.

It did not last long. When it had gone, he sat quietly, staring at the hollow desk and the hollow wall beyond it. The sounds from the traffic below were dream noises. The curl of smoke spiraling up from the wastebasket was dream smoke.

"I hope you don't think you're real," Tweedledum said scornfully.

He noticed that the smoke had changed to orange flame. The curtain caught fire. Presently he would waken.

Someone screamed. Miss Anstruther, his secretary, stood in the doorway, pointing. After that, there was confusion, shouting, and the spurting of a fire extinguisher.

The flames died. The smoke vanished.

"Oh, dear," Miss Anstruther said, wiping a smudge from her nose. "It's lucky I came in when I did, Mr. Dawson. You had your nose in that book–"

"Yeah," Dawson said. "I didn't even notice. I'd better speak to Mr. Carruthers about throwing matches in the wastebaskets."

Instead, he telephoned Hendricks. The psychiatrist could see him in an hour. Dawson passed the time with a crossword puzzle, and, at ten, went upstairs and stripped. Hendricks used stethoscope, blood-pressure gadget, and other useful devices.

"Well?"

"You're all right."

"Sound as a nut, eh?"

"A nut?" Hendricks said. "Come on. Let's have it. What happened?"

Dawson told him. "It's like epilepsy. I don't know when I'll have these attacks. They've never lasted long so far, but they might. And afterward–the dream feeling hangs over. I knew very well that there was a fire in the wastebasket, but it wasn't a real fire."

"Daydreams are apt to carry over a bit. Reorientation isn't always instantaneous."

Dawson chewed on a fingernail. "Sure, but–suppose Carruthers was falling out of a window. I wouldn't have tried to stop him. Hell, I'd have walked off a roof myself. I'd have known it wouldn't have hurt me. It's a *dream*."

"Do you feel you're dreaming now?"

"No," Dawson said, "not now, of course! It's only during these attacks, and afterward–"

"You felt that hard object under your hand?"

"Yeah. And the smell. There was something else, too."

"What?"

"I don't know."

"Move that object. It's a compulsion, in four-bit words. And don't worry about it."

"Not even if I walk off a roof?"

"Stay away from roofs for a while," Hendricks said. "Once you find out the meaning of this symbolism, you'll be cured."

"And if I don't, I'll get secondary delusions."

"You've been reading up on it, eh? Look. If you think you're the richest man in the world, and you haven't got a dime in your pocket, how'll you rationalize that?"

"I don't know," Dawson said. "Maybe I'm eccentric."

Hendricks shook his head, his plump cheeks bobbing. "No, you'll develop the logical delusion–a supplementary one–that you're the victim of an organized plot to rob you. Catch? Don't try to assign phony meanings to your dusty windowpane. Don't start thinking a little man named Alice is popping out of the woodwork with a windowpane tucked under his arm. Or that the glass-blowers' union wants to persecute you. Just find the real meaning behind the symbolism. As I told you. Move that gadget under your hand. Don't simply be passive about it."

"O.K.," Dawson said, "I'll move it. If I can."

He dreamed that night, but it was a typical dream. The familiar hallucination didn't emerge. Instead, he found himself standing on a gibbet, a rope about his neck. Hendricks came rushing up, waving a paper roll tied with a blue ribbon. "You're reprieved!" the psychiatrist shouted. "Here's your pardon, signed by the Governor!" He thrust the roll into Dawson's hands. "Open it," he ordered urgently. "Untie the ribbon." Dawson didn't want to, but Hendricks kept insisting. He pulled at the ribbon. As he did, he saw that it was tied to a long cord that snaked across the platform and vanished from sight beneath it. A bolt clicked. He felt the trap door quiver under his feet. By pulling at the ribbon, he had opened the drop; he was falling.

He woke up, sweating. The room was dark and silent. Cursing under his breath, Dawson got up and took a cool shower. He had not had nightmares for years.

There were, after that, two more interviews with Hendricks. Each time the psychiatrist probed more deeply. But the refrain never altered. *Recognize the symbol. Move your hand. Remember.*

On the third day, as Dawson sat waiting in Hendricks' outer office, he remembered.

The familiar, leaden, sick inertia swept over him. Desperately he tried to focus on the buildings outside the window. But he could not battle the tide. At the last moment Hendricks' advice occurred to him, and, as he felt the cold, hard object under his palm, he made a tremendous effort to move his hand.

To the left, something told him. *To the left.*

It was hard to battle that lethargy, that smothering, dusty suffocation of despair. And it was hard to move. But he strained to send the impulse down his arm, into stiff fingers, and the effort told. He felt something click into place, and–and . . .

He remembered.

The last thing before . . .

Before what?

"Vital therapy," a voice said. *"We grow fewer yearly. And we must guard against that plague."*

Karestly ran an eight-fingered hand over his sweating, bald head. "The tests show you need it, Dawsao."

"I hadn't–"

"You wouldn't know, of course. It'd be imperceptible except by the instruments. But you need the therapy, that's certain."

"I can't spare the time," Dawsao said. "The simplification formulas are just beginning to clear up. How long must I stay in the vorkyl?"

"Half a year," Karestly said. "It doesn't matter."

"And Pharr went in last month."

"He needed it."

Dawsao stared at the wall, made a mental signal, and opaqueness faded to translucence and transparency. He could see the City.

Karestly said, "You'd never vorkyled before. You're one of the youngest. It isn't bad. It's stimulating, curative, and necessary."

"But I feel normal."

"The machines don't lie. The emotion factor is wrong. Listen to me, Dawsao. I'm a great deal older than you, and I've been in the vorkyl twelve times."

Dawsao stared. "Where to?"

"Different eras each time. The one best fitted for my particular warp. Once it was Brazil, in 1890. Another time, Restoration London. And the Second Han Empire. I had plenty to do. I spent ten years in Brazil, building a rubber empire."

"Rubber?"

Karestly smiled. "A substance–it was important at that time. I kept busy. It's fine therapy. In those days, the only therapy they knew involved painting, construction–visual and tangible, not the emotional and psychic therapy we use. However, their minds weren't developed."

"I hate the idea of being shut up in a five-sensed body," Dawsao said.

"You wouldn't know any better. There's the artificial mnemonic angle. Your life-force will take possession of the body that's created for you at the therapeutic epoch we choose, and you'll have a full set of false memories, created especially for that period. You'll probably begin as a child. There may be temporal compression, so you'll be able to live thirty or forty years in a half year of our time."

"I still don't like it."

"Time travel," Karestly said, "is the best therapy known today. You live in a new environment, with a new set of values. And *that's* the vital part. You get away from the current herd instinct that's caused all the trouble."

"But—" Dawsao said. "But! Only four thousand of us still sane, in all the world! And unless we work fast—"

"We're not immune. The whole trouble is that for hundreds of generations the race has followed false values, which conflicted with the primary instincts. Overcomplication plus oversimplification, both in the wrong places. We haven't kept pace with our growing mentality. There was a man—Clemens—who owned a mechanical typesetter that was perfect except for one thing. It was too complicated. When it worked, it was ideal, but it kept breaking down."

"Old stuff," Dawsao said. "I know the trouble. The machines are so enormously complicated now that humans can't keep up with them."

"We're solving it," Karestly said. "Slowly but surely. There are four thousand of us. And we know the right therapy now. After you've had six months in the vorkyl, you'll be a new man. You'll find temporal therapy is foolproof and absolutely certain."

"I hope so. I want to get back to my work."

"If you went back to it now, you'd be insane in six months," Karestly pointed out. "Temporal travel is like preventive serum shots. You'll be occupied; we'll send you back to the twentieth century."

"That far back?"

"That period's indicated, in your case. You'll be given a complete set of artificial memories, and, while you're in the past, you'll have no consciousness of reality. Of *this* reality, I mean."

"Well . . ." Dawsao said.

"Come on." Karestly rose and floated toward the transporter-disk. "The vorkyl's ready for you. The matrix is set. All you have to do is—"

Dawsao got into the case. It closed behind him. He took a last look at Karestly's friendly face and tightened his hand on the control. He moved it toward the right.

Then he was Fred Dawson, with a complete set of artificial memories, in the orphan asylum in Illinois.

But now he lay in the vorkyl, his nose against dusty glassocene that smelled of dead flies, and the vitiated air tore at his throat as he tried to breathe. All was in gray semidarkness around him. He sent out a frantic thought-command.

Somewhere light grew. The distant wall faded to transparency. He could see the City.

It had changed. It was older. And a heaped pile of dust made a canopy atop the vorkyl in which he rested.

The immense, red sun washed the City in bloody gloom. There was no sign of organized activity. Figures moved here and there in the ruins. He could not make out what they were doing.

He looked for the Administration Building, the last stronghold of the race. It had altered, too. A long time must have passed since he had entered the vorkyl. For ruin had touched the great tower, and the white, naked shapes that crawled up and down the structure showed no sign of intelligence. The last light had gone out, then. The tide of madness had engulfed the four thousand.

He used his seventh sense of perception, and his guess was confirmed. In all the world, there was no sanity. The herd instinct had triumphed.

And he could not breathe. That suffocating horror was a reality now. The last oxygen left in the sealed case was rapidly being absorbed by his now-active lungs. He could, of course, open the vorkyl–

To what?

Dawsao moved his hand. The control swung to the right again.

He was sitting in the psychiatrist's outer office. The receptionist was at her desk, scribbling something; she didn't look at him. The white light of morning sunshine made patterns on the rug.

The reality–

"You may go in now, Mr. Dawson."

Dawson stood up and walked into Hendricks' sanctum. He shook hands, muttered something, and sank into a chair.

Hendricks referred to his charts.

"O.K., Fred," he said. "Feel up to another word-association test? You're looking a bit better."

"Am I?" Dawson said. "Maybe I know what the symbol represents now."

Hendricks looked at him sharply. "Do you?"

"Maybe it isn't a symbol at all. Maybe it's a reality."

Then the familiar sensation came back, the dusty, suffocating claustrophobia, and the windowpane, and the brownish, dry smell, and the sense of terrible urgency. But there was nothing to be done about it now, nothing at all. He waited. In a moment it was gone again, and he looked across the desk at Hendricks, who was saying something about the danger of secondary delusions, of rationalizing.

"It's a matter of finding the right sort of therapy," insisted the hollow man.

CONSIDER HER WAYS

by John Wyndham

THERE WAS nothing but myself.

I hung in a timeless, spaceless, forceless void that was neither light, nor dark. I had entity, but no form; awareness, but no senses; mind, but no memory. I wondered, is this—this nothingness—my soul? And it seemed that I had wondered that always, and should go on wondering it forever. . . .

But, somehow, timelessness ceased. I became aware that there *was* a force: that I was being moved, and that spacelessness had, therefore, ceased, too. There was nothing to show that I moved; I knew simply that I was being drawn. I felt happy because I knew there was something or someone to whom I wanted to be drawn. I had no other wish than to turn like a compass needle, and then fall through the void. . . .

But I was disappointed. No smooth, swift fall followed. Instead, other forces fastened on me. I was pulled this way, and then that. I did not know how I knew it; there was no outside reference, no fixed point, no direction, even; yet I could feel that I was tugged hither and thither, as though against the resistance of some inner gyroscope. It was as if one force were in command of me for a time, only to weaken and lose me to a new force. Then I would seem to slide towards an unknown point, until I was arrested, and diverted upon another course. I wafted this way and that, with the sense of awareness continually growing firmer; and I wondered whether rival forces were fighting for me, good and evil, perhaps, or life and death.

The sense of pulling back and forth became more definite until I was almost jerked from one course to another. Then abruptly, the feeling of struggle finished. I had a sense of travelling faster and faster still, plunging like a wandering meteorite that had been trapped at last. . . .

"All right," said a voice. "Resuscitation was a little retarded, for some reason. Better make a note of that on her card. What's the number? Oh, only her fourth time. Yes, certainly make a note. It's all right. Here she comes!"

It was a woman's voice speaking, with a slightly unfamiliar accent. The surface I was lying on shook under me. I opened my eyes, saw the ceiling moving along above me, and let them close. Presently, another voice, again with an unfamiliar intonation, spoke to me:

"Drink this," she said.

A hand lifted my head, and a cup was pressed against my lips. After I had drunk the stuff I lay back with my eyes closed again. I dozed for a little while, and came out of it feeling stronger. For some minutes I lay looking up at the ceiling and wondering vaguely where I was. I could not recall any ceiling that was painted like this pinkish shade of cream. Then, suddenly, while I was still gazing up at the ceiling, I was shocked, just as if something had hit my mind a sharp blow. I was frighteningly aware that it was not just the pinkish ceiling that was unfamiliar—*everything* was unfamiliar. Where there should have been memories there was just a great gap. I had no idea who I was, or where I was; I could recall nothing of how or why I came to be here. . . . In a rush of panic I tried to sit up, but a hand pressed me back, and presently held the cup to my lips again.

"You're quite all right. Just relax," the same voice told me, reassuringly.

I wanted to ask questions, but somehow I felt immensely weary, and everything was too much trouble. The first rush of panic subsided, leaving me lethargic. I wondered what had happened to me—had I been in an accident, perhaps? Was this the kind of thing that happened when one was badly shocked? I did not know, and now for the moment I did not care: I was being looked after. I felt so drowsy that the questions could wait.

I suppose I dozed, and it may have been for a few minutes, or for an hour. I know only that when I opened my eyes again I felt calmer—more puzzled than alarmed—and I lay for a time without moving. I had recovered enough grasp now to console myself with the thought that if there had been an accident, at least there was no pain.

Presently I gained a little more energy, and, with it, curiosity to know where I was. I rolled my head on the pillow to see more of the surroundings.

A few feet away I saw a contrivance on wheels, something between a bed and a trolley. On it, asleep with her mouth open, was the most enormous woman I had ever seen. I stared, wondering whether it was some kind of cage over her to take the weight of the covers that gave her the mountainous look, but the movement of her breathing soon showed me that it was not. Then I looked beyond her and saw two more trolleys, both supporting equally enormous women.

I studied the nearest one more closely, and discovered to my surprise that she was quite young–not more than twenty-two, or twenty-three, I guessed. Her face was a little plump, perhaps, but by no means overfat; indeed, with her fresh, healthy young colouring and her short-cropped gold curls, she was quite pretty. I fell to wondering what curious disorder of the glands could cause such a degree of anomaly at her age.

Ten minutes or so passed, and there was a sound of brisk, businesslike footsteps approaching. A voice inquired:

"How are you feeling now?"

I rolled my head to the other side, and found myself looking into a face almost level with my own. For a moment I thought its owner must be a child, then I saw that the features under the white cap were certainly not less than thirty years old. Without waiting for a reply she reached under the bedclothes and took my pulse. Its rate appeared to satisfy her, for she nodded confidently.

"You'll be all right now, Mother," she told me.

I stared at her blankly.

"The car's only just outside the door there. Do you think you can walk to it?" she went on.

Bemusedly, I asked: "What car?"

"Why, to take you home, of course," she said, with professional patience. "Come along now." And she pulled away the bedclothes.

I started to move, and looked down. What I saw there held me fixed. I lifted my arm. It was like nothing so much as a plump, white bolster with a ridiculous little hand attached at the end. I stared at it in horror. Then I heard a far-off scream as I fainted. . . .

When I opened my eyes again there was a woman–a normal-sized woman–in a white overall with a stethoscope round her neck, frowning at me in perplexity. The white-capped woman I had taken for a child stood beside her, reaching only a little above her elbow.

"–I don't know, Doctor," she was saying. "She just suddenly screamed, and fainted."

"What is it? What's happened to me? I know I'm not like this–I'm not, I'm not," I said, and I could hear my own voice wailing the words.

The doctor went on looking puzzled.

"What does she mean?" she asked.

"I've no idea, Doctor," said the small woman. "It was quite sudden, as if she'd had some kind of shock–but I don't know why."

"Well, she's been passed and signed off, and, anyway, she can't stay here. We need the room," said the doctor. "I'd better give her a sedative."

"But what's happened? Who am I? There's something terribly wrong. I know I'm not like this. P-please t-tell me–" I implored her, and then somehow lost myself in a stammer and a muddle.

The doctor's manner became soothing. She laid a hand gently on my shoulder.

"That's all right, Mother. There's nothing to worry about. Just take things quietly. We'll soon have you back home."

Another white-capped assistant, no taller than the first, hurried up with a syringe, and handed it to the doctor.

"No!" I protested. "I want to know where I am. Who am I? Who are you? What's happened to me?" I tried to slap the syringe out of her hand, but both the small assistants flung themselves on my arm, and held on to it while she pressed in the needle.

It was a sedative, all right. It did not put me out, but it detached me. An odd feeling: I seemed to be floating a few feet outside myself and considering me with an unnatural calmness. I was able, or felt I was able, to evaluate matters with intelligent clarity. . . .

Evidently I was suffering from amnesia. A shock of some kind had caused me to "lose my memory," as it is often put. Obviously it was only a very small part of my memory that had gone–just the personal part, who I was, what I was, where I lived–all the mechanism for day-to-day getting along seemed to be intact: I'd not forgotten how to talk, or how to think, and I seemed to have quite a well-stored mind to think with.

On the other hand there was a nagging conviction that everything about me was somehow *wrong*. I *knew*, somehow, that I'd never before seen the place I was in; I *knew*, too, that there was something queer about the presence of the two small nurses; above all, I *knew*, with absolute certainty, that this massive form lying here was not mine. I could not recall what face I ought to see in a mirror, not even whether it would be dark or fair, or old or young, but there was no shadow of doubt in my mind that whatever it was like, it had never topped such a shape as I had now. And there were the other enormous young women, too. Obviously, it could not be a matter of glandular disorder in all of us, or there'd not be this talk of sending me "home," wherever that might be. . . .

I was still arguing the situation with myself in, thanks no doubt to the sedative, a most reasonable-seeming manner, though without making any progress at all, when the ceiling above my head began to move again, and I realized I was being wheeled along. Doors opened at the end of the room, and the trolley tilted a little beneath me as we went down a gentle ramp beyond.

At the foot of the ramp, an ambulancelike car, with pink coachwork polished until it gleamed, was waiting with the rear doors open. I observed interestedly that I was playing a part in a routine procedure. A team of eight diminutive attendants carried out the task of transferring me from the trolley to a sprung couch in the ambulance as if it were a kind of drill. Two of them lingered after the rest to tuck in my coverings and place another pillow behind my head. Then they got out, closing the doors behind them, and in a minute or two we started off.

It was at this point—and possibly the sedative helped in this, too—that I began to have an increasing sense of balance and a feeling that I was perceiving the situation. Probably there *had* been an accident, as I had suspected, but obviously my error, and the chief cause of my alarm, proceeded from my assumption that I was a stage farther on than I actually was. I had assumed that after an interval I had recovered consciousness in these baffling circumstances, whereas the true state of affairs must clearly be that I had *not* recovered consciousness. I must still be in a suspended state, very likely with concussion, and this was a dream, or hallucination. Presently, I should wake up in conditions that would at least be sensible, if not necessarily familiar.

I wondered now that this consoling and stabilizing thought had not occurred to me before, and decided that it was the alarming sense of detailed reality that had thrown me into panic. It had been astonishingly stupid of me to be taken in to the extent of imagining that I was really a kind of Gulliver among rather oversize Lilliputians. It was quite characteristic of most dreams, too, that I should lack a clear knowledge of my identity, so we did not need to be surprised at that. The thing to do was to take an intelligent interest in all I observed: the whole thing must be chock-full of symbolic content which it would be most interesting to work out later.

The discovery quite altered my attitude and I looked about me with a new attention. It struck me as odd right away that there was so much circumstantial detail, and all of it in focus–there was none of that sense of foreground in sharp relief against a muzzy, or even nonexistent, background that one usually meets in a dream. Everything was presented with a most convincing, three-dimensional solidity. My own sensations, too, seemed perfectly valid. The injection, in particular, had been quite acutely authentic. The illusion of reality fascinated me into taking mental notes with some care.

The interior of the van, or ambulance, or whatever it was, was finished in the same shell pink as the outside–except for the roof, which was powder blue with a scatter of small silver stars. Against the front partition were mounted several cupboards, with plated handles. My couch, or stretcher, lay along the left side; on the other were two fixed seats, rather small, and upholstered in a semi-glazed material to match the colour of the rest. Two long windows on each side left little solid wall. Each of them was provided with curtains of a fine net, gathered back now in pink braid loops, and had a roller blind furled above it. Simply by turning my head on the pillow I was able to observe the passing scenery–though somewhat jerkily, for either the springing of the vehicle scarcely matched its appointments, or the road surface was bad: whichever the cause, I was glad my own couch was independently and quite comfortably sprung.

The external view did not offer a great deal of variety save in its hues. Our way was lined by buildings standing back behind some twenty yards of tidy lawn. Each block was three storeys high, about fifty yards long, and had a tiled roof of somewhat low pitch, suggesting a vaguely Italian influence. Structurally the blocks appeared identical, but each was differently coloured, with contrasting window-frames and doors, and carefully considered, uniform curtains. I could see no one behind the windows; indeed there appeared to be no one about at all except here and there a woman in overalls mowing a lawn, or tending one of the inset flower beds.

Farther back from the road, perhaps two hundred yards away, stood larger, taller, more utilitarian-looking blocks, some of them with high, factory-type chimneys. I thought they might actually be factories of some kind, but at the distance, and because I had no more than fugitive views of them between the foreground blocks, I could not be sure.

The road itself seldom ran straight for more than a hundred yards at a stretch, and its windings made one wonder whether the builders had not been more concerned to follow a contour line than a direction. There was little other traffic, and what there was consisted of lorries, large or small, mostly large. They were painted in one primary colour or other, with only a five-fold combination of letters and figures on their sides for further identification. In design they might have been any lorries anywhere.

We continued this uneventful progress at a modest pace for some twenty minutes, until we came to a stretch where the road was under repair. The car slowed, and the workers moved to one side, out of our way. As we crawled forward over the broken surface I was able to get a good look at them. They were all women or girls dressed in denimlike trousers, sleeveless singlets, and working boots. All had their hair cut quite short, and a few wore hats. They were tall and broad-shouldered, bronzed and healthy-looking. The biceps of their arms were like a man's, and the shafts of their picks and shovels rested in the hard, strong hands of manual toilers.

They watched with concern as the car edged its way on to the rough patch, but when it drew level with them they transferred their attention, and jostled and craned to look inside at me.

They smiled widely, showing strong white teeth in their browned faces. All of them raised their right hands, making some sign to me, still smiling. Their goodwill was so evident that I smiled back. They walked along, keeping pace with the crawling car, looking at me expectantly while their smiles faded into puzzlement. They were saying something but I could not hear the words. Some of them insistently repeated the sign. Their disappointed look made it clear that I was expected to respond with more than a smile. The only way that occurred to me was to raise my own right hand in imitation of their gesture. It was at least a qualified success; their faces brightened though a rather puzzled look remained. Then the car lurched on to the made-up road again, and their still somewhat troubled faces slid back as we speeded up to our former sedate pace. More dream symbols, of course—but certainly not one of the stock symbols from the book. What on earth, I wondered, could a party of friendly Amazons, equipped with navvying implements instead of bows, stand for in my subconscious? Something frustrated, I imagined. A suppressed desire to dominate? I did not seem to be getting much farther along that line when we passed the last of the variegated but nevertheless monotonous blocks, and ran into open country.

The flower beds had shown me already that it was spring, and now I was able to look on healthy pastures, and neat arable fields already touched with green; there was a haze like green smoke along the trim hedges, and some of the trees in the tidily placed spinneys were in young leaf. The sun was shining with a bright benignity upon the most precise countryside I have ever seen; only the cattle dotted about the fields introduced a slight disorder into the careful dispositions. The farmhouses themselves were part of the pattern: hollow squares of neat buildings with an acre or so of vegetable garden on one side, an orchard on another, and a rickyard on a third. There was a suggestion of a doll's landscape about it–Grandma Moses, but tidied up and rationalized. I could see no random cottages, casually sited sheds, or unplanned outgrowths from the farm buildings. And what, I asked myself, should we conclude from this rather pathological exhibition of tidiness? That I was a more uncertain person than I had supposed, one who was subconsciously yearning for simplicity and security? Well, well. . . .

An open lorry which must have been travelling ahead of us turned off down a lane bordered by beautifully laid hedges, towards one of the farms. There were half a dozen young women in it, holding implements of some kind: Amazons, again. One of them, looking back, drew the attention of the rest to us. They raised their hands in the same sign that the others had made, and then waved cheerfully. I waved back.

Rather bewildering, I thought: Amazons for domination *and* this landscape, for passive security: the two did not seem to tie up very well.

We trundled on, at our unambitious pace of twenty miles an hour or so, for what I guessed to be three-quarters of an hour, with the prospect changing very little. The country undulated gently and appeared to continue like that to the foot of a line of low, blue hills many miles away. The tidy farmhouses went by with almost the regularity of milestones, though with something like twice the frequency. Occasionally there were working parties in the fields; more rarely, one saw individuals busy about the farm, and others hoeing with tractors, but they were all too far off for me to make out any details. Presently, however, came a change.

Off to the left of the road, stretching back at right angles to it for more than a mile, appeared a row of trees. At first I thought it just a wood, but then I noticed that the trunks were evenly spaced, and the trees themselves topped and pruned until they gave more the impression of a high fence.

The end of it came to within twenty feet of the road, where it turned, and we ran along beside it for almost half a mile until the car slowed, turned to the left and stopped in front of a pair of tall gates. There were a couple of toots on the horn.

The gates were ornamental, and possibly of wrought iron under their pink paint. The archway that they barred was stucco-covered, and painted the same colour.

Why, I inquired of myself, this prevalence of pink, which I regard as a namby-pamby colour, anyway? Flesh colour? Symbolic of an ardency for the flesh which I had insufficiently gratified? I scarcely thought so. Not pink. Surely a burning red . . . I don't think I know anyone who can be really ardent in a pink way. . . .

While we waited, a feeling that there was something wrong with the gatehouse grew upon me. The structure was a single-storey building, standing against the left, inner side of the archway, and coloured to match it. The woodwork was pale blue, and there were white net curtains at the windows. The door opened, and a middle-aged woman in a white blouse-and-trouser suit came out. She was bare-headed, with a few grey locks in her short, dark hair. Seeing me, she raised her hand in the same sign the Amazons had used, though perfunctorily, and walked over to open the gates. It was only as she pushed them back to admit us that I suddenly saw how small she was–certainly not over four feet tall. And that explained what was wrong with the gatehouse: it was built entirely to her scale. . . .

I went on staring at her and her little house as we passed. Well, what about that? Mythology is rich in gnomes and "little people," and they are fairly pervasive of dreams, too, so somebody, I am sure, must have decided that they are a standard symbol of something, but for the moment I did not recall what it was. Would it be repressed philoprogenitiveness, or was that too unsubtle? I stowed that away, too, for later contemplation and brought my attention back to the surroundings.

We were on our way, unhurriedly, along something more like a drive than a road, with surroundings that suggested a compromise between a public garden and a municipal housing estate. There were wide lawns of an unblemished velvet green, set here and there with flower beds, delicate groups of silver birch, and occasional, larger, single trees. Among them stood pink, three-storey blocks, dotted about, seemingly to no particular plan.

A couple of the Amazon types in singlets and trousers of a faded rust-red were engaged in planting out a bed close beside the drive, and we had to pause while they dragged their handcart full of tulips on to the grass to let us pass. They gave me the usual salute and amiable grin as we went by.

A moment later I had a feeling that something had gone wrong with my sight, for as we passed one block we came in sight of another. It was white instead of pink, but otherwise exactly similar to the rest—except that it was scaled down by at least one-third. . . .

I blinked at it and stared hard, but it continued to seem just the same size.

A little farther on, a grotesquely huge woman in pink draperies was walking slowly and heavily across a lawn. She was accompanied by three of the small, white-suited women looking, in contrast, like children, or very animated dolls; one was involuntarily reminded of tugs fussing round a liner.

I began to feel swamped: the proliferation and combination of symbols was getting well out of my class.

The car forked to the right, and presently we drew up before a flight of steps leading to one of the pink buildings—a normal-sized building, but still not free from oddity, for the steps were divided by a central balustrade; those to the left of it were normal, those to the right, smaller and more numerous.

Three toots on the horn announced our arrival. In about ten seconds half a dozen small women appeared in the doorway and came running down the right-hand side of the steps. A door slammed as the driver got out and went to meet them. When she came into my range of view I saw that she was one of the little ones, too, but not in white as the rest were; she wore a shining pink suit like a livery that exactly matched the car.

They had a word together before they came round to open the door behind me, then a voice said brightly: "Welcome, Mother Orchis. Welcome home."

The couch, or stretcher, slid back on runners, and between them they lowered it to the ground. One young woman whose blouse was badged with a pink St. Andrew's cross on the left breast leaned over me. She inquired considerately: "Do you think you can walk, Mother?"

It did not seem the moment to inquire into the form of address. I was obviously the only possible target for the question.

"Walk?" I repeated. "Of course I can walk." And I sat up, with about eight hands assisting me.

"Of course" had been an overstatement. I realized that by the time I had been heaved to my feet. Even with all the help that was going on around me it was an exertion which brought on heavy breathing. I looked down at the monstrous form that billowed under my pink draperies, with sickly revulsion and a feeling that whatever this particular mass of symbolism disguised, it was likely to prove a distasteful revelation later on. I tried a step. "Walk" was scarcely the word for my progress. It felt like, and must have looked like, a slow series of forward surges. The women, at little more than my elbow height, fluttered about me like a flock of anxious hens. Once started, I was determined to go on, and I progressed with a kind of wave-motion, first across a few yards of gravel, and then, with ponderous deliberation, up the left-hand side of the steps.

There was a perceptible sense of relief and triumph all round as I reached the summit. We paused there a few moments for me to regain my breath, then we moved on into the building. A corridor led straight ahead, with three or four closed doors on each side; at the end it branched right and left. We took the left arm, and, at the end of it, I came face to face, for the first time since the hallucination had set in, with a mirror.

It took every volt of my resolution not to panic again at what I saw in it. The first few seconds of my stare were spent in fighting down a leaping hysteria.

In front of me stood an outrageous travesty: an elephantine female form, looking the more huge for its pink swathings. Mercifully, they covered everything but the head and hands, but these exposures were themselves another kind of shock, for the hands, though soft and dimpled and looking utterly out of proportion, were not uncomely, and the head and face were those of a girl.

She was pretty, too. She could not have been more than twenty-one, if that. Her curling fair hair was touched with auburn lights, and cut in a kind of bob. The complexion of her face was pink and cream, her mouth was gentle, and red without any artifice. She looked back at me, and at the little women anxiously clustering round me, from a pair of blue-green eyes beneath lightly arched brows. And this delicate face, this little Fragonard, was set upon that monstrous body: no less outrageously might a blossom of freesia sprout from a turnip.

When I moved my lips, hers moved; when I bent my arm, hers bent; and yet, once I got the better of that threatening panic, she ceased to be a reflection. She was nothing like me, so she must be a stranger whom I was observing, though in a most bewildering way. My panic and revulsion gave way to sadness, an aching pity for her.

I could weep for the shame of it. I did. I watched the tears brim over on her lower lids; mistily, I saw them overflow.

One of the little women beside me caught hold of my hand. "Mother Orchis, dear, what's the matter?" she asked, full of concern.

I could not tell her: I had no clear idea myself. The image in the mirror shook her head, with tears running down her cheeks. Small hands patted me here and there; small, soothing voices encouraged me onward. The next door was opened for me and I was led into the room beyond, amid concerned fussing.

We entered a place that struck me as a cross between a boudoir and a ward. The boudoir impression was sustained by a great deal of pink—in the carpet, coverlets, cushions, lampshades, and filmy window curtains; the ward motif, by an array of six divans, or couches, one of which was unoccupied.

It was a large enough room for three couches, separated by a chest, chair and table for each, to be arranged on either side without an effect of crowding, and the open space in the middle was still big enough to contain several expansive easy chairs and a central table bearing an intricate flower arrangement. A not displeasing scent faintly pervaded the place, and from somewhere came the subdued sound of a string quartet in a sentimental mood. Five of the bed-couches were already mountainously occupied. Two of my attendant party detached themselves and hurried ahead to turn back the pink satin cover on the sixth.

Faces from all the five other beds were turned towards me. Three of them smiling in welcome, the other two less committal.

"Hallo, Orchis," one of them greeted me in a friendly tone. Then, with a touch of concern she added: "What's the matter, dear? Did you have a bad time?"

I looked at her. She had a kindly, plumply pretty face, framed by light-brown hair as she lay back against a cushion. The face looked about twenty-three or twenty-four years old. The rest of her was a huge mound of pink satin. I couldn't make any reply, but I did my best to return her smile as we passed.

Our convoy hove to by the empty bed. After some preparation and positioning I was helped into it by all hands, and a cushion was arranged behind my head.

The exertion of my journey from the car had been considerable, and I was thankful to relax. While two of the little women pulled up the coverlet and arranged it over me, another produced a handkerchief and dabbed gently at my cheeks. She encouraged me:

"There you are, dear. Safely home again now. You'll be quite all right when you've rested a bit. Just try to sleep for a little."

"What's the matter with her?" inquired a forthright voice from one of the other beds. "Did she make a mess of it?"

The little woman with the handkerchief–she was the one who wore the St. Andrew's cross and appeared to be in charge of the operation–turned her head sharply.

"There's no need for that tone, Mother Hazel. Of course Mother Orchis had four beautiful babies–didn't you, dear?" she added to me. "She's just a bit tired after the journey, that's all."

"H'mph," said the girl addressed, in an unaccommodating tone, but she made no further comment.

A degree of fussing continued. Presently the small woman handed me a glass of something that looked like water, but had unsuspected strength. I spluttered a little at the first taste, but quickly felt the better for it. After a little more tidying and ordering, my retinue departed leaving me propped against my cushion, with the eyes of the five other monstrous women dwelling upon me speculatively.

An awkward silence was broken by the girl who had greeted me as I came in.

"Where did they send you for your holiday, Orchis?"

"Holiday?" I asked blankly.

She and the rest stared at me in astonishment.

"I don't know what you're talking about," I told them.

They went on staring, stupidly, stolidly.

"It can't have been much of a holiday," observed one, obviously puzzled. "I'll not forget my last one. They sent me to the sea, and gave me a little car so that I could get about everywhere. Everybody was lovely to us, and there were only six Mothers there, including me. Did you go by the sea, or in the mountains?"

They were determined to be inquisitive, and one would have to make some answer sooner or later. I chose what seemed the simplest way out for the moment.

"I can't remember," I said. "I can't remember a thing. I seem to have lost my memory altogether."

That was not very sympathetically received, either.

"Oh," said the one who had been addressed as Hazel, with a degree of satisfaction. "I thought there was something. And I suppose you can't even remember for certain whether your babies were Grade One this time, Orchis?"

"Don't be stupid, Hazel," one of the others told her. "Of course they were Grade One. If they'd not been, Orchis wouldn't be back here now–she'd have been re-rated as a Class Two Mother, and sent to Whitewich." In a more kindly tone she asked me: "When did it happen, Orchis?"

"I–I don't know," I said. "I can't remember anything before this morning at the hospital. It's all gone entirely."

"Hospital!" repeated Hazel, scornfully.

"She must mean the Centre," said the other. "But do you mean to say you can't even remember *us,* Orchis?"

"No," I admitted, shaking my head. "I'm sorry, but everything before I came round in the Hosp–in the Centre is all blank."

"That's queer," Hazel said, in an unsympathetic tone. "Do they know?"

One of the others took my part.

"Of course they're bound to know. I expect they don't think that remembering or not has anything to do with having Grade One babies. And why should it, anyway? But look, Orchis–"

"Why not let her rest for a bit," another cut in. "I don't suppose she's feeling too good after the Centre, and the journey, and getting in here. I never do myself. Don't take any notice of them, Orchis, dear. You just go to sleep for a bit. You'll probably find it's quite all right when you wake up."

I accepted her suggestion gratefully. The whole thing was far too bewildering to cope with at the moment; moreover, I did feel exhausted. I thanked her for her advice, and lay back on my pillow. In so far as the closing of one's eyes can be made ostentatious, I made it so. What was more surprising was that, if one can be said to sleep within an hallucination or a dream, I slept. . . .

In the moment of waking, before opening my eyes, I had a flash of hope that I should find the illusion had spent itself. Unfortunately, it had not. A hand was shaking my shoulder gently, and the first thing that I saw was the face of the little women's leader, close to mine.

In the way of nurses, she said: "There, Mother Orchis, dear. You'll be feeling a lot better after that nice sleep, won't you?"

Beyond her, two more of the small women were carrying a short-legged bed tray towards me. They set it down so that it bridged me, and was convenient to reach. I stared at the load on it. It was, with no exception, the most enormous and nourishing meal I had ever seen put before one person. The first sight of it revolted me–but then I became aware of a schism within, for it did not revolt the physical form that I occupied: that, in fact, had a watering mouth, and was eager to begin. An inner part of me marvelled in a kind of semi-detachment while the rest consumed two or three fish, a whole chicken, some slices of meat, a pile of vegetables, fruit hidden under mounds of stiff cream, and more than a quart of milk, without any sense of surfeit. Occasional glances showed me that the other "Mothers" were dealing just as thoroughly with the contents of their similar trays.

I caught one or two curious looks from them, but they were too seriously occupied to take up their inquisition again at the moment. I wondered how to fend them off later, and it occurred to me that if only I had a book or a magazine I might be able to bury myself effectively, if not very politely, in it.

When the attendants returned I asked the badged one if she could let me have something to read. The effect of such a simple request was astonishing: the two who were removing my tray all but dropped it. The one beside me gaped for an amazed moment before she collected her wits. She looked at me, first with suspicion, and then with concern.

"Not feeling quite yourself yet, dear?" she suggested.

"But I am," I protested. "I'm quite all right now."

The look of concern persisted, however.

"If I were you I'd try to sleep again," she advised.

"But I don't want to. I'd just like to read quietly," I objected.

She patted my shoulder, a little uncertainly.

"I'm afraid you've had an exhausting time, Mother. Never mind. I'm sure it'll pass quite soon."

I felt impatient. "What's wrong with wanting to read?" I demanded.

She smiled a smug, professional-nurse smile.

"There, there, dear. Just you try to rest a little more. Why, bless me, what on earth would a Mother want with knowing how to read?"

With that she tidied my coverlet, and bustled away, leaving me to the wide-eyed stares of my five companions. Hazel gave a kind of contemptuous snigger; otherwise there was no audible comment for several minutes.

I had reached a stage where the persistence of the hallucination was beginning to wear away my detachment. I could feel that under a little more pressure I should be losing my confidence and starting to doubt its unreality. I did not at all care for its calm continuity.

Inconsequent exaggerations and jumps, foolish perspectives, indeed any of the usual dream characteristics would have been reassuring, but, instead, it continued to present obvious nonsense, with an alarming air of conviction and consequence. Effects, for instance, were unmistakably following causes. I began to have an uncomfortable feeling that were one to dig deep enough one might begin to find logical causes for the absurdities, too. The integration was far too good for mental comfort—even the fact that I had enjoyed my meal as if I were fully awake, and was consciously feeling the better for it, encouraged the disturbing quality of reality.

"Read!" Hazel said suddenly, with a scornful laugh. "And write, too, I suppose?"

"Well, why not?" I retorted.

They all gazed at me more attentively than ever, and then exchanged meaning glances among themselves. Two of them smiled at one another. I demanded irritably: "What on earth's wrong with that? Am I supposed not to be able to read or write, or something?"

One said kindly, soothingly: "Orchis, dear. Don't you think it would be better if you were to ask to see the doctor? Just for a checkup?"

"No," I told her flatly. "There's nothing wrong with me. I'm just trying to understand. I simply ask for a book, and you all look at me as if I were mad. Why?"

After an awkward pause the same one said humouringly, and almost in the words of the little attendant: "Orchis, dear, do try to pull yourself together. What sort of good would reading and writing be to a Mother? How could they help her to have better babies?"

"There are other things in life besides having babies," I said, shortly.

If they had been surprised before, they were thunderstruck now. Even Hazel seemed bereft of suitable comment. Their idiotic astonishment exasperated me and made me suddenly sick of the whole nonsensical business. Temporarily, I *did* forget to be the detached observer of a dream.

"Damn it," I broke out. "What *is* all this rubbish? Orchis! Mother Orchis!—for God's sake! Where am I? Is this some kind of lunatic asylum?"

I stared at them, angrily, loathing the sight of them, wondering if they were all in some spiteful complicity against me. Somehow I was quite convinced in my own mind that whoever, or whatever, I was, I was not a mother. I said so, forcibly, and then, to my annoyance, burst into tears.

For lack of anything else to use, I dabbed at my eyes with my sleeve. When I could see clearly again I found that four of them were looking at me with kindly concern. Hazel, however, was not.

"I said there was something queer about her," she told the others, triumphantly. "She's mad, that's what it is."

The one who had been most kindly disposed before, tried again: "But, Orchis, *of course* you are a Mother. You're a Class One Mother—with three births registered. Twelve fine Grade One babies, dear. You *can't* have forgotten that!"

For some reason I wept again. I had a feeling that something was trying to break through the blankness in my mind; but I did not know what it was, only that it made me feel intensely miserable.

"Oh, this is cruel, cruel! Why can't I stop it? Why won't it go away and leave me?" I pleaded. "There's a horrible cruel mockery here—but I don't understand it. What's wrong with me? I'm not obsessional—I'm not—I—oh, can't somebody help me . . . ?"

I kept my eyes tight shut for a time, willing with all my mind that the whole hallucination should fade and disappear.

But it did not. When I looked again they were still there, their silly, pretty faces gaping stupidly at me across the revolting mounds of pink satin.

"I'm getting out of this," I said.

It was a tremendous effort to raise myself to a sitting position. I was aware of the rest watching me, wide-eyed, while I made it. I struggled to get my feet round and over the side of the bed, but they were all tangled in the satin coverlet and I could not reach to free them. It was the true, desperate frustration of a dream. I heard my voice pleading: "Help me! Oh, Donald, darling, please help me. . . ."

And suddenly, as if the word "Donald" had released a spring, something seemed to click in my head. The shutter in my mind opened, not entirely, but enough to let me know who I was. I understood, suddenly, where the cruelty had lain.

I looked at the others again. They were still staring half bewildered, half alarmed. I gave up the attempt to move, and lay back on my pillow again.

"You can't fool me any more," I told them. "I know who I am now."

"But, Mother Orchis—" one began.

"Stop that," I snapped at her. I seemed to have swung suddenly out of self-pity into a kind of masochistic callousness. "I am *not* a mother," I said harshly. "I am just a woman who, for a short time, had a husband, and who hoped—but only hoped—that she would have babies by him."

A pause followed that; a rather odd pause, where there should have been at least a murmur. What I had said did not seem to have registered. The faces showed no understanding; they were as uncomprehending as dolls.

Presently, the most friendly one seemed to feel an obligation to break up the silence. With a little vertical crease between her brows: "What," she inquired tentatively, "what is a husband?"

I looked hard from one face to another. There was no trace of guile in any of them; nothing but puzzled speculation such as one sometimes sees in a child's eyes. I felt close to hysteria for a moment; then I took a grip of myself. Very well, then, since the hallucination would not leave me alone, I would play it at its own game, and see what came of that. I began to explain with a kind of dead-pan, simple-word seriousness:

"A husband is a man whom a woman takes. . . ."

Evidently, from their expressions I was not very enlightening. However, they let me go on for three or four sentences without interruption. Then, when I paused for breath, the kindly one chipped in with a point which she evidently felt needed clearing up:

"But what," she asked, in evident perplexity, "what is a man?"

A cool silence hung over the room after my exposition. I had an impression I had been sent to Coventry, or semi-Coventry, by them, but I did not bother to test it. I was too much occupied trying to force the door of my memory further open, and finding that beyond a certain point it would not budge.

I knew now that I was Jane. I had been Jane Summers, and had become Jane Waterleigh when I had married Donald.

I was—had been—twenty-four when we were married; just twenty-five when Donald was killed, six months later. And there it stopped. It seemed like yesterday, but I couldn't tell. . . .

Before that, everything was perfectly clear. My parents and friends, my home, my school, my training, my job, as Dr. Summers, at the Wraychester Hospital. I could remember my first sight of Donald when they brought him in one evening with a broken leg—and all that followed. . . .

I could remember now the face that I ought to see in a looking-glass—and it was certainly nothing like that I had seen in the corridor outside—it should be more oval, with a complexion looking faintly sun-tanned; with a smaller, neater mouth; surrounded by chestnut hair that curled naturally; with brown eyes rather wide apart and perhaps a little grave as a rule.

I knew, too, how the rest of me should look—slender, long-legged, with small, firm breasts—a nice body, but one that I had simply taken for granted until Donald gave me pride in it by loving it. . . .

I looked down at the repulsive mound of pink satin, and shuddered. A sense of outrage came welling up. I longed for Donald to comfort and pet me and love me and tell me it would be all right; that I wasn't as I was seeing myself at all, and that it *really was* a dream. At the same time I was stricken with horror at the thought that he should ever see me gross and obese like this. And then I remembered that Donald would never see me again at all—never any more—and I was wretched and miserable, and the tears trickled down my cheeks again.

The five others just went on looking at me, wide-eyed and wondering. Half an hour passed, still in silence, then the door opened to admit a whole troop of the little women, all in white suits. I saw Hazel look at me, and then at the leader. She seemed about to speak, and then to change her mind. The little women split up, two to a couch. Standing one on each side, they stripped away the coverlet, rolled up their sleeves, and set to work at massage.

At first it was not unpleasant, and quite soothing. One lay back and relaxed. Presently, however, I liked it less; soon I found it offensive.

"Stop that!" I told the one on the right, sharply.

She paused, smiled at me amiably, though a trifle uncertainly, and then continued.

"I said stop it," I told her, pushing her away.

Her eyes met mine. They were troubled and hurt, although a professional smile still curved her mouth.

"I mean it," I added, curtly.

She continued to hesitate, and glanced across at her partner on the farther side of the bed.

"You, too," I told the other. "That'll do."

She did not even pause in her rhythm. The one on the right plucked a decision and returned. She restarted just what I had stopped. I reached out and pushed her, harder this time. There must have been a lot more muscle in that bolster of an arm than one would have supposed. The shove carried her half across the room, and she tripped and fell.

All movement in the room suddenly ceased. Everybody stared, first at her, and then at me. The pause was brief. They all set to work again. I pushed away the girl on the left, too, though more gently. The other one picked herself up. She was crying and she looked frightened, but she set her jaw doggedly and started to come back.

"You keep away from me, you little horrors," I told them threateningly.

That checked them. They stood off, and looked miserably at one another. The one with the badge of seniority fussed up.

"What's the trouble, Mother Orchis?" she inquired.

I told her. She looked puzzled.

"But that's quite right," she expostulated.

"Not for me. I don't like it, and I won't have it," I replied.

She stood awkwardly, at a loss.

Hazel's voice came from the other side of the room:

"Orchis is off her head. She's been telling us the most disgusting things. She's quite mad."

The little woman turned to regard her, and then looked inquiringly at one of the others. When a girl confirmed with a nod and an expression of distaste she turned back to me, giving me a searching inspection.

"You two go and report," she told my discomfited masseuses.

They were both crying now, and they went wretchedly down the room together. The one in charge gave me another thoughtful look, and then followed them.

A few minutes later all the rest had packed up and gone. The six of us were alone again. It was Hazel who broke the ensuing silence.

"That was a bitchy piece of work. The poor little devils were only doing their job," she observed.

"If that's their job, I don't like it," I told her.

"So you just get them a beating, poor things. But I suppose that's the lost memory again. You wouldn't remember that a Servitor who upsets a Mother is beaten, would you?" she added sarcastically.

"Beaten?" I repeated, uneasily.

"Yes, beaten," she mimicked. "But you don't care what becomes of them, do you? I don't know what's happened to you while you were away, but whatever it was it seems to have produced a thoroughly nasty result. I never did care for you, Orchis, though the others thought I was wrong. Well, now we all know."

None of the rest offered any comment. The feeling that they shared her opinion was strong, but luckily I was spared confirmation by the opening of the door.

The senior attendant re-entered with half a dozen small myrmidons, but this time the group was dominated by a handsome woman of about thirty. Her appearance gave me immense relief. She was neither little, nor Amazonian, nor was she huge. Her present company made her look a little overtall, perhaps, but I judged her at about five foot ten; a normal, pleasant-featured young woman with brown hair, cut somewhat short, and a pleated black skirt showing beneath a white overall. The senior attendant was almost trotting to keep up with her longer steps, and was saying something about delusions and "only back from the Centre today, Doctor."

The woman stopped beside my couch while the smaller women huddled together, looking at me with some misgiving. She thrust a thermometer into my mouth and held my wrist. Satisfied on both these counts, she inquired:

"Headache? Any other aches or pains?"

"No," I told her.

She regarded me carefully. I looked back at her.

"What–?" she began.

"She's mad," Hazel put in from the other side of the room. "She says she's lost her memory and doesn't know us."

"She's been talking about horrid, disgusting things," added one of the others.

"She's got delusions. She thinks she can read and write," Hazel supplemented.

The doctor smiled at that.

"Do you?" she asked me.

"I don't see why not–but it should be easy enough to prove," I replied brusquely.

She looked startled, a little taken aback, then she recovered her tolerant half-smile.

"All right," she said, humouring me.

She pulled a small note-pad out of her pocket and offered it to me, with a pencil. The pencil felt a little odd in my hand; the fingers did not fall into place readily on it, nevertheless I wrote:

"I'm only too well aware that I have delusions–and that you are part of them."

Hazel tittered as I handed the pad back.

The doctor's jaw did not actually drop, but her smile came right off. She looked at me very hard indeed. The rest of the room, seeing her expression, went quiet, as though I had performed some startling feat of magic. The doctor turned towards Hazel.

"What sort of things has she been telling you?" she inquired.

Hazel hesitated, then she blurted out:

"Horrible things. She's been talking about two human sexes–just as if we were like the animals. It was disgusting!"

The doctor considered a moment, then she told the senior attendant:

"Better get her along to the sick bay. I'll examine her there."

As she walked off there was a rush of little women to fetch a low trolley from the corner to the side of my couch. A dozen hands assisted me on to it, and then wheeled me briskly away.

"Now," said the doctor grimly, "let's get down to it. Who told you all this stuff about two human sexes? I want her name."

We were alone in a small room with a gold-dotted pink wallpaper. The attendants, after transferring me from the trolley to a couch again, had taken themselves off. The doctor was sitting with a pad on her knee and a pencil at the ready. Her manner was that of an unbluffable inquisitor.

I was not feeling tactful. I told her not to be a fool.

She looked staggered, flushed with anger for a moment, and then took a hold on herself. She went on:

"After you left the Clinic you had your holiday, of course. Now, where did they send you?"

"I don't know," I replied. "All I can tell you is what I told the others–that this hallucination, or delusion, or whatever it is, started in that hospital place you call the Centre."

With resolute patience she said:

"Look here, Orchis. You were perfectly normal when you left here six weeks ago. You went to the Clinic and had your babies in the ordinary way. *But* between then and now somebody has been filling your head with all this rubbish–and teaching you to read and write as well. Now you are going to tell me who that somebody was. I warn you that you won't get away with this loss of memory nonsense with me. If you are able to remember this nauseating stuff you told the others, then you're able to remember where you got it from."

"Oh, for heaven's sake talk sense," I told her.

She flushed again.

"I can find out from the Clinic where they sent you, and I can find out from the Rest Home who were your chief associates while you were there, but I don't want to waste time following up all your contacts, so I'm asking you to save trouble by telling me now. You might just as well. We don't want to have to *make* you talk," she concluded, ominously.

I shook my head.

"You're on the wrong track. As far as I am concerned this whole hallucination, including my connection with this Orchis, began somehow at the Centre–how it happened I can't tell you, and what happened to her before that just isn't there to be remembered."

She frowned, obviously disturbed.

"What hallucination?" she inquired, carefully.

"Why, this fantastic setup–and you, too." I waved my hand to include it all. "This revolting great body, all those little women, everything. Obviously it is all some projection of the subconscious–and the state of my subconscious is worrying me, for it's certainly no wish-fulfilment."

She went on staring at me, more worried now.

"Who on earth has been telling you about the subconscious and wish-fulfilments?" she asked, uncertainly.

"I don't see why, even in an hallucination, I am expected to be an illiterate moron," I replied.

"But a Mother doesn't know anything about such things. She doesn't need to."

"Listen," I said. "I've told you, as I've told those poor grotesques in the other room, that I am *not* a Mother. What I am is just an unfortunate M.B. who is having some kind of nightmare."

"M.B.?" she inquired, vaguely.

"Bachelor of Medicine. I practise medicine," I told her.

She went on looking at me curiously. Her eyes wandered over my mountainous form, uncertainly.

"You are claiming to be a doctor?" she said, in an odd voice.

"Colloquially–yes," I agreed.

There was indignation mixed with bewilderment as she protested: "But this is sheer nonsense! You were brought up and developed to be a Mother. You *are* a Mother. Just look at you!"

"Yes," I said bitterly. "Just look at me!"

There was a pause.

"It seems to me," I suggested at last, "that, hallucination or not, we shan't get much farther simply by going on accusing one another of talking nonsense. Suppose you explain to me what this place is, and who you think I am. It might jog my memory."

She countered that. "Suppose," she said, "that first you tell me what you *can* remember. It would give me more idea of what is puzzling you."

"Very well," I agreed, and launched upon a potted history of myself as far as I could recollect it–up to the time, that is to say, when Donald's aircraft crashed.

It was foolish of me to fall for that one. Of course, she had no intention of telling me anything. When she had listened to all I had to say, she went away, leaving me impotently furious.

I waited until the place quietened down. The music had been switched off. An attendant had looked in to inquire, with an air of polishing off the day's duties, whether there was anything I wanted, and presently there was nothing to be heard. I let a margin of half an hour elapse, and then struggled to get up–taking it by very easy stages this time. The greatest part of the effort was to get on to my feet from a sitting position, but I managed it at the cost of heavy breathing. Presently I crossed to the door, and found it unfastened. I held it a little open, listening. There was no sound of movement in the corridor, so I pulled it wide open, and set out to discover what I could about the place. All the doors of the rooms were shut. Putting my ear close to them I could hear regular, heavy breathing behind some but there were no other sounds in the stillness. I kept on, turning several corners, until I recognized the front door ahead of me. I tried the latch, and found that it was neither barred nor bolted. I paused again, listened for some moments, and then pulled it open and stepped outside.

The parklike garden stretched out before me, sharp-shadowed in the moonlight. Through the trees to the right was a glint of water, to the left was a house similar to the one behind me, with not a light showing in any of its windows.

I wondered what to do next. Trapped in this huge carcass, all but helpless in it, there was very little I could do, but I decided to go on and at least find out what I could while I had the chance. I went forward to the edge of the steps that I had earlier climbed from the ambulance, and started down them cautiously, holding on to the balustrade.

"Mother," said a sharp, incisive voice behind me. "What are you doing?"

I turned and saw one of the little women, her white suit gleaming in the moonlight. She was alone. I made no reply, but took another step down. I could have wept at the outrage of the heavy, ungainly body, and the caution it imposed on me.

"Come back. Come back at once," she told me.

I took no notice. She came pattering down after me and laid hold of my draperies.

"Mother," she said again. "You must come back. You'll catch cold out here."

I started to take another step, and she pulled at the draperies to hold me back. I leant forward against the pull. There was a sharp tearing sound as the material gave. I swung round, and lost my balance. The last thing I saw was the rest of the flight of steps coming up to meet me. . . .

As I opened my eyes a voice said:

"That's better, but it was very naughty of you, Mother Orchis. And lucky it wasn't a lot worse. Such a silly thing to do. I'm ashamed of you–really I am."

My head was aching, and I was exasperated to find that the whole stupid business was still going on; altogether, I was in no mood for reproachful drip. I told her to go to hell. Her small face goggled at me for a moment, and then became icily prim. She applied a piece of lint and plaster to the left side of my forehead, in silence, and then departed, stiffly.

Reluctantly, I had to admit to myself that she was perfectly right. What on earth had I been expecting to do–what on earth *could* I do, encumbered by this horrible mass of flesh? A great surge of loathing for it and a feeling of helpless frustration brought me to the verge of tears again. I longed for my own nice, slim body that pleased me and did what I asked of it. I remembered how Donald had once pointed to a young tree swaying in the wind, and introduced it to me as my twin sister. And only a day or two ago. . . .

Then, suddenly, I made a discovery which brought me struggling to sit up. The blank part of my mind had filled up. I could remember everything. . . . The effort made my head throb, so I relaxed and lay back once more, recalling it all, right up to the point where the needle was withdrawn and someone swabbed my arm. . . .

But what had happened after that? Dreams and hallucinations I had expected . . . but not the sharp-focused, detailed sense of reality . . . not this state which was like a nightmare made solid. . . .

What, what in heaven's name, had they done to me . . . ?

I must have fallen asleep again, for when I opened my eyes there was daylight outside, and a covey of little women had arrived to attend to my toilet.

They spread their sheets dexterously and rolled me this way and that with expert technique as they cleaned me up. I suffered their industry patiently, feeling the fresher for it, and glad to discover that the headache had all but gone.

When we were almost at the end of our ablutions there came a peremptory knock, and without invitation two figures, dressed in black uniforms with silver buttons, entered. They were the Amazon type, tall, broad, well set up, and handsome. The little women dropped everything and fled with squeaks of dismay into the far corner of the room where they cowered in a huddle.

The two gave me the familiar salute. With an odd mixture of decision and deference one of them inquired:

"You are Orchis–Mother Orchis?"

"That's what they're calling me," I admitted.

The girl hesitated, then, in a tone rather more pleading than ordering, she said:

"I have orders for your arrest, Mother. You will please come with us."

An excited, incredulous twittering broke out among the little women in the corner. The uniformed girl quelled them with a look.

"Get the Mother dressed and make her ready," she commanded.

The little women came out of their corner hesitantly, directing nervous, propitiatory glances toward the pair. The second one told them briskly, though not altogether unkindly:

"Come along now. Jump to it."

They jumped.

I was almost swathed in my pink draperies again when the doctor strode in. She frowned at the two in uniform.

"What's all this? What are you doing here?" she demanded.

The leader of the two explained.

"Arrest!" exclaimed the doctor. "Arrest a Mother! I never heard such nonsense. What's the charge?"

The uniformed girl said, a little sheepishly:

"She is accused of Reactionism."

The doctor simply stared at her.

"A Reactionist Mother! What'll you people think of next? Go on, get out, both of you."

The young woman protested:

"We have our orders, Doctor."

"Rubbish. There's no authority. Have you ever heard of a Mother being arrested?"

"No, Doctor."

"Well, you aren't going to make a precedent now. Go on."

The uniformed girl hesitated unhappily, then an idea occurred to her.

"If you would let me have a signed refusal to surrender the Mother . . . ?" she suggested helpfully.

When the two had departed, quite satisfied with their piece of paper, the doctor looked at the little women gloomily.

"You can't help tattling, you servitors, can you? Anything you happen to hear goes through the lot of you like a fire in a cornfield, and makes trouble all round. Well, if I hear any more of this I shall know where it comes from." She turned to me. "And you, Mother Orchis, will in future please restrict yourself to yes-and-no in the hearing of these nattering little pests. I'll see you again shortly. We want to ask you some questions," she added, and went out, leaving a subdued, industrious silence behind her.

She returned just as the tray which held my gargantuan breakfast was being removed, and not alone. The four women who accompanied her, and looked as normal as herself, were followed by a number of little women lugging in chairs which they arranged beside my couch. When they had departed, the five women, all in white overalls, sat down and regarded me as if I were an exhibit. One appeared to be much the same age as the first doctor, two nearer fifty, and one sixty, or more.

"Now, Mother Orchis," said the doctor, with an air of opening the proceedings, "it is quite clear that something highly unusual has taken place. Naturally we are interested to understand just what and, if possible, why. You don't need to worry about those police this morning–it was quite improper of them to come here at all. This is simply an inquiry–a scientific inquiry–to establish what has happened."

"You can't want to understand more than I do," I replied. I looked at them, at the room about me, and finally at my massive prone form. "I am aware that all this must be an hallucination, but what is troubling me most is that I have always supposed that any hallucination must be deficient in at least one dimension–must lack reality to some of the senses. But this does not. I have all my senses, and can use them. Nothing is insubstantial: I am trapped in flesh that is very palpably too, too solid. The only striking deficiency, so far as I can see, is reason–even symbolic reason."

The four other women stared at me in astonishment. The doctor gave them a sort of now-perhaps-you'll-believe-me glance, and then turned to me again.

"We'll start with a few questions," she said.

"Before you begin," I put in, "I have something to add to what I told you last night. It has come back to me."

"Perhaps the knock when you fell," she suggested, looking at my piece of plaster. "What were you trying to do?"

I ignored that. "I think I'd better tell you the missing part–it might help–a bit, anyway."

"Very well," she agreed. "You told me you were–er–married, and that your–er–husband was killed soon afterwards." She glanced at the others; their blankness of expression was somehow studious. "It was the part after that that was missing," she added.

"Yes," I said. "He was a test pilot," I explained to them. "It happened six months after we were married–only one month before his contract was due to expire.

"After that, an aunt took me away for some weeks. I don't suppose I'll ever remember that part very well–I–I wasn't noticing anything very much. . . .

"But then I remember waking up one morning and suddenly seeing things differently, and telling myself that I couldn't go on like that. I knew I must have some work, something that would keep me busy.

"Dr. Hellyer, who is in charge of the Wraychester Hospital where I was working before I married, told me that he would be glad to have me with them again. So I went back, and worked very hard, so that I did not have much time to think. That would be about eight months ago, now.

"Then one day Dr. Hellyer spoke about a drug that a friend of his had succeeded in synthesizing. I don't think he was really asking for volunteers, but I offered to try it out. From what he said it sounded as if the drug might have some quite important properties. It struck me as a chance to do something useful. Sooner or later, someone would try it, and as I didn't have any ties and didn't care very much what happened, anyway, I thought I might as well be the one to try it."

The spokesman doctor interrupted to ask:

"What was this drug?"

"It's called chuinjuatin," I told her. "Do you know it?"

She shook her head. One of the others put in:

"I've heard the name. What is it?"

"It's a narcotic," I told her. "The original form is in the leaves of a tree that grows chiefly in the south of Venezuela. The tribe of Indians who live there discovered it somehow, like others did quinine and mescalin. And in much the same way they use it for orgies. Some of them sit and chew the leaves—they have to chew about six ounces of them—and gradually they go into a zombielike, trance state. It lasts three or four days during which they are quite helpless and incapable of doing the simplest thing for themselves, so that other members of the tribe are appointed to look after them as if they were children, and to guard them.

"It's necessary to guard them because the Indian belief is that chuinjuatin liberates the spirit from the body, setting it free to wander anywhere in space and time, and the guardian's most important job is to see that no other wandering spirit shall slip into the body while the true owner is away. When the subjects recover they claim to have had wonderful mystical experiences. There seem to be no physical ill effects, and no craving results from it. The mystical experiences, though, are said to be intense, and clearly remembered.

"Dr. Hellyer's friend had tested his synthesized chuinjuatin on a number of laboratory animals and worked out the dosage, and tolerances, and that kind of thing, but what he could not tell, of course, was what validity, if any, the reports of the mystical experiences had. Presumably they were the product of the drug's influence on the nervous system—but whether that effect produced a sensation of pleasure, ecstasy, awe, fear, horror, or any of a dozen more, it was impossible to tell without a human guinea pig. So that was what I volunteered for."

I stopped. I looked at their serious, puzzled faces, and at the billow of pink satin in front of me.

"In fact," I added, "it appears to have produced a combination of the absurd, the incomprehensible, and the grotesque."

They were earnest women, these, not to be sidetracked. They were there to disprove an anomaly—if they could.

"I see," said the spokeswoman with an air of preserving reasonableness, rather than meaning anything. She glanced down at a paper on which she had made a note from time to time.

"Now, can you give us the time and date at which this experiment took place?"

I could, and did, and after that the questions went on and on and on. . . .

The least satisfactory part of it from my point of view was that even though my answers caused them to grow more uncertain of themselves as we went on, they did at least get them; whereas when I put a question it was usually evaded, or answered perfunctorily, as an unimportant digression.

They went on steadily, and only broke off when my next meal arrived. Then they went away, leaving me thankfully in peace—but little the wiser. I half expected them to return, but when they did not I fell into a doze from which I was awakened by the incursion of a cluster of the little women, once more. They brought a trolley with them, and in a short time were wheeling me out of the building on it —but not by the way I had arrived. This time we went down a ramp where another, or the same, pink ambulance waited at the bottom. When they had me safely loaded aboard, three of them climbed in, too, to keep me company. They were chattering as they did so, and they kept it up inconsequently, and mostly incomprehensibly, for the whole hour and a half of the journey that ensued.

The countryside differed little from what I had already seen. Once we were outside the gates there were the same tidy fields and standardized farms. The occasional built-up areas were not extensive and consisted of the same types of blocks close by, and we ran on the same, not very good, road surfaces. There were groups of the Amazon types, and, more rarely, individuals, to be seen at work in the fields; the sparse traffic was lorries, large or small, and occasional buses, but with never a private car to be seen. My illusion, I reflected, was remarkably consistent in its details. Not a single group of Amazons, for instance, failed to raise its right hands in friendly, respectful greeting to the pink car.

Once, we crossed a cutting. Looking down from the bridge I thought at first that we were over the dried bed of a canal, but then I noticed a post leaning at a crazy angle among the grass and weeds: most of its attachments had fallen off, but there were enough left to identify it as a railway signal.

We passed through one concentration of identical blocks which was in size, though in no other way, quite a town, and then, two or three miles farther on, ran through an ornamental gateway into a kind of park.

In one way it was not unlike the estate we had left, for everything was meticulously tended; the lawns like velvet, the flower beds vivid with spring blossoms, but it differed essentially in that the buildings were not blocks. They were houses, quite small for the most part, and varied in style, often no larger than roomy cottages. The place had a subduing effect on my small companions; for the first time they left off chattering, and gazed about them with obvious awe.

The driver stopped once to inquire the way of an overalled Amazon who was striding along with a hod on her shoulder. She directed us, and gave me a cheerful, respectful grin through the window, and presently we drew up again in front of a neat little two-storey Regency-style house.

This time there was no trolley. The little women, assisted by the driver, fussed over helping me out, and then half supported me into the house, in a kind of buttressing formation.

Inside, I was manoeuvred with some difficulty through a door on the left, and found myself in a beautiful room, elegantly decorated and furnished in the period style of the house. A white-haired woman in a purple silk dress was sitting in a wing chair beside a wood fire. Both her face and her hands told of considerable age, but she looked at me from keen, lively eyes.

"Welcome, my dear," she said, in a voice which had no trace of the quaver I half expected.

Her glance went to a chair. Then she looked at me again, and thought better of it.

"I expect you'd be more comfortable on the couch," she suggested.

I regarded the couch–a genuine Georgian piece, I thought–doubtfully.

"Will it stand it?" I wondered.

"Oh, I think so," she said, but not too certainly.

The retinue deposited me there carefully, and stood by, with anxious expressions. When it was clear that though it creaked it was probably going to hold, the old lady shooed them away, and rang a little silver bell. A diminutive figure, a perfect parlour maid three foot ten in height, entered.

"The brown sherry, please, Mildred," instructed the old lady. "You'll take sherry, my dear?" she added to me.

"Y-yes–yes, thank you," I said faintly. After a pause I added: "You will excuse me, Mrs.–er–Miss–?"

"Oh, I should have introduced myself. My name is Laura–not Miss, or Mrs., just Laura. You, I know, are Orchis–Mother Orchis."

"So they tell me," I owned distastefully.

We studied one another. For the first time since the hallucination had set in I saw sympathy, even pity, in someone else's eyes. I looked round the room again, noticing the perfection of details.

"This is–I'm not mad, am I?" I asked.

She shook her head slowly, but before she could reply the miniature parlour maid returned, bearing a cut-glass decanter and glasses on a silver tray. As she poured out a glass for each of us I saw the old lady glance from her to me and back again, as though comparing us. There was a curious, uninterpretable expression on her face. I made an effort.

"Shouldn't it be Madeira?" I suggested.

She looked surprised, and then smiled, and nodded appreciatively. "I think you have accomplished the purpose of this visit in one sentence," she said.

The parlour maid left, and we raised our glasses. The old lady sipped at hers and then placed it on an occasional table beside her.

"Nevertheless," she went on, "we had better go into it a little more. Did they tell you why they have sent you to me, my dear?"

"No," I shook my head.

"It is because I am a historian," she informed me. "Access to history is a privilege. It is not granted to many of us nowadays–and then somewhat reluctantly. Fortunately, a feeling that no branches of knowledge should be allowed to perish entirely still exists–though some of them are pursued at the cost of a certain political suspicion." She smiled deprecatingly, and then went on. "So when confirmation is required it is necessary to appeal to a specialist. Did they give you any report on their diagnosis?"

I shook my head again.

"I thought not. So like the profession, isn't it? Well, I'll tell you what they told me on the telephone from the Mothers' Home, and we shall have a better idea of what we are about. I was informed that you have been interviewed by several doctors whom you have interested, puzzled–and I suspect, distressed–very much, poor things. None of them has more than a minimum smattering of history, you see. Well, briefly, two of them are of the opinion that you are suffering from delusions of a schizophrenic nature: and three are inclined to think you are a genuine case of transferred personality. It is an extremely rare condition. There are not more than three reliably documented cases, and one that is more debatable, they tell me; but of those confirmed two are associated with the drug chuinjuatin, and the third with a drug of very similar properties.

"Now, the majority of three found your answers coherent for the most part, and felt that they were authentically circumstantial. That is to say that nothing you told them conflicted directly with what they know, but, since they know so little outside their professional field, they found a great deal of the rest both hard to believe and impossible to check. Therefore I, with my better means of checking, have been asked for my opinion."

She paused, and looked me thoughtfully over.

"I rather think," she added, "that this is going to be one of the most curiously interesting things that has happened to me in my quite long life. Your glass is empty, my dear."

"Transferred personality," I repeated wonderingly as I held out my glass. "Now, if *that* were possible—"

"Oh, there's no doubt about the *possibility*. Those three cases I mentioned are fully authenticated."

"It might be that—almost," I admitted. "At least, in some ways it might be—but not in others. There *is* this nightmare quality. *You* seem perfectly normal to me, but look at me, myself—and at your little maid! There's certainly an element of delusion. I *seem* to be here, like this, and talking to you—but it can't really be so, so where am I?"

"I can understand, better than most, I think, how unreal this must seem to you. In fact, I have spent so much of my time in books that it sometimes seems unreal to me—as if I did not quite belong anywhere. Now, tell me, my dear, when were you born?"

I told her. She thought for a moment.

"H'm," she said. "George the Sixth—but you'd not remember the second big war?"

"No," I agreed.

"But you might remember the coronation of the next monarch? Whose was that?"

"Elizabeth—Elizabeth the Second. My mother took me to see the procession," I told her.

"Do you remember anything about it?"

"Not a lot really—except that it rained, nearly all day," I admitted.

We went on like that for a little while, then she smiled reassuringly.

"Well, I don't think we need any more to establish our point. I've heard about that coronation before—at second hand. It must have been a wonderful scene in the abbey." She mused for a moment, and gave a little sigh. "You've been very patient with me, my dear. It is only fair that you should have your turn—but I'm afraid you must prepare yourself for some shocks."

"I think I must be inured after my last thirty-six hours or what has appeared to be thirty-six hours," I told her.

"I doubt it," she said, looking at me seriously.

"Tell me," I asked her. "Please explain it all—if you can."

"Your glass, my dear. Then I'll get the crux of it over." She poured for each of us, then she asked:

"What strikes you as the oddest feature of your experience, so far?"

I considered. "There's so much—"

"Might it not be that you have not seen a single man?" she suggested.

I thought back. I remembered the wondering tone of one of the Mothers asking: "What is a man?"

"That's certainly one of them," I agreed. "Where are they?"

She shook her head, watching me steadily.

"There aren't any, my dear. Not any more. None at all."

I simply went on staring at her. Her expression was perfectly serious and sympathetic. There was no trace of guile there, or deception, while I struggled with the idea. At last I managed:

"But—but that's impossible! There must be some somewhere. . . . You couldn't—I mean, how?—I mean. . . ." My expostulation trailed off in confusion.

She shook her head.

"I know it must seem impossible to you, Jane—may I call you Jane? But it is so. I am an old woman now, nearly eighty, and in all my long life I have never seen a man—save in old pictures and photographs. Drink your sherry, my dear. It will do you good." She paused. "I'm afraid this upsets you."

I obeyed, too bewildered for further comment at the moment, protesting inwardly, yet not altogether disbelieving, for certainly I had not seen one man, nor sign of any. She went on quietly, giving me time to collect my wits.

"I can understand a little how you must feel. I haven't had to learn all my history entirely from books, you see. When I was a girl, sixteen or seventeen, I used to listen a lot to my grandmother. She was as old then as I am now, but her memory of her youth was still very good. I was able almost to see the places she talked about–but they were part of such a different world that it was difficult for me to understand how she felt. When she spoke about the young man she had been engaged to, tears would roll down her cheeks, even then–not just for him, of course, but for the whole world that she had known as a girl. I was sorry for her, although I could not really understand how she felt. How should I? But now that I am old, too, and have read so much, I am perhaps a little nearer to understanding her feelings, I think." She looked at me curiously. "And you, my dear. Perhaps you, too, were engaged to be married?"

"I was married–for a little time," I told her.

She contemplated that for some seconds, then:

"It must be a very strange experience to be owned," she remarked reflectively.

"Owned?" I exclaimed in astonishment.

"Ruled by a husband," she explained sympathetically.

I stared at her.

"But it–it wasn't like that–it wasn't like that at all," I protested. "It was–" But there I broke off, with tears too close. To sheer her away I asked:

"But what happened? What on earth happened to the men?"

"They all died," she told me. "They fell sick. Nobody could do anything for them, so they died. In little more than a year they were all gone–all but a very few."

"But surely–surely everything would collapse?"

"Oh, yes. Very largely it did. It was very bad. There was a dreadful lot of starvation. The industrial parts were the worst hit, of course. In the more backward countries and in rural areas women were able to turn to the land and till it to keep themselves and their children alive, but almost all the large organizations broke down entirely. Transport ceased very soon: petrol ran out, and no coal was being mined. It was quite a dreadful state of affairs because although there were a great many women, and they had outnumbered the men, in fact, they had only really been important as consumers and spenders of money. So when the crisis came it turned out that scarcely any of them knew how to do any of the important things because they had nearly all been owned by men, and had to lead their lives as pets and parasites."

I started to protest, but her frail hand waved me aside.

"It wasn't their fault–not entirely," she explained. "They were caught up in a process, and everything conspired against their escape. It was a long process, going right back to the eleventh century, in southern France. The Romantic conception started there as an elegant and amusing fashion for the leisured classes. Gradually, as time went on, it permeated through most levels of society, but it was not until the latter part of the nineteenth century that its commercial possibilities were intelligently perceived, and not until the twentieth that it was really exploited.

"At the beginning of the twentieth century women were starting to have their chance to lead useful, creative, interesting lives. But that did not suit commerce: it needed them much more as mass consumers than as producers—except on the most routine levels. So Romance was adopted and developed as a weapon against their further progress and to promote consumption, and it was used intensively.

"Women must never for a moment be allowed to forget their sex, and to compete as equals. Everything had to have a 'feminine angle' which must be different from the masculine angle, and be dinned in without ceasing. It would have been unpopular for manufacturers actually to issue an order 'back to the kitchen,' but there were other ways. A profession without a difference, called 'housewife,' could be invented. The kitchen could be glorified and made more expensive; it could be made to seem desirable, and it could be shown that the way to realize this heart's desire was through marriage. So the presses turned out, by the hundred thousand a week, journals which concentrated the attention of women ceaselessly and relentlessly upon selling themselves to some man in order that they might achieve some small, uneconomic unit of a home upon which money could be spent.

"Whole trades adopted the romantic approach and the glamour was spread thicker and thicker in the articles, the write-ups, and most of all in the advertisements. Romance found a place in everything that women might buy from underclothes to motorcycles, from 'health' foods to kitchen stoves, from deodorants to foreign travel, until soon they were too bemused to be amused any more.

"The air was filled with frustrated moanings. Women maundered in front of microphones yearning only to 'surrender,' and 'give themselves,' to adore and to be adored. The cinema most of all maintained the propaganda, persuading the main and important part of their audience, which was female, that nothing in life was worth achieving but dewy-eyed passivity in the strong arms of Romance. The pressure became such that the majority of young women spent all their leisure time dreaming of Romance, and the means of securing it. They were brought to a state of honestly believing that to be owned by some man and set down in a little brick box to buy all the things that the manufacturers wanted them to buy would be the highest form of bliss that life could offer."

"But–" I began to protest again. The old lady was now well launched, however, and swept on without a check.

"All this could not help distorting society, of course. The divorce rate went up. Real life simply could not come near to providing the degree of romantic glamour which was being represented as every girl's proper inheritance. There was probably, in the aggregate, more disappointment, disillusion, and dissatisfaction among women than there had ever been before. Yet, with this ridiculous and ornamental ideal grained-in by unceasing propaganda, what could a conscientious idealist do but take steps to break up the short-weight marriage she had made, and seek elsewhere for the ideal which was hers, she understood, by right?

"It was a wretched state of affairs brought about by deliberately promoted dissatisfaction; a kind of rat-race with, somewhere safely out of reach, the glamorized romantic ideal always luring. Perhaps an exceptional few almost attained it, but, for all except those very few, it was a cruel, tantalizing sham on which they spent themselves, and of course their money, in vain."

This time I did get in my protest.

"But it wasn't like that. Some of what you say may be true–but that's all the superficial part. It didn't feel a bit like the way you put it. I was in it. I *know*."

She shook her head reprovingly.

"There is such a thing as being too close to make a proper evaluation. At a distance we were able to see more clearly. We can perceive it for what it was–a gross and heartless exploitation of the weaker-willed majority. Some women of education and resolution were able to withstand it, of course, but at a cost. There must always be a painful price for resisting majority pressure–even they could not always altogether escape the feeling that they might be wrong, and that the rat-racers were having the better time of it.

"You see, the great hopes for the emancipation of women with which the century had started had been outflanked. Purchasing power had passed into the hands of the ill-educated and highly suggestible. The desire for Romance is essentially a selfish wish, and when it is encouraged to dominate every other it breaks down all corporate loyalties. The individual woman thus separated from, and yet at the same time thrust into competition with, all other women was almost defenceless; she became the prey of organized suggestion. When it was represented to her that the lack of certain goods or amenities would be fatal to Romance she became alarmed and, thus, eminently exploitable. She could only believe what she was told, and spent a great deal of time worrying about whether she was doing all the right things to encourage Romance. Thus, she became, in a new, subtler way, more exploited, more dependent, and less creative than she had ever been before."

"Well," I said, "this is the most curiously unrecognizable account of my world that I have ever heard–it's like something copied, but with all the proportions wrong. And as for 'less creative'–well, perhaps families were smaller, but women still went on having babies. The population was still increasing."

The old lady's eyes dwelt on me a moment.

"You are undoubtedly a thought-child of your time, in some ways," she observed. "What makes you think there is anything creative about having babies? Would you call a plant pot creative because seeds grow in it? It is a mechanical operation–and, like most mechanical operations, is most easily performed by the least intelligent. Now, bringing up a child, educating, helping her to become a *person,* that *is* creative. But unfortunately, in the time we are speaking of, women had, in the main, been successfully conditioned into bringing up their daughters to be unintelligent consumers, like themselves."

"But," I said helplessly, "I *know* the time. It's my time. This is all distorted."

"The perspective of history must be truer," she told me again, unimpressed, and went on: "But if what happened *had* to happen, then it chose a fortunate time to happen. A hundred years earlier, even fifty years earlier, it would very likely have meant extinction. Fifty years later might easily have been too late–it might have come upon a world in which *all* women had profitably restricted themselves to domesticity and consumership. Luckily, however, in the middle of the century some women were still entering the professions, and by far the greatest number of professional women was to be found in medicine–which is to say that they were only really numerous in, and skilled in, the very profession which immediately became of vital importance if we were to survive at all.

"I have no medical knowledge, so I cannot give you any details of the steps they took. All I can tell you is that there was intensive research on lines which will probably be more obvious to you than they are to me.

"A species, even our species, has great will to survive, and the doctors saw to it that the will had the means of expression. Through all the hunger, and the chaos, and the other privations, babies somehow continued to be born. That had to be. Reconstruction could wait: the priority was the new generation that would help in the reconstruction, and then inherit it. So babies were born: the girl babies lived, the boy babies died. That was distressing, and wasteful, too, and so, presently, only girl babies were born—again, the means by which that could be achieved will be easier for you to understand than for me.

"It is, they tell me, not nearly so remarkable as it would appear at first sight. The locust, it seems, will continue to produce female locusts without male, or any other kind of assistance; the aphis, too, is able to go on breeding alone and in seclusion, certainly for eight generations, perhaps more. So it would be a poor thing if we, with all our knowledge and powers of research to assist us, should find ourselves inferior to the locust and the aphis in this respect, would it not?"

She paused, looking at me somewhat quizzically for my response. Perhaps she expected amazed—or possibly shocked—disbelief. If so, I disappointed her: technical achievements have ceased to arouse simple wonder since atomic physics showed how the barriers fall before the pressure of a good brains team. One can take it that most things are possible: whether they are desirable, or worth doing, is a different matter—and one that seemed to me particularly pertinent to her question. I asked her:

"And what is it that you have achieved?"

"Survival," she said simply.

"Materially," I agreed, "I suppose you have. But when it has cost all the rest, when love, art, poetry, excitement, and physical joy have all been sacrificed to mere continued existence, what is left but a soulless waste? What reason is there any longer for survival?"

"As to the reason, I don't know—except that survival is a desire common to all species. I am quite sure that the *reason* for that desire was no clearer in the twentieth century than it is now. But, for the rest, why should you assume that they are gone? Did not Sappho write poetry? And your assumption that the possession of a soul depends upon a duality of sexes surprises me: it has so often been held that the two are in some sort of conflict, has it not?"

"As an historian who must have studied men, women, and motives you should have taken my meaning better," I told her.

She shook her head, with reproof. "You are so much the conditioned product of your age, my dear. They told you, on all levels, from the works of Freud to that of the most nugatory magazines for women, that it was sex, civilized into romantic love, that made the world go round—and you believed them. But the world continues to go round for others, too—for the insects, the fish, the birds, the animals—and how much do you suppose they know of romantic love, even in brief mating seasons? They hoodwinked you, my dear. Between them they channelled your interests and ambitions along courses that were socially convenient, economically profitable, and almost harmless."

I shook my head.

"I just don't believe it. Oh, yes, you know something of my world —from the outside. But you don't understand it, or feel it."

"That's your conditioning, my dear," she told me calmly.

Her repeated assumption irritated me. I asked:

"Suppose I were to believe what you say, what is it, then, that *does* make the world go round?"

"That's simple, my dear. It is the will to power. We have that as babies; we have it still in old age. It occurs in men and women alike. It is more fundamental, and more desirable, than sex; I tell you, you were misled—exploited, sublimated for economic convenience.

"After the disease had struck, women ceased, for the first time in history, to be an exploited class. Without male rulers to confuse and divert them they began to perceive that all true power resides in the female principle. The male had served only one brief useful purpose; for the rest of his life he was a painful and costly parasite.

"As they became aware of power, the doctors grasped it. In twenty years they were in full control. With them were the few women engineers, architects, lawyers, administrators, some teachers, and so on, but it was the doctors who held the keys of life and death. The future was in their hands and, as things began gradually to revive, they, together with the other professions, remained the dominant class and became known as the Doctorate. It assumed authority; it made the laws; it enforced them.

"There was opposition, of course. Neither the memory of the old days, nor the effect of twenty years of lawlessness, could be wiped out at once, but the doctors had the whip hand—any woman who wanted a child had to come to them, and they saw to it that she was satisfactorily settled in a community. The roving gangs dwindled away, and gradually order was restored.

"Later on, they faced better-organized opposition. There was a party which contended that the disease which had struck down the men had run its course, and the balance could, and should, be restored—they were known as Reactionists, and they became an embarrassment.

"Most of the Council of the Doctorate still had clear memories of a system which used every weakness of women, and had been no more than a mere civilized culmination of their exploitation through the ages. They remembered how they themselves had only grudgingly been allowed to qualify for their careers. They were now in command: they felt no obligation to surrender their power and authority, and eventually, no doubt, their freedom to a creature whom they had proved to be biologically, and in all other ways, expendable. They refused unanimously to take a step that would lead to corporate suicide, and the Reactionists were proscribed as a subversive criminal organization.

"That, however, was just a palliative. It quickly became clear that they were attacking a symptom and neglecting the cause. The Council was driven to realize that it had an unbalanced society at its hands—a society that was capable of continuity, but was in structure, you might say, little more than the residue of a vanished form. It could not continue in that truncated shape, and as long as it tried to disaffection would increase. Therefore, if power was to become stable, a new form suitable to the circumstances must be found.

"In deciding the shape it should take, the natural tendencies of the little-educated and uneducated woman were carefully considered—such qualities as her feeling for hierarchical principles and her disposition to respect artificial distinctions. You will no doubt recollect that in your own time any fool of a woman whose husband was ennobled or honoured at once acquired increased respect and envy from other women though she remained the same fool; and also, that any gathering or society of unoccupied women would soon become obsessionally enmeshed in the creation and preservation of social distinctions. Allied to this is the high value they usually place upon a feeling of security. Important, too, is the capacity for devoted self-sacrifice, and slavery to conscience within the canons of any local convention. We are naturally very biddable creatures. Most of us are happiest when we are being orthodox, however odd our customs may appear to an outsider; the difficulty in handling us lies chiefly in establishing the required standards of orthodoxy.

"Obviously, the broad outline of a system which was going to stand any chance of success would have to provide scope for these and other characteristic traits. It must be a scheme where the interplay of forces would preserve equilibrium and respect for authority. The details of such an organization, however, were less easy to determine.

"An extensive study of social forms and orders was undertaken but for several years every plan put forward was rejected as in some way unsuitable. The architecture of that finally chosen was said, though I do not know with how much truth, to have been inspired by the Bible–a book at that time still unprohibited, and the source of much unrest–I am told that it ran something like: 'Go to the ant, thou sluggard; consider her ways.'

"The Council appears to have felt that this advice, suitably modified, could be expected to lead to a state of affairs which would provide most of the requisite characteristics.

"A four-class system was chosen as the basis, and strong differentiations were gradually introduced. These, now that they have become well established, greatly help to ensure stability–there is scope for ambition within one's class, but none for passing from one class to another. Thus, we have the Doctorate–the educated ruling class, fifty percent of whom are actually of the medical profession. The Mothers, whose title is self-explanatory. The Servitors, who are numerous and, for psychological reasons, small. The Workers, who are physically and muscularly strong, to do the heavier work. All the three lower classes respect the authority of the Doctorate. Both the employed classes revere the Mothers. The Servitors consider themselves more favoured in their tasks than the Workers; and the Workers tend to regard the puniness of the Servitors with a semi-affectionate contempt.

"So you see a balance has been struck, and though it works somewhat crudely as yet, no doubt it will improve. It seems likely, for instance, that it would be advantageous to introduce subdivisions into the Servitor class before long, and the police are thought by some to be put at a disadvantage by having no more than a little education to distinguish them from the ordinary Worker. . . ."

She went on explaining with increasing detail while the enormity of the whole process gradually grew upon me.

"Ants!" I broke in suddenly. "The ant nest! You've taken *that* for your model?"

She looked surprised, either at my tone, or the fact that what she was saying had taken so long to register.

"And why not?" she asked. "Surely it is one of the most enduring social patterns that nature has evolved—though of course some adaptation—"

"You're—are you telling me that only the Mothers have children?" I demanded.

"Oh, members of the Doctorate do, too, when they wish," she assured me.

"But—but—"

"The Council decides the ratios," she went on to explain. "The doctors at the clinic examine the babies and allocate them suitably to the different classes. After that, of course, it is just a matter of seeing to their specialized feeding, glandular control, and proper training."

"But," I objected wildly, "what's it *for?* Where's the sense in it? What's the good of being alive, like that?"

"Well, what *is* the sense in being alive? You tell me," she suggested.

"But we're *meant* to love and be loved, to have babies we love by people we love."

"There's your conditioning again; glorifying and romanticizing primitive animalism. Surely you consider that we are superior to the animals?"

"Of course I do, but—"

"Love, you say, but what can you know of the love there can be between mother and daughter when there are no men to introduce jealousy? Do you know of any purer sentiment than the love of a girl for her little sisters?"

"But you don't understand," I protested again. "How should you understand a love that colours the whole world? How it centres in your heart and reaches out from there to pervade your whole being, how it can affect everything you are, everything you touch, everything you hear. . . . It can hurt dreadfully, I know, oh, I know, but it can run like sunlight in your veins. . . . It can make you a garden out of a slum; brocade out of rags; music out of a speaking voice. It can show you a whole universe in someone else's eyes. Oh, you don't understand . . . you don't know . . . you can't. . . . Oh,

Donald, darling, how can I show her what she's never even guessed at . . . ?"

There was an uncertain pause, but presently she said:

"Naturally, in your form of society it was necessary for you to be given such a conditioned reaction, but you can scarcely expect us to surrender our freedom, to connive at our own resubjection, by calling our oppressors into existence again."

"Oh, you *won't* understand. It was only the more stupid men and women who were continually at war with one another. Lots of us were complementary. We were pairs who formed units."

She smiled. "My dear, either you are surprisingly ill-informed on your own period, or else the stupidity you speak of was astonishingly dominant. Neither as myself, nor as an historian, can I consider that we should be justified in resurrecting such a state of affairs. A primitive stage of our development has now given way to a civilized era. Woman, who is the vessel of life, had the misfortune to find man necessary for a time, but now she does no longer. Are you suggesting that such a useless and dangerous encumbrance ought to be preserved, out of sheer sentimentality? I will admit that we have lost some minor conveniences–you will have noticed, I expect, that we are less inventive mechanically, and tend to copy the patterns we have inherited; but that troubles us very little; our interests lie not in the inorganic, but in the organic and the sentient. Perhaps men could show us how to travel twice as fast, or how to fly to the moon, or how to kill more people more quickly; but it does not seem to us that such kinds of knowledge would be good payment for re-enslaving ourselves. No, our kind of world suits us better–all of us except a few Reactionists. You have seen our Servitors. They are a little timid in manner, perhaps, but are they oppressed, or sad? Don't they chatter among themselves as brightly and perkily as sparrows? And the Workers–those you called the Amazons–don't they look strong, healthy, and cheerful?"

"But you're robbing them all–robbing them of their birthright."

"You mustn't give me cant, my dear. Did not your social system conspire to rob a woman of her 'birthright' unless she married? You not only let her know it, but you socially rubbed it in: here, our Servitors and Workers do not know it, and they are not worried by a sense of inadequacy. Motherhood is the function of the Mothers, and understood as such."

I shook my head. "Nevertheless, they *are* being robbed. A woman has a right to love–"

For once she was a little impatient as she cut me short.

"You keep repeating to me the propaganda of your age. The love you talk about, my dear, existed in your little sheltered part of the world by polite and profitable convention. You were scarcely ever allowed to see its other face, unglamorized by Romance. *You* were never openly bought and sold, like livestock; *you* never had to sell yourself to the first-comer in order to live; *you* did not happen to be one of the women who through the centuries have screamed in agony and suffered and died under invaders in a sacked city—nor were you ever flung into a pit of fire to be saved from them; *you* were never compelled to suttee upon your dead husband's pyre; *you* did not have to spend your whole life imprisoned in a harem; *you* were never part of the cargo of a slave ship; *you* never retained your own life only at the pleasure of your lord and master. . . .

"That is the other side—the age-long side. There is going to be no more of such things. They are finished at last. Dare you suggest that we should call them back, to suffer them all again?"

"But most of these things had already gone," I protested. "The world was getting better."

"Was it?" she said. "I wonder if the women of Berlin thought so when it fell? Was it, indeed? Or was it on the edge of a new barbarism?"

"But if you can only get rid of evil by throwing out the good too, what is there left?"

"There is a great deal. Man was only a means to an end. We needed him in order to have babies. The rest of his vitality accounted for all the misery in the world. We are a great deal better off without him."

"So you really consider that you've improved on nature?" I suggested.

"Tcha!" she said, impatient with my tone. "Civilisation *is* improvement on nature. Would you want to live in a cave, and have most of your babies die in infancy?"

"There are some things, some fundamental things—" I began, but she checked me, holding up her hand for silence.

Outside, the long shadows had crept across the lawns. In the evening quiet I could hear a choir of women's voices singing, a little distance away. We listened for some minutes until the song was finished.

"Beautiful!" said the old lady. "Could angels themselves sing more sweetly! They sound happy enough, don't they? Our own lovely children—two of my granddaughters are there among them. They *are* happy, and they've reason to be happy; they're not growing up into a world where they must gamble on the goodwill of some man to keep them; they'll never need to be servile before a lord and master; they'll never stand in danger of rape and butchery, either. Listen to them!"

Another song had started and came lilting lightly to us out of the dusk.

"Why are you crying?" the old lady asked me as it ended.

"I know it's stupid—I don't really believe any of this is what it seems to be—so I suppose I'm crying for all you would have lost if it were true," I told her. "There should be lovers out there under the trees; they should be listening hand in hand to that song while they watch the moon rise. But there are no lovers now, there won't be any more. . . ." I looked back at her.

"Did you ever read the lines: 'Full many a flower is born to blush unseen, and waste its sweetness on the desert air'? Can't you feel the forlornness of this world you've made? Do you *really* not understand?" I asked.

"I know you've only seen a little of us, but do *you* not begin to understand what it can be like when women are no longer forced to fight one another for the favours of men?" she countered.

We talked on while the dusk gave way to darkness and the lights of other houses started to twinkle through the trees. Her reading had been wide. It had given her even an affection for some periods of the past, but her approval of her own era was unshaken. She felt no aridity in it. Always it was my "conditioning" which prevented me from seeing that the golden age of woman had begun at last.

"You cling to too many myths," she told me. "You speak of a full life, and your instance is some unfortunate woman hugging her chains in a suburban villa. Full life, fiddlesticks! But it was convenient for the traders that she could be made to think so. A truly full life would be an exceedingly short one, in any form of society."

And so on . . .

At length, the little parlour maid reappeared to say that my attendants were ready to leave when it should be convenient. But there was one thing I very much wanted to know before I left. I put the question to the old lady.

"Please tell me. How did it—how could it—happen?"

"Simply by accident, my dear—though it was the kind of accident that was entirely the product of its time. A piece of research which showed unexpected, secondary results, that's all."

"But how?"

"Rather curiously—almost irrelevantly, you might say. Did you ever hear of a man called Perrigan?"

"Perrigan?" I repeated. "I don't think so, it's an uncommon name."

"It became very commonly known indeed," she assured me. "Doctor Perrigan was a biologist, and his concern was the extermination of rats—particularly the brown rat, which used to do a great deal of expensive damage.

"His approach to the problem was to find a disease which would attack them fatally. In order to produce it he took as his basis a virus infection often fatal to rabbits—or, rather, a group of virus infections that were highly selective, and also unstable since they were highly liable to mutation. Indeed, there was so much variation in the strains that when infection of rabbits in Australia was tried, it was only at the sixth attempt that it was successful; all the earlier strains died out as the rabbits developed immunity. It was tried in other places, too, though with indifferent success until a still more effective strain was started in France, and ran through the rabbit population of Europe.

"Well, taking some of these viruses as a basis, Perrigan induced new mutations by irradiation and other means, and succeeded in producing a variant that would attack rats. That was not enough, however, and he continued his work until he had a strain that had enough of its ancestral selectivity to attack only the brown rat, and with great virulence.

"In that way he settled the question of a long-standing pest, for there are no brown rats now. But something went amiss. It is still an open question whether the successful virus mutated again, or whether one of his earlier experimental viruses was accidentally liberated by escaped 'carrier' rats, but that's academic. The important thing is that somehow a strain capable of attacking human beings got loose, and that it was already widely disseminated before it was traced—also, that once it was free, it spread with devastating speed; too fast for any effective steps to be taken to check it.

"The majority of women were found to be immune; and of the ten percent or so whom it attacked over eighty percent recovered. Among men, however, there was almost no immunity, and the few recoveries were only partial. A few men were preserved by the most elaborate precautions but they could not be kept confined forever, and in the end the virus, which had a remarkable capacity for dormancy, got them too."

Inevitably several questions of professional interest occurred to me, but for an answer she shook her head.

"I'm afraid I can't help you there. Possibly the medical people will be willing to explain," she said, but her expression was doubtful.

I manoeuvred myself into a sitting position on the side of the couch.

"I see," I said. "Just an accident–yes, I suppose one could scarcely think of it happening in any other way."

"Unless," she remarked, "unless one were to look upon it as divine intervention."

"Isn't that a little impious?"

"I was thinking of the Death of the Firstborn," she said reflectively.

There did not seem to be an immediate answer to that. Instead, I asked:

"Can you honestly tell me that you never have the feeling that you are living in a dreary kind of nightmare?"

"Never," she said. "There *was* a nightmare–but it's over now. Listen!"

The voices of the choir, reinforced now by an orchestra, reached us distantly out of the darkened garden. No, they were not dreary: they even sounded almost exultant–but then, poor things, how were they to understand . . . ?

My attendants arrived and helped me to my feet. I thanked the old lady for her patience with me and her kindness. But she shook her head.

"My dear, it is I who am indebted to you. In a short time I have learnt more about the conditioning of women in a mixed society than all my books were able to tell me in the rest of my long life. I hope, my dear, that the doctors will find some way of enabling you to forget it, and live happily here with us."

At the door I paused and turned, still helpfully shored up by my attendants.

"Laura," I said, using her name for the first time. "So many of your arguments are right–yet, over all, you're, oh, so *wrong*. Did you never read of lovers? Did you never, as a girl, sigh for a Romeo who would say: 'It is the east, and Laura is the sun!'?"

"I think not. Though I have read the play. A pretty, idealized tale –I wonder how much heartbreak it has given to how many would-be

Juliets? But I would set a question against yours, my dear Jane. Did you ever see Goya's cycle of pictures called 'The Horrors of War'?"

The pink car did not return me to the "Home." Our destination turned out to be a more austere and hospital-like building where I was fussed into a bed in a room alone. In the morning, after my massive breakfast, three new doctors visited me. Their manner was more social than professional, and we chatted amiably for half an hour. They had evidently been fully informed on my conversation with the old lady, and they were not averse to answering my questions. Indeed, they found some amusement in many of them, though I found none, for there was nothing consolingly vague in what they told me–it all sounded too disturbingly practicable, once the technique had been worked out. At the end of that time, however, their mood changed. One of them, with an air of getting down to business, said:

"You will understand that you present us with a problem. Your fellow Mothers, of course, are scarcely susceptible to Reactionist disaffection–though you have in quite a short time managed to disgust and bewilder them considerably–but on others less stable your influence might be more serious. It is not just a matter of what you may say, your difference from the rest is implicit in your whole attitude. You cannot help that, and, frankly, we do not see how you, as a woman of education, could possibly adapt yourself to the placid, unthinking acceptance that is expected of a Mother. You would quickly feel frustrated beyond endurance. Furthermore, it is clear that the conditioning you have had under your system prevents you from feeling any goodwill towards ours."

I took that straight–simply as a judgement without bias. Moreover, I could not dispute it. The prospect of spending the rest of my life in pink, scented, soft-musicked illiteracy, interrupted, one gathered, only by the production of quadruplet daughters at regular intervals, would certainly have me violently unhinged in a very short time.

"And so–what?" I asked. "Can you reduce this great carcass to normal shape and size?"

She shook her head. "I imagine not–though I don't know that it has ever been attempted. But even if it were possible, you would be just as much of a misfit in the Doctorate–and far more of a liability as a Reactionist influence."

I could understand that, too.

"What, then?" I inquired.

She hesitated, then she said gently:

"The only practicable proposal we can make is that you should agree to a hypnotic treatment which will remove your memory."

As the meaning of that came home to me I had to fight off a rush of panic. After all, I told myself, they were being reasonable with me. I must do my best to respond sensibly. Nevertheless, some minutes must have passed before I answered, unsteadily:

"You are asking me to commit suicide. My mind *is* my memories: they are me. If I lose them I shall die, just as surely as if you were to kill my–this body."

They did not dispute that. How could they?

There is just one thing that makes my life worth living–knowing that you loved me, my sweet, sweet Donald. It is only in my memory that you live now. If you ever leave there you will die again–and forever.

"No!" I told them. "No! No!"

At intervals during the day small servitors staggered in under the weight of my meals. Between their visits I had only my thoughts to occupy me, and they were not good company.

"Frankly," one of the doctors had put it to me, not unsympathetically, "we can see no alternative. For years after it happened the annual figures of mental breakdowns were our greatest worry–even though the women then could keep themselves fully occupied with the tremendous amount of work that had to be done, so many of them could not adjust. And we can't even offer you work."

I knew that it was a fair warning she was giving me–and I knew that, unless the hallucination which seemed to grow more real all the time could soon be induced to dissolve, I was trapped.

During the long day and the following night I tried my hardest to get back to the objectivity I had managed earlier, but I failed. The whole dialectic was too strong for me now; my senses too consciously aware of my surroundings; the air of consequence and coherence too convincingly persistent. . . .

When they had let me have twenty-four hours to think it over, the same trio visited me again.

"I think," I told them, "that I understand better now. What you are offering me is painless oblivion, in place of a breakdown followed by oblivion–and you see no other choice."

"We don't," admitted the spokeswoman, and the other two nodded. "But, of course, for the hypnosis we shall need your cooperation."

"I realize that," I told her, "and I also see now that in the circumstances it would be obstinately futile to withhold it. So I–I–yes, I'm willing to give it–but on one condition."

They looked at me questioningly.

"It is this," I explained, "that you will try one other course first. I want you to give me an injection of chuinjuatin. I want it in precisely the same strength as I had it before–I can tell you the dose.

"You see, whether this is an intense hallucination, or whether it is some kind of projection which makes it seem very similar, it must have something to do with that drug. I'm sure it must–nothing remotely like this has ever happened to me before. So, I thought that if I could repeat the condition–or, would you say believe myself to be repeating the condition?–there may be just a chance . . . I don't know. It may be simply silly . . . but even if nothing comes of it, it can't make things worse in any way now, can it? So, will you let me try it . . . ?"

The three of them considered for some moments.

"I can see no reason why not . . ." said one.

The spokeswoman nodded.

"I shouldn't think there'll be any difficulty with authorization in the circumstances," she agreed. "If you want to try, well, it's fair to let you, but–I'd not count on it too much. . . ."

In the afternoon half a dozen small servitors arrived, bustling round, making me and the room ready, with anxious industry. Presently there came one more, scarcely tall enough to see over the trolley of bottles, trays and phials which she pushed to my bedside.

The three doctors entered together. One of the little servitors began rolling up my sleeve. The doctor who had done most of the talking looked at me, kindly, but seriously.

"This is a sheer gamble, you know that?" she said.

"I know. But it's my only chance. I'm willing to take it."

She nodded, picked up the syringe, and charged it while the little servitor swabbed my monstrous arm. She approached the bedside, and hesitated.

"Go on," I told her. "What is there for me here, anyway?"

She nodded, and pressed in the needle. . . .

Now, I have written the foregoing for a purpose. I shall deposit it with my bank, where it will remain unread unless it should be needed.

I have spoken of it to no one. The report on the effect of chuinjuatin—the one that I made to Dr. Hellyer where I described my sensation as simply one of floating in space—was false. The foregoing was my true experience.

I concealed it because after I came round, when I found that I was back in my own body in my normal world, the experience haunted me as vividly as if it had been actuality. The details were too sharp, too vivid, for me to get them out of my mind. It overhung me all the time, like a threat. It would not leave me alone. . . .

I did not dare to tell Dr. Hellyer how it worried me—he would have put me under treatment. If my other friends did not take it seriously enough to recommend treatment, too, then they would have laughed over it, and amused themselves at my expense interpreting the symbolism. So I kept it to myself.

As I went over parts of it again and again in detail, I grew angry with myself for not asking the old lady for more facts, things like dates, and details that could be verified. If, for instance, the thing should, by her account, have started two or three years ago, then the whole sense of threat would fall to pieces: it would all be discredited. But it had not occurred to me to ask that crucial question. . . . And then, as I went on thinking about it, I remembered that there was one, just one, piece of information that I could check, and I made inquiries. I wish now that I had not, but I felt forced to. . . .

So I have discovered that:

There *is* a Dr. Perrigan, he *is* a biologist, he *does* work with rabbits and rats. . . .

He is quite well known in his field. He has published papers on pest control in a number of journals. It is no secret that he is evolving new strains of myxomatosis intended to attack rats; indeed, he has already developed a group of them and calls them mucosimorbus, though he has not yet succeeded in making them either stable or selective enough for general use. . . .

But I had never heard of this man or his work until his name was mentioned by the old lady in my "hallucination." . . .

I have given a great deal of thought to this whole matter. What sort of experience is it that I have recorded above? If it should be a kind of pre-vision of an inevitable, predestined future, then nothing anyone could do would change it. But that does not seem to me to make sense: it is what has happened, and is happening now, that determines the future. Therefore, there must be a great number of *possible* futures, each a possible consequence of what is being done now. It seems to me that under chuinjuatin I saw *one* of those futures. . . .

It was, I think, a warning of what *may* happen—unless it is prevented. . . .

The whole idea is so repulsive, so misconceived, it amounts to such a monstrous aberration of the normal course, that failure to heed the warning would be neglect of duty to one's kind.

I shall, therefore, on my own responsibility and without taking any other person into my confidence, do my best to ensure that such a state as I have described *cannot* come about.

Should it happen that any other person is unjustly accused of doing, or of assisting me to do, what I intend to do, this document must stand in his defence. That is why I have written it.

It is my own unaided decision that Dr. Perrigan must not be permitted to continue his work.

(Signed) JANE WATERLEIGH

The solicitor stared at the signature for some moments; then he nodded. "And so," he said, "she then took the car and drove over to Perrigan's—with this tragic result.

"From the little I do know of her, I'd say that she probably did her best to persuade him to give up his work—though she can scarcely have expected any success with that. It is difficult to imagine a man who would be willing to give up the work of years on account of what must sound to him like a sort of gipsy's warning. So, clearly, she went there prepared to fall back on direct action, if necessary. It looks as if the police are quite right when they suppose her to have shot him deliberately; but not so right when they suppose that she burnt the place down to hide evidence of the crime. The statement makes it pretty obvious that her main intention in doing that was to wipe out Perrigan's work."

He shook his head. "Poor girl! There's a clear conviction of duty in her last page or two: the sort of simplified clarity that drives martyrs on, regardless of consequences. She has never denied that she did it. What she wouldn't tell the police is *why* she did it."

He paused again, before he added: "Anyway, thank goodness for this document. It ought at least to save her life. I should be very surprised indeed if a plea of insanity could fail, backed up by this." He tapped the pile of manuscript with his finger. "It's a lucky thing she put off her intention of taking it to her bank."

Dr. Hellyer's face was lined and worried.

"I blame myself most bitterly for the whole thing," he said. "I ought never to have let her try the damned drug in the first place, but I thought she was over the shock of her husband's death. She was trying to keep her time fully occupied, and she was anxious to volunteer. You've met her enough to know how purposeful she can be. She saw it as a chance to contribute something to medical knowledge–which it was, of course. But I ought to have been more careful, and I ought to have seen afterwards that there was something wrong. The real responsibility for this thing runs right back to me."

"H'm," said the solicitor. "Putting that forward as a main line of defence isn't going to do you a lot of good professionally, you know, Hellyer."

"Possibly not. I can look after that when we come to it. The point is that I hold a responsibility for her as a member of my staff, if for no other reason. It can't be denied that if I had refused her offer to take part in the experiment, this would not have happened. Therefore it seems to me that we ought to be able to argue a state of temporary insanity; that the balance of her mind was disturbed by the effects of the drug which I administered. And if we can get that as a verdict it will result in detention at a mental hospital for observation and treatment–perhaps quite a short spell of treatment."

"I can't say. We can certainly put it up to counsel and see what he thinks of it."

"It's valid, too," Hellyer persisted. "People like Jane don't do murder if they are in their right minds, not unless they're really in a corner, then they do it more cleverly. Certainly they don't murder perfect strangers. Clearly, the drug caused an hallucination sufficiently vivid to confuse her to a point where she was unable to make a proper distinction between the actual and the hypothetical. She got into a state where she believed the mirage was real, and acted accordingly."

"Yes. Yes, I suppose one might put it that way," agreed the solicitor. He looked down again at the pile of paper before him. "The whole account is, of course, unreasonable," he said, "and yet it is pervaded throughout with such an air of reasonableness. I wonder. . . ." He paused pensively, and went on: "This expendability of the male, Hellyer. She doesn't seem to find it so much incredible as undesirable. That seems odd in itself to a layman who takes the natural order for granted, but would you, as a medical scientist, say it was–well, not impossible, in theory?"

Dr. Hellyer frowned.

"That's very much the kind of question one wants more notice of. It would be very rash to proclaim it *impossible.* Considering it purely as an abstract problem, I can see two or three lines of approach. . . . Of course, if an utterly improbable situation were to arise calling for intensive research–research, that is, on the sort of scale they tackled the atom–well, who can tell . . . ?" He shrugged.

The solicitor nodded again.

"That's just what I was getting at," he observed. "Basically it is only just such a little way off the beam; quite near enough to possibility to be faintly disturbing. Mind you, as far as the defence is concerned, her air of thorough conviction, taken in conjunction with the near-plausibility of the thing, will probably help. But, for my part, it is just that nearness that is enough to make me a trifle uneasy."

The doctor looked at him rather sharply.

"Oh, come! Really now! A hard-boiled solicitor, too! Don't tell me you're going in for fantasy-building. Anyway, if you are, you'll have to conjure up another one. If Jane, poor girl, has settled one thing, it is that there's no future in this particular fantasy. Perrigan's finished with, and all his work's gone up in smoke and fire."

"H'm," said the solicitor again. "All the same, it would be more satisfactory if we knew of some way other than this"–he tapped the pile of papers–"some other way in which she is likely to have acquired some knowledge of Perrigan and his work. There is, as far as one knows, *no* other way in which he can have come into her orbit at all–unless, perhaps, she takes an interest in veterinary subjects?"

"She doesn't. I'm sure of that," Hellyer told him, shaking his head.

"Well that, then, remains one slightly disturbing aspect. And there is another. You'll think it foolish of me, I'm sure–and no doubt time will prove you right to do so–but I have to admit I'd be feeling just a bit easier in my mind if Jane had been just a bit more thorough in her inquiries before she went into action."

"Meaning–?" asked Dr. Hellyer, looking puzzled.

"Only that she does not seem to have found out that there is a son. But there is, you see. He appears to have taken quite a close interest in his father's work, and is determined that it shan't be wasted. In fact he has already announced that he will do his best to carry it on with the very few specimens that were saved from the fire. . . .

"Laudably filial, no doubt. All the same it does disturb me a little to find that he, also, happens to be a D.Sc., a biochemist and that, very naturally, his name, too, is Perrigan. . . ."

AN ORNAMENT TO HIS PROFESSION

by Charles L. Harness

> *The world has different owners at sunrise. . . . Even your own garden does not belong to you.*
>
> ANNE LINDBERGH

CONRAD PATRICK reached over and shut off the alarm. The dream of soft flesh and dark hair faded into six o'clock of a Friday morning. Patrick lay there a moment, pushing Lilas out of his thoughts, keeping his mind dark with the room, his body numb.

To move was to accept wakefulness, and this was unthinkable, for wakefulness must lead to knowledge, and then the problem barbs would begin to do their ulcerous work in his brain. They would begin, one by one, until all were in hideous clamor. None of them seemed ever to get really solved, and getting rid of one didn't necessarily mean he had solved it. More often, getting rid of it just meant he had found some sort of neutralizing paralysis, or that he had once more increased his pain threshold.

Patrick got up heavily, found his robe and slippers, and stumbled into the bathroom, where he turned on the light and surveyed his face with overt distaste. It was a heavy, fleshy face, and the red hair and mustache were awry. He was not exactly thin, but not really fat, either. His cheeks and stomach showed the effects of myriad beers in convivial company. He considered these beers, these cheerful hours, one by one, going back, in a mirrored moment of wonder and gratitude. He considered what life would have been like without them, and as the realization hit, his forehead creased uneasily. He scowled, dashed water over his eyes, and reached for a towel.

"Patrick," he muttered to himself in the mirror, "it's Friday. Another day has begun, and still the company hasn't found you out."

Patrick no longer knew exactly what he meant by this routine, which he had started some years before, when he was the newest chemical patent attorney with Hope Chemicals. He had first been a chemist, but not a very good one, and then, after he and Lilas had got married, he had gone to law school at night. After he got his LLB he had discovered, with more fatalism than dismay, that he was not a very good lawyer, either. Yet, all was by no means lost. He was accepted by Hope's Patent Department. And not just barely accepted; he was accepted as an excellent chemical patent attorney. He found this incredible, but he did not fight it. And finally, he deliberately masked his supposed deficiencies; when he was in the company of chemists, he spoke as a lawyer, and when with lawyers, he was a chemist. And when with the chemical patent lawyers, he didn't mind being just a fifty-fifty chemist-lawyer. They had his problem, too. It was like group therapy. Patent lawyers had a profound sympathy for each other.

From the beginning he had thrown himself into his work with zest. And now, with Lilas and the baby gone, his work was not just an opiate; it was a dire necessity.

He got the kettle boiling in the kitchen. There was now a pink glow in the east. He looked out the kitchen window and almost smiled. It was going to be a beautiful morning. He made the coffee quickly, four spoons of coffee powder in his pint mug, took the first bitter, exhilarating sip, tightened his robe about him, stepped out the kitchen door, and padded off down the garden path, holding his coffee mug carefully.

This again was all part of his morning routine. Today, of course, there was a special reason. Theoretically the house and grounds were ready and waiting for the little party tonight, but it would do no harm to take a look around, down by the pool.

The flagstone path lay down a grassy slope and was lined with azaleas. He and Lilas had put them in together. At the foot of the slope was a tiny stream, fed mostly by a spring half a mile away, on his neighbor's property. In this little stream Patrick had contrived a series of pools by dint of fieldstone and mortar, slapped together with such indolence into the stream side that the result was a pleasing but entirely accidental naturalness. These little pools were bordered with water cress, cat-o'-nine-tails, arrowhead, water iris, and lovely things with names he could no longer remember. He and Lilas had splurged one summer and bought all manner of water plants by mail. They had got very muddy planting them, and they had sorrowed over those that had died the next spring or that the baby had happily yanked. And then suddenly everything had begun to grow like weeds, and in a wild way, it was all very pretty.

The path along the stream led toward a grassy sward. Patrick stopped on the path a moment and listened. Yes, there it was, very faint, like a tinkling of tiny bells. He held his breath. Around the turn of the path, and so far invisible, was the bench. He and Lilas used to sit here, overlooking the lily pond. Only then, of course, it wasn't the lily pond, but the baby's wading pool. It was . . . how long ago? . . . that she had splashed in the pool and her baby delight had shattered the garden peace. And that was what he heard now. And he could hear Lilas' answering laughter. This had happened to him on many past mornings. To him, it was not a conjured thing; it was faint, very far away, but it was real.

He began to walk again, and rounded the bend in the path. But as soon as the pool and the bench came in view, the sounds stopped abruptly. He had tried to deal with the phenomenon logically. This led him to various alternative conclusions, neither of which he completely disbelieved: (a) he was subject to hallucinations; (b) Lilas and the baby were really there.

Patrick sighed and looked about him. Here, all within a few steps of each other, were the lily pool, the benches, the outdoor grill, and the arbor. The arbor was a simple structure, framed with two-by-fours, bordered with lilacs that had never bloomed, and which enclosed his "work table." This was a stone-topped table with a drawer, which contained writing materials and a few scribbled pages.

He looked into the arbor. From somewhere up in the ceiling of honeysuckle there was a flutter of wings. Sparrows. The "room" seemed to concentrate the odor of grass clippings, fresh from yesterday's mowing. Patrick glanced over at the stone table and permitted himself the habitual morning question: Would he have a few moments to work on his article? This was followed by a prompt companion thought. He was being stupid even to think about it. In three years he had not even finished the first chapter. And already the Court of Customs and Patent Appeals had wrought far-reaching revisions in the law of prior printed publication. Maybe he should pick another subject. An article he could do quickly, get into print quickly, before the court could hand down a modifying decision. Somehow, there must be a way to get this thing off dead center. A top-flight professional in any field ought to publish. Not that he was really that good. Still, as Francis Bacon had said, a man owed a debt to his profession.

He opened the drawer and pulled out the sheaf of papers. But he knew that he wasn't going to work on it this morning. A breeze fluttered the sheets. His eye cast about for a paperweight and found the candle-bottle—a stub of candle sticking in the neck of a wine bottle, used when he sat here at night and did not want to use the floodlights. He put the bottle on the papers.

Glumly he accepted his first inadequacy of the day. No use trying to hold the others back. The line forms to the right. The magic was gone from the morning; so be it. Let them come. He finished off his coffee. In his own garden he was a match for all of them. He felt girded and armored.

They came.

One. His department was about to lose a secretary—Sullivan's Miss Willow. He hadn't told Sullivan. But maybe Sullivan knew already. Maybe even Miss Willow knew. These things always seemed to get around. He didn't mind interdepartmental promotions for the girls. He'd used it himself on occasion. But he didn't like the way Harvey Jayne was using company personnel policy to pressure him. And right now was a bad time to lose a secretary, with all those Neol cases to get out. As an army travels on its stomach, so his Patent Department traveled on its typewriters, or, more exactly, on the flying fingers of its stenographers as applied to the keys of those typewriters, "thereby to produce," as they say in patentese, a daily avalanche of specifications, amendments, appeals, contracts, and opinions.

He halfway saw an angle here. Maybe he could boomerang the whole thing back on Harvey Jayne. Have to be careful, though. Jayne was a vice-president.

Two, and getting worse. Jayne wanted publication clearance for the "Neol Technical Manual," and he wanted it today. It had to be cleared for legal form, proofread, and back to the printers tonight, because bright and early Monday morning twenty-five crisp and shining copies, smelling beautifully of printer's ink, had to be on that big table in the Directors' Room. Monday, the Board was going to vote on whether the company would build a six-million-dollar Neol plant.

Three, and still worse. John Fast, Neol pilot plant manager, wanted the Patent Department to write a very special contract. Consideration, soul of the party of the first part, in return for, inter alia, guarantee of success with Neol. It was impossible, and there was something horrid and sick in it, and yet Patrick was having the contract written by Sullivan, his contract expert, and in fact the first draft should be ready this morning. He was *not* going to refer Fast to the company psychiatrist. At least not yet. Maybe in two or three weeks, after Fast was through helping Sullivan get those new Neol cases on file in the

Patent Office, he might casually mention this situation to the psychiatrist. Why did it always happen this way? Nobody could just go quietly insane without involving him. Forever and ever people like John Fast sought him out, involved him, and laid their madness upon him, like a becoming mantle.

Fourth, and absolutely and unendurably the worst. The patent structure for the whole Neol process was in jeopardy. The basic patent application, bought by the company from an "outside" inventor two years before, was now known to Patrick, and to several of the senior attorneys in his department, to be a phony, a hoax, a thing discovered to have been created in ghastly jest—by a man in his own department. This was the thing that really got him. He could think of nothing, no way to deal with it. The jester, Paul Bleeker, was the son of Andy Bleeker, his old boss and good friend. (Did anybody have any real friends at this crazy place any more?) And that was really why he had to come up with an answer. It would kill Andy if this got out. Certainly, he and both Bleekers would probably have to resign. After that there would come the slow, crushing hearings of the Committee on Disbarment.

Problems.

Was this why he couldn't write, why he couldn't even get started? He blinked, shook his head. Only then did he realize that he was still staring, unseeing, at the handwritten notes in front of him.

He leafed slowly through the scribblings. How long ago had he started the article? Months? Nearly three years ago, in fact. He had wanted to do something comprehensive, to attain some small measure of fame. This was the real reason lawyers wrote. Or was it? Some time soon, he'd have to re-examine this thing, lay bare his real motives. It was just barely conceivable it would be something quite unpleasant. He gave a last morose look at the title page, "The College Thesis as Prior Art in Chemical Patent Interferences," and put the papers back in the envelope. He just didn't know how to put this thing back on the rails. Fundamentally he must be just plain lazy.

But time was wasting. He looked at his wristwatch, put the papers back, closed the drawer, and walked out to the lily pond again.

It was in the same wet sparkle of sunlight that he remembered his baby daughter, splashing in naked glee that warm summer day so many months ago. Lilas had stood there and called the baby out of the pool to get dressed, for that fatal Saturday afternoon trip to the shopping center. And his daughter had climbed out of the pool, ignored the tiny terry-cloth robe, and dashed dripping wet into her father's arms. At least her front got dried as he held her writhing wetness against his shirt, patting her dancing little bottom with the palm of his hand.

Slowly he sat down again. It must have been that sunbeam on the pool. It was going to be bad. He began to shudder. He wanted to scream. He bent over and buried his face in his hands. For a time he breathed in noisy rasps. Finally he stood up again, wiped his gray face on the sleeve of his robe, and started back up the garden path to the house. He would have to be on his way to the office. As soon as he got to the office, he would be all right.

'Tis all a Chequer-board of
Nights and Days
Where Destiny with Men for
Pieces plays . . .
OMAR KHAYYAM

Patrick sometimes had the impression that he was just a pawn on Alec Cord's chessboard. Cord was always looking seven moves deep, and into a dozen alternate sequences. Patrick sighed. He had long suspected that they were all smarter than he was, certainly each doing his job better than Patrick could do it. It was only the trainees that he could really teach anything anymore, and even here he had to fight to find the time. Nothing about it made sense. The higher you rose in the company, the less you knew about anything, and the more you had to rely on the facts and appraisals developed by people under you. They could make a better patent search than he; they could write a better patent specification, and do it faster; they could draft better and more comprehensive infringement opinions. In a gloomy moment he had wondered whether it was the same way throughout the company, and if so, why had the company nevertheless grown into the Big Ten of the American chemical industry. But he never figured it out.

He looked up at his lieutenant. "I understand it was the crucial game, in the last round. If you beat Gadsen, you won the tournament, and if he beat you, he won."

"Didn't realize you followed the sports page, Con," said Alec Cord.

"Gadsen had white, and opened with the Ruy Lopez. You defended with Marshall's Counter Gambit. They gave the score in the paper. Somebody said it was identical, move for move, with a game between Marshall and Capablanca, in 1918, when Marshall first pulled his gambit on Capablanca."

"I wouldn't know."

"That's a surprise. They say you even had an article in *Chess Review* last year on the Marshall Counter Gambit."

Cord was silent. Patrick took a new tack. "Gadsen's that Examiner in Group 170, the one handling your Neol cases?"

"That's right."

"Including the basic case, the one we know now is the phony? The one our whole Neol plant depends on?"

"The very one."

"The one you would have given just about anything, even the Annual D.C. Chess Tournament, for Gadsen to allow?"

"All right, Con. But it's not what you think. I didn't throw the tournament. And Gadsen didn't throw the allowance. We didn't discuss it at all. I admit I let him win that game, but there wasn't any deal. It would have to occur to him, with no help from me, that there was something he owed me. He could have done it either way, and I'd have had no kick. Maybe he'd have given the allowance anyhow. In fact, for all you know, maybe he allowed the case despite the game, and not because of it."

"I won't argue the point, Alec. We may never know. Anyhow, the thing I came to see you about is this." He handed the other a legal-size sheet.

Cord's eyes widened. "An interference!"

"So maybe Gadsen allowed the claims just to set you up for an interference."

"Maybe. But not likely. If he were going to do that, he would have just sent the interference notice, this thing, without the allowance."

"Any ideas who the other party is?"

"Probably Du Santo. We've been picking up their foreign patents in the quick-issue countries, like Belgium. We'll know for sure after the inventors file their preliminary statements. Which brings me to the next question: How can we file a preliminary statement sworn to by a phony inventor who doesn't even exist?"

"I don't know. I want you to figure out something after we talk to Paul Bleeker."

"Take it from the beginning, Paul," said Patrick.

Paul Bleeker's face rippled with misery.

Cord said: "Maybe I'd better go."

"Stay put," said Patrick shortly. "Paul, you understand why we have to have Alec in on this. You're emotionally involved. You might not be able to do what has to be done. Alec has to listen to everything, so he and I together can plan what to do. You trust him, don't you?"

The young man nodded.

"It began as sort of a joke . . . ?" prompted Patrick.

"Yes, a joke," said Paul. "When I was a freshman in law school. Harvey Jayne and those others were teasing Dad. That was when Dad was still Director of the Research Division, before they promoted him."

The light was dawning. Patrick sat up. "They were teasing him about the Research Division?"

"Yes, then Mr. Jayne said Dad's Research Division was essential, but only to verify outside inventions he bought."

"So you decided to booby-trap Mr. Jayne?"

"Yes."

"You then wrote those patent attorneys in Washington?"

"Yes, I mailed them the examples for the patent application. They took them and changed them around a little bit, the same way we do here in the Patent Department. They added the standard gobbledygook at the front, and eight or ten claims at the back. They sent the final draft back to me for execution. The standard procedure. They sent me a bill for three hundred dollars. I paid that out of the money Mr. Jayne sent them, when he bought the invention. I still have the rest—four thousand and seven hundred dollars. I haven't spent any of it." He looked uncertainly at Patrick. "You won't tell Dad about this, will you?"

"Certainly not." Patrick looked at him with genuine curiosity. "But how were you able to make the oath? What notary would notarize the signature of 'Percy B. Shelley'?"

"Absolutely any, Con. They all just assume you are who you say you are, so long as you pay the fee."

Patrick was momentarily shaken. "But that's the whole idea of notarizing, to make the inventor swear he's truly the inventor, the person named in the oath."

Cord smiled faintly. "Not all notaries waive identification, Con."

"Well," said Patrick, "now we've committed perjury, sworn falsely to the United States Patent Office. So far, all they can do to you, Paul, besides disbarring you, followed by imprisonment in the Federal

Penitentiary, is to strike your Shelley case from the files in the Patent Office."

The young man was silent.

Cord said: "Harvey Jayne bought the patent application only after he knew it worked. The whole thing depended on whether John Fast could reproduce it in the lab. Paul, how could you be so sure it would work?"

"If John did it right, it couldn't *not* work. I copied the examples right out of something in the library. Somebody's college thesis."

Patrick brightened. "Alec?"

Cord shook his head. "Nothing like that ever turned up in our literature searches. We hit the Dissertation Abstracts, all the way back to the beginning."

Patrick turned back to Paul Bleeker. "You'll have to tell us more about this thesis. What was the name of the student? We'd also like the name of the university, and the year. In fact, anything and everything you can remember."

"All I can remember is these runs, tucked away in the back pages. They didn't really seem pertinent to the main body of the thesis. Other than that, I can't remember anything."

"You must have seen the title page," pressed Patrick.

"I guess so."

"You could identify it if you saw the thesis again?"

"Sure, but it's gone."

"Gone?"

"The library just had it on loan. They have hundreds come in, this way. Our people keep them awhile, then send them back. You know the procedure."

"There must be some record."

Cord shook his head. "We've checked all the inter-library loans for the past five years. We found nothing. If Paul's memory is correct on the facts, that it *was* within the last five years, and the library *did* have it on loan, we are led to the conclusion that the thesis was done by somebody here at Hope, and lent on a personal basis to the library, without any formal record."

Patrick groaned. "Our own inventor, here all the time? That's all we need. He'll scream. He'll take it to court. We've got to find him first, before he finds us." He turned to Cord. "Alec, add it all up for us, will you?"

"It admits of precise calculation," said Cord, "in the manner of a chess combination. There are two primary variations. Each of these has several main subvariations. None of them is really difficult. The only problem is to recognize that our tactics are absolutely controlled, move by move, by events as they develop."

Patrick raised his hand. "Not so fast. Let's take the main angles. The primary variations."

"First primary. We do nothing. If we're senior party in the interference, this means we take no testimony, but rely purely on our filing date. Chances: better than even. If we're junior party, we lose hands down.

"Second primary. We fight. Firstly, this gives subvariant A. With Paul's help we find the real inventor. We buy his invention from him, and, if he hasn't already published, we file a good and true application for him. We enter a motion to substitute the new case for Paul's case, and then we expressly abandon Paul's case. If this inventor actually has published in the way Paul remembers, this gives subvariant B. We find that thesis, then we move to dissolve the interference, contending that the sole count is unpatentable over the disclosures in the thesis."

Patrick twisted his mustache nervously. "However you state it, we wind up with no chance of a patent. Maybe we can live with that. Perhaps we can forego a patent-based monopoly. But there's one thing we *must* have—and that's the right to build the plant, free and clear from interference or infringement of anybody else's patent. Can we tell the Board we have that right? The Board wants to know. They're going to vote on it Monday. And I don't think we can tell them anything . . . not yet. The economics and market are there. Everything hangs on the patent situation. Bleeker says the vote will be to build, if the patent picture is clear. We're holding the whole thing up in our shop right here." He turned back to Cord. "Alec, take it from the college thesis. Run the variations off from that."

"Variation One," said Cord, "the thesis is a good reference. This means it adequately describes the invention, that it was at least typewritten, that it was placed on the shelves at the University Library, available to all who might ask for it, and that all of this was done more than one year before either Paul or his opponent filed their respective cases. This would support the motion to dissolve. Both parties would lose, and neither would get a patent, fraudulent or otherwise. With no basic patent to be infringed, it follows that anybody could build a Neol plant. Paul's application would be given a prompt final rejection and would be transferred to the abandoned files in the Patent Office. Then it would lie buried until destroyed under the twenty-year rule. Nobody would ever learn about it.

"Variation Two. The thesis for some reason is not citable as a good, sufficient, and competent reference under the Patent Office rules. For example, we might not find it in time, or if we do find it, it might really present substantial differences from Paul's disclosure. Even if we are senior party, we will not be able to negotiate a settlement of the interference without grave danger of discovery of what Paul did. If we turn out to be junior party, it's even more certain we can't settle the interference, but there's actually less risk of being found out, if only because the opposition won't talk to us."

Patrick's mouth dropped. "All right. We always come back to the thesis. We've got to find it. If we find it, we can build a Neol plant. If we can't find it, we can't build a plant, and even worse things will probably happen to a number of people in this company." He turned to Cord. "Have you and Paul exhausted every possibility, every lead?"

Cord nodded glumly. Paul Bleeker bent over and put his face in his hands.

Patrick sighed. He thought, "I'll have to do it the hard way. Tonight." He said, "Paul, you'll be over tonight, won't you?"

"Yes, Con."

"Thanks, fellows. Paul, would you ask Sullivan to come in?"

He must needes goe whom the devill doth drive.
JOHN HEYWOOD

Patrick smiled at Sullivan. "Good morning, Mike. How are those Neol cases coming?"

"We're in good shape. John Fast and I will need a couple of more weeks, though. It's a whole series of cases. Covers the catalysts, the whole pilot-plant setup, the vapor phase job, everything. John and I get together every morning and dictate this stuff to Willow. She types her notes in the afternoon. Except that as of now she's about a week behind in transcription. If she left right now, the Neol patent cases would be in quite a hole."

Patrick met Sullivan's studied gaze noncommittally. "He knows," he thought. "They all know about Willow." He said easily, "I guess you're right. How about John? Will he stick with your program?"

Sullivan shrugged his shoulders. "He'd better. We need him. But, like I said, he needs us, too. And he insisted that you approve the contract. Do you want to see it?"

Patrick shifted uncomfortably. "It's nearly ten o'clock. He'll be here in a minute. You can read it to both of us, then."

Sullivan smiled. "You're getting off easy."

Patrick said, "I know what you're thinking, Mike. And you're right. We *are* going to turn him over to the psychiatrist. But not just yet. Not until you get these last three Neol disclosures written up. Another couple of weeks won't hurt him."

Sullivan's smile deepened.

Patrick said, "Medically, it certainly can't hurt to humor him."

Sullivan laughed. "Con, you're a sham, a fraud, and a hypocrite. Preserve him long enough for him to file his cases, then let him drop dead."

Patrick bridled. "That's putting it a little strong. If I thought for a moment . . ."

"Oh, come off it, Con. We're all on edge with this thing. Anyhow, you can take comfort in the thought that the Patent Department has simply ground out one more contract, one out of a hundred a year, doing their daily hacking, what they are paid to do, and therefore what they rejoice in doing. If you look at it that way, you have served your client to the very best of your ability, and at night you can sleep with sound conscience."

Patrick growled, "If I didn't need you—"

Sullivan held up his hand. "Speak of the devil—"

"Come in," called Patrick.

John Fast entered the room. He was an average-looking man, average size, of an average grayness. His face was almost without expression, perhaps a little sad. There was something unnerving in his eyes. They were acquainted with—

"Horror?" thought Patrick, wondering. No. That was too simple. John Fast was acquainted with the sub-elements of horror, with the building stones of terror, and with the unrest of darkness. And this was the man whom he would need tonight. "Hello, John," he said genially. "I hear your Neol cases are going a mile a minute."

"Going nicely, Con, thanks." Fast looked at Sullivan, then back at Patrick. "Is my contract ready?"

"Contract? Yes, of course, the contract. Mike and I have been going over it. Before we read it to you, though, we'd like to make sure we've covered everything. Now Mike here has heard your story, but I haven't. I'd like to hear it from you, straight, exactly the way it happened."

"It's a long story, Con."

"We've got lots of time."

"All right, then." Fast took a deep breath; his eyes grew distant. "I think it began with the ozonator. You know what ozone smells like? It's sharp, electric. In certain concentrations it's hard to distinguish from chlorine or sulfur dioxide. You know how the Bible talks about brimstone? Brimstone is sulfur, but there wasn't any surfur in Palestine. The old prophets were just trying to identify an odor that was there long before they learned about sulfur. This creature moves in an atmosphere of ozone. He moves around in time and space, and to do this he applies an electrical field on the space-time continuum. Ozone is sort of a by-product, the same as when you run an electric motor. So this thing moves around in a fog of ozone. Not only that, ozone seems to attract him, the way nectar attracts bees.

"For a long time I didn't really realize he was around. And then last week I met him. It might have been an accident. But with all this Freudian theory, maybe there's no such thing as an accident. Maybe, on the subconscious level, I did it deliberately. Anyhow, you know we have a big structural formula of pentacyclopropane drawn in white paint on the floor of the pilot plant. This makes a star, with the methylene groups as the five points. It is also a pentagram—a star-like geometric design used in certain . . . rituals. Within the history of the United States, people have been burnt for making a pentagram. The stage was set. Just one more thing was needed: the Lord's Prayer recited backwards. This was provided. I'm a steady churchgoer. Bible class on Sunday mornings. Last Sunday I took my office tape recorder to Bible class. Yes, we said the Lord's Prayer. It was still on the tape when I was going to dictate my monthly progress report. I rewound the tape, so there it was, everything going backwards on audio. I was inside the pentagram. And suddenly, there–it–was, on the other side. I was so scared I was petrified. I wasn't surprised. Just scared. Maybe that means I knew what I was doing. So we stared at each other. Except I wasn't sure what I was staring at. But it was definitely a shape, with arms, head, eyes . . ."

"You were tired," said Patrick. "You know how fatigue can induce hallucinations."

"It's not that simple, Con. There–*was*–there *is*–something there, some kind of elemental force. It's a being, an intelligent being. And powerful, in strange ways. It can . . . alter the laws of chemistry and physics. I got it to increase the yield of terpineol—'Neol.' At first, by about ten percent. Then another ten percent. It was easy. And then last night we started up the pilot plant. We ran the C-10 through first, cold, just to flush the lines and check the flowmeters. We got the ozonator tied in about midnight. Now you understand the ozone won't start reacting with the C-10 until you hit about one sixty F., and we'd planned to turn steam into the jacket after the ozone concentration had built up to about five percent. But the reactor began to warm up. It hit one sixty in a matter of seconds. The two technicians on shift were scared. They ran over behind the explosion mat. I stayed put. I knew what was going on. *He* was doing it. I wanted to know how far he could push it. I shunted the C-10 through the flowmeter. I switched in the product receiver. It took about thirty minutes to feed one pound mole of C-10 . . . exactly one hundred and thirty pounds. I shut everything off. I had been watching the product scales all along, so I knew what it was going to be. It was one hundred fifty-four pounds, one pound mole of Neol, exactly. Yield: one hundred percent of theory.

"They came out from behind the mats, then. They looked at the graphs. Nobody believed the graphs. They looked for a weighing error. They knew it couldn't happen. So I told them to check the meters. The meters were all right. I knew there was nothing wrong with the meters. Then we started another run. The reaction didn't start cold this time. So we turned the steam into the jacket. That was supposed to start the reaction. We usually start getting terpineol in the receiver at about one sixty. We watched it for a good hour. Not a drop of product. Just C-10 going in, C-10 coming out. We couldn't explain it. We were making ozone. The ozonator was O.K. We had the right concentration of C-10, the right temperature, mole ratio, space velocity, everything was right. But not a gram of terpineol was coming out. *He* wanted to *show* me, you understand, that he could control it either way. But he was going to leave it up to me which way it went. I didn't want to decide right then. I didn't know what to do. Just then I didn't even know how I could tell him, if I did decide. So we simply shut down and knocked off.

"I went home, but I couldn't sleep. I tried to think it through. And I guess I did think it through. This *being* can put me through. With him on my side I can do anything. There's no position in this corporation I couldn't have. And *that* would just be a starter. I don't know where the end would be. So I want to make the deal. I know exactly what I want. And what *he* wants. He wants, well, he wants *me*. Not my body, really, or anything like that. It's more like something mental. He wants to take it from me a little at a time, like a parasitical drain. But it wouldn't affect me physically or mentally. In fact, I'd get sharper all the time. And whatever it is, it would go so slowly, day by day, that I wouldn't notice it. This goes on for years. I'll even have a normal life expectancy. When he's got all of it, I'll die. And that's the deal. The next thing is to get it down on paper. Something he and I can both sign. A binding contract. It doesn't matter whether you believe he exists. Call him the Devil if you like. And call the thing I'm giving him my soul. A lot of people who believe in God don't believe the Devil exists. And some of them don't believe in souls, either. Although, as I said, it isn't really that simple."

There was a long silence.

"The contract?" prompted Fast.

Patrick nodded, as in a dream, to Sullivan.

Sullivan began: "This Agreement, made as of this blank day of blank, in the year of our Lord—"

"Not 'of our Lord,'" said Fast.

"Quite so," said Sullivan. "I'll fix that." He continued: ". . . By and between John Fast, hereinafter sometimes referred to as 'Fast,' and His Satanic Majesty, hereinafter sometimes referred to as 'The Devil,' Witnesseth: Whereas Fast is desirous of certain improvements in his present circumstances; and Whereas The Devil is able to cause and bring about said improvements; now therefore, in consideration of the mutual promises herein contained, and for other good and valuable consideration, the receipt of which is hereby acknowledged, the parties agree as follows: Article One. The Devil shall promptly cause the Hope Chemical Company to erect a plant for the production of terpineol, hereinafter referred to as 'Neol,' and to make Fast the manager thereof. The Devil shall, with all deliberate speed, cause Fast to become a world-famous chemist, rich, respected, and to win at least two Nobel prizes. Without limiting the generality of the foregoing, The Devil will immediately enter upon the performance, and will continue same, for the full term of this Agreement, of every obligation set forth on Exhibit A, annexed hereto, and incorporated by reference herein."

Sullivan looked up at Fast. "You wrote out the list?"

"Right here."

"Mark it 'Exhibit A,'" said Sullivan. He continued. "Article Two. Fast hereby assigns, grants, conveys, sets over, and transfers all his right, title, and interest in and to his soul, to the said Devil, on the death of Fast; provided, however, that Fast shall live until the age of seventy, and that during said period The Devil shall have met faithfully, and in a good and workmanlike manner, all his obligations, both general and specific, as above set forth."

Patrick nodded. "That's fine."

"We had to change some of our 'boiler-plate' clauses," said Sullivan. "Others we had to leave out altogether. For example, we thought it best to omit completely the 'Force Majeure' clause, whereby the Devil is relieved from his obligation to perform, if prevented by an Act of God, but can nevertheless require you to perform, that is, give up your soul!"

"Logical," agreed Fast.

"And we had to change the 'construction and validity' clause. Ordinarily we provide that our contracts shall be construed, and their validity determined, under the laws of the state of New York. However, we think that under New York law the contract might be held invalid, as having an immoral object, and hence unenforceable by either side. So we changed it to Hawaiian law."

"Yes," said Fast. "It's all ready to sign, then?"

"Right there, there're lines for the signature of both, ah, parties," said Sullivan. "Are we to understand, John, that the Devil will actually affix his signature to this document, in real pen and ink?"

"I sign in blood," said Fast calmly. "How *he* signs, I'm not really sure. All I know is, he'll do something, maybe make a special appearance, to let me know that he accepts."

"I see," said Patrick. (He saw nothing.) He asked curiously, "But why do you think you need the Devil? An energetic man with a solid technical background and a high I.Q. in a big, growing chemical company doesn't need assistance such as this."

Fast looked at him in surprise. "Coming from you, Con, that's a very strange question."

"How is that?"

"I accept aid from any source, because I am totally committed. But so are you, and therefore, you, too, will accept assistance without asking the cost, or to whom the payment will be made."

Patrick felt a flurry of confusion. "And to what am I totally committed?"

"To your patents. Did you not know?"

Patrick had to think about this. Finally, he shook his head, not in denial, but to admit incomprehension. "Well," he defended. "It's my job."

Fast's mouth, immobile and cryptic as the Mona Lisa's, seemed almost to smile. "Yes, but only because you have contracted for it. So you see, what I have done is not a particularly strange thing. You . . . everyone . . . has entered into his own private contract, with something. My only difference is that I have put mine in writing. This does not necessarily mean that I am more honest than you. Perhaps I am merely more perceptive.

"True, my deal is with the Devil. But is that immoral? Morality is relative. *My* action, *my* way of life, has to be evaluated against the background of *your* action, and *your* way of life. You think me immoral, if not insane. Yet you wrote this contract for me. Why? Because you want to keep me happy. And why do you want to keep me happy? So that I'll keep your patents coming. Therefore you've made your own contract–with your patents. You resolve all questions of sin, virtue, and morality in light of the effect on your patents. With you, nothing can be sinful–even an assignment to hell–if it helps your terpineol patents. Before you judge my contract, take a look at your own."

Patrick stared at the gray man. Finally he smiled uneasily. "Whatever you say, John."

"And now I'll do *you* a favor, Con. Change the name."

"Change what name?"

"Neol. It's wrong."

"What's wrong with it?"

"The sound; wrong altogether. If you should ever have to . . . call . . . anyone with it, it wouldn't do it. Also, you ought to have five letters, exactly, one letter for each point of the pentagram. Correct symbology is essential."

"Whom would I be calling?" said Patrick. "And why?"

"You know . . . for your patents."

Patrick looked blank, then frowned, then finally he smiled. "All right, John. Whether or not you're a mystic, I'll give you 'x-plus,' for mystification."

After Fast had gone, Patrick and Sullivan stared at each other.

"Do *you* believe any of that?" said Patrick.

"I believe he *thinks* he saw something. A kind of self-hypnosis."

"How about the yield. You know one hundred percent of theory is impossible."

"No, Con, I don't know that. And neither do you. Within experimental errors, he may well have got one hundred percent. And even if he didn't, he really might have got fairly close to it. A pilot plant always does much better than a bench scale unit. You just naturally expect the yield to be high. All the variables are optimized, easily controlled."

"So you think he just hypnotized himself into seeing the devil?"

"Why not? Actually, he's an accomplished amateur hypnotist. I'm told he is quite a parlor performer, if you can catch him."

"I know. He'll be at the party tonight for something like that. But he's wrong about me. I'm *not* totally committed to my patents. It's my job, the same as it's your job. John Fast doesn't know what he's saying."

Sullivan's eyes twinkled wickedly. "You're absolutely right, Con. There are *some* things you would not resort to, even to save the Neol patent position. You would *not* sell your own grandmother into white slavery even if it would win the interference and solve the whole problem." He paused, then added maliciously, "Would you, Con?"

Patrick snorted. "Don't tempt me!"

"Are you going to change the name?" asked Sullivan.

" 'Neol'?"

"You know what I mean."

"Well, maybe. There's nothing really wrong with 'Neol.' "

"Except that John Fast thinks it's wrong."

". . . Without saying how to make it right," added Patrick. "I want to think about it. And I might change it, just to be ornery."

That which we call a rose
By any other name would smell as sweet.
SHAKESPEARE

Patrick sat in his office, looking at the proofs of the "Neol Technical Manual," and thinking hard. This was Harvey Jayne's manual, and Jayne was trying to steal Miss Willow. But Jayne needed Patent Department clearance for his manual. Right away, this suggested possibilities. This morning, he had it nearly figured. And then John Fast had decided the name was wrong. And what difference did it make to John Fast? He wasn't even going to ask, because tonight he was going to need the man.

But *could* he change the name? How sacred was this manual to Jayne?

Patrick considered the matter.

He knew, certainly, that a technical manual prepared and published by an American chemical giant was like nothing else in the world of books. It was the strange child of the mating of the laboratory with Madison Avenue, midwifed by the corporate public-relations committee. It told all. It was rich in history, process descriptions, flow sheets, rotogravures, chemical equations, and nomographs. It was comprehensive, and its back pages were filled with thousands of arrogant footnotes. The stockholders of Hope Chemical were given the impression that the sole function of the "Neol Technical Manual" was to incite an unendurable craving for Neol in the hearts of purchasing agents throughout the country. But Patrick knew that the compiler privately harbored other motives. For that man, Harvey Jayne, it represented an opportunity for creativity that comes only when the company builds a new plant; it could not happen to Jayne twice in one lifetime.

In this manual, Harvey Jayne would have a ready-made solace for whatever disasters might lie ahead. His wife might on occasion fail to recognize his greatness; his son might fail in school; he might, alas, even be laterally transferred within the company. Yet, withal, his faith in himself would be restored, and the blood brought back into his cheeks, when he gets out his old Technical Manual, to read a little in it, to fondle its worn covers, and to look at the pictures. So doing, Harvey Jayne might murmur, with tears in his eyes, as did Jonathan Swift, rereading *Gulliver's Travels,* "God, what genius!"

So, thought Patrick, this volume will be cherished forever by Harvey Jayne. He will keep it in his office bookcase, with a spare in his den at home. When he transfers, it will be carefully packed. Years later, for presentation at his retirement dinner, his lieutenants will borrow his last copy from his wife, or perhaps steal one from the company library. They will have it bound in the company colors, blue and gold; and the chairman of the board, the president, and numerous fellow vice-presidents will autograph its pages.

Now, brooded Patrick, the whole of this immense and immemorial undertaking, this monster, this manual, centers around the product trademark, which is as essential to it as the proton to the atom, the protoplasmic nucleus to the growing cell. The manual is known by this name. Once thus baptized, the name is sacred. And to deny this book its name, to suggest that its name is wrong, that it should have another name, is to invite the visitation of the Furies, for this is desecration, a charge so sinister that it must rank with defamation of motherhood, or with being against J. Edgar Hoover.

Yes, there were possibilities. For personal disaster. He could not change the name of the manual. And yet he was going to. Why? he wondered. Why am I going to do this? I am as crocked as John Fast. His mind floundered, searching. I have to fight Harvey Jayne, that's why. No. That's not why. It's something else. John Fast said the name was wrong. The new name should have five letters. He tugged briefly at his mustache, then leaned over to the intercom.

Books cannot always please.
George Crabbe

"Con," said Cord, "it's not really bad. A few editorial changes should do the job."

Patrick's face was a blank. "How about 'Neol'?"

"It's clear. The closest thing is 'Neolan,' registered for textiles."

Patrick brightened. "Clear? It's a clear case of infringement!"

Cord stared at him. "What . . . what did you say?"

"I said it infringes. And I hasten to add, Cord, my boy, that you look quite strange, with your mouth open." He reached for the phone and dialed Jayne.

"Oh, hi there, Harvey. . . . No, I didn't call to protest about Miss Willow. We're really grateful you can do something for her, Harvey. Her place is with you, Harvey. On one condition . . . It's this, Harvey, that you double her raise. She's worth every bit of it. Good, Harvey, splendid you see it our way. . . . Tech manual, Harvey? Yes, we're looking at it right now. No, Harvey, I'm afraid we can't do that. There's a very close prior registration that will probably kill Neol as a trademark. No, Harvey, please get that out of your head. Miss Willow has nothing to do with it. She will transfer with our very best wishes. . . . That is indeed your privilege, Harvey. If you want to present the manual to the Board on Monday morning without Patent Department clearance, go right ahead. It would, of course, be my duty to give Andrew Bleeker a memo itemizing my objections, absolving the Patent Department of all responsibility for the content of the manual. There will be carbons, of course, to . . . You will? Why, that's fine, Harvey." He hung up. "He's coming over."

"I'm amazed," said Cord dryly.

"Keep your fingers crossed on Willow."

"But you said the louse could have her, with a double raise," said Cord.

"Alec, you wouldn't believe me if I told you what is about to happen. So I won't waste time. We have only a few minutes before Harvey is due to show. So—*Cord.*"

"Yes, Con?"

"I didn't address you. I merely stated your name. It turns crisply from the tongue, like honest bacon in the griddle. A fine name. Cord, Cord, Cord. A good word to say. Here, I'll write it, too. Flows easily on paper. Cord looks good. Listens good. Charming. A man's name is the best thing about him. Like Narcissus. Hello there, you beautiful name!"

Cord flushed red. "Con, for goodness' sake. It isn't at all remarkable!"

"Yes, my boy, it is . . . to you." He leered at his lieutenant. "A man's name is his most enchanting possession. For you, for me, for Harvey Jayne, for anybody."

"So?"

"That's how we find a substitute for Neol. We will derive us a new word, from 'Jayne.' Harvey will find it irresistible. And it will be a good trademark. Think of the trouble American Cyanamid had, trying to find a trademark for their acrylic fiber. They finally named it after the project leader, Arthur Cresswell. They called it 'Creslan.' And Cluett-Peabody, naming their 'Sanforize' process for preshrunk fabric after the inventor, Sanford. And think of how many of Willard Dow's products are 'Dow' something or other, 'Dowicide,' for example. And look at Monsanto's 'Santowax;' 'Santowhite,' 'Santomerse.' And Du Pont's 'Duponol,' and W. R. Grace's 'Grex' polyethylene. So we'll name our terpineol after Harvey Jayne. 'Jayne-ol.' Of course not exactly 'Jayne-ol.' We'll have to fix it so he won't recognize it. Some phonetic equivalent."

"He'll recognize it, Con. It'll just make him madder."

"No, I don't think he will. A man has a selfish complex on his own name. He loves it, and he doesn't want other people to have it. He has trouble remembering people who have similar names. So if we do this right, he won't recognize it when he hears it. It'll fascinate him, but he won't understand why. He'll approve it on the spot. But first, we'll have to work him over, soften him up a little. So listen carefully to what you have to do."

"Harvey," said Patrick, "you're making us revise our company leaflet on trademarks."

"I didn't know you had one," said Harvey Jayne suspiciously.

"It lists everything that shouldn't be done—all possible error. At least it *did*. Now, you've added a few more. We'll have to revise."

"This brochure. You wouldn't happen to have a copy—"

Patrick handed him the leaflet. "Brand-new edition, just off the press this afternoon."

Jayne read slowly. " 'The trademark should be capitalized, and preferably set in distinctive type. If the trademark is registered in the United States Patent Office, follow it with the registration symbol, ®. If no application for registration has been filed, or, if filed, not yet granted, then use an asterisk after the trademark, with footnote identification. Hope Chemical Company's trademark for . . .' " He looked up. "I'm not sure I follow your reasoning on this particular point. For example, I didn't capitalize 'neol.' I don't care whether it's capitalized or not. And I didn't say 'trademark' every time I said 'neol.' I just said plain old neol. I want it to become so familiar to our customers that they'll think of it as a household word."

Patrick shook his head sadly. "Harvey, I understand your viewpoint, and I deeply sympathize. Such charity and philanthropy are all too infrequent in this hatchet-hearted corporation."

"Charity? Philanthropy?"

"Yes. Really touching. Gets me *here*." Patrick struck his fist to his chest. "You want to give the trademark to the general public, including our competitors. Come one, come all, anybody can use this name, which isn't a trademark any more, because Harvey doesn't want it spelled with a capital."

"I don't see how spelling it lower case prevents it from being a trademark."

"It converts it into the *thing itself*. Remember 'cellophane'? It used to be Du Pont's trademark for transparent wrappings, and it was spelled with a capital 'C.' And then it became so well known that the newspapers and magazines began spelling it lower case, and they never mentioned it was Du Pont's brand of anything, because everybody by that time thought of cellophane only as the transparent wrapping itself. It had become the common name of the thing itself; it had become *generic*. Now anybody can sell his own transparent wrapping and call it 'cellophane.' Cellophane has now joined the list of irresistible trademarks that are wide open to the public: shredded wheat, mineral oil, linoleum, escalator, aspirin, milk of magnesia."

"Anything else wrong?"

"Several other points. On the title page, you ought to say 'Copyright, Hope Chemical Company.' "

"But how can I say 'Copyright' before we publish? I thought you just said you couldn't do that. You said we couldn't say Neol was registered."

"I won't try to explain it, Harvey. That's the way it has worked out historically."

"Anything else?"

"We don't like your trademark, 'Neol,'" said Patrick. "We think it infringes at least one mark already registered. Besides which, it's a weak mark, made up of weak syllables."

"What . . . what are you saying?" sputtered Jayne. "There's nothing wrong with 'Neol.' How can it be weak?"

"Look at it this way," said Patrick smoothly. "Fashions in trademarks come and go, like women's hats. At the moment, the ad people are conditioned to think in terms of certain well-worn prefixes and suffixes. The suffix is supposed to classify the product as a liquid, a solid, a plastic, a synthetic fiber, a flooring compound, soap, deodorant, toothpaste, and so on. True, they have their differences, but these are minuscule. The pack of them are so much alike you'd take them for a children's *a capella* choir."

"That's probably true for most trademarks," said Harvey Jayne smugly, "but not for 'Neol.' 'Neol' was selected by our computer, which was programmed to synthesize words from certain mellifluous-sounding syllables and to discard everything harsh. And not only that, but to present a final list of one hundred names graded according to final audial acceptance. 'Neol' headed the list."

Patrick shook his head pityingly. "Look, Harvey, when you use a computer, you've got two and a half strikes against you from the start. In the first place, the only marks the computer can grind out will be made up of these forbidden syllables we've already ruled out. And secondly, no computer can zero in on the gray area between the legally acceptable 'suggestive' marks and the legally unacceptable 'descriptive' marks. Even the courts have a hard time with this concept. To demonstrate this, we are going to decomputerize 'Neol' for you."

"De . . . computerize . . . ?"

"Yes, our decomputer takes a computerized trademark and tells us whether it's too close to known marks or names to be registrable."

"May I see it, this decomputer?"

"You could, but that won't be necessary. It's so simple, I'll just describe it to you briefly. It consists of two cylinders, rotating on the same shaft, one next to the other. On the left cylinder we have prefixes; on the right, suffixes. All our syllables were compiled from trademarks in the chemical and plastics fields. When a new trademark comes in, we break it down into syllables and see if it's in our decomputer. If it's not here, we search it in the Trademark Division of the Patent Office, in Washington."

"What syllables do you have on your, ah, decomputer?" said Jayne uneasily.

"Really only the extremely common ones. For prefixes, things like 'ray,' 'hy,' 'no,' 'ko,' 'kor,' 'di,' 'so,' 'ro,' the 'par-per-pro' set, 'vel,' 'val,' and of course, 'neo.'"

"Neo, you said?"

"Yes, 'neo,' which is simply the Greek variant of 'new,' which again frequently comes out as 'nu,' or in the Latin form, 'novo.'"

"And I presume 'ol' is among your proscribed suffixes?" demanded Jayne bitterly.

"Yes, that's 'ol,' from Latin, 'oleum,' oil. So that gives us 'Neol,' or 'new oil.'"

Jayne frowned and looked at his notes. "Well, how about 'Neolan'? Or do you have 'lan' in your suffices, too?"

"Yes, indeed. But there again, we consider 'lan' as a species of the 'on' family, from 'rayon,' of course. Between vowels, 'on' takes a consonant, so you would come out with 'lin,' 'lan,' 'lon,' and so you have 'neolan.'"

Jayne threw up his hands. "Well, then, you fellows just do whatever you have to do, to fix this. Say the right words over it. Do your legal mumbo jumbo."

Patrick studied Jayne quietly for a moment. "Harvey. I'm going to do something I shouldn't. I'll clear a trademark–no, not Neol. Some other mark."

Jayne looked dubious. "*We* would have to originate it. Our ad people have to screen these things. All kinds of image and audio requirements."

"Impossible, Harvey. This is not a job for the agency. All they can do is put together syllables to skirt along the fringes of what they think your customers will almost but not quite recognize. The way they draw up those lists, they practically guarantee their mark will be weak. Leave them out of this. I'll give you a mark I will guarantee *you* will like and that will not infringe any existing mark."

"But if it isn't on my list, how can you be so sure I'll like it?"

Patrick smiled. "We've never lost a customer."

"Probably it will be very similar to a trademark on my list."

Patrick picked up the list and scanned it briefly. "No, I think not. But we're wasting time. Let's move on to the next item."

"Next item?"

"Payment."

"Charge my department."

"You don't quite understand, Harvey. Let's go over it again. I'm promising you a clean, desirable trademark. I'm giving you a guarantee—on something that as yet doesn't even exist. I don't have to do it. This is above and beyond the call of duty. A big favor to you."

"So?"

"If the company gets sued, you're in the clear, but it's a black eye for me. They'll say Hope needs a younger man in their Patent Department. Patrick is slipping. And then the next time it happens, I'm out on my ear. So I'm taking a chance, and I want payment."

Jayne was suspicious. "Like what?"

"We need not be crass. You could offer a prize for a suitable mark."

"And *you* would win it?"

"The Patent Department would win it."

"Go on," said Jayne acidly.

"The prize couldn't be money."

"I can see that. As you say, crass. How about wall-to-wall carpeting?"

"No."

"A conference room . . ."

"Not that, either."

"Electric typewriters . . ."

"Not exactly what I had in mind."

"Then what *do* you want?"

Patrick leaned over and murmured, "Willow."

Jayne was silent for a moment. Finally he said, "I don't know what to say. It's cheap, shoddy, not in character with you, Con. Furthermore, I don't make the rules. This promotion program is a company policy. It's not anything you or I have anything to do with. I need a secretary. I have a vacancy. I either fill it by promoting a girl from the lab, or I go outside. I think it's a good policy."

"So do I," said Patrick morosely. "I hate to do this."

"You don't have to do it. In fact, you're being absolutely unreasonable. If you insist on doing this to me, I'll have to take it up with Andrew Bleeker."

"If you do that, you could get me in trouble."

"As you say, I would hate to have to do it."

"At the same time, you will also have to mention to Bleeker that you couldn't get the manual out in time for the Board. You won't have to tell him why, though. He'll be first on my list of carbons of my trademark infringement report to you. He will not be happy."

The room became very quiet. The pale drift of typewriters ebbed and flowed in the outer bays.

Jayne's restraint was massive. "You win."

"Thank you, Harvey. And now, just so we won't have any misunderstandings, when Miss Willow comes back to us from having been your secretary, she'll keep her double raise?"

"I thought that she was never leaving you. How can she come back to you?"

"It's all over the place, Harvey, that she's being transferred to you. If we kept her here, she'd be entitled to think that we cheated her out of a raise. So we have to get her transferred to you on the books, get her double raise, and then transferred back to us on the books. Physically, of course, there would seem to be no reason for her to transfer . . . that is, clean out her desk, or anything like that."

"So that not only I don't get a secretary, Willow gets two raises."

"But you get a clean bill of health for your manual."

"And a good trademark?"

"Absolutely." Patrick was solemn. "We can pick one here and now. We guarantee we can get the trademark application on file this afternoon. All we need is a more exotic name—one not made out of these garden-variety building units. A really *beautiful* name."

Cord picked up the cue. "How about some foreign words that mean 'beautiful'?"

"Well, there's a thought. Harvey, what do you think?"

Jayne shrugged his shoulders. "Like what?"

"*Pulchra*—Latin for 'pretty,'" said Cord.

"Hard to do anything with it," said Patrick. "What else?"

"*Kallos*—'beautiful' in Greek."

Patrick looked doubtful.

"*Bel?*" said Cord.

"That's a little better. What is it in Italian?"

"*Bella.*"

"Still not quite right," said Patrick.

"You could take a big jump. 'Beautiful' in German is *schoen.* You'd have to Anglicize the accent a little, give it a long 'a.'"

"Ah yes. 'Shane.' *Shane!*" Patrick's eyes lit up. "I really like that. Harvey?"

"Not bad. Shane. Hm-m-m. Yes, I must admit, there's something about it. Something tantalizing."

"I hear it, too, Harvey."

Cord's eyes rolled upward briefly.

"How long will it take to search it out in the Washington trademarks?" demanded Jayne.

"We can do it this afternoon. My man will call in, any minute now, and we'll tell him to go ahead."

"I'll take it," said Jayne.

"Good enough. If it's clear in the Trademark Division, we'll get the application on file this afternoon."

Jayne looked surprised. "You'll have to have labels made up. Then you'll have to make a bona fide sale in interstate commerce. And then have the trademark application executed by Andy Bleeker. I don't think you can do all that in three hours. And I won't pay off on a phony."

"Of course not." Patrick smiled angelically as the other left.

In the early afternoon Patrick walked across the court to the terpineol pilot plant and into the cramped dusty office of John Fast. As he stepped inside, his eyes were drawn immediately across the cubicle, beyond Fast's desk, to a large painting, in black and white, hanging on the wall behind Fast. He poised at the doorway, slack-jawed, staring at this . . . thing.

Within the plain black frame were two figures, one large, and, in front, a smaller. The outlines of the larger figure seemed initially luminous, hazy, then, even as he squinted, perplexed and uneasy, the lines seemed to crystallize, and suddenly a face took form, with eyes, a mouth, and arms. The arms were reaching out, enfolding the figure in front, a man wearing a medieval velvet robe and feathered beret.

Unaccountably, Patrick shivered. His eyes dropped, and found themselves locked with those of John Fast, unquestioning, waiting.

Fast murmured, "It is an oversize reproduction of Harry Clarke's pen-and-ink drawing, the end piece of Bayard Taylor's translation of Goethe."

"What is it?" blurted Patrick.

"Mephistopheles, taking Faust," said John Fast.

Patrick took a deep breath and got his voice under control. "Very effective." He paused. "John, I'm here to ask a favor."

Fast was silent.

"I understand you have a certain skill in the art of hypnosis."

Fast's great dark eyes washed like tides at Patrick. "That's not quite the right word. But perhaps the result is similar."

"I'll come to the point. All this is highly confidential. Our basic terpineol patent application is in interference in the Patent Office. We intend to dissolve the interference by a motion contending that the interference count is unpatentable over the prior art. This prior art is a college thesis. The problem is, Paul Bleeker is the only one who has seen the thesis, and he can't remember anything about it. Is it possible for him to remember, under hypnosis?"

"It's possible," said Fast, "but by no means a certainty."

"But isn't it true that everyone records, somewhere on his cerebrum, everything he has ever experienced?"

"Possibly. But that doesn't necessarily mean we can remember it all. Recall is a complicated process. The theory in fashion today is the 'see-all-forget-nearly-all' theory. In this one, every bit of incoming sensation is recorded and filed away in your subconscious. But to bring it up again, you not only have to call for it, you also have to walk it out, holding it by the hand, chopping along with a mental machete to clear away all the subconscious blocks along its path. Persistence will turn up many a forgotten item in this way. But if it's quite old, there may be so many blocks that it will never be able to penetrate the conscious mind. In this case you have to get down there with it, in your far subconscious—take a good look at it, and then holler out to somebody what you see. Hypnosis is the accepted procedure. In the hands of an expert, all kinds of oddities can be turned up in this way: stimuli the subject barely had time to receive; or things, which, if recalled on a conscious level, would be intolerable."

"I want you to try it on Paul Bleeker tonight."

Fast hesitated a moment. "I gather you renamed 'Neol'?"

Patrick's eyebrows arched. "Yes. How did you know?"

"It was best for your patents, and you always do what's best for your patents."

" 'Neol' was a poor trademark," said Patrick doggedly. "That was the only reason we changed."

"What is the new name?" asked Fast.

And now Patrick hesitated. He found himself unwilling to answer this question. Suddenly, he almost disliked John Fast. He shook himself. "'Shane,'" he said curtly.

Tiny iridescent lights seemed to sparkle from somewhere deep in the eyes of the other.

"Well?" demanded Patrick.

"Exquisite," murmured Fast. "I will do this thing for you. It may involve something more than hypnotism. You understand that, don't you?"

"Of course."

"No, you don't. You can't, at least not yet. But no matter. If Paul is willing, I will do it for you anyway. Since you are totally committed, it cannot be otherwise."

Those who have lost an infant are never, as it were, without an infant child. They are the only persons who, in one sense, retain it always.

LEIGH HUNT

Andrew Bleeker swung his swivel chair slowly back and forth as he motioned to the two chairs nearest his desk.

Patrick said cheerfully, "Good afternoon, Andy."

Harvey Jayne grunted. He was not cheerful.

Bleeker's eyes flickered broodingly at Patrick's face. He had a horror of these nasty internecine arguments. Patrick beamed back, and Bleeker sighed. "I'll come to the point, Con. There seems to be some question about the way you handled Harvey's Neol manual."

"Really? I realize I wasn't able to satisfy him completely, but I didn't think he felt strongly enough about it to take it to the head office."

"What was the problem, Con?"

Harvey rose out of his chair. "Andy, let *me* state–"

"Con?" said Bleeker quietly.

"I sort of blackmailed him, Andy. I pressured him into giving one of our secretaries a double raise, out of *his* budget. In return I got him a good trademark, made an infringement search on it, and got the trademark application on file in the Patent Office, all within four hours. He still has time to get his brochure proofs corrected and back to the printers tonight. But it isn't the Neol Manual anymore. We changed the trademark to 'Shane.'"

"'Shane'?"

"Harvey picked it out, all by himself."

"You don't say," murmured Bleeker.

"The name is all right," grumbled Jayne. "It's the trademark *application* I'm protesting. It's a fraud, a phony. Andy, you perjured yourself when you made oath that the company had used the trademark in commerce. The mark didn't even exist until a few hours ago, and I know for a fact our shipping department hasn't mailed out anything labeled 'Shane' across a state line. It has to be interstate commerce, you know. But there hasn't been any shipment at all. Not one of the packages has left the Patent Department. I just checked."

Bleeker hunched his shoulders and began to swing his chair in slow oscillations. "Con?"

"He has the facts very nearly straight, Andy, but his inference is wrong. There was no fraud. When you signed the declaration, you did not commit perjury."

"But doesn't the form say that the goods have been shipped in interstate commerce? Didn't I sign something to that effect?"

"The trademark application simply asks for the date of first use in commerce. The statute defines commerce as that commerce regulated by Congress. *That's* been settled for over a hundred and fifty years. Congress controls commerce between the states and territories, commerce between the United States and foreign countries, and commerce with the Indian tribes."

"But we didn't ship in interstate commerce," said Jayne.

"That's right," said Patrick.

"Nor in foreign commerce?" asked Bleeker.

"No, Andy."

"That leaves—"

"The Indians," said Patrick.

"Apaches," said Jayne acidly, "disguised as patent attorneys."

"Not exactly Apaches, Harvey," said Patrick. "But we do have a lawful representative of the Sioux tribe, duly accredited to the Bureau of Indian Affairs in Washington. Commerce is with the Sioux, through their representative. A sale to her is a sale to the tribe. If you checked on the packages, you probably noticed that one was on her desk."

"Her desk," rasped Jayne. "This . . . Indian . . . *you mean—"*

"Miss Green Willow, late of the Sioux reservation? Of course. Drives a hard bargain. We finally settled on fifteen cents for the gallon jug of terpineol. Her people back in Wyoming will make it into soap for the tourists."

Bleeker seemed suddenly to have problems with his face, and this was detectable largely by the efforts he was making to freeze his mouth in an expression of polite inquiry. Then his cheeks turned crimson, his stomach jumped, and he hastily swiveled his chair away from his visitors.

There was a long silence. Jayne looked from Bleeker's back to Patrick's earnest innocence. He was bewildered.

Finally Bleeker's chair swung around again. His eyes looked watery, but his voice was under control. "Harvey, can't we be satisfied to leave it this way?"

Jayne stood up. "Whatever you say, Andy." He refused to look at Patrick.

Bleeker smiled. "Well, gentlemen."

Jayne walked stiffly out the door. Patrick started to follow.

"Just a minute, Con," said Bleeker. He motioned Patrick back inside. "Close the door."

"Yes, Andy?"

Bleeker grinned. "One day, Con, they'll get you. They'll nail you to the wall. They'll hang you up by the thumbs. You have got to stop this. Is Willow really an Indian?"

"Certainly, she is." Patrick was plaintive. "Doesn't *any*body trust me? The arrangement is legal."

"Of course, of course," soothed Bleeker. "I was just thinking, how convenient to have your own Indian when you need a quick trademark registration. It's like having a notary public in your office."

"All our secretaries are notaries," said Patrick, puzzled.

Bleeker sighed. "Of course. They would be. I stepped into that one, didn't I?"

"What?"

"Never mind." Bleeker's chair began its slow rhythm again. "How's that chess player getting along? Alec Cord?"

"He made second place in the D.C. annual."

"He's still not in your league, though, Con. Nobody, absolutely nobody, can equal your brand of chess."

Patrick squirmed. "I don't even know the moves, Andy."

"And your contract man, Sullivan? Can he write as good a contract as you?"

"Much better," said Patrick.

"Did he write the contract that bound you to the Hope Patent Department?"

"What do you mean, Andy?"

"Oh, never mind. I don't know what I mean. I don't think I'll ever understand you patent fellows. Take Paul. Chemists become lawyers; lawyers never become chemists. Paul can't—or won't—explain it. There's probably something profound in this, but I've never been able to unravel it. Does it mean chemists have the intellect and energy to rise to advocacy, but that lawyers could never rise further into the realm of science? Or does it mean that the law is the best of all professions, that once in the law, other disciplines are attainted?"

Bleeker's chair began to swivel slowly again. Patrick knew what was coming. He got everything under control.

"How *is* Paul the patent lawyer?" asked Bleeker.

"A competent man," said Patrick carefully. "We're glad you sent him around to us."

Bleeker was almost defensive. "You know why I did it, Con. There's nobody else in the company I could trust to make him toe the mark. Really make him. You know what I mean."

"Sure, Andy, I know. He's a bright kid. I would have hired him anyway. Quit worrying about him. Just let him do a good job, day by day. Same as I did when I worked for you."

"I worked you hard, Con. Make Paul work hard."

"He works hard, Andy."

"And there's one more thing, Con. You switched trademarks. Neol to . . . Shane, you said?"

"That's right. Neol is a poor trademark. Shane is better."

"That's another thing Jayne is going to hold against you, Con. Switching marks on his cherished manual."

"It isn't really that bad, Andy." Patrick marveled at the older man's technique. At no time during the conversation had Bleeker asked Patrick whether the Patent Department was going to approve the terpineol plant, nor in fact had he asked him anything at all about the terpineol patent situation, even though they both knew this was vital to Bleeker's future in the company. And yet the questions and the pressure were there, all the same, and the questions were being asked by their very obvious omission. Patrick decided to meet the matter with directness. He said simply: "We haven't completely resolved the patent problem, Andy. But we certainly hope to have the answer for you well before the Board meeting Monday morning. With luck, we may even have it tonight."

Bleeker murmured absently, "That's fine, Con."

Patrick started to get up, but Bleeker stopped him with a gesture.

"Shane," said Bleeker thoughtfully. "Very curious." His eyes became contemplative. "Perhaps you never realized it, Con, but we regarded your wife as an outstanding scientist. *You* were wise, however, to take up law in night school."

Patrick nodded, wondering.

"We got interested in her," continued Bleeker, "when she was just finishing up her master's degree at State. I think we still have her thesis around somewhere. Old Rohberg made a special trip to drive her up for her interview. She was so pretty, I made her an offer on the spot. My only error was in turning her over to you for the standard lab tour. You louse."

Patrick smiled, his face warmly reminiscent.

Bleeker studied the other man carefully. "What was the name of your little girl?"

"Shan."

"Odd name."

"Lilas picked it. It's short for *'chandelle,'* French for 'candle.' Lilas was French, you know. Lilas Blanc. White lilac. And Shan was our little candle. The wallpaper in the nursery was designed with a candle print. The lights above her crib were artificial candles. We painted fluorescent candles inside her crib. She would pat them every night before I tucked her in."

Bleeker cleared his throat. "Con, sooner or later somebody's going to tell Harvey Jayne that you renamed Neol after your baby daughter."

Patrick didn't get it. He stared back, stupidly. "After . . . Shan?"

"Well, didn't you? Shan . . . Shane . . . ?"

Patrick felt his insides collapsing. "But I didn't . . ." he blurted. "It didn't occur to me." Then his mouth twisted into a lopsided smile. "At least, consciously. But there it is, isn't it? So maybe you're right, Andy. I really walked into that one. There I was, telling Cord that Jayne's mental blocks wouldn't let him see why he liked Shane. The same rule applied to me, although I don't want my daughter's name on terpineol, plastered on tank cars, warehouses, stationery, magazine ads. Too late now. Botched the whole thing."

Bleeker regarded him gravely. "Con, how long has it been now, since the . . . accident?"

"Three years."

"You're still a young man, Con. Relatively speaking. Our young ladies think it's about time you got back into circulation."

"You might be right, Andy."

Bleeker coughed. "You're just being agreeable to avoid an argument. Believe me, Con, it's one thing to remember the dead. It's an altogether different thing to have your every waking thought controlled by your memories. You ought to get away from that place."

Patrick was shocked. "Move? From the garden? The house? It has our bedroom. Shan's room. How about Lilas? How about Shan? They're *buried* there. Their ashes—"

"Ashes?"

"They were cremated. Lilas wanted it that way. I spread the ashes in the lilacs."

The older man looked at him with compassion. "Then release *them,* Con. *Let them go!*"

"I *can't,* Andy." Patrick's face twisted. "They're all I have. Can't you understand?"

"I guess I do, Con. I guess I do. I'm sorry. None of my business, really."

On this night of all nights in the year,
Ah, what demon has tempted me here?
EDGAR ALLAN POE, *Ulalume*

The evening was warm, and along about ten o'clock the party drifted down into the garden.

Patrick, as usual drinking only beer, was, for all practical purposes, cold sober, a condition that enhanced rather than alleviated an unexplainable and growing sense of anxiety. The nearness of the lilacs, usually a thing of nostalgic pleasure, somehow contributed to his edginess. He was startled to note that several clusters were on the verge of opening. He started to call Cord's attention to this, then thought better of it. And then he wondered, "Why didn't I? What's the matter with me? What's going on?"

The group was in the arbor now. He would have to get on with it, the reason why they were all here. Paul Bleeker and John Fast knew what they were supposed to do. All he had to do was to ask them to start. Paul was already seated at the stone table. As he watched, Paul pulled the table drawer out in an idle exploratory gesture.

"My notes for a patent law article I started . . . a couple of years ago," said Patrick wryly. "I just can't seem to get back to it."

"Then perhaps you should be thankful," said Fast.

"What do you mean?"

"A professional man writes for a variety of reasons," said Fast. "I'm working now on my 'Encyclopedia of Oxidative Reactions.' I know why I'm writing it. And I know why you're not writing, Con. It's because life has been kind to you. Let it stay that way."

Paul Bleeker broke in. "You say a professional man writes for a variety of reasons, John. Name one. Why do you write?"

Fast's dark eyes turned on Paul Bleeker. "You have heard it said, a man owes a debt to his profession. This may be true. But no professional man pays his debt by writing for the profession. If he is an independent, say a consulting engineer, or a partner in a law firm, or a history professor in a big university, he publishes because it's part of his job to advertise himself and his establishment. There's very little money in it *per se.* If he's a rising young man in a corporate research or corporate law department, he writes for the reputation. It helps him move up. If his own company doesn't recognize him, their competitors will. But if he's already at the top of his department in his company, he has none of these incentives. But he doesn't need them. If such a man writes, he has behind him the strongest force known to the human mind."

"And what might that be?"

"Guilt," said Fast quietly. "He writes to hide from the things he has done in the name of his profession. It gives him a protective cocoon to burrow into. A smoke screen to hide behind."

"In the name of the patent system," said Patrick firmly, "I've committed every crime known to man. And still I can't get started."

"You've done very little, really," said Fast in his nearly inaudible monotone. "But when you really have done something, you'll know it. You won't have to wonder or conjecture. Then, you'll begin to write. It'll come instantly. No floundering. No lost motion. You'll leap to it. The words, pages, and chapters will pour out in a torrent. It will be your salvation, your sure escape."

They stared at him. Cord laughed nervously. "So why do *you* write, John? What is your unspeakable crime?"

Fast turned his great black eyes on the other, almost unseeing. "I cannot tell you, my friend. And you wouldn't believe me if I did tell you. Anyhow, it can never happen to you." He looked away to Patrick. "But to you, Con, it could happen. And it could happen soon. Tonight. In this place."

Patrick laughed shakily. "Well, now, John. You know how careful I am. Nothing is going to happen to me. It's spare time I need to start writing, not penitence."

Fast looked at him gravely. "You do not weep. You smile. Before the Nazarene called Lazarus up, He wept." His toneless eyes seemed almost sad. "How can I explain this to you. Then let it be done. I have placed the Shane manual at the five angles of the pentagram. I think they are waiting."

"They?" stammered Patrick. "Oh yes, of course. The fellows. Perhaps we should begin."

"What's that smell?" called Sullivan.

"It's a terpineol," said Fast, sniffing a moment. "Like 'Shane.' Maybe a mixture of alpha and gamma terpineols." He snapped his fingers. "Of course!"

"Of course . . . *what?"* said Patrick. His voice was under control, but he felt his armpits sweating copiously.

"The mixture . . . very correctly balanced, I'd say. Just right for synthetic oil of lilac."

Patrick was struck dumb.

"That's very odd," said Sullivan. "Con's lilacs are not open yet."

"The odor must be coming from somewhere."

"Maybe we're all tired," said Cord. "Breeds hallucinations, you know."

Patrick looked at him in wonder.

"It's hard to convince anybody that odor can have a supra-chemical source," said Fast.

Cord laughed incredulously. "You mean there's something out there that is synthesizing oil of lilac . . . or Shane . . . or whatever it is?"

"We are so accustomed to thinking of the impact of odors *on* people that we don't think too much about the creation of odors *by* people. Actually, of course, everyone has his characteristic scent, and it's generally not unpleasant, at least under conditions of reasonable cleanliness. In this, man is not really basically different from the other animals. But man—or rather, a certain few extraordinary people—seem to have the ability, quite possibly involuntary, of evoking odors that could not possibly have come from the human sweat gland."

"Evoking?" said Sullivan.

"No other word seems to describe the phenomenon. Chemically speaking, in the sense of detectable air-borne molecules dissolving in the olfactory mucosa, the presence of odor is indeed arguable. On the other hand, in the strictly neuro-psychic sense, that an 'odor' response has been received in the cerebrum there can be no real doubt. The phenomenon has been reported and corroborated by entire groups. The 'odor of sanctity' of certain saints and mystics seems to fall in this category. Thomas Aquinas radiated the scent of male frankincense. Saint John of the Cross had a strong odor of lilies. When the tomb of Saint Theresa of Avila—the 'great' Theresa—was opened in 1583, the scent of violets gushed out. And more recently, the odor of roses has been associated with Saint Theresa of Lisieux—the 'little' Theresa." He looked at Patrick. "I think—everyone is ready."

Patrick wiped his face with his handkerchief. "Go ahead," he said hoarsely.

Ma chandelle est morte . . .
FRENCH NURSERY RHYME

Paul Bleeker was seated in the iron chair at the stone table. John Fast faced him, from one side. The others stood behind Paul.

"You are in a long dark tunnel," said John Fast quietly. "Just now everything is pitch black. But your eyes are beginning to adjust."

There was absolute silence. Then Fast's voice droned on. "In a little while, far ahead of you, you will be able to see the tunnel opening. It will be a tiny disk of light. When you see this little light, I want you to nod your head gently."

From far down stream drifted the plaintive call of a whippoorwill.

Paul Bleeker's eyes were heavy, glazed. His stony slump in the iron chair was broken only by his slow rhythmic breathing.

"You now see the little light—the mouth of the tunnel," monotoned Fast. "Nod your head."

"Candle," whispered Paul.

Patrick started, then recovered himself instantly.

Fast picked it up smoothly. "Watch the candle," he said. "Soon it will start to move toward you. It is beginning to move."

"Closer," murmured Paul.

In a flash of feverish ingenuity Patrick stepped forward, seized the wine bottle and its stub of candle from the stone table, struck his lighter, then lit the candle. He replaced the bottle on the table front. The flame wavered a moment, then flickered up. Patrick stole a glance at Paul's face. It was frozen, impassive.

Fast continued gravely: "Soon you will have enough light to see that you are sitting at your desk in the library. In a moment you will see the piles of books on the tables nearby. There are several books on your desk. There's a big book just in front of you. Now the candle is close enough."

"Close," murmured Paul.

The hair on Patrick's scalp was rising. The odor of lilacs was stifling. And he then noticed that the lilacs were opening, all around him. He somehow realized that lilacs do not bloom in minutes. It was a botanical impossibility. He could almost hear the tender calyxes folding back.

Fast continued. "You are opening the front cover. You are looking at the title page. It is typewritten. It is a thesis. You are able to read everything. You can see the name clearly. The name of the student is–"

Patrick heard gasps behind him, and his eyes suddenly came into focus. Beyond Paul, on the far edge of the stone table, beyond the candle, he saw the two figures. They were wavering, silent, indistinct, but they were there. The larger one would just about reach his chin. The eyes of the small one came barely to the table edge.

He wanted to scream, but nothing would come out of his throat.

The taller figure was leaning over the table toward Paul, and she was holding something . . . an open book. But neither figure was looking at Paul. Both of them were looking at him. He knew them.

In this frozen moment his nose twitched. The scent of lilacs wavered, then was suddenly smothered by something sharp, acrid. Patrick recognized it, without thinking. It was ozone. And as if in confirmation of its olfactory trademark, a luminous . . . thing . . . was taking shape behind the two figures. Suddenly it acquired a face, then eyes. Then arms, reaching out, encircling.

Patrick had a horrid, instantaneous flash of recognition. The portrait in John Fast's office. Mephistopheles taking Faust.

"The name of the student is Lilas Blanc," said Paul Bleeker metallically. "State U–"

"Oh, God, *no!*" screamed Patrick.

The candle blew out instantly. Paul struggled in his chair. "Hey, what . . . where?" He knocked the chair over getting up.

The voices rose up around Patrick in the darkness.

He dropped in a groaning heap on the grass. "Lilas, Shan, forgive me. I didn't know." But he must have known. All along.

And now his mind began to swing like a pendulum, faster and faster, finally oscillating in a weird rhythm of patterns so bewildering and contradictory that he could hardly follow them. His mind said to him, they escaped. It said to him, they did not escape. It said to him, they were there. It said, nothing was there. And then it started again. His throat constricted, his teeth bit the turf, and by brazen command his thoughts slowed their wounded flailing. He ceased to ask, to wonder. And finally he refused to think at all.

He heard Cord's firm voice. Somebody found the light switch. There were querulous whispers. And then there was something on his back. Some of them had dropped their jackets on him. A man's hand lingered briefly on his shoulder. It was a gentle, even affectionate gesture, and he recognized the touch as that of a man accustomed to tucking small children into their beds at night. He had used the same touch, many times, and long ago.

And now the sound of footsteps fading. And then, motors starting. And finally nothing, just the splash of the little falls, the crickets, and, far away, the whippoorwill.

He did not want to move. He wanted only never to have been born.

He closed his eyes, and sleep locked him in.

I hold every man a debtor to his profession; from the which, as men of course do seek to receive countenance and profit, so ought they of duty to endeavor themselves by way of amends to be a help and ornament thereunto.

FRANCIS BACON,
Preface to *Maxims of the Law*

It was early morning, and with the pink of dawn on his cheek, waking was instantaneous. His mind was clear and serene as he threw the jackets aside and got to his feet. He rubbed his eyes, stretched with enormous gusto, and walked over to the lily pond. A green frog was sitting on a pad of the yellow lotus, but jumped in as Patrick bent over to splash water on his face. He dried his face on his shirt-tail, which was flopping out over his belt.

The sun was now barely over the little hill, and a shaft of light was slicing into the pond. Patrick considered this phenomenon briefly, then peered into the bottom of the pool for the refracted beam. There was some kind of rule of optics—law of sines. Somebody's law. Check into it. Meanwhile, there was work to be done. Important work.

He walked into the arbor, picked up the overturned iron chair, sat down at the stone table, and pulled a pencil and paper pad out of the drawer. After a moment, he began to write; slowly, at first.

"Ex parte Gulliksen revisited. The typewritten college thesis as a prior printed publication. This decision from the Patent Office Board of Appeals in . . ."

Then faster and faster. ". . . essential, of course, that the thesis be available to the public. This requirement is satisfied by . . ."

Now, he was writing furiously, and the pages were accumulating.

He was going to make it. Just a question of staying with it, now, and it would give him complete protection. No need to worry about what to work on *after* this article, either. He knew he could turn out a text. No trouble at all. Or even an encyclopedia. Patrick, "Chemical Patent Practice," four volumes. He could see it now. Red vinyl covers, gilt lettering.

The stack of sheets torn from his pad was now quite bulky. He pushed the pile to the table corner, and in so doing knocked the bottle and candle unheeding to the ground and into the withering lilacs. Already he could visualize his "Preface to the First Edition." It should be something special, based perhaps on a precisely apt quotation. What was that thing from Bacon? He frowned, puzzled. No. There was something not quite right about *that*. But never mind. Plenty of others. Somehow, somewhere, there would be a word for him.

THE THIRD LEVEL

by Jack Finney

THE PRESIDENTS of the New York Central and the New York, New Haven and Hartford railroads will swear on a stack of timetables that there are only two. But I say there are three, because I've *been* on the third level at Grand Central Station. Yes, I've taken the obvious step: I talked to a psychiatrist friend of mine, among others. I told him about the third level at Grand Central Station, and he said it was a waking-dream wish fulfillment. He said I was unhappy. That made my wife kind of mad, but he explained that he meant the modern world is full of insecurity, fear, war, worry, and all the rest of it, and that I just want to escape. Well, hell, who doesn't? Everybody I know wants to escape, but they don't wander down into any third level at Grand Central Station.

But that's the reason, he said, and my friends all agreed. Everything points to it, they claimed. My stamp collecting, for example—that's a "temporary refuge from reality." Well, maybe, but my grandfather didn't need any refuge from reality; things were pretty nice and peaceful in his day, from all I hear, and he started my collection. It's a nice collection, too, blocks of four of practically every U.S. issue, first-day covers, and so on. President Roosevelt collected stamps, too, you know.

Anyway, here's what happened at Grand Central. One night last summer I worked late at the office. I was in a hurry to get uptown to my apartment, so I decided to subway from Grand Central because it's faster than the bus.

Now, I don't know why this should have happened to me. I'm just an ordinary guy named Charley, thirty-one years old, and I was wearing a tan gabardine suit and a straw hat with a fancy band—I passed a dozen men who looked just like me. And I wasn't trying to escape from anything; I just wanted to get home to Louisa, my wife.

I turned into Grand Central from Vanderbilt Avenue and went down the steps to the first level, where you take trains like the Twentieth Century. Then I walked down another flight to the second level, where the suburban trains leave from, ducked into an arched doorway heading for the subway—and got lost. That's easy to do. I've been in and out of Grand Central hundreds of times, but I'm always bumping into new doorways and stairs and corridors. Once I got into a tunnel about a mile long and came out in the lobby of the Roosevelt Hotel. Another time I came up in an office building on Forty-sixth Street, three blocks away.

Sometimes I think Grand Central is growing like a tree, pushing out new corridors and staircases like roots. There's probably a long tunnel that nobody knows about feeling its way under the city right now, on its way to Times Square, and maybe another to Central Park. And maybe—because for so many people through the years Grand Central *has* been an exit, a way of escape—maybe that's how the tunnel I got into . . . but I never told my psychiatrist friend about that idea.

The corridor I was in began angling left and slanting downward and I thought that was wrong, but I kept on walking. All I could hear was the empty sound of my own footsteps and I didn't pass a soul. Then I heard that sort of hollow roar ahead that means open space, and people talking. The tunnel turned sharp left; I went down a short flight of stairs and came out on the third level at Grand Central Station. For just a moment I thought I was back on the second level, but I saw the room was smaller, there were fewer ticket windows and train gates, and the information booth in the center was wood and old-looking. And the man in the booth wore a green eyeshade and long black sleeve-protectors. The lights were dim and sort of flickering. Then I saw why: they were open-flame gaslights.

There were brass spittoons on the floor, and across the station a glint of light caught my eye: a man was pulling a gold watch from his vest pocket. He snapped open the cover, glanced at his watch, and frowned. He wore a dirty hat, a black four-button suit with tiny lapels, and he had a big, black, handle-bar mustache. Then I looked around and saw that everyone in the station was dressed like 1890 something; I never saw so many beards, sideburns and fancy mustaches in my life. A woman walked in through the train gate; she wore a dress with leg-of-mutton sleeves and skirts to the top of her high-buttoned shoes. Back of her, out on the tracks, I caught a glimpse of a locomotive, a very small Currier & Ives locomotive with a funnel-shaped stack. And then I knew.

To make sure, I walked over to a newsboy and glanced at the stack of papers at his feet. It was the *World;* and the *World* hasn't been published for years. The lead story said something about President Cleveland. I've found that front page since, in the Public Library files, and it was printed June 11, 1894.

I turned toward the ticket windows knowing that here—on the third level at Grand Central—I could buy tickets that would take Louisa and me anywhere in the United States we wanted to go. In the year 1894. And I wanted two tickets to Galesburg, Illinois.

Have you ever been there? It's a wonderful town still, with big old frame houses, huge lawns, and tremendous trees whose branches meet overhead and roof the streets. And in 1894, summer evenings were twice as long, and people sat out on their lawns, the men smoking cigars and talking quietly, the women waving palm-leaf fans, with the fireflies all around, in a peaceful world. To be back there with the First World War still twenty years off, and World War II over forty years in the future . . . I wanted two tickets for that.

The clerk figured the fare—he glanced at my fancy hatband, but he figured the fare—and I had enough for two coach tickets, one way. But when I counted out the money and looked up, the clerk was staring at me. He nodded at the bills. "That ain't money, mister," he said, "and if you're trying to skin me you won't get very far," and he glanced at the cash drawer beside him. Of course the money was old-style bills, half again as big as the money we use nowadays, and different-looking. I turned away and got out fast. There's nothing nice about jail, even in 1894.

And that was that. I left the same way I came, I suppose. Next day, during lunch hour, I drew $300 out of the bank, nearly all we had, and bought old-style currency (that *really* worried my psychiatrist friend). You can buy old money at almost any coin dealer's, but you have to pay a premium. My $300 bought less than $200 in old-style bills, but I didn't care; eggs were thirteen cents a dozen in 1894.

But I've never again found the corridor that leads to the third level at Grand Central Station, although I've tried often enough.

Louisa was pretty worried when I told her all this and didn't want me to look for the third level any more, and after a while I stopped; I went back to my stamps. But now we're *both* looking, every weekend, because now we have proof that the third level is still there. My friend Sam Weiner disappeared! Nobody knew where, but I sort of suspected because Sam's a city boy, and I used to tell him about

Galesburg—I went to school there—and he always said he liked the sound of the place. And that's where he is, all right. In 1894.

Because one night, fussing with my stamp collection, I found—well, do you know what a first-day cover is? When a new stamp is issued, stamp collectors buy some and use them to mail envelopes to themselves on the very first day of sale; and the postmark proves the date. The envelope is called a first-day cover. They're never opened; you just put blank paper in the envelope.

That night, among my oldest first-day covers, I found one that shouldn't have been there. But there it was. It was there because someone had mailed it to my grandfather at his home in Galesburg; that's what the address on the envelope said. And it had been there since July 18, 1894—the postmark showed that—yet I didn't remember it at all. The stamp was a six-cent, dull brown, with a picture of President Garfield. Naturally, when the envelope came to Granddad in the mail, it went right into his collection and stayed there—till I took it out and opened it.

The paper inside wasn't blank. It read:

941 Willard Street
July 18, 1894
Galesburg, Illinois

Charley:

I got to wishing that you were right. Then I got to *believing* you were right. And, Charley, it's true: I found the third level! I've been here two weeks, and right now, down the street at the Dalys', someone is playing a piano, and they're all out on the front porch singing *Seeing Nellie Home*. And I'm invited over for lemonade. Come on back, Charley and Louisa. Keep looking till you find the third level! It's worth it, believe me!

The note is signed Sam.

At the stamp and coin store I go to, I found out that Sam bought $800 worth of old-style currency. That ought to set him up in a nice little hay, feed, and grain business; he always said that's what he really wished he could do, and he certainly can't go back to his old business. Not in Galesburg, Illinois, in 1894. His old business? Why, Sam was my psychiatrist.

ONE ORDINARY DAY, WITH PEANUTS

by Shirley Jackson

MR. JOHN PHILIP JOHNSON shut his front door behind him and came down his front steps into the bright morning with a feeling that all was well with the world on this best of all days, and wasn't the sun warm and good, and didn't his shoes feel comfortable after the resoling, and he knew that he had undoubtedly chosen the precise very tie which belonged with the day and the sun and his comfortable feet, and, after all, wasn't the world just a wonderful place? In spite of the fact that he was a small man, and the tie was perhaps a shade vivid, Mr. Johnson irradiated this feeling of well-being as he came down the steps and onto the dirty sidewalk, and he smiled at people who passed him, and some of them even smiled back. He stopped at the newsstand on the corner and bought his paper, saying "*Good* morning" with real conviction to the man who sold him the paper and the two or three other people who were lucky enough to be buying papers when Mr. Johnson skipped up. He remembered to fill his pockets with candy and peanuts, and then he set out to get himself uptown. He stopped in a flower shop and bought a carnation for his buttonhole, and stopped almost immediately afterward to give the carnation to a small child in a carriage, who looked at him dumbly, and then smiled, and Mr. Johnson smiled, and the child's mother looked at Mr. Johnson for a minute and then smiled too.

When he had gone several blocks uptown, Mr. Johnson cut across the avenue and went along a side street, chosen at random; he did not follow the same route every morning, but preferred to pursue his eventful way in wide detours, more like a puppy than a man intent upon business. It happened this morning that halfway down the block a moving van was parked, and the furniture from an upstairs apartment stood half on the sidewalk, half on the steps, while an amused group of people loitered, examining the scratches on the tables and the worn spots on the chairs, and a harassed woman, trying to watch a young child and the movers and the furniture all at the same time, gave the clear impression of endeavoring to shelter her private life from the people staring at her belongings. Mr. Johnson stopped, and for a moment joined the crowd, and then he came forward and, touching his hat civilly, said, "Perhaps I can keep an eye on your little boy for you?"

The woman turned and glared at him distrustfully, and Mr. Johnson added hastily, "We'll sit right here on the steps." He beckoned to the little boy, who hesitated and then responded agreeably to Mr. Johnson's genial smile. Mr. Johnson brought out a handful of peanuts from his pocket and sat on the steps with the boy, who at first refused the peanuts on the grounds that his mother did not allow him to accept food from strangers; Mr. Johnson said that probably his mother had not intended peanuts to be included, since elephants at the circus ate them, and the boy considered, and then agreed solemnly. They sat on the steps cracking peanuts in a comradely fashion, and Mr. Johnson said, "So you're moving?"

"Yep," said the boy.

"Where you going?"

"Vermont."

"Nice place. Plenty of snow there. Maple sugar, too; you like maple sugar?"

"Sure."

"Plenty of maple sugar in Vermont. You going to live on a farm?"

"Going to live with Grandpa."

"Grandpa like peanuts?"

"Sure."

"Ought to take him some," said Mr. Johnson, reaching into his pocket. "Just you and Mommy going?"

"Yep."

"Tell you what," Mr. Johnson said. "You take some peanuts to eat on the train."

The boy's mother, after glancing at them frequently, had seemingly decided that Mr. Johnson was trustworthy, because she had devoted herself wholeheartedly to seeing that the movers did not—what movers rarely do, but every housewife believes they will—crack a leg from her good table, or set a kitchen chair down on a lamp. Most of the furniture was loaded by now, and she was deep in that nervous stage when she knew there was something she had forgotten to pack—hidden away in the back of a closet somewhere, or left at a neighbor's and forgotten, or on the clothesline—and was trying to remember under stress what it was.

"This all, lady?" the chief mover said, completing her dismay.

Uncertainly, she nodded.

"Want to go on the truck with the furniture, sonny?" the mover asked the boy, and laughed. The boy laughed too and said to Mr. Johnson, "I guess I'll have a good time at Vermont."

"Fine time," said Mr. Johnson, and stood up. "Have one more peanut before you go," he said to the boy.

The boy's mother said to Mr. Johnson, "Thank you so much; it was a great help to me."

"Nothing at all," said Mr. Johnson gallantly. "Where in Vermont are you going?"

The mother looked at the little boy accusingly, as though he had given away a secret of some importance, and said unwillingly, "Greenwich."

"Lovely town," said Mr. Johnson. He took out a card, and wrote a name on the back. "Very good friend of mine lives in Greenwich," he said. "Call on him for anything you need. His wife makes the best doughnuts in town," he added soberly to the little boy.

"Swell," said the little boy.

"Goodbye," said Mr. Johnson.

He went on, stepping happily with his new-shod feet, feeling the warm sun on his back and on the top of his head. Halfway down the block he met a stray dog and fed him a peanut.

At the corner, where another wide avenue faced him, Mr. Johnson decided to go on uptown again. Moving with comparative laziness, he was passed on either side by people hurrying and frowning, and people brushed past him going the other way, clattering along to get somewhere quickly. Mr. Johnson stopped on every corner and waited patiently for the light to change, and he stepped out of the way of anyone who seemed to be in any particular hurry, but one young lady came too fast for him, and crashed wildly into him when he stooped to pat a kitten which had run out onto the sidewalk from an apartment house and was now unable to get back through the rushing feet.

"Excuse me," said the young lady, trying frantically to pick up Mr. Johnson and hurry on at the same time, "terribly sorry."

The kitten, regardless now of danger, raced back to its home. "Perfectly all right," said Mr. Johnson, adjusting himself carefully. "You seem to be in a hurry."

"Of course I'm in a hurry," said the young lady. "I'm late."

She was extremely cross and the frown between her eyes seemed well on its way to becoming permanent. She had obviously awakened late, because she had not spent any extra time in making herself look pretty, and her dress was plain and unadorned with collar or brooch, and her lipstick was noticeably crooked. She tried to brush past Mr. Johnson, but, risking her suspicious displeasure, he took her arm and said, "Please wait."

"Look," she said ominously. "I ran into you and your lawyer can see my lawyer and I will gladly pay all damages and all inconveniences suffered therefrom but please this minute let me go because *I am late.*"

"Late for what?" said Mr. Johnson; he tried his winning smile on her but it did no more than keep her, he suspected, from knocking him down again.

"Late for work," she said between her teeth. "Late for my employment. I have a job and if I am late I lose exactly so much an hour and I cannot really afford what your pleasant conversation is costing me, be it *ever* so pleasant."

"I'll pay for it," said Mr. Johnson. Now these were magic words, not necessarily because they were true, or because she seriously expected Mr. Johnson to pay for anything, but because Mr. Johnson's flat statement, obviously innocent of irony, could not be, coming from Mr. Johnson, anything but the statement of a responsible and truthful and respectable man.

"What *do* you mean?" she asked.

"I said that since I am obviously responsible for your being late I shall certainly pay for it."

"Don't be silly," she said, and for the first time the frown disappeared. "*I* wouldn't expect you to pay for anything—a few minutes ago I was offering to pay *you.* Anyway," she added, almost smiling, "it *was* my fault."

"What happens if you don't go to work?"

She stared. "I don't get paid."

"Precisely," said Mr. Johnson.

"What do you mean, precisely? If I don't show up at the office exactly twenty minutes ago I lose a dollar and twenty cents an hour, or two cents a minute or . . ." She thought. ". . . Almost a dime for the time I've spent talking to you."

Mr. Johnson laughed, and finally she laughed, too. "You're late already," he pointed out. "Will you give me another four cents worth?"

"I don't understand why."

"You'll see," Mr. Johnson promised. He led her over to the side of the walk, next to the buildings, and said, "Stand here," and went out into the rush of people going both ways. Selecting and considering, as one who must make a choice involving perhaps whole years of lives, he estimated the people going by. Once he almost moved, and then at the last minute thought better of it and drew back. Finally, from half a block away, he saw what he wanted, and moved out into the center of the traffic to intercept a young man, who was hurrying, and dressed as though he had awakened late, and frowning.

"Oof," said the young man, because Mr. Johnson had thought of no better way to intercept anyone than the one the young woman had unwittingly used upon him. "Where do you think you're going?" the young man demanded from the sidewalk.

"I want to speak to you," said Mr. Johnson ominously.

The young man got up nervously, dusting himself and eying Mr. Johnson. "What for?" he said. "What'd *I* do?"

"That's what bothers me most about people nowadays," Mr. Johnson complained broadly to the people passing. "No matter whether they've done anything or not, they always figure someone's after them. About what you're going to do," he told the young man.

"Listen," said the young man, trying to brush past him, "I'm late, and I don't have any time to listen. Here's a dime, now get going."

"Thank you," said Mr. Johnson, pocketing the dime. "Look," he said, "what happens if you stop running?"

"I'm late," said the young man, still trying to get past Mr. Johnson, who was unexpectedly clinging.

"How much do you make an hour?" Mr. Johnson demanded.

"A communist, are you?" said the young man. "Now will you please let me—"

"No," said Mr. Johnson insistently, "*how* much?"

"Dollar fifty," said the young man. "And *now* will you—"

"You like adventure?"

The young man stared, and, staring, found himself caught and held by Mr. Johnson's genial smile; he almost smiled back and then repressed it and made an effort to tear away. "I got to *hurry*," he said.

"Mystery? Like surprises? Unusual and exciting events?"

"You selling something?"

"Sure," said Mr. Johnson. "You want to take a chance?"

The young man hesitated, looked longingly up the avenue toward what might have been his destination and then, when Mr. Johnson said, "I'll pay for it," with his own peculiar and convincing emphasis, turned and said, "Well, okay. But I got to *see* it first, what I'm buying."

Mr. Johnson, breathing hard, led the young man over to the side where the girl was standing; she had been watching with interest Mr. Johnson's capture of the young man and now, smiling timidly, she looked at Mr. Johnson as though prepared to be surprised at nothing.

Mr. Johnson reached into his pocket and took out his wallet. "Here," he said, and handed a bill to the girl. "This about equals your day's pay."

"But no," she said, surprised in spite of herself. "I mean, I *couldn't.*"

"Please do not interrupt," Mr. Johnson told her. "And *here,*" he said to the young man, "this will take care of *you.*" The young man accepted the bill dazedly, but said, "Probably counterfeit" to the young woman out of the side of his mouth. "Now," Mr. Johnson went on, disregarding the young man, "what is your name, miss?"

"Kent," she said helplessly. "Mildred Kent."

"Fine," said Mr. Johnson. "And you, sir?"

"Arthur Adams," said the young man stiffly.

"Splendid," said Mr. Johnson. "Now, Miss Kent, I would like you to meet Mr. Adams. Mr. Adams, Miss Kent."

Miss Kent stared, wet her lips nervously, made a gesture as though she might run, and said, "How do you do?"

Mr. Adams straightened his shoulders, scowled at Mr. Johnson, made a gesture as though he might run, and said, "How do you do?"

"Now *this,*" said Mr. Johnson, taking several bills from his wallet, "should be enough for the day for both of you. I would suggest, perhaps, Coney Island—although I personally am not fond of the place—or perhaps a nice lunch somewhere, and dancing, or a matinee, or even a movie, although take care to choose a really *good* one; there are *so* many bad movies these days. You might," he said, struck with an inspiration, "visit the Bronx Zoo, or the Planetarium. Anywhere, as a matter of fact," he concluded, "that you would like to go. Have a nice time."

As he started to move away Arthur Adams, breaking from his dumbfounded stare, said, "But see here, mister, you *can't* do this. Why—how do you know—I mean, *we* don't even know—I mean, how do you know we won't just take the money and not do what you said?"

"You've taken the money," Mr. Johnson said. "You don't have to follow any of my suggestions. You may know something you prefer to do—perhaps a museum, or something."

"But suppose I just run away with it and leave her here?"

"I know you won't," said Mr. Johnson gently, "because you remembered to ask *me* that. Goodbye," he added, and went on.

As he stepped up the street, conscious of the sun on his head and his good shoes, he heard from somewhere behind him the young man saying, "Look, you know you don't *have* to if you don't want to," and the girl saying, "But unless *you* don't want to . . ." Mr. Johnson smiled to himself and then thought that he had better hurry along; when he wanted to he could move very quickly, and before the young woman had gotten around to saying, "Well, *I* will if *you* will," Mr. Johnson was several blocks away and had already stopped twice, once to help a lady lift several large packages into a taxi and once to hand a peanut to a seagull. By this time he was in an area of large stores and many more people and he was buffeted constantly from either side by people hurrying and cross and late and sullen. Once he offered a peanut to a man who asked him for a dime, and once he offered a peanut to a bus driver who had stopped his bus at an intersection and had opened the window next to his seat and put out his head as though longing for fresh air and the comparative quiet of the traffic. The man wanting a dime took the peanut because Mr. Johnson had wrapped a dollar bill around it, but the bus driver took the peanut and asked ironically, "You want a transfer, Jack?"

On a busy corner Mr. Johnson encountered two young people—for one minute he thought they might be Mildred Kent and Arthur Adams—who were eagerly scanning a newspaper, their backs pressed against a storefront to avoid the people passing, their heads bent together. Mr. Johnson, whose curiosity was insatiable, leaned onto the storefront next to them and peeked over the man's shoulder; they were scanning the "Apartments Vacant" columns.

Mr. Johnson remembered the street where the woman and her little boy were going to Vermont and he tapped the man on the shoulder and said amiably, "Try down on West Seventeen. About the middle of the block, people moved out this morning."

"Say, what do you—" said the man, and then, seeing Mr. Johnson clearly, "Well, thanks. Where did you say?"

"West Seventeen," said Mr. Johnson. "About the middle of the block." He smiled again and said, "Good luck."

"Thanks," said the man.

"Thanks," said the girl as they moved off.

"Goodbye," said Mr. Johnson.

He lunched alone in a pleasant restaurant, where the food was rich, and only Mr. Johnson's excellent digestion could encompass two of their whipped-cream-and-chocolate-and-rum-cake pastries for dessert. He had three cups of coffee, tipped the waiter largely, and went out into the street again into the wonderful sunlight, his shoes still comfortable and fresh on his feet. Outside he found a beggar staring into the windows of the restaurant he had left and, carefully looking through the money in his pocket, Mr. Johnson approached the beggar and pressed some coins and a couple of bills into his hand. "It's the price of the veal cutlet lunch plus tip," said Mr. Johnson. "Goodbye."

After his lunch he rested; he walked into the nearest park and fed peanuts to the pigeons. It was late afternoon by the time he was ready to start back downtown, and he had refereed two checker games and watched a small boy and girl whose mother had fallen asleep and awakened with surprise and fear which turned to amusement when she saw Mr. Johnson. He had given away almost all of his candy, and had fed all the rest of his peanuts to the pigeons, and it was time to go home. Although the late-afternoon sun was pleasant, and his shoes were still entirely comfortable, he decided to take a taxi downtown.

He had a difficult time catching a taxi, because he gave up the first three or four empty ones to people who seemed to need them more; finally, however, he stood alone on the corner and–almost like netting a frisky fish–he hailed desperately until he succeeded in catching a cab which had been proceeding with haste uptown and seemed to draw in toward Mr. Johnson against its own will.

"Mister," the cab driver said as Mr. Johnson climbed in, "I figured you was an omen, like. I wasn't going to pick you up at all."

"Kind of you," said Mr. Johnson ambiguously.

"If I'd of let you go it would of cost me ten bucks," said the driver.

"Really?" said Mr. Johnson.

"Yeah," said the driver. "Guy just got out of the cab, he turned around and gave me ten bucks, said take this and bet it in a hurry on a horse named Vulcan, right away."

"Vulcan?" said Mr. Johnson, horrified. "A fire sign on a Wednesday?"

"What?" said the driver. "Anyway, I said to myself if I got no fare between here and there I'd bet the ten, but if anyone looked like they needed the cab I'd take it as a omen and I'd take the ten home to the wife."

"You were very right," said Mr. Johnson heartily. "This is Wednesday, you would have lost your money. Monday, yes, or even Saturday. But never never never a fire sign on a Wednesday. Sunday would have been good, now."

"Vulcan don't run on Sunday," said the driver.

"You wait till another day," said Mr. Johnson. "Down this street, please, driver. I'll get off on the next corner."

"He *told* me Vulcan, though," said the driver.

"I'll tell you," said Mr. Johnson, hesitating with the door of the cab half open. "You take that ten dollars and I'll give you another ten dollars to go with it, and you go right ahead and bet that money on any Thursday on any horse that has a name indicating . . . let me see, Thursday . . . well, grain. Or any growing food."

"Grain?" said the driver. "You mean a horse named, like Wheat or something?"

"Certainly," said Mr. Johnson. "Or, as a matter of fact, to make it even easier, any horse whose name includes the letters C, R, L. Perfectly simple."

"Tall Corn?" said the driver, a light in his eye. "You mean a horse named, like, Tall Corn?"

"Absolutely," said Mr. Johnson. "Here's your money."

"Tall Corn," said the driver. "Thank *you,* mister."

"Goodbye," said Mr. Johnson.

He was on his own corner and went straight up to his apartment. He let himself in and called "Hello?" and Mrs. Johnson answered from the kitchen, "Hello, dear, aren't you early?"

"Took a taxi home," Mr. Johnson said. "I remembered the cheesecake, too. What's for dinner?"

Mrs. Johnson came out of the kitchen and kissed him; she was a comfortable woman, and smiling as Mr. Johnson smiled. "Hard day?" she asked.

"Not very," said Mr. Johnson, hanging his coat in the closet. "How about you?"

"So-so," she said. She stood in the kitchen doorway while he settled into his easy chair and took off his good shoes and took out the paper he had bought that morning. "Here and there," she said.

"I didn't do so badly," Mr. Johnson said. "Couple young people."

"Fine," she said. "I had a little nap this afternoon, took it easy most of the day. Went into a department store this morning and accused the woman next to me of shoplifting, and had the store detective pick her up. Sent three dogs to the pound—*you* know, the usual thing. Oh, and listen," she added, remembering.

"What?" asked Mr. Johnson.

"Well," she said, "I got onto a bus and asked the driver for a transfer, and when he helped someone else first I said that he was impertinent, and quarreled with him. And then I said why wasn't he in the army, and I said it loud enough for everyone to hear, and I took his number and I turned in a complaint. Probably got him fired."

"Fine," said Mr. Johnson. "But you do look tired. Want to change over tomorrow?"

"I *would* like to," she said. "I could do with a change."

"Right," said Mr. Johnson. "What's for dinner?"

"Veal cutlet."

"Had it for lunch," said Mr. Johnson.

BERNIE THE FAUST

by William Tenn

BERNIE THE FAUST—that's what Ricardo calls me. I don't know what I am.

Here I am, I'm sitting in my little nine-by-six office. I'm reading notices of government-surplus sales. I'm trying to decide where lies a possible buck and where lies nothing but more headaches.

So the office door opens. This little guy with a dirty face, wearing a very dirty, very wrinkled Palm Beach suit, he walks into my office, and he coughs a bit and he says: "Would you be interested in buying a twenty for a five?"

That was it. I mean, that's all I had to go on.

I looked him over and I said, *"Wha-at?"*

He shuffled his feet and coughed some more. "A twenty," he mumbled. "A twenty for a five."

I made him drop his eyes and stare at his shoes. They were lousy, cracked shoes, lousy and dirty like the rest of him. Every once in a while his left shoulder hitched up in a kind of tic. "I give you twenty," he explained to his shoes, "and I buy a five from you with it. I wind up with five, you wind up with twenty."

"How did you get into the building?"

"I just came in," he said, a little mixed up.

"You just *came in.*" I put a nasty, mimicking note in my voice. "Now you just go right back downstairs and come the hell out. There's a sign in the lobby—NO BEGGARS ALLOWED."

"I'm not begging." He tugged at the bottom of his jacket. It was like a guy trying to straighten out his slept-in pajamas. "I want to sell you something. A twenty for a five. I give you—"

"You want me to call a cop?"

He looked very scared. "No. Why should you call a cop? I haven't done anything to make you call a cop!"

"I'll call a cop in just a second. I'm giving you fair warning. I just phone down to the lobby and they'll have a cop up here fast. They don't want beggars in this building. This is a building for business."

He rubbed his hand against his face, taking a little dirt off, then he rubbed the hand against the lapel of his jacket and left the dirt there. "No deal?" he asked. "A twenty for a five? You buy and sell things. What's the matter with my deal?"

I picked up the phone.

"All right," he said, holding up the streaky palm of his hand. "I'll go. I'll go."

"You better. And shut the door behind you."

"Just in case you change your mind." He reached into his dirty, wrinkled pants pocket and pulled out a card. "You can get in touch with me here. Almost any time during the day."

"Blow," I told him.

He reached over, dropped the card on my desk, on top of all the surplus notices, coughed once or twice, looked at me to see if maybe I was biting. No? No. He trudged out.

I picked the card up between the nails of my thumb and forefinger and started to drop it into the wastebasket.

Then I stopped. A card. It was just so damned out of the ordinary—a slob like that with a card. A card, yet.

For that matter, the whole play was out of the ordinary. I began to be a little sorry I hadn't let him run through the whole thing. After all, what was he trying to do but give me an offbeat sales pitch? I can always use an offbeat sales pitch. I work out of a small office, I buy and sell, but half my stock is good ideas. I'll use ideas, even from a bum.

The card was clean and white, except where the smudge from his fingers made a brown blot. Written across it in a kind of ornate handwriting were the words *Mr. Ogo Eksar*. Under that was the name and the telephone number of a hotel in the Times Square area, not far from my office. I knew that hotel: not expensive, but not a fleabag either—somewhere just under the middle line.

There was a room number in one corner of the card. I stared at it and I felt kind of funny. I really didn't know.

Although, come to think of it, why couldn't a panhandler be registered at a hotel? "Don't be a snob, Bernie," I told myself.

Twenty for five. What kind of panhandling pitch would follow it? I couldn't get it out of my mind!

There was only one thing to do. Ask somebody about it. Ricardo? A big college professor, after all. One of my best contacts.

He'd thrown a lot my way–a tip on the college building program that was worth a painless fifteen hundred, an office-equipment disposal from the United Nations, stuff like that. And any time I had any questions that needed a college education, he was on tap. All for the couple, three hundred he got out of me in commissions.

I looked at my watch. Ricardo would be in his office now, marking papers or whatever it is he does there. I dialed his number.

"Ogo Eksar?" he repeated after me. "Sounds like a Finnish name. Or maybe Estonian. From the eastern Baltic, I'd say."

"Forget that part," I said. "This is all I care about." And I told him about the twenty-for-five offer.

He laughed. "That thing again!"

"Some old hustle that the Greeks pulled on the Egyptians?"

"No. Something the Americans pulled. And not a con game. During the Depression, a New York newspaper sent a reporter around the city with a twenty-dollar bill which he offered to sell for exactly one dollar. There were no takers. The point being that even with people out of work and on the verge of starvation, they were so intent on not being suckers that they turned down an easy profit of nineteen-hundred percent."

"Twenty for one? This was twenty for five."

"Oh, well, you know, Bernie, inflation," he said, laughing again. "And these days it's more likely to be a television show."

"Television? You should have seen the way the guy was dressed!"

"Just an extra, logical touch to make people refuse to take the offer seriously. University research people operate much the same way. A few years back, a group of sociologists began an investigation of the public's reaction to sidewalk solicitors in charity drives. You know, those people who jingle little boxes on street corners: HELP THE TWO-HEADED CHILDREN, RELIEF FOR FLOOD-RAVAGED ATLANTIS? Well, they dressed up some of their students–"

"You think he was on the level, then, this guy?"

"I think there is a good chance that he was. I don't see why he would have left his card with you, though."

"That I can figure–now. If it's a TV stunt, there must be a lot of other angles wrapped up in it. A giveaway show with cars, refrigerators, a castle in Scotland, all kinds of loot."

"A giveaway show? Well, yes–it could be."

I hung up, took a deep breath, and called Eksar's hotel. He was registered there all right. And he'd just come in.

I went downstairs fast and took a cab. Who knew what other connections he'd made by now?

Going up in the elevator, I kept wondering. How did I go from the twenty-dollar bill to the real big stuff, the TV giveaway stuff, without letting Eksar know that I was on to what it was all about? Well, maybe I'd be lucky. Maybe he'd give me an opening.

I knocked on the door. When he said "Come in," I went in. But for a second or two I couldn't see a thing.

It was a little room, like all the rooms in that hotel, little and smelly and stuffy. But he didn't have the lights on, any electric lights. The window shade was pulled all the way down.

When my eyes got used to the dark, I was able to pick out this Ogo Eksar character. He was sitting on the bed, on the side nearest me. He was still wearing that crazy rumpled Palm Beach suit.

And you know what? He was watching a program on a funny little portable TV set that he had on the bureau. Color TV. Only it wasn't working right. There were no faces, no pictures, nothing but colors chasing around. A big blob of red, a big blob of orange and a wiggly border of blue and green and black. A voice was talking from it, but all the words were fouled up: *"Wah-wah, de-wah, de-wah."*

Just as I went in, he turned it off. "Times Square is a bad neighborhood for TV," I told him. "Too much interference."

"Yes," he said. "Too much interference." He closed up the set and put it away. I wished I'd seen it when it was working right.

Funny thing, you know? I would have expected a smell of liquor in the room, I would have expected to see a couple of empties in the tin trash basket near the bureau. Not a sign.

The only smell in the room was a smell I couldn't recognize. I guess it was the smell of Eksar himself, concentrated.

"Hi," I said, feeling a little uncomfortable because of the way I'd been with him back in the office. So rough I'd been.

He stayed on the bed. "I've got the twenty," he said. "You've got the five?"

"Oh, I guess I've got the five, all right," I said, looking in my wallet hard and trying to be funny. He didn't say a word, didn't even invite me to sit down. I pulled out a bill. "O.K.?"

He leaned forward and stared, as if he could see—in all that dimness—what kind of a bill it was. "O.K.," he said. "But I'll want a receipt. A notarized receipt."

Well, what the hell, I thought, a notarized receipt. "Then we'll have to go down. There's a druggist on Forty-fifth."

"Let's go," he said, getting to his feet with several small coughs that came one, two, three, four, right after one another.

On the way to the druggist, I stopped in a stationery store and bought a book of blank receipts. I filled out most of one right there. New York, N.Y., and the date. *Received from Mr. Ogo Eksar the sum of twenty dollars for a five-dollar bill bearing the serial number* . . . "That O.K.?" I asked him. "I'm putting in the serial number to make it look as if you want that particular bill, you know, what the lawyers call the value-received angle."

He screwed his head around and read the receipt. Then he checked the serial number of the bill I was holding. He nodded.

We had to wait for the druggist to get through with a couple of customers. When I signed the receipt, he read it to himself, shrugged and went ahead and stamped it with his seal.

I paid him the two bits; I was the one making the profit.

Eksar slid a crisp new twenty to me along the counter. He watched while I held it up to the light, first one side, then the other.

"Good bill?" he asked.

"Yes. You understand: I don't know you, I don't know your money."

"Sure. I'd do it myself with a stranger." He put the receipt and my five-dollar bill in his pocket and started to walk away.

"Hey," I said. "You in a hurry?"

"No." He stopped, looking puzzled. "No hurry. But you've got the twenty for a five. We made the deal. It's all over."

"All right, so we made the deal. How about a cup of coffee?"

He hesitated.

"It's on me," I told him. "I'll be a big shot for a dime. Come on, let's have a cup of coffee."

Now he looked worried. "You don't want to back out? I've got the receipt. It's all notarized. I gave you a twenty, you gave me a five. We made a deal."

"It's a deal, it's a deal," I said, shoving him into an empty booth. "It's a deal, it's all signed, sealed and delivered. Nobody's backing out. I just want to buy you a cup of coffee."

His face cleared up, all the way through that dirt. "No coffee. Soup. I'll have some mushroom soup."

"Fine, fine. Soup, coffee, I don't care. I'll have coffee."

I sat there and studied him. He hunched over the soup and dragged it into his mouth, spoonful after spoonful, the living picture of a bum who hadn't eaten all day. But pure essence of bum, triple-distilled, the label of a fine old firm.

A guy like this should be lying in a doorway trying to say no to a cop's night stick, he should be coughing his alcoholic guts out. He shouldn't be living in a real honest-to-God hotel, or giving me a twenty for a five, or eating anything as respectable as mushroom soup.

But it made sense. A TV giveaway show, they want to do this, they hire a damn good actor, the best money can buy, to toss their dough away. A guy who'll be so good a bum that people'll just laugh in his face when he tries to give them a deal with a profit.

"You don't want to buy anything else?" I asked him.

He held the spoon halfway to his mouth and stared at me suspiciously. "Like what?"

"Oh, I don't know. Like maybe you want to buy a ten for a fifty. Or a twenty for a hundred dollars?"

He thought about it, Eksar did. Then he went back to his soup, shoveling away. "That's no deal," he said contemptuously. "What kind of deal is that?"

"Excuse me for living. I just thought I'd ask. I wasn't trying to take advantage of you." I lit a cigarette and waited.

My friend with the dirty face finished the soup and reached for a paper napkin. He wiped his lips. I watched him: he didn't smudge a spot of the grime around his mouth. He just blotted up the drops of soup. He was dainty in his own special way.

"Nothing else you want to buy? I'm here, I've got time right now. Anything else on your mind, we might as well look into it."

He balled up the paper napkin and dropped it into the soup plate. It got wet. He'd eaten all the mushrooms and left the soup.

"The Golden Gate Bridge," he said all of a sudden.

I dropped the cigarette. "What?"

"The Golden Gate Bridge. The one in San Francisco. I'll buy that. I'll buy it for . . ." He lifted his eyes to the fluorescent fixtures in the ceiling and thought for a couple of seconds. ". . . Say a hundred and a quarter. A hundred and twenty-five dollars. Cash on the barrel."

"Why the Golden Gate Bridge?" I asked him like an idiot.

"That's the one I want. You asked me what else I wanted to buy—well, that's what else. The Golden Gate Bridge."

"What's the matter with the George Washington Bridge? It's right here in New York, it's across the Hudson River. Why buy something all the way out on the Coast?"

He grinned at me as if he admired my cleverness. "Oh, no," he said, twitching his left shoulder hard. Up, down, up, down. "I know what I want. The Golden Gate Bridge in San Francisco. A hundred and a quarter. Take it or leave it."

"I'll take it. If that's what you want, you're the doctor. But look—all I can sell you is my share of the Golden Gate Bridge, whatever equity in it I may happen to own."

He nodded. "I want a receipt. Put that down on the receipt."

I put it down on the receipt. And back we went. The druggist notarized the receipt, shoved the stamping outfit into the drawer under the counter and turned his back on us. Eksar counted out six twenties and one five from a big roll of bills, all of them starchy new. He put the roll back into his pants pocket and started away again.

"More coffee?" I asked, catching up. "A refill on the soup?"

He turned a very puzzled look at me and kind of twitched all over. "Why? What do you want to sell now?"

I shrugged. "What do you want to buy? You name it. Let's see what other deals we can work out."

This was all taking one hell of a lot of time, but I had no complaints. I'd made a hundred and forty dollars in fifteen minutes. Say a hundred and thirty-eight fifty, if you deducted expenses such as notary fees, coffee, soup—all legitimate expenses, all low. I had no complaints.

But I was waiting for the big one. There had to be a big one.

Of course, it could maybe wait until the TV program itself. They'd be asking me what was on my mind when I was selling Eksar all that crap, and I'd be explaining, and they'd start handing out refrigerators and gift certificates for Tiffany's and . . .

Eksar had said something while I was away in cloudland. Something damn unfamiliar. I asked him to say it again.

"The Sea of Azov," he told me. "In Russia. I'll give you three hundred and eighty dollars for it."

I'd never heard of the place. I pursed my lips and thought for a second. A funny amount—three hundred and eighty. And for a whole damn sea. I tried an angle.

"Make it four hundred and you've got a deal."

He began coughing his head off, and he looked mad. "What's the matter," he asked between coughs, "three hundred and eighty is a bad price? It's a small sea, one of the smallest. It's only fourteen thousand square miles. And do you know what the maximum depth is?"

I looked wise. "It's deep enough."

"Forty-nine feet," Eksar shouted. "That's all, forty-nine feet! Where are you going to do better than three hundred and eighty for a sea like that?"

"Take it easy," I said, patting his dirty shoulder. "Let's split the difference. You say three eighty, I want four hundred. How about leaving it at three ninety?" I didn't really care: ten bucks more, ten bucks less. But I wanted to see what would happen.

He calmed down. "Three hundred and ninety dollars for the Sea of Azov," he muttered to himself, a little sore at being a sucker, at being taken. "All I want is the sea itself; it's not as if I'm asking you to throw in the Kerch Strait, or maybe a port like Taganrog or Osipenko . . ."

"Tell you what." I held up my hands. "I don't want to be hard. Give me my three ninety and I'll throw in the Kerch Strait as a bonus. Now how about that?"

He studied the idea. He sniffled. He wiped his nose with the back of his hand. "All right," he said finally. "It's a deal. Azov *and* the Kerch Strait for three hundred ninety."

Bang! went the druggist's stamp. The bangs were getting louder.

Eksar paid me with six fifties, four twenties and a ten, all new-looking bills from that thick roll in his pants pocket.

I thought about the fifties still on the roll, and I felt the spit start to ball up in my mouth.

"O.K.," I said. "Now what?"

"You still selling?"

"For the right price, sure. You name it."

"There's lots of stuff I could use," he sighed. "But do I need it right now? That's what I have to ask myself."

"Right now is when you've got a chance to buy it. Later—who knows? I may not be around, there may be other guys bidding against you, all kinds of things can happen." I waited awhile, but he just kept scowling and coughing. "How about Australia?" I suggested. "Could you use Australia for, say, five hundred bucks? Or Antarctica? I could give you a real nice deal on Antarctica."

He looked interested. "Antarctica? What would you want for it? No—I'm not getting anywhere. A little piece here, a little piece there. It all costs so much."

"You're getting damn favorable prices, buddy, and you know it. You couldn't do better buying at wholesale."

"Then how about wholesale? How much for the whole thing?"

I shook my head. "I don't know what you're talking about. What whole thing?"

He looked impatient. "The whole thing. The world. Earth."

"Hey," I said. "That's a lot."

"Well, I'm tired of buying a piece at a time. Will you give me a wholesale price if I buy it all?"

I shook my head, kind of in and out, not yes, not no. Money was coming up, the big money. This was where I was supposed to laugh in his face and walk away. I didn't even crack a smile. "For the whole planet–sure, you're entitled to a wholesale price. But what is it, I mean, exactly *what* do you want to buy?"

"Earth," he said, moving close to me so that I could smell his stinking breath. "I want to buy Earth. Lock, stock and barrel."

"It's got to be a good price. I'll be selling out completely."

"I'll make it a good price. But this is the deal. I pay two thousand dollars, cash. I get Earth, the whole planet, and you have to throw in some stuff on the Moon. Fishing rights, mineral rights and rights to buried treasure. How about it?"

"It's a hell of a lot."

"I know it's a lot," he agreed. "But I'm paying a lot."

"Not for what you're asking. Let me think about it."

This was the big deal, the big giveaway. I didn't know how much money the TV people had given him to fool around with, but I was pretty sure two thousand was just a starting point. Only what was a sensible, businesslike price for the whole world?

I mustn't be made to look like a penny-ante chiseler on TV. There was a top figure Eksar had been given by the program director.

"You really want the whole thing," I said, turning back to him, "the Earth and the Moon?"

He held up a dirty hand. "Not all the Moon. Just those rights on it. The rest of the Moon you can keep."

"It's still a lot. You've got to go a hell of a lot higher than two thousand dollars for any hunk of real estate that big."

Eksar began wrinkling and twitching. "How–how much higher?"

"Well, let's not kid each other. This is the big time now! We're not talking about bridges or rivers or seas. This is a whole world and part of another that you're buying. It takes dough. You've got to be prepared to spend dough."

"How much?" He looked as if he were jumping up and down inside his dirty Palm Beach suit. People going in and out of the store kept staring at us. "How *much?*" he whispered.

"Fifty thousand. It's a damn low price. And you know it."

Eksar went limp all over. Even his weird eyes seemed to sag. "You're crazy," he said in a low, hopeless voice. "You're out of your head."

He turned and started for the revolving door, walking in a kind of used-up way that told me I'd really gone over the line. He didn't look back once. He just wanted to get far, far away.

I grabbed the bottom of his filthy jacket and held on tight.

"Look, Eksar," I said, fast, as he pulled. "I went over your budget, way over, I can see that. But you know you can do better than two thousand. I want as much as I can get. What the hell, I'm taking time out to bother with you. How many other guys would?"

That got him. He cocked his head, then began nodding. I let go of his jacket as he came around. We were connecting again!

"Good. You level with me, and I'll level with you. Go up a little higher. What's your best price? What's the best you can do?"

He stared down the street, thinking, and his tongue came out and licked at the side of his dirty mouth. His tongue was dirty, too. I mean that! Some kind of black stuff, grease or grime, was all over his tongue.

"How about," he said after a while, "how about twenty-five hundred? That's as high as I can go. I don't have another cent."

He was like me: he was a natural bargainer.

"You can go to three thousand," I urged. "How much is three thousand? Only another five hundred. Look what you get for it. Earth, the whole planet, and fishing and mineral rights and buried treasure, all that stuff on the Moon. How's about it?"

"I can't. I just can't. I wish I could." He shook his head as if to shake loose all those tics and twitches. "Maybe this way. I'll go as high as twenty-six hundred. For that, will you give me Earth and just fishing rights and buried-treasure rights on the Moon? You keep the mineral rights. I'll do without them."

"Make it twenty-eight hundred and you can have the mineral rights, too. You want them, I can tell you do. Treat yourself. Just two hundred bucks more, and you can have them."

"I can't have everything. Some things cost too much. How about twenty-six fifty, without the mineral rights and without the buried-treasure rights?"

We were both really swinging now. I could feel it.

"This is my absolutely last offer," I told him. "I can't spend all day on this. I'll go down to twenty-seven hundred and fifty, and not a penny less. For that, I'll give you Earth and just fishing rights on the Moon. Or just buried-treasure rights. You pick whichever one you want."

"All right," he said. "You're a hard man; we'll do it your way."

"Twenty-seven fifty for the Earth and either fishing or buried-treasure rights on the Moon?"

"No, twenty-seven even, and no rights on the Moon. I'll forget about that. Twenty-seven even and all I get is the Earth."

"Deal!" I sang out, and we struck hands. We shook on it.

Then, with my arm around his shoulders—what did I care about the dirt on his clothes when the guy was worth twenty-seven hundred dollars to me?—we marched back to the drugstore.

"I want a receipt," he reminded me.

"Right," I said. "But I put the same stuff on it: that I'm selling you whatever equity I own or have a right to sell. You're getting a lot for your money."

"You're getting a lot of money for what you're selling," he came right back. I liked him. Twitches and dirt or not, he was my kind of guy.

We got back to the druggist for notarization, and, honest, I've never seen a man look more disgusted in my life. "Business is good, huh?" he said. "You two are sure hotting it up."

"Listen, you," I told him. "You just notarize." I showed the receipt to Eksar. "This the way you want it?"

He studied it, coughing. "Whatever equity you own or have a right to sell. All right. And put in, you know, in your capacity as sales agent, your professional capacity."

I changed the receipt and signed it. The druggist notarized.

Eksar brought that lump of money out of his pants pocket. He counted out fifty-four crisp new fifties and laid them on the glass counter. Then he picked up the receipt, folded it and put it away. He started for the door.

I grabbed up the money and went with him. "Anything else?"

"Nothing else," he said. "It's all over. We made our deal."

"I know, but we might find something else, another item."

"There's nothing else to find. We made our deal." And his voice told me he really meant it. It didn't have a trace of the tell-me-more whine that you've got to hear before there's business.

I came to a stop and watched him push out through the revolving door. He went right out into the street and turned left and kept moving, all fast, as if he was in a hell of a hurry.

There was no more business. O.K. I had thirty-two hundred and thirty dollars in my wallet that I'd made in one morning.

But how good had I really been? I mean, what was the top figure in the show's budget? How close had I come to it?

I had a contact who maybe could find out–Morris Burlap.

Morris Burlap is in business like me, only he's a theatrical agent, sharp, real sharp. Instead of selling a load of used copper wire, say, or an option on a corner lot in Brooklyn, he sells talent. He sells a bunch of dancers to a hotel in the mountains, a piano player to a bar, a disc jockey or a comic to late-night radio. The reason he's called Morris Burlap is because of these heavy Harris-tweed suits he wears winter and summer, every day in the year. They reinforce the image, he says.

I called him from a telephone booth near the entrance and filled him in on the giveaway show. "Now, what I want to find out–"

"Nothing to find out," he cut in. "There's no such show, Bernie."

"There sure as hell is, Morris. One you haven't heard of."

"There's no such show. Not in the works, not being rehearsed, not anywhere. Look: before a show gets to where it's handing out this kind of dough, it's got to have a slot, it's got to have air time all bought. And before it even buys air time, a packager has prepared a pilot. By then I'd have gotten a casting call–I'd have heard about it a dozen different ways. Don't try to tell me my business, Bernie; when I say there's no such show, there's no such show."

So damn positive he was. I had a crazy idea all of a sudden and turned it off. No. Not that. No.

"Then it's a newspaper or college research thing, like Ricardo said?"

He thought it over. I was willing to sit in that stuffy telephone booth and wait; Morris Burlap has a good head. "Those damn documents, those receipts, newspapers and colleges doing research don't operate that way. And nuts don't either. I think you're being taken, Bernie. How you're being taken, I don't know, but you're being taken."

That was enough for me. Morris Burlap can smell a hustle through sixteen feet of rock-wool insulation. He's never wrong. Never.

I hung up, sat, thought. The crazy idea came back and exploded.

A bunch of characters from outer space, say they want Earth.

They want it for a colony, for a vacation resort, who the hell knows what they want it for? They got their reasons. They're strong enough and advanced enough to come right down and take over. But they don't want to do it cold. They need a legal leg.

All right. These characters from outer space, maybe all they had to have was a piece of paper from just one genuine, accredited human being signing the Earth over to them. No, that couldn't be right. *Any* piece of paper? Signed by *any* Joe Jerk?

I jammed a dime into the telephone and called Ricardo's college. He wasn't in. I told the switchboard girl it was very important; she said, all right, she'd ring around and try to spot him.

All that stuff, I kept thinking, the Golden Gate Bridge, the Sea of Azov–they were as much a part of the hook as the twenty-for-a-five routine. There's one sure test of what an operator is really after: when he stops talking, closes up shop and goes away.

With Eksar, it had been the Earth. All that baloney about extra rights on the Moon! They were put in to cover up the real thing he was after, for extra bargaining power.

That's how Eksar had worked on me. It was like he'd made a special study of how I operate. From me alone, he had to buy.

But why me?

All that stuff on the receipt, about my equity, about my professional capacity, what the hell did it mean? I don't own Earth; I'm not in the planet-selling business. You have to own a planet before you can sell it. That's law.

So what could I have sold Eksar? I don't own any real estate. Are they going to take over my office, claim the piece of sidewalk I walk on, attach the stool in the diner where I have my coffee?

That brought me back to my first question. Who was this "they"? Who the holy hell were "they"?

The switchboard girl finally dug up Ricardo. He was irritated. "I'm in the middle of a faculty meeting, Bernie. Call you back?"

"Just listen a second," I begged. "I'm in something, I don't know whether I'm coming or going. I've got to have some advice."

Talking fast–I could hear a lot of big-shot voices in the background–I ran through the story from the time I'd called him in the morning. What Eksar looked like and smelled like, the funny portable color TV he had, the way he'd dropped all those Moon rights and gone charging off once he'd been sure of the Earth. What Morris Burlap had said, the suspicions I'd been building up, everything.

"Only thing is–" I laughed a little to show that maybe I wasn't really serious about it–"who am I to make such a deal, huh?"

He seemed to be thinking hard for a while. "I don't know, Bernie, it's possible. It does fit together. There's the UN aspect."

"UN aspect? Which UN aspect?"

"The UN aspect of the situation. The–uh–study of the UN on which we collaborated two years ago." He was using double talk because of the college people around him. But I got it. I got it.

Eksar must have known all along about the deal that Ricardo had thrown my way, getting rid of old, used-up office equipment for the United Nations here in New York. They'd given me what they called an authorizing document. In a file somewhere there was a piece of paper, United Nations stationery, saying that I was their authorized sales agent for surplus, secondhand equipment and installations.

Talk about a legal leg!

"You think it'll stand up?" I asked Ricardo. "I can see how the Earth is secondhand equipment and installations. But surplus?"

"International law is a tangled field, Bernie. And this might be even more complex. You'd be wise to do something about it."

"But what? What should I do, Ricardo?"

"Bernie," he said, sounding sore as hell, "I told you I'm in a faculty meeting, damn it! A *faculty* meeting!" And he hung up.

I ran out of the drugstore like a wild man and grabbed a cab back to Eksar's hotel.

What was I most afraid of? I didn't know: I was so hysterical. This thing was too big-time for a little guy like me, too damn dangerously big-time. It would put my name up in lights as the biggest sell-out sucker in history. Who could ever trust me again to make a deal? I had the feeling like somebody had asked me to sell him a snapshot, and I'd said sure, and it turned out to be a picture of the Nike Zeus, you know, one of those top-secret atomic missiles. Like I'd sold out my country by mistake. Only this was worse: I'd sold out my whole goddamn world. I had to buy it back–I had to!

When I got to Eksar's room, I knew he was about ready to check out. He was shoving his fully portable TV in one of those cheap leather grips they sell in chain stores. I left the door open, for the light.

"We made our deal," he said. "It's over. No more deals."

I stood there, blocking his way. "Eksar," I told him, "listen to what I figured out. First, you're not human. Like me, I mean."

"I'm a hell of a lot more human than you, buddy boy."

"Maybe. But you're not from Earth–that's my point. Why you need Earth–"

"I *don't* need it. I'm an agent. I represent someone."

And there it was, straight out, you are right, Morris Burlap! I stared into his fish eyes, now practically pushing into my face. I wouldn't get out of the way. "You're an agent for someone," I repeated slowly. "Who? What do they want Earth for?"

"That's their business. I'm an agent. I just buy for them."

"You work on a commission?"

"I'm not in business for my health."

You sure as hell aren't in it for your health, I thought. *That cough, those tics and twitches–* Then I realized what they meant. This wasn't the kind of air he was used to. Like if I go up to Canada, right away I'm down with diarrhea. It's the water or something.

The dirt on his face was a kind of suntan oil! A protection against our sunlight. Blinds pulled down, face smeared over–and dirt all over his clothes so they'd fit in with his face.

Eksar was no bum. He was anything but. I was the bum. Think fast, Bernie, I said to myself. This guy took you, and big!

"How much you work on–ten percent?" No answer: he leaned against me, and he breathed and he twitched. "I'll top any deal you have, Eksar. You know what I'll give you? Fifteen percent! I hate to see a guy running back and forth for a lousy ten percent."

"What about ethics?" he said hoarsely. "I got a client."

"Look who's bringing up ethics! A guy goes out to buy the whole damn Earth for twenty-seven hundred! You call that ethics?"

Now he got sore. He set down the grip and punched his fist into his hand. "No, I call that business. A deal. I offer, you take. You go away happy, you feel you made out. All of a sudden, here you are back, crying you didn't mean it, you sold too much for the price. Too bad! I got ethics: I don't screw my client for a crybaby."

"I'm not a crybaby. I'm just a poor schnook trying to scratch out a living. Here, I'm up against a big-time operation from another world with all kinds of angles and gimmicks going for him."

"You had these angles, these gimmicks, you wouldn't use them?"

"Certain things I wouldn't do. Don't laugh, Eksar, I mean it. I wouldn't hustle a guy in an iron lung. I wouldn't hustle a poor schnook with a hole-in-the-wall office to sell out his entire planet."

"You really sold," he said. "That receipt will stand up anywhere.

And we got the machinery to make it stand up. Once my client takes possession, the human race is finished, it's kaput, forget about it. And you're Mr. Patsy."

It was hot in that hotel-room doorway, and I was sweating like crazy. But I was feeling better. All of a sudden, I'd got the message that Eksar wanted to do business with me. I grinned at him.

He changed color a little under all that dirt. "What's your offer, anyway?" he asked, coughing. "Name a figure."

"*You* name one. You got the property, I got the dough."

"Aah!" he grunted impatiently, and pushed me out of the way. He was *strong!* I ran after him to the elevator.

"How much you want, Eksar?" I asked him as we were going down.

A shrug. "I got a planet, and I got a buyer for it. You, you're in a jam. The one in a pickle is the one who's got to tickle."

The louse! For every one of my moves, he knew the countermove.

He checked out and I followed him into the street. Down Broadway we went, me offering him the thirty-two hundred and thirty he'd paid me, him saying he couldn't make a living out of shoving the same amount of money back and forth all day. "Thirty-four?" I offered. "I mean, you know, thirty-four fifty?" He just kept walking.

If I didn't get him to name a figure, any figure, I'd be dead.

I ran in front of him. "Eksar, let's stop hustling each other. If you didn't want to sell, you wouldn't be talking to me in the first place. You name a figure. Whatever it is, I'll pay it."

That got a reaction. "You mean it? You won't try to chisel?"

"How can I chisel? I'm over a barrel."

"O.K., then. I'll give you a break and save myself a long trip back to my client. What's fair for you and fair for me and fair all around? Let's say eight thousand even?"

Eight thousand–it was almost exactly what I had in the bank. He knew my bank account cold, up to the last statement.

He knew my thoughts cold, too. "You're going to do business with a guy," he said, between coughs, "you check into him a little. You got eight thousand and change. It's not much for saving a guy's neck."

I was boiling. "Not much? Then let me set you straight, you Florence goddamn Nightingale! You're not getting it! A little skin I know maybe I have to give up. But not every cent I own, not for you, not for Earth, not for anybody!"

A cop came up close to see why I was yelling, and I had to calm down until he went away again. "Help! Police! Aliens invading us!"

I almost screamed out. What would the street we were standing on look like in ten years if I didn't talk Eksar out of that receipt?

"Eksar, your client takes over Earth waving my receipt–I'll be hung high. But I've got only one life, and my life is buying and selling. I can't buy and sell without capital. Take my capital away, and it makes no difference to me who owns Earth and who doesn't."

"Who the hell do you think you're kidding?" he said.

"I'm not kidding anybody. Honest, it's the truth. Take my capital away, and it makes no difference if I'm alive or if I'm dead."

That last bit of hustle seemed to have reached him. Listen, there were practically tears in my eyes the way I was singing it. How much capital did I need, he wanted to know–five hundred? I told him I couldn't operate one single day with less than seven times that. He asked me if I was really seriously trying to buy my lousy little planet back–or was today my birthday and I was expecting a present from him? "Don't give your presents to me," I told him. "Give them to fat people. They're better than going on a diet."

And so we went. Both of us talking ourselves blue in the face, swearing by everything, arguing and bargaining, wheeling and dealing. It was touch and go who was going to give up first.

But neither of us did. We both held out until we reached what I'd figured pretty early we were going to wind up with, maybe a little bit more.

Six thousand, one hundred and fifty dollars.

That was the price over and above what Eksar had given me. The final deal. Listen, it could have been worse.

Even so, we almost broke up when we began talking payment.

"Your bank's not far. We could get there before closing."

"Why walk myself into a heart attack? My check's good as gold."

"Who wants a piece of paper? I want cash. Cash is definite."

Finally, I managed to talk him into a check. I wrote it out; he took it and gave me the receipts, all of them. Every last receipt I'd signed. Then he picked up his little satchel and marched away.

Straight down Broadway, without even a goodbye. All business, Eksar was, nothing but business. He didn't look back once.

All business. I found out next morning he'd gone right to the bank and had my check certified before closing time. What do you think of that? I couldn't do a damn thing: I was out six thousand, one hundred and fifty dollars. Just for talking to someone.

Ricardo said I was a Faust. I walked out of the bank, beating my head with my fist, and I called up him and Morris Burlap and asked them to have lunch with me. I went over the whole story with them in an expensive place that Ricardo picked out. "You're a Faust," he said.

"What Faust?" I asked him. "Who Faust? How Faust?"

So naturally he had to tell us all about Faust. Only I was a new kind of Faust, a twentieth-century-American one. The other Fausts, they wanted to know everything. I wanted to own everything.

"But I didn't wind up owning," I pointed out. "I got taken. Six thousand, one hundred and fifty dollars' worth I got taken."

Ricardo chuckled and leaned back in his chair. "O my sweet gold," he said under his breath. "O my sweet gold."

"What?"

"A quotation, Bernie. From Marlowe's *The Tragical History of Dr. Faustus.* I forget the context, but it seems apt. *'O my sweet gold.'* "

I looked from him to Morris Burlap, but nobody can ever tell when Morris Burlap is puzzled. As a matter of fact, he looks more like a professor than Ricardo, him with those thick Harris tweeds and that heavy, thinking look. Ricardo is, you know, a bit too natty.

The two of them added up to all the brains and sharpness a guy could ask for. That's why I was paying out an arm and a leg for this lunch, on top of all my losses with Eksar.

"Morris, tell the truth. You understand him?"

"What's there to understand, Bernie? A quote about the sweet gold? It might be the answer, right there."

Now I looked at Ricardo. He was eating away at a creamy Italian pudding. Two bucks even, those puddings cost in that place.

"Let's say he was an alien," Morris Burlap said. "Let's say he came from somewhere in outer space. O.K. Now what would an alien want with U.S. dollars? What's the rate of exchange out there?"

"You mean he needed it to buy some merchandise here on Earth?"

"That's exactly what I mean. But what *kind* of merchandise, that's the question. What could Earth have that he'd want?"

Ricardo finished the pudding and wiped his lips with a napkin. "I think you're on the right track, Morris," he said, and I swung my attention back to him. "We can postulate a civilization far in advance of our own. One that would feel we're not quite ready to know about them. One that has placed primitive little Earth strictly off limits—a restriction only desperate criminals dare ignore."

"From where come criminals, Ricardo, if they're so advanced?"

"Laws produce law-breakers, Bernie, like hens produce eggs. Civilization has nothing to do with it. I'm beginning to see Eksar now. An unprincipled adventurer, a star-man version of those cutthroats who sailed the South Pacific a hundred years or more ago. Once in a while, a ship would smash upon the coral reefs, and a bloody opportunist out of Boston would be stranded for life among primitive, backward tribesmen. I'm sure you can fill in the rest."

"No, I can't. And if you don't mind, Ricardo–"

Morris Burlap said he'd like another brandy. I ordered it. He came as close to smiling as Morris Burlap ever does and leaned toward me confidentially. "Ricardo's got it, Bernie. Put yourself in this guy Eksar's position. He racks up his spaceship on a dirty little planet which it's against the law to be near in the first place. He can make some half-assed repairs with merchandise that's available here–but he has to buy the stuff. Any noise, any uproar, and he'll be grabbed for a Federal rap in outer space. Say you're Eksar, what do you do?"

I could see it now. "I'd peddle and I'd parlay. Copper bracelets, strings of beads, dollars–whatever I had to lay my hands on to buy the native merchandise, I'd peddle and I'd parlay in deal after deal. Maybe I'd start with a piece of equipment from the ship, then I'd find some novelty item that the natives would go for. But all this is *Earth* business know-how, *human* business know-how."

"Bernie," Ricardo told me, "Indians once traded pretty little shells for beaver pelts at the exact spot where the stock exchange now stands. Some kind of business goes on in Eksar's world, I assure you, but its simplest form would make one of our corporate mergers look like a game of potsy on the sidewalk."

Well, I'd wanted to figure it out. "So I was marked as his fish all the way. I was screwed and blued and tattooed," I mumbled, "by a hustler superman."

Ricardo nodded. "By a businessman's Mephistopheles fleeing the thunderbolts of heaven. He needed to double his money one more time and he'd have enough to repair his ship. He had at his disposal a fantastic sophistication in all the ways of commerce."

"What Ricardo's saying," came an almost soft voice from Morris Burlap, "is the guy who beat you up was a whole lot bigger than you."

My shoulders felt loose, like they were sliding down off my arms. "What the hell," I said. "You get stepped on by a horse or you get stepped on by an elephant. You're still stepped on."

I paid the check, got myself together and went away.

Then I began to wonder if maybe this was really the story after all. They both enjoyed seeing me up there as an interplanetary jerk. Ricardo's a brilliant guy, Morris Burlap's sharp as hell, but so what? Ideas, yes. Facts, no.

So here's a fact.

My bank statement came at the end of the month with that canceled check I'd given Eksar. It had been endorsed by a big store in the Cortlandt Street area. I know that store. I've dealt with them. I went down and asked them about it.

They handle mostly marked-down, surplus electronic equipment. That's what they said Eksar had bought. A walloping big order of transistors and transformers, resistors and printed circuits, electronic tubes, wiring, tools, gimmicks like that. All mixed up, they said, a lot of components that just didn't go together. He'd given the clerk the impression that he had an emergency job to do—and he'd take as close as he could get to the things he actually needed. He'd paid a lot of money for freight charges: delivery was to some backwoods town in northern Canada.

That's a fact, now, I have to admit it. But here's another one.

I've dealt with that store, like I said. Their prices are the lowest in the neighborhood. And why is it, do you think, they can sell so cheap? There's only one answer: because they buy so cheap. They buy at the lowest prices; they don't give a damn about quality: all they want to know is, how much mark-up? I've personally sold them job lots of electronic junk that I couldn't unload anywhere else, condemned stuff, badly wired stuff, stuff that was almost dangerous—it's a place to sell to when you've given up on making a profit because you yourself have been stuck with inferior merchandise in the first place.

You get the picture? It makes me feel rosy all over.

There is Eksar out in space, the way I see it. He's fixed up his ship, good enough to travel, and he's on his way to his next big deal. The motors are humming, the ship is running, and he's sitting there with a big smile on his dirty face: he's thinking how he took me, how easy it was.

He's laughing his head off.

All of a sudden, there's a screech and a smell of burning. That circuit that's running the front motor, a wire just got touched through the thin insulation, the circuit's tearing the hell out of itself. He gets scared. He turns on the auxiliaries. The auxiliaries don't go on—you know why? The vacuum tubes he's using have come to the end of their rope; they didn't have much juice to start with. *Blooie!* That's the rear motor developing a short circuit. *Kapow!* That's a defective transformer melting away in the middle of the ship.

And there he is, millions of miles from nowhere, empty space all around him, no more spare parts, tools that practically break in his hands–and not a single, living soul he can hustle.

And here am I, in my office, thinking about it, and *I'm* laughing my head off. Because it's just possible, it just could happen, that what goes wrong with his ship is one of the half dozen or so job lots of really bad electronic equipment that I personally, me, Bernie the Faust, that I sold to that surplus store at one time or another.

That's all I'd ask. Just to have it happen that way.

Faust. He'd have Faust from me then. Right in the face, Faust. On the head, splitting it open, Faust. Faust I'd give him!

The only trouble is I'll never know. All I know for sure is that I'm the only guy in history who sold the whole goddamn planet.

And bought it back.

LIGHT OF OTHER DAYS

by Bob Shaw

LEAVING THE village behind, we followed the heady sweeps of the road up into a land of slow glass.

I had never seen one of the farms before and at first found them slightly eerie—an effect heightened by imagination and circumstance. The car's turbine was pulling smoothly and quietly in the damp air so that we seemed to be carried over the convolutions of the road in a kind of supernatural silence. On our right the mountain sifted down into an incredibly perfect valley of timeless pine, and everywhere stood the great frames of slow glass, drinking light. An occasional flash of afternoon sunlight on their wind bracing created an illusion of movement, but in fact the frames were deserted. The rows of windows had been standing on the hillside for years, staring into the valley, and men only cleaned them in the middle of the night when their human presence would not matter to the thirsty glass.

They were fascinating, but Selina and I didn't mention the windows. I think we hated each other so much we both were reluctant to sully anything new by drawing it into the nexus of our emotions. The holiday, I had begun to realize, was a stupid idea in the first place. I had thought it would cure everything, but, of course, it didn't stop Selina being pregnant and, worse still, it didn't even stop her being angry about being pregnant.

Rationalizing our dismay over her condition, we had circulated the usual statements to the effect that we would have *liked* having children—but later on, at the proper time. Selina's pregnancy had cost us her well-paid job and with it the new house we had been negotiating and which was far beyond the reach of my income from poetry. But the real source of our annoyance was that we were face to face with the realization that people who say they want children later always mean they want children never. Our nerves were thrumming with the knowledge that we, who had thought ourselves so unique, had fallen into the same biological trap as every mindless rutting creature which ever existed.

The road took us along the southern slopes of Ben Cruachan until we began to catch glimpses of the gray Atlantic far ahead. I had just cut our speed to absorb the view better when I noticed the sign spiked to a gatepost. It said: "SLOW GLASS—Quality High, Prices Low —J. R. Hagan." On an impulse I stopped the car on the verge, wincing slightly as tough grasses whipped noisily at the body-work.

"Why have we stopped?" Selina's neat, smoke-silver head turned in surprise.

"Look at that sign. Let's go up and see what there is. The stuff might be reasonably priced out here."

Selina's voice was pitched high with scorn as she refused, but I was too taken with my idea to listen. I had an illogical conviction that doing something extravagant and crazy would set us right again.

"Come on," I said, "the exercise might do us some good. We've been driving too long anyway."

She shrugged in a way that hurt me and got out of the car. We walked up a path made of irregular, packed clay steps nosed with short lengths of sapling. The path curved through trees which clothed the edge of the hill and at its end we found a low farmhouse. Beyond the little stone building tall frames of slow glass gazed out towards the voice-stilling sight of Cruachan's ponderous descent towards the waters of Loch Linnhe. Most of the panes were perfectly transparent but a few were dark, like panels of polished ebony.

As we approached the house through a neat cobbled yard a tall middle-aged man in ash-colored tweeds arose and waved to us. He had been sitting on the low rubble wall which bounded the yard, smoking a pipe and staring towards the house. At the front window of the cottage a young woman in a tangerine dress stood with a small boy in her arms, but she turned disinterestedly and moved out of sight as we drew near.

"Mr. Hagan?" I guessed.

"Correct. Come to see some glass, have you? Well, you've come to the right place." Hagan spoke crisply, with traces of the pure highland which sounds so much like Irish to the unaccustomed ear. He had one of those calmly dismayed faces one finds on elderly roadmenders and philosophers.

"Yes," I said. "We're on holiday. We saw your sign."

Selina, who usually has a natural fluency with strangers, said nothing. She was looking towards the now empty window with what I thought was a slightly puzzled expression.

"Up from London, are you? Well, as I said, you've come to the right place–and at the right time, too. My wife and I don't see many people this early in the season."

I laughed. "Does that mean we might be able to buy a little glass without mortgaging our home?"

"Look at that now," Hagan said, smiling helplessly. "I've thrown away any advantage I might have had in the transaction. Rose, that's my wife, says I never learn. Still, let's sit down and talk it over." He pointed at the rubble wall then glanced doubtfully at Selina's immaculate blue skirt. "Wait till I fetch a rug from the house." Hagan limped quickly into the cottage, closing the door behind him.

"Perhaps it wasn't such a marvelous idea to come up here," I whispered to Selina, "but you might at least be pleasant to the man. I think I can smell a bargain."

"Some hope," she said with deliberate coarseness. "Surely even you must have noticed that ancient dress his wife is wearing? He won't give much away to strangers."

"Was that his wife?"

"Of course that was his wife."

"Well, well," I said, surprised. "Anyway, try to be civil with him. I don't want to be embarrassed."

Selina snorted, but she smiled whitely when Hagan reappeared and I relaxed a little. Strange how a man can love a woman and yet at the same time pray for her to fall under a train.

Hagan spread a tartan blanket on the wall and we sat down, feeling slightly self-conscious at having been translated from our city-oriented lives into a rural tableau. On the distant slate of the loch, beyond the watchful frames of slow glass, a slow-moving steamer drew a white line towards the south. The boisterous mountain air seemed almost to invade our lungs, giving us more oxygen than we required.

"Some of the glass farmers around here," Hagan began, "give strangers, such as yourselves, a sales talk about how beautiful the autumn is in this part of Argyll. Or it might be spring, or the winter. I don't do that–any fool knows that a place which doesn't look right in summer never looks right. What do you say?"

I nodded compliantly.

"I want you just to take a good look out towards Mull, Mr. . . ."

"Garland."

". . . Garland. That's what you're buying if you buy my glass, and it never looks better than it does at this minute. The glass is in perfect phase, none of it is less than ten years thick–and a four-foot window will cost you two hundred pounds."

"Two hundred!" Selina was shocked. "That's as much as they charge at the Scenedow shop in Bond Street."

Hagan smiled patiently, then looked closely at me to see if I knew enough about slow glass to appreciate what he had been saying. His price had been much higher than I had hoped–but *ten years thick!* The cheap glass one found in places like the Vistaplex and Pane-orama stores usually consisted of a quarter of an inch of ordinary glass faced with a veneer of slow glass perhaps only ten or twelve months thick.

"You don't understand, darling," I said, already determined to buy. "This glass will last ten years and it's in phase."

"Doesn't that only mean it keeps time?"

Hagan smiled at her again, realizing he had no further necessity to bother with me. "Only, you say! Pardon me, Mrs. Garland, but you don't seem to appreciate the miracle, the genuine honest-to-goodness miracle, of engineering precision needed to produce a piece of glass in phase. When I say the glass is ten years thick it means it takes light ten years to pass through it. In effect, each one of those panes is ten light-years thick–more than twice the distance to the nearest star–so a variation in actual thickness of only a millionth of an inch would . . ."

He stopped talking for a moment and sat quietly looking towards the house. I turned my head from the view of the loch and saw the young woman standing at the window again. Hagan's eyes were filled with a kind of greedy reverence which made me feel uncomfortable and at the same time convinced me Selina had been wrong. In my experience husbands never looked at wives that way, at least, not at their own.

The girl remained in view for a few seconds, dress glowing warmly, then moved back into the room. Suddenly I received a distinct, though inexplicable, impression she was blind. My feeling was that Selina and I were perhaps blundering through an emotional interplay as violent as our own.

"I'm sorry," Hagan continued, "I thought Rose was going to call me for something. Now, where was I, Mrs. Garland? Ten light-years compressed into a quarter of an inch means . . ."

I ceased to listen, partly because I was already sold, partly because

I had heard the story of slow glass many times before and had never yet understood the principles involved. An acquaintance with scientific training had once tried to be helpful by telling me to visualize a pane of slow glass as a hologram which did not need coherent light from a laser for the reconstitution of its visual information, and in which every photon of ordinary light passed through a spiral tunnel coiled outside the radius of capture of each atom in the glass. This gem of, to me, incomprehensibility not only told me nothing, it convinced me once again that a mind as nontechnical as mine should concern itself less with causes than effects.

The most important effect, in the eyes of the average individual, was that light took a long time to pass through a sheet of slow glass. A new piece was always jet black because nothing had yet come through, but one could stand the glass beside, say, a woodland lake until the scene emerged, perhaps a year later. If the glass was then removed and installed in a dismal city flat, the flat would–for that year–appear to overlook the woodland lake. During the year it wouldn't be merely a very realistic but still picture–the water would ripple in sunlight, silent animals would come to drink, birds would cross the sky, night would follow day, season would follow season. Until one day, a year later, the beauty held in the subatomic pipelines would be exhausted and the familiar gray cityscape would reappear.

Apart from its stupendous novelty value, the commercial success of slow glass was founded on the fact that having a scenedow was the exact emotional equivalent of owning land. The meanest cave dweller could look out on misty parks–and who was to say they weren't his? A man who really owns tailored gardens and estates doesn't spend his time proving his ownership by crawling on his ground, feeling, smelling, tasting it. All he receives from the land are light patterns, and with scenedows those patterns could be taken into coal mines, submarines, prison cells.

On several occasions I have tried to write short pieces about the enchanted crystal but, to me, the theme is so ineffably poetic as to be, paradoxically, beyond the reach of poetry–mine at any rate. Besides, the best songs and verse had already been written, with prescient inspiration, by men who had died long before slow glass was discovered. I had no hope of equaling, for example, Moore with his:

Oft in the stilly night,
Ere slumber's chain has bound me,
Fond Memory brings the light,
Of other days around me . . .

It took only a few years of slow glass to develop from a scientific curiosity to a sizable industry. And much to the astonishment of us poets—those of us who remain convinced that beauty lives though lilies die—the trappings of that industry were no different from those of any other. There were good scenedows which cost a lot of money, and there were inferior scenedows which cost rather less. The thickness, measured in years, was an important factor in the cost but there was also the question of *actual* thickness, or phase.

Even with the most sophisticated engineering techniques available thickness control was something of a hit-and-miss affair. A coarse discrepancy could mean that a pane intended to be five years thick might be five and a half, so that light which entered in summer emerged in winter; a fine discrepancy could mean that noon sunshine emerged at midnight. These incompatibilities had their peculiar charm—many night workers, for example, liked having their own private time zones—but, in general, it cost more to buy scenedows which kept closely in step with real time.

Selina still looked unconvinced when Hagan had finished speaking. She shook her head almost imperceptibly and I knew he had been using the wrong approach. Quite suddenly the pewter helmet of her hair was disturbed by a cool gust of wind, and huge clean tumbling drops of rain began to spang round us from an almost cloudless sky.

"I'll give you a check now," I said abruptly, and saw Selina's green eyes triangulate angrily on my face. "You can arrange delivery?"

"Aye, delivery's no problem," Hagan said, getting to his feet. "But wouldn't you rather take the glass with you?"

"Well, yes—if you don't mind." I was shamed by his readiness to trust my scrip.

"I'll unclip a pane for you. Wait here. It won't take long to slip it into a carrying frame." Hagan limped down the slope towards the seriate windows, through some of which the view towards Linnhe was sunny, while others were cloudy and a few pure black.

Selina drew the collar of her blouse closed at her throat. "The least he could have done was invite us inside. There can't be so many fools passing through that he can afford to neglect them."

I tried to ignore the insult and concentrated on writing the check. One of the outsize drops broke across my knuckles, splattering the pink paper.

"All right," I said, "let's move in under the eaves till he gets back." You worm, I thought as I felt the whole thing go completely wrong.

I just had to be a fool to marry you. A prize fool, a fool's fool—and now that you've trapped part of me inside you I'll never ever, never ever, *never ever* get away.

Feeling my stomach clench itself painfully, I ran behind Selina to the side of the cottage. Beyond the window the neat living room, with its coal fire, was empty but the child's toys were scattered on the floor. Alphabet blocks and a wheelbarrow the exact color of freshly pared carrots. As I stared in, the boy came running from the other room and began kicking the blocks. He didn't notice me. A few moments later the young woman entered the room and lifted him, laughing easily and wholeheartedly as she swung the boy under her arm. She came to the window as she had done earlier. I smiled self-consciously, but neither she nor the child responded.

My forehead prickled icily. *Could they both be blind?* I sidled away.

Selina gave a little scream and I spun towards her.

"The rug!" she said. "It's getting soaked."

She ran across the yard in the rain, snatched the reddish square from the dappling wall and ran back, towards the cottage door. Something heaved convulsively in my subconscious.

"Selina," I shouted. "Don't open it!"

But I was too late. She had pushed open the latched wooden door and was standing, hand over mouth, looking into the cottage. I moved close to her and took the rug from her unresisting fingers.

As I was closing the door I let my eyes traverse the cottage's interior. The neat living room in which I had just seen the woman and child was, in reality, a sickening clutter of shabby furniture, old newspapers, cast-off clothing and smeared dishes. It was damp, stinking and utterly deserted. The only object I recognized from my view through the window was the little wheelbarrow, paintless and broken.

I latched the door firmly and ordered myself to forget what I had seen. Some men who live alone are good housekeepers; others just don't know how.

Selina's face was white. "I don't understand. I don't understand it."

"Slow glass works both ways," I said gently. "Light passes out of a house as well as in."

"You mean . . . ?"

"I don't know. It isn't our business. Now steady up—Hagan's coming back with our glass." The churning in my stomach was beginning to subside.

Hagan came into the yard carrying an oblong, plastic-covered frame. I held the check out to him, but he was staring at Selina's face. He seemed to know immediately that our uncomprehending fingers had rummaged through his soul. Selina avoided his gaze. She was old and ill-looking, and her eyes stared determinedly towards the nearing horizon.

"I'll take the rug from you, Mr. Garland," Hagan finally said. "You shouldn't have troubled yourself over it."

"No trouble. Here's the check."

"Thank you." He was still looking at Selina with a strange kind of supplication. "It's been a pleasure to do business with you."

"The pleasure was mine," I said with equal, senseless formality. I picked up the heavy frame and guided Selina towards the path which led to the road. Just as we reached the head of the now slippery steps Hagan spoke again.

"Mr. Garland!"

I turned unwillingly.

"It wasn't my fault," he said steadily. "A hit-and-run driver got them both, down on the Oban road six years ago. My boy was only seven when it happened. I'm entitled to keep something."

I nodded wordlessly and moved down the path, holding my wife close to me, treasuring the feel of her arms locked around me. At the bend I looked back through the rain and saw Hagan sitting with squared shoulders on the wall where we had first seen him.

He was looking at the house, but I was unable to tell if there was anyone at the window.

THE GAME OF RAT AND DRAGON

by Cordwainer Smith

PINLIGHTING IS a hell of a way to earn a living. Underhill was furious as he closed the door behind himself. It didn't make much sense to wear a uniform and look like a soldier if people didn't appreciate what you did.

He sat down in his chair, laid his head back in the headrest and pulled the helmet down over his forehead.

As he waited for the pin-set to warm up, he remembered the girl in the outer corridor. She had looked at it, then looked at him scornfully.

"Meow." That was all she had said. Yet it had cut him like a knife.

What did she think he was—a fool, a loafer, a uniformed nonentity? Didn't she know that for every half hour of pinlighting, he got a minimum of two months' recuperation in the hospital?

By now the set was warm. He felt the squares of space around him, sensed himself at the middle of an immense grid, a cubic grid, full of nothing. Out in that nothingness, he could sense the hollow aching horror of space itself and could feel the terrible anxiety which his mind encountered whenever it met the faintest trace of inert dust.

As he relaxed, the comforting solidity of the Sun, the clockwork of the familiar planets and the Moon rang in on him. Our own solar system was as charming and as simple as an ancient cuckoo clock filled with familiar ticking and with reassuring noises. The odd little moons of Mars swung around their planet like frantic mice, yet their regularity was itself an assurance that all was well. Far above the plane of the ecliptic, he could feel half a ton of dust more or less drifting outside the lanes of human travel.

Here there was nothing to fight, nothing to challenge the mind, to tear the living soul out of a body with its roots dripping in effluvium as tangible as blood.

Nothing ever moved in on the Solar System. He could wear the pin-set forever and be nothing more than a sort of telepathic astronomer, a man who could feel the hot, warm protection of the Sun throbbing and burning against his living mind.

Woodley came in.

"Same old ticking world," said Underhill. "Nothing to report. No wonder they didn't develop the pin-set until they began to planoform. Down here with the hot Sun around us, it feels so good and so quiet. You can feel everything spinning and turning. It's nice and sharp and compact. It's sort of like sitting around home."

Woodley grunted. He was not much given to flights of fantasy.

Undeterred, Underhill went on, "It must have been pretty good to have been an ancient man. I wonder why they burned up their world with war. They didn't have to planoform. They didn't have to go out to earn their livings among the stars. They didn't have to dodge the Rats or play the Game. They couldn't have invented pinlighting because they didn't have any need of it, did they, Woodley?"

Woodley grunted, "Uh-huh." Woodley was twenty-six years old and due to retire in one more year. He already had a farm picked out. He had gotten through ten years of hard work pinlighting with the best of them. He had kept his sanity by not thinking very much about his job, meeting the strains of the task whenever he had to meet them and thinking nothing more about his duties until the next emergency arose.

Woodley never made a point of getting popular among the Partners. None of the Partners liked him very much. Some of them even resented him. He was suspected of thinking ugly thoughts of the Partners on occasion, but since none of the Partners ever thought a complaint in articulate form, the other pinlighters and the Chiefs of the Instrumentality left him alone.

Underhill was still full of the wonder of his job. Happily he babbled on, "What does happen to us when we planoform? Do you think it's sort of like dying? Did you ever see anybody who had his soul pulled out?"

"Pulling souls is just a way of talking about it," said Woodley. "After all these years, nobody knows whether we have souls or not."

"But I saw one once. I saw what Dogwood looked like when he came apart. There was something funny. It looked wet and sort of sticky as if it were bleeding and it went out of him–and you know what they did to Dogwood? They took him away, up in that part of the hospital where you and I never go–way up at the top part where the others are, where the others always have to go if they are alive after the Rats of the Up-and-Out have gotten them."

Woodley sat down and lit an ancient pipe. He was burning something called tobacco in it. It was a dirty sort of habit, but it made him look very dashing and adventurous.

"Look here, youngster. You don't have to worry about that stuff. Pinlighting is getting better all the time. The Partners are getting better. I've seen them pinlight two Rats forty-six million miles apart in one and a half milliseconds. As long as people had to try to work the pin-sets themselves, there was always the chance that with a minimum of four hundred milliseconds for the human mind to set a pinlight, we wouldn't light the Rats up fast enough to protect our planoforming ships. The Partners have changed all that. Once they get going, they're faster than Rats. And they always will be. I know it's not easy, letting a Partner share your mind–"

"It's not easy for them, either," said Underhill.

"Don't worry about them. They're not human. Let them take care of themselves. I've seen more pinlighters go crazy from monkeying around with Partners than I have ever seen caught by the Rats. How many do you actually know of them that got grabbed by Rats?"

Underhill looked down at his fingers, which shone green and purple in the vivid light thrown by the tuned-in pin-set, and counted ships. The thumb for the *Andromeda,* lost with crew and passengers, the index finger and the middle finger for *Release Ships* 43 and 56, found with their pin-sets burned out and every man, woman, and child on board dead or insane. The ring finger, the little finger, and the thumb of the other hand were the first three battleships to be lost to the Rats–lost as people realized that there was something out there *underneath space itself* which was alive, capricious and malevolent.

Planoforming was sort of funny. It felt like–

Like nothing much.

Like the twinge of a mild electric shock.

Like the ache of a sore tooth bitten on for the first time.

Like a slightly painful flash of light against the eyes.

Yet in that time, a forty-thousand-ton ship lifting free above Earth disappeared somehow or other into two dimensions and appeared half a light-year or fifty light-years off.

At one moment, he would be sitting in the Fighting Room, the pin-set ready and the familiar Solar System ticking around inside his head. For a second or a year (he could never tell how long it really was, subjectively), the funny little flash went through him and then he was loose in the Up-and-Out, the terrible open spaces between the stars, where the stars themselves felt like pimples on his telepathic mind and the planets were too far away to be sensed or read.

Somewhere in this outer space, a gruesome death awaited, death and horror of a kind which Man had never encountered until he reached out for interstellar space itself. Apparently the light of the suns kept the Dragons away.

Dragons. That was what people called them. To ordinary people, there was nothing, nothing except the shiver of planoforming and the hammer blow of sudden death or the dark spastic note of lunacy descending into their minds.

But to the telepaths, they were Dragons.

In the fraction of a second between the telepaths' awareness of a hostile something out in the black, hollow nothingness of space and the impact of a ferocious, ruinous psychic blow against all living things within the ship, the telepaths had sensed entities something like the Dragons of ancient human lore, beasts more clever than beasts, demons more tangible than demons, hungry vortices of aliveness and hate compounded by unknown means out of the thin tenuous matter between the stars.

It took a surviving ship to bring back the news–a ship in which, by sheer chance, a telepath had a light beam ready, turning it out at the innocent dust so that, within the panorama of his mind, the Dragon dissolved into nothing at all and the other passengers, themselves non-telepathic, went about their way not realizing that their own immediate deaths had been averted.

From then on, it was easy–almost.

Planoforming ships always carried telepaths. Telepaths had their sensitiveness enlarged to an immense range by the pin-sets, which were telepathic amplifiers adapted to the mammal mind. The pin-sets in turn were electronically geared into small dirigible light bombs. Light did it.

Light broke up the Dragons, allowed the ships to reform three-dimensionally, skip, skip, skip, as they moved from star to star.

The odds suddenly moved down from a hundred to one against mankind to sixty to forty in mankind's favor.

This was not enough. The telepaths were trained to become ultra-sensitive, trained to become aware of the Dragons in less than a millisecond.

But it was found that the Dragons could move a million miles in just under two milliseconds and that this was not enough for the human mind to activate the light beams.

Attempts had been made to sheath the ships in light at all times. This defense wore out.

As mankind learned about the Dragons, so too, apparently, the Dragons learned about mankind. Somehow they flattened their own bulk and came in on extremely flat trajectories very quickly.

Intense light was needed, light of sunlike intensity. This could be provided only by light bombs. Pinlighting came into existence.

Pinlighting consisted of the detonation of ultravivid miniature photonuclear bombs, which converted a few ounces of a magnesium isotope into pure visible radiance.

The odds kept coming down in mankind's favor, yet ships were being lost.

It became so bad that people didn't even want to find the ships because the rescuers knew what they would see. It was sad to bring back to Earth three hundred bodies ready for burial and two hundred or three hundred lunatics, damaged beyond repair, to be wakened, and fed, and cleaned, and put to sleep, wakened and fed again until their lives were ended.

Telepaths tried to reach into the minds of the psychotics who had been damaged by the Dragons, but they found nothing there beyond vivid spouting columns of fiery terror bursting from the primordial id itself, the volcanic source of life.

Then came the Partners.

Man and Partner could do together what Man could not do alone. Men had the intellect. Partners had the speed.

The Partners rode their tiny craft, no larger than footballs, outside the spaceships. They planoformed with the ships. They rode beside them in their six-pound craft ready to attack.

The tiny ships of the Partners were swift. Each carried a dozen pinlights, bombs no bigger than thimbles.

The pinlighters threw the Partners–quite literally threw–by means of mind-to-firing relays direct at the Dragons.

What seemed to be Dragons to the human mind appeared in the form of gigantic Rats in the minds of the Partners.

Out in the pitiless nothingness of space, the Partners' minds responded to an instinct as old as life. The Partners attacked, striking with a speed faster than Man's, going from attack to attack until the Rats or themselves were destroyed. Almost all the time, it was the Partners who won.

With the safety of the interstellar skip, skip, skip of the ships, commerce increased immensely, the population of all the colonies went up, and the demand for trained Partners increased.

Underhill and Woodley were a part of the third generation of pinlighters and yet, to them, it seemed as though their craft had endured forever.

Gearing space into minds by means of the pin-set, adding the Partners to those minds, keying up the mind for the tension of a fight on which all depended—this was more than human synapses could stand for long. Underhill needed his two months' rest after half an hour of fighting. Woodley needed his retirement after ten years of service. They were young. They were good. But they had limitations.

So much depended on the choice of Partners, so much on the sheer luck of who drew whom.

Father Moontree and the little girl named West entered the room. They were the other two pinlighters. The human complement of the Fighting Room was now complete.

Father Moontree was a red-faced man of forty-five who had lived the peaceful life of a farmer until he reached his fortieth year. Only then, belatedly, did the authorities find he was telepathic and agree to let him late in life enter upon the career of pinlighter. He did well at it, but he was fantastically old for this kind of business.

Father Moontree looked at the glum Woodley and the musing Underhill. "How're the youngsters today? Ready for a good fight?"

"Father always wants a fight," giggled the little girl named West. She was such a little little girl. Her giggle was high and childish. She looked like the last person in the world one would expect to find in the rough, sharp dueling of pinlighting.

Underhill had been amused one time when he found one of the most sluggish of the Partners coming away happy from contact with the mind of the girl named West.

Usually the Partners didn't care much about the human minds with which they were paired for the journey. The Partners seemed to take the attitude that human minds were complex and fouled up beyond belief, anyhow. No Partner ever questioned the superiority of the human mind, though very few of the Partners were much impressed by that superiority.

The Partners liked people. They were willing to fight with them. They were even willing to die for them. But when a Partner liked an individual the way, for example, that Captain Wow or the Lady

May liked Underhill, the liking had nothing to do with intellect. It was a matter of temperament, of feel.

Underhill knew perfectly well that Captain Wow regarded his, Underhill's, brains as silly. What Captain Wow liked was Underhill's friendly emotional structure, the cheerfulness and glint of wicked amusement that shot through Underhill's unconscious thought patterns, and the gaiety with which Underhill faced danger. The words, the history books, the ideas, the science—Underhill could sense all that in his own mind, reflected back from Captain Wow's mind, as so much rubbish.

Miss West looked at Underhill. "I bet you've put stickum on the stones."

"I did not!"

Underhill felt his ears grow red with embarrassment. During his novitiate, he had tried to cheat in the lottery because he got particularly fond of a special Partner, a lovely young mother named Murr. It was so much easier to operate with Murr and she was so affectionate toward him that he forgot pinlighting was hard work and that he was not instructed to have a good time with his Partner. They were both designed and prepared to go into deadly battle together.

One cheating had been enough. They had found him out and he had been laughed at for years.

Father Moontree picked up the imitation-leather cup and shook the stone dice which assigned them their Partners for the trip. By senior rights, he took first draw.

He grimaced. He had drawn a greedy old character, a tough old male whose mind was full of slobbering thoughts of food, veritable oceans full of half-spoiled fish. Father Moontree had once said that he burped cod-liver oil for weeks after drawing that particular glutton, so strongly had the telepathic image of fish impressed itself upon his mind. Yet the glutton was a glutton for danger as well as for fish. He had killed sixty-three Dragons, more than any other Partner in the service, and was quite literally worth his weight in gold.

The little girl West came next. She drew Captain Wow. When she saw who it was, she smiled.

"I *like* him," she said. "He's such fun to fight with. He feels so nice and cuddly in my mind."

"Cuddly, hell," said Woodley. "I've been in his mind, too. It's the most leering mind in this ship, bar none."

"Nasty man," said the little girl. She said it declaratively, without reproach.

Underhill, looking at her, shivered.

He didn't see how she could take Captain Wow so calmly. Captain Wow's mind *did* leer. When Captain Wow got excited in the middle of a battle, confused images of Dragons, deadly Rats, luscious beds, the smell of fish, and the shock of space all scrambled together in his mind as he and Captain Wow, their consciousnesses linked together through the pin-set, became a fantastic composite of human being and Persian cat.

That's the trouble with working with cats, thought Underhill. It's a pity that nothing else anywhere will serve as Partner. Cats were all right once you got in touch with them telepathically. They were smart enough to meet the needs of the fight, but their motives and desires were certainly different from those of humans.

They were companionable enough as long as you thought tangible images at them, but their minds just closed up and went to sleep when you recited Shakespeare or Colegrove, or if you tried to tell them what space was.

It was sort of funny realizing that the Partners who were so grim and mature out here in space were the same cute little animals that people had used as pets for thousands of years back on Earth. He had embarrassed himself more than once while on the ground saluting perfectly ordinary non-telepathic cats because he had forgotten for the moment that they were not Partners.

He picked up the cup and shook out his stone dice.

He was lucky–he drew the Lady May.

The Lady May was the most thoughtful Partner he had ever met. In her, the finely bred pedigree mind of a Persian cat had reached one of its highest peaks of development. She was more complex than any human woman, but the complexity was all one of emotions, memory, hope and discriminated experience–experience sorted through without benefit of words.

When he had first come into contact with her mind, he was astonished at its clarity. With her he remembered her kittenhood. He remembered every mating experience she had ever had. He saw in a half-recognizable gallery all the other pinlighters with whom she had been paired for the fight. And he saw himself radiant, cheerful and desirable.

He even thought he caught the edge of a longing–

A very flattering and yearning thought: *What a pity he is not a cat.*

Woodley picked up the last stone. He drew what he deserved–a sullen, scared old tomcat with none of the verve of Captain Wow.

Woodley's Partner was the most animal of all the cats on the ship, a low, brutish type with a dull mind. Even telepathy had not refined his character. His ears were half chewed off from the first fights in which he had engaged.

He was a serviceable fighter, nothing more.

Woodley grunted.

Underhill glanced at him oddly. Didn't Woodley ever do anything but grunt?

Father Moontree looked at the other three. "You might as well get your Partners now. I'll let the Scanner know we're ready to go into the Up-and-Out."

Underhill spun the combination lock on the Lady May's cage. He woke her gently and took her into his arms. She humped her back luxuriously, stretched her claws, started to purr, thought better of it, and licked him on the wrist instead. He did not have the pin-set on, so their minds were closed to each other, but in the angle of her mustache and in the movement of her ears, he caught some sense of gratification she experienced in finding him as her Partner.

He talked to her in human speech, even though speech meant nothing to a cat when the pin-set was not on.

"It's a damn shame, sending a sweet little thing like you whirling around in the coldness of nothing to hunt for Rats that are bigger and deadlier than all of us put together. You didn't ask for this kind of fight, did you?"

For answer, she licked his hand, purred, tickled his cheek with her long fluffy tail, turned around and faced him, golden eyes shining.

For a moment, they stared at each other, man squatting, cat standing erect on her hind legs, front claws digging into his knee. Human eyes and cat eyes looked across an immensity which no words could meet, but which affection spanned in a single glance.

"Time to get in," he said.

She walked docilely into her spheroid carrier. She climbed in. He saw to it that her miniature pin-set rested firmly and comfortably against the base of her brain. He made sure that her claws were padded so that she could not tear herself in the excitement of battle.

Softly he said to her, "Ready?"

For answer, she preened her back as much as her harness would permit and purred softly within the confines of the frame that held her.

He slapped down the lid and watched the sealant ooze around the seam. For a few hours, she was welded into her projectile until a workman with a short cutting arc would remove her after she had done her duty.

He picked up the entire projectile and slipped it into the ejection tube. He closed the door of the tube, spun the lock, seated himself in his chair, and put his own pin-set on.

Once again he flung the switch.

He sat in a small room, *small, small, warm, warm,* the bodies of the other three people moving close around him, the tangible lights in the ceiling bright and heavy against his closed eyelids.

As the pin-set warmed, the room fell away. The other people ceased to be people and became small glowing heaps of fire, embers, dark red fire, with the consciousness of life burning like old red coals in a country fireplace.

As the pin-set warmed a little more, he felt Earth just below him, felt the ship slipping away, felt the turning Moon as it swung on the far side of the world, felt the planets and the hot, clear goodness of the Sun which kept the Dragons so far from mankind's native ground.

Finally, he reached complete awareness.

He was telepathically alive to a range of millions of miles. He felt the dust which he had noticed earlier high above the ecliptic. With a thrill of warmth and tenderness, he felt the consciousness of the Lady May pouring over into his own. Her consciousness was as gentle and clear and yet sharp to the taste of his mind as if it were scented oil. It felt relaxing and reassuring. He could sense her welcome of him. It was scarcely a thought, just a raw emotion of greeting.

At last they were one again.

In a tiny remote corner of his mind, as tiny as the smallest toy he had ever seen in his childhood, he was still aware of the room and the ship, and of Father Moontree picking up a telephone and speaking to a Scanner captain in charge of the ship.

His telepathic mind caught the idea long before his ears could frame the words. The actual sound followed the idea the way that thunder on an ocean beach follows the lightning inward from far out over the seas.

"The Fighting Room is ready. Clear to planoform, sir."

Underhill was always a little exasperated the way that Lady May experienced things before he did.

He was braced for the quick vinegar thrill of planoforming, but he caught her report of it before his own nerves could register what happened.

Earth had fallen so far away that he groped for several milliseconds before he found the Sun in the upper rear right-hand corner of his telepathic mind.

That was a good jump, he thought. This way we'll get there in four or five skips.

A few hundred miles outside the ship, the Lady May thought back at him, "O warm, O generous, O gigantic man! O brave, O friendly, O tender and huge Partner! O wonderful with you, with you so good, good, good, warm, warm, now to fight, now to go, good with you . . ."

He knew that she was not thinking words, that his mind took the clear amiable babble of her cat intellect and translated it into images which his own thinking could record and understand.

Neither one of them was absorbed in the game of mutual greetings. He reached out far beyond her range of perception to see if there was anything near the ship. It was funny how it was possible to do two things at once. He could scan space with his pin-set mind and yet at the same time catch a vagrant thought of hers, a lovely, affectionate thought about a son who had had a golden face and a chest covered with soft, incredibly downy white fur.

While he was still searching, he caught the warning from her.

We jump again!

And so they had. The ship had moved to a second planoform. The stars were different. The sun was immeasurably far behind. Even the nearest stars were barely in contact. This was good Dragon country, this open, nasty, hollow kind of space. He reached farther, faster, sensing and looking for danger, ready to fling the Lady May at danger wherever he found it.

Terror blazed up in his mind, so sharp, so clear, that it came through as a physical wrench.

The little girl named West had found something–something immense, long, black, sharp, greedy, horrific. She flung Captain Wow at it.

Underhill tried to keep his own mind clear. "Watch out!" he shouted telepathically at the others, trying to move the Lady May around.

At one corner of the battle, he felt the lustful rage of Captain Wow as the big Persian tomcat detonated lights while he approached the streak of dust which threatened the ship and the people within.

The lights scored near-misses.

The dust flattened itself, changing from the shape of a sting-ray into the shape of a spear.

Not three milliseconds had elapsed.

Father Moontree was talking human words and was saying in a voice that moved like cold molasses out of a heavy jar, "C-a-p-t-a-i-n." Underhill knew that the sentence was going to be "Captain, move fast!"

The battle would be fought and finished before Father Moontree got through talking.

Now, fractions of a millisecond later, the Lady May was directly in line.

Here was where the skill and speed of the Partners came in. She could react faster than he. She could see the threat as an immense Rat coming direct at her.

She could fire the light bombs with a discrimination which he might miss.

He was connected with her mind, but he could not follow it.

His consciousness absorbed the tearing wound inflicted by the alien enemy. It was like no wound on Earth–raw, crazy pain which started like a burn at his navel. He began to writhe in his chair.

Actually he had not yet had time to move a muscle when the Lady May struck back at their enemy.

Five evenly spaced photonuclear bombs blazed out across a hundred thousand miles.

The pain in his mind and body vanished.

He felt a moment of fierce, terrible, feral elation running through the mind of the Lady May as she finished her kill. It was always disappointing to the cats to find out that their enemies whom they sensed as gigantic space Rats disappeared at the moment of destruction.

Then he felt her hurt, the pain and the fear that swept over both of them as the battle, quicker than the movement of an eyelid, had come and gone. In the same instant, there came the sharp and acid twinge of planoform.

Once more the ship went skip.

He could hear Woodley thinking at him. "You don't have to bother much. This old son of a gun and I will take over for a while."

Twice again the twinge, the skip.

He had no idea where he was until the lights of the Caledonia space board shone below.

With a weariness that lay almost beyond the limits of thought, he threw his mind back into rapport with the pin-set, fixing the Lady May's projectile gently and neatly in its launching tube.

She was half dead with fatigue, but he could feel the beat of her heart, could listen to her panting, and he grasped the grateful edge of a thanks reaching from her mind to his.

They put him in the hospital at Caledonia.

The doctor was friendly but firm. "You actually got touched by that Dragon. That's as close a shave as I've ever seen. It's all so quick that it'll be a long time before we know what happened scientifically, but I suppose you'd be ready for the insane asylum now if the contact had lasted several tenths of a millisecond longer. What kind of cat did you have out in front of you?"

Underhill felt the words coming out of him slowly. Words were such a lot of trouble compared with the speed and the joy of thinking, fast and sharp and clear, mind to mind! But words were all that could reach ordinary people like this doctor.

His mouth moved heavily as he articulated words, "Don't call our Partners cats. The right thing to call them is Partners. They fight for us in a team. You ought to know we call them Partners, not cats. How is mine?"

"I don't know," said the doctor contritely. "We'll find out for you. Meanwhile, old man, you take it easy. There's nothing but rest that can help you. Can you make yourself sleep, or would you like us to give you some kind of sedative?"

"I can sleep," said Underhill. "I just want to know about the Lady May."

The nurse joined in. She was a little antagonistic. "Don't you want to know about the other people?"

"They're okay," said Underhill. "I knew that before I came in here."

He stretched his arms and sighed and grinned at them. He could see they were relaxing and were beginning to treat him as a person instead of a patient.

"I'm all right," he said. "Just let me know when I can go see my Partner."

A new thought struck him. He looked wildly at the doctor. "They didn't send her off with the ship, did they?"

"I'll find out right away," said the doctor. He gave Underhill a reassuring squeeze of the shoulder and left the room.

The nurse took a napkin off a goblet of chilled fruit juice.

Underhill tried to smile at her. There seemed to be something wrong with the girl. He wished she would go away. First she had started to be friendly and now she was distant again. It's a nuisance being telepathic, he thought. You keep trying to reach even when you are not making contact.

Suddenly she swung around on him.

"You pinlighters! You and your damn cats!"

Just as she stamped out, he burst into her mind. He saw himself a radiant hero, clad in his smooth suede uniform, the pin-set crown shining like ancient royal jewels around his head. He saw his own face, handsome and masculine, shining out of her mind. He saw himself very far away and he saw himself as she hated him.

She hated him in the secrecy of her own mind. She hated him because he was–she thought–proud, and strange, and rich, better and more beautiful than people like her.

He cut off the sight of her mind and, as he buried his face in the pillow, he caught an image of the Lady May.

"She *is* a cat," he thought. "That's all she is–a *cat!*"

But that was not how his mind saw her–quick beyond all dreams of speed, sharp, clever, unbelievably graceful, beautiful, wordless and undemanding.

Where would he ever find a woman who could compare with her?

BECALMED IN HELL

by Larry Niven

I COULD feel the heat hovering outside. In the cabin it was bright and dry and cool, almost too cool, like a modern office building in the dead of summer. Beyond the two small windows it was as black as it ever gets in the solar system, and hot enough to melt lead, at a pressure equivalent to three hundred feet beneath the ocean.

"There goes a fish," I said just to break the monotony.

"So how's it cooked?"

"Can't tell. It seems to be leaving a trail of bread crumbs. Fried? Imagine that, Eric! A fried jellyfish."

Eric sighed noisily. "Do I have to?"

"You have to. Only way you'll see anything worthwhile in this—this—" Soup? Fog? Boiling maple syrup?

"Searing black calm."

"Right."

"Someone dreamed up that phrase when I was a kid, just after the news of the Mariner II probe. An eternal searing black calm, hot as a kiln, under an atmosphere thick enough to keep any light or any breath of wind from ever reaching the surface."

I shivered. "What's the outside temperature now?"

"You'd rather not know. You've always had too much imagination, Howie."

"I can take it, Doc."

"Six hundred and twelve degrees."

"I can't take it, Doc!"

This was Venus, planet of Love, favorite of the science-fiction writers of three decades ago. Our ship hung below the Earth-to-Venus hydrogen fuel tank, twenty miles up and all but motionless in the syrupy air. The tank, nearly empty now, made an excellent blimp. It would keep us aloft as long as the internal pressure matched the external. That was Eric's job, to regulate the tank's pressure by regulating the temperature of the hydrogen gas. We had collected air samples after each ten-mile drop from three hundred miles on down, and temperature readings for shorter intervals, and we had dropped the small probe. The data we had got from the surface merely confirmed in detail our previous knowledge of the hottest world in the solar system.

"Temperature just went up to six-thirteen," said Eric. "Look, are you through bitching?"

"For the moment."

"Good. Strap down. We're taking off."

"Oh frabjous day!" I started untangling the crash webbing over my couch.

"We've done everything we came to do. Haven't we?"

"Am I arguing? Look, I'm strapped down."

"Yeah."

I knew why he was reluctant to leave. I felt a touch of it myself. We'd spent four months getting to Venus in order to spend a week circling her and less than two days in her upper atmosphere, and it seemed a terrible waste of time.

But he was taking too long. "What's the trouble, Eric?"

"You'd rather not know."

He meant it. His voice was a mechanical, inhuman monotone; he wasn't making the extra effort to get human expression out of his "prosthetic" vocal apparatus. Only a severe shock would affect him that way.

"I can take it," I said.

"Okay. I can't feel anything in the ramjet controls. Feels like I've just had a spinal anesthetic."

The cold in the cabin drained into me, all of it. "See if you can send motor impulses the other way. You could run the rams by guess-and-hope even if you can't feel them."

"Okay." One split second later, "They don't. Nothing happens. Good thinking though."

I tried to think of something to say while I untied myself from the couch. What came out was, "It's been a pleasure knowing you, Eric. I've liked being half of this team, and I still do."

"Get maudlin later. Right now, start checking my attachments. Carefully."

I swallowed my comments and went to open the access door in the cabin's forward wall. The floor swayed ever so gently beneath my feet.

Beyond the four-foot-square access door was Eric. Eric's central nervous system, with the brain perched at the top and the spinal cord coiled in a loose spiral to fit more compactly into the transparent glass-and-sponge-plastic housing. Hundreds of wires from all over the ship led to the glass walls, where they were joined to selected nerves which spread like an electrical network from the central coil of nervous tissue and fatty protective membrane.

Space leaves no cripples; and don't call Eric a cripple, because he doesn't like it. In a way he's the ideal spaceman. His life support system weighs only half what mine does, and takes up a twelfth as much room. But his other prosthetic aids take up most of the ship. The ramjets were hooked into the last pair of nerve trunks, the nerves which once moved his legs, and dozens of finer nerves in those trunks sensed and regulated fuel feed, ram temperature, differential acceleration, intake aperture dilation, and spark impulse.

These connections were intact. I checked them four different ways without finding the slightest reason why they shouldn't be working.

"Test the others," said Eric.

It took a good two hours to check every trunk nerve connection. They were all solid. The blood pump was chugging along, and the fluid was rich enough, which killed the idea that the ram nerves might have "gone to sleep" from the lack of nutrients or oxygen. Since the lab is one of his prosthetic aids, I let Eric analyze his own blood sugar, hoping that the "liver" had goofed and was producing some other form of sugar. The conclusions were appalling. There was nothing wrong with Eric–inside the cabin.

"Eric, you're healthier than I am."

"I could tell. You look worried, son, and I don't blame you. Now you'll have to go outside."

"I know. Let's dig out the suit."

It was in the emergency tools locker, the Venus suit that was never supposed to be used. NASA had designed it for use at Venusian ground level. Then they had refused to okay the ship below twenty miles until they knew more about the planet. The suit was a segmented armor job. I had watched it being tested in the heat-and-pressure box at Cal Tech, and I knew that the joints stopped moving after five hours and wouldn't start again until they had been cooled. Now I opened the locker and pulled the suit out by the shoulders and held it in front of me. It seemed to be staring back.

"You still can't feel anything in the ramjets?"

"Not a twinge."

I started to put on the suit, piece by piece like medieval armor.

Then I thought of something else. "We're twenty miles up. Are you going to ask me to do a balancing act on the hull?"

"No! Wouldn't think of it. We'll just have to go down."

The lift from the blimp tank was supposed to be constant until takeoff. When the time came Eric could get extra lift by heating the hydrogen to higher pressure, then cracking a valve to let the excess out. Of course he'd have to be very careful that the pressure was higher in the tank, or we'd get Venusian air coming in, and the ship would fall instead of rising. Naturally that would be disastrous.

So Eric lowered the tank temperature and cracked the valve, and down we went.

"Of course there's a catch," Eric said.

"I know."

"The ship stood the pressure twenty miles up. At ground level it'll be six times that."

"I know."

We fell fast, with the cabin tilted forward by the drag on our tail fins. The temperature rose gradually. The pressure went up fast. I sat at the window and saw nothing, nothing but black, but I sat there anyway and waited for the window to crack. NASA had refused to okay the ship below twenty miles.

Eric said, "The blimp tank's okay, and so's the ship, I think. But will the cabin stand up to it?"

"I wouldn't know."

"Ten miles."

Five hundred miles above us, unreachable, was the atomic ion engine that was to take us home. We couldn't get to it on the chemical rocket alone. The rocket was for use after the air became too thin for the ramjets.

"Four miles. Have to crack the valve again."

The ship dropped.

"I can see ground," said Eric.

I couldn't. Eric caught me straining my eyes and said, "Forget it. I'm using deep infrared, and getting no detail."

"No vast, misty swamps with weird, terrifying monsters and man-eating plants?"

"All I see is hot, bare dirt."

But we were almost down, and there were no cracks in the cabin wall. My neck and shoulder muscles loosened. I turned away from the window. Hours had passed while we dropped through the poisoned, thickening air. I already had most of my suit on. Now I screwed on my helmet and three-fingered gauntlets.

"Strap down," said Eric. I did.

We bumped gently. The ship tilted a little, swayed back, bumped again. And again, with my teeth rattling and my armor-plated body rolling against the crash webbing. "Damn," Eric muttered. I heard the hiss from above. Eric said, "I don't know how we'll get back up."

Neither did I. The ship bumped hard and stayed down, and I got up and went to the airlock.

"Good luck," said Eric. "Don't stay out too long." I waved at his cabin camera. The outside temperature was seven hundred and thirty.

The outer door opened. My suit refrigerating unit set up a complaining whine. With an empty bucket in each hand, and with my headlamp blazing a way through the black murk, I stepped out onto the right wing.

My suit creaked and settled under the pressure, and I stood on the wing and waited for it to stop. It was almost like being under water. My headlamp beam went out thick enough to be solid, penetrating no more than a hundred feet. The air couldn't have been that opaque, no matter how dense. It must have been full of dust, or tiny droplets of some fluid.

The wing ran back like a knife-edged running board, widening toward the tail until it spread into a tail fin. The two tail fins met back of the fuselage. At the tail fin tip was the ram, a big sculptured cylinder with an atomic engine inside. It wouldn't be hot because it hadn't been used yet, but I had my counter anyway.

I fastened a line to the wing and slid to the ground. As long as we were *here* . . . The ground turned out to be a dry, reddish dirt, crumbly, and so porous that it was almost spongy. Lava etched by chemicals? Almost anything would be corrosive at this pressure and temperature. I scooped one pailful from the surface and another from underneath the first, then climbed up the line and left the buckets on the wing.

The wing was terribly slippery. I had to wear magnetic sandals to stay on. I walked up and back along the two-hundred-foot length of the ship, making a casual inspection. Neither wing nor fuselage showed damage. Why not? If a meteor or something had cut Eric's contact with his sensors in the rams, there should have been evidence of a break in the surface.

Then, almost suddenly, I realized that there was an alternative.

It was too vague a suspicion to put into words yet, and I still had to finish the inspection. Telling Eric would be very difficult if I was right.

Four inspection panels were set into the wing, well protected from the reentry heat. One was halfway back on the fuselage, below the lower edge of the blimp tank, which was molded to the fuselage in such a way that from the front the ship looked like a dolphin. Two more were in the trailing edge of the tail fin, and the fourth was in the ram itself. All opened, with powered screwdriver on recessed screws, on junctions of the ship's electrical system.

There was nothing out of place under any of the panels. By making and breaking contacts and getting Eric's reactions, I found that his sensation ended somewhere between the second and third inspection panels. It was the same story on the left wing. No external damage, nothing wrong at the junctions. I climbed back to ground and walked slowly beneath the length of each wing, my headlamp tilted up. No damage underneath.

I collected my buckets and went back inside.

"A bone to pick?" Eric was puzzled. "Isn't this a strange time to start an argument? Save it for space. We'll have four months with nothing else to do."

"This can't wait. First of all, did you notice anything I didn't?" He'd been watching everything I saw and did through the peeper in my helmet.

"No. I'd have yelled."

"Okay. Now get this.

"The break in your circuits isn't inside, because you get sensation up to the second wing inspection panels. It isn't outside because there's no evidence of damage, not even corrosion spots. That leaves only one place for the flaw."

"Go on."

"We also have the puzzle of why you're paralyzed in both rams. Why should they both go wrong at the same time? There's only one place in the ship where the circuits join."

"What? Oh, yes, I see. They join through me."

"Now let's assume for the moment that you're the piece with the flaw in it. You're not a piece of machinery, Eric. If something's wrong with you it isn't medical. That was the first thing we covered. But it could be psychological."

"It's nice to know you think I'm human. So I've slipped a cam, have I?"

"Slightly. I think you've got a case of what used to be called trigger anesthesia. A soldier who kills too often sometimes finds that his right index finger or even his whole hand has gone numb, as if it were no longer a part of him. Your comment about not being a machine is important, Eric. I think that's the whole problem. You've never really believed that any part of the ship is a part of *you.* That's intelligent, because it's true. Every time the ship is redesigned you get a new set of parts, and it's right to avoid thinking of a change of model as a series of amputations." I'd been rehearsing this speech, trying to put it so that Eric would have no choice but to believe me. Now I know that it must have sounded phony. "But now you've gone too far. Subconsciously you've stopped believing that the rams can *feel* like a part of you, which they were designed to do. So you've persuaded yourself that you don't feel anything."

With my prepared speech done, and nothing left to say, I stopped talking and waited for the explosion.

"You make good sense," said Eric.

I was staggered. "You agree?"

"I didn't say that. You spin an elegant theory, but I want time to think about it. What do we do if it's true?"

"Why . . . I don't know. You'll just have to cure yourself."

"Okay. Now here's *my* idea. I propose that you thought up this theory to relieve yourself of responsibility for getting us home alive. It puts the whole problem in my lap, metaphorically speaking."

"Oh, for–"

"Shut up. I haven't said you're wrong. That would be an *ad hominem* argument. We need time to think about this."

It was lights-out, four hours later, before Eric would return to the subject.

"Howie, do me a favor. Assume for a while that something mechanical is causing all our trouble. I'll assume it's psychosomatic."

"Seems reasonable."

"It is reasonable. What can you do if I've gone psychosomatic? What can I do if it's mechanical? I can't go around inspecting myself. We'd each better stick to what we know."

"It's a deal." I turned him off for the night and went to bed.

But not to sleep.

With the lights off it was just like outside. I turned them back on. It wouldn't wake Eric. Eric never sleeps normally, since his blood doesn't accumulate fatigue poisons, and he'd go mad from being awake all the time if he didn't have a Russian sleep-inducer plate near his cortex. The ship could implode without waking Eric when his sleep inducer's on. But I felt foolish being afraid of the dark.

While the dark stayed outside it was all right.

But it wouldn't stay there. It had invaded my partner's mind. Because his chemical checks guard him against chemical insanities like schizophrenia, we'd assumed he was permanently sane. But how could any prosthetic device protect him from his own imagination, his own misplaced common sense?

I couldn't keep my bargain. I knew I was right. But what could I do about it?

Hindsight is wonderful. I could see exactly what our mistake had been. Eric's and mine and the hundreds of men who had built his life support after the crash. There was nothing left of Eric then except the intact central nervous system, and no glands except the pituitary. "We'll regulate his blood composition," they said, "and he'll always be cool, calm and collected. No panic reactions from Eric!"

I know a girl whose father had an accident when he was forty-five or so. He was out with his brother, the girl's uncle, on a fishing trip. They were blind drunk when they started home, and the guy was riding on the hood while the brother drove. Then the brother made a sudden stop. Our hero left two important glands on the hood ornament.

The only change in his sex life was that his wife stopped worrying about late pregnancy. His *habits* were developed.

Eric doesn't need adrenal glands to be afraid of death. His emotional patterns were fixed long before the day he tried to land a moonship without radar. He'd grab any excuse to believe that I'd fixed whatever was wrong with the ram connections.

But he was counting on me to do it.

The atmosphere leaned on the windows. Not wanting to, I reached out to touch the quartz with my fingertips. I couldn't feel the pressure. But it was there, inexorable as the tide smashing a rock into sand grains. How long would the cabin hold it back?

If some broken part were holding us here, how could I have missed finding it? Perhaps it had left no break in the surface of either wing. But how?

That was an angle.

Two cigarettes later I got up to get the sample buckets. They were empty, the alien dirt safely stored away. I filled them with water and put them in the cooler, set the cooler for 40° Absolute, then turned off the lights and went to bed.

The morning was blacker than the inside of a smoker's lungs. What Venus really needs, I decided, philosophizing on my back, is to lose 99 percent of her air. That would give her a bit more than half as much air as Earth, which would lower the greenhouse effect enough to make the temperature livable. Drop Venus' gravity to near zero for a few weeks and the work would do itself.

The whole damn universe is waiting for us to discover antigravity.

"Morning," said Eric. "Thought of anything?"

"Yes." I rolled out of bed. "Now don't bug me with questions. I'll explain everything as I go."

"No breakfast?"

"Not yet."

Piece by piece I put my suit on, just like one of King Arthur's gentlemen, and went for the buckets only after the gauntlets were on. The ice, in the cold section, was in the chilly neighborhood of absolute zero. "This is two buckets of ordinary ice," I said, holding them up. "Now let me out."

"I should keep you here till you talk," Eric groused. But the doors opened and I went out onto the wing. I started talking while I unscrewed the number two right panel.

"Eric, think a moment about the tests they run on a manned ship before they'll let a man walk into the life system. They test every part separately and in conjunction with other parts. Yet if something isn't working, either it's damaged or it wasn't tested right. Right?"

"Reasonable." He wasn't giving away anything.

"Well, nothing caused any damage. Not only is there no break in the ship's skin, but no coincidence could have made both rams go haywire at the same time. So something wasn't tested right."

I had the panel off. In the buckets the ice boiled gently where it touched the surfaces of the glass buckets. The blue ice cakes had cracked under their own internal pressure. I dumped one bucket into the maze of wiring and contacts and relays, and the ice shattered, giving me room to close the panel.

"So I thought of something last night, something that wasn't tested. Every part of the ship must have been in the heat-and-pressure box, exposed to artificial Venus conditions, but the ship as a whole, a unit, couldn't have been. It's too big." I'd circled around to the left wing and was opening the number-three panel in the trailing edge. My remaining ice was half water and half small chips; I sloshed these in and fastened the panel. "What cut your circuits must have been the heat or the pressure or both. I can't help the pressure, but I'm cooling these relays with ice. Let me know which ram gets its sensation back first, and we'll know which inspection panel is the right one."

"Howie. Has it occurred to you what the cold water might do to those hot metals?"

"It could crack them. Then you'd lose all control over the ramjets, which is what's wrong right now."

"Uh. Your point, partner. But I still can't feel anything."

I went back to the airlock with my empty buckets swinging, wondering if they'd get hot enough to melt. They might have, but I wasn't out that long. I had my suit off and was refilling the buckets when Eric said, "I can feel the right ram."

"How extensive? Full control?"

"No, I can't feel the temperature. Oh, here it comes. We're all set, Howie."

My sigh of relief was sincere.

I put the buckets in the freezer again. We'd certainly want to take off with the relays cold. The water had been chilling for perhaps twenty minutes when Eric reported, "Sensation's going."

"What?"

"Sensation's going. No temperature, and I'm losing fuel feed control. It doesn't stay cold long enough."

"Ouch! Now what?"

"I hate to tell you. I'd almost rather let you figure it out for yourself."

I had. "We go as high as we can on the blimp tank, then I go out on the wing with a bucket of ice in each hand–"

We had to raise the blimp tank temperature to almost eight hundred degrees to get pressure, but from then on we went up in good shape. To sixteen miles. It took three hours.

"That's as high as we go," said Eric. "You ready?"

I went to get the ice. Eric could see me; he didn't need an answer. He opened the airlock for me.

Fear I might have felt, or panic, or determination or self-sacrifice –but there was nothing. I went out feeling like a used zombie.

My magnets were on full. It felt as if I was walking through shallow tar. The air was thick, though not as heavy as it had been down there. I followed my headlamp to the number-two panel, opened it, poured ice in and threw the bucket high and far. The ice was in one cake. I couldn't close the panel. I left it open and hurried around to the other wing. The second bucket was filled with exploded chips; I sloshed them in and locked the number-two left panel and came back with both hands free. It still looked like limbo in all directions, except where the headlamp cut a tunnel through the darkness, and–my feet were getting hot. I closed the right panel on boiling water and sidled back along the hull into the airlock.

"Come in and strap down," said Eric. "Hurry!"

"Gotta get my suit off." My hands had started to shake from reaction. I couldn't work the clamps.

"No you don't. If we start right now we may get home. Leave the suit on and come in."

I did. As I pulled my webbing shut, the rams roared. The ship shuddered a little, then pushed forward as we dropped from under the blimp tank. Pressure mounted as the rams reached operating speed. Eric was giving it all he had. It would have been uncomfortable even without the metal suit around me. With the suit on it was torture. My couch was afire from the suit, but I couldn't get breath to say so. We were going almost straight up.

We had gone twenty minutes when the ship jerked like a galvanized frog. "Ram's out," Eric said calmly. "I'll use the other." Another lurch as we dropped the dead one. The ship flew on like a wounded penguin, but still accelerating.

One minute . . . two . . .

The other ram quit. It was as if we'd run into molasses. Eric blew off the ram and the pressure eased. I could talk.

"Eric."

"What?"

"Got any marshmallows?"

"*What?* Oh, I see. Is your suit tight?"

"Sure."

"Live with it. We'll flush the smoke out later. I'm going to coast above some of this stuff, but when I use the rocket it'll be savage. No mercy."

"Will we make it?"

"I think so. It'll be close."

The relief came first, icy cold. Then the anger. "No more inexplicable numbnesses?" I asked.

"No. Why?"

"If any come up you'll be sure and tell me, won't you?"

"Are you getting at something?"

"Skip it." I wasn't angry any more.

"I'll be damned if I do. You know perfectly well it was mechanical trouble, you fool. You fixed it yourself!"

"No. I convinced you I must have fixed it. You needed to believe the rams *should* be working again. I gave you a miracle cure, Eric. I just hope I don't have to keep dreaming up new placebos for you all the way home."

"You thought that, but you went out on the wing sixteen miles up?" Eric's machinery snorted. "You've got guts where you need brains, Shorty."

I didn't answer.

"Five thousand says the trouble was mechanical. We let the mechanics decide after we land."

"You're on."

"Here comes the rocket. Two, one—"

It came, pushing me down into my metal suit. Sooty flames licked past my ears, writing black on the green metal ceiling, but the rosy mist before my eyes was not fire.

The man with the thick glasses spread a diagram of the Venus ship and jabbed a stubby finger at the trailing edge of the wing. "Right around here," he said. "The pressure from outside compressed the wiring channel a little, just enough so there was no room for the wire to bend. It had to act as if it were rigid, see? Then when the heat expanded the metal these contacts pushed past each other."

"I suppose it's the same design on both wings?"

He gave me a queer look. "Well, naturally."

I left my check for $5000 in a pile of Eric's mail and hopped a plane for Brasilia. How he found me I'll never know, but the telegram arrived this morning.

HOWIE COME HOME ALL IS FORGIVEN
DONOVANS BRAIN

I guess I'll have to.

APOLOGY TO INKY

by Robert M. Green, Jr.

WALTON ULSTER, between sleep and waking, heard a car horn go "ah-ooga," and thought: *that's a sound that's getting to be passé.* Even the boop-boop-a-doop horn, in spite of the teen-age sports with their roadsters, was getting to be passé, along with the biplane—

Walton snapped awake.

It was a wrenching brain-battering awakening. He had not been deeply asleep, if he had been asleep at all, but he had been more than thirty years back, or down, in time, and to rocket in an instant from 1931 to 1965 was enough to give anyone a case of psychological bends.

Walton looked out the window of the bus and studied the highway traffic. There was not a car in sight older than 1950. Some humorist could have installed an "ah-ooga" horn from a junkyard Model T, but Walton wouldn't have heard it here in the back of the bus, with the wheels singing directly under his feet and the cold-air jet humming and burbling into his ear.

An "ah-ooga" horn would be charming really. Very much *in.* Like vintage cars. Walton weighed the idea of buying one and writing a concerto for it. It would have to be one of those gimmicky, show-off pieces that struts its hour on the stage shouting, "Hey, look at me! What a brash, outrageous piece of affrontery am I!"

Walton remembered the time when he would have sneered at such blatant self-advertisement passing itself off as music, but that was when he was so full of music himself that it vibrated at his very fingertips, when he could say "to hell with the orchestration; let them play it on jew's-harps and frisco slide whistles and it will come out good; set it up for trained seals with bicycle horns; I don't care."

All right. But that was before the dreams—the waking dreams and sleeping dreams—and the shrill rising voices within him that cried out his guilt and left no room for music. His talent was barren now and he knew it, but a man who had been famous for his pride—arrogance, gall, conceit; what you will—could not turn humble all at once and bow meekly to denigrating truth.

If all he had left was a bag of tricks with which to titillate the novelty seekers, the tricks were good tricks—duet for garden hose and bagpipe, sonata for piano with tissue paper over the strings, "Borborygmy in Harmony" with taped sounds of authentic belches and belly rumbles, "Alley Cat Chorale" featuring tapes of honest-to-God alley cats yowling over a percussion base consisting of shoes being thrown against a sheet of galvanized steel—arresting though sterile manipulations of sound that enraged just about everybody and kept Walton's name in the newspapers.

That sort of thing would have to suffice for the present. Somehow someday, soon God willing, he would surely find a way to recharge his talent. Then he would go back to filling the air with glory, and he would damn well sue any conductor who presumed to perform even a part of any single smart-aleck opus from this interlude of bleakness.

The talent-recharging trick, he was certain, was to put his finger on the specific moments of past time into which he seemed to be slipping in his waking dreams—the times which seemed to invoke at least the aura of the guilt for which as yet he could find no name—and then to find a link or common denominator for these fragments of time. The moments he was groping for, he was just about certain by now, were in the spring of 1931 and the winter of 1944.

Therefore, of course, Moira Hendricks had to be the common denominator. The more he thought about Moira these days—after twenty years of dogged effort not to think about her at all—the stronger became the pull of his dreams. He would hear a plane overhead and look up wondering whether it was a monoplane or a biplane, or, by a marvelous stroke of luck, a Ford Trimotor. He would find himself searching magazine racks for *Ballyhoo,* or *Judge,* or *College Humor*. He would twiddle the dial on the radio until his exasperated wife asked him what in the world he was looking for, and would realize with an embarrassed start that he was idly hoping to catch Ruth Etting singing "Shine on, Harvest Moon."

Those were the 1931 moments.

Then he would put his hand to his shirt collar and think, *Oh my God, I've forgotten to put on my collar insignia!* He would automatically reach for nonexistent crutches before getting up from his chair. He would hear—actually hear—Frank Sinatra singing "I'm gonna buy a paper doll that I can call my own." He would say to his wife, "Hey, you didn't throw away Dick Tracy, did you? How am I ever going to know whether Flat Top sizzled him with that flame thrower?" He would hear, from far-off jukeboxes, the bossy right hand, saucy left hand and mocking voice of Fats Waller, and catch himself thinking, boozily, sentimentally, *See? See? He didn't die after all.*

Those were the 1944 moments.

But most significantly, the more he thought about Moira, the more he brooded about guilt, and the surer he became that whatever it was he was guilty of, she was the victim of it. If so, she was the one who could tell him. That was why he was making this trip. It wasn't going to be easy. He couldn't come out flatly and ask her if he had done anything to her about which he ought to feel guilty. Old friends, old loves could alter drastically in twenty years, but he doubted that Moira would ever lose her knack for puncturing tension with a gay little crack and making him feel like a self-dramatizing, rather pompous fake. Oddly, though he had had occasion to resent this knack of Moira's, it was part of her charm. It had kept him on his toes, and she had never punctured him except when he deserved puncturing. He had indeed lapsed on occasion into pomposity. It was still a bad habit of his, particularly with no Moira in his life to keep him in check, and he was going to have to guard against it when he met her.

It had been Walton's plan to take the bus clear down into Cincinnati, then pick up a Hamilton bus that would take him up to Glendale, some fourteen miles north of the city. Now as he looked out the window and saw the gateway to Sharon Park, he realized that his bus was coming into Sharonville, which is also some fourteen miles north of Cincinnati, but only about three miles east of Glendale. It struck him as ridiculous to ride twenty-eight miles in a bus just to go three miles. It was an easy walk from Sharonville to Glendale. He had done it hundreds of times when he was a kid.

He got off the bus at Sharon Avenue, which leads to Glendale. A few other people were getting off at the same place, so he had time to change his mind and jump back aboard, back to the gentle, phony zephyrs of the air conditioner, as the 114-degree July heat slapped him in the face. But what the heck; he had no luggage; he'd walked farther than three miles on hotter days, back in the 1931 he was seeking to rediscover, and besides he could stand to lose a few pounds around the midriff.

First of all, he went into a drugstore telephone booth to call Moira at her mother's home.

"You didn't answer my letter," he said. "But I came anyway."

"Well, you told me you would if you didn't hear from me." The voice of the beloved, as though twenty years had never been. It was as crisply cool as ever. No nonsense. Walton's hands were shaking. "I was expecting you, Walton."

"I wasn't sure my letter reached you."

"You might have known I'd still be in Mother's clutches."

"But when Aunt Jane told me you were Mrs. Moira Buntline, I sort of wondered–"

"Boy, you really are out of touch. I married Billy seventeen years ago. I'm sure you were on the invitation list."

"Not if your mother had anything to do with it. Billy Buntline. I'll be damned. I never would have matched you two."

"Neither would Mother. After a while Billy came to see it her way. It was as simple as that. No children. No settlement. He's married to Gladys Mallon now."

"That I can see."

"You wouldn't recognize her. She's fat and alcoholic."

"No! Well, look, Moira, I'd better hang up. I've got a little walk ahead of me."

"Where are you calling from?"

"Sharonville. Nothing like a healthy hike–"

"Walton, you nut. In this heat?"

"I've done it a million times."

"You're not getting any younger. The miles are longer these days."

"I'm in pretty good shape, Moira."

"And the belts are shorter these days too. Your Aunt Jane tells me you're fat as a pig. Look, don't come here. Mother is still Mother, only more so. Call me from Igler's when you get to Glendale, and I'll meet you there."

Her hair was long, her foot was light
And her eyes were wild.

And her tongue was tart as ever. "Fat as a pig." As he hung up, Walton felt that sweet, long-forgotten throbbing ache within his rib cage that Tin Pan Alley still ascribed to the heart, though it was more likely an endocrine reaction. Moira forever. How liltingly she put you in your place. How he had ranted at it, how he had hoity-toitied at it, and how he had needed it. He had really brimmed over in those days–the days of Moira. He had brimmed over with music, with love, with inchoate philosophy, with hair-trigger perceptions. That was fine so long as it was on the level; Moira was with him, encouraging him, occasionally pruning the rank overgrowth. He was full of glory in those days, and Moira was involved in the glory. It was only when he was overweening and pretentious that she cut him down to size, but an arrogant young man with notions of being an artist can't always know when he is pretentious.

That was why twenty years ago he had fled from Moira and all his glory. But he was not so simpleminded as to think that he could flee back and recapture Moira and glory. There was more to it than that. Somehow he must also recapture himself—a scared kid with a dog—no, *two* dogs—an angry Army captain with crutches and shards of phonograph records. He didn't know how, or, really, why this was to be accomplished.

Walton wasn't wearing a summer suit. He didn't own one, to begin with, and wouldn't have worn one anyway, since it had been damp and windy in New York when he left there yesterday. He had forgotten about those southern Ohio summers.

He took off his suit coat, draped it over his arm, and began walking west on Sharon Avenue. Whether or not they really made the miles longer these days, they certainly did make the highways narrower. He remembered Sharon as a fine, wide road, with plenty of room on both sides for boys and dogs to ramble and for cars to park. Cars to park. Right up there on the left, just this side of the railroad tracks and in front of the locomotive roundhouse was where the Model A Ford was parked with a flat tire. The guilty Model A. The murderer of Inky. With a flat tire. Served it right.

No. There was no Model A there now. You couldn't even park a bicycle there without tying up traffic all the way to Glendale. Traffic was pretty nearly jammed up anyway. The road was wide enough for a comfortable flow of two-way traffic, but it didn't seem to be. Everything seemed hemmed in, squeezed together by some invisible pressure; Walton was bucking this pressure by sheer physical effort in order to stay out of the way of the laboring, monoxide-fuming cars. The heat pressed him down from above. Claustrophobia qualms fluttered through him, but he soothed himself with the assurance that he would soon be out of Sharonville and in wide-open farm country. Maybe if he tried Boy Scout pace—fifty steps walking, fifty running—he would be out of this unseen dungeon before the walls closed in and crushed him.

A silly notion. He was barely past the old Sharonville roundhouse, and already his shirt was drenched in sweat; his feet, as in a dream, seemed to be dragging through thick gelatin. It was still early in the afternoon, but the mixture of haze, heat waves, exhaust fumes, diesel smoke, and sweat streaks on the lenses of his glasses distorted and darkened everything around him. Suddenly, above the sounds of automobile tires and motors, he heard the voice of a boy, across the street and behind him, calling: "Here, Slimmy! Here, Slimmy!"

Walton looked over his shoulder. He couldn't have heard properly, over the highway noises. Possibly, without being fully aware of it, he had seen the liver-colored Chesapeake Bay retriever out of the corner of his eye, and the name "Slimmy" had merely leaped to his mind. The kid in the green sweater, kneeling by the absurdly right-angled high-bottomed Model A Ford, might have been calling "Here, Spot," or "Here, Rover." Besides, there was only one Slimmy, as Walton had found out after a number of experiences with other Chesapeake Bay retrievers.

Or possibly it was the setting, the background, because he had seen it in dream after dream. The old roundhouse was out of true, just as it was in the dreams, and might easily, as in some of the dreams, turn into a Rhenish castle which you entered to find everything upholstered in green and be waited upon by smiling servants dressed as Pullman porters.

The Model A Ford with the flat front tire was also out of the dreams. The boy in the green sweater, with Slimmy (Spot? Rover?) at his elbow, was squatting by the tire. He was doing something to it, but Walton couldn't see what. Spot-Rover was sniffing at the tire just as Slimmy sniffed it in the dreams, sniffing Inky's blood, still bright red and gleaming in the April sunlight, though Inky had been dead since St. Patrick's Day.

Whatever it was that the boy and dog were doing, it was damned dangerous. They were on the left side, the highway side of the car. With all that hemmed-in traffic.

Walton shouted a warning, then turned to cross the street in order to give the boy some avuncular advice. Just then, a parade of three monster diesel trucks blocked him and cut off his view of boy, dog, and Model A Ford.

Walton shrugged and resumed his walk. It would have been out of character for him to butt in. He was an inveterate minder of his own business; the kid undoubtedly would have suggested to him that he continue as such.

He noticed that he was weaving slightly. Damned carbon monoxide. Plus heat waves. Plus too vivid a recollection of a recurrent dream.

That was it! The dream! His motives had not been avuncular after all. He had simply wanted to see what crucial thing the boy was doing to that automobile tire, and the diesel trucks had forbidden him, just as blurring of focus or sudden awakening always forbade him in his dreams to see what was being done to the tire. Good Lord, had it come now to hallucinations in broad daylight?

He looked back toward the roundhouse. He knew the rule about hallucination. You merely had to utter, or even think "hallucination," and it would vanish. No. The boy and the dog and the Model A were still there. But from where he stood, the car looked too rounded and sloping to be a Model A, the boy's sweater looked more brown than green, and the dog looked more like a collie than a Chesapeake Bay. Damned glasses. Walton had nothing to wipe them with, except a dirty, sweat-sopping handkerchief.

He walked on.

Hallucination or not, the thing to do was to present it to Moira as such. He had been wondering how, in the face of her inevitable scorn, he was going to broach the subject of the dreams. One of Moira's most engaging traits had been the trace of witch in her. Her crisp and merry practicality, her brusque impatience with emotional flatulence had been an acquired camouflage for an occult spirit sensitive to ghosts, bodiless voices in the dark, and nasty, vengeful pre-Olympian demigods. There had been madness in that big, creaky old house of the Hendrickses. You saw it staring bleakly out of stiff ancestral portraits.

Walton supposed that she had inherited from her father—certainly not her savage vampire mother—the mother wit that gave her the arms and armor that had saved her and probably would always save her from being drawn wholly into her shadowy interior world—her witch world. She had succeeded in keeping everyone but Walton himself from seeing inside this armor. Maybe she had, through wishful thinking, seen some nonexistent quality in Walton, but inevitably he had failed her in the role of demon lover. He had gradually become enraptured with her voices in long unlit corridors, her deals with black powers. He had become, in fact, hooked.

I set her on my prancing steed,
And nothing else saw all day long,
For sidelong would she bend, and sing
A faery's song.

But he could come only as far as the gates of her world. No ghosts ever talked to him. He could only deal with her world in a poetic sense, and Moira's ghosts were not poetry; they were Tom, Dick and Harry. Poetry was dangerous to Walton; it led him to excesses, to the verge of utter sappiness. But only to the verge. At the crucial moment Moira's needle of matter-of-fact would pop the balloon. Damned witch.

Anyway, Inky wasn't in this handily contrived "hallucination," as he so often–implausibly–was, in the dreams. He wouldn't have to mention Inky, which was a blessing. Moira might be venomous about Inky.

No, that was unfair. It wasn't Moira, but Moira's mother who had destroyed Inky with the Model A Ford. Inky, pointless, clumsy black mongrel, always subordinate to Slimmy, had been a member of his inviolate boy's world, had been one of the components of love that glued that world together, and without Inky there had been nothing left for a boy to do but kick his way through the shatterable dome of someone else's world. Not to destroy. Just to get in there and perhaps to find new components of love. But the very entry into another world was and had to be an act of destruction. Moira's mother had been the shatterable dome, and he had shattered this dome by doing some secret thing to a punctured tire with bloodstains still on it. But Moira had been the component of love inside the dome, and he had found her. And what secret thing had he done to her? And why the fingers pointing at him?

Outside of Sharonville, where the open fields had been, Walton found himself more hemmed in than before–by factories and by concrete overpasses and underpasses for highways he remembered as bucolic lovers' lanes. One bridge, once reasonably broad, had now become too narrow to accommodate both foot and vehicular traffic. Maybe it didn't matter. Maybe no one walked any more–not out this way to be sure.

It seemed that the only way for a man on foot to cross this bridge was to wait for a hiatus in the traffic and then run like hell. As Walton was standing there in woozy befuddlement, a slow rattletrap truck approached the bridge, heading in the direction of Glendale. The tailgate was down, and Walton, forgetting the dignity fitting to his age and increasing portliness, leaped aboard. No doubt the driver would see him soon enough through his rear-view mirror, but he surely wouldn't stop on the bridge, and Walton had no intention of staying on the truck after the bridge was crossed. His conscience would be clear. He would still have walked from Sharonville to Glendale; no one would count a tiny ferry trip across an otherwise unfordable obstacle.

He was sitting on the tailgate, facing to the rear, when the cold came. Suddenly he was struggling to put on his suit jacket and huddle in it, whistling breathily over a shivering jaw. The tune he was whistling was "Mairzy Doats and Doazy Doats and Little Lamzy Divey; a Kiddly Divey Too; Wouldn't You?" That was a tune he hadn't heard for twenty years or so. He wouldn't have remembered all the words yesterday, but he did at this moment.

Walton knew it wasn't as cold as it seemed to be. These broiling humid days could trick you sometimes. A change of wind, a sudden downdraft of high cool air might lower the temperature no more than five degrees and yet feel positively wintry against your sweat-soaked body.

Right behind the truck was a big black old car. Walton was no good at guessing makes or vintages of cars, but he guessed that this was a pre-World War II model–1939 or '40–and a Packard. In truth, Walton could barely tell a Packard from a jeep. Moreover his eyes, unpampered by spectacles, watered and blurred in the sudden drop of temperature.

But in the dream–the other dream–it was always a Packard, only he was *inside* it. The car behind him then was no hallucination, but the Packardness of it surely was, and for the first time Walton began to wonder if his coming back here for the first time after so many years to the scene of his crimes (?) was not going to make things worse instead of better.

Walton could see clearly the flashing black eyes and tight angry lips of the young woman who was driving; he could see her blue-black hair, set in a long, barbaric version of a page-boy bob and spreading out onto her shoulders from under a pale blue babushka to lend splendor to a pathetic old dyed squirrel coat. Next to her he could see the gesticulating Army captain, bundled up in his greatcoat, his crutches propped up beside him against the back of the seat.

Once again the dream was taking the place of objective vision. Walton proved it. He closed his eyes and still saw the Packard, the young woman and the gesticulating captain. He would palm this one off on Moira too as a hallucination. She would take it seriously and perhaps revel in it, but Walton didn't dare take it seriously, and far from revelling in it he steeled himself to fight it. This sort of thing was nothing to him but a cold grey warning–an intimation of creeping psychosis.

He blinked several times and pounded his forehead with the heel of his hand; his objective eyesight gradually got the better of his psychic eyesight, and what he saw in the car back there was the figures of two people only vaguely discernible through the blur of his drenched eyes and the glint of afternoon sunlight on the car's windshield. The person driving appeared to be a woman all right, but surely not in babushka and dyed squirrel coat, at this time of year, despite the sudden illusion of chill. The man might or might not be a soldier. He seemed to be wearing some kind of visored hat (did they wear those in today's Army?), but it could be a sports cap or boating cap.

The man was indeed gesticulating. Goddamn it, he was breaking phonograph records. Goddamn it, he was nothing of the sort. That was the goddamn dream again. The hell it was. You could see the labels clearly. Harry James, Bunny Berigan, Benny Goodman, Artie Shaw, Count Basie, Jimmy Lunceford, Duke Ellington. That, of course, proved it was all a crock, because even without blur or glint, even with good glasses or 20/20 vision, you couldn't read those labels from this distance, and under the present circumstances, Walton couldn't even have made out the silhouette of an uplifted phonograph record.

The records weren't all that important. Except for some of the Basies and Ellingtons, they weren't records he would spend money on today, but there was a time when they had been to him what Chapman's Homer had been to Keats.

It hadn't been only the music. Those records had been a bond between him and Moira. They were a background for long summer evenings of chaste necking on moonlit lawns, of spinning moonlit plans for a–then conceivable–wildly romantic and interminable future. Therefore at a certain insane yet perfectly lucid moment in a frosty-windowed Packard which was burning up its OPA gas coupons for a week, it had become necessary for a flaming Army captain to smash some records he had loved in order to break a bond he had loved. But no Waller records. Fats was scarcely cold in his grave. And this was the reason for the grab of an out-of-focus dream that now no longer needed to wait on sleep.

Suddenly the man (?) in the car made some sort of violent gesture. There seemed to be some movement of the crutches, if they were crutches, which they damn well had better not be or ding, ding, here comes the wagon. The big car went into a skid and hit the side of the bridge, not hard enough to do more than crumple a fender, but hard enough to stop the car. Since he was now across the bridge, he jumped off the tailgate of the truck and started back to see if anyone was hurt.

The car suddenly backed away from the guard rail and shot ahead so quickly that Walton had to straddle the rail to keep from being grazed. As it passed him he had a quick glimpse of the fortyish woman at the wheel. She was wearing a sleeveless lavender summer dress. The car had tail fins. It was probably a Cadillac of mid-50s vintage; certainly not a pre-World War II Packard. The surprise zephyr had passed, and heat waves thrummed again on Walton's temples.

He took his coat off again and tied the sleeves loosely around his waist. Forward march. Hut-two. That was the ticket. Head up, shoulders back, chest out, belly in. Hut-hoo-hreep-hope. My head is bloody but unbowed.

He could still feel the rage of the Army captain who wasn't there. He always woke up still trembling with it after the dream. But what was it all about?

Walton remembered his days of brooding at the Army hospital, while he was waiting for the retirement board to meet and turn him loose.

Before the war he had somehow acquired a Macedonian bagpipe, softer and more sweetly plaintive in tone than the Scottish Highland pipe, and he had seized on the idea of using it as instrumental accompaniment for a choral setting of Keats's "Grecian Urn." *Therefore, ye soft pipes, play on.* He had worked out a simple ground melody for the bagpipe, but Army life had swallowed him up before he could put down the bagpipe variations or any of the voice parts. In North Africa, a shell fragment in the kneecap set him free again.

For three months after his first hospitalization he was able to do nothing but torture his original ground melody into labored, wooden variations, and drudge away at the architecture of chord progressions. Finally, in October, when he was about to be retired from an Army general hospital in Texas, the muse began to take grudging pity on him; little by little the melodies started to come back.

Clumping around the hospital ward on his crutches, he pieced together a jigsaw picture of the future that would be thrust upon him if he went with the drift of things. In a few days he would be out of the Army. In a few months he would be free of his crutches, limping up and down the city streets looking for a job. In a year or so he would be married to Moira, and within five years he would have children, pediatricians, mortgages, commutation tickets, crab grass —and no melodies, ever again.

This was unthinkable; this was suicide. The only alternative was to stand up to the dismay and anger of his mother and father and uncles and aunts, and renounce the world for his melodies. Renouncing the world might mean the renunciation of Moira, but this was not up to him; it was up to Moira. He would live in the modern equivalent of a city garret, and he would earn rent and grocery money by teaching harmony and counterpoint or by playing piano in a cocktail lounge. If Moira loved him enough to live this life with him, wholly *with* him, undeviatingly on his side, his renunciation would be sweet. If not, it would be agony, at least at first, but a necessary agony.

Moira had gotten out the old puncturing needle just once too often. She had made him look and feel like an overdramatic egoist. She had laughed gaily at his garret. It was a bright and lilting laugh that pretended not to be what it really was—a sneer at the melodies that spangled the dome of his world—a sneer, somehow, at Inky.

The shards of the phonograph records were Inky's broken body. He had picked up a whole disk—Artie Shaw's "Begin the Beguine," Moira's favorite—and seen blood on it, on hub and spokes and tire.

But if this was the way it had really happened, then he, Walton, was in the right and Moira in the wrong. Why, then, the voices and pointing fingers in the dark?

Walton marched bravely up a gradual hill where, at this time of year, fields of corn and wheat once purred with joy in green and gold under the heat, and cottonwood fringes blinked from green to silver at the hint of a breeze. Now, on both sides of Sharon Avenue, there were rows of small homes and desperate lawns clinging to bare survival through the mercy of whirling sprinklers.

At the edge of Glendale, completely obliterating a monstrous field through which he, Caesar, and Inky, Labienus, had once pursued Slimmy, the noble Vercingetorix, in a forest of weeds, was a vast, functional high school.

Ahead of Walton, the land sloped gradually down to Albion Creek, which ran perpendicular to Sharon Avenue, then gradually up. Most of Glendale, including the village center, was on the far slope, though from where Walton stood it looked more like a woods than a village. Home was more than home; it was an oasis, and thank God the skyline was unchanged. Farthest to the left was the pointed spire of the Presbyterian church; next, looking taller because it was at the top of the slope, was the flat-topped, English Gothic steeple of the Episcopal church; then, looming like a mystic druid stronghold, the cone-topped cylinder of the old stone and concrete water tower, all covered with ivy.

Covered with ivy! How in hell could he see, with or without his glasses, ivy more than a mile away? How, for that matter, could he see a water tower that had been torn down more than thirty years ago?

He blinked his eyes and punched his temple, and the tower, properly, vanished. Got to keep making these little corrections. Got to ward off the little guys in the white suits.

Up ahead of him to the right, on this side of Albion Creek, was the new (new in 1930) water tower, functional and ivyless: a giant kettle perched on daddy-long-legs. He saw a boy with a green sweater turn off the highway and stroll toward the tower, through the trees. The boy was followed by a liver-colored dog. Possibly a Chesapeake Bay retriever. Slimmy. And a black, ungainly, huge-pawed–Oh no, oh no. Pound the old temple. Blink the old eyes. Correct every last little detail.

Walton wondered if there was anything nowadays to attract a kid and a dog to the water tower. There used to be a lovely dump, with rusted old auto bodies to climb into and bottles and jugs to throw at rats and sometimes a treasure to take home–a chair, for example, with only one leg broken, which would help furnish that always projected but somehow never built secret clubhouse.

Walton knew that if he followed the boy he would come to no dump at all but to trim lawns, and probably to neat walks or drives, with, no doubt, flowers planted along the borders. He hadn't been near the new water tower in over thirty years, and he had no intention of going near it now, but there were respectable, landscaped, tree-shadowed homes with two-car garages along this part of Sharon Avenue today, possibly inhabited by some of the same guys with whom he had bottled rats to death in the old days, and it stood to reason that the presence of a lovely dump would be intolerable.

He wondered if anyone was looking out a window at him, saying: "Why that looks like little Walton Ulster." It was more likely, since he had not been able to shave today and since dust had glued itself to his sweat-drenched shirt, that anyone seeing him out here on the highway would say, "Who is that fat bum waddling along out there?"

Knotty skirted the dump, trying not to make himself conspicuous. Maybe there would be some kids with 22s, shooting at tin cans, or, with luck, rats, and if they didn't see him they might shoot in his direction. He knew he would be too yellow to stand up in front of a firing squad, but it would be kind of nice to be hit by a stray bullet if you didn't really expect it but just sort of idly hoped for it.

There just wasn't any other way out of the mess he was in, except maybe a disease like tuberculosis which would get him off to a sanitarium somewhere so he could start all over again. People would be sorry for him, and they would forgive him for some of the things they were bound to find out about pretty soon. They would never find out the whole thing about Mrs. Hendricks. Maybe she wouldn't be killed instantly. Maybe she would live long enough to talk, and Moira Hendricks would rat and tell somebody everything she knew, but everybody knew there was insanity in the Hendricks family, and it would be Moira's word against the word of a poor sick kid wasting away in a sanitarium.

There was a guy he knew in high school in Cincinnati who had TB. His family was too poor to send him to a sanitarium, and he was probably at home or in the General Hospital. Knotty's freshman class at Walnut Hills, or anyway the kids in Knotty's home room, had all chipped in to help pay for the guy's doctor's bills or medicine or something like that. His sister was a senior, and maybe Knotty could get her to take him to visit her brother. It would look very sweet and thoughtful, and Knotty could make some kind of deal with the guy. Suppose, say, the guy had a bowl by his bed to spit in, and Knotty could take it home and rub the glop all over a lot of needle pricks on the back of his hand. Or he could–ik–drink it.

Aw, but heck, you couldn't get tuberculosis in two weeks. Or maybe you could get the germ, but you couldn't get anything that showed enough on the outside so you could get your mother to take you to a doctor for an examination. In two weeks the jig would be up. The April report card would be out, and it wouldn't be a good idea to forge his father's signature again. He had done an expert job on the March report card and his father had been too busy to notice what time of month it was, but just the other day he had said, "Isn't it a pretty long time between marking periods? It seems to me there was snow on the ground the last time I signed one of yours." Knotty had squeaked through that one by reminding his father of a freak snowstorm that had come a few days after St. Patrick's Day. Naturally, his father hadn't marked it on his calendar, and it could just as easily have occurred March 21 as March 19 or 20, but he had frowned and shrugged and said, "Well, time can fool you. Particularly when you're on the road a lot. I'll have to write something on my memo pad for April 30th."

Boy, that was really going to be a report card. Knotty was going to have to go some to explain the "incomplete" in Math and Latin. He just couldn't tell the truth: that he had been cutting those classes for two solid months.

A guy could get into one of these things without meaning any harm, but it was just about impossible to get out. He only meant to cut that one class in Math the day he was supposed to bring in three homework make-up assignments or get sent to the principal's office. He didn't know why he was still afraid to be sent to the principal's office, but he was. Well, it was a simple enough matter to go to the nurse just before class and groan a little. His sinuses were always pretty badly congested at this time of year anyway, and if he didn't really have a headache, he had a perfect right to one; it wasn't hard to persuade the nurse to give him some aspirin and make him lie down for an hour or so. The only trouble was that he had met another guy in the nurse's office–a sophomore Knotty knew in the orchestra–who had a pretty good idea for a hit tune, but just couldn't get anywhere with the verse or the release; so by the time he and Knotty had something worked out that really sounded smoo-oo-ooth, two hours had gone by, and Knotty had cut Latin class too. The Math teacher was a sour-faced fat woman, all covered with chalk dust. She just looked down her nose at the guys like Knotty who couldn't get Math. But the Latin was a nice old maidy auntie sort of lady who was always being *disappointed* in Knotty, which was worse than having someone look down her nose at him. Well, naturally, Knotty had planned to catch up on his Latin and Math that night, but, naturally, he had some more work to do on this song, and–well–by the third or fourth day of this sort of thing he was just plain scared to go face his Latin and Math teachers. What's more, the homework kept piling up until there was more than he could make up in a hundred years. About the middle of March he had thought maybe if he went up to somebody and made a clean breast of everything, he would get yelled at a little and then things would get worked out some way, but he kept putting it off and putting it off, and when he finally forged his father's signature to the report card he was too deep in crime to figure a way out.

Well, there weren't going to be any stray bullets for Knotty today, because there was nobody out shooting in the dump. Knotty picked up an armload of bottles of different sizes: tough blue milk-of-magnesia bottles, elegant green mineral-water bottles, brown cod-liver-oil bottles, pop bottles, castor-oil bottles. With Slimmy cavorting wildly around him, tail flagrantly up and thrashing, Knotty walked through the line of trees that fringed Albion Creek, into a foliage-vaulted otherworld. He lined up his bottles beside the creek. This time of year there was plenty of water in the creek, and the stink of sewage was not as bad as it would be by July or August. He sat down and began experimenting with various levels of water in his bottles, blowing across the mouths of the bottles, pouring out or adding a little water, then blowing again, until he had, for each bottle, the precise tone he wanted. Slimmy sat down beside him and whined each time he produced a tone. It was probably true that the musical notes bothered the dog's ears, but they didn't drive him away.

When he was satisfied with the tone of each bottle, Knotty placed them in a row in front of him, the deepest-toned bottle farthest to the left, the next deepest-toned beside it, and so on up, from left to right, to the little shrill medicine bottles.

"Okay, Slimmy," he said. "This is gonna be an ode for Inky."

Slim pricked up his ears at the sound of the familiar name.

"That's right, Slimmer. You were the best, but we always loved old Inker, didn't we? We used to make fun of him because he was clumsy and couldn't do half the things you did, but we loved old Inker. Didn't we, Slimmy boy? This is gonna be an ode to tell old Inker we're sorry for all the times we teased him, 'cause we never had a chance to tell him when he was alive. Did we, Slimmy boy?"

Slim whimpered and bathed Knotty's face with his tongue.

The "ode" was in reality a dirge. For mechanical reasons it had to be. In order to go from one note to another, you had to put a different bottle to your lips at the same time you put down the last bottle you had blown and groped for the next one you would need. Knotty was dextrous, but not dextrous enough to produce a trill or a grace note or a liquid arpeggio; however, by overblowing the deep-toned bottles, he could produce a sudden jump from a solemn moan to a wild shrill wail. All in all, the music he forced from his bottles was majestic, and fitting to the green-willow, bird-twittering cathedral in which it was played. Assuredly Inky got the message.

After a few minutes the constant blowing made Knotty dizzy, and he stopped for a rest. Once more he went back in his mind to his unsolvable problems, and found himself, to his surprise, chuckling. People were always saying, "Someday you'll look back on this and laugh," and now, unaccountably, it *was* "someday" and he *was* looking back and laughing, with some scorn, at the pathetic molehills a damfool thirteen-year-old kid seemed to think were mountains.

Well, what he was doing to Mrs. Hendricks' flat tire wasn't any molehill, but the grownups who were watching him do it as they drove by in their cars, they didn't know what he was doing, and they never would. Some things were all right if they were necessary and you didn't get caught.

He knew what all those grownups were thinking. "Golly, what I wouldn't give to be a boy again and wander along the highway with a good old dog like that."

And what he, Knotty, was thinking about the grownups, here and now in his green-willow April cathedral, was "I've got something you haven't got." This was true, for all of a sudden he knew exactly what new turn of melody to blow on his bottles in memory of Inky.

That was the trick. You had to know exactly what the next note *had* to be. If you had to force it or puzzle it out, it was no good, and you might as well quit playing till it came to you. It was like the chicken laying the egg; the chicken didn't plan on it or work at it; when the egg was there to be laid, what else could the chicken do with it but lay it?

Knotty blew a long-drawn-out steamboat whistle hoot on his biggest bottle, a half-gallon jug that had contained something vile-smelling. He wished he had a *gallon* jug; his melody line was sweetening now, and he felt it needed the seasoning of a really full-bellied bass. But unbroken gallon jugs were almost impossible to find in this dump. They were too tempting as targets for boys with rocks, air rifles or 22s.

After finishing the tune, he smashed each bottle, one at a time, starting with the littlest bottle, going from right to left. He didn't know why he did this, but it seemed to be a necessary part of the ritual.

He stood up and turned to leave his arcade. Sitting on the stump of a lightning-struck willow tree was an old old man, maybe eighty or even ninety—a jowly old man, almost bald, with a writing pad in his lap and a funny-looking pencil in his hand.

"I believe I've got every note," said the old man. "Thank you very much."

"Golly," said Knotty. "You mean you were writing down that stuff I was playing?"

"From start to finish. Let's see. Your title for the tune is—uh—"

"Ode to Inky," said Knotty.

"Oh yes. Good old Inky. Tell me: does it invoke Inky? I mean, does it bring him back? Do you see him?"

"Oh, *heck* no. It's just sort of a memory–well–like an apology to Inky. I mean–well–Slimmy and me–that is, when Inky was alive, we never–"

"I know, I know. Nobody ever does. That's the guilt that makes the world go round. Don't wallow in it though. Guilt is really another form of pride, but you won't understand this until you're a great deal older, and I won't try to explain it to you. 'Apology to Inky.' Don't you think that's a better title than 'Ode'?"

"Well, golly, I never– Well, sure, I guess so. I just never thought about it as a real composition–like written down and all that."

" 'Apology to Inky' is the title then. 'Apology to Inky' by–uh–"

"Retslu Notlaw. That's my *nom de plume,* sort of. We used to have a gang a couple of years ago, and all the guys did their names that way. Mine was the only one that stuck." Knotty looked over the old man's shoulder as he wrote in his pad. "Say, gee, what kind of an Eversharp is that you got there? The writing looks like ink."

"It's called a ball-point pen," said the old man, quickly pocketing it. "I don't think I ought to show it to you. You're getting too far ahead of yourself."

"I don't get it," said Knotty. "Say, how come you found this place? How come Slimmy didn't let me know you were here?"

"Slimmy knows me," said the old man. "I think I would have liked it if he had jumped up and licked my face."

"Huh?"

"In any event, this place is no stranger to me. I can almost see the trees that used to be here. The alameda of willows. The glorious tin cans and rusty axles. And the rats."

"I don't get it."

"For your sake, I hope not. Forgive a moderately insane old man. And accept my humble gratitude for 'Apology to Inky.' "

"Gee, I wish you could stick around. You've got me all mixed up."

"You were worse mixed up before you saw me. Remember that. Now, I really can't stay. I have an engagement with my hair shirt."

"Wait a sec, please. What are you going to do with the music you wrote down?"

The old man had already stepped out of sight through the fringe of willows. Knotty ran after him, out into the open dump, but could see no sign of anyone.

"Oh, shoot," he said. "I did the Inky tune better than ever. I wish

I could see it the way he wrote it down. I never told him I just make it up as I go along, and it won't be anywheres near as good tomorrow."

Walton Ulster gasped with pleasure as the cool air of Igler's Drug Store embraced him and caressed his sopping shirt. He looked around, wondering if he would see a familiar face behind one of the counters, when he heard her voice.

"Walton Ulster: I'd hardly recognize you."

There she was, sitting at one of the tables, sipping Coke through a straw. Beware! Beware! Her flashing eyes, her floating hair! Impossible that she should have aged not a single day in twenty years. It must be a miracle of make-up, he thought, but it was certainly invisible to the naked eye. Witchcraft?

He strode toward her, with both hands outstretched, and she looked up at him with startled hostility.

"Walton! It *is* you, isn't it?"

The voice came from *behind* him.

He spun around. She was sitting at the counter, sipping hot black coffee. She had aged some, but not much. There were little lines at the corners of her eyes and on her neck, her lips were a trifle thinner than they had been, and her hair, still long but not barbarian, was salted attractively with gray. She had made no attempt to hide behind heavy make-up, lipstick or dye. Her figure was youthful, and Walton would have bet she wasn't wearing a girdle.

"My God, Moira, you're a damned handsome woman. If I didn't know better I wouldn't believe you were over thirty."

"I wish I could say the same for you. Aunt Jane is right. You're fat as a pig."

"I guess I could lose a few pounds. The doctor says I'm not dangerously overweight."

"Oh, shut up, Walton, you sensitive plant. Give me a kiss."

He put his lips to hers, intending nothing more serious than a kissing-cousin's peck, but the surprisingly soft responsiveness of her lips, enhanced by a sudden, rather embarrassing vision of the girl with the wild black hair drinking Coke at the table just behind him, made him, momentarily, drunk. He pressed Moira to him.

She threw her head back, laughing gently.

"Decorum's the word, old boy. Here in Igler's anyway."

"I don't understand myself," he said. "The years just seemed to blow away."

"You'd better watch it. You'll get picked up as a dirty old man. What's with the hot number at the table back there?"

"You won't believe it, Moira. She was the first person I saw when I came in here, and I thought she was you. Do you have a dry handkerchief I can clean my glasses with?"

"It's a good thing you didn't accost her. She's jumpy about something. I saw her pour something out of a flask into her Coke. Here, will a Kleenex do?"

Walton began to polish his glasses.

"Join me in a cup of coffee," said Moira.

"I couldn't, I'm parboiled. Oh, for a glass of ice cold beer."

"Mercy. In Igler's?"

"Let's go over to Bob Heine's. I can unbutton a few more buttons on my shirt and put my feet on the table. Or is that too disreputable for you?"

"It isn't Heine's any more. It's very reputable now. Very in. Lots of decor, fine cuisine, waiters with uniforms, early American hitching posts, steel engravings. . . ."

"Beer on tap?"

"The best. It's called the Iron Horse, if that gives you any kind of a picture."

"I have a picture of beer."

"Oh, I don't know, Walton. I suppose they'd be too nice to refuse to serve you, but I won't go there with you. Not until you've had a shower and put on a clean shirt with a tie."

"Can Glendale support a place like that?"

"Progress, old boy. Oh, the village itself hasn't changed much. Same old winding roads and trees and lawns. But we're surrounded by industry now, and that means bright young executives putting the best foot forward. If you were a bright young executive, would you take a customer to lunch in a place like Heine's?"

"We had lovely afternoons there. I wish they'd suspend progress long enough for people like me to catch up with ourselves." He put on his glasses and turned to look at the girl at the table.

"She does look remarkably like you, Moira."

"I had a squirrel coat like that once, but I wouldn't have dreamed of wearing it out on the hottest day of summer."

Being a normal male, Walton had not noticed what Moira was wearing until just this moment. Her sleeveless lavender summer dress was just right for her and just right for the weather.

"What kind of a car do you drive, Moira?"

"A '54 Cadillac. It's a souvenir of my pointless liaison with the Buntline money. Billy let me have it after the divorce, which was unnecessary, but sweet."

"That's a picture of Billy Buntline. Unnecessary but sweet."

"I didn't know you had claws under those darling pink paddies of yours, Walton. It really *was* sweet. I couldn't afford another car, and I can get another five years out of this one with judicious replacement of withering parts here and there."

"What were you doing out on Sharon Avenue this afternoon?"

"Looking for you, you vaunting ass. When you told me you were going to walk all the way from Sharonville in this heat—and at your age too—my first thought was 'let him learn the hard way.' Then I had a picture of you lying lobster-red by the highway; so I told Mother some cock-and-bull story and came out to find you."

"You drove right by me."

"I drove by a portly, sweaty hobo lurching along in the curb. I saw no connection between him and Walton Ulster, distinguished New York music critic and *enfant terrible* of the concert hall. For heaven's sake, join me in something. Cherry Coke?"

"My favorite used to be vanilla phosphate. On second thought, I think I'll have a lime Coke. Do you suppose that girl would let us look at her flask for a few rapturous seconds."

The boy in the green sweater came in. The liver-colored dog sat patiently on the sidewalk just outside the door.

"Good heavens, Walton," Moira whispered. "That boy looks just like you when you were thirteen or fourteen."

"I was never that skinny," said Walton.

The boy came up to the counter and ordered a vanilla phosphate. Walton ordered his lime Coke. It suddenly occurred to him that the people behind the counters astonishingly resembled the people of 1931. He knew that if they were still alive, Mr. Igler and Miss Katie would be over a hundred now, Miss Tillie and Miss Frances would be in their sixties or seventies, and Wilbur at least in his late fifties. *I'm not hallucinating,* he thought. *I'm only seeing imaginary resemblances my subconscious wants to see.* Be Nonchalant. Light a Murad. Were there Murads any more? Just for fun he asked the one who looked like Wilbur to bring him a Murad, and Wilbur did. He took one out and lit it—nonchalantly. It was too strong for a taste long since cravenly conditioned to filter cigarettes.

Moira said, "I'll be darned. The things they can come up with."

"It's stale. Probably been sitting here for thirty years."

Some other boys came in and joined the kid with the green sweater. They ordered phosphates of various flavors and sat down by the window to flip through the movie magazines. There had been a time when Mr. Igler endured this sort of imposition.

"Hey. Here's a picture of Joan Crawford. She's my dream queen."

"Mine's Janet Gaynor. She's like a real kind of a girl."

"Hey. It says maybe Doug Fairbanks is quitting the movies."

"That's a heck of a note. Hey. Did you know Edward G. Robinson is really a nice guy in real life?"

Moira said, "Why so dreamy?"

"I was just listening to the kids."

"You must have super-ears. I can't hear a word from here. Look, Walton, I really do love seeing you, but I have a tyrannical invalid for a mother and she expects me home. What is it you wanted to talk to me about?"

"Well, for one thing, your mother. After all these years you had to tell her a cock-and-bull story just to meet me for a few minutes in Igler's?"

"You know she hasn't been rational since the accident. She has always held you to blame. You and that black mutt."

"Moira, I ought to tell you; after more than thirty years, my temples still throb at the sound of the word 'mutt.' "

"I apologize, Walton. We don't need to drag that business out into the light of day again."

"Yes we do. That's just it. I'm fouled up, Moira, and I'm trying to grope my way into the past to find some answers that might help. You're the key, Moira. What happened to us?"

"What could be simpler. 'Us' was lovely, but 'us' was out of the question. You were a pretty far-out boy. You were dedicated, determined on poverty, and all in all, a lovable–God, how lovable–sap. I was a bird-brained debutante dreaming of an escape from my mother, a Cadillac, and a rich husband–in that order. Well, I got the Cadillac and the rich husband, and I still have the Cadillac. Next question."

Walton frowned. Was Moira making this up to save face?

"That's not the way it was at all," he said. "I was an arrogant, pompous cad. I treated you like dirt. Why? How?"

"You were all of that when you wanted to be. I didn't mind much. You always got over it pretty quickly. So. Now. You've had a successful career. You have a charming wife and lovely children. Aunt Jane keeps me posted. But you say you're fouled up."

"Please don't rush me, Moira. Let me collect my thoughts."

Four girls in their early teens came in, wearing the green and white uniforms of Hillsdale School for young ladies. They walked haughtily past the boys, hiding their secret smiles, and went to the corner where, Walton knew, the Hit-of-the-Week records were on display. The boys ambled over to join them, some swaggering, some slouching, all projecting huge indifference.

Girl: "The one I liked best was 'The moon and you appear to be/ so near and yet so far from me.' "

Another girl: " 'I'm through with love; I'll never fall again/said adieu to love; don't ever call again.' That's my theme song."

Another girl: " 'I am just a lonesome lover.' That's mine."

Boy: "Nerts on Rudy Vallee. He sings like a girl."

Another boy: "Bing Crosby sings okay."

Girl: "Oh, he's divine."

Boy: "What about Maurice Chevalier? He makes me sick."

Girl: "My mother thinks he's divine."

Boy in green sweater: "Ooooogh! So does mine. You wanta know who my favorite is? My favorite is Elmer Zilch."

(Laughter.)

Walton tensed, waiting for the phone of doom to ring. He was almost relieved when it did. The one who looked like Mr. Igler answered it and went to the teen-age girl with the wildest, longest, blackest hair of all to tell her the call was for her.

Just then, an Army captain, his greatcoat buttoned to his throat, came in on crutches, looked around almost timidly, then walked over to the young lady with the dyed squirrel-fur coat. She glowered at her empty Coke glass, refusing to look at him, but he sat down anyway.

The young lady spoke through her teeth, still refusing to look at him. "Did you have a good time at Bob Heine's? Did you search your soul, or did you just get loaded?"

"I just had a couple of slow, slo-o-ow beers. Give me a break, Mo. To err is human; to forgive, divine."

Teen-age girl (in background): "I have a divine idea. Let's go to my place and play Truth'n'Consequences."

Another girl: "Divine!"

Boy in green sweater: "Swell. Wait till Moira gets off the phone and we'll all go."

First girl: "Divine."

The young lady with the dyed squirrel-fur coat deigned now to look at the captain. "I'm not divine," she said. "I'm not the one to do the forgiving anyway. You behaved like a brat, but I might have known you would when the message finally seeped through the rock wall of your ego. You simply can't take a hint unless it's delivered with a baseball bat."

"Hint? What are you talking about?"

"How can an intelligent man be so dense? Even before you went into the Army, I tried to tell you in as nice a way as possible. What did you do with the letters I sent you? Just glance at them and throw them away? Didn't you ever try to read between the lines? I didn't want to hurt you but you've been making it difficult for both of us. You have your plans; fine! Well, I have mine too, and they don't include you. I can't make it any blunter than that. I'm sorry, Wall. I'm really very fond of you."

Walton wished he could stop up his ears without making a spectacle of himself. He hated overhearing this conversation. It was all wrong–cockeyed–out of true. The man should be the one to strike, not the girl.

The captain said, almost whining, "Oh, Mo. Mo. It can't be like this. I swear to God, I've really got it inside of me now. We could be great together. I've got it."

Walton took another sip of his cherry Coke. "The truth is, Moira," he said, "I just haven't got it. I haven't had it for I don't know how many years. I make a fair living teaching and writing reviews, and I attract attention with my outrageous bag of instrumental tricks, but tap me with a rubber mallet and all you'll get is a hollow boing."

"What about your wife?"

"That's all over, Moira. It's been over for a long time, but now that the kids are in college we're ready to make it legal. Everything will be civilized. I haven't any right to be bitter. My God, it wasn't her fault she was loaded with dough. It wasn't her fault I turned out to be a hollow man, and a damned resentful, boorish hollow man at that. She's been more than patient."

"You don't have to tell me," said Moira. "I know the combination. So you married money too?"

"More than that. She was–still is–a very sexy broad. She believed in me. We had our moments of romance. But you're right. It was a lousy combination. We should have known it at the start."

"Did you smash phonograph records?"

"Worse."

"Whose side are the children on?"

"It hasn't come to that. I suppose if it does, they'll stand up for their mother. But they're good, level-headed kids. They won't be estranged from either of us. Fact, they'll probably be relieved. Divorce solves a lot of unacknowledged problems. Not that it will really solve mine."

"What *will?*"

"I told you, Moira. I've got to catch up with myself, recapture my past. I have the feeling I once did something dreadful, too dreadful to be carried in my memory–something having to do with you and me. I've got to work my way back to it. With your help. I've got to find a name for it, and, please God, purge myself of it."

"All right, Walton, I want you to listen to me, and, damn it, take me seriously, or I'll bounce something off your head. To begin with, forget all that jazz about Hell having no fury like a woman scorned. I've had plenty of experience in swallowing my pride. I've even come to find it rather nutritious. For Pete's sake, Walton Ulster, why don't we undo all this silly damn nonsense and get married to each other?"

Walton looked at her in amazement. "You know, it's the funniest darn thing, but I was just about to say the same thing. It hadn't occurred to me till just now. But–hadn't there ought to be a courtship? Flowers? Candy? Serenades?"

There was a commotion among the teen-agers. The girl with the long black hair was weeping and ranting.

"It's all your fault, Knotty. You killed her. You and that–that *damn* mutt of yours."

"Inky didn't have anything to do with it," said the boy in the green sweater.

"Don't you dare talk to me, you *murderer*. Don't ever talk to me again."

She fled from the store.

"Golly, Knotty," said a boy. "What did *you* have to do with it?"

Girl: "She isn't really *dead,* is she?"

Walton strode over to the group of youngsters. He gripped the green-sweatered boy by the upper arms and said through his teeth, "What *did* you have to do with it?"

"Ow," said the boy with the green sweater.

"You fixed the wheel, didn't you?"

"You can't prove anything," said Knotty.

Mr. Igler came up, tapped Walton on the shoulder and beckoned him to a private corner of the store.

"I don't know why you're making this your business, mister, but I'd better set you straight. Something very serious has–"

"I know. Mrs. Hendricks has been in an auto accident. She's not dead."

"How in the deuce could *you* know *that?*"

Play it cool.

"I overheard the kids," Walton lied.

"Well, you're right. She's not dead, and Doc Allen thinks she'll probably pull through. The shame of it is, her brain will probably be affected some, and—do you know Mrs. Hendricks?"

"Quite well."

"A handsome woman. But her head went through the windshield."

"God, her face!" said Walton. "That's terrible."

"But it doesn't have a blessed thing to do with Knotty over there. I don't know what little Moira was fussing about. Upset, I guess. Well, it's only natural. But Knotty didn't do anything."

"How in the world could *you* know *that?*"

"Well, plenty of people saw the accident. She was in her old Model T, and her brother was driving."

"Ducky Cook?"

"That's right. The soft-headed one. If they had drivers' licenses in Ohio, he wouldn't be allowed to drive. Well, what's done—"

"Wait. You said the Model T. You mean the Model A, don't you?"

"Nope. The tin lizzie. The *new* Ford had a flat tire out on Sharon Avenue. She came in here and phoned for Ducky to come pick her up in the *old* Ford and drive out to change the tire. They weren't far from here when it happened. A big black dog ran out in the road and Mrs. Hendricks grabbed the steering wheel to swerve the car away from it. Smashed right into an iron street-light pole. Ducky was killed right away. In some ways, I guess *that's* a blessing."

Knotty's voice became shrill.

"All right, all right," he shouted. "I fixed the wheel!"

Mr. Igler and Walton hurried over to the cluster of youngsters. Mr. Igler was scolding, "That's enough of that, young man. This is nothing to joke about."

"I'm not joking. I fixed the wheel."

"Aw, go on," said one of the boys. "You wouldn't even know *how* to fix a wheel. What did you do?"

"All right, I'll tell you," said Knotty. "I don't care. I wrote the Lord's Prayer backwards all around the tire. All of it."

Everyone but Walton roared with laughter.

"All right," said Knotty, his voice trembling. "You wouldn't like it if I wrote the Lord's Prayer backwards on something of yours. It's not funny. 'Nema. Reve dna reverof, yrolg eht—' "

"Oh boy. Oh wow. You're nertzy."

"You oughta be in a padded cell in Longview."

Knotty turned red. Tears came to his eyes, and he ran out of the store.

Walton wondered if he ought to run after the boy and tell him about the Model T. He couldn't ask Moira for advice.

He decided against it. *Ding, ding; here comes the wagon.*

"What was that rumpus about?" asked Moira.

"Automobile accident. Little girl's mother was badly hurt."

"The poor dear. What was the little boy so excited about?"

"Oh, kid stuff. You never can tell."

"I swear, he looked just like you as a little boy. What moved you to horn in?"

"Kid's probably one of my second cousins. I had an impulse to go over and introduce myself and find out what he was mixed up in. I'm glad I didn't, now that I think of it. I love my relatives, but I don't dare let any one of them know I'm in town. I'd be stuck for the next two days paying duty calls on uncles and aunts and cousins and friends, and I've got a deadline to meet in New York."

"Not much time for all that courtship you were talking about."

"Come to New York with me. We'll do the town. Please, Moira."

"I'd love it, Walton, but there's always Mother. Damn! For one wild, delirious moment there I actually forgot Mother. *We* can't get married, Walton. We can't even have an affair."

"Moira, look. One of the reasons I married Nancy was that I wasn't cut out to be a monk. I took the soft, fat way out, and if I wasn't hollow to begin with, *that* did the job. I need a hair shirt, Moira–something to beat me down from time to time, to force humility on me. Come to New York *with* your mother, Moira. All *three* of us will do the town."

"Isn't it wonderful, Walton, that we can sit here like this without a drop of dutch courage between us and be honest with each other. It's a new kick for me. God, how I've needed it."

"This isn't a build-up to one of those histrionic abnegation scenes? Wringing of the hands. 'No, Walton; I must bear alone the burden of my mother. I cannot allow you to make this sacrifice.'"

"All right, Walton. You needn't pitch so hard. I've had my own share of sacrifice until it's coming out my ears; so maybe it *is* your turn. Marriage is still an open question then. But not New York. That's *out* of the question. Mother can't leave the house, and I can't leave her alone in it for very long. Oh, she's not so far gone that she doesn't know who she is and where she is–And, by the way, that's the answer to your next question: Why don't I put her in an institution?"

"That wasn't going to be my next question. I don't condone torture. I'll accept your mother as she is. I'll turn the other cheek a hundred times a day. I know it won't be idyllic, but I'm old enough not to believe in idylls, and maybe someday she'll come to accept *me,* if not as a member of the family, at least as a useful and familiar accessory around the house."

There was a crash behind them. The captain was on his feet, his chair lying on the floor behind him, shouting: "You don't fool me for a minute. Your damn mother has poisoned your mind against me. You want to know what I think? She's just putting on an act. She was a run-of-the-mill neurotic until she killed my dog, and ever since then she's been hiding behind this phony brain injury. She's been loading all her guilt onto me! She's got you right where she wants you."

The young lady stiffened. "Well! The very idea!"

"Don't get on your high horse. If she's really as nutty as everyone says she is, why don't you have her put away?"

"Well, if you're going to have another tantrum, I'm leaving."

"I'll beat you to it. I'm going over to Bob Heine's and really tie one on this time. See you around one of these years."

He marched out, turning up the collar of his greatcoat as the door closed behind him.

"Was that it?" Walton asked.

"Was what it?"

"Now, don't tell me you didn't hear that little interchange."

"I didn't hear the words. I heard an angry voice; that's all. My God, Walton, you've got sharp ears. Does that go with having perfect pitch?"

"It goes with being hollow. Like a little pitcher. Look, Moira, a little while ago I heard the little girl who was over in the corner telling the little boy in the green sweater it was all his fault that her mother was in an accident. Just now, I heard our stiff-necked friend, the captain, telling his lady friend that her mother was unloading her own guilt on him. Do you want to marry a man who hallucinates in broad daylight?"

"Don't be silly, Walton. You're in some kind of a crisis, and you're reading your own memories into everything you hear. Your little dramas aren't unique. Neither are mine."

"Did your mother really feel guilty about Inky?"

"That was your black mongrel, wasn't it. You don't think Mother ran over it on purpose?"

"Of course not."

"I wish you could make her realize that, but of course it's too late. She's not very–uh–reachable. I never knew myself what you really thought, and I didn't dare ask. You were too young to know what you were doing, and I was too young to understand what the death of one mongrel dog can mean to a little boy. I did forgive you though for standing there that horrible day shouting 'murderer' at Mother. I even stopped having dreams about it. But Mother didn't."

"But, Moira, I never did that."

"You were beside yourself, Walton. You were standing there looking at the dead dog in the street, and Mother and I were in the car, both of us trying to think of something kind to say. I didn't realize it then, but Mother had been–well–eccentric ever since Daddy died. She couldn't stand to be upset. I know she *meant* to be kind, but any kind of emotional crisis just brought out the poison in her. What she said was true enough, but–"

"She said Inky was a mutt. She said I ought to be grateful I still had a fine thoroughbred like Slimmy, and she hoped I wouldn't waste time grieving over a no-good mutt."

"I know. It was terrible. She was beside herself too, and she had no control over her words. She could see how unhappy you were, and it tore her to pieces. All she was trying to say was 'damn you, child, don't stand there being unhappy in front of me and making me unhappy. I've got enough to be unhappy about.'"

"I know, I know. So I called her a murderer. I didn't remember that. I do remember thinking it."

"You have a handy forgettory. I wish Mother did."

"Why is it that when we're old enough not to be able to hurt anyone very much, we finally learn how to refrain?"

The young lady behind them stood up and put on her dyed squirrel-fur coat. She said to Miss Frances, "Charge it to me," and walked out. An old man, jowly and almost bald, bowed to her outside on the sidewalk.

"Are you up to facing Mother today, Walton?" asked Moira.

"Might as well be today. I ought to buy a clean shirt somewhere first. Can you sneak me in the back door to shave and change before the ordeal?"

"We'll work something out. Then afterwards it's drinks and duck à l'orange at the Iron Horse. Deal?"

"Deal. If you can get away from Mother that long."

Outside, the young lady was saying to the jowly old man, "Well, the windshield was frosted, and when I saw you there on the side of the bridge I had an illusion that there was an extra traffic lane on the right side of the bridge. It's the funniest thing, I had this idea you were someone I knew, someone who had something to tell me. Something important. I pulled over to the right, and then–bang!"

"Did the captain see me too?"

"Maybe. I don't know. I can't imagine what I thought you had to tell me."

The old man chuckled. "I can't either. A man my age gives out a lot of advice, but it's hardly ever solicited and it never does any good. Well, it's been a pleasure, ma'am."

As the young lady was getting into her car, Walton said to the old man, "I know a piece of advice you could have given her. You could have told her to march right over to Bob Heine's and join a certain captain in about twenty salubrious belts of bourbon."

"Good Lord, Walton. *Bob Heine's?*" said Moira. "And what an old buttinsky you've turned into."

"Perfectly all right, ma'am," said the old man. "Mr. Ulster and I are acquainted."

Walton peered at the old man.

"Why, yes. Yes," he said. "The freemasonry of the mad."

Ding, ding!

The old man looked reflectively in the direction of the Iron Horse, cat-cornered across the village square.

"Bob Heine's," he said. "Oh yes, of course. You'd hardly recognize the village now."

"Oh, I don't know," said Walton. "The outskirts have changed a lot, but once you're in the village everything looks pretty much the same. A little remodeling here and there, but–"

"Of course. I wasn't thinking. It wasn't till 1983 they tore down the–"

"Easy does it," Walton hissed. "Ding, ding."

"That's right," said the old man. "Pardon the senility of an octogenarian. 'Play it cool.' That's the expression, isn't it?"

"Not too easy in weather like this," said Walton, wiping his forehead with the sleeve of his shirt.

"As for the advice you were talking about," said the old man. "It would be an act of cruelty. Those young people would destroy each other in about two years."

Walton glanced nervously at Moira.

"Oh, not you two. Not you two," said the old man. "You've both been through the purifier's flame. If benedictions are in order, please accept mine."

A gun-metal-blue sports car that looked like a water bug pulled up to the curb and a hollow-cheeked, deep-eyed, but still strangely beautiful old lady put her head out the window.

"I've been looking all over for you, Wally. Mother is worried about you. Where on earth have you been?"

"Oh, alone and palely loitering," said the old man. "The sedge is withered from the lake, and no birds sing."

The old lady laughed.

"Don't mind him," she said. "He would like me to be the Belle Dame Sans Merci. There's a bit of witch in me, but I'm not that."

"Okay, okay," said the old man, opening the car door on her side. "Take me to your elfin grot."

"You're a dirty old man," said the old lady.

"Move over," said the old man. "You're too decrepit to drive."

The old man climbed in the bug car beside his wife, and took her hand.

"Can you imagine?" he said to Walton. "Here I am eighty-five years old and ought to be lounging in slippered ease, but I've got a mother-in-law a hundred and five years old and I spend my days pushing her around in a wheelchair like a dutiful son."

"Oh, you *know* you and Mother get along *beautifully.*"

"Of course," said the old man, winking at Walton. "It's the freemasonry of the mad. She fusses at me and pampers me and depends upon me. I fuss at her and pamper her and depend upon her. We're both of us making something up to each other, something that happened so long ago we ought to have made it up by now. But you see, every day is yesterday all over again. By the way, you didn't happen to see a boy in a green sweater trailed by a liver-colored dog?"

"He was in Igler's a little while ago, but he's not there now."

"Oh well," said the old man, "I know where he lives. Maybe I can catch him before he reaches home."

"You and that boy," said the old lady. "One of these days I'm going to turn you in for child molestation. That is, if you ever find him."

"Oh, I found him. This afternoon." The old man laughed, put the palm of his hand on the old lady's face and gave it a gentle shove.

"Wife beater," she said.

"Be happy, you two," the old man called to Walton and Moira. "Be patient. You'll find it. You'll find it."

He drove away.

"Good Lord, what was that all about?" asked Moira.

Knotty dragged his feet along the sidewalk leading to home. He started to worry a little stone with his foot, intending halfheartedly to see if he could kick it all the way home, but he lost interest after the fourth kick. Well, he knew what Mom was going to say. "Where have you been and what did you do, darling?" "Well, Mom, I just happened to hike to Sharonville and I just happened to see Mrs. Hendricks' car by the side of the road with a flat tire and I just happened to–"

Oboyoboyoboy.

Aw, to heck with everybody.

This screwy little cart that looked just like a waterbug came to a stop beside him, and there was this same old old man he had seen earlier by the dump. There was an old old woman with him.

"Oh, hi," he said listlessly.

"Look, Knotty," said the old man. "I've done a lot of thinking about this score. Does the instrumentation really matter? I mean, does it have to be bottles?"

"Well, it doesn't *haf* to, I guess, but you'd have to make it different if you played it on an accordion or a piano, say. I mean, you'd want to put in some fast notes and stuff. And on a harmonica, you'd want to blow in some chords."

"I'm glad you called my attention to that," said the old man. "Stupid of me not to have thought of it myself. All right. Bottles it is. I did think though that some kind of bass *harmony–*"

"Yeh, yeah," said Knotty, enthusiastic now. "Cellos would be swell, don't you think? Just a bunch of cellos."

"Cellos *would* be swell," said the old old man.

"Will I get to hear it?"

"You'll get to hear it, Knotty. Be patient. Don't hold your breath. And, say, Knotty–"

"Yeah?"

"I kind of think Inky will like it."

"Shucks. Dogs don't like music. It hurts their ears."

THE DEMOLISHED MAN

by Alfred Bester

In the endless universe there is nothing new, nothing different. What may appear exceptional to the minute mind of man may be inevitable to the infinite Eye of God. This strange second in a life, that unusual event, those remarkable coincidences of environment, opportunity, and encounter . . . all may be reproduced over and over on the planet of a sun whose galaxy revolves once in two hundred million years and has revolved nine times already.

There are and have been worlds and cultures without end, each nursing the proud illusion that it is unique in space and time. There have been men without number suffering from the same megalomania; men who imagined themselves unique, irreplaceable, irreproducible. There will be more . . . more plus infinity. This is the story of such a time and such a man . . .

The Demolished Man.

1

Explosion! Concussion! The vault doors burst open. And deep inside, the money is racked ready for pillage, rapine, loot. Who's that? Who's inside the vault? Oh God! The Man With No Face! Looking. Looming. Silent. Horrible. Run . . . Run . . .

Run, or I'll miss the Paris Pneumatique and that exquisite girl with her flower face and figure of passion. There's time if I run. But that isn't the Guard before the gate. Oh Christ! The Man With No Face. Looking. Looming. Silent. Don't scream. Stop screaming . . .

But I'm not screaming. I'm singing on a stage of sparkling marble while the music soars and the lights burn. But there's no one out there in the amphitheater. A great shadowed pit . . . empty except for one spectator. Silent. Staring. Looming. The Man With No Face.

And this time his scream had sound.

Ben Reich awoke.

He lay quietly in the hydropathic bed while his heart shuddered and his eyes focused at random on objects in the room, simulating a calm he could not feel. The walls of green jade, the nightlight in the porcelain mandarin whose head nodded interminably if you touched him, the multi-clock that radiated the time of three planets and six satellites, the bed itself, a crystal pool flowing with carbonated glycerine at ninety-nine point nine Fahrenheit.

The door opened softly and Jonas appeared in the gloom, a shadow in puce sleeping suit, a shade with the face of a horse and the bearing of an undertaker.

"Again?" Reich asked.

"Yes, Mr. Reich."

"Loud?"

"Very loud, sir. And terrified."

"God damn your jackass ears," Reich growled. "I'm never afraid."

"No, sir."

"Get out."

"Yes, sir. Good night, sir." Jonas stepped back and closed the door.

Reich shouted: "Jonas!"

The valet reappeared.

"Sorry, Jonas."

"Quite all right, sir."

"It isn't all right." Reich charmed him with a smile. "I'm treating you like a relative. I don't pay enough for the privilege."

"Oh no, sir."

"Next time I yell at you, yell right back. Why should I have all the fun?"

"Oh, Mr. Reich . . ."

"Do that and you get a raise." The smile again. "That's all, Jonas. Thank you."

"Thank you, sir." The valet withdrew.

Reich arose from the bed and toweled himself before the cheval mirror, practicing the smile. "Make your enemies by choice," he muttered, "not by accident." He stared at the reflection: the heavy shoulders, narrow flanks, long corded legs . . . the sleek head with wide eyes, chiseled nose, small sensitive mouth scarred by implacability.

"Why?" he asked. "I wouldn't change looks with the devil. I wouldn't change places with God. Why the screaming?"

He put on a gown and glanced at the clock, unaware that he was noting the time panorama of the solar system with an unconscious skill that would have baffled his ancestors. The dials read:

A.D. 2301

VENUS	EARTH	MARS
Mean Solar Day 22	February 15	Duodecember 35
Noon + 09	0205 Greenwich	2220 Central Syrtis

MOON	IO	GANYMEDE	CALLISTO	TITAN	TRITON
2D3H	1D1H	6D8H	13D12H	15D3H	4D9H
		(eclipsed)		(transit)	

Night, noon, summer, winter . . . without bothering to think Reich could have rattled off the time and season for any meridian on any body in the solar system. Here in New York it was a bitter winter morning after a bitter night of dreaming. He would give himself a few minutes of analysis with the Esper psychiatrist he retained. The screaming had to stop.

"E for Esper," he muttered. "Esper for Extra Sensory Perception . . . For Telepaths, Mind Readers, Brain Peepers. You'd think a mind-reading doctor could stop the screaming. You'd think an Esper M.D. would earn his money and peep inside your head and stop the screaming. Those damned mindreaders are supposed to be the greatest advance since Homo sapiens evolved. E for Evolution. Bastards! E for Exploitation!"

He yanked open the door, shaking with fury.

"But I'm not afraid!" he shouted. "I'm never afraid."

He stepped down the corridor, clacking his sandals sharply on the silver floor, ke-tat-ke-tat-ke-tat-ke-tat, indifferent to the slumber of his house staff, unaware that this early-morning skeletal clack awakened twelve hearts to hatred and dread. He thrust open the door of his analyst's suite, entered and at once lay down on the couch.

Carson Breen, Esper Medical Doctor 2, was already awake and ready for him. As Reich's staff analyst he slept the "nurse's sleep" in which he remained *en rapport* with his patient and could only be awakened by his needs. That one scream had been enough for Breen. Now he was seated alongside the couch elegant in embroidered gown (his job paid twenty thousand credits a year) and sharply alert (his employer was generous but demanding).

"Go ahead Mr. Reich."

"The Man With No Face again," Reich growled.

"Nightmares?"

"You lousy blood-sucker, peep me and find out. No. Sorry. Childish of me. Yes, nightmares again. I was trying to rob a bank. Then I was trying to catch a train. Then someone was singing. Me, I think. I'm trying to give you the pictures best I can. I don't think I'm leaving anything out . . ." There was a long pause. Finally Reich blurted: "Well? You peep anything?"

"You persist that you cannot identify The Man With No Face, Mr. Reich?"

"How can I? I never see it. All I know is—"

"I think you can. You simply will not."

"Listen," Reich burst out in guilty rage. "I pay you twenty thousand. If the best you can do is make idiotic statements . . ."

"Do you mean that, Mr. Reich, or is it simply a part of the general anxiety syndrome?"

"There is no anxiety," Reich shouted. "I'm not afraid. I'm never—" He stopped himself, realizing the inutility of ranting while the deft mind of the peeper searched underneath his overturning words. "You're wrong anyway," he said sulkily. "I don't know who it is. It's a Man With No Face. That's all."

"You've been rejecting the essential points, Mr. Reich. You must be made to see them. We'll try a little free association. Without words, please. Just think. Robbery . . ."

"Jewels – watches – diamonds – stocks – bonds – sovereigns – counterfeiting – cash – bullion – dort . . ."

"What was that last again?"

"Slip of the mind. Meant to think bort . . . uncut gem stones."

"It was not a slip. It was a significant correction; or, rather, alteration. Let's continue. Pneumatique . . ."

"Long – car – compartments – air-conditioned . . . That doesn't make sense."

"It does, Mr. Reich. A phallic pun. Read 'Heir' for 'air' and you'll see it. Continue, please."

"You peepers are too damned smart. Let's see. Pneumatique . . . *train – underground – compressed air – ultra sonic speed – 'We Transport You Into Transports,' slogan of the— What the devil is the name of that company? Can't remember. Where'd the notion come from anyway?"*

"From the pre-conscious, Mr. Reich. One more trial and you'll begin to understand. Amphitheater . . ."

"Seats – pits – balcony – boxes – stalls – horse stalls – Martian horses – Martian Pampas . . ."

"And there you have it, Mr. Reich. Mars. In the past six months, you've had ninety-seven nightmares about The Man With No Face. He's been your constant enemy, frustrator, and inspirer of terror in dreams that contain three common denominators . . . Finance, Transportation, and Mars. Over and over again . . . The Man With No Face, and Finance, Transportation, and Mars."

"That doesn't mean anything to me."

"It must mean something, Mr. Reich. You must be able to identify this terrifying figure. Why else would you attempt to escape by rejecting his face?"

"I'm not rejecting anything."

"I offer as further clues the altered word 'dort' and the forgotten name of the company that coined the slogan 'We Transport You Into–' "

"I tell you I don't know who it is." Reich arose abruptly from the couch. "Your clues don't help. I can't make any identification."

"The Man With No Face does not fill you with fear because he's faceless. You know who he is. You hate him and fear him, but you know who he is."

"You're the peeper. You tell me."

"There's a limit to my ability, Mr. Reich. I can read your mind no deeper without help."

"What do you mean, help? You're the best E.M.D. I could hire. If–"

"You're neither thinking nor meaning that, Mr. Reich. You deliberately hired a 2nd Class Esper in order to protect yourself in such an emergency. Now you're paying the price of your caution. If you want the screaming to stop, you'll have to consult one of the 1st Class men . . . Say, Augustus Tate or Gart or Samuel @kins . . ."

"I'll think about it," Reich muttered and turned to go. As he opened the door, Breen called: "By the way . . . 'We Transport You Into Transports' is the slogan of the D'Courtney Cartel. How does that tie in with the alteration of 'bort' to 'dort'? Think it over."

"The Man With No Face!"

Without staggering, Reich slammed the door across the path from his mind to Breen and then lurched down the corridor toward his own suite. A wave of savage hatred burst over him. *"He's right. It's D'Courtney who's giving me the screams. Not because I'm afraid of him. I'm afraid of myself. Known all along. Known it deep down inside. Known that once I faced it I'd have to kill that D'Courtney bastard. It's no face because it's the face of murder."*

Fully dressed and in his wrong mind, Reich stormed out of his apartment and descended to the street where a Monarch Jumper picked him up and carried him in one graceful hop to the giant tower that housed the hundreds of floors and thousands of employees of Monarch's New York Office. Monarch Tower was the central nervous system of an incredibly vast corporation, a pyramid of transportation, communication, heavy industry, manufacture, sales distribution, research, exploration, importation. Monarch Utilities & Resources, Inc., bought and sold, traded and gave, made and destroyed. Its pattern of subsidiaries and holding companies was so complex that it demanded the full-time services of a 2nd Class Esper Accountant to trace the labyrinthine flow of its finances.

Reich entered his office, followed by his chief (Esper 3) secretary and her staff, bearing the litter of the morning's work.

"Dump it and jet," he growled.

They deposited the papers and recording crystals on his desk and departed hastily but without rancor. They were accustomed to his rages. Reich seated himself behind his desk, trembling with a fury that was already goring D'Courtney. Finally he muttered: "I'll give the bastard one more chance."

He unlocked his desk, opened the drawer safe and withdrew the Executive's Code Book, restricted to the executive heads of the firms listed quadruple A-1-* by Lloyds. He found most of the material he required in the middle pages of the book:

QQBA . . . . PARTNERSHIP
RRCB . . . . BOTH OUR
SSDC . . . . BOTH YOUR
TTED . . . . MERGER
UUFE . . . . INTERESTS
VVGF . . . . INFORMATION
WWHG . . . . ACCEPT OFFER
XXIH . . . . GENERALLY KNOWN
YYJI . . . . SUGGEST
ZZKJ . . . . CONFIDENTIAL
AALK . . . . EQUAL
BBML . . . . CONTRACT

Marking his place in the code book, Reich flipped the v-phone on and said to the image of the interoffice operator: "Get me Code."

The screen dazzled and cut to a smoky room cluttered with books and coils of tape. A bleached man in a faded shirt glanced at the screen, then leaped to attention.

"Yes, Mr. Reich?"

"Morning, Hassop. You look like you need a vacation." *Make your enemies by choice.* "Take a week at Spaceland. Monarch expense."

"Thank you, Mr. Reich. Thank you very much."

"This one's confidential. To Craye D'Courtney. Send—" Reich consulted the Code Book. "Send YYJI TTED RRCB UUFE AALK QQBA. Get the answer to me like rockets. Right?"

"Right, Mr. Reich. I'll jet."

Reich cut off the phone. He jabbed his hand once into the pile of papers and crystals on his desk, picked up a crystal and dropped it into the play-back. His chief secretary's voice said: "Monarch gross off two point one one three four percent. D'Courtney gross up two point one one three oh percent . . ."

"God damn him!" Reich growled. "Out of my pocket into his." He snapped off the play-back and arose in an agony of impatience. It would take hours for the reply to come. His whole life hung on D'Courtney's reply. He left his office and began to roam through the floors and departments of Monarch Tower, pretending the remorseless personal supervision he usually exercised. His Esper secretary unobtrusively accompanied him like a trained dog.

"*Trained bitch!*" Reich thought. Then aloud: "I'm sorry. Did you peep that?"

"Quite all right, Mr. Reich. I understand."

"Do you? I don't. Damn D'Courtney!"

In Personnel they were testing, checking, and screening the usual mass of job applicants—clerks, craftsmen, specialists, middle-bracket executives, top-echelon experts. All of the preliminary elimination was done with standardized tests and interviews, and never to the satisfaction of Monarch's Esper Personnel Chief, who was stalking through the floor in an icy rage when Reich entered. The fact that Reich's secretary had sent an advance telepathic announcement of the visit made no difference to him.

"I have allotted ten minutes per applicant for my final screening interview," the Chief was snapping to an assistant. "Six per hour, forty-eight per day. Unless my percentage of final rejections drops below thirty-five, I am wasting my time; which means you are wasting Monarch's time. I am not employed by Monarch to screen out the obviously unsuitable. That is your work. See to it." He turned to Reich and nodded pedantically. "Good morning, Mr. Reich."

"Morning. Trouble?"

"Nothing that cannot be handled once this staff understands that Extra Sensory Perception is not a miracle but a skill subject to wage-hour limitations. And what is your decision on Blonn, Mr. Reich?"

Secretary: "He hasn't read your memo yet."

"May I point out, young woman, that unless I am used with maximum efficiency I am wasted. The Blonn memo has been on Mr. Reich's desk for three days."

"Who the hell is Blonn?" Reich asked.

"First, the background, Mr. Reich: There are approximately one hundred thousand (100,000) 3rd Class Espers in the Esper Guild. An Esper 3 can peep the conscious level of a mind—can discover what a subject is thinking at the moment of thought. A 3rd is the lowest class of telepath. Most of Monarch's security positions are held by 3rds. We employ over five hundred . . ."

"He knows all this. Everybody does. Get to the point, long-wind!"

"Permit me, if I may, to arrive at the point in my own way. Next, there are approximately ten thousand 2nd Class Espers in the Guild," the Personnel Chief continued frostily. "They are experts like myself who can penetrate beneath the conscious level of the mind to the preconscious. Most 2nds are in the professional class—physicians, lawyers, engineers, educators, economists, architects and so on."

"And you all cost a fortune," Reich growled.

"Why not? We have a unique service to sell. Monarch appreciates the fact. Monarch employs over one hundred 2nds at present."

"Will you get to the point?"

"Finally there are less than a thousand 1st Class Espers in the Guild. The 1sts are capable of deep peeping, through the conscious and preconscious layers down to the unconscious—the lowest levels of the mind. Primordial basic desires and so forth. These, of course, hold premium positions. Education, specialized medical service . . . analysts like Tate, Gart, @kins, Moselle . . . criminologists like Lincoln Powell of the Psychotic Division . . . Political Analysts, State Negotiators, Special Cabinet Advisors, and so on. Thus far Monarch Utilities has never had occasion to hire a 1st."

"And?" Reich muttered.

"The occasion has arisen, Mr. Reich, and I believe Blonn may be available. Briefly . . ."

"It says here."

"Briefly, Mr. Reich, Monarch is hiring so many Espers that I have suggested we set up a special Esper Personnel Department, headed by a 1st like Blonn, to devote itself exclusively to interviewing telepaths."

"He's wondering why you can't handle it."

"I have given you the background to explain why I cannot handle the job, Mr. Reich. I am a 2nd Class Esper. I can telepath normal applicants rapidly and efficiently, but I cannot handle other Espers with the same speed and economy. All Espers are accustomed to using mind blocks of varying effectiveness depending on their rating. It would take me one hour per 3rd for an efficient screening interview. It would take me three hours per 2nd. I could not possibly peep through the mind block of a 1st. We must hire a 1st like Blonn for this work. The cost will be enormous, of course, but the necessity is urgent."

"What's so urgent?" Reich said.

"For heaven's sake! Don't give him that picture! That isn't diversion. It's waving a red flag. He's sore enough now."

"I have my job to do, Madam." To Reich, the Chief said: "The fact is, sir, we are not hiring the best Espers. The D'Courtney Cartel has been taking the cream of the Espers away from us. Over and over again, through lack of proper facilities, we have been mousetrapped by D'Courtney into bidding for inferior people while D'Courtney has quietly appropriated the best."

"Damn you!" Reich shouted. "Damn D'Courtney. All right. Set it up. And tell this Blonn to start mousetrapping D'Courtney. You'd better start, too."

Reich tore out of Personnel and over to Sales-city. The same unpleasant information was waiting for him. Monarch Utilities & Resources was losing the gut-fight with the D'Courtney Cartel. It was losing the fight in every sector-city—Advertising, Engineering, Research, Public Relations. There was no escaping the certainty of defeat. Reich knew his back was to the wall.

He returned to his own office and paced in a fury for five minutes. "It's no use," he muttered. "I know I'll have to kill him. He won't accept merger. Why should he? He's licked me and he knows it. I'll have to kill him and I'll need help. Peeper help."

He flipped on the v-phone and told the operator: "Recreation."

A sparkling lounge appeared on the screen, decorated in chrome and enamel, equipped with game tables and a bar dispenser. It appeared to be and was used as a recreation center. It was, in fact, headquarters of Monarch's powerful espionage division. The Recreation Director, a bearded scholar named West, looked up from a chess problem, then rose to attention.

"Good morning, Mr. Reich."

Warned by the formal "Mister," Reich said: "Good morning, Mr. West. Just a routine check. Paternalism, you know. How's amusement these days?"

"Modulated, Mr. Reich. However, I must complain, sir. I think there's entirely too much gambling going on." West stalled in a fussy voice until two bona fide Monarch clerks innocently finished their drinks and departed. Then he relaxed and slumped into his chair. "All clear, Ben. Shoot."

"Has Hassop broken the confidential code yet, Ellery?"

The peeper shook his head.

"Trying?"

West smiled and nodded.

"Where's D'Courtney?"

"En route to Terra, aboard the *Astra.*"

"Know his plans? Where he'll be staying?"

"No. Want a check?"

"I don't know. It depends . . ."

"Depends on what?" West glanced at him curiously. "I wish the Telepathic Pattern could be transmitted by phone, Ben. I'd like to know what you're thinking at."

Reich smiled grimly. "Thank God for the phone. At least we've got that protection from mind readers. What's your attitude on crime, Ellery?"

"Typical."

"Of anybody?"

"Of the Guild. The Guild doesn't like it, Ben."

"So what's so hot about the Esper Guild? You know the value of money, success . . . Why don't you clever-up? Why do you let the Guild do your thinking?"

"You don't understand. We're born in the Guild. We live with the Guild. We die in the Guild. We have the right to elect Guild officers, and that's all. The Guild runs our professional lives. It trains us, grades us, sets ethical standards, and sees that we stick to them. It protects us by protecting the layman, the same as medical associations. We have the equivalent of the Hippocratic Oath. It's called the Esper Pledge. God help any of us if we break it . . . as I judge you're suggesting I should."

"Maybe I am," Reich said intently. "Maybe I'm hinting it could be worth your while to break the peeper pledge. Maybe I'm thinking in terms of money . . . more than you or any 2nd Class peeper ever sees in a lifetime."

"Forget it, Ben. Not interested."

"So you bust your pledge. What happens?"

"We're ostracized."

"That's all? Is that so awful? With a fortune in your pocket? Smart peepers have broken with the Guild before. They've been ostracized. So what? Clever-up, Ellery."

West smiled wryly: "You wouldn't understand, Ben."

"Make me understand."

"Those ousted peepers you mention . . . like Jerry Church. They weren't so smart. It's like this . . ." West considered. "Before surgery really got started, there used to be a handicapped group called deaf mutes."

"No-hear no-talk?"

"That's it. They communicated by a manual sign language. That meant they couldn't communicate with anybody but deaf mutes. Understand? They had to live in their own community or they couldn't live at all. A man goes crazy if he can't talk to friends."

"So?"

"Some of them started a racket. They'd tax the more successful deaf mutes for weekly hand-outs. If the victim refused to pay, they'd ostracize him. The victim always paid. It was a choice of paying or living in solitary until he went mad."

"You mean you peepers are like deaf mutes?"

"No, Ben. You normals are the deaf mutes. If we had to live with you alone, we'd go mad. So leave me alone. If you're nursing something dirty, I don't want to know."

West cut off the phone in Reich's face. With a roar of rage, Reich snatched up a gold paperweight and hurled it into the crystal screen. Before the shattered fragments finished flying, he was in the corridor and on his way out of the building.

His peeper secretary knew where he was going. His peeper chauffeur knew where he wanted to go. Reich arrived in his apartment and was met by his peeper house supervisor who at once announced early luncheon and dialed the meal to Reich's unspoken demands. Feeling slightly less violent, Reich stalked into his study and turned to his safe, a shimmer of light in the corner.

It was simply a honeycomb paper rack tuned out of temporal phase with a single-cycle beat. Each second when the safe phase and the temporal phase coincided, the rack pulsed with a brilliant glow. The safe could only be opened by the pore-pattern of Reich's left index finger, which was irreproducible.

Reich placed the tip of his finger in the center of the glow. It faded and the honeycomb rack appeared. Holding his finger in place, he reached up and took down a small black notebook and a large red envelope. He removed his index finger and the safe pulsed out of phase again.

Reich flipped through the pages of the notebook . . . ABDUCTION . . . ANARCHISTS . . . ARSONISTS . . . BRIBERY (PROVEN) . . . BRIBERY (POTENTIAL) . . . Under (POTENTIAL) he found the names of fifty-seven prominent people. One of them was Augustus Tate, Esper Medical Doctor I. He nodded with satisfaction.

He tore open the red envelope and examined its contents. It contained five sheets of closely written pages in a handwriting that was centuries old. It was a message from the founder of Monarch Utilities and the Reich clan. Four of the pages were lettered: PLAN A, PLAN B, PLAN C, PLAN D. The fifth was headed INTRODUCTION. Reich read the ancient spidery cursive slowly:

To those who come after me: The test of intellect is the refusal to belabor the obvious. If you have opened this letter we understand one another. I have prepared four general murder plans which may help you. I bequeath them to you as part of your Reich inheritance. They are outlines. The details must be filled in by yourself as your time, your environment, and necessity require.

Caution: The essence of murder never changes. In every era it remains the conflict of the killer against society with the victim as the prize. And the ABC of conflict with society remains constant. Be audacious, be brave, be confident and you will not fail. Against these assets society can have no defense.

GEOFFRY REICH

Reich leafed through the plans slowly, filled with admiration for the first of his line who had had the forethought to prepare for every possible emergency. The plans were outdated but they kindled imagination; and ideas began forming and crystallizing to be considered, discarded, and instantly replaced. One phrase caught his attention:

If you believe yourself a natural killer, avoid planning too carefully. Leave most to your instinct. Intellect may fail you, but the killer instinct is invincible.

"The killer instinct," Reich breathed. "By God, I've got that."

The phone chimed once and then the automatic switched on. There was a quick chatter and tape began to stutter out of the recorder. Reich strode to the desk and examined it. The message was short and deadly: CODE TO REICH: REPLY WWHG.

"WWHG. 'Offer refused.' Refused! REFUSED! I knew it!" Reich shouted. "All right, D'Courtney. If you won't let it be merger, then I'll make it murder."

2

Augustus Tate, E.M.D. I, received Cr. 1,000 per hour of analysis—not a high fee considering that a patient rarely required more than an hour of the doctor's devastating time; but it placed his income at Cr. 8,000 a day or well over Cr. 2 million a year. Few people knew what proportion of that income was paid into the Esper Guild for the education of other telepaths and the furthering of the Guild's Eugenic Plan to bring Extra-Sensory Perception to everyone in the world.

Augustus Tate knew, and the 95 percent he paid was a sore point with him. Consequently, he belonged to "The League of Esper Patriots," an extreme right-wing political group within the Guild, dedicated to the preservation of the autocracy and incomes of the upper-grade Espers. It was this membership that placed him in Ben Reich's BRIBERY (POTENTIAL) category. Reich marched into Tate's exquisite consultation room, glanced once at Tate's tiny frame—a figure slightly out of proportion but carefully realigned by tailors. Reich sat down and grunted: "Peep me quick."

He glared in concentration at Tate while the elegant little peeper examined him with a glittering eye and spoke in quick bursts: "You're Ben Reich of Monarch. Ten-billion credit firm. Think I should know you. I do. You're involved in a death struggle with the D'Courtney Cartel. Right? You're savagely hostile toward D'Courtney. Right? Offered merger this morning. Coded message: YYJI TTED RRCB UUFE AALK QQBA. Offer refused. Right? In desperation you have resolved to—" Tate broke off abruptly.

"Go ahead," Reich said.

"To murder Craye D'Courtney as the first step in taking over his cartel. You want my help. . . . Mr. Reich, this is ridiculous! If you keep on thinking like this, I'll have to commit you. You know the law."

"Clever-up, Tate. You're going to help me break the law."

"No, Mr. Reich. I'm not in a position to help you."

"You say that? A 1st Class Esper? And I'm supposed to believe it? I'm supposed to believe you're incapable of outwitting any man, any group, the whole world?"

Tate smiled. "Sugar for the fly," he said. "A characteristic device of—"

"Peep me," Reich interrupted. "It'll save time. Read what's in my mind. Your gift. My resources. An unbeatable combination. My God! It's lucky for the world I'm willing to stop at one murder. Together we could rape the universe."

"No," Tate said with decision. "This won't do. I'll have to commit you, Mr. Reich."

"Wait. Want to find out what I'm offering you? Read me deeper. How much am I willing to pay? What's my top limit?"

Tate closed his eyes. His mannequin face tightened painfully. Then his eyes opened in surprise. "You can't be serious," he exclaimed.

"I am," Reich grunted. "And what's more, you know it's an offer in good faith, don't you?"

Tate nodded slowly.

"And you're aware that Monarch plus D'Courtney can make the offer good."

"I almost believe you."

"You can believe me. I've been financing your League of Esper Patriots for five years. If you've peeped me deep enough you know why. I hate the damned Esper Guild as much as you do. Guild ethics are bad for business—lousy for making money. Your League is the organization that can break the Esper Guild some day."

"I've got all that," Tate said sharply.

"With Monarch and D'Courtney in my pocket I can do better than help your faction break the Guild. I can make you president of a new Esper Guild for life. That's an unconditional guarantee. You can't do it alone, but you can do it with me."

Tate closed his eyes and murmured: "There hasn't been a successful premeditated murder in seventy-nine years. Espers make it impossible to conceal intent before murder. Or, if Espers have been evaded before the murder, they make it impossible to conceal the guilt afterwards."

"Esper evidence isn't admitted in court."

"True, but once an Esper discovers guilt he can always uncover objective evidence to support his peeping. Lincoln Powell, the Prefect of the Police Psychotic Division, is deadly." Tate opened his eyes. "D'you want to forget this conversation?"

"No," Reich growled. "Look it over with me first. Why have murders failed? Because mind readers patrol the world. What can stop a mind reader? Another one. But no killer ever had the sense to hire a good peeper to run interference for him; or if he had the sense, he couldn't make the deal. I've made the deal."

"Have you?"

"I'm going to fight a war," Reich continued. "I'm going to fight one sharp skirmish with society. Let's look at it as a problem in strategy and tactics. My problem's simply the problem of any army. Audacity, bravery, and confidence aren't enough. An army needs Intelligence. A war is won with Intelligence. I need you for my G-2."

"Agreed."

"I'll do the fighting. You'll provide the Intelligence. I'll have to know where D'Courtney will be, where I can strike, when I can strike. I'll take care of the killing myself, but you'll have to tell me when and where the opportunity will be."

"Understood."

"I'll have to invade first—cut through the defensive network surrounding D'Courtney. That means reconnaissance from you. You'll have to check the normals, spot the peepers, warn me and block their mind-reading if I can't avoid them. I'll have to retreat after the killing through another network of normals and peepers. You'll have to help me fight a rear-guard action. You'll have to remain on the scene after the murder. You'll find out whom the police suspect and why. If I know suspicion is directed against myself, I can divert it. If I know it's directed against someone else, I can clinch it. I can fight this war and win this war with your Intelligence. Is that the truth? Peep me."

After a long pause, Tate said, "It's the truth. We can do it."

"Will you do it?"

Tate hesitated, then nodded with finality. "Yes. I'll do it."

Reich took a deep breath. "Right. Now here's the course I'm plotting. I think I can set up the killing with an old game called 'Sardine.' It will give me the opportunity to get at D'Courtney, and I've figured out a trick to kill him; I know how to fire an antique explosive gun without bullets."

"Wait," Tate interrupted sharply. "How are you going to keep all this intent concealed from stray peepers? I can only screen you when I'm with you. I won't be with you all the time."

"I can work up a temporary mind-block. There's a songwriter down on Melody Lane I can swindle into helping me."

"It may work," Tate said after a moment's peeping. "But one thing occurs to me. Suppose D'Courtney is protected? Do you expect to shoot it out with his bodyguards?"

"No. I'm hoping it won't be necessary. A physiologist named Jordan has just developed visual knock-out drops for Monarch. We intended using it for strike riots. I'll use it on D'Courtney's guards."

"I see."

"You'll be working with me all along–doing reconnaissance and intelligence, but I need one piece of information first. When D'Courtney comes to town he's usually the guest of Maria Beaumont."

"The Gilt Corpse?"

"The same. I want you to find out if D'Courtney intends staying with her this trip. Everything depends on that."

"Easy enough. I can locate D'Courtney's destination and plans for you. There's to be a social gathering tonight at Lincoln Powell's house. D'Courtney's physician will probably be there. He's on Terra for a week's visit. I'll start the reconnaissance through him."

"And you're not afraid of Powell?"

Tate smiled contemptuously. "If I were, Mr. Reich, would I trust myself in this bargain with you? Make no mistake. I'm no Jerry Church."

"Church!"

"Yes. Don't act surprised. Church, the 2nd. He was kicked out of the Guild ten years ago for that little junket of his with you."

"Damn you. Got that from my mind, eh?"

"Your mind and history."

"Well, it won't repeat itself this time. You're tougher and smarter than Church. Need anything special for Powell's party? Women? Clothes? Jewels? Money? Just call on Monarch."

"Nothing, but thank you very much."

"Criminal but generous, that's me." Reich smiled as he arose to go. He did not offer to shake hands.

"Mr. Reich!" Tate called suddenly.

Reich turned at the door.

"The screaming will continue. The Man With No Face is not a symbol of murder."

"What? Oh Christ! The nightmares? Still? You goddamned peeper. How did you get that? How did you–"

"Don't be a fool. D'you think you can play games with a 1st?"

"Who's playing, you bastard? What about the nightmares?"

"No, Mr. Reich, I won't tell you. I doubt if anyone but a 1st can tell you, and naturally you would not dare to consult another after this conference."

"For God's sake, man! Are you going to help me?"

"No, Mr. Reich." Tate smiled malevolently. "That's my little weapon. It keeps us on a parity basis. Balance of power, you understand. Mutual dependence ensures mutual faith. Criminal but peeper –that's me."

Like all upper-grade Espers, Lincoln Powell, Ph.D.1, lived in a private house. It was not a question of conspicuous consumption, but rather a problem of privacy. Although thought transmission was too faint to penetrate masonry, the average plastic apartment unit was too flimsy to block this transmission. Life in any such multiple dwelling was life in an inferno of naked emotion for an Esper.

Powell, the Police Prefect, could afford a small limestone maisonette on Hudson Ramp overlooking the North River. There were only four rooms–upstairs a bedroom and study, downstairs a living room and kitchen. There was no servant in the house. Like most upper-grade Espers, Powell required large quantities of solitude. He preferred to do for himself. He was in the kitchen, checking over the refreshment dials in preparation for the party, whistling a plaintive, crooked tune.

He was a slender man in his late thirties, tall, loose, slow-moving. His wide mouth seemed perpetually on the verge of laughter, but at the moment he wore an expression of sad disappointment. He was lecturing himself on the follies and stupidities of his worst vice.

The essence of the Esper is his responsiveness. His personality always takes color from his surroundings. The trouble with Powell was an enlarged sense of humor, and his response was invariably exaggerated. He had attacks of what he called "Dishonest Abe" moods. Someone would ask Lincoln Powell an innocent question, and Dishonest Abe would answer. His fervent imagination would cook up the wildest tall story and he would deliver it with straight-faced sincerity. He could not suppress the liar in him.

Only this afternoon, Police Commissioner Crabbe had inquired about a routine blackmail case, and simply because he'd mispronounced a name, Powell had been inspired to fabricate a dramatic account involving a make-believe crime, a daring midnight raid, and the heroism of an imaginary Lieutenant Kopenick. Now the Commissioner wanted to award Lieutenant Kopenick a medal.

"Dishonest Abe," Powell muttered bitterly. "You give me a stiff pain."

The house bell chimed. Powell glanced at his watch in surprise (it was too early for company) and then directed *Open* in C-sharp at the TP lock-sensor. It responded to the thought pattern, as a tuning fork will vibrate to the right note, and the front door slid open.

Instantly came a familiar sensory impact: Snow/mint/tulips/taffeta.

"Mary Noyes. Come to help the bachelor prepare for the party? **Blessings!**"

"Hoped you'd need me, Linc."

"Every host needs a hostess. Mary, what am I going to do for canapes$^{S.O.S.}$*?"*

"Just invented a new recipe. I'll make it for you. Roast chutney &."

"&?"

"That's telling, my love."

She came into the kitchen, a short girl physically, but tall and swaying in thought; a dark girl exteriorly, but frost white in pattern. Almost a nun in white, despite the swarthy texture of externals; but the mind is the reality. You are what you think.

"I wish I could rethink, darling. Have my psyche reground!"

"Change your (I kiss you as you are) self, Mary?"

"If I only (You never really do, Linc) could. I'm so tired of tasting you tasting mint every time we meet."

"Next time I'll add brandy and ice. Shake well. Voila! Stinger-Mary."

"Do that. Also ~~SNOW~~."

"Why strike out the snow? I love snow."

"But I love you."

"And I love you, Mary."

"Thanks, Linc." But he said it. He always said it. He never thought it. She turned away quickly. The tears within her scalded him.

"Again, Mary?"

"Not again. Always. Always." And the deeper levels of her mind cried: *"I love you, Lincoln. I love you. Image of my father: Symbol of security: Of warmth: Of protecting passion: Do not reject me always . . . always . . . forever . . ."*

"Listen to me, Mary . . ."

"Don't talk. Please, Linc. Not in words. I couldn't bear it if words came between us."

"You're my friend, Mary. Always. For every disappointment. For every elation."

"But not for love."

"No, dear heart. Don't let it hurt you so. Not for love."

"I have enough love, God pity me, for both of us."

"One, God pity us, is not enough for both, Mary."

"You must marry an Esper before you're forty, Linc. The Guild insists on that. You know it."

"I know it."

"Then let friendship answer. Marry me, Lincoln. Give me a year, that's all. One little year to love you. I'll let you go. I won't cling. I won't make you hate me. Darling, it's so little to ask . . . so little to give . . ."

The doorbell chimed. Powell looked at Mary helplessly. "Guests," he murmured and directed *Open* in C-sharp at the TP lock-sensor. At the same instant she directed *Close* a fifth above. The harmonies meshed and the door remained shut.

"Answer me first, Lincoln."

"I can't give you the answer you want, Mary."

The doorbell chimed again.

He took her shoulders firmly, held her close and looked deep into her eyes. *"You're a 2nd. Read me as deeply as you can. What's in my mind? What's in my heart? What's my answer?"*

He removed all blocks. The thundering plunging depths of his mind cascaded over her in a warm, frightening torrent . . . terrifying yet magnetic and desirable; but . . . "Snow. Mint. Tulips. Taffeta," she said wearily. *"Go meet your guests, Mr. Powell. I'll make your canapes. It's all I'm good for."*

He kissed her once, then turned toward the living room and

opened the front door. Instantly, a fountain of brilliance sparkled into the house, followed by the guests. The Esper party began.

Frankly   Canapes?   Why,
Ellery,   Thanks,   delicious.   Yes,
I   Mary, they're   Tate,
don't   I'm
think   treating
We   you'll   Canapes?   D'Courtney.
brought   be   I
Galen   working   expect
along   for   him
to   Monarch   in
help him celebrate.   much   town
He's   longer.   very
just   The   shortly.
taken his Guild Exam
If   is   and
you're   just   been
interested   about   classed
Powell, we're ready   2nd.
to
run rule
you   Monarch's
for   espionage
Guild   Canapes?   unethical.
president.
Canapes?
Why, yes.
Thank
Canapes?   you,
Mary . . .

"@kins! Chervil! Tate! Have a heart! Will you people take a look at the pattern(?) we've been weaving . . ."

The TP chatter stopped. The guests considered for a moment, then burst into laughter.

"This reminds me of my days in the kindergarten. A little mercy for your host, please. I'll jump my tracks, if we keep on weaving this mish-mash. Let's have some order. I don't even ask for beauty."

"Just name the pattern, Linc."

"What'll you have?"

"Basket-weave? Math curves? Music? Architectural design?"

"Anything. Anything. Just so long as you don't make my brains itch."

Sorry, Lincoln. We weren't party-minded Enough
Tate thought Esper
but Alan men
I'm Seaver remaining
Not that a pres was ever elected still unmarried
at coming can
liberty but ruin
To be generous, I feel Al's a man to loa the
reveal don't Guild's
anything TP entire
about him eugenic
D'Courtney is arriving according to plan
yet

There was another burst of laughter when Mary Noyes was left hanging with that unreticulated "yet." The doorbell chimed again, and a Solar Equity Advocate 2 entered with his girl. She was a demure little thing, surprisingly attractive outwardly, and new to the company. Her TP pattern was naïve and not deeply responsive. Obviously a 3rd.

"Greetings. Greetings. Abject apologies for the delay. Orange blossoms & wedding rings are the excuse. I proposed on the way over."

"And I'm afraid I accepted," the girl said, smiling.

"Don't talk," the lawyer shot at her. *"This isn't a 3rd Class brawl, I told you not to use words."*

"I forgot," she blurted again, and then heated the room with her fright and shame. Powell stepped forward and took the girl's trembling hand.

"Ignore him, he's a 2nd-come-lately snob. I'm Lincoln Powell, your host. I Sherlock for the cops. If your fiancé beats you, I'll help him regret it. Come and meet your fellow freaks . . ." He conducted her around the room. *"This is Gus Tate, a quack-one. Next to him, Sam & Sally @kins. Sam's another of the same. She's a baby-sitter-two. They're just in from Venus. Here on a visit . . ."*

"H-How–*I mean, how do you do?"*

"That fat man sitting on the floor is Wally Chervil, architect-two. The blonde sitting in his (lap)² is June, his wife. June's an editor-

two. That's their son, Galen, talking to Ellery West. Gally's a tech-undergrad-three . . ."

Young Galen Chervil indignantly started to point out that he'd just been classed 2nd and hadn't needed to use words in over a year. Powell cut him off and below the girl's perceptive threshold explained the reason for the deliberate mistake.

"Oh," said Galen. "Yep, brother and sister 3rds, that's us. And am I glad you're here. These deep peepers were beginning to scare me."

"Oh, I don't know. I was scared at first, but I'm not any more."

"And this is your hostess, Mary Noyes."

"Hello. Canapes?"

"Thank you. They look delicious, Mrs. Powell."

"Now how about a game?" Powell interposed quickly. *"Rebus, anyone?"*

Outside, huddled in the shadow of the limestone arch, Jerry Church pressed against the garden door of Powell's house, listening with all his soul. He was cold, silent, immobile, and starved. He was resentful, hating, contemptuous, and starved. He was an Esper 2 and starved. The bend sinister of ostracism was the source of his hunger.

Through the thin maple panel filtered the multiple TP pattern of the party—a weaving, ever-changing, exhilarating design. And Church, Esper 2, living on a submarginal diet of words for the past ten years, was starved for his own people—for the Esper world he had lost.

"The reason I mentioned D'Courtney is that I've just come across a case that might be similar."

That was Augustus Tate, sucking up to @kins.

"Oh really? Very interesting. I'd like to compare notes. Matter of fact, I made the trip to Terra because D'Courtney is coming here. Too bad D'Courtney won't—well, be available." @kins was obviously being discreet and it smelled as though Tate was after something. Maybe not, Church speculated, but there was some elegant block and counter-blocking going on, like duelists fencing with complicated electrical circuits.

"Look here, peeper. I think you've been pretty snotty to that poor girl."

"Listen to him shoot off his mind," Church muttered. "Powell, that holy louse who had me kicked out, preaching down his big nose at the lawyer."

"Poor girl? You mean dumb girl, Powell. My God! How gauche can you get?"

"She's only a 3rd. Be fair."

"She gives me a pain."

"Do you think it's decent . . . marrying a girl when you feel that way about her?"

"Don't be a romantic ass, Powell. We've got to marry peepers. I might as well settle for a pretty face."

The Rebus game was going on in the living room. The Noyes girl was busy building a camouflaged image with an old poem:

The vast,
sea and
is out Glimmering
calm in the stand,
tonight, tranquil bay. England
The Come to the window; of
tide sweet is the night cliffs
is air. Only the
full from the gone;
the long line is
moon of spray and
lies Gleams
fair light
Upon the straits;—on the French coast the

What the devil was that? An eye in a glass? Eh? Oh. Not a glass. A stein. Eye in a stein. Einstein. Easy.

"What d'you think of Powell for the job, Ellery?" That was Chervil with his phony smile and his big fat pontifical belly.

"For Guild president?"

"Yes."

"Damned efficient man. Romantic but efficient. The perfect candidate if only he'd get married."

"That's the romance in him. He's having trouble locating a girl."

"Don't all you deep peepers? Thank God I'm not a 1st."

And then a smash of glass crashing in the kitchen and Preacher Powell again, lecturing that little snot, Gus Tate.

"Never mind the glass, Gus. I had to drop it to cover for you. You're radiating anxiety like a nova."

"The devil I am, Powell."

"The devil you're not. What's all this about Ben Reich?"

The little man was really on guard. You could feel his mental shell hardening.

"Ben Reich? What brought him up?"

"You did, Gus. It's been moiling in your mind all evening. I couldn't help reading it."

"Not me, Powell. You must be tuning another TP."

Image of a horse laughing.

"Powell, I swear I'm not–"

"Are you mixed up with Reich, Gus?"

"No." But you could feel the blocks bang down into place.

"Take a hint from an old hand, Gus. Reich can get you into trouble. Be careful. Remember Jerry Church? Reich ruined him. Don't let it happen to you."

Tate drifted back to the living room; Powell remained in the kitchen, calm and slow-moving, sweeping up broken glass. Church lay frozen against the back door, suppressing the seething hatred in his heart. The Chervil boy was showing off for the lawyer's girl, singing a love ballad and paralleling it with a visual parody. College stuff. The wives were arguing violently in sine curves. @kins and West were interlacing cross-conversation in a fascinating intricate pattern of sensory images that made Church's starvation keener.

"Would you like a drink, Jerry?"

The garden door opened. Powell stood silhouetted in the light, a bubbling glass in his hand. The stars lit his face softly. The deep hooded eyes were compassionate and understanding. Dazed, Church climbed to his feet and timidly took the proffered drink.

"Don't report this to the Guild, Jerry. I'll catch hell for breaking the taboo. I'm always breaking rules. Poor Jerry . . . We've got to do something for you. Ten years is too long."

Suddenly Church hurled the drink in Powell's face, then turned and fled.

3

At nine Monday morning, Tate's mannequin face appeared on the screen of Reich's v-phone.

"Is this line secure?" he asked sharply.

In answer Reich simply pointed to the Warranty Seal.

"All right," Tate said. "I think I've done the job for you. I peeped @kins last night. But before I report, I must warn you. There's a chance of error when you deep peep a first. @kins blocked pretty carefully."

"I understand."

"Craye D'Courtney arrives from Mars on the *Astra* next Wednesday morning. He will go at once to Maria Beaumont's townhouse where he will be a secret and hidden guest for exactly one night. No more."

"One night," Reich muttered. "And then? His plans?"

"I don't know. Apparently D'Courtney is planning some form of drastic action–"

"Against me!" Reich growled.

"Perhaps. According to @kins, D'Courtney is under some kind of violent strain and his adaptation pattern is shattering. The Life Instinct and Death Instinct have defused. He is regressing under the emotional bankruptcy very rapidly."

"God damn it! My life depends on this," Reich raged. "Talk straight."

"It's quite simple. Every man is a balance of two opposed drives–the Life Instinct and the Death Instinct. Both drives have the identical purpose–to win Nirvana. The Life Instinct fights for Nirvana by smashing all opposition. The Death Instinct attempts to win Nirvana by destroying itself. Usually both instincts fuse in the adapted individual. Under strain they defuse. That's what's happening to D'Courtney."

"Yes, by God! And he's jetting for me!"

"@kins will see D'Courtney Thursday morning in an effort to dissuade him from whatever he contemplates. @kins is afraid of it and determined to stop it. He made a flying trip from Venus to cut D'Courtney off."

"He won't have to stop it. I'll stop it myself. He won't have to protect me. I'll protect myself. It's self-defense, Tate–not murder! Self-defense! You've done a good job. This is all I need."

"You need much more, Reich. Among other things, time. This is Monday. You'll have to be ready by Wednesday."

"I'll be ready," Reich growled. "You'd better be ready too."

"We can't afford to fail, Reich. If we do–it's Demolition. You realize that?"

"Demolition for both of us. I realize that." Reich's voice began to crack. "Yes, Tate, you're in this with me, and I'm in it straight to the finish–all the way to Demolition."

He planned all through Monday, audaciously, bravely, with confidence. He penciled the outlines as an artist fills a sheet with delicate tracery before the bold inking-in; but he did no final inking. That was to be left for the killer instinct on Wednesday. He put the plan away and slept Monday night . . . and awoke screaming, dreaming again of The Man With No Face.

Tuesday afternoon, Reich left Monarch Tower early and dropped in at the Century Audio-bookstore on Sheridan Place. It specialized mostly in piezo-electric crystal recordings—tiny jewels mounted in elegant settings. The latest vogue was brooch-operas for M'lady. ("She Shall Have Music Wherever She Goes.") Century also had shelves of obsolete printed books.

"I want something special for a friend I've neglected," Reich told the salesman.

He was bombarded with merchandise.

"Not special enough," he complained. "Why don't you people hire a peeper and save your clients this trouble? How quaint and old-fashioned can you get?" He began sauntering around the shop, tailed by a retinue of anxious clerks.

After he had dissembled sufficiently, and before the worried manager could send out for a peeper salesman, Reich stopped before the bookshelves.

"What's this?" he inquired in surprise.

"Antique books, Mr. Reich." The sales staff began explaining the theory and practice of the archaic visual book while Reich slowly searched for the tattered brown volume that was his goal. He remembered it well. He had glanced through it five years ago and made a note in his little black opportunity book. Old Geoffry Reich wasn't the only Reich who believed in preparedness.

"Interesting. Yes. Fascinating. What's this one?" Reich pulled down the brown volume. "'Let's Play Party.' What's the date on it? Not really. You mean to say they had parties that long ago?"

The staff assured him that the ancients were very modern in many astonishing ways.

"Look at the contents," Reich chuckled. "'Honeymoon Bridge' . . . 'Prussian Whist' . . . 'Post Office' . . . 'Sardine.' What in the world could that be? Page ninety-six. Let's have a look."

Reich flipped pages until he came to a bold-face heading: HILARIOUS MIXED PARTY GAMES. "Look at this," he laughed, pretending surprise. He pointed to the well-remembered paragraph.

SARDINE

One player is selected to be It. All the lights are extinguished and the It hides anywhere in the house. After a few minutes, the players go to find the It, hunting separately. The first one who finds him does not reveal the fact but hides with him wherever he may be. Successively each player finding the Sardines joins them until all are hidden in one place and the last player, who is the loser, is left to wander alone in the dark.

"I'll take it," Reich said. "It's exactly what I need."

That evening he spent three hours carefully defacing the remains of the volume. With heat, acid, stain, and scissors, he mutilated the game instructions; and every burn, every cut, every slash was a blow at D'Courtney's writhing body. When his proxy murders were finished, he had reduced every game to incomplete fragments. Only "Sardine" was left intact.

Reich wrapped the book, addressed it to Graham, the appraiser, and dropped it into the airslot. It went off with a puff and a bang and returned an hour later with Graham's official sealed appraisal. Reich's mutilations had not been detected.

He had the book gift-wrapped with the appraisal enclosed (as was the custom) and slotted it to Maria Beaumont's house. Twenty minutes later came the reply: "Darling! Darling! Darling! I thot you'd forgoten (evidently Maria had written the note herself) little ol sexy me. How 2 divine. Come to Beaumont House tonite. We're having a party. We'll play games from your sweet gift." There was a portrait of Maria centered in the star of a synthetic ruby enclosed in the message capsule. A nude portrait, naturally.

Reich answered: "Devastated. Not tonight. One of my millions is missing."

She answered: "Wednesday, you clever boy. I'll give you one of mine."

He replied: "Delighted to accept. Will bring guest. I kiss all of yours." And went to bed.

And screamed at The Man With No Face.

Wednesday morning, Reich visited Monarch's Science-city ("Paternalism, you know") and spent a stimulating hour with its bright young men. He discussed their work and their glowing futures if they would only have faith in Monarch. He told the ancient dirty joke about the celibate pioneer who made the emergency landing on the hearse in deep space (and the corpse said: "I'm just one of the tourists!") and the bright young men laughed subserviently, feeling slightly contemptuous of the boss.

This informality enabled Reich to drift into the Restricted Room and pick up one of the visual knock-out capsules. They were cubes of copper, half the size of fulminating caps, but twice as deadly. When they were broken open, they erupted a dazzling blue flare that ionized the rhodopsin—the visual purple in the retina of the eye —blinding the victim and abolishing his perception of time and space.

Wednesday afternoon, Reich went over to Melody Lane in the heart of the theatrical district and called on Psych-Songs, Inc. It was run by a clever young woman who had written some brilliant jingles for his sales division and some devastating strike-breaking songs for Propaganda back when Monarch needed everything to smash last year's labor fracas. Her name was Duffy Wyg&. To Reich she was the epitome of the modern career girl—the virgin seductress.

"Well, Duffy?" He kissed her casually. She was as shapely as a sales curve, pretty, but a trifle too young.

"Well, Mr. Reich?" She looked at him oddly. "Some day I'm going to hire one of those Lonely-Heart Peepers to case your kiss. I keep thinking you don't mean business."

"I don't."

"Dog."

"A man has to make up his mind early, Duffy. If he kisses girls he kisses his money goodbye."

"You kiss me."

"Only because you're the image of the lady on the credit."

"Pip," she said.

"Pop," he said.

"Bim," she said.

"Bam," he said.

"I'd like to kill the bem who invented that fad," Duffy said darkly. "All right, handsome. What's your problem?"

"Gambling," Reich said. "Ellery West, my Rec director, is complaining about the gambling in Monarch. Says there's too much. Personally I don't care."

"Keep a man in debt and he's afraid to ask for a raise."

"You're entirely too smart, young lady."

"So you want a no-gamble-type song?"

"Something like that. Catchy. Not too obvious. More a delayed action than a straight propaganda tune. I'd like the conditioning to be more or less unconscious."

Duffy nodded and made quick notes.

"And make it a tune worth hearing. I'll have to listen to God knows how many people singing and whistling and humming it."

"You louse. All my tunes are worth hearing."

"Once."

"That's a thousand extra on your tab."

Reich laughed. "Speaking of monotony . . ." he continued smoothly.

"Which we weren't."

"What's the most persistent tune you ever wrote?"

"Persistent?"

"You know what I mean. Like those advertising jingles you can't get out of your head."

"Oh. Pepsis, we call 'em."

"Why?"

"Dunno. They say because the first one was written centuries ago by a character named Pepsi. I don't buy that. I wrote one once . . ." Duffy winced in recollection. "Hate to think of it even now. Guaranteed to obsess you for a month. It haunted me for a year."

"You're rocketing."

"Scout's honor, Mr. Reich. It was 'Tenser, Said the Tensor.' I wrote it for that flop show about the crazy mathematician. They wanted nuisance value and they sure got it. People got so sore they had to withdraw it. Lost a fortune."

"Let's hear it."

"I couldn't do that to you."

"Come on, Duffy. I'm really curious."

"You'll regret it."

"I don't believe you."

"All right, pig," she said, and pulled the punch panel toward her. "This pays you back for that no-guts kiss."

Her fingers and palm slipped gracefully over the panel. A tune of utter monotony filled the room with agonizing, unforgettable banality. It was the quintessence of every melodic cliché Reich had ever heard. No matter what melody you tried to remember, it invariably led down the path of familiarity to "Tenser, Said the Tensor." Then Duffy began to sing:

Eight, sir; seven, sir;
Six, sir; five, sir;
Four, sir; three, sir;
Two, sir; one!

Tenser, said the Tensor.
Tenser, said the Tensor.
Tension, apprehension,
And dissension have begun.

"Oh my God!" Reich exclaimed.

"I've got some real gone tricks in that tune," Duffy said, still playing. "Notice the beat after 'one'? That's a semicadence. Then you get another beat after 'begun.' That turns the end of the song into a semicadence, too, so you can't ever end it. The beat keeps you running in circles, like: Tension, apprehension, and dissension have begun. RIFF. Tension, apprehension, and dissension have begun. RIFF. Tension, appre–"

"You little devil!" Reich started to his feet, pounding his palms on his ears. "I'm accursed. How long is this affliction going to last?"

"Not more than a month."

"Tension, apprehension, and diss–I'm ruined. Isn't there any way out?"

"Sure," Duffy said. "It's easy. Just ruin me." She pressed herself against him and planted an earnest young kiss. "Lout," she murmured. "Pig. Boob. Dolt. When are you going to drag me through the gutter? Clever-up, dog. Why aren't you as smart as I think you are?"

"I'm smarter," he said and left.

As Reich had planned, the song established itself firmly in his mind and echoed again and again all the way down to the street. *Tenser, said the Tensor. Tenser, said the Tensor. Tension, apprehension, and dissension have begun. RIFF.* A perfect mind-block for a non-Esper. What peeper could get past that? *Tension, apprehension, and dissension have begun.*

"Much smarter," murmured Reich, and flagged a Jumper to Jerry Church's pawnshop on the Upper West Side.

Tension, apprehension, and dissension have begun.

Despite all rival claims, pawnbroking is still the oldest profession. The business of lending money on portable security is the most ancient of human occupations. It extends from the depths of the past to the uttermost reaches of the future, as unchanging as the pawnbroker's shop itself. You walked into Jerry Church's cellar store, crammed and littered with the debris of time, and you were in a museum of eternity. And even Church himself, wizened, peering, his face blackened and bruised by the internal blows of suffering, embodied the ageless moneylender.

Church shuffled out of the shadows and came face to face with Reich, standing starkly illuminated in a patch of sunlight slanting across the counter. He did not start. He did not acknowledge Reich's identity. Brushing past the man who for ten years had been his mortal enemy, he placed himself behind the counter and said: "Yes, please?"

"Hello, Jerry."

Without looking up, Church extended his hand across the counter. Reich attempted to clasp it. It was snatched away.

"No," Church said with a snarl that was half hysterical laugh. "Not that, thank you. Just give me what you want to pawn."

It was the peeper's sour little trap, and he had tumbled into it. No matter.

"I haven't anything to pawn, Jerry."

"As poor as that? How the mighty have fallen. But we must expect it, eh? We all fall. We all fall." Church glanced sidelong at him, trying to peep him. Let him try. *Tension, apprehension, and dissension have begun.* Let him get through the crazy tune rattling in his head.

"All of us fall," Church said. "All of us."

"I expect so, Jerry. I haven't yet. I've been lucky."

"I wasn't lucky," the peeper leered. "I met you."

"Jerry," Reich said patiently. "I've never been your bad luck. It was your own luck that ruined you. Not–"

"You God damned bastard," Church said in a horribly soft voice. "You God damned eater of slok. May you rot before you die. Get out of here. I want nothing to do with you. Nothing! Understand?"

"Not even my money?" Reich withdrew ten gleaming sovereigns from his pocket and placed them on the counter. It was a subtle touch. Unlike the credit, the sovereign was the coin of the underworld. *Tension, apprehension, and dissension have begun* . . .

"Least of all your money. I want your heart cut open. I want your blood spilling on the ground. I want the maggots eating the eyes out of your living head . . . But I don't want your money."

"Then what do you want, Jerry?"

"I told you!" the peeper screamed. "I told you! You God damned lousy–"

"What do you want, Jerry?" Reich repeated coldly, keeping his eyes on the wizened man. *Tension, apprehension, and dissension have begun.* He could still control Church. It didn't matter that

Church had been a 2nd. Control wasn't a question of peeping. It was a question of personality. *Eight, sir; seven, sir; six, sir; five, sir . . .* He always had . . . He always would control Church.

"What do you want?" Church asked sullenly.

Reich snorted. "You're the peeper. You tell me."

"I don't know," Church muttered after a pause. "I can't read it. There's crazy music mixing everything up . . ."

"Then I'll have to tell you. I want a gun."

"A what?"

"G-u-n. Gun. Ancient weapon. It propels projectiles by explosion."

"I haven't anything like that."

"Yes, you do, Jerry. Keno Quizzard mentioned it to me some time ago. He saw it. Steel and collapsible. Very interesting."

"What do you want it for?"

"Read me, Jerry, and find out. I haven't anything to hide. It's all quite innocent."

Church screwed up his face, then quit in disgust. "Isn't worth the trouble," he mumbled and shuffled off into the shadows. There was a distant slamming of metal drawers. Church returned with a compact nodule of tarnished steel and placed it on the counter alongside the money. He pressed a stud and the lump of metal sprang open into steel knuckle rings, revolver and stiletto. It was a twentieth-century knife-pistol–the quintessence of murder.

"What do you want it for?" Church asked again.

"You're hoping it's something that can lead to blackmail, eh?" Reich smiled. "Sorry. It's a gift."

"A dangerous gift." The ostracized peeper gave him that sidelong glance of snarl and laugh. "Ruination for someone else, eh?"

"Not at all, Jerry. It's a gift for a friend of mine. Dr. Augustus Tate."

"Tate!" Church stared at him.

"Do you know him? He collects old things."

"I know him. I know him." Church began to chuckle asthmatically. "But I'm beginning to know him better. I'm beginning to feel sorry for him." He stopped laughing and shot a penetrating glance at Reich. "Of course. This will make a lovely gift for Gus. A perfect gift for Gus. Because it's loaded."

"Oh? Is it loaded?"

"Oh yes indeed. It's loaded. Five lovely cartridges." Church cackled again. "A gift for Gus." He touched a cam. A cylinder snapped out of the side of the gun displaying five chambers filled with brass cartridges. He looked from the cartridges to Reich. "Five serpent's teeth to give to Gus."

"I told you this was innocent," Reich said in a hard voice. "We'll have to pull those teeth."

Church stared at him in astonishment, then he trotted down the aisle and returned with two small tools. Quickly he wrenched each of the bullets from the cartridges. He slid the harmless cartridge cases back into the chambers, snapped the cylinder home and then placed the gun alongside the money.

"All safe," he said brightly. "Safe for dear little Gus." He looked at Reich expectantly. Reich extended both hands. With one he pushed the money toward Church. With the other he drew the gun toward himself. At that instant, Church changed again. The air of chirpy madness left him. He grasped Reich's wrists with iron claws and bent across the counter with blazing intensity.

"No, Ben," he said, using the name for the first time. "That isn't the price. You know it. Despite that crazy song in your head, I know you know it."

"All right, Jerry," Reich said steadily, never relaxing his hold on the gun. "What is the price? How much?"

"I want to be reinstated," the peeper said. "I want to get back into the Guild. I want to be alive again. That's the price."

"What can I do? I'm not a peeper. I don't belong to the Guild."

"You're not helpless, Ben. You've got ways and means. You could get to the Guild. You could have me reinstated."

"Impossible."

"You can bribe, blackmail, intimidate . . . bless, dazzle, fascinate. You can do it, Ben. You can do it for me. Help me, Ben. I helped you, once."

"I paid through the nose for that help."

"And I? What did I pay?" the peeper screamed. "I paid with my life!"

"You paid with your stupidity."

"For God's sake, Ben. Help me. Help me or kill me. I'm dead already. I just haven't the guts to commit suicide."

After a pause, Reich said brutally: "I think the best thing for you, Jerry, would be suicide."

The peeper flung himself back as though he had been branded. In his bruised face his eyes stared glassily at Reich.

"Now tell me the price," Reich said.

Quite deliberately, Church spat on the money, then leveled a glance of burning hatred at Reich. "There will be no charge," he said, and turned and disappeared into the shadows of the cellar.

4

Until it was destroyed for reasons lost in the misty confusion of the late twentieth century, the Pennsylvania Station in New York City was, unknown to millions of travelers, a link in time. The interior of the giant terminal was a replica of the mighty Baths of Caracalla in ancient Rome. So also was the sprawling mansion of Madame Maria Beaumont, known to her thousand most intimate enemies as the Gilt Corpse.

As Ben Reich glided down the east ramp with Dr. Tate at his side and murder in his pocket, he communicated with his senses in staccato spurts. The sight of the guests on the floor below . . . The glitter of uniforms, of dress, of phosphorescent flesh, of beams of pastel light swaying on stilt legs . . . *Tenser, said the Tensor* . . .

The sound of voices, of music, of annunciators, of echoes . . . *Tension, apprehension, and dissension* . . . The wonderful potpourri of flesh and perfume, of food, of wine, of gilt ostentation . . . *Tension, apprehension* . . .

The gilt trappings of death . . . Of something, by God, which has failed for seventy years . . . A lost art . . . As lost as phlebotomy, chirurgery, alchemy . . . I'll bring death back. Not the hasty, crazy killing of the psychotic, the brawler . . . but the normal, deliberate, planned, cold-blooded–

"For God's sake!" Tate murmured. "Be careful, man. Your murder's showing."

Eight, sir; seven, sir . . .

"That's better. Here comes one of the peeper secretaries. He screens the guests for crashers. Keep singing."

A slender, willowy young man, all gush, all cropped golden hair, all violet blouse and silver culottes: "Dr. Tate! Mr. Reich! I'm speechless. Actually. I can't utter word one. Come in! Come in!"

Six, sir; five, sir . . .

Maria Beaumont clove through the crowd, arms outstretched, eyes outstretched, naked bosom outstretched . . . her body transformed by pneumatic surgery into an exaggerated East Indian figure with puffed hips, puffed calves and puffed gilt breasts. To Reich she was the painted figurehead of a pornographic ship—the famous Gilt Corpse.

"Ben, darling creature!" She embraced him with pneumatic intensity, contriving to press his hand into her cleavage. "It's too too wonderful."

"It's too too plastic, Maria," he murmured in her ear.

"Have you found that lost million yet?"

"Just laid hands on it now, dear."

"Be careful, audacious lover. I'm having every morsel of this divine party recorded."

Over her shoulder, Reich shot a glance at Tate. Tate shook his head reassuringly.

"Come and meet everybody who's everybody," Maria said. She took his arm. "We'll have ages for ourselves later."

The lights in the groined vaults overhead changed again and shifted up the spectrum. The costumes changed color. Skin that had glowed with pink nacre now shone with eerie luminescence.

On his left flank, Tate gave the prearranged signal: Danger! Danger! Danger!

Tension, apprehension, and dissension have begun. RIFF. Tension, apprehension, and dissension have begun . . .

Maria was introducing another effete, all gush, all cropped copper hair, all fuchsia blouse and Prussian blue culottes.

"Larry Ferar, Ben. My other social secretary. Larry's been dying to meet you."

Four, sir; three, sir . . .

"Mr. Reich! But too thrilled. I can't utter word one."

Two, sir; one!

The young man accepted Reich's smile and moved on. Still circling in convoy, Tate gave Reich a reassuring nod. Again the overhead lights changed. Portions of the guests' costumes appeared to dissolve. Reich, who had never succumbed to the fashion of wearing ultraviolet windows in his clothes, stood secure in his opaque suit, watching with contempt the quick roving eyes around him, searching, appraising, comparing, desiring.

Tate signaled: Danger! Danger! Danger!

Tenser, said the Tensor . . .

A secretary appeared at Maria's elbow. "Madame," he lisped, "a slight contretemps."

"What is it?"

"The Chervil boy. Galen Chervil."

Tate's face constricted.

"What about him?" Maria peeped through the crowd.

"Left of the fountain. An impostor, Madame. I have peeped him. He has no invitation. He's a college student. He bet he could crash the party. He intends to steal a picture of you as proof."

"Of me!" Maria said, staring through the windows in young Chervil's clothes. "What does he think of me?"

"Well, Madame, he's extremely difficult to probe. I think he'd like to steal more from you than your picture."

"Oh, would he?" Maria cackled delightedly.

"He would, Madame. Shall he be removed?"

"No." Maria glanced once more at the muscular young man, then turned away. "He'll get his proof."

"And it won't be stolen," Reich said.

"Jealous! Jealous!" she squawked. "Let's dine."

In response to Tate's urgent sign, Reich stepped aside momentarily.

"Reich, you've got to give it up."

"What the hell . . . ?"

"The Chervil boy."

"What about him?"

"He's a 2nd."

"God damn!"

"He's precocious, brilliant. . . . I met him at Powell's last Sunday. Maria Beaumont never invites peepers to her house. I'm only in on your pass. I was depending on that."

"And this peeper kid has to be the one to crash. God damn!"

"Give it up, Reich."

"Maybe I can stay away from him."

"Reich, I can block the social secretaries. They're only 3rds. But I can't guarantee to handle them and a 2nd too . . . even if he is only a kid. He's young. He may be too nervous to do any clever peeping. But I can't promise."

"I'm not quitting," Reich growled. "I can't. I'll never get a chance like this again. Even if I knew I could, I wouldn't quit. I couldn't. I've got the stink of D'Courtney in my nostrils. I–"

"Reich, you'll never–"

"Don't argue. I'm going through with it." Reich turned his scowl full on Tate's nervous face. "I know you're looking for a chance to squirm out of this; but you won't. We're trapped in this together, right down the line, from here to Demolition."

He shaped his distorted face into a frozen smile and rejoined his hostess on a couch alongside one of the tables. It was still the custom for couples to feed one another at these affairs but the gesture that had originated in Oriental courtesy and generosity had degenerated into erotic play. The morsels of food were accompanied by tongue touched to fingers and were as often offered between the lips. The wine was tasted mouth to mouth. Sweets were given more intimately.

Reich endured it all with a seething impatience, waiting for the vital word from Tate. Part of Tate's Intelligence work was to locate D'Courtney's hiding place in the house. He watched the little peeper drift through the crowd of diners, probing, prying, searching, until he at last returned with a negative shake of his head and gestured toward Maria Beaumont. Clearly Maria was the only source of information, but she was now too excited by sensuality to be easily probed. It was another in a never-ending series of crises that had to be met by the killer instinct. Reich arose and crossed toward the fountain. Tate intercepted him.

"What are you up to, Reich?"

"Isn't it obvious? I've got to get the Chervil boy off her mind."

"How?"

"Is there any way but one?"

"For God's sake, Reich, don't go near the boy."

"Get out of my way." Reich radiated a burst of savage compulsion that made the peeper recoil. He signaled in fright and Reich tried to control himself. "It's taking chances, I know, but the odds aren't as long as you think. In the first place he's young and green. In the second place he's a crasher and scared. In the third place, he can't be flying full jets or he wouldn't have let the fag secretaries peep him so easily."

"Have you got any conscious control? Can you double-think?"

"I've got that song on my mind and enough trouble to make doublethinking a pleasure. Now get the hell out of the way and stand by to peep Maria Beaumont."

Chervil was eating alone alongside the fountain, clumsily attempting to appear to belong.

"Pip," said Reich.

"Pop," said Chervil.

"Bim," said Reich.

"Bam," said Chervil.

With the latest fad in informality disposed of, Reich eased himself down alongside the boy. "I'm Ben Reich."

"I'm Gally Chervil. I mean . . . Galen. I—" He was visibly impressed by the name of Reich.

Tension, apprehension, and dissension . . .

"That damned song," Reich muttered. "Heard it for the first time the other day. Can't get it out of my mind. Maria knows you're a phony, Chervil."

"Oh no!"

Reich nodded. *Tension, apprehension . . .*

"Should I start running?"

"Without the picture?"

"You know about that too? There must be a peeper in the house."

"Two of them. Her social secretaries. People like you are their job."

"What about that picture, Mr. Reich? I've got fifty credits riding on the line. You ought to know what a bet means. You're a gamb— I mean, financier."

"Glad I'm not a peeper, eh? Never mind. I'm not insulted. See that arch? Go straight through and turn right. You'll find a study. The walls are lined with Maria's portraits, all in synthetic stones. Help yourself. She'll never miss one."

The boy leaped up, scattering food. "Thanks, Mr. Reich. Some day I'll do you a favor."

"Such as?"

"You'd be surprised. I happen to be a—" He caught himself and blushed. "You'll find out, sir. Thanks again." He began weaving his way across the floor toward the study.

Four, sir; three, sir; two, sir; one!

Reich returned to his hostess.

"Naughty lover," she said. "Who've you been feeding? I'll tear her eyes out."

"The Chervil boy," Reich answered. "He asked me where you keep your pictures."

"Ben! You didn't tell him!"

"Sure did," Reich grinned. "He's on his way to get one now. Then he'll take off. You know I'm jealous."

She leaped from the couch and sailed toward the study.

"Bam," said Reich.

By eleven o'clock, the ritual of dining had aroused the company to a point of intensity that required solitude and darkness for release. Maria Beaumont had never failed her guests, and Reich hoped she would not fail tonight. She had to play the Sardine game. He knew it when Tate returned from the study with concise directions for locating the hidden D'Courtney.

"I don't know how you got away with it," Tate whispered. "You're broadcasting bloodlust on every wavelength of the TP band. He's here. Alone. No servants. Only two bodyguards provided by Maria. @kins was right. He's dangerously sick . . ."

"To hell with that. I'll cure him. Where is he?"

"Go through the west arch. Turn right. Upstairs. Through overpass. Turn right. Picture Gallery. Door between paintings of the Rape of Lucrece and the Rape of the Sabine Women . . ."

"Sounds typical."

"Open the door. Up a flight of steps to an anteroom. Two guards in the anteroom. D'Courtney's inside. It's the old wedding suite her grandfather built."

"By God! I'll use that suite again. I'll marry him to murder. And I'll get away with it, little Gus. Don't think I won't."

The Gilt Corpse began to clamor for attention. Flushed and shining with perspiration, standing in the glare of a pink light on the dais between the two fountains, Maria clapped her hands for silence. Her moist palms beat together, and the echoes roared in Reich's ears: Death. Death. Death.

"Darlings! Darlings! Darlings!" she cried. "We're going to have so much fun tonight. We're going to provide our own entertainment." A subdued groan went up from the guests and a drunken voice shouted: "I'm just one of the tourists."

Through the laughter, Maria said: "Naughty lovers, don't be disappointed. We're going to play a wonderful old game; and we're going to play it in the dark."

The company cheered up as the overhead lights began to dim and disappear. The dais still blazed, and in the light, Maria produced a tattered volume. Reich's gift.

Tension . . .

Maria turned the pages slowly, blinking at the unaccustomed print.

Apprehension . . .

"It's a game," Maria cried, "called 'Sardine.' Isn't that too adorable?"

She took the bait. She's on the hook. In three minutes I'll be invisible. Reich felt his pockets. The gun. The rhodopsin. *Tension, apprehension, and dissension have begun.*

"One player," Maria read, "is selected to be It. That's going to be me. All the lights are extinguished and the It hides anywhere in the house." As Maria struggled through the directions, the great hall was reduced to pitch-darkness with the exception of the single pink beam on the stage.

"Successively each player finding the Sardine joins them until all are hidden in one place, and the last player, who is the loser, is left to wander alone in the dark." Maria closed the book. "And, darlings, we're all going to feel sorry for the loser because we're going to play this funny old game in a darling new way."

As the last light on the dais melted away, Maria stripped off her gown and displayed the astonishing nude body that was a miracle of pneumatic surgery.

"We're going to play Sardine like this!" she cried.

The last light blinked out. There was a roar of exultant laughter and applause, followed by a multiple whisper of cloth drawn across skin. Occasionally there came the sound of a rip, then muttered exclamations and more laughter.

Reich was invisible at last. He had half an hour to slip up into the house, find and kill D'Courtney, and then return to the game. Tate was committed to pinning the peeper secretaries out of the line of his attack. It was safe. It was foolproof except for the Chervil boy. He had to take that chance.

He crossed the main hall and jostled into bodies at the west arch. He went through the arch into the music room and turned right, groping for the stairs.

At the foot of the stairs he was forced to climb over a barrier of bodies with octopus arms that tried to pull him down. He ascended the stairs, seventeen eternal steps, and felt his way through a close tunnel overpass papered with velour. Suddenly he was seized and a woman crushed herself against him.

"Hello, Sardine," she whispered in his ear. Then her skin became aware of his clothes. "Owww!" she exclaimed, and felt the hard outlines of the gun in his breast pocket. "What's that?" He slapped her hand away. "Clever-up, Sardine," she giggled. "Get out of the can."

He divested himself of her and bruised his nose against the dead end of the overpass. He turned right, opened a door and found himself in a vaulted gallery over fifty feet long. The lights were extinguished here too, but the luminescent paintings, glowing under ultraviolet spotlights, filled the gallery with a virulent glow. It was empty.

Between a livid Lucrece and a horde of Sabine Women was a flush door of polished bronze. Reich stopped before it, removed the tiny

Rhodopsin Ionizer from his back pocket and attempted to poise the copper cube between his thumbnail and forefinger. His hands were trembling violently. Rage and hatred boiled inside him, and his death lust shot image after image of an agonized D'Courtney through his mind's eye.

"Christ!" he cried. "He'd do it to me. He's tearing at my throat. I'm fighting for survival." He made his orisons in fanatical multiples of three and nine. "Stand by me, dear Christ! Today, tomorrow, and yesterday. Stand by me! Stand by me! Stand by me!"

His fingers steadied. He poised the rhodopsin cap, then thrust open the bronze door, revealing nine steps mounting to an anteroom. Reich snapped his thumbnail against the copper cube as though he were trying to flip a penny to the moon. As the rhodopsin cap flew up into the anteroom, Reich averted his eyes. There was a cold purple flash. Reich leaped up the stairs like a tiger. The two Beaumont House guards were seated on the bench where he had caught them. Their faces were sagging, their vision destroyed, their time sense abolished.

If anyone entered and found the guards before he was finished, he was on the road to Demolition. If the guards revived before he was finished, he was on the road to Demolition. No matter what happened, it was a final gamble with Demolition. Leaving the last of his sanity behind him, Reich pushed open a jeweled door and entered the wedding suite.

5

Reich found himself in a spherical room designed as the heart of a giant orchid. The walls were curling orchid petals, the floor was a golden calyx; the chairs, tables and couches were orchid and gold. But the room was old. The petals were faded and peeling; the golden tile floor was ancient and the tessellations were splitting. There was an old man lying on the couch, musty and wilted, like a dried weed. It was D'Courtney, stretched out like a corpse.

Reich slammed the door in rage. "You're not dead already, you bastard," he exploded. "You can't be dead."

The faded man started up, stared, then arose painfully from the couch, his face breaking into a smile.

"Still alive," Reich cried exultantly.

D'Courtney stepped toward Reich, smiling, his arms outstretched as though welcoming a prodigal son. Alarmed again, Reich growled: "Are you deaf?"

The old man shook his head.

"You speak English," Reich shouted. "You can hear me. You can understand me. I'm Reich. Ben Reich of Monarch."

D'Courtney nodded, still smiling. His mouth worked soundlessly. His eyes glistened with sudden tears.

"What the hell is the matter with you? I'm Ben Reich. Ben Reich! Do you know me? Answer me."

D'Courtney shook his head and tapped his throat. His mouth worked again. Rusty sounds came; then words as faint as dust: "Ben . . . Dear Ben . . . Waited so long. Now . . . Can't talk. My throat . . . Can't talk." Again he attempted to embrace Reich.

"Arrgh! Keep off, you crazy idiot." Bristling, Reich stepped around D'Courtney like an animal, his hackles raised, the murder boiling in his blood.

D'Courtney's mouth formed the words: "Dear Ben . . ."

"You know why I'm here. What are you trying to do? Make love to me?" Reich laughed. "You crafty old pimp. Am I supposed to turn soft for your chewing?" His hand lashed out. The old man reeled back from the slap and fell into an orchid chair that looked like a wound.

"Listen to me–" Reich followed D'Courtney and stood over him. He began to shout incoherently. "This payoff's been on the fire for years. And you want to rob me with a Judas kiss. Does murder turn the other cheek? If it does, embrace me, brother killer. Kiss death! Teach death love. Teach Godliness and shame and blood and–No. Wait. I–" He stopped short and shook his head like a bull trying to cast off a halter of delirium.

"Ben," D'Courtney whispered in horror. "Listen, Ben . . ."

"You've been at my throat for ten years. There was room enough for both of us. Monarch and D'Courtney. All the room in time and space, but you wanted my blood, eh? My heart. My guts in your lousy hands. The Man With No Face!"

D'Courtney shook his head in bewilderment. "No, Ben. No . . ."

"Don't call me Ben. I'm no friend of yours. Last week I gave you one more chance to wash in decency. Me. Ben Reich. I asked for armistice. Begged for peace. Merger. I begged like a screaming woman. My father would spit on me if he were alive. Every fighting Reich would blacken my face with contempt. But I asked for peace, didn't I? Eh? Didn't I?" Reich prodded D'Courtney savagely. "Answer me."

D'Courtney's face was blanched and staring. Finally he whispered: "Yes. You asked . . . I accepted."

"You what?"

"Accepted. Waiting for years. Accepted."

"Accepted!"

D'Courtney nodded. His lips formed the letters: "WWHG."

"What? WWHG? Acceptance?"

The old man nodded again.

Reich shrieked with laughter. "You clumsy old liar. That's refusal. Denial. Rejection. War."

"No, Ben. No . . ."

Reich reached down and yanked D'Courtney to his feet. The old man was frail and light, but his weight bruised Reich's arm, and the touch of the old skin burned Reich's fingers.

"So it's to be war, is it? Death?"

D'Courtney shook his head and tried to make signs.

"No merger. No peace. Death. That's the choice, eh?"

"Ben . . . No."

"Will you surrender?"

"Yes," D'Courtney whispered. "Yes, Ben. Yes."

"Liar. Clumsy old liar." Reich laughed. "But you're dangerous. I can see it. Protective mimicry. That's your trick. You imitate the idiots and trap us at your leisure. But not me. Never."

"I'm not . . . your enemy, Ben."

"No," Reich spat. "You're not because you're dead. You've been dead ever since I came into this orchid coffin. Man With No Face! Can you hear me screaming for the last time? You're finished forever!"

Reich tore the gun out of his breast pocket. He touched the stud and it opened like a red steel flower. A faint groan escaped from D'Courtney when he saw the weapon. He backed away in horror. Reich caught him and held him fast. D'Courtney twisted in Reich's grasp, his face pleading, his eyes glazed and rheumy. Reich transferred his grasp to the back of D'Courtney's thin neck and wrenched the head toward him. He had to fire through the open mouth for the trick to work.

At that instant, one of the orchid petals swung open, and a half-dressed girl burst into the room. In a blaze of surprise, Reich saw the corridor behind her, a bedroom door standing open at the far end; the girl, nude under a frost silk gown hastily thrown on, yellow hair flying, dark eyes wide in alarm . . . A lightning flash of wild beauty.

"Father!" she screamed. "For God's sake! Father!"

She ran toward D'Courtney. Reich swung quickly between them, never relaxing his hold on the old man. The girl stopped short, backed away, then darted to the left around Reich, screaming. Reich pivoted and cut viciously at her with the stiletto. She eluded him but was driven back on the couch. Reich thrust the point of the stiletto between the old man's teeth and forced his jaws open.

"No!" she cried. "No! For the love of Christ! Father!"

She stumbled around the couch and ran toward her father again. Reich thrust the gun muzzle into D'Courtney's mouth and pulled the trigger. There was a muffled explosion and a gout of blood spurted from the back of D'Courtney's head. Reich let the body drop and leaped for the girl. He caught her while she fought and screamed.

Reich and the girl were screaming together. Reich shook with galvanic spasms that forced him to release the girl. The girl fell forward to her knees and crawled to the body. She moaned in pain as she snatched the gun from the mouth where it still hung. Then she crouched over the twitching body, silent, fixed, staring into the waxen face.

Reich gasped for breath and beat his knuckles together painfully. When the roaring in his ears subsided, he propelled himself toward the girl, trying to arrange his thoughts and make split-second alterations in his plans. He had never counted on a witness. No one mentioned a daughter. God damn Tate! He would have to kill the girl. He—

She turned and shot a terror-stricken glance over her shoulder. Again that lightning flash of yellow hair, dark eyes, dark brows, wild beauty. She leaped to her feet, darted out of his sodden grasp, ran to the jeweled door, flung it open and ran into the anteroom. As the door slowly closed, Reich had a glimpse of the guards still slumped on the bench and the girl running silently down the stairs with the gun in her hands . . . with Demolition in her hands.

Reich started. The clogged blood began pounding through his veins again. He reached the door in three strides, ran through and tore down the steps to the picture gallery. It was empty but the door to the overpass was just closing. And still no sound from her. Still no alarm. How long before she started screaming the house down?

He raced down the gallery and entered the overpass. It was still pitch-dark. He blundered through, reached the head of the stairs that led down to the music room and paused again. Still no sound. No alarm.

He went down the steps. The dark silence was terrifying. Why didn't she scream? Where was she? Reich crossed toward the west arch and knew he was at the edge of the main hall by the quiet splash of the fountains. Where was the girl? In all that black silence, where was she? And the gun! Christ! The tricked gun!

A hand touched his arm. Reich jerked in alarm. Tate whispered: "I've been standing by. It took you exactly—"

"You son of a bitch!" Reich burst out. "There was a daughter. Why didn't you—"

"Be quiet," Tate snapped. "Let me peep it." After fifteen seconds of burning silence, he began to tremble. In a terrified voice he whined: "My God. Oh, my God . . ."

His terror was the catalyst. Reich's control returned. He began thinking again. "Shut up," he growled. "It isn't Demolition yet."

"You'll have to kill her too, Reich. You'll—"

"Shut up. Find her, first. Cover the house. You got her pattern from me. Locate her. I'll be waiting at the fountain. Jet!"

He flung Tate from him and staggered to the fountain. At the jasper rim he bent and bathed his burning face. It was burgundy. Reich wiped his face and ignored the muffled sounds that came from the other side of the basin. Evidently some other person or persons unknown were bathing in wine.

He considered swiftly. The girl must be located and killed. If she still had the gun when Tate found her, the gun would be used. If she didn't? What? Strangle her? No . . . The fountain. She was naked under that silk gown. It could be stripped off. She could be found drowned in the fountain . . . just another guest who had bathed in wine too long. But it had to be soon . . . soon . . . soon . . . Before this damned Sardine game was ended. Where was Tate? Where was the girl?

Tate came blundering up through the darkness, his breath wheezing.

"Well?"

"She's gone."

"You weren't gone long enough to find a louse. If this is a double-cross—"

"Who could I cross? I'm on the same road you are. I tell you her pattern's nowhere in the house. She's gone."

"Anyone notice her leave?"

"No."

"Christ! Out of the house!"

"We'd better leave too."

"Yes, but we can't run. Once we get out of here, we'll have the rest of the night to find her, but we've got to leave as though nothing's happened. Where's the Gilt Corpse?"

"In the projection room."

"Watching a show?"

"No. Still playing Sardine. They're packed in there like fish in a can. We're almost the last out here in the house."

"Wandering alone in the dark, eh? Come on."

He gripped Tate's shaking elbow and marched him toward the projection room. As he walked he called plaintively: "Hey . . . Where is everybody? Maria! Ma-ri-aaa! Where's everybody?"

Tate emitted a hysterical sob. Reich shook him roughly. "Play up! We'll be out of here in five minutes. Then you can start worrying."

"But if we're trapped in here, we won't be able to get the girl. We'll—"

"We won't be trapped. ABC, Gus. Audacious, brave, and confident." Reich pushed open the door of the projection room. There was darkness in here, too, but the heat of many bodies. "Hey," he called. "Where is everybody? I'm all alone."

No answer.

"Maria. I'm all alone in the dark."

A muffled sputter, then a burst of laughter.

"Darling, darling, darling!" Maria called. "You've missed all the fun, poor dear."

"Where are you, Maria? I've come to say good night."

"Oh, you can't be leaving."

"Sorry, dear. It's late. I've got to swindle a friend tomorrow. Where are you, Maria?"

"Come up on the stage, darling."

Reich walked down the aisle, felt for the steps and mounted the stage. He felt the cool perimeter of the projection globe behind him. A voice called: "All right. Now we've got him. Lights!"

White light flooded the globe and blinded Reich. The guests seated in the chairs around the stage started to whoop with laughter, then howled in disappointment.

"Oh, Ben, you cheat," Maria screeched. "You're still dressed. That isn't fair. We've been catching everybody divinely *flagrante*."

"Some other time, Maria dear." Reich extended his hand before him and began the graceful bow of farewell. "Respectfully, Madame, I give you my thanks for—" He broke off in amazement. On the gleaming white lace of his cuff an angry red spot appeared.

In stunned silence, Reich saw a second, then a third red splotch appear on the lace. He snatched his hand back and a red drop spattered on the stage before him, to be followed by a slow, inexorable stream of gleaming crimson droplets.

"That's blood!" Maria screamed. "That's blood! There's someone upstairs bleeding. For God's sake, Ben . . . You can't leave me now. Lights! Lights! Lights!"

6

At 12:30 A.M., the Emergency Patrol arrived at Beaumont House in response to precinct notification: "GZ. Beaumont. YLP-R," which, translated, meant: "An Act or Omission forbidden by law has been reported at Beaumont House, 9 Park South."

At 12:40, the Park precinct captain arrived in response to Patrol report: "Criminal Act, possible Felony-AAA."

At 1:00 A.M., Lincoln Powell arrived at Beaumont House in response to a frantic call from a deputy inspector: "I tell you, Powell, it's Felony Triple-A. I'll swear it is. The wind's been knocked out of me. I don't know whether to be grateful or scared; but I know none of us is equipped to handle it."

"What can't you handle?"

"Look here, Powell. Murder's abnormal. Only a distorted TP pattern can produce death by violence. Right?"

"Yes."

"Which is why there hasn't been a successful Triple-A in over seventy years. A man can't walk around with a distorted pattern, maturing murder, and go unnoticed these days. He'd have as much chance of going unnoticed as a man with three heads. You peepers always pick 'em up before they go into action."

"We try to . . . when we contact them."

"And there are too many peeper screens to pass in normal living these days for you to be avoided. A man would have to be a hermit to do that. How can a hermit kill?"

"How indeed?"

"Now here's a killing that must have been carefully planned . . .

and the killer was never noticed. Never reported. Even by Maria Beaumont's peeper secretaries. That means there couldn't have been anything to notice. He must have a passable pattern and yet be abnormal enough to murder. How the hell can we resolve a paradox like that?"

"I see. Any prospects?"

"We've got a payload of inconsistencies to iron out. One, we don't know what killed D'Courtney. Two, his daughter's disappeared. Three, somebody robbed D'Courtney's guards of one hour and we can't figure how. Four–"

"Don't count any higher. I'll be right over."

The great hall of Beaumont House blazed with harsh white light. Uniformed police were everywhere. The white-smocked technicians from Lab were scurrying like beetles. In the center of the hall, the party guests (dressed) were assembled in a rough corral, milling like a herd of terrified steers at a slaughterhouse.

As Powell came down the east ramp, tall and slender, black and white, he felt the wave of hostility that greeted him. He reached out quickly to Jackson Beck, police Inspector 2: *"What's the situation, Jax?"*

"Scramble."

Switching to their informal police code of scrambled images, reversed meanings and personal symbols, Beck continued: *"Peepers here. Play it safe."* In a microsecond he brought Powell up to date.

"I see. Nasty. What's everybody doing lumped out on the floor? You staging something?"

"The villain-friend act."

"Necessary?"

"It's a rotten crowd. Pampered. Corrupt. They'll never cooperate. You'll have to do some tricky coaxing to get anything out of them; and this case is going to need it. I'll be the villain. You be their friend."

"Right. Good work. Start recording."

Halfway down the ramp, Powell halted. The humor departed from his mouth. The friendliness disappeared from his deep dark eyes. An expression of shocked indignation appeared on his face.

"Beck," he snapped. His voice cracked through the echoing hall. There was dead silence. Every eye turned in his direction.

Inspector Beck faced Powell. In a brutal voice, he said: "Here, sir."

"Are you in charge, Beck?"

"I am, sir."

"And is this your concept of the proper conduct of an investigation? To herd a group of innocent people together like cattle?"

"They're not innocent," Beck growled. "A man's been killed."

"All in this house are innocent, Beck. They will be presumed to be innocent and treated with every courtesy until the truth is uncovered."

"What?" Beck sneered. "This gang of liars? Treated with courtesy? This rotten, lousy, high-society pack of hyenas . . ."

"How dare you! Apologize at once."

Beck took a deep breath and clenched his fists angrily.

"Inspector Beck, did you hear me? Apologize to these ladies and gentlemen at once."

Beck glared at Powell, then turned to the staring guests. "My apologies," he mumbled.

"And I'm warning you, Beck," Powell snapped. "If anything like this happens again, I'll break you. I'll send you straight back to the gutter you came from. Now get out of my sight."

Powell descended to the floor of the hall and smiled at the guests. Suddenly he was again transformed. His bearing conveyed the subtle suggestion that he was at heart one of them. There was even a tinge of fashionable corruption in his diction.

"Ladies and gentlemen: Of course I know you all by sight. I'm not that famous, so let me introduce myself. Lincoln Powell, Prefect of the Psychotic Division. Prefect and Psychotic. Two antiquated titles, eh? We won't let them bother us." He advanced toward Maria Beaumont with hand outstretched. "Dear Madame Maria, what an exciting climax for your wonderful party. I envy all of you. You'll make history."

A pleased rustle ran through the guests. The lowering hostility began to fade. Maria took Powell's hand dazedly, mechanically beginning to preen herself.

"Madame . . ." He confused and delighted her by kissing her brow with paternal warmth. "You've had a trying time, I know. These boors in uniform."

"Dear Prefect . . ." She was a little girl, clinging to his arm. "I've been so terrified."

"Is there a quiet room where we can all be comfortable and endure this exasperating experience?"

"Yes. The study, dear Prefect Powell." She was actually beginning to lisp.

Powell snapped his fingers behind him. To the captain who

stepped forward, he said: "Conduct Madame and her guests to the study. No guards. The ladies and gentlemen are to be left in privacy."

"Mr. Powell, sir . . ." The captain cleared his throat. "About Madame's guests. One of them arrived after the felony was reported. An attorney, Mr. ¼maine."

Powell found Jo ¼maine, Attorney-at-Law 2, in the crowd. He shot him a telepathic greeting.

"Jo?"

"Hi."

"What brings you to this Blind Tiger?"

"Business. Called by my cli(Ben Reich)ent."

"That shark? Makes me suspicious. Wait here with Reich. We'll get squared off."

"That was an effective act with Beck."

"Hell. You cracked our scramble?"

"Not a chance. But I know you two. Gentle Jax playing a thick cop is one for the books."

Beck broke in from across the hall where he was apparently sulking: *"Don't give it away, Jo."*

"Are you crazy?" It was as though ¼maine had been requested not to smash every sacred ethic of the Guild. He radiated a blast of indignation that made Beck grin.

All this during the second in which Powell again kissed Maria's brow with chaste devotion and gently disengaged himself from her tremulous grasp.

"Ladies and gentlemen: we'll meet again in the study."

The crowd of guests moved off, conducted by the captain. They were chattering with renewed animation. It was all beginning to take on the aspect of a fabulous new form of entertainment. Through the buzz and the laughter, Powell felt the iron elbows of a rigid telepathic block. He recognized those elbows and permitted his astonishment to show.

"Gus! Gus Tate!"

"Oh. Hello, Powell."

"You? Lurking & Slinking?"

"Gus?" Beck popped out. *"Here? I never tagged him."*

"What the devil are you hiding for?"

Chaotic response of anger, chagrin, fear of lost reputation, self-deprecation, shame—

"Sign off, Gus. Your pattern's trapped in a feedback. Won't do

you any harm to let a little scandal rub off on you. Make you more human. Stay here & help. Got a hunch I can use another 1st. This one is going to be a Triple-A stinker."

After the hall cleared, Powell examined the three men who remained with him. Jo ¼maine was a heavy-set man, thick, solid, with a shining bald head and a friendly blunt-featured face. Little Tate was nervous and twitchy—more so than usual.

And the notorious Ben Reich. Powell was meeting him for the first time. Tall, broad-shouldered, determined, exuding a tremendous aura of charm and power. There was kindliness in that power, but it was corroded by the habit of tyranny. Reich's eyes were fine and keen, but his mouth seemed too small and sensitive and looked oddly like a scar. A magnetic man, with something vague inside him that was repellent.

He smiled at Reich. Reich smiled back. Spontaneously, they shook hands.

"Do you take everybody off guard like this, Reich?"

"The secret of my success," Reich grinned. He understood Powell's meaning. They were *en rapport.*

"Well, don't let the other guests see you charm me. They'll suspect collusion."

"Not you, they won't. You'll swindle them, Powell. You'll make 'em all feel they're in collusion with you."

They smiled again. An unexpected chemotropism was drawing them together. It was dangerous. Powell tried to shake it off. He turned to ¼maine: "Now then, Jo?"

"About the peeping, Linc . . ."

"Keep it up on Reich's level," Powell interrupted. "We're not going to pull any fast ones."

"Reich called me in to represent him. No TP, Linc. This has got to stay on the objective level. I'm here to see that it does. I'll have to be present at every examination."

"You can't stop peeping, Jo. You've got no legal right. We can dig out all we can—"

"Provided it's with the consent of the examinee. I'm here to tell you whether you've got that consent or not."

Powell looked at Reich. "What happened?"

"Don't you know?"

"I'd like your version."

Jo ¼maine snapped: "Why Reich's in particular?"

"I'd like to know why he hollered so quick for a lawyer. Is he mixed up in this mess?"

"I'm mixed up in plenty," Reich grinned. "You don't run Monarch without building a stockpile of secrets that have got to be protected."

"But murder isn't one of them?"

"Get out of there, Linc!"

"Stop throwing blocks, Jo. I'm just peeping around a little because I like the guy."

"Well, like him on your own time . . . not mine."

"Jo doesn't want me to love you," Powell smiled to Reich. "I wish you hadn't called a lawyer. It makes me suspicious."

"Isn't that an occupational disease?" Reich laughed.

"No." Dishonest Abe took over and answered smoothly. "You'd never believe it, but the occupational disease of detectives is Laterality. That's right-handedness or left-handedness. Most detectives suffer from strange changes of Laterality. I was naturally left-handed until the Parsons Case when I–"

Abruptly, Powell choked off his lie. He took two steps away from his fascinated audience and sighed deeply. When he turned back to them, Dishonest Abe was gone.

"I'll tell you about that another time," he said. "Tell me what happened after Maria and the guests saw the blood dripping down on your cuff."

Reich glanced at the bloodstains on his cuff. "She yelled bloody murder and we all went tearing upstairs to the Orchid Suite."

"How could you find your way in the dark?"

"It was light. Maria yelled for lights."

"You didn't have any trouble locating the suite with the light on, eh?"

Reich smiled grimly. "I didn't locate the suite. It was secret. Maria had to lead the way."

"There were guards there–knocked out or something?"

"That's right. They looked dead."

"Like stone, eh? They hadn't moved a muscle?"

"How would I know?"

"How indeed?" Powell looked hard at Reich. "What about D'Courtney?"

"He looked dead too. Hell, he was dead."

"And everybody was standing around staring?"

"Some were in the rest of the suite, looking for the daughter."

"That's Barbara D'Courtney. I thought nobody knew D'Courtney and his daughter were in the house. Why look for her?"

"We didn't know. Maria told us and we looked."

"Surprised to find her gone?"

"We were beyond surprise."

"Any idea where she went?"

"Maria said she'd killed the old man and rocketed."

"Would you buy that?"

"I don't know. The whole thing was crazy. If the girl was lunatic enough to sneak out of the house without a word and go running naked through the streets, she may have had her father's scalp in her hand."

"Would you permit me to peep you on all this for background and detail?"

"I'm in the hands of my lawyer."

"The answer is no," ¼maine said. "A man's got the constitutional right to refuse Esper Examination without prejudice to himself. Reich is refusing."

"And I'm in one hell of a mess," Powell sighed and shrugged. "Well, let's start the investigation."

They turned and walked toward the study. Across the hall, Beck scrambled into police code and asked: *"Linc, why'd you let Reich make a monkey out of you?"*

"Did he?"

"Sure he did. That shark can stiff you any time."

"Well, you better get your knife ready, Jax. This shark is ripe for Demolition."

"What?"

"Didn't you hear the slip when he was busy stiffing me? Reich didn't know there was a daughter. Nobody did. He didn't see her. Nobody did. He could infer that the murder made her run out of the house. Anybody could. But how did he know she was naked?"

There was a moment of stunned silence, and then, as Powell went through the north arch into the study, a broadcast of fervent admiration followed him: *"I bow, Linc. I bow to the Master."*

The "study" of Beaumont House was constructed on the lines of a Turkish bath. The floor was a mosaic of jacinth, spinel and sunstone. The walls, cross-hatched with gold wire cloisons, were glittering with inset synthetic stones—ruby, emerald, garnet, chrysolite, amethyst, topaz—all containing various portraits of the owner. There were scatter rugs of velvet, and scores of chairs and lounges.

Powell entered the room and walked directly to the center, leaving Reich, Tate, and ¼maine behind him. The buzz of conversation stopped, and Maria Beaumont struggled to her feet. Powell motioned her to remain seated. He looked around him, accurately gauging the mass psyche of the assembled sybarites and measuring the tactics he would have to use. At length he began.

"The law," he remarked, "makes the silliest damned fuss about death. People die by the thousands every day; but simply because someone has had the energy and enterprise to assist old D'Courtney to his demise, the law insists upon turning him into an enemy of the people. I think it's idiotic, but please don't quote me."

He paused and lit a cigarette. "You all know, of course, that I'm a peeper. Probably this fact has alarmed some of you. You imagine that I'm standing here like some mind-peeping monster, probing your mental plumbing. Well . . . Jo ¼maine wouldn't let me if I could. And frankly, if I could, I wouldn't be standing here. I'd be standing on the throne of the universe practically indistinguishable from God. I notice that none of you have commented on that resemblance so far."

There was a ripple of laughter. Powell smiled disarmingly and continued: "No, mass mind-reading is a trick no peeper can perform. It's difficult enough to probe a single individual. It's impossible when dozens of TP patterns are confusing the picture. And when a group of unique, highly individual people like yourselves is gathered, we find ourselves completely at your mercy."

"And he said *I* had charm," Reich muttered.

"Tonight," Powell went on, "you were playing a game called 'Sardine.' I wish I had been invited, Madame. You must remember me next time . . ."

"I will," Maria called. "I will, dear Prefect."

"In the course of that game, old D'Courtney was killed. We're almost positive it was premeditated murder. We'll be certain after Lab has finished its work. But let's assume that it is a Triple-A Felony. That will enable us to play another game—a game called 'Murder.'"

There was an uncertain response from the guests. Powell continued on the same casual course, carefully turning the most shocking crime in seventy years into a morsel of unreality.

"In the game of 'Murder,'" he said, "a make-believe victim is killed. A make-believe detective must discover who killed the victim. He asks questions of the make-believe suspects. Everyone must tell the truth, except the killer, who is permitted to lie. The detective compares stories, deduces who is lying, and uncovers the killer. I thought you might enjoy playing this game."

A voice asked: "How?"

Another called: "I'm just one of the tourists."

More laughter.

"A murder investigation," Powell smiled, "explores three facets of a crime. First, the motive. Second, the method. Third, the opportunity. Our Lab people are taking care of the second two. The first we can discover in our game. And if we do, we'll be able to crack the second two problems that have Lab stumped now. Did you know that they can't figure out what killed D'Courtney? Did you know that D'Courtney's daughter has disappeared? She left the house while you were playing 'Sardine.' Did you know that D'Courtney's guards were mysteriously short-circuited? Yes, indeed. Somebody robbed them of a full hour in time. We'd all like to know just how."

They were hanging at the very edge of the trap, breathless, fascinated. It had to be sprung with infinite caution.

"Death, disappearance, and time-theft—we can find out all about them through motive. I'll be the make-believe detective. You'll be the make-believe suspects. You'll tell me the truth . . . all except the killer, of course. We'll expect him to lie. But we'll trap him and bring this party to a triumphant finish if you'll give me permission to make a telepathic examination of each of you."

"Oh!" cried Maria in alarm.

"Wait, Madame. Understand me. All I want is your permission. I won't have to peep. Because, you see, if all the innocent suspects grant permission, then the one who refuses must be the guilty. He alone will be forced to protect himself from peeping."

"Can he pull that?" Reich whispered to ¼maine.

¼maine nodded.

"Just picture the scene for a moment." Powell was building the drama for them, turning the room into a stage. "I ask formally: 'Will you permit me to make a TP examination?' Then I go around this room." He began a slow circuit, bowing to each of the guests in turn. "And the answers come . . . 'Yes . . . Yes . . . Of course . . . Why not? . . . Certainly . . . Yes . . . Yes . . .' And then suddenly a dramatic pause." Powell stopped before Reich, erect, terrifying. "'You, sir,' I repeat. 'Will you give me your permission to peep?'"

They all watched, hypnotized. Even Reich was aghast, transfixed by the pointing finger and the fierce scowl.

"Hesitation. His face flushes red, then ghastly white as the blood drains out. You hear the tortured refusal: 'No!' . . ." The Prefect turned and enveloped them all with an electrifying gesture: "And in that thrilling moment, we know we have captured the killer!"

He almost had them. Almost. It was daring, novel, exciting; a sudden display of ultraviolet windows through clothes and flesh into the soul. But Maria's guests had bastardy in their souls . . . perjury . . . adultery–the Devil. And the shame within all of them rose up in terror.

"No!" Maria cried. They all shot to their feet and shouted, "No! No! No!"

"It was a beautiful try, Linc, but there's your answer. You'll never get motive out of these hyenas."

Powell was still charming in defeat. "I'm sorry, ladies and gentlemen, but I really can't blame you. Only a fool would trust a cop." He sighed. "One of my assistants will tape the oral statements from those of you who care to make statements. Mr. ¼maine will be on hand to advise and protect you."

He glanced dolefully at ¼maine. *"And louse me."*

"Don't pull at my heart-strings like that, Linc. This is the first Triple-A Felony in over seventy years. I've got my career to watch. This can make me."

"I've got my own career to watch, Jo. If my department doesn't crack this, it can break me."

"Then it's every peeper for himself. Here's thinking at you, Linc."

"Hell," Powell said. He winked at Reich and sauntered out of the room.

Lab was finished in the orchid Wedding Suite. De Santis, abrupt, testy, harassed, handed Powell the reports and said in an overwrought voice: "This is a bitch!"

Powell looked down at D'Courtney's body. "Suicide?" he snapped. He was always peppery with De Santis, who was comfortable in no other relationship.

"Tcha! Not a chance. No weapon."

"What killed him?"

"We don't know."

"You still don't know? You've had three hours!"

"We don't know," De Santis raged. "That's why it's a bitch."

"Why, he's got a hole in his head you could jet through."

"Yes, yes, yes, of course. Entry above the uvula. Exit below the fontanelle. Death instantaneous. But what produced the wound? What drilled the hole through his skull? Go ahead, ask me."

"Hard ray?"

"No burn."

"Crystallization?"

"No freeze."

"Nitro vapor charge?"

"No ammonia residue."

"Acid?"

"Too much shattering. Acid spray might needle a wound like that, but it couldn't burst the back of his skull."

"Thrusting weapon?"

"You mean a dirk or a knife?"

"Something like that."

"Impossible. Have you any idea how much force is necessary to penetrate like this? Couldn't be done."

"Well . . . I've just about exhausted penetrating weapons. No, wait. What about a projectile?"

"How's that?"

"Ancient weapon. They used to shoot bullets with explosives. Noisy and smelly."

"Not a chance here."

"Why?"

"Why?" De Santis spat. "Because there's no projectile. None in the wound. None in the room. Nothing nowhere."

"Damnation!"

"I agree."

"Have you got anything for me? Anything at all?"

"Yes. He was eating candy before his death. Found a fragment of gel in his mouth–bit of standard candy wrapping."

"And?"

"No candy in the suite."

"He might have eaten it all."

"No candy in his stomach. Anyway, he wouldn't be eating candy, with his throat."

"Why not?"

"Psychogenic cancer. Bad. He couldn't talk, let alone eat gook."

"Hell and damnation. We need that weapon . . . whatever it is."

Powell fingered the sheaf of field reports, staring at the waxen body, whistling a crooked tune. He remembered hearing an audio-book once about an Esper who could read a corpse . . . like that old myth about photographing the retina of a dead eye. He wished it could be done.

"Well," he sighed at last. "They licked us on motive, and they've licked us on method. Let's hope we can get something on opportunity, or we'll never bring Reich down."

"What Reich? Ben Reich? What about him?"

"It's Gus Tate I'm worried about most," Powell murmured. "If he's mixed up in this . . . What? Oh, Reich? He's the killer, De Santis. I slicked Jo ¼maine down in Maria Beaumont's study. Reich made a slip. I staged an act and misdirected Jo while I peeped to make sure. This is off the record, of course, but I got enough to convince me Reich's our man."

"Holy Christ!" De Santis exclaimed.

"But that's a long way from convincing a court. We're a long way from Demolition, brother. A long, long way."

Moodily, Powell took leave of the Lab Chief, loafed through the anteroom and descended to field headquarters in the picture gallery.

"And I like the guy," he muttered.

In the picture gallery outside the Orchid Suite where temporary headquarters had been set up, Powell and Beck met for a conference. Their mental exchange took exactly thirty seconds in the lightning tempo typical of telepathic talk:

Well, it's Reich for Demolition, Jax. We tripped him up in that talk, and I sneaked a peep in Maria's study just to make sure. Ben's our boy.

You'll never prove it, Linc.

Can the guards help?

Not a chance. They've lost one solid hour. De Santis says their retinal rhodopsin was destroyed. That's the visual purple—what you see with in your eye. As far

Uh-huh.

as the guards are concerned, they were on duty and alert. Nothing happened until the mob suddenly blew in, and Maria was screeching at them for falling asleep on the job—which they emphatically swear they did not.

Nothing much!

And how the Gilt Corpse can screech.

But we know it was Reich.

You know it was Reich. Nobody else does.

He went up there while the guests were playing the Sardine game. He destroyed the guards' visual purple some way and robbed them of an hour of time. He went into the Orchid Suite and killed D'Courtney. The girl got mixed up in it, somehow, which is why she ran.

How?

How did he kill D'Courtney?

And last of all: why did he kill D'Courtney?

I don't know. I don't know any of the answers . . . yet.

You'll never get a Demolition that way.

That I do know.

You've got to show motive, method, and opportunity, objectively. All you've got is a peeper's knowledge that Reich killed D'Courtney.

Uh-huh.

Uh-huh.

Did you peep how or why?

Couldn't get in deep enough—not with Jo ¼maine watching me.

And you'll probably never get in. Jo's too careful.

Hell & Damnation! Jackson, we need the girl.

Barbara D'Courtney?

Yes. She's the key. If she can tell us what she saw and why she ran, we'll satisfy a court. Collate everything we've got so far and file it. It won't do us any good without the girl. Let everyone go. They won't do us any good without the girl. We'll have to backtrack on Reich—see what collateral evidence we can dig up, but—

I agree.

Right.

I'm beginning to hate her.

But it won't help without that goddamn girl.

Times like this, Mr. Beck, I hate women too. For Christ's sake, why are they all trying to get me married?

Image of a horse laughing.

Sar(censored)castic retort.

Sar(censored)donic reply.

(censored)

Having had the last word, Powell got to his feet and left the picture gallery. He crossed the overpass, descended to the music room and entered the main hall. He saw Reich, ¼maine, and Tate standing alongside the fountain, deep in conversation. Once again he fretted over the frightening problem of Tate. If the little peeper really was mixed up with Reich, as Powell had suspected at his party the week before, he might be mixed up in this killing.

The idea of a 1st Class Esper, a pillar of the Guild, participating in murder was unthinkable; yet, if actually the fact, a son of a bitch to prove. Nobody ever got anything from a 1st without full consent. And if Tate was (incredible . . . impossible . . . 100-1 against) working with Reich, Reich himself might prove impregnable. Resolving on one last propaganda attack before he was forced to resort to police work, Powell turned toward the group.

He caught their eyes, and directed a quick command to the peepers: *"Jo. Gus. Jet off. I want to say something to Reich I don't want you to hear. I won't peep him or record his words. That's a pledge."*

¼maine and Tate nodded, muttered to Reich and quietly departed. Reich watched them go with curious eyes and then looked at Powell. "Scare 'em off?" he inquired.

"Warned them off. Sit down, Reich."

They sat on the edge of the basin, looking at each other in a friendly silence.

"No," Powell said after a pause, "I'm not peeping you."

"Didn't think you were. But you did in Maria's study, eh?"

"Felt that?"

"No. Guessed. It's what I would have done."

"Neither of us is very trustworthy, eh?"

"Pfutz!" Reich said emphatically. "We don't play girl's rules. We play for keeps, both of us. It's the cowards and weaklings and sore losers who hide behind rules and fair play."

"What about honor and ethics?"

"We've got honor in us, but it's our own code—not the make-believe rules some frightened little man wrote for the rest of the frightened little men. Every man's got his own honor and ethics, and so long as he sticks to 'em, who's anybody else to point the finger? You may not like his ethics, but you've no right to call him unethical."

Powell shook his head sadly. "You're two men, Reich. One of them's fine; and the other's rotten. If you were all killer, it wouldn't be so bad. But there's half louse and half saint in you, and that makes it worse."

"I knew it was going to be bad when you winked," Reich grinned. "You're tricky, Powell. You really scare me. I never can tell when the punch is coming or which way to duck."

"Then for God's sake stop ducking and get it over with," Powell said. His voice burned. His eyes burned. Once again he terrified Reich with his intensity. "I'm going to lick you on this one, Ben. I'm going to strangle the lousy killer in you, because I admire the saint. This is the beginning of the end, for you. You know it. Why don't you make it easier for yourself?"

For an instant, Reich wavered on the verge of surrender. Then he mustered himself to meet the attack. "And give up the best fight of my life? No. Never in a million years, Linc. We're going to slug this out straight down to the finish."

Powell shrugged angrily. They both arose. Instinctively, their hands met in the four-way clasp of final farewell.

"I lost a great partner in you," Reich said.

"You lost a great man in yourself, Ben."

"Enemies?"

"Enemies."

It was the beginning of Demolition.

7

The Police Prefect of a city of seventeen and one half millions cannot be tied down to a desk. He does not have files, memoranda, notes, and reels of red tape. He has three Esper secretaries, memory wizards all, who carry within their minds the minutiae of his business. They accompany him around headquarters like a triple index. Surrounded by his flying squad (nicknamed Wynken, Blynken, and Nod by the staff) Powell jetted through Centre Street, assembling the material for his fight.

To Commissioner Crabbe he laid out the broad outlines once more. "We need motive, method, and opportunity, Commissioner. We've got possible opportunity so far, but that's all. You know Old Man Mose. He's going to insist on hard-fact evidence."

"Old Man who?" Crabbe looked startled.

"Old Man Mose," Powell grinned. "That's our nickname for the Mosaic Multiplex Prosecution Computer. You wouldn't want us to use his full name, would you? We'd strangle."

"That confounded adding machine!" Crabbe snorted.

"Yes, sir. Now, I'm ready to go all out on Ben Reich and Monarch to get that evidence for Old Man Mose. I want to ask you a straight question. Are you willing to go all out too?"

Crabbe, who resented and hated all Espers, turned purple and shot up from the ebony chair behind the ebony desk in his ebony-and-silver office. "What the hell is that supposed to mean, Powell?"

"Don't sound for undercurrents, sir. I'm merely asking if you're tied to Reich and Monarch in any way. Will you be embarrassed when the heat's on? Will it be possible for Reich to come to you and get our rockets cooled?"

"No, it will not, damn you."

"Sir," Wynken shot at Powell. *"On December 4th last, Commissioner Crabbe discussed the Monolith Case with you. Extract follows:*

POWELL: There's a tricky financial angle to this business, Commissioner. Monarch may hold us up with a Demurrer.

CRABBE: Reich's given me his word he won't; and I can always depend on Ben Reich. He backed me for County Attorney.

"End quote."

"Right, Wynk. I thought there was something in Crabbe's file."

Powell switched his tactics and glared at Crabbe. "What the devil are you trying to hand me? What about your campaign for County D. A.? Reich backed you for that, didn't he?"

"He did."

"And I'm supposed to believe he hasn't continued supporting you?"

"Damn you, Powell– Yes, you are. He backed me then. He has not supported me since."

"Then I have the beacon on the Reich murder?"

"Why do you insist that Ben Reich killed that man? It's ridiculous. You've got no proof. Your own admission."

Powell continued to glare at Crabbe.

"He didn't kill him. Ben Reich wouldn't kill anybody. He's a fine man who–"

"Do I have your beacon on this murder?"

"All right, Powell. You do."

"But with strong reservations. Make a note, boys. He's scared to death of Reich. Make another note. So am I."

To his staff, Powell said: "Now look–you all know what a cold-blooded monster Old Man Mose is. Always screaming for facts–facts–evidence–unassailable proof. We'll have to produce evidence to convince that damned machine he ought to prosecute. To do that we're going to pull the Rough & Smooth on Reich. You know the method. We'll assign a clumsy operative and a slick one to every subject. The cluck won't know the smoothie is on the job. Neither will the subject. After he's shaken the rough tail he'll imagine he's clear. That makes it a cinch for the slicker. And that's what we're going to do to Reich."

"Check," said Beck.

"Go through every department. Pull out a hundred low-grade cops. Put 'em in plainclothes and assign 'em to the Reich case. Go up to Lab and get hold of every crackpot tracer-robot that's been submitted in the last ten years. Put all the gadgets to work on the Reich case. Make this whole package a rough tail–the kind he won't have any trouble shaking, but the kind he'll have to work to shake."

"Any specific areas?" Beck inquired.

"Why were they playing 'Sardine'? Who suggested the game? The Beaumont's secretaries went on record that Reich couldn't be peeped because he had a song kicking around in his skull. What song? Who wrote it? Where'd Reich hear it? Lab says the guards were blasted with some kind of visual purple ionizer. Check all research on that sort of thing. What killed D'Courtney? Let's have lots of weapon research. Backtrack on Reich's relations with D'Courtney. We know they were commercial rivals. Were they deadly enemies? Was it a profitable murder? A terrified murder? What and how much does Reich stand to win by D'Courtney's death?"

"Jesus!" Beck exclaimed. "All this rough? We'll louse the case, Linc."

"Maybe. I don't think so. Reich's a successful man. He's had a string of victories that's made him cocky. I think he'll bite. He'll imagine he's outsmarting us every time he outmaneuvers one of our decoys. Keep him thinking that. We're going to run into some brutal public relations. The news'll tear us apart. But play along with it. Rave. Rant. Make outraged statements. We're all going to be blundering outwitted cops . . . and while Reich's eating himself fat on that diet–"

"You'll be eating Reich," Beck grinned. "What about the girl?"

"She's the one exception to the rough routine. We level with her. I want a description and photo sent to every police officer in the country within one hour. On the bottom of the stat we announce that the man who locates her will automatically be jumped five grades."

"Sir: Regulations forbid elevation of more than three ranks at any time." Thus spake Nod.

"To hell with regulations," Powell snapped. "Five grades to the man who finds Barbara D'Courtney. I've got to get that girl."

In Monarch Tower, Ben Reich shoved every piezo crystal off his desk into the startled hands of his secretaries.

"Get the hell out of here and take all this slok with you," he growled. "From now on the office coasts without me. Understand? Don't bother me."

"Mr. Reich, we'd understood you were contemplating taking over the D'Courtney interests now that Craye D'Courtney's dead. If you–"

"I'm taking care of that right now. That's why I don't want to be bothered. Now beat it. Jet!"

He herded the terrified squad toward the door, pushed them out, slammed the door and locked it. He went to the phone, punched

BD-12,232 and waited impatiently. After too long a time, the image of Jerry Church appeared against a background of pawnshop debris.

"You?" Church snarled and reached for the cut-off.

"Me. On business. Still interested in reinstatement?"

Church stared. "What about it?"

"You've made yourself a deal. I'm starting action on your reinstatement at once. And I can do it, Jerry. I own the league of Esper Patriots. But I want a lot in return."

"For God's sake, Ben. Anything. Just ask me."

"That's what I want."

"Anything?"

"And everything. Unlimited service. You know the price I'm paying. Are you selling?"

"I'm selling, Ben. Yes."

"And I want Keno Quizzard too."

"You can't want him, Ben. He isn't safe. Nobody gets anything from Quizzard."

"Set up a meeting. Same old place. Same time. This is like it used to be, eh, Jerry? Only this time it's going to have a happy ending."

The usual line was assembled in the anteroom of the Esper Guild Institute when Lincoln Powell entered. The hopeful hundreds, all ages, all sexes, all classes, each dreaming that he had the magic quality that could make life the fulfillment of fantasy, unaware of the heavy responsibility that quality entailed. The naïveté of those dreams always made Powell smile. *Read minds and make a killing on the market . . .* (Guild Law forbade speculation or gambling by peepers.) *Read minds and know the answers to all exam questions . . .* (That was a schoolboy, unaware that Esper proctors were hired by Examination Boards to prevent that kind of peeper-cheating.) *Read minds and know what people really think of me . . . Read minds and know which girls are willing . . . Read minds and be like a King . . .*

At the desk, the receptionist wearily broadcast on the widest TP band: *If you can hear me, please go through the door on the left marked* EMPLOYEES ONLY. *If you can hear me, please go through the door on the left marked* EMPLOYEES ONLY *. . .*

To an assured young socialite with a checkbook in her hand, she was saying: "No, Madame. The Guild does not charge for training and instruction, your offer is worthless. Please go home, Madame. We can do nothing for you."

Deaf to the basic test of the Guild, the woman turned away angrily, to be succeeded by the schoolboy.

If you can hear me, please go through the door on the left . . .

A young Negro suddenly detached himself from the line, glanced uncertainly at the receptionist, and then walked to the door marked EMPLOYEES ONLY. He opened it and entered. Powell was excited. Latent Espers turned up infrequently. He'd been fortunate to arrive at this moment.

He nodded to the receptionist and followed the Latent through the door. Inside, two of the Guild staff were enthusiastically shaking the surprised man's hand and patting him on the back. Powell joined them for a moment and added his congratulations. It was always a happy day for the Guild when they unearthed another Esper.

Powell walked down the corridor toward the president's suite. He passed a kindergarten where thirty children and ten adults were mixing speech and thought in a frightful patternless mish-mash. Their instructor was patiently broadcasting: *"Think, class. Think. Words are not necessary. Think. Remember to break the speech reflex. Repeat the first rule after me . . ."*

And the class chanted: "Eliminate the Larynx."

Powell winced and moved on. The wall opposite the kindergarten was covered by a gold plaque on which was engraved the sacred words of the Esper Pledge:

I will look upon him who shall have taught me this Art as one of my parents. I will share my substance with him, and I will supply his necessities if he be in need. I will regard his offspring even as my own brethren and I will teach them this Art by precept, by lecture, and by every mode of teaching; and I will teach this Art to all others. The regimen I adopt shall be for the benefit of mankind according to my ability and judgment, and not for hurt or wrong. I will give no deadly thought to any, though it be asked of me.

Whatsoever mind I enter, there will I go for the benefit of man, refraining from all wrongdoing and corruption. Whatsoever thoughts I see or hear in the mind of man which ought not to be made known, I will keep silence thereon, counting such things to be as sacred secrets.

In the lecture hall, a class of 3rds was earnestly weaving simple basket patterns while they discussed current events. There was one little overdue 2nd, a twelve-year-old, who was adding zigzag ad libs to the dull discussion and peaking every zig with a spoken word. The words rhymed and were barbed comments on the speakers. It was amusing and amazingly precocious.

Powell found the president's suite in an uproar. All the office doors were open, and clerks and secretaries were scurrying. Old

T'sung H'sai, the president, a portly mandarin with shaven skull and benign features, stood in the center of his office and raged. He was so angry he was shouting, and the shock of the articulated words made his staff shake.

"I don't care what the scoundrels call themselves," T'sung H'sai roared. "They're a gang of selfish, self-seeking reactionaries. Talk to me about purity of the race, will they? Talk to me about aristocracy, will they? I'll talk to them. I'll fill their ears. Miss Prinn! Miss Pr-i-nnnnn!"

Miss Prinn crept into T'sung's office, horrified at the prospect of oral dictation.

"Take a letter to these devils. To the League of Esper Patriots. Gentlemen. . . . *Good morning, Powell. Haven't seen you in eons . . . How's Dishonest Abe?* The organized campaign of your clique to cut down Guild taxation and appropriations for the education of Espers and the dissemination of Esper training to mankind is conceived in a spirit of treachery and fascism. Paragraph . . ."

T'sung wrenched himself from his diatribe and winked profoundly at Powell. *"And have you found the peeper of your dreams yet?"*

"Not yet, sir."

"Confound you, Powell. Get married!" T'sung bellowed. "I don't want to be stuck with this job forever. Paragraph, Miss Prinn: You speak of the hardships of taxation, of preserving the aristocracy of Espers, of the unsuitability of the average man for Esper training . . . *What do you want, Powell?"*

"I want to use the grapevine, sir."

"Well don't bother me. Speak to my #2 girl. Paragraph, Miss Prinn: Why don't you come out into the open? You parasites want Esper powers reserved for an exclusive class so you can turn the rest of the world into a host for your blood-sucking! You leeches want to—"

Powell tactfully closed the door and turned to T'sung's second secretary, who was quaking in a corner.

"Are you really scared?"

Image of an eye winking.

Image of a question mark quaking.

"When Papa T'sung blows his top we like him to think we're petrified. Makes him happier. He hates to be reminded that he's a Santa Claus."

"Well, I'm Santa Claus too. Here's something for your stocking."

Powell dropped the official police description and portrait of Barbara D'Courtney on the secretary's desk.

"What a beautiful girl!" she exclaimed.

"I want this sent out on the grapevine. Marked urgent. A reward goes with it. Pass the word that the peeper who locates Barbara D'Courtney for me will have his Guild taxes remitted for a year."

"Jeepers!" the secretary sat bolt upright. *"Can you do that?"*

"I think I'm big enough in Council to swing it."

"This'll make the grapevine jump."

"I want it to jump. I want every peeper to jump. If I want anything for Xmas, I want that girl."

Quizzard's Casino had been cleaned and polished during the afternoon break—the only break in a gambler's day. The EO and Roulette tables were brushed, the Birdcage sparkled, the Hazard and Bank Crap boards gleamed green and white. In crystal globes, the ivory dice glistened like sugar cubes. On the cashier's desk, sovereigns, the standard coin of gambling and the underworld, were racked in tempting stacks. Ben Reich sat at the billiard table with Jerry Church and Keno Quizzard, the blind croupier. Quizzard was a giant pulplike man, fat, with flaming red beard, dead white skin, and malevolent dead white eyes.

"Your price," Reich told Church, "you know already. And I'm warning you, Jerry. If you know what's good for you, don't try to peep me. I'm poison. If you get into my head you're getting into Demolition. Think about it."

"Jesus," Quizzard murmured in his sour voice. "As bad as that? I don't hanker for a Demolition, Reich."

"Who does? What do you hanker for, Keno?"

"A question." Quizzard reached back and with sure fingers pulled a rouleau of sovereigns off the desk. He let them cascade from one hand to the other. "Listen to what I hanker for."

"Name the best price you can figure, Keno."

"What's it for?"

"To hell with that. I'm buying unlimited service with expenses paid. You tell me how much I've got to put up to get it—guaranteed."

"That's a lot of service."

"I've got a lot of money."

"You got a hundred Ms laying around?"

"One hundred thousand. Right? That's the price."

"For the love of . . ." Church popped upright and stared at Reich. "A hundred thousand?"

"Make up your mind, Jerry," Reich growled. "Do you want money or reinstatement?"

"It almost worth– No. Am I crazy? I'll take reinstatement."

"Then stop drooling." Reich turned to Quizzard. "The price is one hundred thousand."

"In sovereigns?"

"What else? Now, d'you want me to put the money up in advance or can we get to work right off?"

"Oh, for Christ's sake, Reich," Quizzard protested.

"Frab that," Reich snapped. "I know you, Keno. You've got an idea you can find out what I want and then shop around for higher bids. I want you committed right now. That's why I let you set the price."

"Yeah," Quizzard said slowly. "I had that idea, Reich." He smiled and the milk-white eyes disappeared in folds of skin. "I still got that idea."

"Then I'll tell you right now who'll buy from you. A man named Lincoln Powell. Trouble is, I don't know what he'd pay."

"Whatever it is, I don't want it," Quizzard spat.

"It's me against Powell, Keno. That's the whole auction. I've placed my bid. I'm still waiting to hear from you."

"It's a deal," Quizzard replied.

"All right," Reich said, "now listen to this. First job. I want a girl. Her name is Barbara D'Courtney."

"The killing?" Quizzard nodded heavily. "I thought so."

"Any objections?"

Quizzard jingled gold from one hand to the other and shook his head.

"I want the girl. She blew out of the Beaumont House last night and no one knows where she landed. I want her, Keno. I want her before the police get her."

Quizzard nodded.

"She's about twenty-five. About five-five. Around a hundred and twenty pounds. Stacked. Thin waist. Long legs . . ."

The fat lips smiled hungrily. The dead white eyes glistened.

"Yellow hair. Black eyes. Heart-shaped face. Full mouth and a kind of aquiline nose. She's got a face with character. It jabs out at you. Electric."

"Clothes?"

"She was wearing a silk dressing gown last time I saw her. Frosty white and translucent . . . like a frozen window. No shoes. No stockings. No hat. No jewelry. She was off her beam. Crazy enough to tear out into the streets and disappear. I want her." Something compelled Reich to add: "I want her undamaged. Understand?"

"With her hauling a freight like that? Have a heart, Reich." Quizzard licked his fat lips. "You don't stand a chance. *She* don't stand a chance."

"That's what a hundred Ms are for. I stand a good chance if you get her fast enough."

"I may have to slush for her."

"Then slush. Check every bawdy house, bagnio, Blind Tiger, and frab-joint in the city. Pass the word down the grapevine. I'm willing to pay. I don't want any fuss. I just want the girl. Understand?"

Quizzard nodded, still jingling the gold. "I understand."

Suddenly Reich reached across the table and slashed Quizzard's fat hands with the edge of his palm. The sovereigns chimed into the air and clattered into the four corners.

"And I don't want any double-cross," Reich growled in a deadly voice. "I want the girl."

8

Seven days of combat.

One week of action and reaction, attack and defense, all fought on the surface while deep below the agitated waters Powell and Augustus Tate swam and circled like silent sharks awaiting the onset of the real war.

A patrol officer, now in plainclothes, believed in the surprise attack. He waylaid Maria Beaumont during a theater intermission, and before her horrified friends bellowed: "It was a frame. You was in cahoots with the killer. You set up the murder. That's why you was playin' that Sardine game. Go ahead and answer me."

The Gilt Corpse squawked and ran. As the rough tail set off in hot pursuit, he was peeped deeply and thoroughly.

Tate to Reich: The cop was telling the truth. His department believes Maria was an accomplice.

Reich to Tate: All right. We'll throw her to the wolves. Let the cops have her.

In consequence, Madame Beaumont was left unprotected. She

took refuge, of all places, in the Loan Brokerage that was the source of the Beaumont fortune. The patrol officer located her there three hours later and subjected her to a merciless grilling in the office of the peeper Credit Supervisor. He was unaware that Lincoln Powell was just outside the office, chatting with the Supervisor.

Powell to staff: She got the game out of some ancient book Reich gave her. Probably purchased at Century. They handle that stuff. Pass the word. Did he ask for it specifically? Also, check Graham, the appraiser. How come the only intact game in the book was 'Sardine'? Old Man Mose'll want to know. And where's that girl?

A traffic officer, now in plainclothes, was going to come through on his big chance with the suave approach. To the manager and staff of the Century Audio-bookstore, he drawled: "I'm in the market for old game books . . . . The kind my very good friend, Ben Reich, asked for last week."

Tate to Reich: I've been peeping around. They're going to check that book you sent Maria.

Reich to Tate: Let 'em. I'm covered. I've got to concentrate on that girl.

The manager and staff carefully explained matters at great length in response to the rough tail's suave questions. Many clients lost patience and left the store. One sat quietly in a corner, too rapt in a crystal recording to realize he was left unattended. Nobody knew that Jackson Beck was completely tone-deaf.

Powell to staff: Reich apparently found the book accidentally. Stumbled over it while he was looking for a present for Maria Beaumont. Pass the word. And where's that girl?

In conference with the agency that handled copy for the Monarch Jumper ("the *only* Family Air-Rocket on the market"), Reich came up with a new advertising program.

"Here's the slant," Reich said. "People always anthropomorphize the products they use. They attribute human characteristics to them. They give 'em pet names and treat 'em like family pets. A man would rather buy a Jumper if he can feel affectionate toward it. He doesn't give a damn for efficiency. He wants to love that Jumper."

"Check, Mr. Reich. Check!"

"We're going to anthropomorphize our Jumper," Reich said. "Let's find a girl and vote her the Monarch Jumper Girl. When a consumer buys one, he's buying the girl. When he handles one, he's handling her."

"Check!" the account man cried. "Your idea has a sense of solar scope that dwarfs us, Mr. Reich. This is a wrap-up and blast!"

"Start an immediate campaign to locate the Jumper Girl. Get every salesman onto it. Comb the city. I want the girl to be about twenty-five. About five-five tall, weighing a hundred and twenty pounds. I want her built. Lots of appeal."

"Check, Mr. Reich. Check."

"She ought to be a blonde with dark eyes. Full mouth. Good strong nose. Here's a sketch of my idea of the Jumper Girl. Look it over, have it reproduced and passed out to your crew. There's a promotion for the man who locates the girl I have in mind."

Tate to Reich: I've been peeping the police. They're sending a man into Monarch to dig up collusion between you and that appraiser, Graham.

Reich to Tate: Let 'em. There isn't anything, and Graham's left town on a buying spree. Something between me and Graham! Powell couldn't be that dumb, could he? Maybe I've been overrating him.

Expense was no object to a squadman, now in plainclothes, who believed in the disguises of plastic surgery. Freshly equipped with mongoloid features, he took a job in Monarch Utilities' Accounting-city and attempted to unearth Reich's financial relations with Graham, the appraiser. It never occurred to him that his intent had been peeped by Monarch's Esper Personnel Chief, reported upstairs, and that upstairs was quietly chuckling.

Powell to staff: Our stooge was looking for bribery recorded in Monarch's books. This should lower Reich's opinion of us by fifty percent; which makes him fifty percent more vulnerable. Pass the word. Where's that girl?

At the board meeting of *The Hour*, the only round-the-clock paper on earth, twenty-four editions a day, Reich announced a new Monarch charity.

"We're calling it 'Sanctuary,'" he said. "We offer aid and comfort and sanctuary to the city's submerged millions in their time of crisis. If you've been evicted, bankrupted, terrorized, swindled . . . If you're frightened for any reason and don't know where to turn . . . If you're desperate . . . Take Sanctuary."

"It's a terrific promotion," the managing editor said, "but it'll cost like crazy. What's it for?"

"Public relations," Reich snapped. "I want this to hit the next edition. Jet!"

Reich left the board room, went down to the street and located a public phone booth. He called "Recreation" and gave careful instructions to Ellery West. "I want a man placed in every Sanctuary office in the city. I want a full description and photo of every applicant relayed to me at once. At once, Ellery. As they come in."

"I'm not asking any questions, Ben, but I wish I could peep you on that."

"Suspicious?" Reich snarled.

"No. Just curious."

"Don't let it kill you."

As Reich left the booth, a man clothed in an air of inept eagerness accosted him.

"Oh, Mr. Reich. Lucky I bumped into you. I just heard about Sanctuary and I thought a human-interest interview with the originator of this wonderful new charity might–"

Lucky he bumped into him! The man was the *Industrial Critic's* famous peeper reporter. Probably tailed him down and–*Tenser, said the Tensor. Tenser, said the Tensor. Tension, apprehension, and dissension have begun.*

"No comment," Reich mumbled. *Eight, sir; seven, sir; six, sir; five, sir . . .*

"What childhood episode in your life brought about the realization of this crying need for–"

Four, sir; three, sir; two, sir; one . . .

"Was there ever a time when you didn't know where to turn? Were you ever afraid of death or murder? Were–"

Tenser, said the Tensor. Tenser, said the Tensor, Tension, apprehension, and dissension have begun.

Reich dove into a Public Jumper and escaped.

Tate to Reich: The cops are really after Graham. They've got their entire Lab looking for the appraiser. God knows what kind of red herring Powell's following, but it's away from you. I think the safety margin's increasing.

Reich to Tate: Not until I've found that girl.

Marcus Graham had left no forwarding address and was pursued by half a dozen impractical tracer-robots dug up by the police lab. They were accompanied by their impractical inventors to various parts of the solar system. In the meantime, Marcus Graham had arrived on Ganymede, where Powell located him at an auction of rare primitive books conducted at breakneck speed by a peeper auctioneer. The books had been part of the Drake estate, inherited by Ben Reich from his mother. They had been unexpectedly dumped on the market.

Powell interviewed Graham in the foyer of the auction room, before a crystal port overlooking the arctic tundra of Ganymede with the belted red-brown bulk of Jupiter filling the black sky. Then Powell took the Fortnighter back to Earth, and Dishonest Abe was inspired by a pretty stewardess to disgrace him. Powell was not a happy man when he arrived at headquarters, and Wynken, Blynken, and Nod did some salacious wynking, blynking and nodding.

Powell to staff: No hope. I don't know why Reich even bothered to decoy Graham to Ganymede with that sale.

Beck to Powell: What about the game book?

Powell to Beck: Reich bought it, had it appraised, and sent it as a gift. It was in bad condition and the only game Maria could select was 'Sardine.' We'll never get Mose to pin anything on Reich with that. I know how that machine's mind works. Damn it! Where's that girl!

Three low-grade operatives in succession were smitten with Miss Duffy Wyg& and retired in disgrace to don their uniforms once more. When Powell finally reached her, she was at the "4,000" Ball. Miss Wyg& was delighted to talk.

Powell to staff: I called Ellery West down at Monarch and he supports Miss Wyg&'s story. West did complain about gambling and Reich bought a psych-song to stop it. It looks like he picked up that mind-block by accident. What about that gimmick Reich used on the guards? And what about that girl?

In response to bitter criticism and loud laughter, Commissioner Crabbe gave an exclusive press interview in which he revealed that Police Laboratories had discovered a new investigation technique which would break the D'Courtney case within twenty-four hours. It involved photographic analysis of the visual purple in the corpse's eyes which would reveal a picture of the murderer. Rhodopsin researchers were being requisitioned by the police.

Unwilling to run the risk of having Wilson Jordan, the physiologist who had developed the Rhodopsin Ionizer for Monarch, picked up and questioned by the police, Reich phoned Keno Quizzard and devised a ruse to get Dr. Jordan off the planet.

"I've got an estate on Callisto," Reich said. "I'll relinquish title and let a court throw it up for grabs. I'll make sure the cards are stacked for Jordan."

"And I tell Jordan?" Quizzard asked in his sour voice.

"We won't be that obvious, Keno. We can't leave a back-trail. Call Jordan. Make him suspicious. Let him find out the rest for himself."

As a result of that conversation, an anonymous person with a sour voice phoned Wilson Jordan and casually attempted to purchase Dr. Jordan's interest in the Drake estate on Callisto for a small sum. The sour voice sounded suspicious to Dr. Jordan, who had never heard of the Drake estate, and he called a lawyer. He was informed that he had just become the probable legatee to half a million credits. The astonished physiologist jetted for Callisto one hour later.

Powell to staff: We've flushed Reich's man into the open. Jordan must be our lead on the rhodopsin angle. He's the only visual physiologist to disappear after Crabbe's announcement. Pass the word to Beck to tail him to Callisto and handle it. What about that girl?

Meanwhile, the slick side of Operation Rough & Smooth was quietly in progress. While Maria Beaumont was occupying Reich's attention with her squawking flight, a bright young attorney from Monarch's legal department was deftly decoyed to Mars and held there anonymously on a valid, if antiquated, vice charge. An astonishing duplication of that young attorney went to work for him.

Tate to Reich: Check your legal department. I can't peep what's going on, but something's fishy. This is dangerous.

Reich brought in an Esper 1 Efficiency Expert, ostensibly for a general checkup, and located the substitution. Then he called Keno Quizzard. The blind croupier produced a plaintiff who suddenly appeared and sued the bright young attorney for barratry. That ended the substitute's connection with Monarch painlessly and legitimately.

Powell to staff: Damn it! We're being licked. Reich's slamming every door in our face. . . . Rough & Smooth. Find out who's doing the legwork for him, and find that girl.

While the squadman was cavorting around Monarch Tower with his brand-new Mongolian face, one of Monarch's scientists who had been badly hurt in a laboratory explosion apparently left the hospital a week early and reported back for duty. He was heavily bandaged, but eager for work. It was the old Monarch spirit.

Tate to Reich: I've finally figured it. Powell isn't dumb. He's running his investigation on two levels. Don't pay any attention to the one that shows. Watch out for the one underneath. I've peeped something about a hospital. Check it.

Reich checked. It took three days and then he called Keno Quizzard again. Monarch was promptly burgled of Cr. 50,000 in laboratory platinum and the Restricted Room was destroyed in the process. The newly returned scientist was unmasked as an imposter, accused of complicity in the crime, and handed over to the police.

Powell to staff: Which means we'll never prove Reich got that rhodopsin stuff from his own lab. How in God's name did he unslick our trick? Can't we do anything on any level? Where's that girl?

While Reich was laughing at the ludicrous robot search for Marcus Graham, his top brass was greeting the Continental Tax Examiner, an Esper 2, who had arrived for a long delayed check on Monarch Utilities & Resources' books. One of the new additions to the Examiner's squad was a peeper ghostwriter who prepared her chief's reports. She was an expert in official work—mainly police work.

Tate to Reich: I'm suspicious of that Examiner's squad. Don't take any chances.

Reich smiled grimly and turned his public books over to the squad. Then he sent Hassop, his Code Chief, to Spaceland on that promised vacation. Hassop obligingly carried a small spool of exposed film with his regular photographic equipment. That spool contained Monarch's secret books, cased in a thermite seal which would destroy all records unless it was properly opened. The only other copy was in Reich's invulnerable safe at home.

Powell to staff: And that just about ends everything. Have Hassop double-tailed; Rough & Smooth. He's probably got vital evidence on him, so Reich's probably got him beautifully protected. Damn it, we're licked. I say it. Old Man Mose would say it. You know it. For Christ's sake! Where is that goddamn missing girl?

Like an anatomical chart of the blood system, colored red for the arteries and blue for the veins, the underworld and overworld spread their networks. From Guild headquarters the word passed to instructors and students, to their families, to their friends, to their friends' friends, to casual acquaintances, to strangers met in business. From Quizzard's Casino the word was passed from croupier to gamblers, to confidence men, to the heavy racketeers, to the light thieves, to hustlers, steerers, and suckers, to the shadowy fringe of the semi-crook and near-honest.

On Friday morning, Fred Deal, Esper 3, awoke, arose, bathed, breakfasted, and departed to his regular job. He was Chief Guard on the floor of the Mars Exchange Bank down on Maiden Lane. Stopping to buy a new commutation ticket at the Pneumatique, he passed the time with an Esper 3, on duty at the Information Desk, who passed Fred the word about Barbara D'Courtney. Fred memorized the TP picture she flashed him. It was a picture framed in credit signs.

On Friday morning, Snim Asj was awakened by his landlady, Chooka Frood, with a loud scream for back rent.

"For chrissakes, Chooka," Snim mumbled. "You already makin' a frabby fortune with 'at loopy yella head girl you pick up. You runnin' a golmine withat spook stuff down-inna basement. Whaddya want from me?"

Chooka Frood pointed out to Snim that: a) The yellow-headed girl was not crazy. She was a genuine medium. b) She (Chooka) did not run rackets. She was a legitimate fortune teller. c) If he (Snim) did not come through with six weeks roof and rolls, she (Chooka) would be able to tell his fortune without any trouble at all. Snim would be out on his asphalt.

Snim arose, and, already dressed, descended into the city to pick up a few credits. It was too early to run up to Quizzard's and work the sob on the more prosperous clients. Snim tried to sneak a ride uptown on the Pneumatique. He was thrown out by the peeper change clerk and walked. It was a long haul to Jerry Church's hock-shop, but Snim had a gold and pearl pocket-pianino up there and he was hoping to cadge Church into advancing another sovereign on it.

Church was absent on business and the clerk could do nothing for Snim. They passed the time. Snim told the sob to the clerk about his bitch landlady crowning herself every day with the new spook-shill she was using in her palm-racket and still trying to milk him when she was rolling. The clerk would not weep even for the price of coffee. Snim departed.

When Jerry Church returned to the hockshop for a brief time-out in his wild quest for Barbara D'Courtney, the clerk reported Snim's visit and conversation. What the clerk did not report, Church peeped. Nearly fainting, he tottered to the phone and called Reich. Reich could not be located. Church took a deep breath and called Keno Quizzard.

Meanwhile, Snim was growing a little desperate. Out of that desperation arose his crazy decision to work the bank-teller graft. Snim trudged downtown to Maiden Lane and cased the banks in that pleasant esplanade around Bomb Inlet. He was not too bright and made the mistake of selecting the Mars Exchange as his battlefield. It looked dowdy and provincial. Snim had not learned that it is only the powerful and efficient institutions that can afford to look second-rate.

Snim entered the bank, crossed the crowded main floor to the row of desks opposite the tellers' cages, and stole a handful of deposit slips and a pen. As Snim left the bank, Fred Deal glanced at him once, then motioned wearily to his staff.

"See that little louse?" He pointed to Snim, who was disappearing through the front door. "He's getting ready to pull the 'Adjustment' routine."

"Want us to send him, Fred?"

"What the hell's the use? He'll only try it on someone else. Let him go ahead with it. We'll pick him up after he's got the money and get a conviction. Stash him for keeps. There's plenty of room in Kingston."

Unaware of this, Snim lurked outside the bank, watching the tellers' cages closely. A solid citizen was making a withdrawal at Cage Z. The teller was passing over big chunks of paper cash. This was the fish. Snim hastily removed his jacket, rolled up his sleeves, and tucked the pen in his ear.

As the fish came out of the bank, counting his money, Snim slipped behind him, darted up and tapped the man's shoulder.

"Excuse me, sir," he said briskly. "I'm from Cage Z. I'm afraid our teller made a mistake and short-counted you. Will you come back for adjustment, please?" Snim waved his sheaf of slips, gracefully swept the money from the fish's fins and turned to enter the bank. "Right this way, sir," he called pleasantly. "You have another hundred coming to you."

As the surprised solid citizen followed him, Snim darted busily across the floor, slipped into the crowd and headed for the side exit. He would be out and away before the fish realized he'd been gutted. It was at this moment that a rough hand grasped Snim's neck. He was swung around face to face with a bank guard. In one chaotic instant, Snim contemplated fight, flight, bribery, pleas, Kingston Hospital, the bitch Chooka Frood and her yellow-headed ghost girl, his pocket-pianino and the man who owned it. Then he collapsed and wept.

The peeper guard flung him to another uniform and shouted: "Take him, boys. I've just made myself a mint!"

"Is there a reward for this little guy, Fred?"

"Not for him. For what's in his head. I've got to call the Guild."

At nearly the same moment late Friday afternoon, Ben Reich and Lincoln Powell received the identical information: "Girl answering to the description of Barbara D'Courtney can be found in Chooka Frood's Fortune Act, 99 Bastion West Side."

9

Bastion West Side, famous last bulwark in the Siege of New York, was dedicated as a war memorial. Its ten torn acres were to be maintained in perpetuity as a stinging denunciation of the insanity that produced the final war. But the final war, as usual, proved to be the next-to-the-final, and Bastion West Side's shattered buildings and gutted alleys were patched into a crazy slum by squatters.

Number 99 was an eviscerated ceramics plant. During the war a succession of blazing explosions had burst among the stock of thousands of chemical glazes, fused them, and splashed them into a wild rainbow reproduction of a lunar crater. Great splotches of magenta, violet, bice green, burnt umber, and chrome yellow were burned into the stone walls. Long streams of orange, crimson, and imperial purple had erupted through windows and doors to streak the streets and surrounding ruins with slashing brush strokes. This became the Rainbow House of Chooka Frood.

The top floors had been patched and subdivided into a warren of cells so complicated and confused that only Chooka understood the pattern of the maze, and even Chooka herself was in doubt at times. A man could drift from cell to cell while the floors were being searched, and easily slip through the meshes of the finest dragnet. This unusual complexity netted Chooka large profits each year.

The lower floors were given over to Chooka's famous Frab Joint, where, for a sufficient sum, a consummate expert graciously MC'd the well-known vices for the hungry and upon occasion invented new vices for the satiated. But the cellar of Chooka Frood's house was the phenomenon that had inspired her most lucrative industry.

The war explosions that had turned the building into a rainbow crater had also fused the ceramic glazes, the metals, glasses, and plastics in the old plant; and a molten conglomerate had oozed down through the floors to settle on the floor of the lowest vault and harden into shimmering pavement, crystal in texture, phosphorescent in color, strangely vibrant and singing.

It was worth the hazardous trip to Bastion West Side. You threaded your way through twisting streets until you reached the streak of jagged orange that pointed to the door of Chooka's Rainbow House. At the door you were met by a solemn person in twentieth-century formal costume who asked: "Frab or Fortune, sir?" If you replied "Fortune" you were conducted to a sepulchral door where you paid a gigantic fee and were handed a phosphor candle. Holding the candle aloft, you walked down a steep stone staircase. At the very bottom it turned sharply and abruptly disclosed a broad, long, arched cellar filled with a lake of singing fire.

You stepped onto the surface of that lake. It was smooth and glassy. Under the surface glowed and flickered a constant play of pastel borealis. At every step the crystal hummed sweet chords, throbbing like the prolonged overtones of bronze bells. If you sat motionless, the floor still sang, responding to vibrations from distant streets.

Around the rim of the cellar, on stone benches, sat the other fortune-seekers, each holding his phosphor candle. You looked at them, sitting silent and awed, and suddenly you realized that each of them looked saintly, glowing with the aura of the floor; and each of them sounded saintly, their bodies echoing the music of the floor. The candles looked like stars on a frosty night.

You joined the throbbing, burning silence and sat quietly, until at last there came the high chime of a silver bell repeated over and over. The entire floor took up the resonance, and the strange relationship of sight and sound made the colors flare up brilliantly. Then, clothed in a cascade of flaming music, Chooka Frood entered the cellar and paced to the center of the floor.

"And there, of course, the illusion ends," Lincoln Powell said to himself. He stared at Chooka's blunt face–the thick nose, flat eyes, and corroded mouth. The borealis flickered around her features and tightly gowned figure, but it could not disguise the fact that although she had ambition, avarice, and ingenuity, she was utterly devoid of sensitivity and clairvoyance.

"Maybe she can act," Powell muttered hopefully.

Chooka stopped in the middle of the floor, looking much like a vulgar Medusa, then lifted her arms in what was intended for a sweeping mystic gesture.

"She can't," Powell decided.

"I am come here to you," Chooka intoned in a hoarse voice, "to help you look into the deeps of your hearts. Look down into your hearts, you which are looking for . . ." Chooka hesitated, then ran on: "You which are looking for revenge on a man named Zerlen from Mars . . . For the love of a red-eyed woman of Callisto . . . For every credit of that rich old uncle in Paris . . . For . . ."

"Why damn me! The woman's a peeper!"

Chooka stiffened. Her mouth hung open.

"You're receiving me, aren't you, Chooka Frood?"

The telepathic answer came in frightened fragments. It was obvious that Chooka Frood's natural ability had never been trained. *"Wha . . . ? Who? Which is . . . you?"*

As carefully as if he were communicating with an infant 3rd, Powell spelled it out: *"Name: Lincoln Powell. Occupation: Police Prefect. Intent: To question a girl named Barbara D'Courtney. I have heard she's participating in your act."* Powell transmitted a picture of the girl.

It was pathetic the way Chooka tried to block. *"Get . . . . out. Out. Out of here. Get. Get out. Out . . ."*

"Why haven't you come to the Guild? Why aren't you in contact with your own people?"

"Get out. Out of here. Peeper! Get out."

"You're a peeper, too. Why haven't you let us train you? What kind of a life is this for you? Mumbo Jumbo . . . Picking sucker brains and turning it all into a Fortune Act. There's real work waiting for you, Chooka."

"Real money?"

Powell repressed the wave of exasperation that rose up in him. It was not exasperation with Chooka. It was anger for the relentless force of evolution that insisted on endowing man with increased powers without removing the vestigial vices that prevented him from using them.

"We'll talk about that later, Chooka. Where's the girl?"

"No girl. There is no girl."

"Don't be an ass, Chooka. Peep the customers with me. That old goat obsessed with the red-eyed woman . . ." Powell explored him gently. *"He's been here before. He's waiting for Barbara D'Courtney to come in. You dress her in sequins. You bring her on in half an hour. He likes her looks. She does some kind of trance routine to music. Her dress is slit open and he likes that. She–"*

"He's crazy. I never–"

"And the woman who was loused by a man named Zerlen? She's seen the girl often. She believes in her. She's waiting for her. Where's the girl, Chooka?"

"No!"

"I see. Upstairs. Where upstairs, Chooka? Don't try to block, I'm deep peeping. You can't mis-direct a 1st–I see. Fourth room on the

left of the angle turn. That's a complicated labyrinth you've got up there, Chooka. Let's have it again to make sure . . ."

Helpless and mortified, Chooka suddenly shrieked: "Get out of here, you goddamn cop! Get the hell out of here!"

"Excuse it, please," said Powell. "I'm on my way."

He rose and left the room.

That entire telepathic investigation took place within the second it took Reich to move from the eighteenth to the twentieth step on his way down to Chooka Frood's rainbow cellar. Reich heard Chooka's furious screech and Powell's reply. He turned and shot up the stairs to the main floor.

As he jostled past the door attendant, he thrust a sovereign into the man's hand and hissed: "I wasn't here. Understand?"

"No one is ever here, Mr. Reich."

He made a quick circuit of the frab rooms. *Tenser, said the Tensor. Tenser, said the Tensor. Tension, apprehension, and dissension have begun.* He brushed past the girls who variously solicited him, then locked himself into the phone booth and punched BD-12,232. Church's anxious face appeared on the screen.

"Well, Ben?"

"We're in a jam. Powell's here."

"Oh my God!"

"Where in hell is Quizzard?"

"He isn't there?"

"I can't locate him."

"But I thought he'd be down in the cellar. He—"

"Powell was in the cellar, peeping Chooka. You can bet Quizzard wasn't there. Where in hell is he?"

"I don't know, Ben. He went down with his wife, and—"

"Look, Jerry. Powell must have found the girl's location. I've got maybe five minutes to beat him to her. Quizzard was supposed to do that for me. He isn't in the cellar. He's nowhere in the Frab Joint. He—"

"He must be upstairs in the coop."

"I was going to figure that for myself. Listen, is there a quick way to get up to the coop? A short cut I can use to beat Powell to her?"

"If Powell peeped Chooka, he peeped the short cut."

"God damn it, I know that. But maybe he didn't. Maybe he was concentrating on the girl. It's a chance I'll have to take."

"Behind the main stairs. There's a marble bas-relief. Turn the woman's head to the right. The bodies separate and there's a door to a vertical pneumatique."

"Right."

Reich hung up, left the booth, and darted to the main stairs. He turned to the rear of the marble staircase, found the bas-relief, twisted the woman's head savagely and watched the bodies swing apart. A steel door appeared. A panel of buttons was set in the lintel. Reich punched TOP, yanked the door open and stepped into the open shaft. Instantly a metal plate jolted up against his soles and with a hiss of air pressure he was lofted eight stories to the top floor. A magnetic catch held the plate while he opened the shaft door and stepped out.

He found himself in a corridor that slanted up at an angle of thirty degrees and leaned to the left. It was floored with canvas. The ceiling glowed at intervals with small flickering globes of radon. The walls were lined with doors, none of them numbered.

"Quizzard!" Reich shouted.

There was no answer.

"Keno Quizzard!"

Still no answer.

Reich ran halfway up the corridor, and then at a venture tried a door. It opened to a narrow cubby entirely filled with an oval bed. Reich tripped over the edge of the bed and fell. He crawled across the foam mattress to a door on the opposite side, thrust it open, and fell through. He found himself on a landing. A flight of steps led down to a round anteroom rimmed with doors. Reich tumbled down the steps and stood, breathing heavily, staring at the circle of doors.

"Quizzard!" he shouted again. "Keno Quizzard!"

There was a muffled reply. Reich spun on his heels, ran to a door and pulled it open. A woman with eyes dyed red by plastic surgery was standing just inside and Reich blundered against her. She burst into unaccountable laughter, raised both fists and beat his face. Blinded and bewildered, Reich backed away from the powerful red-eyed woman, reached for the door, apparently missed it and seized the knob of another, for when he backed out of the room it was not into the circular foyer. His heels caught in three inches of plastic quilting. He tumbled over backwards, slamming the door as he fell and struck his head a stunning blow against the edge of a porcelain stove.

When his vision cleared he found himself staring up into the angry face of Chooka Frood.

"What the hell are you doing in my room?" Chooka screamed.

Reich shot to his feet. "Where is she?" he said.

"You get to hell out of here, Ben Reich."

"I asked you where is she? Barbara D'Courtney. Where is she?"

Chooka turned her head and yelled: "Magda!"

The red-eyed woman came into the room. She held a neuron scrambler in her hand and she was still laughing; but the gun was trained on his skull and never wavered.

"Get out of here," Chooka repeated.

"I want the girl, Chooka. I want her before Powell gets her. Where is she?"

"Get him out of here, Magda!" Chooka screamed.

Reich clubbed the woman across the eyes with the back of his hand. She fell backward, dropping the gun, and twitched in a corner, still laughing. Reich ignored her. He picked up the scrambler and rammed it against Chooka's temple.

"Where's the girl?"

"You go to hell, you–"

Reich pulled the trigger back into first notch. The radiation charged Chooka's nervous system with a low induction current. She stiffened and began to tremble. Her skin glistened with sudden sweat, but she still shook her head. Reich yanked the trigger back to second notch. Chooka's body was thrown into a break-bone ague. Her eyes started. Her throat emitted the brute groans of a tortured animal. Reich held her in it for five seconds, then cut the gun.

"Third notch is death notch," he growled. "The Big D. I don't give a curse, Chooka. It's Demolition for me one way or the other if I don't get that girl. Where is she?"

Chooka was almost completely paralyzed. "Through . . . door, she croaked. "Fourth room . . . Left . . . After turn."

Reich dropped her. He ran across the bedroom, through the door, and came to a corkscrewed ramp. He mounted it, took a sharp turn, counted doors and stopped before the fourth on the left. He listened for an instant. No sound. He thrust open the door and entered. There was an empty bed, a single dresser, an empty closet, a single chair.

"Gulled, by God!" he cried. He stepped to the bed. It showed no sign of use. Neither did the closet. As he turned to leave the room, he yanked at the middle dresser drawer and tore it open. It contained a frost white silk gown and a stained steel object that looked like a malignant flower. It was the murder weapon; the knife-pistol.

"My God!" Reich breathed. "Oh my God."

He snatched up the gun and inspected it. Its chambers still contained the emasculated cartridges. The one that had blown the top of Craye D'Courtney's head out was still in place under the hammer.

"It isn't Demolition yet," Reich muttered. "Not by a damned sight. No, by Christ, not by a damned sight!" He folded up the knife-pistol and thrust it into his pocket. At that moment he heard the sound of distant laughter—a sour laugh. Quizzard's laugh.

Reich stepped quickly to the twisted ramp and followed the sound of the laughter to a plush door hung open on brass hinges and deep set in the wall. Gripping the scrambler at the alert with the trigger set for Big D, Reich stepped through the door. There was a hiss of compressed air and it closed behind him.

He was in a small round room, walled and ceilinged in midnight velvet. The floor was transparent crystal, and gave a clear uninterrupted view of a boudoir on the floor below. It was Chooka's Voyeur Chamber.

In the boudoir, Quizzard sat in a deep chair, his blind eyes glazing. The D'Courtney girl was perched on his lap wearing an astonishing slit gown of sequins. She sat quietly, her yellow hair smooth, her deep dark eyes staring placidly into space, while Quizzard fondled her brutally.

"How does she look?" Quizzard's sour voice came distinctly. "How does she feel?"

He was speaking to a small faded woman who stood across the boudoir from him with her back against the wall and an incredible expression of agony on her face. It was Quizzard's wife.

"How does she look?" the blind man repeated.

"She doesn't know what's happening," the woman answered.

"She knows," Quizzard shouted. "She isn't that far gone. Don't tell me she don't know what's happening. Christ! If I only had my eyes!"

The woman said: "I'm your eyes, Keno."

"Then look for me. Tell me!"

Reich cursed and aimed the scrambler at Quizzard's head. It could kill through the crystal floor. It could kill through anything. It was going to kill now. Then Powell entered the boudoir.

The woman saw him at once. She emitted a bloodcurdling scream: "Run, Keno! Run!" She thrust herself from the wall and darted toward Powell, her hands clawing at his eyes. Then she tripped and fell prone. Apparently, the fall knocked her unconscious, for she never moved. As Quizzard surged up from the chair with the girl in his arms, his blind eyes staring, Reich came to the appalled conclusion that the woman's fall was no accident; for Quizzard suddenly dropped in his tracks. The girl tumbled out of his arms and fell into the chair.

There was no doubt that Powell had accomplished this on a TP level, and for the first time in their war, Reich was afraid of Powell—physically afraid. Again he aimed the scrambler, this time at Powell's head as the peeper walked to the chair.

Powell said: "Good evening, Miss D'Courtney."

Reich muttered: "Goodbye, Mr. Powell," and tried to hold his trembling hand steady on Powell's skull.

Powell said: "Are you all right, Miss D'Courtney?" When the girl failed to answer, he bent down and stared into her blank, placid face. He touched her arm and repeated: "Are you all right, Miss D'Courtney? Miss D'Courtney! Do you need help?"

At the word "help" the girl whipped upright in the chair in a listening attitude. Then she thrust out her legs and leaped from the chair. She ran past Powell in a straight line, stopped abruptly and reached out as though grasping a doorknob. She turned the knob, thrust an imaginary door open and burst forward, yellow hair flying, dark eyes wide with alarm . . . A lightning flash of wild beauty.

"Father!" she screamed. "For God's sake! Father!"

She ran forward, then stopped short and backed away as though eluding someone. She darted to the left and ran in a half circle, screaming wildly, her eyes fixed.

"No!" she cried. "No! For the love of Christ! Father!"

She ran again, then stopped and struggled with imaginary arms that held her. She fought and screamed, her eyes still fixed, then stiffened and clapped her hands to her ears as though a violent sound had pierced them. She fell forward to her knees and crawled across the floor, moaning in pain. Then she stopped, snatched at something on the floor, and remained crouched on her knees, her face once again placid, doll-like and dead.

With sickening certainty, Reich knew what the girl had just done. She had relived the death of her father. She had relived it for Powell. And if he had peeped her . . .

Powell went to the girl and raised her from the floor. She arose as gracefully as a dancer, as serenely as a somnambulist. The peeper put his arm around her and took her to the door. Reich followed him all the way with the muzzle of the scrambler, waiting for the best shooting angle. He was invisible. His unsuspecting enemies were below him, easy targets for the death notch. He could win safety with a shot. Powell opened the door, then suddenly swung the girl around, held her close to him and looked up. Reich caught his breath.

"Go ahead," Powell called. "Here we are. An easy shot. One for the both of us. Go ahead!" His lean face was suffused with anger. The heavy jet brows scowled over the dark eyes. For half a minute he stared up at the invisible Reich, waiting, hating, daring. At last Reich lowered his eyes and turned his face away from the man who could not see him.

Then Powell took the docile girl through the door and closed it quietly behind him, and Reich knew he had permitted safety to slip through his fingers. He was halfway to Demolition.

10

Conceive of a camera with a lens distorted into wild astigmatism so that it can only photograph the same picture over and over–the scene that twisted it into shock. Conceive of a bit of recording crystal, traumatically warped so that it can only reproduce the same fragment of music over and over, the one terrifying phrase it cannot forget.

"She's in a state of hysterical recall," Dr. Jeems of Kingston Hospital explained to Powell and Mary Noyes in the living room of Powell's house. "She responds to the key word 'help' and relives one terrifying experience."

"The death of her father," Powell said.

"Oh? I see. Outside of that . . . Catatonia."

"Permanent?" Mary Noyes asked.

Young Doctor Jeems looked surprised and indignant. He was one of the brighter young men of Kingston Hospital despite the fact that he was not a peeper, and was fanatically devoted to his work. "In this day and age? Nothing is permanent except physical death, Miss Noyes, and up at Kingston we've started working on that. Investigating death from the symptomatic point of view, we've actually–"

"Later, Doctor," Powell interrupted. "No lectures tonight. We've got work. Can I use the girl?"

"Use her how?"

"Peep her."

Jeems considered. "No reason why not. I gave her the Déjà Eprouvé Series for catatonia. That shouldn't get in the way."

"The Déjà Eprouvé Series?" Mary asked.

"A great new treatment," Jeems said excitedly. "Developed by Gart–one of your peepers. Patient goes into catatonia. It's an escape. Flight from reality. The conscious mind cannot face the conflict between the external world and its own unconscious. It wishes it had never been born. It attempts to revert back to the foetal stage. You understand?"

Mary nodded. "So far."

"All right. Déjà Eprouvé is an old nineteenth-century psychiatric term. Literally, it means: 'something already experienced, already tried.' Many patients wish for something so strongly that finally the wish makes them imagine that the act or the experience in which they never engaged has already happened. Get it?"

"Wait a minute," Mary began slowly. "You mean I–"

"Put it this way," Jeems interrupted briskly. "Pretend you had a burning wish to . . . oh, say, to be married to Powell here and have a family. Right?"

Mary flushed. In a rigid voice she said: "Right." For a moment Powell yearned to blast this well-meaning, clumsy young Normal.

"Well," Jeems continued in blithe ignorance. "If you lost your balance you might come to believe that you'd married Powell and had three children. That would be Déjà Eprouvé. Now what we do is synthesize an artificial Déjà Eprouvé for the patient. We make the catatonic wish to escape come true. We make the experience they desire actually happen. We dissociate the mind from the lower levels, send it back to the womb, and let it pretend it's being born to a new life all over again. Got that?"

"Got it." Mary tried to smile as her control returned.

"On the surface of the mind . . . in the conscious level . . . the patient goes through development all over again at an accelerated rate. Infancy, childhood, adolescence, and finally maturity."

"You mean Barbara D'Courtney is going to be a baby . . . learn to speak . . . walk . . . ?"

"Right. Right. Right. Takes about three weeks. By the time she catches up with herself, she'll be ready to accept the reality she's trying to escape. She'll have grown up to it, so to speak. Like I said, this is only on the conscious level. Below that, she won't be touched. You can peep her all you like. Only trouble is . . . she must be pretty scared down there. Mixed up. You'll have trouble getting what you want. Of course, that's your specialty. You'll know what to do."

Jeems stood up abruptly. "Got to get back to the shop." He made for the front door. "Delighted to be of service. Always delighted to be called in by peepers. I can't understand the recent hostility toward you people." He was gone.

"Ummm. That was a significant parting note."

"What'd he mean, Linc?"

"Our great & good friend, Ben Reich. Reich's been backing an Anti-Esper campaign. You know . . . peepers are clannish, can't be trusted, never become patriots, Interplanetary conspirators, eat little Normal babies, &c."

"Ugh! And he's supporting the League of Patriots too. He's a disgusting, dangerous man."

"Dangerous but not disgusting, Mary. He's got charm. That's what makes him doubly dangerous. People always expect villains to look villainous. Well, maybe we can take care of Reich before it's too late. Bring Barbara down, Mary."

Mary brought the girl downstairs and seated her on the low dais. Barbara sat like a calm statue. Mary had dressed her in blue leotards and combed her blond hair back, tying it into a fox-tail with blue ribbon. Barbara was polished and shining; a lovely waxwork doll.

"Lovely outside; mangled inside. Damn Reich!"

"What about him?"

"I told you, Mary. I was so mad at Chooka Frood's coop, I handed it to that red slug Quizzard and his wife. And when I peeped Reich upstairs, I threw it in his teeth. I—"

"What did you do to Quizzard?"

"Basic Neuro-Shock. Come up to the Lab sometime and we'll show you. It's new. If you make 1st we'll teach you. It's like the scrambler but psychogenic."

"Fatal?"

"Forgotten the Pledge? Of course not."

"And you peeped Reich through the floor? How?"

"TP reflection. The Voyeur Chamber wasn't wired for sound. It had open acoustical ducts. Reich's mistake. He was transmitting down the channel and I swear I was hoping he had the guts to shoot. I was going to blast him with a Basic that would have made Case History."

"Why didn't he shoot?"

"I don't know, Mary. I don't know. He thought he had every reason to kill us. He thought he was safe . . . Didn't know about the Basic, even though Quizzard's Decline & Fall jolted him . . . But he couldn't."

"Afraid?"

"Reich's no coward. He wasn't afraid. He just couldn't. I don't know why. Maybe next time it'll be different. That's why I'm keeping Barbara D'Courtney in my house. She'll be safe here."

"She'll be safe in Kingston Hospital."

"But not quiet enough for the work I've got to do."

"?"

"She's got the detailed picture of the murder locked up in her hysteria. I've got to get at it . . . piece by piece. When I've got it, I've got Reich."

Mary arose. *"Exit Mary Noyes."*

"Sit down, peeper! Why d'you think I called you? You're staying here with the girl. She can't be left alone. You two can have my bedroom. I'll convert the study for myself."

"Choke it, Linc. Don't jet off like that. You're embarrassed. Let's see if I can't maybe thread-needle through that mind block."

"Listen—"

"No you don't, Mr. Powell." Mary burst into laughter. *"So that's it. You want me for a chaperone. Victorian word, isn't it? So are you, Linc. Positively atavistic."*

"I brand that as a lie. In toffy circles I'm known as the most progressive—"

"And what's that image? Oh. Knights of the Round Table. Sir Galahad Powell. And there's something underneath that. I—" Suddenly she stopped laughing and turned pale.

"What'd you dig?"

"Forget it."

"Oh, come on, Mary."

"Forget it, Linc. And don't peep me for it. If you can't reach it yourself, you'd better not get it second-hand. Especially from me."

He looked at her curiously for a moment, then shrugged. *"All right, Mary. Then we'd better go to work."*

To Barbara D'Courtney he said: "Help, Barbara."

Instantly she whipped upright on the dais in a listening attitude, and he probed delicately. Sensation of bedclothes . . . Voice calling dimly . . . *Whose voice, Barbara?* Deep in the preconscious she answered: "Who is that?" *A friend, Barbara.* "There's no one. No one. I'm alone." And she was alone, racing down a corridor to thrust a door open and burst into an orchid room to see—*What, Barbara?* "A man. Two men." *Who?* "Go away. Please go away. I don't like voices. There's a voice screaming. Screaming in my ears . . ." And she was screaming while instincts of terror made her dodge from a dim figure that clutched at her to keep her from her father. She turned and circled. *What is your father doing, Barbara?* "He– No. You don't belong here. There's only the three of us. Father and me and–" And the dim figure caught her. A flash of his face. No more. *Look again, Barbara. Sleek head. Wide eyes. Small chiseled nose. Small sensitive mouth. Like a scar. Is that the man? Look at the picture. Is that the man?* "Yes. Yes. Yes." And then all was gone.

And she was kneeling again, placid, doll-like, dead.

Powell wiped perspiration from his face and took the girl back to the dais. He was badly shaken–worse than Barbara D'Courtney. Hysteria cushioned the emotional impact for her. He had nothing. He was reliving her terror, her horror, her torture, naked and unprotected.

"It was Ben Reich, Mary. Did you get the picture, too?"

"Couldn't stay in long enough, Linc. Had to run for cover."

"It was Reich, all right. Only question is, how in hell did he kill her father? What did he use? Why didn't old D'Courtney put up a fight to defend himself? Have to try again. I hate to do this to her . . ."

"I hate you to do this to yourself."

"Have to." He took a deep breath and said: "Help, Barbara."

Again she whipped upright on the dais in a listening attitude. He slipped in quickly. *Gently, dear. Not so fast. There's plenty of time.* "You again?" *Remember me, Barbara?* "No. No. I don't know you. Get out." *But I'm part of you, Barbara. We're running down the corridor together. See? We're opening the door together. It's so much easier, together. We help each other.* "We?" *Yes, Barbara, you and I.* "But why don't you help me now?" *How can I, Barbara?* "Look at Father! Help me stop him. Stop him. Stop him. Help me scream. Help me! For pity's sake, help me!"

She knelt again, placid, doll-like, dead.

Powell felt a hand under his arm and realized he was not supposed to be kneeling too. The body before him slowly disappeared; the orchid room disappeared, and Mary Noyes was straining to raise him.

"You first this time," she said grimly.

He shook his head and tried to help Barbara D'Courtney. He fell to the floor.

"All right, Sir Galahad. Cool awhile."

Mary raised the girl and led her to the dais. Then she returned to Powell. *"Ready for help now, or don't you think it's manly?"*

"The word is virile. Don't waste your time trying to help me up. I need brain power. We're in trouble."

"What'd you peep?"

"D'Courtney wanted to be murdered."

"No!"

"Yep. He wanted to die. For all I know he may have committed suicide in front of Reich. Barbara's recall is confused. That point's got to be cleared up. I'll have to see D'Courtney's physician."

"That's Sam @kins. He and Sally went back to Venus last week."

"Then I'll have to make the trip. Do I have time to catch the ten-o'clock rocket? Call Idlewild."

Sam @kins, E.M.D. 1, received Cr. 1,000 per hour of analysis. The public knew that Sam earned two million credits per year, but it did not know that Sam was efficiently killing himself with charity work. @kins was one of the burning lights of the Guild long-range education plan, and leader of the Environment Clique which believed that telepathic ability was not a congenital characteristic, but rather a latent quality of every living organism which could be developed by suitable training.

As a result, Sam's desert house in the brilliant arid mesa outside Venusburg was overrun by charity cases. He invited everyone in the low-income brackets to trek their problems out to him, and while he was solving them, he was carefully attempting to foster telepathy in his patients. Sam's reasoning was quite simple. If, say, peeping were a question of developing unused muscles, it might well be that the majority of people had been too lazy or lacked opportunity to do so. But when a man is caught up in the press of a crisis, he cannot afford to be lazy; and Sam was there to offer opportunity and training. So far, his results had been the discovery of 2% Latent Espers, which was under the average of the Guild Institute interviews. Sam remained undiscouraged.

Powell found him charging through the rock garden of his desert home vigorously destroying desert flowers under the impression that he was cultivating, and conducting simultaneous conversations with a score of depressed people who followed him about like puppies. The perpetual clouds of Venus radiated dazzling light. Sam's bald head was burned pink. He was snorting and shouting at plants and patients alike.

"Damn it! Don't you tell me that's a glow-wort. It's a weed. Don't I know a weed when I see it? Hand me the rake, Bernard."

A small man in black handed him the rake and said: "My name is Walter, Dr. @kins."

"And that's your whole trouble," @kins grunted, tearing out a clump of rubbery red. It changed colors in prismatic hysteria and emitted a plaintive wail which proved it was neither weed nor glow-wort but the disconcerting pussywillow of Venus.

@kins eyed it with disfavor, watching the collapsing air bladders cry. Then he glared at the small man. "Semantic escape, Bernard. You live in terms of the label, not the object. It's your escape from reality. What are you running away from, Bernard?"

"I was hoping you'd tell me, Dr. @kins," Walter replied.

Powell stood quietly, enjoying the spectacle. It was like an illustration from a primitive Bible. Sam, an ill-tempered Messiah, glowering at his humble disciples. Around them the glittering silica stones of the rock garden, crawling with the dry motley-colored Venus plants. Overhead, the blinding nacre glow; and in the background, as far as the eye could reach, the red, purple, and violet Badlands of the planet.

@kins snorted at Walter/Bernard: "You remind me of the redhead. Where is that make-believe courtesan anyway?"

A pretty redheaded girl jostled through the crowd and smirked: "Here I am, Dr. @kins."

"Well, don't preen yourself because I labeled you." @kins frowned at her and continued on the TP level: *"You're delighted with yourself because you're a woman, aren't you? It's your substitute for living. It's your fantasy. 'I'm a woman,' you tell yourself. 'Therefore, men desire me. It's enough to know that thousands of men could have me if I'd let them. That makes me real.' Nonsense! You can't escape that way. Sex isn't make-believe. Life isn't make-believe. Virginity isn't an apotheosis."*

@kins waited impatiently for a response, but the girl merely smirked and postured before him. Finally he burst out: *"Didn't any of you hear what I told her?"*

"I did, teacher."

"Lincoln Powell! No! What are you doing here? Where'd you sneak up from?"

"From Terra, Sam. Came for a consultation and can't stay long. Got to jet back on the next rocket."

"Couldn't you phone Interplanetary?"

"It's complicated, Sam. Has to be done peeper-wise. It's the D'Courtney case."

"Oh. Ah. Hm. Right. Be with you in a minute. Go get something to drink." @kins let out a warning blast. *"SALLY. COMPANY."*

One of @kins' flock unaccountably flinched and Sam turned on the man excitedly. "You heard that, didn't you?"

"No sir. I didn't hear nothing."

"Yes you did. You picked up a TP broadcast."

"No, Dr. @kins."

"Then why did you jump?"

"A bug bit me."

"It did not," @kins roared. "There are no bugs in my garden. You heard me yell to my wife." And then he began a frightful racket. *"YOU CAN ALL HEAR ME. DON'T SAY YOU CAN'T. DON'T YOU WANT TO BE HELPED? ANSWER ME. GO AHEAD. ANSWER ME!"*

Powell found Sally @kins in the cool, spacious living room of the house. The ceiling was open to the sky. It never rained on Venus. A plastic dome was enough to provide shade from the sky that blazed through the seven-hundred-hour-long Venus day. And when the seven hundred hour night began its deadly chill, the @kinses simply packed up and returned to their heated city unit in Venusburg. Everyone on Venus lived in thirty-day cycles.

Sam came bouncing into the living room and engulfed a quart of ice water. *"Ten credits down the drain, black market,"* he shot at Powell. *"You know that? We've got a water black market on Venus. And what the devil are the police doing about it? Never mind, Linc. I know it's out of your jurisdiction. What's with D'Courtney?"*

Powell presented the problem. Barbara D'Courtney's hysterical recall of the death of her father was susceptible of two interpretations. Either Reich had killed D'Courtney, or merely been a witness to D'Courtney's suicide. Old Man Mose would insist on that being cleared up.

"I see. The answer is yes. D'Courtney was suicidal."

"Suicidal? How?"

"He was crumbling. His adaptation pattern was shattering. He was regressing under emotional exhaustion and on the verge of self-destruction. That's why I rushed over to Terra to cut him off."

"Hmmm. That's a blow, Sam. Then he could have blown the back of his head out, eh?"

"What? Blown the back of his head out?"

"Yes. Here's the picture. We don't know what the weapon was, but—"

"Wait a minute. Now I can give you something definite. If D'Courtney died that way he certainly did not commit suicide."

"Why not?"

"Because he had a poison fixation. He was set on killing himself with narcotics. You know suicides, Linc. Once they've fixed on a particular form of death, they never change it. D'Courtney must have been murdered."

"Now we're jetting places, Sam. Tell me, why was D'Courtney set on suicide by poison?"

"You supposed to be funny? If I knew, he wouldn't have been. I'm not too happy about all this, Powell. Reich turned my case into a failure. I could have saved D'Courtney. I—"

"You made any guesses why D'Courtney's pattern was crumbling?"

"Yes. He was trying to take drastic action to escape deep guilt sensations."

"Guilt about what?"

"His child."

"Barbara? How? Why?"

"I don't know. He was fighting irrational symbols of abandonment . . . desertion . . . shame . . . loathing . . . cowardice. We were going to work on that. That's all I know."

"Could Reich have figured and counted on all this? That's something Old Man Mose is going to fuss about. When we present him the case."

"Reich might have guessed— No. Impossible. He'd need expert help to—"

"Hold it, Sam. You've got something hidden under that. I'd like to get it if I can . . ."

"Go ahead. I'm wide open."

"Don't try to help me. You're just mixing everything. Easy, now . . . association with festivity . . . party . . . conversation at— my party. Last month. Gus Tate, an expert himself, but needing help on a similar patient of his own, he said. If Tate needed help, you reasoned, Reich certainly would need help." Powell was so upset he spoke aloud. "Well how about that peeper?"

"How about what?"

"Gus Tate was at the Beaumont party the night D'Courtney was killed. He came with Reich, but I kept hoping—"

"Linc, I don't believe it!"

"Neither did I, but there it is. Little Gus Tate was Reich's expert. Little Gus laid it out for him. He pumped you and turned his information over to a killer. Good old Gus. What price the Esper Pledge now?"

"What price Demolition!" @kins answered fiercely.

From somewhere inside the house came an announcement from Sally @kins: *"Linc. Phone."*

"Hell! Mary's the only one who knows I'm here. Hope nothing's happened to the D'Courtney girl."

Powell loped down a hall toward the v-phone alcove. In the distance he saw Beck's face on the screen. His lieutenant saw him at the same moment and waved excitedly. He began talking before Powell was within earshot.

". . . gave me your number. Lucky I caught you, boss. We've got twenty-six hours."

"Wait a minute. Take it from the top, Jax."

"Your rhodopsin man, Dr. Wilson Jordan, is back from Callisto. Now a man of property by courtesy of Ben Reich. I came back with him. He's on earth for twenty-six hours to settle his affairs, and then he rockets back to Callisto to live on his brand-new estate forever. If you want anything from him, you'd better come quick."

"Will Jordan talk?"

"Would I call you Interplanetary if he would? No, boss. He's got money-measles. Also he's grateful to Reich who (I am now quoting) generously stepped out of the legal picture in favor of Dr. Jordan and justice. If you want anything, you'd better come back to Terra and get it yourself."

"And this," Powell said, "is our Guild Laboratory, Dr. Jordan."

Jordan was impressed. The entire top floor of the Guild building was devoted to laboratory research. It was a circular floor, almost a thousand feet in diameter, domed with a double layer of controlled quartz that could give graded illumination from full to total darkness, including monochrome light to within one tenth of an angstrom. Now, at noon, the sunlight was modulated slightly so that it flooded the tables and benches, the crystal and silver apparatus, the coveralled workers with a gentle peach radiance.

"Shall we stroll?" Powell suggested pleasantly.

"I haven't much time, Mr. Powell, but . . ." Jordan hesitated.

"Of course not. Very kind of you to give us an hour, but we need you desperately."

"If it's anything to do with D'Courtney," Jordan began.

"Who? Oh yes. The murder. Whatever put that into your mind?"

"I've been hounded," Jordan said grimly.

"I assure you, Dr. Jordan. We're asking for research guidance, not information on a murder case. What's murder to a scientist? We're not interested."

Jordan unfolded a little. "Very true. You have only to look at this laboratory to realize that."

"Shall we tour?" Powell took Jordan's arm. To the entire laboratory he broadcast: *"Stand by, peepers! We're pulling a fast one."*

Without interrupting their work, the lab technicians responded with loud razzberries. And amid a hail of derisory images came the raucous cry of a backbiter: *"Who stole the weather, Powell?"* This apparently referred to an obscure episode in Dishonest Abe's lurid career which no one had ever succeeded in peeping, but which never failed to make Powell blush. It did not fail now. A silent cackle filled the room.

"No. This is serious, peepers. My whole case hangs on something I've got to coax out of this man."

Instantly the silent cackle was stilled.

"This is Dr. Wilson Jordan," Powell announced. *"He specializes in visual physiology and he's got information I want him to volunteer. Let's make him feel paternal. Please fake obscure visual problems and beg for help. Make him talk."*

They came by ones, by twos, in droves. A redheaded researcher, actually working on a problem of a transistor which would record the TP impulse, hastily invented the fact that TP optical transmission was astigmatic and humbly requested enlightenment. A pair of pretty girls, engrossed in the infuriating dead end of long-range telepathic communication, demanded of Dr. Jordan why transmission of visual images always showed color aberration, which it did not. The Japanese team, experts on the Extrasensory Node, center of TP perceptivity, insisted that the Node was in circuit with the optic nerve (it wasn't within two millimeters of same) and besieged Dr. Jordan with polite hissings and specious proofs.

At 1:00 P.M., Powell said: "I'm sorry to interrupt, Doctor, but your hour is finished and you've got important business to—"

"Quite all right. Quite all right," Jordan interrupted. "Now my dear doctor, if you would try a transection of the optic—" &c.

At 1:30 P.M. Powell gave the time signal again. "It's half past one, Dr. Jordan. You jet at five. I really think—"

"Plenty of time. Plenty of time. Women and rockets, you know. There's always another. The fact is, my dear sir, your admirable work contains one significant flaw. You have never checked the living Node with a vital dye. Ehrlich Röt, perhaps, or Gentian Violet. I would suggest . . ." &c.

At 2:00 P.M. a buffet luncheon was served without interrupting the feast of reason.

At 2:30 P.M., Dr. Jordan, flushed and ecstatic, confessed that he loathed the idea of being rich on Callisto. No scientists there. No meetings of the minds. Nothing on the level of this extraordinary seminar.

At 3:00 P.M., he confided to Powell how he had inherited his foul estate. Seemed that Craye D'Courtney originally owned it. The old Reich (Ben's father) must have swindled it one way or another, and placed it in his wife's name. When she died, it went to her son. That thief Ben Reich must have had conscience qualms, for he threw it into open court, and by some legal hokey-pokey Wilson Jordan came up with it.

"And he must have plenty more on his conscience," Jordan said. "The things I saw when I worked for him! But all financiers are crooks. Don't you agree?"

"I don't think that's true of Ben Reich," Powell replied, striking the noble note. "I rather admire him."

"Of course. Of course," Jordan agreed hastily. "After all, he does have a conscience. That's admirable indeed. I wouldn't want him to think that I–"

"Naturally." Powell became a fellow-conspirator and captivated Jordan with a grin. "As fellow scientists we can deplore; but as men of the world we can only praise."

"You *do* understand." Jordan shook Powell's hand effusively.

And at 4:00 P.M., Dr. Jordan informed the genuflecting Japanese that he would gladly volunteer his most secret work on Visual Purple to these fine youngsters to aid them in their own research. He was handing on the torch to the next generation. His eyes moistened and his throat choked with sentiment as he spent twenty minutes carefully describing the Rhodopsin Ionizer he had developed for Monarch.

At 5:00 P.M., the Guild scientists escorted Dr. Jordan by launch to his Callisto rocket. They filled his stateroom with gifts and flowers; they filled his ears with grateful testimonials, and he accelerated toward Jupiter's fourth satellite with the pleasant knowledge that he had materially benefited science and never betrayed that fine and generous patron, Mr. Benjamin Reich.

Barbara was in the living room on all fours, crawling energetically. She had just been fed and her face was eggy.

"Hajajajajaja," she said. "Haja."

"Mary! Come quick! She's talking!"

"No!" Mary ran in from the kitchen. *"What'd she say?"*

"She called me Dada."

"Haja," said Barbara. "Hajajajahajaja."

Mary blasted him with scorn. *"She said nothing of the kind. She said Haja."* She returned to the kitchen.

"She meant Dada. Is it her fault if she's too young to articulate?" Powell knelt alongside Barbara. "Say Dada, baby. *Dada? Dada? Say Dada."*

"Haja," Barbara replied with an enchanting drool.

Powell gave it up. He went down past the conscious level to the preconscious.

Hello, Barbara.

"You again?"

Remember me?

"I don't know."

Sure you do. I'm the guy who pries into your private little turmoil down here. We fight it out together.

"Just the two of us?"

Just the two of us. Do you know who you are? Would you like to know why you're buried way down here in this solitary existence?

"I don't know. Tell me."

Well, dear infant, once upon a time you were like this before—an entity merely existing. Then you were born. You had a mother and a father. You grew up into a lovely girl with blond hair and dark eyes and a sweet graceful figure. You traveled from Mars to Earth with your father and you were—

"No. There's no one but you. Just the two of us together in the darkness."

There was your father, Barbara.

"There was no one. There is no one else."

I'm sorry, dear. I'm really sorry, but we must go through the agony again. There's something I have to see.

"No. No . . . please. It's just the two of us alone together. Please, dear spook . . ."

It'll be just the two of us together, Barbara. Stay close, dear. There was your father in the other room . . . the orchid room . . . and suddenly we heard something . . . Powell took a deep breath and cried: "Help. Barbara. Help!"

And they whipped upright in a listening attitude. Sensation of bedclothes. Cool floor under running feet and the endless corridor until at last they burst through the door into the orchid room and screamed and dodged the startled grasp of Ben Reich while he raised something to father's mouth. Raised what? Hold that image. Photograph it. Christ! That horrible muffled explosion. The back of the head burst out and the loved, the adored, the worshipped figure crumpling unbelievably, tearing at their hearts while they moaned and crawled across the floor to snatch a malignant steel flower from the waxen—

"Get up, Linc! For heaven's sake!"

Powell found himself dragged to his feet by Mary Noyes. The air was crackling with indignation.

"Can't I leave you alone for a minute? Idiot!"

"Have I been kneeling here long, Mary?"

"At least a half hour. I came in and found you two like this . . ."

"I got what I was after. It was a gun, Mary. An ancient explosive weapon. Clear picture. Take a look."

"Mmmmm. That's a gun?"

"Yes."

"Where'd Reich get it? Museum?"

"I don't think so. I'm going to play a long shot. Kill two birds. Leave me at the phone."

Powell lurched to the phone and dialed BD-12,232. Presently, Church's twisted face appeared on the screen.

"Hi, Jerry."

"Hello . . . Powell." Cautious. Guarded.

"Did Gus Tate buy a gun from you, Jerry?"

"Gun?"

"Explosive weapon. Twentieth-century style. Used in the D'Courtney murder."

"No!"

"Yes indeed. I think Gus Tate is our killer, Jerry. I was wondering if he bought the gun from you. I'd like to bring the picture of the gun over and check with you." Powell hesitated and then stressed the next words gently: "It'd be a big help, Jerry, and I'll be extremely appreciative. Extremely. Wait for me. I'll be up in half an hour."

Powell hung up. He looked at Mary. Image of an eye winking. *"That ought to give little Gus time to hustle over to Church's place."*

"Why Gus? I thought Ben Reich was–" She caught the picture Powell had sketched in at @kins' house. *"Oh. I see. It's a trap for both Tate and Church. Church sold the gun to Reich."*

"Maybe. It's a long shot. But he does run a hockshop, and that's next door to a museum."

"And Tate helped Reich use the gun on D'Courtney? I don't believe it."

"Almost a certainty, Mary."

"So you're playing one against the other."

"And both against Reich. We've failed on the objective level all the way down the line. From here on in it's got to be peeper tricks or I'm through."

"But suppose you can't play them against Reich? What if they call Reich in?"

"They can't. We lured Reich out of town. Scared Keno Quizzard into running for his life, and Reich's out somewhere trying to cut him off and gag him."

"You really are a thief, Linc. I bet you did steal the weather."

"No," he said. "Dishonest Abe did." He blushed, kissed Mary, kissed Barbara D'Courtney, blushed again and left the house in confusion.

11

The pawnshop was in darkness. A single lamp burned on the counter, sending out its sphere of soft light. As the three men spoke, they leaned in and out of the illumination, their faces and gesticulating hands suddenly appearing and disappearing in staccato eclipses.

"No," Powell said sharply. "I didn't come here to peep anybody. I'm sticking to straight talk. You two peepers may consider it an insult to have words addressed to you. I consider it evidence of good faith. While I'm talking, I'm not peeping."

"Not necessarily," Tate answered. His gnome face popped into the light. "You've been known to finesse, Powell."

"Not now. Check me. What I want from you two, I want objectively. I'm working on a murder. Peeping isn't going to do me any good."

"What do you want, Powell?" Church cut in.

"You sold a gun to Gus Tate."

"The hell he did," Tate said.

"Then why are you here?"

"Am I supposed to take an outlandish accusation like that lying down?"

"Church called you because he sold you the gun and he knows how it was used."

Church's face appeared. "I sold no gun, peeper, and I don't know how any gun was used. That's my objective evidence. Eat it."

"Oh, I'll eat it," Powell chuckled. "I know you didn't sell the gun to Gus. You sold it to Ben Reich."

Tate's face came back into the light. "Then why'd you–"

"Why?" Powell stared into Tate's eyes. "To get you here for a talk, Gus. Let it wait a minute. I want to finish with Jerry." He turned toward Church. "You had the gun, Jerry. It's the kind of thing you would have. Reich came here for it. It's the only place he could come. You did business together before. I haven't forgotten the Chaos Swindle."

"God damn you!" Church shouted.

"It swindled you out of the Guild," Powell continued. "You risked and lost everything for Reich–just because he asked you to peep and squeal on four members of the Stock Exchange. He made a million out of that swindle–just by asking a dumb peeper for a favor."

"He paid for that favor!" Church cried.

"And now all I'm asking for is the gun," Powell answered quietly.

"Are you offering to pay?"

"You know me better than that, Jerry. I threw you out of the Guild because I'm mealy-mouthed Preacher Powell, didn't I? Would I make a shady offer?"

"Then what are you paying for the gun?"

"Nothing, Jerry. You'll have to trust me to do the fair thing; but I'm making no promises."

"I've got a promise," Church muttered.

"You do? Ben Reich, probably. He's long on promise. Sometimes he's short on delivery. You'll have to make up your mind. Trust me or trust Ben Reich. What about the gun?"

Church's face disappeared from the light. After a pause, he spoke from the darkness. "I sold no gun, Peeper, and I don't know how any gun was used. That's my objective evidence for the court."

"Thanks, Jerry." Powell smiled, shrugged, and turned again to Tate. "I just want to ask you one question, Gus. Skipping over the fact that you're Ben Reich's accessory . . . that you pumped Sam @kins about D'Courtney and got the orbits set for him . . . Skipping over the fact that you went to the Beaumont party with Reich, ran interference for him and've been running interference ever since–"

"Wait a minute, Powell–"

"Don't get panicky, Gus. All I want to know is whether I've guessed Reich's bribe correctly. He couldn't bribe you with money. You make too much. He couldn't bribe you with position. You're one of the top peepers in the Guild. He must have bribed you with power, eh? Is that it?"

Tate was peeping him hysterically, and the calm assurance he found in Powell's mind; the casual acceptance of Tate's ruin as an accomplished fact jolted the little peeper with a series of shocks too sudden for adjustment. And he was communicating his panic to Church. All this Powell had planned in preparation for one crucial moment that was to come later.

"Reich could offer you power in his world," Powell continued conversationally, "but it isn't likely. He wouldn't give up any of his own, and you wouldn't want any of his kind. So he must have offered you power in the Esper world. How could he do that? Well, he finances the League of Esper Patriots. My guess is he offered you power through the League. A *coup d'état,* maybe? A dictatorship in the Guild? Probably you're a member of the League."

"Listen, Powell . . ."

"That's my guess, Gus." Powell's voice hardened. "And I've got a hunch I can make my guess good. Did you imagine we'd let you and Reich smash the Guild as easily as that?"

"You'll never prove anything. You'll–"

"Prove? What?"

"Your word against mine. I–"

"You little fool. Haven't you ever been at a peeper trial? We don't run 'em like a court of law, where you swear and then I swear and then a jury tries to figure who's lying. No, little Gus. You stand up there before the board and all the 1sts start probing. You're a 1st, Gus. Maybe you could block two . . . possibly three . . . But not all. I tell you, you're dead."

"Wait a minute, Powell. Wait!" The mannequin face was twitching with terror. *"The Guild takes confession into account. Confession before the fact. I'll give you everything right now. Everything. It was an aberration. I'm sane now. Tell the Guild. When you get mixed*

up with a damned psychotic like Reich, you fall into his pattern. You identify yourself with it. But I'm out of it. Tell the Guild. Here's the whole picture. He came to me with a nightmare about a Man With No Face. He–"

"He was a patient?"

"Yes. That's how he trapped me. He dragooned me! But I'm out of it now. Tell the Guild I'm cooperating. I've recanted. I'm volunteering everything. Church is your witness."

"I'm not witness," Church shouted. "You dirty squealer. After Ben Reich promised–"

"Shut up. You think I want permanent exile? Like you? You were crazy enough to trust Reich. Not me, thank you. I'm not that crazy."

"You whining yellow peeper. Do you think you'll get off? Do you think you'll–"

"I don't give a damn!" Tate cried. "I don't take that kind of medicine for Reich. I'll bust him first. I'll walk into court and sit on the witness stand and do everything I can to help Powell. Tell that to the Guild, Linc. Tell them that–"

"You'll do nothing of the kind," Powell snapped.

"What?"

"You were trained by the Guild. You're still in the Guild. Since when does a peeper squeal on a patient?"

"It's the evidence you need to get Reich, isn't it?"

"Sure, but I'm not taking it from you. I'm not letting any peeper disgrace the rest of us by walking into court and blabbing."

"It could mean your job if you don't get him."

"To hell with my job. I want it, and I want Reich . . . but not at this price. Any peeper can be a right pilot when the orbit's easy; but it takes guts to hold to the Pledge when the heat's on. You ought to know. You didn't have the guts. Look at you now."

"But I want to help you, Powell."

"You can't help me. Not at the price of ethics."

"But I was an accessory!" Tate shouted. "You're letting me off. Is that ethics? Is that–?"

"Look at him," Powell laughed. "He's begging for Demolition. No, Gus. We'll get you when we get Reich. But I can't get him through you. I'll play this according to the Pledge." He turned and left the circle of light. As he walked through the darkness toward the front door, he waited for Church to take the bait. He had played the entire scene for this moment alone . . . but so far there was no action on his hook.

As Powell opened the door, flooding the pawnshop with the cold argent street light, Church suddenly called: "Just a minute."

Powell stopped, silhouetted against the door. "Yes?"

"What have you been handing Tate?"

"The Pledge, Jerry. You ought to remember it."

"Let me peep you on that."

"Go ahead. I'm wide open." Most of Powell's blocks opened. What was not good for Church to discover was carefully jumbled and camouflaged with tangential associations and a kaleidoscopic pattern, but Church certainly could not locate a suspicious block.

"I don't know," Church said at last. "I can't make up my mind."

"About what, Jerry? I'm not peeping you."

"About you and Reich and the gun. God knows, you're a mealy-mouthed preacher, but I think maybe I'd be smarter to trust you."

"That's nice, Jerry. I told you, I can't make any promises."

"Maybe you're the kind that doesn't have to make promises. Maybe the whole trouble with me is that I've always been looking for promises instead of–"

At that moment, Powell's restless radar picked up death out on the street. He whirled and slammed the door. *"Get off the floor. Quick."* He took three steps back toward the globe of light and vaulted onto the counter. *"Up here with me. Jerry, Gus. Quick, you fools!"*

A queasy shuddering seized the pawnshop and shook it into horrible vibration. Powell kicked the light globe and extinguished it.

"Jump for the ceiling light bracket and hold on. It's a Harmonic gun. Jump!" Church gasped and leaped up into the darkness. Powell gripped Tate's shaking arm. *"Too short, Gus? Hold out your hands. I'll toss you."* He flung Tate upward and followed himself, clawing for the steel spider arms of the bracket. The three hung in space, cushioned against the murderous vibrations enveloping the store . . . vibrations that created shattering harmonics in every substance in contact with the floor. Glass, steel, stone, plastic–all screeched and burst apart. They could hear the floor cracking, and the ceiling thundered. Tate groaned.

"Hang on, Gus. It's one of Quizzard's killers. Careless bunch. They've missed me before."

Tate blacked out. Powell could sense every conscious synapse losing hold. He probed for Tate's lower levels: *"Hang on. Hang on. HOLD. HOLD. HOLD!"*

Destruction loomed up in the little peeper's subconscious and in that instant Powell realized that no Guild conditioning could ever have prevented Tate from destroying himself. The death compulsion struck. Tate's hands relaxed and he dropped to the floor. The vibrations ceased an instant later, but in that second Powell heard the thick, gravid choke of bursting flesh. Church heard it too and started to scream.

"Quiet, Jerry! Not yet. Hang on!"

"D-did you hear him? DID YOU HEAR HIM?"

"I heard. We're not safe yet. Hang on!"

The pawnshop door opened a slit. A razor edge of light shot in and searched the floor. It found a broad red and gray organic puddle of flesh, blood, and bones, hovered for three seconds, then blinked out. The door closed.

"All right, Jerry. They think I'm dead again. You can have your hysterics now."

"I can't get down, Powell. I can't step on . . ."

"I don't blame you." Powell held himself with one hand, took Church's arm and swung him toward the counter. Church dropped and shuddered. Powell followed him and fought hard against nausea.

"Did you say that was one of Quizzard's killers?"

"Sure. He owns a squad of psychgoons. Every time we round 'em up and send 'em to Kingston, Quizzard gets another batch. They follow the dope trail to his place."

"But what have they got against you? I–"

"Clever-up, Jerry. They're Ben's deputies. Ben's getting panicky."

"Ben? Ben Reich? But it was in my shop. I might have been here."

"You were here. What the hell difference did that make?"

"Reich wouldn't want me killed. He–"

"Wouldn't he?" Image of a cat smiling.

Church took a deep breath. Suddenly he exploded: "The son of a bitch! The goddamn son of a bitch!"

"Don't feel like that, Jerry. Reich's fighting for his life. You can't expect him to be too careful."

"Well, I'm fighting, too, and that bastard's made up my mind for me. Get ready, Powell. I'm opening up. I'm going to give you everything."

After he finished with Church and returned from headquarters and the Tate nightmare, Powell was grateful for the sight of the blond urchin in his home. Barbara D'Courtney had a black crayon in her right hand and a red crayon in her left. She was energetically scribbling on the walls, her tongue between her teeth and her dark eyes squinted in concentration.

"Baba!" he exclaimed in a shocked voice. "What are you doing?"

"Drawrin pitchith," she lisped. "Nicth pitchith for Dada."

"Thank you, sweetheart," he said. "That's a lovely thought. Now come and sit with Dada."

"No," she said, and continued scribbling.

"Are you my girl?"

"Yeth."

"Doesn't my girl always do what Dada asks?"

She thought that one over. "Yeth," she said. She deposited the crayons in her pocket, her bottom on the couch alongside Powell, and her grubby paws in his hands.

"Really, Barbara," Powell murmured. "That lisping is beginning to worry me. I wonder if your teeth need braces?"

The thought was only half a joke. It was difficult to remember that this was a woman seated alongside him. He looked into the deep dark eyes shining with the empty brilliance of a crystal glass awaiting its fulfilling measure of wine.

Slowly he probed through the vacant conscious levels of her mind to the turbulent preconscious, heavily hung with obscuring clouds like a vast dark nebula in the heavens. Behind the clouds was the faint flicker of light, isolated and childlike, that he had grown to like. But now, as he threaded his way down, that flicker of light was the faint spicule of a star that burned with the hot roar of a nova.

Hello, Barbara. You seem to–

He was answered with a burst of passion that made him backtrack fast.

"Hey, Mary!" he called. "Come quick!"

Mary Noyes popped out of the kitchen. "You in trouble again?"

"Not yet. Soon maybe. Our patient's on the mend."

"I haven't noticed any difference."

"Come on inside with me? She's made contact with her Id. Down on the lowest level. Almost had my brains burned out."

"What do you want? A chaperone? Someone to protect the secrets of her sweet girlish passions?"

"Are you comic? I'm the one who needs protection. Come and hold my hand."

"You've got both of yours in hers."

"Just a figure of speech." Powell glanced uneasily at the calm doll face before him and the cool relaxed hands in his. "Let's go."

He went down the black passages again toward the deep-seated furnace that was within the girl . . . that is within every man . . . the timeless reservoir of psychic energy, reasonless, remorseless, seething with the never-ending search for satisfaction. He could sense Mary Noyes mentally tiptoeing behind him. He stopped at a safe distance.

Hi, Barbara.

"Get out!"

This is the spook.

Hatred lashed out at him.

You remember me?

The hatred subsided into the turbulence to be replaced by a wave of hot desire.

"Linc, you'd better jet. If you get trapped inside that pleasure-pain chaos, you're gone."

"I'd like to locate something."

"You can't find anything in there except raw love and raw death."

"I want her relations with her father. I want to know why he had those guilt sensations about her."

"Well, I'm getting out."

The furnace fumed over again. Mary fled.

Powell teetered around the edge of the pit, feeling, exploring, sensing. It was like an electrician gingerly touching the ends of exposed wires to discover which of them did not carry a knock-out charge. A blazing bolt surged near him. He touched it, was stunned, and stepped aside to feel a blanket of instinctual self-preservation choke him. He relaxed, permitted himself to be drawn down into a vortex of associations and began sorting. He struggled to maintain his frame of reference that was crumbling in that chaos of energy.

Here were the somatic messages that fed the cauldron; cell reactions by the incredible billion, organic cries, the muted drone of muscle tone, sensory subcurrents, blood flow, the wavering superheterodyne of blood pH—all whirling and churning in the balance pattern that formed the girl's psyche. The never-ending make-and-break of synapses contributed a crackling hail of complex rhythms. Packed in the changing interstices were broken images, half-symbols, partial references . . . the ionized nuclei of thought.

Powell caught part of a plosive image, followed it to the letter P . . . to the sensory association of a kiss, then by cross-circuit to the infant's sucking reflex at the breast . . . to an infantile memory of . . . her mother? No. A wet-nurse. That was encrusted with parental associations . . . Negation. Minus Mother . . . Powell dodged an associated flame of infantile rage and resentment, the Orphan's Syndrome. He picked up P again, searched for a related Pa . . . Papa . . . Father.

Abruptly he was face to face with himself.

He stared at the image, teetered on the verge of disintegration, then scrambled back to sanity.

Who the hell are you?

The image smiled beautifully and was gone.

P . . . Pa . . . Papa . . . Father. Heat-of-love-and-devotion-associated-with . . . He was face to face with his image again. This time it was nude, powerful; its outlines haloed with an aura of love and desire. Its arms outstretched.

Get lost. You embarrass me.

The image disappeared. *Damn it! Has she fallen in love with me?*

"Hi, spook."

There was her picture of herself, pathetically caricatured, the blond hair in strings, the dark eyes like blotches, the lovely figure drawn into flat, ungracious planes. It faded, and abruptly the image of Powell-Powerful-Protective-Paternal rushed at him, torrentially destructive. He stayed with it, grappling. The back of the head was D'Courtney's face. He followed the Janus image down to a blazing channel of doubles, pairs, linkages and duplicities to—Reich? Imposs— Yes, Ben Reich and the caricature of Barbara, linked side to side like Siamese twins, brother and sister from the waist upward, their legs turning and twisting separately in a sea of complexity below. B linked to B. B&B. Barbara & Ben. Half joined in blood. Half—

"Linc!"

A call far off. Directionless.

"Lincoln!"

It could wait a second. That amazing image of Reich had to—

"Lincoln Powell! This way, you fool!"

"Mary?"

"I can't find you."

"Be out in a few minutes."

"Linc, this is the third time I've tried to locate you. If you don't come out now, you're lost."

"The third time?"

"In three hours. Please, Linc . . . While I've got the strength."

He permitted himself to wander upward. He could not find upward. The timeless, spaceless chaos roared around him. The image of Barbara D'Courtney appeared, now a caricature of the sexual siren.

"Hi, spook."

"Lincoln, for the love of God!"

In momentary panic, he plunged in any direction until his peeper training reasserted itself. Then the Withdrawal Technique went into automatic operation. The blocks banged down in steady sequence, each barrier a step backward toward the light. Halfway up, he sensed Mary alongside him. She stayed with him until he was once more in his living room, seated alongside the urchin, her hands in his. He dropped the hands as though they were red hot.

"Mary, I located the weirdest association with Ben Reich. Some kind of linkage that–"

Mary had an iced towel. She slapped his face with it smartly. He realized that he was shaking.

"Only trouble is . . . Trying to make sense out of fragments in the Id is like trying to run a qualitative analysis in the middle of a sun."

The towel flicked again.

"You aren't working with unit elements. You're working with ionized particles." He dodged the towel and stared at Barbara. *"My God, Mary, I think this poor kid's in love with me."*

Image of a cockeyed turtledove.

"No kidding. I kept meeting myself down there. I–"

"And what about you?"

"Me?"

"Why do you think you refused to send her to Kingston Hospital?" she said. "Why do you think you've been peeping her twice a day since you brought her here? Why did you have to have a chaperone? I'll tell you, Mr. Powell . . ."

"Tell me what?"

"You're in love with her. You've been in love with her since you found her at Chooka Frood's."

"Mary!"

She stung him with a vivid picture of himself and Barbara D'Courtney and that fragment she had peeped days ago . . . the fragment that had made her turn pale with jealousy and anger. Powell knew it was true.

"Mary, dear . . ."

"Never mind me. To hell with me. You're in love with her, and the girl isn't a peeper. She isn't even sane. How much of her are you in love with? One tenth? What part of her are you in love with? Her face? Her subconscious? What about the other ninety percent? Will you love that when you find it? Damn you! I wish I'd let you stay inside her mind until you rotted!" She turned away and began to cry.

"Mary, for the love of–"

"Shut up," she sobbed. "Damn you, shut up! I . . . There's a message for you. From headquarters. You're to jet for Spaceland as soon as possible. Ben Reich's there, and they've lost him. They need you. Everybody needs you. So why should I complain?"

12

It was years since Powell had last visited Spaceland. He sat in the police launch that had picked him off the luxury ship *Holiday Queen,* and as the launch dropped, Powell stared through the port at Spaceland glittering below like a patchwork quilt worked in silver and gold. He smiled as he always did at the identical image that came to him each time he saw the playground in space. It was a vision of a shipload of explorers from a far galaxy, strange creatures, solemn and studious, who stumbled on Spaceland and researched it. He always tried to imagine how they'd report it and always failed.

"It's a job for Dishonest Abe," he muttered.

Spaceland had started several generations back with a flat plate of asteroid rock half a mile in diameter. A mad health cultist had raised a transparent hemisphere of Air-Gel on the plate, installed an atmosphere generator, and started a colony. From that, Spaceland had grown into an irregular table in space, extending hundreds of miles. Each new entrepreneur had simply tacked another mile or so onto the shelf, raised his own transparent hemisphere, and gone into business. By the time engineers got around to advising Spaceland that the spherical form was more efficient and economical, it was too late to change. The table just went on proliferating.

As the launch swung around, the sun caught Spaceland at an angle, and Powell could see the hundreds of hemispheres shimmering against the blue-black of space like a mass of soap bubbles on a checkered table. The original health colony was now in the center and still in business. The others were hotels, amusement parks, health resorts, nursing homes, and even a cemetery. On the Jupiter side of the table was the giant fifty-mile hemisphere that covered the Spaceland Nature Reservation which guaranteed more natural history and more weather per square mile than any natural planet.

"Let's have the story," Powell said.

The police sergeant gulped. "We followed instructions," he said. "Rough tail on Hassop. Slickie following him. The rough got taken out by Reich's girl . . ."

"It was a girl, eh?"

"Yeah. Cute little trick named Duffy Wyg&."

"Damnation!" Powell jerked bolt upright. The sergeant stared at him. "Why, I questioned that girl myself. I never–" He caught himself. "Seems like I did some lousing myself. Shows you. When you meet a pretty girl . . ." He shook his head.

"Well, like I say," the sergeant continued, "she takes out the rough, and just when the slickie moves in, Reich jets into Spaceland with a commotion."

"Like?"

"Private yacht. Has a crash in space and limps in hollerin' emergency. One killed. Three injured, including Reich. Front of the yacht stove in. Derelict or meteor stray. They take Reich to the hospital where we figure he's planted for a little. When we turn around, Reich's gone. Hassop too. I grab a peeper interpreter and go looking in four languages. No dice."

"Hassop's luggage?"

"Gone likewise."

"Damnation! We've got to pinch Hassop and that luggage. They're our motive. Hassop is Monarch's Code Chief. We need him for that last message Reich sent to D'Courtney and the reply . . ."

"Monday before the murder?"

"Yes. That exchange probably ignited the killing. And Hassop may have Reich's financial records with him. They can probably tell a court why Reich had a hell of a motive for murdering D'Courtney."

"Such as, for instance?"

"The talk around Monarch is that D'Courtney had Reich with his back to the wall."

"You got method and opportunity?"

"Yes and no. I opened up Jerry Church and got everything, but it's ticklish. We can show Reich had the opportunity. It'll stand if the other two stand. We can show the murder method. It'll stand if the other two stand. Same goes for Reich's motive. They're like three wigwam poles. Each of them needs the other two. No one can stand alone. That's Old Man Mose's opinion. And that's why we need Hassop."

"I'll swear they ain't left Spaceland. That efficient I still am."

"Don't hang your head because Reich outsmarted you. He's outsmarted plenty. Me included."

The sergeant shook his head gloomily.

"I'll start peeping Spaceland for Reich and Hassop at once," Powell said as the launch drifted down for the passage through the airlock, "but I want to check a hunch first. Show me the corpse."

"What corpse?"

"From Reich's crash."

In the police mortuary, displayed on an air cushion in the stasis-freeze, the corpse was a mangled figure with dead white skin and a flaming red beard.

"Uh-huh," Powell muttered. "Keno Quizzard."

"You know him?"

"A gimpster. Was working for Reich and turned too hot to be useful. What'll you bet the crash was a cover-up for a killing."

"Hell!" the cop exploded, "those two other guys are hurt bad. Reich might have been faking. Admitted. But the yacht was ruined, and those two other guys–"

"So they were hurt. And the yacht was ruined. So what? Quizzard's mouth is shut for keeps and Reich's that much safer. Reich took care of him. We'll never prove it, but we won't have to if we locate Hassop. That'll be enough to walk friend Reich into Demolition."

Wearing the fashionable spray-gun tights (Spaceland sport clothes were being painted on, this year), Powell began a lightning tour of the bubbles–Victoria Hotel, Sportsman's Hotel, Magic, Home From Home, Ye New Neu Babblesberg, The Martian (very chic), the Venusberg (very bawdy), and the other dozens. . . . Powell struck up conversations with strangers, described his dear old friends in half a dozen languages, and peeped gently to make sure they had the precise picture of Reich and Hassop before they answered. And then the answers. Negative. Always negative.

The peepers were easy–and Spaceland was filled with them, at work and at play–but always the reply was negative.

A revival meeting at Solar Rheims–hundreds of chanting, genuflecting devotees participating in a kind of hopped-up Midsummer Morn festival. Reply negative. Sailing Races in Mars From Home–cat boats and sloops skipping over the water in long hops like scaled stones. Reply negative. The Plastic Surgery Resort . . . hundreds of bandaged faces and bodies. Reply negative, Free-Flight Polo. Reply negative. Hot Sulphur Springs. White Sulphur Springs. Black Sulphur Springs. No Sulphur Springs—replies negative.

Discouraged and depressed, Powell dropped into Solar Dawn Cemetery. The cemetery looked like an English garden—all flagged paths and oak, ash and elm trees with tiny little plots of green grass. Muted music from costumed robot string quartets sawing away in strategic pavilions. Powell began to smile.

There was a faithful reproduction of the Notre Dame Cathedral in the center of the cemetery. It was painstakingly labeled: Ye Wee Kirk O Th'Glen. From the mouth of one of the gargoyles in the tower, a syrupy voice roared: "SEE THE DRAMA OF THE GODS PORTRAYED IN VIBRANT ROBOT-ACTION IN YE WEE KIRK O TH' GLEN. MOSES ON MT. SINAI, THE CRUCIFIXION OF CHRIST, MOHAMMED AND THE MOUNTAIN, LAO TSE AND THE MOON, THE REVELATION OF MARY BAKER EDDY, THE ASCENSION OF OUR LORD BUDDHA, THE UNVEILING OF THE TRUE AND ONLY GOD GALAXY . . ." Pause, and then a little more matter-of-factly: "OWING TO THE SACRED NATURE OF THIS EXHIBIT, ADMISSION IS BY TICKET ONLY. TICKETS MAY BE PURCHASED FROM THE BAILIFF." Pause. Then another voice, injured and pleading: "ATTENTION ALL WORSHIPERS. ATTENTION ALL WORSHIPERS. NO LOUD TALKING OR LAUGHTER . . . PLEASE!" A click, and another gargoyle began in another language. Powell burst out laughing.

"You ought to be ashamed of yourself," a girl said behind him.

Without turning, Powell replied: "I'm sorry. 'No loud talking or laughter.' But don't you think this is the most ludicrous—" Then the pattern of her psyche hit him and he spun around. He was face to face with Duffy Wyg&.

"Well, Duffy!" he said.

Her frown changed to a look of perplexity, then to a quick smile. "Mr. Powell!" she exclaimed. "The boy sleuth. You still owe me a dance."

"I owe you an apology," Powell said.

"Delighted. Can't have enough of them. What's this one for?"

"Underestimating you."

"The story of my life." She linked arms and drew him along the path. "Tell me how reason has finally prevailed. You took another look at me, and—?"

"I realized you're the cleverest person Ben Reich has working for him."

"I am clever. I did do some work for Ben . . . but your compliment seems to have deep brooding undertones. Is there something?"

"The tail we had on Hassop."

"Just a little more accent on the down-beat, please."

"You took out our tail, Duffy. Congratulations."

"Ah-ha! Hassop is your pet horse. A childhood accident robbed him of a horse's crowning glory. You substituted an artificial one which–"

"Clever-up, Duffy. That isn't going to travel far."

"Then, boy wonder, will you ream your tubes?" Her pert face looked up at him, half serious, half amused. "What in hell are you talking about?"

"I'll spell it out. We had a tail on Hassop. A tail is a shadow, a spy, a secret agent assigned to the duty of following and watching a suspect . . ."

"Contents noted. What's a Hassop?"

"A man who works for Ben Reich. His Code Chief."

"And what did I do to your spy?"

"Following instructions from Ben Reich, you captivated the man, enravished him, turned him into a derelict from duty, kept him at a piano all day, day after day, and–"

"Wait a minute!" Duffy spoke sharply. "I know that one. The little bem. Let's square this off. He was a cop?"

"Now, Duffy, if–"

"I asked a question."

"He was a cop."

"Following this Hassop?"

"Yes."

"Hassop . . . Bleached man? Dusty hair? Dusty blue eyes?"

Powell nodded.

"The louse," Duffy muttered. "The lowdown louse!" She turned on Powell furiously. "And you think I'm the kind that does his dirty work, do you! Why, you–you peeper! You listen to me, Powell. Reich asked me to do him a favor. Said there was a man up here working on an interesting musical code. Wanted me to check him. How the hell was I supposed to know he was your goon? How was I supposed to know your goon was masquerading as a musician?"

Powell stared at her. "Are you claiming that Reich tricked you?"

"What else?" She glared back. "Go ahead and peep me. If Reich wasn't in the Reservation you could peep that double-crossing–"

"Hold it!" Powell interrupted sharply. He slipped past her conscious barrier and peeped her precisely and comprehensively for ten seconds. Then he turned and began to run.

"Hey!" Duffy yelled. "What's the verdict?"

"Medal of Honor," Powell called over his shoulder. "I'll pin it on as soon as I bring a man back alive."

"I don't want a man. I want you."

"That's your trouble, Duffy. You want anybody."

"Whooooo?"

"An-y-bod-y."

"NO LOUD TALKING OR LAUGHTER . . . PLEASE!"

Powell found his police sergeant in the Spaceland Globe Theater where a magnificent Esper actress stirred thousands with her moving performances–performances that owed as much to her telepathic sensitivity to audience response as to her exquisite command of stage technique. The cop, immune to the star's appeal, was gloomily inspecting the house, face by face. Powell took his arm and led him out.

"He's in the Reservation," Powell told him. "Took Hassop with him. Took Hassop's luggage too. Perfect alibi. He was shaken up by the crash and he needs a rest. Also company. He's eight hours ahead of us."

"The Reservation, huh?" the sergeant pondered. "Twenty-five hundred square miles of more damned animals, geography, and weather than you ever see in three lives."

"What's the odds Hassop has a fatal accident, if he hasn't had one already?"

"No takers at any price."

"If we want to get Hassop out we'll have to grab a helio and do some fast hunting."

"Uh-uh. No mechanical transportation allowed in the Reservation."

"This is an emergency. Old Man Mose has got to have Hassop!"

"Go let that damn machine argue with the Spaceland Board. You could get special permission in maybe three, four weeks."

"By which time Hassop'd be dead and buried. What about radar or sonar? We could work out Hassop's pattern and–"

"Uh-uh. No mechanical devices outside of cameras allowed in the Reservation."

"What the hell plays with that Reservation?"

"Hundred percent guaranteed pure nature for the eager beavers. You go in at your own risk. Element of danger adds spice to your trip. Get the picture? You battle the elements. You battle the wild animals. You feel primitive and refreshed again. That's what the ads say."

"What do they do in there? Rub sticks together?"

"Sure. You hike on your own feet. You carry your own food. You take one defensive barrier screen with you so's the bears don't eat you. If you want a fire you got to build it. If you want to hunt animals, you got to make your own weapons. If you want to catch fish, likewise. You versus nature. And they make you sign a release in case nature wins."

"Then how are we going to find Hassop?"

"Sign a release and go hike for him."

"The two of us? Cover twenty-five hundred square miles of geography? How many squadmen can you spare?"

"Maybe ten."

"Adding up to two hundred and fifty square miles per cop. Impossible."

"Maybe you could persuade the Spaceland Board– No. Even if you could, we wouldn't be able to get the Board together in under a week. Wait a minute! Could you get 'em together by peeping 'em? Send out urgent messages or something? How do you peepers work that anyway?"

"We can only pick you up. We can't transmit to anybody except another peeper, so– Hey! Ho! That's an idea!"

"What's an idea?"

"Is a human being a mechanical device?"

"Nope."

"Is he a civilized invention?"

"Not lately."

"Then I'm going to do some fast co-opting and take my own radar into the Reservation."

Which is why a sudden craving for nature overtook a prominent lawyer in the midst of delicate contractual negotiations in one of Spaceland's luxurious conference rooms. The same craving also came upon the secretary of a famous author, a judge of domestic relations, a job analyst screening applicants for the United Hotel Association, an industrial designer, an efficiency engineer, the chairman of Amalgamated Union's Grievance Committee, Titan's Superintendent of Cybernetics, a secretary of Political Psychology, two Cabinet members, five parliamentary leaders, and scores of other Esper clients of Spaceland at work and at play.

They filed through the Reservation Gate in a unified mood of holiday festivity and assorted gear. Those that had gotten word on the grapevine early enough were in sturdy camping clothes. Others were not; and the astonished gate guards, checking and inspecting for illicit baggage, saw one lunatic in full diplomatic regalia march through with a pack on his back. But all the nature-lovers carried detailed maps of the Reservation carefully zoned into sectors.

Moving swiftly, they spread out and beat forward across the miniature continent of weather and geography. The TP band crackled as comments and information swept up and down the line of living radar in which Powell occupied the central position.

"Hey. No fair, I've got a mountain dead ahead."

"Snowing here. Full b-b-blizzard."

"Swamps and (ugh!) mosquitoes in my sector."

"Hold it. Party ahead, Linc. Sector 21."

"Shoot a picture."

"Here it is . . ."

"Sorry. No sale."

"Party ahead, Linc. Sector 9."

"Let's have the picture."

"Here it comes . . ."

"Nope. No sale."

"Party ahead, Linc. Sector 17."

"Shoot a picture."

"Hey! It's a goddamn bear!"

"Don't run! Negotiate!"

"Party ahead, Linc. Sector 12."

"Shoot a picture."

"Here it comes . . ."

"No sale."

"AAAAAAA-choo!"

"That the blizzard?"

"No. I'm a cloudburst."

"Party ahead, Linc. Sector 41."

"Shoot a picture."

"Here it is."

"Not them."

"How do you climb a palm tree?"

"You shinny up."

"Not up. Down."

"How'd you get up, your honor?"

"I don't know. A moose helped me."

"Party ahead, Linc. Sector 37."

"Let's have the picture."

"Here it comes."

"No sale."

"Party ahead, Linc. Sector 60."

"Go ahead."

"Here's the picture . . ."

"Pass 'em by."

"How long do we have to keep on traveling?"

"They're at least eight hours ahead."

"No. Correction, peepers. They've got eight hours start but they may not be eight hours ahead."

"Spell that out, will you, Linc?"

"Reich may not have trekked straight ahead. He may have circled around to a favorite spot close to the gate."

"Favorite for what?"

"For murder."

"Excuse me. How does one persuade a cat not to devour one?"

"Use political psychology."

"Use your barrier screen, Mr. Secretary."

"Party ahead, Linc. Sector 1."

"Shoot a picture, Mr. Superintendent."

"Here it is."

"Pass 'em by, sir. That's Reich and Hassop."

"What!"

"Don't make a fuss. Don't make anybody suspicious. Just pass 'em by. When you're out of sight, circle around to Sector 2. Everybody head back for the gate and go home. All my thanks. From here on I'll take it alone."

"Leave us in on the kill, Linc."

"No. This needs finesse. I don't want Reich to know I'm abducting Hassop. It's all got to look logical and natural and unimpeachable. It's a swindle."

"And you're the thief to do it."

"Who stole the weather, Powell?"

The departing peepers were propelled by a hot blush.

This particular square mile of Reservation was jungle, humid, swampy, overgrown. As darkness fell, Powell slowly wormed his way toward the glimmering campfire Reich had built in a clearing alongside a small lake. The water was infested with hippo, crocodile, and swambat. The trees and terrain swarmed with life. The entire jungle was a savage tribute to the brilliance of Reservation ecologists who could assemble and balance nature on the point of a pin. And in tribute to that nature, Reich's defensive barrier screen was in full operation.

Powell could hear mosquitoes whine as they batted against the outer rim of the barrier, and there was an intermittent hail of larger insects caroming off the invisible wall. Powell could not risk operating his own. The screens hummed slightly and Reich had keen ears. He inched forward and peeped.

Hassop was at ease, relaxed, just a little beglamoured by the idea of intimacy with his puissant chief, just a little intoxicated by the knowledge that his film cannister contained Ben Reich's fate. Reich, working feverishly on a crude, powerful bow, was planning the accident that would eliminate Hassop. It was that bow and the sheaf of fire-tipped arrows alongside Reich that had eaten up the eight hours start on Powell. You can't kill a man in a hunting accident unless you go hunting.

Powell lifted his knees and crawled forward, his senses pinpointed on Reich's perception. He froze again as ALARM clanged in Reich's head. Reich leaped to his feet, bow ready, a featherless arrow at half cock, and peered intently into the darkness.

"What is it, Ben?" Hassop murmured.

"I don't know. Something."

"Hell. You've got your barrier, haven't you?"

"I keep forgetting." Reich sank back and built up the fire; but he was not forgetting the barrier. The wary instinct of the killer was warning him, vaguely, persistently. . . . And Powell could only marvel at the intricate survival mechanism of the human mind. He peeped Reich again. Reich was mechanically resorting to the tune block he associated with crisis: *Tenser, said the Tensor. Tenser, said the Tensor. Tension, apprehension, and dissension have begun.* Behind that there was turmoil; a mounting resolution to kill quickly . . . kill savagely . . . destroy now and arrange the evidence later . . .

As Reich reached for the bow, his eyes carefully averted from Hassop, his mind intent on the throbbing heart that was his target, Powell drove forward urgently. Before he had moved ten feet, ALARM tripped again in Reich's mind and the big man was on his feet once more. This time he whipped a burning branch from the fire and hurled the flare toward the blackness where Powell was concealed. The idea and execution came so quickly that Powell could not anticipate the action. He would have been fully illumined if Reich had not forgotten the barrier. It stopped the flaming branch in mid-flight and dropped it to the ground.

"Christ!" Reich cried, and swung around abruptly at Hassop.

"What is it, Ben?"

In answer, Reich drew the arrow back to the lobe of his ear and held the point on Hassop's body. Hassop scrambled to his feet.

"Ben, watch out! You're shooting at me!"

Hassop leaped to one side unexpectedly as Reich let the arrow fly.

"Ben! For the love of–" Suddenly Hassop realized the intent. He turned with a strangulated cry and ran from the fire as Reich notched another arrow. Running desperately, Hassop smashed into the barrier and staggered back from the invisible wall as an arrow shot past his shoulder and shattered.

"Ben!" he screamed.

"You son of a bitch," Reich growled, and notched another shaft.

Powell leaped forward and reached the edge of the barrier. He could not pass it. Inside, Hassop ran screaming across the far side while Reich stalked him with half-cocked bow, closing in for the kill. Hassop again smashed into the barrier, fell, crawled, and regained his feet to dart off again like a cornered rat, Reich following him doggedly.

"Jesus!" Powell muttered. He stepped back into the darkness, thinking desperately. Hassop's screams had aroused the jungle, and there was a roaring and an echoing rumble in his ears. He reached out on the TP band, sensing, touching, feeling. There was nothing but blind fear, blind rage, blind instinct around him. The hippos, sodden and viscid; the crocodiles, deaf, angry, hungry; swambats, as furious as rhinoceroses whose size they doubled. A quarter mile off were the faint broadcasts of elephant, wapiti, giant cats . . .

"It's worth the chance," Powell said to himself. "I've got to bust that barrier. It's the only way."

He set his blocks on the upper levels, masking everything except the emotional broadcast, and transmitted: *fear, fear, terror, fear*– driving the emotion down to its most primitive level–*Fear. Fear. Terror. Fear.* FEAR – FLIGHT – TERROR – *FEAR – FLIGHT – TERROR* – **Flight!**

Every bird in every roost awoke screaming. The monkeys

screamed back and shook thousands of branches in sudden flight. A barrage of sucking explosions sounded from the lake as the herd of hippos surged up from the shallows in blind terror. The jungle was shaken by the earsplitting trumpetings of elephants and the crashing thunder of their stampede. Reich heard and froze in his tracks, ignoring Hassop, who still ran and sobbed and screamed from wall to wall of the barrier.

The hippos hit the barrier first in a blind, blundering rush. They were followed by the swambats and the crocodiles. Then came the elephants. Then the wapiti, the zebra, the gnu–heavy, pounding herds. There had never been such a stampede in the history of the Reservation. Nor had the manufacturers of the defense barrier screen ever anticipated such a concerted mass attack. Reich's barrier went down with a sound like scissored glass.

The hippos trampled the fire, scattered it and extinguished it. Powell darted through the darkness, seized Hassop's arm, and dragged the crazed creature across the clearing to the piled packs. A wild hoof sent him reeling, but he held on to Hassop and located the precious film cannister. In the frantic blackness Powell could sort the frenzied TP broadcasts of the stampeding animals. Still dragging Hassop, he threaded his way out of the main stream. Behind the thick bole of a *lignum vitae* Powell paused to catch his breath and settle the cannister safely in his pocket. Hassop was still sobbing. Powell sensed Reich, a hundred feet away, back against a fever tree, bow and arrows clutched in his stricken hands. He was confused, furious, terrified–but still safe. Above all, Powell wanted to keep him safe for Demolition.

Unhitching his own defensive barrier screen, Powell tossed it across the clearing toward the embers of the fire where Reich would surely find it. Then he turned and led the numb, unresisting Code Chief toward the gate.

13

The Reich case was ready for final submission to the District Attorney's office. Powell hoped it was also ready for that cold-blooded cynical monster of facts and evidence, Old Man Mose.

Powell and his staff assembled in Mose's office. A round table had been set up in the center, and on it was constructed a transparent model of the key rooms of Beaumont House, inhabited by miniature android models of the *dramatis personae*. The lab's model division had done a superlative job, and actually had characterized the leading players. The tiny Reich, Tate, Beaumont, and others moved with the characteristic gaits of their originals. Alongside the table was massed the documentation the staff had prepared, ready for presentation to the machine.

Old Man Mose himself occupied the entire circular wall of the giant office. His multitudinous eyes winked and glared coldly. His multitudinous memories whirred and hummed. His mouth, the cone of a speaker, hung open in a kind of astonishment at human stupidity. His hands, the keys of a multiflex typewriter, poised over a roll of tape, ready to hammer out logic. Mose was the Mosaic Multiplex Prosecution Computer of the District Attorney's office, whose awful decisions controlled the preparation, presentation, and prosecution of every police case.

"We won't bother Mose to start with," Powell told the D.A. "Let's take a look at the models and check them against the Crime Schedule. Your staff has the time sheets. Just watch them while the dolls go through the motions. If you catch anything our gang's missed, make a note and we'll kick it around."

He nodded to De Santis, the harassed Lab Chief, who inquired in an overwrought voice: "One to one?"

"That's a little fast. Make it one to two. Half slow motion."

"The androids look unreal at that tempo," De Santis snarled. "It can't do them justice. We slaved for two weeks and now you—"

"Never mind. We'll admire them later."

De Santis verged on mutiny, then touched a button. Instantly the model was illumined and the dolls came to life. Acoustics had faked a background. There was a hint of music, laughter, and chatter. In the main hall of Beaumont House, a pneumatic model of Maria Beaumont slowly climbed to a dais with a tiny book in her hands.

"The time is 11:09 at that point," Powell said to the D.A.'s staff. "Watch the clock above the model. It's geared to synchronize with the slow motion."

In rapt silence, the legal division studied the scene and jotted notes while the androids reproduced the actions of the fatal Beaumont party. Once again Maria Beaumont read the rules of the Sardine game from the dais in the main hall of Beaumont House. The lights dimmed and went out. Ben Reich slowly threaded his way through the main hall to the music room, turned right, mounted the stairs to the Picture Gallery, passed through the bronze doors leading to the Orchid Suite, blinded and stunned the Beaumont guards, and then entered the suite.

And again Reich met D'Courtney face to face, closed with him, drew a deadly knife-pistol from his pocket and with the blade pried D'Courtney's mouth open while the old man hung weak and unresisting. And again a door of the Orchid Suite burst open to reveal Barbara D'Courtney in a frost-white transparent dressing gown. And she and Reich feinted and dodged until Reich suddenly blew the back of D'Courtney's head out with a shot through the mouth.

"Got the material from the D'Courtney girl," Powell murmured. "Peeped her. It's authentic."

Barbara D'Courtney crawled to the body of her father, seized the gun and suddenly dashed out of the Orchid Suite, followed by Reich. He pursued her down into the darkened house and lost her as she darted out through the front entrance into the street. Then Reich met Tate and they marched to the projection room, pretending to play Sardine. The drama came to an end at last with the stampede of the guests up to the Orchid Suite where the dolls burst in and crowded around the tiny dead body. There they froze in a grotesque little tableau.

There was a long pause while the legal staff digested the drama.

"All right," Powell said. "That's the picture. Now let's feed the data to Mose for an opinion. First, opportunity. You won't deny that the Sardine game provided Reich with perfect opportunity?"

"How'd Reich know they were going to play Sardine?" the D.A. muttered.

"Reich bought the book and sent it to Maria Beaumont. He provided his own Sardine game."

"How'd he know she'd play the game?"

"He knew she liked games. Sardine was the only legible game in the book."

"I don't know . . ." The D.A. scratched his head. "Mose takes a lot of convincing. Feed it to him. Won't do any harm."

The office door banged open and Commissioner Crabbe marched in as though heading a parade.

"Mr. Prefect Powell," Crabbe pronounced formally.

"Mr. Commissioner?"

"It has come to my attention, sir, that you are perverting that mechanical brain for the purpose of implicating my good friend, Ben Reich, in the foul and dastardly murder of Craye D'Courtney. Mr. Powell, such a purpose is grotesque. Ben Reich is an honorable and leading citizen of our country. Furthermore, sir, I have never approved of that mechanical brain. You were chosen by the electorate to exercise your intellectual powers, not bow in slavery to that—"

Powell nodded to Beck, who began feeding the punched data into Mose's ear. "You're absolutely right, Commissioner. Now, about the method. First question: How'd Reich knock out the guards. De Santis?"

"And furthermore, gentlemen . . ." Crabbe continued.

"Rhodopsin ionizer," De Santis spat. He picked up a plastic sphere and tossed it to Powell, who exhibited it. "Man named Jordan developed it for Reich's private police. I've got the empiric processing formula ready for the computer, and the sample we mocked up. Anybody care to try it?"

The D.A. looked dubious. "I don't see the use. Mose can make up his own mind about that."

"In addition to which, gentlemen . . ." Crabbe summarized.

"Oh come on," De Santis said with unpleasant cheerfulness. "You'll never believe us unless you see it for yourself. It doesn't hurt. Just makes you *non compos* for six or seven—"

The plastic bulb shattered in Powell's fingers. A vivid blue light flared under Crabbe's nose. Caught in mid-oration, the Commissioner collapsed like an empty sack. Powell looked around in horror.

"Good heavens!" he exclaimed. "What *have* I done? That bulb simply melted in my fingers." He looked at De Santis and spoke severely. "You made the covering too thin, De Santis. Now see what you've done to Commissioner Crabbe."

"What *I've* done!"

"Feed that data to Mose," the D.A. said in a voice rigid with control. "This I know he'll buy."

They made the Commissioner's body comfortable in a deep chair. "Now, the murder method," Powell continued. "Kindly watch this, gentlemen. The hand is quicker than the eye." He exhibited a revolver from the police museum. From the chambers he removed the shells, and from one of the shells he extracted the bullet. "This is what Reich did to the gun Jerry Church gave him before the murder. Pretended to make it safe. A phony alibi."

"Phony, hell! That gun is safe. Is that Church's evidence?"

"It is. Look at your sheet."

"Then you don't have to bother Mose with the problem." The D.A. threw his papers down in disgust. "We haven't got a case."

"Yes, we have."

"How can a cartridge kill without a bullet? Your sheet doesn't say anything about Reich reloading."

"He reloaded."

"He did not," De Santis spat. "There was no projectile in the wound or the room. There was nothing."

"There was everything. It was easy once I figured the clue."

"There was no clue!" De Santis shouted.

"Why, you located it, De Santis. That bit of candy gel in D'Courtney's mouth. Remember? And no candy in the stomach."

De Santis glared, Powell grinned. He took an eyedropper and filled a gel capsule with water. He pressed it into the open end of the cartridge above the charge and placed the cartridge in the gun. He raised the gun, aimed at a small wooden block on the edge of the model table, and pulled the trigger. There was a dull, flat explosion and the block leaped into fragments.

"For the love of– That was a trick!" the D.A. exclaimed. "There was something in that shell besides water." He examined the fragments of wood.

"No, there was not. You can shoot an ounce of water with a powder charge. You can shoot it with enough muzzle velocity to blow out the back of a head if you fire through the soft roof of the mouth. That's why Reich had to shoot through the mouth. That's why De Santis found the bit of gel. That's why he found nothing else. The projectile was gone."

"Give it to Mose," the D.A. said faintly. "By God, Powell, I'm beginning to think we've got a case."

"All right. Now, motive. We picked up Reich's business records, and Accounting's gone through them. D'Courtney had Reich with his back to the wall. With Reich it was 'if you can't lick 'em, join 'em.' He tried to join D'Courtney. He failed. He murdered D'Courtney. Will you buy that?"

"Sure I'll buy it. But will Old Man Mose? Feed it in and let's see."

They fed in the last of the punched data, warmed the computer up from 'Idle' to 'Run,' and kicked him into it. Mose's eyes blinked in hard meditation; his stomach rumbled softly; his memories began to hiss and stutter. Powell and the others waited with mounting suspense. Abruptly, Mose hiccupped. A soft bell began to "Ping-Ping-Ping-Ping-Ping-Ping–" and Mose's type began to flail the virgin tape under it.

"IF IT PLEASE THE COURT," Mose said, "WITH PLEADERING OF NON VULTS AND DEMURERS, LEGAL SIGNATURES. SS. LEADING CASE HAY V. COHOES AND THE RULE IN SHELLEY'S CASE. URP."

"What the–" Powell looked at Beck.

"He gets kittenish," Beck explained.

"At a time like this!"

"Happens now and then. We'll try him again."

They filled the computer's ear again, held the warmup for a good five minutes and then kicked him into it. Once again his eyes blinked, his stomach growled, his memories hissed, and Powell and the two staffs waited anxiously. A month's hard work hung on this decision. The type-hammers began to fall.

"BRIEF #921,088. SECTION C-1. MOTIVE," Mose said. "PASSION MOTIVE FOR CRIME INSUFFICIENTLY DOCUMENTED. CF STATE V. HANRAHAN, 1202 SUP. COURT 19, AND SUBSEQUENT LINE OF LEADING CASES."

"Passion motive?" Powell muttered. "Is Mose crazy? It's a profit motive. Check C-1, Beck."

Beck checked. "No mistake here."

"Try him again."

They ran the computer through it a third time. This time he spoke to the point: "BRIEF #921,088. SECTION C-1. MOTIVE. PROFIT MOTIVE FOR CRIME INSUFFICIENTLY DOCUMENTED. CF STATE V. ROYAL 1197 SUP. COURT 388."

"Didn't you punch C-1 properly?" Powell inquired.

"We got everything in that we could," Beck replied.

"Excuse me," Powell said to the others, "I've got to peep this out with Beck. You don't mind, I hope." He turned to Beck: *"Open up, Jackson. I smelled an evasion in them last words. Let me have it . . ."*

"Honestly, Linc, I'm not aware of any–"

"If you were aware, it wouldn't be an evasion. It'd be a downright lie. Now lemme see . . . Oh. Of course! Idiot. You don't have to be ashamed because Code's a little slow." Powell spoke aloud to the staffs: "Beck's missing one small datum point. Code's still working with Hassop upstairs trying to bust Reich's private code. So far all we've got is the knowledge that Reich offered merger and was refused. We haven't got the definite offer and refusal yet. That's what Mose wants. A cautious monster."

"If you didn't bust the code, how do you know the offer was made and refused?" the D.A. asked.

"Got that from Reich himself through Gus Tate. It was one of the last things Tate gave me before he was murdered. I tell you what, Beck. Add an assumption to the tape. Assuming that our merger evidence is unassailable—which it is—what does Mose think of the case?"

Beck hand-punched a strip, spliced it to the main problem and fed it in again. By now well warmed up, the Mosaic Multiplex Computer answered in thirty seconds: "BRIEF #921,088. ACCEPTING ASSUMPTION, PROBABILITY OF SUCCESSFUL PROSECUTION 97.0099%."

Powell's staff grinned and relaxed. Powell tore the tape out of the typewriter and presented it to the D.A. with a flourish. "And there's your case, Mr. District Attorney. Sewn up and delivered."

"By God!" the D.A. said. "Ninety-seven percent! Jesus, we haven't had one in the ninety bracket all my term. I thought I was lucky when I broke seventy. Ninety-seven percent . . . Against Ben Reich himself! Jesus!" He looked around at his staff in a kind of wild surmise. "We'll make goddamn history!"

The office door opened and two perspiring men darted in waving manuscript.

"Here's Code now," Powell said. "You bust it?"

"We busted it," they said, "and now you're busted, Powell. The whole case is busted."

"What? What the hell are you talking about?"

"Reich knocked off D'Courtney because D'Courtney wouldn't merge, didn't he? He had a nice fat profit motive for killing D'Courtney, didn't he? In a pig's eye he did."

"Oh God!" Beck groaned.

"Reich sent YYJI TTED RRCB UUFE AALK QQBA to D'Courtney. That reads: SUGGEST MERGER BOTH OUR INTERESTS EQUAL PARTNERSHIP."

"Damn it, that's what I've said all along. And D'Courtney replied: WWHG. That was a refusal. Reich told Tate. Tate told me."

"D'Courtney answered WWHG. That reads: ACCEPT OFFER."

"The hell it does!"

"The hell it don't. WWHG. ACCEPT OFFER. It was the answer Reich wanted. It was the answer that gave Reich every reason for keeping D'Courtney alive. You'll never convince any court in the solar system that Reich had a motive for murdering D'Courtney. Your case is washed out."

Powell stood stock-still for half a minute, his fists clenched, his face working. Suddenly he turned on the model, reached in and pulled out the android figure of Reich. He twisted its head off. He went to

Mose, yanked out the tapes of punched data, crumpled them into a wad and hurled the wad across the room. He strode to Crabbe's recumbent figure and launched a tremendous kick at the seat of the chair. While the staffs watched in an appalled silence, the chair and Commissioner overturned to the floor.

"God damn you! You're always sitting in that God damned chair!" Powell cried in a shaking voice and stormed out of the office.

14

Explosion! Concussion! The cell doors burst open. And far outside, freedom is waiting in the cloak of darkness and flight into the unknown. . . .

Who's that? Who's outside the cell block? Oh God! Oh Christ! The Man With No Face! Looking. Looming. Silent. Run! Escape! Fly! Fly. . . .

Fly through space. There's safety in the solitude of this silver-lined launch jetting to the deeps of the distant unknown. . . . The hatch door! Opening. But it can't. There's no one on this launch to swing it slowly, ominously . . . Oh God! The Man With No Face! Looking. Looming. Silent . . .

But I am innocent, your honor. Innocent. You will never prove my guilt, and I will never stop pleading my case though you pound your gavel until you deafen my ears and—oh Christ! On the bench. In wig and gown. The Man With No Face. Looking. Looming. Quintessence of vengeance . . .

The pounding gavel dissolved to knuckles on the stateroom door. The steward's voice called: "Over New York, Mr. Reich. One hour to debarkation. Over New York, Mr. Reich." The knuckles went on hammering on the door.

Reich found his voice. "All right," he croaked. "I hear you."

The steward departed. Reich climbed out of the liquid bed and found his legs giving way. He clutched at the wall and cursed himself upright. Still in the grip of the nightmare's terror, he went into the bathroom, depilated, showered, steamed, and air-washed for ten minutes. He was still reeling. He stepped into the massage alcove and punched "Glow-Salt." Two pounds of moistened, scented salt were sprayed on his skin. As the massage buffers were about to begin, Reich suddenly decided he needed coffee. He stepped out of the alcove to ring Service.

There was a dull concussion and Reich was hurled to his face by the force of the explosion in the alcove. His back was slashed by flying particles. He darted into the bedroom, seized his traveling case, and turned like an animal at bay, his hands automatically opening the case and groping for the cartridge of detonation bulbs he always carried. There was no cartridge in the case.

Reich pulled himself together. He was aware of the bite of salt in the cuts in his back and the streaming blood. He was aware that he was no longer trembling. He went back into the bathroom, shut off the massage buffers and inspected the alcove wreckage. Someone had removed the cartridge from his case during the night and planted a bulb in each of the massage buffers. The empty cartridge lay behind the alcove. Only a split-second miracle had saved his life . . . from whom?

He inspected his stateroom door. The lock had evidently been gaffed by a past master. It showed no sign of tampering. But who? Why?

"Son of a bitch!" Reich growled. With iron nerve he returned to the bathroom, washed off the salt and blood, and sprayed his back with coagulant. He dressed, had his coffee, and descended to the Staging Hall, where, after a savage skirmish with the peeper customs man (*Tension, apprehension, and dissension have begun!*), he boarded the Monarch launch that was waiting to take him down to the city.

From the launch he called Monarch Tower. His secretary's face appeared on the screen.

"Any news of Hassop?" Reich asked.

"No, Mr. Reich. Not since you called from Spaceland."

"Give me Recreation."

The screen herringboned and then disclosed the chrome lounge of Monarch. West, bearded and scholarly, was carefully binding sheets of typescript into plastic volumes. He looked up and grinned.

"Hello, Ben."

"Don't look so cheerful, Ellery," Reich growled. "Where the hell is Hassop? I thought you'd surely—"

"Not my problem any more, Ben."

"What are you talking about?"

West displayed the volumes. "Just finishing up my work. History of my career with Monarch Utilities and Resources for your files. Said career ended this morning at nine o'clock."

"What!"

"Yep. I warned you, Ben. The Guild's just ruled Monarch out of bounds for me. Company espionage is unethical."

"Listen, Ellery, you can't quit now. I'm on a hook and I need you bad. Someone tried to booby-trap me on the ship this morning. I beat it by an eyelash. I've got to find out who it is. I need a peeper."

"Sorry, Ben."

"You don't have to work for Monarch. I'll put you under personal contract for private service. The same contract Breen has."

"Breen? A 2nd? The analyst?"

"Yes. My analyst."

"Not any more."

"What!"

West nodded. "The ruling came down today. No more exclusive practice. It limits the service of peepers. We've got to be dedicated to the most good for the most people. You've lost Breen."

"It's Powell!" Reich shouted. "Using every dirty peeper trick he can dig out of the slime to bitch me. He's trying to nail me to the D'Courtney cross, the sneaking peeper! He—"

"Sign off, Ben. Powell had nothing to do with it. Let's break it off friendly, eh? We've always kept it pleasant. Let's break it pleasant. What do you say?"

"I say go to hell!" Reich roared and cut the connection. To the launch pilot he said in the same tone: "Take me home!"

Reich burst into his penthouse apartment, once again awakening the hearts of his staff to terror and hatred. He hurled his traveling case at his valet and went immediately to Breen's suite. It was empty. A crisp note on the desk repeated the information West had already given him. Reich strode to his own rooms, went to the phone and dialed Gus Tate. The screen cleared and displayed a sign: SERVICE PERMANENTLY DISCONTINUED. Reich stared, broke the connection and dialed Jerry Church. The screen cleared and displayed a sign: SERVICE PERMANENTLY DISCONTINUED.

Reich snapped the contact key up, paced the study uncertainly, then went to the shimmer of light in the corner that was his safe. He switched the safe into temporal phase, revealing the honeycomb paper rack, and reached for the small red envelope in the upper left-hand pigeonhole. As he touched the envelope he heard the faint click. He doubled up and spun away, his face buried in his arms.

There was a blinding flash of light and a heavy explosion. Something brutal punched Reich in the left side, hurled him across the study and slammed him against the wall. Then a hail of debris followed. He struggled to his feet, bellowing in bewilderment and fury, stripping the ripped clothes from his left side to examine the state of his body. He was badly slashed, and a particularly excruciating pain indicated at least one broken rib.

He heard his staff come running down the corridor and roared: "Keep out! You hear me? Keep out! All of you!"

He stumbled through the wreckage and began sorting over the remains of his safe. He found the neuron scrambler he had taken from Chooka Frood's red-eyed woman. He found the malignant steel flower that was the knife-pistol that had killed D'Courtney. It still contained four unfired shells loaded with water and sealed with gel. He thrust both into the pocket of a new jacket, got a fresh cartridge of detonation bulbs from his desk, and tore out of the room, ignoring the servants who stared at him in astonishment.

Reich swore feverishly all the way down from the tower apartment to the cellar garage, where he deposited his private Jumper key in the call slot and waited for the little car. When it came out of storage with the key in the door, another tenant was approaching and even at a distance was staring. Reich turned the key and yanked open the door to jump in. There was a low-pressure *rrrrrrip*. Reich hurled himself to the ground. The Jumper tank exploded. By some freak, it failed to burst into flame. It erupted a shattering geyser of raw fuel and fragments of twisting metal. Reich crawled frantically, reached the exit ramp, and ran for his life.

On the street level, torn, bleeding, rank with creosote fuel, he searched frantically for a Public Jumper. He couldn't find a coin Jumper. He managed to flag a piloted machine.

"Where to?" the driver asked.

Reich dabbed dazedly at the blood and oil that smeared him. "Chooka Frood!" he croaked in a hysterical voice.

The cab hopped him to 99 Bastion West.

Reich thrust past the protesting doorman, the indignant reception clerk, and Chooka Frood's highly paid *chargé d'affaires* to the private office, a Victorian room furnished with stained-glass lamps, overstuffed sofas and a roll-top desk. Chooka was seated at the desk, wearing a dingy smock and a dingy expression that changed to alarm when Reich yanked the scrambler out of his pocket.

"For God's sake, Reich!" she exclaimed.

"Here I am, Chooka," he said hoarsely. "So let's have the trial run before we feed it to the dice. I used this scrambler on you once before. I'm warmed up for it again. You warmed me up, Chooka."

She shot up from the desk and screamed: "Magda!"

Reich caught her by the arm and hurled her across the office. She sideswiped the couch and fell across it. The red-eyed bodyguard came running into the office. Reich was ready for her. He clubbed her across the back of the neck, and as she fell forward, he ground his heel into her back and slammed her flat on the floor. The woman twisted and clawed at his leg. Ignoring her, he spat at Chooka: "Let's get it squared off. Why the booby-traps?"

"What are you talking about?" Chooka cried.

"What the hell do I look like I'm talking about? Read the blood, lady. I've skinned out of three obituaries running. How long can my luck hold out?"

"Make sense, Reich! I can't–"

"I'm talking about the big D, Chooka, D for death. I came in here and strong-armed the D'Courtney girl out of you. I beat hell out of your girl-friend and I beat hell out of you. So you got frabbed off and set those traps. Right?"

Chooka shook her head dazedly.

"Three of them so far. On the ship coming back from Spaceland. In my study. In my Jumper. How many more, Chooka?"

"It wasn't me, Reich. So help me. I–"

"It has to be you, Chooka. You're the only one with a gripe and the only one who hires gimpsters. That adds up to you, so let's get it squared off." He slapped the safety off the scrambler. "I've got no time for a two-bit hater with coffin-queer friends."

"For God's sake!" Chooka screamed. "What the hell have I got against you? So you roughhoused a little. So you mugged Magda. You wasn't the first. You ain't gonna be the last. Use your head!"

"I used it. If it isn't you, who else?"

"Keno Quizzard. He hires gimpsters too. I heard you and him–"

"Quizzard's out. Quizzard's dead. Who else?"

"Church."

"He hasn't got the guts. If he had he would have tried it ten years ago. Who else?"

"How do I know? There's hundreds hate you enough."

"There's thousands, but who could get into my safe? Who could break a phase combination and–"

"Maybe nobody broke into your safe. Maybe somebody broke into your head and peeped the combination. Maybe–"

"Peeped!"

"Yeah. Peeped. Maybe you added Church up wrong . . . Or some other peeper what's got a eager reason for filling your coffin."

"My God . . ." Reich whispered. "Oh my God . . . Yes."

"Church?"

"No. Powell."

"The cop?"

"The cop. Powell. Yes. Mr. Holy Lincoln Powell. Yes!" The words began pouring out of Reich in a torrent. "Yes, Powell! The son of a bitch is fighting dirty because I've licked him clean. He can't get a case together. He's got nothing but booby-trapping left."

"You're crazy, Reich."

"Am I? Why the hell did he take Ellery West away from me, and Breen? He knows the only defense I've got against a booby-trap is a peeper. It's Powell!"

"But a cop, Reich? A cop?"

"Sure a cop!" Reich shouted. "Why not a cop? He's safe. Who'd suspect him? It's smart. It's what I'd do myself. All right . . . Now I'm going to booby-trap him!"

He kicked the red-eyed woman from him, went to Chooka and yanked her to her feet. "Call Powell."

"What?"

"Call Powell," he yelled. "Lincoln Powell. Call him at his house. Tell him to come down here right away."

"No, Reich . . ."

He shook her. "Listen to me, frab-head. Bastion West is owned by the D'Courtney Cartel. Now that old D'Courtney's dead, I'm going to own the cartel, which means I'll own Bastion. I'll own this house. I'll own you, Chooka. You want to stay in business? Call Powell!"

She stared at his livid face, feebly peeping him, slowly realizing that what he said was true.

"But I got no excuse, Reich."

"Wait a minute. Wait a minute." Reich thought, then yanked the knife-pistol from his pocket and shoved it into Chooka's hands. "Show him this. Tell him the D'Courtney girl left it here."

"What is it?"

"The gun that killed D'Courtney."

"For the love of— Reich!"

Reich laughed. "It won't do him any good. By the time he's got it, he'll be booby-trapped. Call him. Show him the gun. Get him down here." He thrust Chooka toward the phone, followed her and stood alongside the screen out of the line of sight. He hefted the scrambler in his hand meaningfully. Chooka understood.

She dialed Powell's number. Mary Noyes appeared on the screen, listened to Chooka, then called Powell. The prefect appeared, his lean face haggard, his dark eyes heavily shadowed.

"I . . . I got something you might want, maybe, Mr. Powell," Chooka stammered. "I just found it. That girl you took outa my house. She left it behind."

"Left what, Chooka?"

"The gun which killed her father."

"No!" Powell's face was suddenly animated. "Let's see it."

Chooka displayed the knife-pistol.

"That's it, by heaven!" Powell exclaimed. "Maybe I'm going to get a break after all. Stay right where you are, Chooka. I'll be down as fast as a Jumper can jet."

The screen blacked out. Reich ground his teeth and tasted blood. He turned, dashed out of the Rainbow House and located a vacant coin Jumper. He dropped a half-credit into the lock, opened the door and lurched in. As he took off with a hissing roar, he clattered against a thirtieth-story cornice and nearly capsized. He realized dazedly that he was in no condition to pilot a Jumper or set a booby-trap.

"Don't try to think," he thought. *"Don't try to plan. Leave it to your instincts. You're a killer. A natural killer. Just wait and kill!"*

Reich fought himself and the controls all the way to Hudson Ramp, and he fought the Jumper down through the crazy, shifting North River winds. The killer instinct prompted him to crash-land in Powell's back garden. He didn't know why. As he pounded the twisted cabin door open, a canned voice spoke: "Your attention, please. You are liable for any damage to this vehicle. Please leave your name and address. If we are forced to trace you, you will be liable for the costs. Thank you."

"I'm going to be liable for a lot more damage," Reich growled. "You're welcome."

He plunged under a heavy clump of forsythia and waited with the scrambler ready. Then he understood why he had crashed. The girl who answered Powell's phone came out of the house and ran down through the garden toward the Jumper. Reich waited. No one else came from the house. The girl was alone. He surged up out of the brush and the girl spun around before she heard him. A peeper.

He pulled the trigger to first notch. She stiffened and trembled—helpless.

At the moment when he was about to pull the trigger all the way back to the big D, instinct stopped him again. Suddenly the booby-trap for Powell came to him. Kill the girl inside the house. Seed her body with detonation bulbs, and leave that bait for Powell. Sweat broke out on the girl's swarthy face. The muscles in her jaws twitched. Reich took her by the arm and led her up the garden to the house. She walked with the stiff-legged gait of a scarecrow.

Inside the house, Reich led the girl through the kitchen to the living room. He found a long, corded modern lounge and thrust the girl down on it. She was fighting him with everything short of her body. He grinned savagely, bent down and kissed her full on the mouth.

"My love to Powell," he said, and stepped back, raising the scrambler. Then he lowered it.

Someone was watching him.

He turned, almost casually, and darted a quick look around the living room. There was no one. He turned back to the girl and asked: "Are you doing that with TP, peeper?" Then he raised the scrambler. Again he lowered it.

Someone was watching him.

This time, Reich prowled around the living room, searching behind chairs, inside closets. There was no one. He checked the kitchen and the bath. No one. He returned to the living room and Mary Noyes. Then he thought of the upper floor. He went to the stairs, started to mount them, and then stopped in mid-stride as though he had been pole-axed.

Someone was watching him.

She was at the head of the stairs, kneeling and peeping through the bannisters like a child. She was dressed like a child in tight little leotards with her hair drawn back and tied with ribbon. She looked at him with the droll, mischievous expression of a child. Barbara D'Courtney.

"Hello," she said.

Reich began to shake.

"I'm Baba," she said.

Reich motioned to her faintly.

She arose at once and came down the stairs, holding on to the bannister carefully. "I'm not s'posed to," she said. "Are you Papa's friend?"

Reich took a deep breath. "I . . . I . . ." he croaked.

"Papa had to go away," she prattled. "But he's coming back right away. He told me. If I'm a good girl, he'll bring me a present. I'm trying, but it's awful hard. Are you good?"

"Your father? Coming b-back? Your *father?*"

She nodded. "Was you playing games with Aunt Mary? You kissed her. I saw it. Papa kisses me. I like it. Does Aunt Mary like it?" She took his hand confidently. "When I grow up I'm going to marry Papa and be his girl for always. Do you have a girl?"

Reich pulled Barbara around and stared into her face. "Are you rocketing?" he said hoarsely. "Do you think I'll fall into that orbit? How much did you tell Powell?"

"That's my papa," she said. "When I ask him why his name is different from my name he looks funny. What's your name?"

"I asked you!" Reich shouted. "How much did you tell him? Who do you think you're fooling with that act? Answer me!"

She looked at him doubtfully, then began to cry, trying to pull away from him. He held on to her.

"Go 'way!" she sobbed. "Let me go!"

"Will you answer me!"

"Let me go!"

He dragged her from the foot of the stairs to the lounge where Mary Noyes still sat paralyzed. He threw the girl alongside her and stepped back again, with the scrambler raised. Suddenly the girl whipped upright in the chair in a listening attitude. Her face lost its childishness and became drawn and taut. She thrust out her legs, leaped from the lounge, ran, stopped abruptly, then appeared to open a door. She ran forward, yellow hair flying, dark eyes wide with alarm—a lightning flash of wild beauty.

"Father!" she screamed. "For God's sake! Father!"

Reich's heart constricted. The girl ran toward him. He stepped forward to catch her. She stopped short, backed away, then darted to the left and ran in a half circle, screaming wildly, her eyes fixed.

"No!" she cried. "No! For the love of Christ! Father!"

Reich pivoted and clutched at the girl. This time he caught her while she fought and screamed. Reich was shouting too. The girl suddenly stiffened and clutched her ears. Reich was back in the Orchid Suite. He heard the explosion and saw the blood and brains gout out of the back of D'Courtney's head. He shook with galvanic spasms that forced him to release the girl. She fell forward to her knees and crawled across the floor. He saw her crouch over the waxen body.

Reich gasped for breath and beat his knuckles together painfully, fighting for control. When the roaring in his ears subsided, he propelled himself toward Barbara, trying to arrange his thoughts and make split-second alterations in his plans. He had never counted on a witness. God damn Powell. He would have to kill the girl. Could he arrange a double murder in the– No. Not murder. Booby-trap. Damn Gus Tate. Wait. He wasn't in Beaumont House. He was . . . in . . .

"Thirty-three Hudson Ramp," Powell said from the front door.

Reich jerked around, crouched automatically and whipped the scrambler up under his left elbow as Quizzard's killers had taught him.

Powell sidestepped. "Don't try it," he said sharply.

"You son of a bitch!" Reich shouted. He wheeled on Powell, who had already crossed him up and again stepped out of the line of fire. "You God damned peeper! You lousy, sleazy son of a–"

Powell faked to the left, reversed, closed with Reich and delivered a six-inch jab to the ulnar nerve complex. The scrambler fell to the floor. Reich clinched–punching, clawing, butting, swearing hysterically. Powell hit him with three lightning blows, nape, navel, and groin. The effect was that of a full spinal block. Reich crashed to the floor, retching, blood streaming from his nose.

"Brother, you only think you know how to gut fight," Powell grunted. He went to Barbara D'Courtney, who still knelt on the floor, and raised her.

"All right, Barbara?" he said.

"Hello, Papa. I had a bad dream."

"I know, baby. I had to give it to you. It was an experiment on that big oaf."

"Gimme a kiss."

He kissed her forehead. "You're growing up fast," he smiled. "You were just baby-talking yesterday."

"I'm growing up because you promised to wait for me."

"It's a promise, Barbara. Can you go upstairs by yourself or do you have to be carried . . . like yesterday?"

"I can go all by own self."

"All right, baby. Go up to your room."

She went to the stairs, took a firm hold on the bannister and climbed up. Just before she reached the top, she darted a glance at Reich and stuck her tongue out. Then she disappeared. Powell crossed to Mary Noyes, checked her pulse, then made her comfortable on the lounge.

"First notch, eh?" he murmured to Reich. "Painful but she'll recover in an hour." He went back to Reich and stared down at him, anger darkening his drawn face. "I ought to pay you back for Mary; but what's the use? It wouldn't teach you anything. You poor bastard . . . you're just no damned good."

"Kill me!" Reich groaned. "Kill me or let me up and by Christ I'll kill you!"

Powell picked up the scrambler and cocked an eye at Reich. "Try flexing your muscles a little. Those blocks shouldn't last more than a few seconds." He sat down with the scrambler in his lap. "You had a tough break. I wasn't out of the house five minutes when I realized Chooka's story was a phony. You put her up to it, of course."

"You're the phony!" Reich shouted. "You and your ethics and your high talk. You and your phony goddamn—"

"She said the gun killed D'Courtney," Powell continued imperturbably. "It did, but no one knows what killed D'Courtney . . . except you and me. I turned around and came back. It was a long take. Almost too long. Try getting up now. You can't be that sick."

Reich struggled up, his breath hissing horribly. Suddenly he dipped into his pocket and brought out the cartridge of detonation bulbs. Powell arched back in the chair and kicked Reich in the chest with his heel. The cartridge went flying. Reich fell back and collapsed on a sofa.

"When will you people learn you can't surprise a peeper?" Powell said. He went to the cartridge and picked it up. "You're quite the arsenal today, aren't you? You're acting more like you're wanted dead or alive than like a free man. Notice I said free. Not innocent."

"Free how long?" Reich said through his teeth. "I never talked about innocence either. But free how long?"

"Forever. I had a perfect case against you. Every detail right. I checked that when I peeped you with Barbara just now. I had every detail except one, and that one flaw blew my case out into deep space. You're a free man, Reich. We've closed your file."

Reich stared. "Closed the file?"

"Yep. No solution. I'm licked. You can disarm, Reich. Go about your business. No one's going to bother you."

"You're a liar! This is one of your peeper tricks. You—"

"Nope. I'll lay it out for you. I know all about you. How much you bribed Gus Tate. What you promised Jerry Church. Where you located that Sardine game. What you did with Wilson Jordan's rhodopsin caps. How you emptied those cartridges for an alibi and then turned them lethal again with a drop of water. So far a perfect chain of evidence. Method and opportunity. But motive was the flaw. The courts demand objective motive and I can't produce it. That sets you free."

"You liar!"

"Of course I could throw this breaking and entering with deadly intent at you . . . but it's too small a charge. Like shooting a popgun after you misfire with a cannon. You could probably beat it, too. My only witnesses would be a peeper and a sick girl. I—"

"You liar," Reich growled. "You hypocrite. You lying peeper. Am I supposed to believe you? Am I supposed to listen to the rest of it? You had nothing, Powell. Nothing! I licked you on every point. That's why you're booby-trapping me. That's why you—" Reich broke off abruptly and beat his forehead. "And this is probably the biggest booby-trap of all. And I fell into it. What a damned fool I am. What a—"

"Shut up," Powell snapped. "When you rave like that I can't peep you. Now what's all this about booby-traps? Think it through."

Reich uttered a ragged laugh. "As if you don't know . . . My stateroom on the liner . . . My gaffed safe . . . My Jumper . . ."

For almost a minute, Powell focused on Reich, peeping, absorbing, digesting. Then his face began to pale and his respiration quicken. "My God!" he exclaimed. "My God!" He leaped to his feet and began pacing distractedly. "That's it. . . . That explains it. And Old Man Mose was right. Passion motive, and we thought he was kittenish. And Barbara's Siamese-twin image. And D'Courtney's guilt. No wonder Reich couldn't kill us at Chooka's. But—the murder isn't important any more. It goes deeper. Far deeper. And it's dangerous. More than I ever dreamed." He stopped, turned and looked at Reich with blazing eyes.

"If I could kill you," he cried, "I'd twist your head off with my hands. I'd tear you apart and hang you on a galactic gallows, and the universe would bless me. Do you know how dangerous you are? Does a plague know its peril? Is death conscious?"

Reich goggled at Powell in bewilderment. The prefect shook his head impatiently. "Why ask you?" he muttered. "You don't know what I'm talking about. You'll never know." He went to a sideboard, selected two brandy ampules and popped them into Reich's mouth. Reich attempted to spit them out. Powell held his jaws shut.

"Swallow them," he said crisply. "I want you to pull yourself together and listen to me. Do you want butylene? Thyric acid? Can you compose yourself without drugs?"

Reich choked on the brandy and sputtered angrily. Powell shook him silent.

"Get this straight," Powell said. "I'm going to show you half the pattern. Try to understand it. The case against you is closed. It's closed because of those booby-traps. If I'd known about them I'd never have started the case. I'd have broken my conditioning and killed you. Try to understand this, Reich."

Reich stopped sputtering.

"I couldn't find a motive for your murder. That's the flaw. When you offered merger to D'Courtney, he accepted. He sent WWHG in answer. That's acceptance. You had no reason to murder him. You had every objective reason to keep him alive."

Reich went white. His head began to wobble crazily. "No. No. WWHG. Offer refused. Refusal. Refusal!"

"Acceptance."

"No. The bastard refused. He–"

"He accepted. When I learned that D'Courtney accepted your offer, I was finished. I knew I couldn't bring a case to court. But I haven't been trying to booby-trap you. I did not gaff your stateroom lock. I did not plant those detonation bulbs. I'm not the man who's trying to murder you. That man is trying to kill you because he knows you're safe from me. He knows you're safe from Demolition. He's always known what I've just discovered–that you're the deadly enemy of our entire future."

Reich tried to speak. He struggled up out of the sofa, gesticulating feebly. Finally he said: "Who is it? Who? Who?"

"He's your ancient enemy, Reich. A man you'll never escape. You'll never be able to run from him . . . hide from him . . . and I pray to God you'll never be able to save yourself from him."

"Who is it, Powell? *Who is it?*"

"The Man With No Face."

Reich emitted a guttural cry of pain. Then he turned and staggered out of the house.

15

Tension, apprehension, and dissension have begun.
Tension, apprehension, and dissension have begun.
Tension, apprehension, and dissension have begun.

"Shut up!" Reich cried.

Eight, sir;
Seven, sir;
Six, sir;
Five, sir:

"For God's sake! Shut up!"

Four, sir;
Three, sir;
Two, sir;
One!

"You've got to think. Why don't you think? What's happened to you? Why don't you think?"

Tension, apprehension, and–

"He was lying. You know he was lying. You were right the first time. A giant booby-trap. WWHG. Refusal. Refusal. But why did he lie? How is that going to help him?"

–dissension have begun.

"The Man With No Face. Breen could have told him. Gus Tate could have told him. Think!"

Tension–

"There is no Man With No Face. It's just a dream. A nightmare!"

Apprehension–

"But the booby-traps? What about the booby-traps? He had me cold in his house. Why didn't he pull the switch? Telling me I'm free. What's he up to? Think!"

Dissension–

A hand touched his shoulder.

"Mr. Reich?"

"What?"

"Mr. Reich!"

"What? Who's that?"

Reich's eyes focused. He became aware that it was raining heavily. He was lying on his side, knees drawn up, arms folded, his cheek buried in mud. He was drenched, shivering with cold. He was in the esplanade of Bomb Inlet. Around him were sighing, sodden trees. A figure was bending over him.

"Who are you?"

"Galen Chervil, Mr. Reich."

"What?"

"Galen Chervil, sir. From Maria Beaumont's party. Can I do you that favor, Mr. Reich?"

"Don't peep me!" Reich cried.

"I'm not, Mr. Reich. We don't usually–" Young Chervil caught himself. "I didn't know you knew I was a peeper. You'd better get up, sir."

He took Reich's arm and pulled. Reich groaned and yanked his arm free. Young Chervil took him under the shoulders and raised him, staring at Reich's frightful appearance.

"Were you mugged, Mr. Reich?"

"What? No. No . . ."

"Accident, sir?"

"No. No, I . . . Oh, for God's sake," Reich burst out, "get the hell away from me!"

"Certainly, sir. I thought you needed help and I owe you a favor, but–"

"Wait," Reich interrupted. "Come back." He grasped the bole of a tree and leaned against it, panting hoarsely. Finally he thrust himself erect and glared at Chervil with bloodshot eyes. "You mean that about the favor?"

"Of course, Mr. Reich."

"No questions asked. No tales told?"

"Certainly not, Mr. Reich."

"My problem's murder, Chervil. I want to find out who's trying to kill me. Will you do me that favor? Will you peep someone for me?"

"I should imagine the police would be able to–"

"The police?" Reich laughed hysterically, then clutched himself in agony as the broken rib caught. "I want you to peep a cop for me, Chervil. A big cop. The Commissioner of cops. D'you understand?" He let go the tree and lurched to Chervil. "I want to visit my friend the Commissioner and ask him a few questions. I want you to be there to tell me the truth. Will you come to Crabbe's office and peep him for me? Will you just do it and forget about it? Will you?"

"Yes, Mr. Reich . . . I will."

"What? An honest peeper! How about that? Come on. Let's jet."

Reich stumbled out of the esplanade with a horrible gait. Chervil followed, overwhelmed by the fury in the man that drove him through injury, through fever, through agony to police headquarters. There, Reich bulled and roared past clerks and guards until the mud-streaked, blood-smeared figure burst into Commissioner Crabbe's elaborate ebony and silver office.

"My God, Reich!" Crabbe was aghast. "It is you, isn't it? Ben Reich?"

"Sit down, Chervil," Reich said. He turned to Crabbe. "It's me. Get a full perspective. I'm half a corpse, Crabbe. The red stuff is blood. The rest is slime. I've had a great day–a glorious day–and I want to know where the hell the police have been? Where's your God Almighty Prefect Powell? Where's your–"

"Half a corpse? What are you telling me, Ben?"

"I'm telling you that I was almost murdered three times today. This boy . . ." Reich pointed to Chervil. "This boy just found me in the Inlet Esplanade more dead than alive. Look at me, for Christ's sake. Look at me!"

"Murdered!" Crabbe thumped his desk emphatically. "Of course. That Powell is a fool. I should never have listened to him. The man who killed D'Courtney is trying to kill you."

Behind his back, Reich motioned savagely to Chervil.

"I told Powell you were innocent. He wouldn't listen to me," Crabbe said. "Even when that infernal adding machine in the District Attorney's office told him you were innocent, he wouldn't listen."

"The machine said I was innocent?"

"Of course it did. There's no case against you. There never was a case against you. And by the sacred Bill of Rights, you'll have the protection from the murderer that any honest law-abiding citizen deserves. I'll see to that at once." Crabbe strode to the door. "And I think this is all I'll need to settle Mr. Powell's hash for good! Don't go, Ben. I want to talk to you about your support for the Solar Senatorship. . . ."

The door opened and slammed. Reich reeled and fought his way back to the world. He looked at three Chervils. "Well?" he muttered. "Well?"

"He's telling the truth, Mr. Reich."

"About me? About Powell?"

"Well . . ." Chervil paused judiciously, weighing the truth.

"Jet, you bastard," Reich groaned. "How long do you think I can keep my fuses from blowing?"

"He's telling the truth about you," Chervil said quickly. "The prosecution computer has declined to authorize any action against you for the D'Courtney murder. Mr. Powell has been forced to abandon the case and . . . well . . . his career is very much in jeopardy."

"Is that true!" Reich staggered to the boy and seized his shoulders. "Is that true, Chervil? I've been cleared? I can go about my business? No one's going to bother me?"

"You've been dropped, Mr. Reich. You can go about your business. No one's going to bother you."

Reich burst into a roar of triumphant laughter. The pain of his bruised and broken body made him groan as he laughed, and his eyes smarted with tears. He pulled himself up, brushed past Chervil and left the Commissioner's office. He was more a Neanderthal vestige as he paraded down headquarters' corridors streaked with blood and mud, laughing and groaning, bearing himself with limping arrogance. He needed a stag's carcass on his shoulders or a cave bear borne in triumph behind him to complete the picture.

"I'll complete the picture with Powell's head," he told himself. "Stuffed and mounted on my wall. I'll complete the picture with the D'Courtney Cartel stuffed into my pockets. By God, give me time, I'll complete a picture with the Galaxy inside the frame!"

He passed through the steel portals of headquarters and stood for a moment on the steps gazing at the rain-swept streets—at the amusement center across the square, block after block blazing under a single mutual transparent dome; at the open shops lining the upper footways, all bustle and brilliance as the city's night shopping began; the towering office buildings in the background, great two-hundred-story cubes; the lace tracery of skyways linking them together; the twinkling running lights of Jumpers bobbing up and down like a plague of crimson-eyed grasshoppers in a field . . .

"And I'll own you!" he shouted, raising his arms to engulf the universe. "I'll own you all! Bodies, passions, and souls!"

Then his eye caught the tall, ominous, familiar figure crossing the square, watching him covertly over its shoulder. A figure of black shadows sparkling with raindrop jewels—looking, looming, silent, horrible. A Man With No Face.

There was a strangled cry. The fuses blew. Like a blighted tree, Reich fell to the ground.

At one minute to nine, ten of the fifteen members of the Esper Guild Council assembled in President T'sung's office. Emergency business required their attention. At one minute after nine, the meeting was adjourned with the business completed. Within those one hundred and twenty Esper seconds, the following took place:

A gavel pounding
A clock face
Hour hand at 9
Minute hand at 59
Second hand at 60

EMERGENCY MEETING

To examine a request for Mass Cathexis with Lincoln Powell as the human canal for the capitalized energy.

(*Consternation*)

T'SUNG: *You can't be serious, Powell. How can you make such a request? What can possibly require such an extraordinary and dangerous measure?*

POWELL: *An astonishing development in the D'Courtney case which I would like you all to examine.*

(*Examination*)

POWELL: *You all know that Reich is our most dangerous enemy. He is supporting the anti-Esper smear campaign. Unless that is blocked we may suffer the usual history of minority groups.*

@KINS: *True enough.*

POWELL: *He is also supporting the League of Esper Patriots. Unless that organization is blocked we may be plunged into a civil war and be lost forever in a morass of internal chaos.*

FRANION: *That's true too.*

POWELL: *But there is an additional development which you have all examined. Reich is about to become a Galactic focal point—a crucial link between the positive past and the probable future. He is on the verge of a powerful reorganization at this moment. Time is of the essence. If Reich can readjust and reorient before I can reach him, he will become immune to our reality, invulnerable to our attack, and the deadly enemy of Galactic reason and reality.*

(*Alarm*)

@KINS: *Surely you're exaggerating, Powell.*

POWELL: *Am I? Inspect the picture with me. Look at Reich's position in time and space. Will not his beliefs become the world's beliefs? Will not his reality become the world's reality? Is he not, in his critical position of power, energy, and intellect, a sure road to utter destruction?*

(*Conviction*)

T'SUNG: *That's true. Nevertheless I'm reluctant to authorize the Mass Cathexis Measure. You will recall that the MCM has invariably destroyed the human energy canal in past attempts. You're too valuable to be destroyed, Powell.*

POWELL: *I must be permitted to run the risk. Reich is one of the rare universe-shakers–a child as yet, but about to mature. And all reality–Espers, Normals, life, the earth, the solar system, the universe itself–all reality hangs precariously on his awakening. He cannot be permitted to awake to the wrong reality. I call the question.*

FRANION: *You're asking us to vote your death.*

POWELL: *It's my death against the eventual death of everything we know. I call the question.*

@KINS: *Let Reich awaken as he will. We have the time and the warning to attack him at another crossroad.*

POWELL: *Question! I call the question!*

(Request granted)
Meeting adjourned
Clock face
Hour hand at 9
Minute hand at 01
Second hand at Demolition

Powell arrived home an hour later. He had made his will, paid his bills, signed his papers, arranged everything. There had been dismay at the Guild. There was dismay when he came home. Mary Noyes read what he had done the instant he entered.

"Linc!"

"No fuss. It's got to be done."

"But–"

"There's a chance it won't kill me. Oh . . . One reminder. Lab wants a brain autopsy soon as I'm dead . . . if I die. I've signed all the papers, but I wish you'd help in case there's trouble. They'd like to have the body before rigor. If they can't get the corpse they'll settle for the head. See to it, will you?"

"Linc!"

"Sorry. Now, you'd better pack and take the baby up to Kingston Hospital. She won't be safe here."

"She isn't a baby any more. She–"

Mary turned and ran upstairs, trailing the familiar sensory impact:

Snow/mint/tulips/taffeta—and now mixed with terror and tears. Powell sighed, then smiled as a highly poised teen-ager appeared at the head of the stairs and came down with grand insouciance. She was wearing a dress and an expression of rehearsed surprise. She paused halfway down to let him take in the dress and the manner.

"Why! It's Mr. Powell, is it not?"

"It is. Good morning, Barbara."

"And what brings you to our little domain this morning?" She came down the rest of the stairs with her fingertips brushing the bannister and tripped on the bottom step. "Oh pip!" she squawked.

Powell caught her. "Pop," he said.

"Bim."

"Bam."

She looked up at him. "You stand right here. I'm going to come down those stairs again and I bet I do it perfect."

"I'll bet you don't."

She turned, trotted up and posed again at the top step. "Dear Mr. Powell, what a scatterbrain you must think me." She began the grand descent. "You must re-evaluate your opinion of me. I am no longer the mere child I was yesterday. I am ages and ages older. You must regard me as an adult from now on." She negotiated the bottom step and regarded him intently. "Re-evaluate? Is that right?"

"Revaluate is sometimes preferred, dear."

"I thought it had an extra sound." Suddenly she laughed, pushed him into a chair, and plumped down on his lap. Powell groaned. "Gently, Barbara. You're ages older and pounds heavier."

"Listen," she said. "What ever made me think you was . . . . Were? Were my father?"

"What's the matter with me as a father?"

"Let's be frank. Real frank."

"Sure."

"Do you feel like a father toward me? Because I don't feel like a daughter toward you."

"Oh? How do you feel?"

"I asked first, so you go first."

"My feelings toward you are those of a loving and dutiful son."

"No. Be serious."

"I have resolved to be a trustworthy son to all women until Vulcan assumes its rightful place in the Community of Planets."

She flushed angrily and got up from his lap. "I wanted you to be serious, because I need advice. But if you—"

"I'm sorry, Barbara. What is it?"

She knelt alongside him and took his hand. "I'm all mixed up about you."

"How?"

She looked into his eyes with the alarming directness of the young. "You know."

After a pause, he nodded. "Yes. I know."

"And you're all mixed up about me, too. I know."

"Yes, Barbara. That's true. I am."

"Is it wrong?"

Powell heaved up from the chair and began pacing unhappily. "No, Barbara, it isn't wrong. It's . . . mistimed."

"I want you to tell me about it."

"Tell you . . . ? Yes, I suppose I'd better. I . . . I'll put it this way, Barbara. The two of us are four people. There's two of you, and two of me."

"Why?"

"You've been sick, dear. So we had to turn you into a baby and let you grow up again. That's why you're two people. The grown-up Barbara inside, and the baby outside."

"And you?"

"I'm two grown-up people. One of them is me . . . Powell . . . The other is a member of the governing Council of the Esper Guild."

"What's that?"

"It doesn't need explaining. It's the part of me that's got me mixed up. God knows, maybe it's the baby part. I don't know."

She considered earnestly, then said slowly, "When I don't feel like a daughter to you . . . which me feels like that?"

"I don't know, Barbara."

"You do know. Why won't you say?" She came to him and put her arms around his neck–a grown-up woman with the manner of a child. "If it isn't wrong, why won't you say? If I love you–"

"Who said anything about love!"

"It's what we're talking about, isn't it? Isn't it? I love you and you love me. Isn't that it?"

"All right," Powell thought desperately. *"Here it is. What are you going to do? Admit the truth?"*

"Yes!" From the stairs. Mary was descending with a traveling case in her hand. *"Admit the truth."*

"She isn't a peeper."

"Forget that. She's a woman and she's in love with you. You're in love with her. Please, Linc, give yourselves a chance."

"A chance for what? An affair if I get out of this Reich mess alive? That's all it could be. You know the Guild won't let us marry Normals."

"She'll settle for that. She'll be grateful to settle for that. Ask me. I know."

"And if I don't come out alive? She'll have nothing . . . Nothing but half a memory of half a love."

"No, Barbara," he said. "That isn't it at all."

"It is," she insisted. "It is!"

"No. It's the baby part of you talking. The baby thinks she's in love with me. The woman is not."

"She'll grow up into the woman."

"And she'll forget all about me."

"You'll make her remember."

"Why should I, Barbara?"

"Because you feel that way about me, too. I know you do."

Powell laughed. "Baby! Baby! Baby! What makes you think I'm in love with you that way? I'm not. I've never been."

"You are!"

"Open your eyes, Barbara. Look at me. Look at Mary. You're ages older, aren't you? Can't you understand? Do I have to explain the obvious?"

"For God's sake, Linc!"

"Sorry, Mary. Got to use you."

"I'm getting ready to say goodbye . . . Maybe for good . . . Do I have to endure this? Isn't it bad enough for me already?"

"Shhhhh. Gently, dear . . ."

Barbara stared at Mary, then at Powell. She shook her head slowly. "You're lying."

"Am I? Look at me." He put his hands on her shoulders and looked into her face. Dishonest Abe came to his assistance. His expression was kind, tolerant, amused, patronizing. "Look at me, Barbara."

"No!" she cried. "Your face is lying. It's . . . It's hateful! I–" She burst into tears and sobbed: "Oh go away. Why don't you go away?"

"We're going away, Barbara," Mary said. She came forward, took the girl's arm and led her to the door.

"There's a Jumper waiting, Mary."

"There's me waiting, Linc. For you. Always. And the Chervils & @kins & Jordans &&&&&&&–"

"I know. I know. I love you all. Kisses. XXXXXX. 𝔅𝔩𝔢𝔰𝔰𝔦𝔫𝔤𝔰 *. . ."*

Image of four-leaf clover, rabbits' feet, horseshoes . . .

Bawdy response of Powell emerging from slok covered with diamonds.

Faint laughter.

Farewell.

He stood in the doorway whistling a crooked, plaintive tune, watching the Jumper disappear into the steel-blue sky boring north toward Kingston Hospital. He was exhausted. A little proud of himself for having made the sacrifice. Intensely ashamed of himself for feeling proud. Clearly melancholic. Should he take a grain of potassium niacate and kick himself up into the manic curve? What the hell was the use? Look at that great foul city of seventeen and one half million souls and not one soul for him. Look at–

The first impulse came. A thin trickle of latent energy. He felt it distinctly and glanced at his watch. Ten-twenty. So soon? So quickly? Good. He'd better get ready.

He turned into the house and darted up the stairs to his dressing room. The impulses came pattering–like the preliminary raindrops before a storm. His psyche began to throb and vibrate as he reached out and absorbed those tiny streams of latent energy. He changed his clothes, dressed for all weather, and–

And what? The pattering had become a drizzle, washing over him, filling his consciousness with ague–with grinding emotional flashes . . . with– Yes, nutrient capsules. Hold on to that. Nutrient. Nutrient. Nutrient! He tumbled down the stairs into the kitchen. Found the plastic bulb, cracked it and swallowed a dozen capsules.

The energy came in torrents now. From each Esper in the city, a trickle of latent power that merged and merged into a stream, a river, a swirling sea of Mass Cathexis directed toward Powell, tuned to Powell. He opened all blocks and absorbed it all. His nervous system superheterodyned and screamed and a turbine in his mind whirled faster and faster with a mounting intolerable whine.

He was out of the house, wandering through the streets, blind, deaf, senseless, immersed in that boiling mass of latent energy–like a ship with sails caught in the nexus of a typhoon, fighting to convert a whirlpool of wind into the motive power that would lead to safety.

So Powell fought to absorb that fearful torrent, to capitalize that latent energy, to cathectize and direct it toward the Demolition of Reich before it was too late, too late, too late, too late, too late . . .

16

ABOLISH THE LABYRINTH.
DESTROY THE MAZE.
DELETE THE PUZZLE.
($X^2 \phi Y^3$d! SPACE/d! TIME)
DISBAND.
(OPERATIONS, EXPRESSIONS, FACTORS, FRACTIONS, POWERS, EXPONENTS, RADICALS, IDENTITIES, EQUATIONS, PROGRESSIONS, VARIATIONS, PERMUTATIONS, DETERMINANTS, AND SOLUTIONS)
EFFACE.
(ELECTRON, PROTON, NEUTRON, MESON AND PHOTON)
ERASE.
(CAYLEY, HENSON, LILLIENTHAL, CHANUTE, LANGLEY, WRIGHT, TURNBUL AND S&ERSON)
EXPUNGE.
(NEBULAE, CLUSTERS, STREAMS, BINARIES, GIANTS, MAIN SEQUENCE, AND WHITE DWARFS)
DISPERSE.
(PISCES, AMPHIBIA, BIRDS, MAMMALS, AND MAN)
ABOLISH.
DESTROY.
DELETE.
DISBAND.
ERASE ALL EQUATIONS.
INFINITY EQUALS ZERO.
THERE IS NO—

"—there is no what?" Reich shouted. "There is no what?" He struggled upward, fighting the bedclothes and the restraining hands. "There is no what?"

"No more nightmares," Duffy Wyg& said.

"Who's that?"

"Me. Duffy."

Reich opened his eyes. He was in a frilly bedroom in a frilly bed with old-fashioned linen and blankets. Duffy Wyg&, starched and fresh, had her hands against his shoulders. Once again she tried to thrust him back against the pillows.

"I'm asleep," Reich said. "I want to wake up."

"You say the nicest things. Lie down and the dream will continue."

Reich fell back. "I was awake," he said somberly. "I was wide awake for the first time in my life. I heard . . . I don't know what I heard. Infinity and zero. Important things. Reality. Then I fell asleep and I'm here."

"Correction," Duffy smiled. "Just for the record. You awoke."

"I'm asleep!" Reich shouted. He sat up. "Have you got a shot? Anything–opium, hemp, somnar, lethettes . . . I've got to wake up, Duffy. I've got to get back to reality."

Duffy bent over him and kissed him hard on the mouth. "How about this? Real?"

"You don't understand. It's all been delusions . . . hallucinations . . . everything. I've got to readjust, reorientate, reorganize . . . Before it's too late, Duffy. Before it's too late, too late, too late . . ."

Duffy threw up her hands. "What the hell's happened to medicine!" she exclaimed. "First that damned doctor scares you into a faint. Then he swears you're patched up . . . and now look at you. Psychotic!" She knelt on the bed and shook a finger against Reich's nose. "One more word out of you and I call Kingston."

"What? Who?"

"Kingston, as in hospital. Where they send people like you."

"No. Who did you say scared me into a faint?"

"A doctor friend."

"In the square in front of police headquarters?"

"X marks the spot."

"Sure?"

"I was with him, looking for you. Your valet told me about the explosion and I was worried. We got to the rescue just in time."

"Did you see his face?"

"See it? I've kissed it."

"What's it look like?"

"It's a face. Two eyes. Two lips. Two ears. One nose. Three chins. Listen, Ben, if this is some more of the awake-asleep-reality-infinity lyrics . . . it ain't commercial."

"And you brought me here?"

"Sure. How could I pass up the opportunity? It's the only way I can get you into my bed."

Reich grinned. He relaxed and said: "Duffy, you may now kiss me."

"Mr. Reich, you already been kissed. Or was that when you were still awake?"

"Forget that. Nightmares. Plain nightmares." Reich burst into laughter. "Why the hell should I worry about having nightmares? I have the rest of the world in my hands. I'll take the dreams too. Didn't you once ask to be dragged through the gutter, Duffy?"

"That was a childish whim. I thought I could meet a better class of people."

"You name the gutter and you can have it, Duffy. Gold gutters . . . Jeweled gutters. You want a gutter from here to Mars? You'll have it. You want to turn the System into a gutter? I'll do it. Christ! I can turn the Galaxy into a gutter if you want it." He jabbed his chest with his thumb. "Want to look at God? Here I am. Go ahead and look."

"Dear man. So modest and so hung-over."

"Drunk? Sure, I'm drunk." Reich thrust his legs out of the bed and stood up, reeling slightly. Duffy came to him at once and he put his arms around her waist for support. "Why shouldn't I be drunk? I've licked D'Courtney. I've licked Powell. I'm forty years old. I've got sixty years of owning the whole world ahead of me. Yes, Duffy . . . the whole damned world!" He began walking around the room with Duffy. It was like a stroll through her ebullient erotic mind. A peeper decorator had reproduced Duffy's psyche perfectly in the decor.

"How'd you like to start a dynasty with me, Duffy?"

"I wouldn't know about starting dynasties."

"You start with Ben Reich. First you marry him. Then—"

"That's enough. When do I start?"

"Then you have children. Boys. Dozens of boys . . ."

"Girls. And only three."

"And you watch Ben Reich take over D'Courtney and merge it with Monarch. You watch the enemies go down . . . like this!" In full stride, Reich kicked the leg of a busty vanity table. It toppled and crashed a score of crystal bottles to the floor.

"After Monarch and D'Courtney become Reich, Incorporated, you watch me eat up the rest . . . the small ones . . . the fleas. Case and Umbrel on Venus. Eaten!" Reich brought his fist down on a torso-shaped side table and smashed it. "United Transaction on Mars. Mashed and eaten!" He crushed a delicate chair. "The GCI Combine on Ganymede, Callisto, and Io . . . Titan Chemical and Atomics . . . And then the smaller lice: the backbiters, the haters, the Guild of Peepers, the moralists, the patriots . . . Eaten! Eaten! Eaten!" He pounded his palm against a marble nude until it toppled from its pedestal and shattered.

"Clever-up, dog," Duffy hung on his neck. "Why waste all that dear violence? Punch me around a little."

He lifted her in his arms and shook her until she squealed. "And parts of the world will taste sweet . . . like you. Duffy; and parts will stink to high heaven . . . but I'll gobble them all." He laughed and crushed her against him. "I don't know much about the God business, but I know what I like. We'll tear it all down, Duffy, and we'll build it all up to suit us . . . You and me and the dynasty."

He carried her to the window, tore away the drapes and kicked open the sashes with a mighty jangle of smashed glass. Outside, the city was in velvet darkness. Only the skyways and streets twinkled with lights, and the scarlet eyes of an occasional Jumper popped up over the jet skyline. The rain had stopped and a slender moon hung in the sky. The night wind came whispering in, cutting through the cloy of the spilled perfume.

"You out there!" Reich roared. "Can you hear me? All of you . . . sleeping and dreaming. You'll dream my dreams from now on. You'll—"

Abruptly he was silent. He relaxed his hold on Duffy and permitted her to slide to the floor alongside him. He seized the sides of the window and poked his head far out into the night, twisting his neck to stare up. When he drew his head back into the room, his face wore a bewildered expression.

"The stars," he mumbled. "Where are the stars?"

"Where are the what?" Duffy wanted to know.

"The stars," Reich repeated. He gestured timidly toward the sky. "The stars. They're gone."

Duffy looked at him curiously. "The what are gone?"

"The stars!" Reich cried. "Look up at the sky. The stars are gone. The constellations are gone! The Great Bear . . . The Little Bear . . . Cassiopeia . . . Draco . . . Pegasus . . . They're all gone! There's nothing but the moon! Look!"

"It's the way it always is," Duffy said.

"It is not! Where are the stars?"

"What stars?"

"I don't know their names . . . Polaris and . . . Vega . . . and . . . How the hell should I know their names? I'm not an astronomer. What's happened to us? What's happened to the stars?"

"What are stars?" Duffy asked.

Reich seized her savagely. "Suns . . . Boiling and blazing with light. Thousands of them. Billions of them . . . shining through the night. What the hell's the matter with you? Don't you understand? There's been a catastrophe in space. The stars are gone!"

Duffy shook her head. Her face was terrified. "I don't know what you're talking about, Ben. I don't know what you're talking about."

He shoved her away, turned and ran to the bathroom and locked himself in. While he was hurriedly bathing and dressing, Duffy pounded on the door and pleaded with him. Finally she broke off, and seconds later he heard her calling Kingston Hospital, using a guarded voice.

"Let her start explaining about the stars," Reich muttered, halfway between anger and terror. He finished his toilette and came out into the bedroom. Duffy cut the phone off hastily and turned to him.

"Ben," she began.

"Wait here for me," he growled. "I'm going to find out."

"Find out about what?"

"About the stars!" he yelled. "The Christ almighty missing stars!"

He flung out of the apartment and rushed down to the street. On the empty footway, he paused and stared up again. There was the moon. There was one brilliant red point of light—Mars. There was another—Jupiter. There was nothing else. Blackness. Blackness. Blackness. It hung over his head, enigmatic, unrelieved, terrifying. It pressed downward, by some trick of the eye, oppressive, stifling, deadly.

He began to run, still staring upward. He turned a corner of the footway and collided with a woman, knocking her flat. He pulled her to her feet.

"You clumsy bastard!" she screamed, adjusting her feathers. Then in an oily voice: "Lookin' for a good time, pilot?"

Reich held her arm. He pointed up. "Look. The stars are gone. Have you noticed? The stars are gone."

"What's gone?"

"The stars. Don't you see? They're gone."

"I don't know what you're talkin' about, pilot. C'mon. Let's have us a ball."

He tore himself away from her claws and ran. Halfway down the footway was a public v-phone alcove. He stepped in and dialed information. The screen lit and a robot voice spoke: "Question?"

"What's happened to the stars?" Reich asked. "When did it happen? It must have been noticed by now. What's the explanation?"

There was a click, a pause, then another click. "Will you spell the word, please."

"Star!" Reich roared. "S-t-a-r. Star!"

Click, pause, click. "Noun or verb?"

"God damn you! Noun!"

Click, pause, click. "There is no information listed under that heading," the canned voice announced.

Reich swore, then fought to control himself. "Where's the nearest observatory to the city?"

"Kindly specify city."

"This city. New York."

Click, pause, click. "The Lunar Observatory at Croton Park is situated thirty miles north. It may be reached by Jumper Route North Coordinate 227. The Lunar Observatory was endowed in the year two thousand–"

Reich slammed down the phone. "No information listed under that heading! My God! Are they all crazy?" He ran out into the streets, searching for a public Jumper. A piloted machine cruised past and Reich signaled. It swooped to pick him up.

"Northco 227," he snapped as he stepped into the cabin. "Thirty miles. The Lunar Observatory."

"Premium trip," the driver said.

"I'll pay it. Jet!"

The cab jetted. Reich restrained himself for five minutes, then began casually: "Notice the sky?"

"Why, mister?"

"The stars are gone."

Sycophantic laugh.

"It's not supposed to be a joke," Reich said. "The stars are gone."

"If it ain't a joke, it needs explaining," the driver said. "What the hell are stars?"

A blasting reply trembled on Reich's lips. Before it could erupt, the cab landed him on the observatory grounds close to the domed roof. He snapped: "Wait for me," and ran across the lawns to the small stone entrance.

The door was ajar. He entered the observatory and heard the low whine of the dome mechanism and the quiet click of the observatory clock. Except for the low glow of the clock light, the room was in darkness. The twelve-inch refractor was in operation. He could see the observer, a dim outline, crouched over the eyepiece of the guiding telescope.

Reich walked toward him, nervous, strained, flinching at the loud clack of his footsteps in the silence. There was a chill in the air.

"Listen," Reich began in a low voice. "Sorry to bother you but you must have noticed. You're in the star business. You have noticed, haven't you? The stars. They're gone. All of them. What's happened? Why hasn't there been any alarm? Why's everybody pretending? My God! The stars! We always take them for granted. And now they're gone. What's happened! Where are the stars?"

The figure straightened slowly and turned toward Reich. "There are no stars," it said.

It was the Man With No Face.

Reich cried out. He turned and ran. He flew out of the door, down the steps and across the lawn to the waiting cab. He blundered against the crystal cabin wall with a crack that dropped him to his knees.

The driver pulled him to his feet. "You all right, Mac?"

"I don't know," Reich groaned. "I wish I did."

"None of my business," the driver said, "but I think you ought to see a peeper. You're talkin' crazy."

"About the stars?"

"Yeah."

Reich gripped the man. "I'm Ben Reich," he said, "Ben Reich of Monarch."

"Yeah, Mac. I recognized you."

"Good. You know what I can do for you if you do me a favor? Money . . . New job . . . Anything you want . . ."

"You can't do nothin' for me, Mac. I already been adjusted at Kingston."

"Better. An honest man. Will you do me a favor for the love of God or anything you love?"

"Sure, Mac."

"Go into that building. Take a look at the man behind the telescope. A good look. Come back and describe him to me."

The driver departed, was gone five minutes, then returned.

"Well?"

"He's just an ordinary guy, Mac. Sixtyish. Got lines in his face kinda deep. His ears stick out and he's got what they call a weak chin. You know. It kinda backslides."

"It's nobody . . . nobody," Reich muttered.

"What?"

"About those stars," Reich said. "You never heard of them? You never saw them? You don't know what I'm talking about?"

"Nope."

"Oh God . . ." Reich moaned. "Sweet God . . ."

"Now don't warp your orbit, Mac." The driver thumped him powerfully on the back. "Tell you something. They taught me plenty up at Kingston. One of them things was . . . Well, sometimes you get a crazy notion. It's brand new, see? But you think you always had it. Like . . . oh . . . for instance, that people always had one eye and now all of a sudden they got two."

Reich stared at him.

"So you run around yellin': 'For Chrissakes, where did they all of a sudden get two eyes everybody?' And they say: 'They always got two eyes.' And you say: 'The hell they did. I distinctly remember everybody got one eye.' And by God you believe it. And they have a hell of a time knockin' the notion outa you." The driver thumped him again. "Seems to me, Mac, like you're on a one-eye kick."

"One eye," Reich muttered. "Two eyes. Tension, apprehension, and dissension have begun."

"What?"

"I don't know. I don't know. I've had a rough time the last month. Maybe . . . Maybe you're right. But—"

"You want to go to Kingston?"

"No!"

"You want to stay here and mope about them stars?"

Abruptly, Reich shouted: "What the hell do I care about the stars!" His fear turned to hot rage. Adrenaline flooded his system, bringing with it a surge of courage and high spirits. He leaped into the cab. "I've got the world. What do I care if a few delusions go with it?"

"That's the way, Mac. Where to?"

"The Royal Palace."

"The which?"

Reich laughed. "Monarch," he said, and roared with laughter all the flight through the dawn to Monarch's soaring tower. But it was a semi-hysterical laughter.

The office ran around-the-clock shifts, and the night staff was in the last drowsy stages of the 12-8 shift when Reich bustled in. Although they had not seen much of him in the past month, the staff was accustomed to these visits, and shifted smoothly into high gear. As Reich went to his desk he was followed by secretaries and sub-secretaries carrying the urgent agenda of the day.

"Let all that wait," he snapped. "Call in the entire staff . . . all department heads and organizational supervisors. I'm going to make an announcement."

The flutter soothed him and recaptured his frame of reference. He was alive again, real again. All this was the only reality–the hustle, the bustle, the annunciator bells, the muted commands, the quick filling of his office with so many awed faces. All this was a preview of the future when bells would ring on planets and satellites and world supervisors would scuttle to his desk with awe on their faces.

"As you all know," Reich began, pacing slowly and darting piercing glances into the faces that watched him, "we of Monarch have been locked in a death struggle with the D'Courtney Cartel. Craye D'Courtney was killed some time ago. There were complications that have just been ironed out. You'll be pleased to hear that the road is open for us now. We can commence operation of Plan AA to take over the D'Courtney Cartel."

He paused, waiting for the excited murmur that should respond to his announcement. There was no response.

"Perhaps," he said, "some of you do not comprehend the size of the job and the importance of the job. Let me put it this way–in terms you'll understand. Those of you that are city supervisors will become continental supervisors. Continental supervisors will become satellite chiefs. Present satellite chiefs will become planetary chiefs. From now on, Monarch will dominate the solar system. From now on all of us must think in terms of the solar system. From now on . . ."

Reich faltered, alarmed by the blank looks around him. He glanced around, then singled out the chief secretary. "What the hell's the matter?" he growled. "There been news I haven't heard yet? Bad news?"

"N-No, Mr. Reich."

"Then what's eating you? This is something we've all been waiting for. What's wrong with it?"

The chief secretary stammered: "We . . . I . . . I'm s-sorry, sir. I d-don't know what y-you're talking about."

"I'm talking about the D'Courtney Cartel."

"I . . . I've n-never heard of the organization, Mr. Reich, sir.

I . . . we . . ." The chief secretary turned around for support. Before Reich's unbelieving eyes the entire staff shook their heads in mystification.

"D'Courtney on Mars!" Reich shouted.

"On where, sir?"

"Mars! Mars! M-a-r-s. One of the ten planets. Fourth from the sun." Gripped by the returning terror, Reich bellowed incoherently. "Mercury, Venus, Earth, Mars, Jupiter, Saturn, Mars! Mars! Mars! A hundred and forty-one million miles from the sun, Mars!"

Again the staff shook their heads. There was a rustle and they backed away slightly from Reich. He darted at the secretaries and tore the sheafs of business papers from their hands. "You've got a hundred memos about D'Courtney on Mars there. You've got to. My God, we've been battling it out with D'Courtney for the last ten years. We–"

He clawed through the papers, throwing them wildly in all directions, filling the office with fluttering snow. There was not one reference to D'Courtney or Mars. There was neither any reference to Venus, Jupiter, the moon, nor the other satellites.

"I've got memos in my desk," Reich shouted. "Hundreds of them. You lousy liars! Look in my desk . . ."

He darted to the desk and yanked out drawers. There was a stunning explosion. The desk burst asunder. Fragments of flying fruitwood slashed the staff, and Reich was hurled back against the window by the desk top which smacked him like a giant's hand.

"The Man With No Face!" Reich cried. "Christ Almighty!" He shook his head feverishly, and clung to the paramount obsession. "Where are the files? I'll show you in the files . . . D'Courtney and Mars and all the rest. And I'll show him, too. The Man With No Face . . . Come on!"

He ran out of his office and burst into the file vaults. He tore out rack after rack, scattering papers, clusters of piezo crystals, ancient wire recordings, microfilm, molecular transcripts. There was no reference to D'Courtney or Mars. There was no reference to Venus, Jupiter, Mercury, the asteroids, the satellites.

And now indeed the office was alive with hustle and bustle, annunciator bells, strident commands. Now the office was stampeding, and three burly gentlemen from Recreation came trotting into the vaults directed by the bleeding secretary, who urged: "You must! You must! I'll take the responsibility!"

"Easy now, easy now, easy now, Mr. Reich," they said with the hissing noise with which hostlers soothe savage stallions. "Easy . . . easy . . . easy . . ."

"Get away from me, you sons of bitches."

"Easy, sir. Easy. It's all right, sir."

They deployed strategically while the hustle and the bustle increased and the bells sounded and voices far off called: "Who's his doctor? Get his doctor. Somebody call Kingston. Did you notify the police? No, don't. No scandal. Get the legal department, will you! Isn't the Infirmary open yet?"

Reich's breath came and went in snarls. He overturned files in the path of the burly gentlemen, put his head down and bulled straight through them. He raced through the office to the outside corridor and the Pneumatique. The door opened; he punched Science-city 57. He stepped into the air shuttle and was shot over to Science, where he stepped out.

He was on the laboratory floor. It was in darkness. Probably the staff imagined he had dropped to the street level. He would have time. Still breathing heavily, he trotted to the lab library, snapped on the lights and went to the reference alcove. A sheet of frosted crystal, cocked like a drafting board, was set before a desk chair. There was a complicated panel of control buttons alongside it.

Reich seated himself and punched READY. The sheet lit up and a canned voice spoke from an overhead speaker.

"Topic?"

Reich punched SCIENCE.

"Section?"

Reich punched ASTRONOMY.

"Question?"

"The universe."

Click-pause-click. "The term universe in its complete physical sense applies to all matter in existence."

"What matter is in existence?"

Click-pause-click. "Matter is gathered into aggregates ranging in size from the smallest atom to the largest collection of matter known to astronomers."

"What is the largest collection of matter known to astronomers?" Reich punched DIAGRAM.

Click-pause-click. "The sun." The crystal plate displayed a dazzling picture of the sun in speeded-up action.

"But what about the others? The stars?"

Click-pause-click. "There are no stars."

"The planets?"

Click-pause-click. "There is the earth." A picture of the revolving earth appeared.

"The other planets? Mars? Jupiter? Saturn . . ."

Click-pause-click. "There are no other planets."

"The moon?"

Click-pause-click. "There is no moon."

Reich took a deep trembling breath. "We'll try it again. Go back to the sun."

The sun appeared again in the crystal. "The sun is the largest collection of matter known to astronomers," the canned voice began. Suddenly it stopped. Click-pause-click. The picture of the sun began to fade slowly. The voice spoke. "There is no sun."

The model disappeared, leaving behind it an after-image that looked up at Reich–looming, silent, horrible–The Man With No Face.

Reich howled. He leaped to his feet, knocking the desk chair backward. He picked it up and smashed it down on that frightful image. He turned and blundered out of the library into the lab, and thence to the corridor. At the Vertical Pneumatique, he punched STREET. The door opened, he staggered in and was dropped fifty-seven stories to the Main Hall of Monarch's Science-city.

It was filled with early workers hurrying to their offices. As Reich pushed past them, he caught the astonished glances at his cut and bleeding face. Then he was aware of a dozen uniformed Monarch guards closing in on him. He ran down the hall and with a frantic burst of speed dodged the guards. He slipped into the revolving doors and whirled through to the footway. There he jerked to a stop as though he had run into white-hot iron. There was no sun.

The street lights were lit; the skyways twinkled; Jumper eyes floated up and down; the shops were blazing. And overhead there was nothing–nothing but a deep, black, fathomless infinity.

"The sun!" Reich shouted. "The sun!"

He pointed upward. The office workers regarded him with suspicious eyes and hurried on. No one looked up.

"The sun! Where's the sun? Don't you understand, you fools? The sun!" Reich plucked at their arms, shaking his fist at the sky. Then the first of the guards came through the revolving door and he took to his heels.

He went down the footway, turned sharp to his right and sprinted through an arcade of brilliant, busy shops. Beyond the arcade was the entrance of a Vertical Pneumatique to the skyway. Reich leaped in. As the door closed behind him, he caught sight of the pursuing guards less than twenty yards off. Then he was lofted seventy stories and emerged on the skyway.

There was a small car-park alongside him, shelved onto the face of Monarch Tower, with a runway leading into the skyway. Reich ran in, flung credits to the attendant and got into a car. He pressed GO. The car went. At the foot of the runway he pressed LEFT. The car turned left and continued. That was all the control he had. Left, right; stop, go. The rest was automatic. Moreover, cars were strictly limited to the skyways. He might spend hours racing in circles high over the city, trapped like a dog in a revolving cage.

The car needed no attention. He glanced alternately over his shoulder and up at the sky. There was no sun—and they went about their business as though there had never been a sun. He shuddered. Was this more of the one-eye kick? Suddenly the car slowed and stopped; and he was marooned in the middle of the skyway, halfway between Monarch Tower and the giant Visiphone & Visigraph Building.

Reich hammered on the control studs. There was no response. He leaped out and raised the tail hood to inspect the pick-up. Then he saw the guards far down the skyway, running toward him, and he understood. These cars were powered by broadcast energy. They'd cut the transmission off at the car-park and were coming after him. Reich turned tail and sprinted toward the V & V Building.

The skyway tunneled through the building and was lined with shops, restaurants, a theater—and there was a travel office! A sure out. He could grab a ticket, get into a one-man capsule and have himself slotted to any of the take-off fields. He needed a little time to reorganize—reorient—and he had a house in Paris. He leaped across the center island, dodged past cars and ran into the office.

It looked like a miniature bank. A short counter. A grilled window protected by burglar-proof plastic. Reich went to the window, pulling money from his pocket. He slapped credits down on the counter and shoved them under the grille.

"Ticket to Paris," he said. "Keep the change. Which way to the capsules? Jet, man! Jet!"

"Paris?" came the reply. "There is no Paris."

Reich stared through the cloudy plastic and saw—looking, looming, silent—the Man With No Face. He spun around twice, heart pounding, skull pounding, located the door and ran out. He ran blindly onto the skyway, shied feebly from an oncoming car, and was struck down into enveloping darkness—

ABOLISH.

DESTROY.

DELETE.

DISBAND.

(MINERALOGY, PETROLOGY, GEOLOGY, PHYSIOGRAPHY)

DISPERSE.

(METEOROLOGY, HYDROLOGY, SEISMOLOGY)

ERASE.

(X^2. ϕY^3 d:SPACE/d:TIME)

EFFACE.

THE SUBJECT WILL BE—

"—will be what?"

THE SUBJECT WILL BE—

"—will be what? What? WHAT?"

A hand was placed over his mouth. Reich opened his eyes. He was in a small tiled room, an emergency police station. He was lying on a white table. Around him were grouped the guards, three uniformed police, unidentified strangers. All were writing carefully in report books, murmuring, shifting confusedly.

The stranger removed his hand from Reich's mouth and bent over him. "It's all right," he said gently. "Easy. I'm a doctor."

"A peeper?"

"What?"

"Are you a peeper? I need a peeper. I need somebody inside my head to prove I'm right. My God! I've got to know I'm right. I don't care about the price. I—"

"What's he want?" a policeman asked.

"I don't know. He said a peeper." The doctor turned back to Reich. "What d'you mean by that? Just tell us. What's a peeper?"

"An Esper! A mind reader. A—"

The doctor smiled. "He's joking. Show of high spirits. Many patients do that. They simulate sang-froid after accidents. We call it gallows humor."

"Listen," Reich said desperately. "Let me up. I want to say something."

They helped him up.

To the police, he said: "My name is Ben Reich. Ben Reich of Monarch. You know me. I want to confess. I want to confess to Lincoln Powell, the police prefect. Take me to Powell."

"Who's Powell?"

"And what y'want to confess?"

"The D'Courtney murder. I murdered Craye D'Courtney last month. In Maria Beaumont's house . . . Tell Powell. I killed D'Courtney."

The police looked at each other in surprise. One of them drifted to a corner and picked up an old-fashioned hand phone: "Captain? Got a character here. Calls himself Ben Reich of Monarch. Wants to confess to some prefect named Powell. Claims he killed a party named Craye D'Courtney last month." After a pause, the policeman called to Reich: "How do you spell that?"

"D'Courtney! Capital D apostrophe capital C-o-u-r-t-n-e-y."

The policeman spelled it out and waited. After another pause, he grunted and hung up. "A nut," he said and stowed his notebook in a pocket.

"Listen–" Reich began.

"Is he all right?" the policeman asked the doctor without looking at Reich.

"Just shaken a little. He's all right."

"Listen!" Reich shouted.

The policeman yanked him to his feet and propelled him toward the door of the station. "All right, buddy. Out!"

"You've got to listen to me! I–"

"You listen to me, buddy. There ain't no Lincoln Powell in the service. There ain't no D'Courtney killing in the books. And we ain't takin' no slok from your kind. Now . . . out!" And he hurled Reich into the street.

The pavement was strangely broken. Reich stumbled, then regained his balance and stood still, numb, lost. It was darker–eternally darker. A few street lights were lit. The skyways were extinguished. The Jumpers had disappeared. There were great gaps shorn in the skyline.

"I'm sick," Reich moaned. "I'm sick. I need help . . ."

He began to lurch down the broken streets with arms clutching his belly.

"Jumper!" he yelled. "Jumper! Isn't there anything in this God-forsaken city? Where is everything? Jumper!"

There was nothing.

"I'm sick . . . sick. Got to get home. I'm sick . . ." Again he shouted: "Isn't there anybody can hear me? I'm sick. I need help . . . Help! . . . Help!"

There was nothing.

He moaned again. Then he tittered—weakly, inanely. He sang in a broken voice: "Eight, sir . . . Five, sir . . . One, sir . . . Tenser, said Tensor . . . Tension . . . 'prehension . . . 'ssension have begun . . ."

He called plaintively: "Where is everybody? Maria! Lights! Mari-aaa! Stop this crazy Sardine game!"

He stumbled.

"Come back!" Reich called. "For God's sake, come back! I'm all alone."

No answer.

He was searching for 9 Park South, looking for the Beaumont Mansion, the site of D'Courtney's death . . . and Maria Beaumont, shrill, decadent, reassuring.

There was nothing.

A bleak tundra. Black sky. Unfamiliar desolation.

Nothing.

Reich shouted once—a hoarse, inarticulate yell of rage and fright.

No answer. Not even an echo.

"For God's sake!" he cried. "Where is everything? Bring it all back! There's nothing but space . . ."

Out of the enveloping desolation, a figure gathered and grew, familiar, ominous, silent . . . The Man With No Face. Reich watched it, paralyzed, transfixed.

Then the figure spoke: "There is no space. There is nothing."

And there was a screaming in Reich's ears that was his voice, and a hammering pulse that was his heart. He was running down a yawning alien path, devoid of life, devoid of space, running before it was too late, too late, too late—running while there was still time, time, time—

He ran headlong into a figure of black shadows. A figure without a face. A figure that said: "There is no time. There is nothing."

Reich backed away. He turned. He fell. He crawled feebly through eternal emptiness shrieking: "Powell! Duffy! Quizzard! Tate! Oh Christ! Where is everybody? Where is everything? For the love of God . . ."

And he was face to face with the Man With No Face, who said: "There is no God. There is nothing."

And now there was no longer escape. There was only a negative infinity and Reich and the Man With No Face. And fixed, frozen, helpless in that matrix, Reich at last raised his eyes and stared deep into the face of his deadly enemy–the man he could not escape . . . the terror of his nightmares . . . the destroyer of his existence . . .

It was . . .

Himself.

D'Courtney.

Both.

Two faces, blending into one. Ben D'Courtney. Craye Reich. D'Courtney-Reich. D'R.

He could make no sound. He could make no move. There was neither time nor space nor matter. There was nothing left but dying thought.

"Father?"

"Son."

"You are me?"

"We are us."

"Father and son?"

"Yes."

"I can't understand. What's happened?"

"You lost the game, Ben."

"The Sardine Game?"

"The Cosmic Game."

"I won. I won. I owned every bit of the world. I–"

"And therefore you lose. We lose."

"Lose what?"

"Survival."

"I don't understand. I can't understand."

"My part of us understands, Ben. You would understand too if you hadn't driven me from you."

"How did I drive you from me?"

"With every rotten, distorted corruption in you."

"You say that? You . . . betrayer, who tried to kill me?"

"That was without passion, Ben. That was to destroy you before you could destroy us. That was for survival. It was to help you lose the world and win the game, Ben."

"What game? What Cosmic Game?"

"The maze . . . the labyrinth . . . all the universe, created as a puzzle for us to solve. The galaxies, the stars, the sun, the planets . . . the world as we knew it. We were the only reality. All the rest

was make-believe—dolls, puppets, stage settings—pretended passions. It was a make-believe reality for us to solve."

"I conquered it. I owned it."

"And you failed to solve it. We'll never know what the solution is, but it's not theft, terror, hatred, lust, murder, rapine. You failed, and it's all been abolished, disbanded . . ."

"But what's to become of us?"

"We are abolished too. I tried to warn you. I tried to stop you. But we failed the test."

"But why? Why? Who are we? What are we?"

"Who knows? Did the seed know who or what it was when it failed to find fertile soil? Does it matter who or what we are? We have failed. Our test is ended. We are ended."

"No."

"Perhaps if we had solved it, Ben, it might have remained real. But it is ended. Reality has turned into might-have-been, and you have awakened at last . . . to nothing."

"We'll go back! We'll try it again!"

"There is no going back. It is ended."

"We'll find a way. There must be a way . . ."

"There is none. It is ended."

It was ended.

Now . . . Demolition.

17

They found the two men next morning, far up the island in the gardens overlooking the old Haarlem Canal. Each had wandered all the night, through footway and skyway, unconscious of his surroundings, yet both were drawn inevitably together like two magnetized needles floating on a weed-choked pond.

Powell was seated cross-legged on the wet turf, his face shriveled and lifeless, his respiration almost gone, his pulse faded. He was clutching Reich with an iron grip. Reich was curled into a tight fetal ball.

They rushed Powell to his home on Hudson Ramp, where the entire Guild Lab team alternately sweated over him and congratulated themselves on the first successful Mass Cathexis Measure in the history of the Esper Guild. There was no hurry for Reich. In due course and with proper procedure, his inert body was transported to Kingston Hospital for Demolition.

There the matter rested for seven days.

On the eighth day, Powell arose, bathed, dressed, successfully defeated his nurses in single combat, and left the house. He made one stop at Sucre et Cie., emerged with a large mysterious parcel and then proceeded to headquarters to make his personal report to Commissioner Crabbe. On the way up, he poked his head into Beck's office.

"Hi, Jax."

"Bless(and curses)ings, Linc."

"Curses?"

"Bet fifty they'd keep you in bed till next Wed."

"You lose. Did Mose back us up on the D'Courtney motive?"

"Lock, stock & barrel. Trial took one hour. Reich's going into Demolition now."

"Good. Well, I'd better go up and s-p-e-l-l it out for Crabbe."

"What you got under your arm?"

"Present."

"For me?"

"Not today. Here's thinking at you."

Powell went up to Crabbe's ebony and silver office, knocked, heard the imperious: "Come!" and entered. Crabbe was properly solicitous, but stiff. The D'Courtney case had not improved his relations with Powell. The denouement had come as an additional blow.

"It was a remarkably complex case, sir," Powell began tactfully. "None of us could understand it, and none of us are to blame. You see, Commissioner, even Reich himself was not consciously aware of why he had murdered D'Courtney. The only one who grasped the case was the prosecution computer, and we thought it was acting kittenish."

"The machine? It understood?"

"Yes, sir. When we ran our final data through the first time, the computer told us that the 'passion motive' was insufficiently documented. We'd all been assuming profit motive. So had Reich. Naturally we assumed the computer was having kinks, and we insisted on computation based on the profit motive. We were wrong."

"And that infernal machine was right?"

"Yes, Commissioner. It was. Reich told himself that he was killing D'Courtney for financial reasons. That was his psychological camouflage for the real passion motive. And it couldn't hold up. He offered merger to D'Courtney. D'Courtney accepted. But Reich was subconsciously compelled to misunderstand the message. He had to. He had to go on believing he murdered for money."

"Why?"

"Because he couldn't face the real motive."

"Which was . . . ?"

"D'Courtney was his father."

"What!" Crabbe stared. "His father? His flesh and blood?"

"Yes, sir. It was all there before us. We just couldn't see it . . . because Reich couldn't see it. That estate on Callisto, for instance. The one that Reich used to decoy Dr. Jordan off the planet. Reich inherited it from his mother, who'd received it from D'Courtney. We all assumed Reich's father had chiseled it out of D'Courtney and placed it in his wife's name. We were wrong. D'Courtney had given it to Reich's mother because they were lovers. It was his love-gift to the mother of his child. Reich was born there. Jackson Beck uncovered all that, once we had the lead."

Crabbe opened his mouth, then closed it.

"And there were so many other signposts. D'Courtney's suicide drive, produced by intense guilt sensations of abandonment. He *had* abandoned his son. It was tearing him apart. Then, Barbara D'Courtney's deep half-twin image of herself and Ben Reich; somehow she knew they were half-brother and -sister. And Reich's inability to kill Barbara at Chooka Frood's. He knew it too, deep down in the unconscious. He wanted to destroy the hateful father who had rejected him, but he could not bring himself to harm his sister."

"But when did you unearth all this?"

"After the case was closed, sir. When Reich attacked me for setting those booby-traps."

"He claimed you did. He— But if you didn't, Powell, who did?"

"Reich himself, sir."

"Reich!"

"Yes, sir. He murdered his father. He discharged his hatred. But his super-ego . . . his conscience, could not permit him to go unpunished for such a horrible crime. Since the police apparently were unable to punish him, his conscience took over. That was the meaning of Reich's nightmare image—the Man With No Face."

"The Man With No Face?"

"Yes, Commissioner. It was the symbol of Reich's real relationship to D'Courtney. The figure had no face because Reich could not accept the truth—that he had recognized D'Courtney as his father. The figure appeared in his dreams when he made the decision to kill his father. It never left him. It was first the threat of punishment for what he contemplated. Then it became the punishment itself for the murder."

"The booby-traps?"

"Exactly. His conscience had to punish him. But Reich had never admitted to himself that he murdered because he hated D'Courtney as the father who had rejected and abandoned him. Therefore, the punishment had to take place on the unconscious level. Reich set those traps for himself without ever realizing it–in his sleep, somnambulistically–during the day, in short fugues–brief departures from conscious reality. The tricks of the mind-mechanism are fantastic."

"But if Reich himself knew none of this . . . how did you get at it, Powell?"

"Well, sir. That was the problem. We couldn't get it by peeping him. He was hostile and you have to have complete cooperation from a subject to get that kind of material. It takes months anyway. Also, if Reich recovered from the series of shocks he'd had, he would be able to readjust, reorient, and become immune to us. That was dangerous, too, because he was in a position of power to rock the solar system. He was one of those rare World-Shakers whose compulsions might have torn down our society and irrevocably committed us to his own psychotic pattern."

Crabbe nodded.

"He very nearly succeeded. These men appear every so often–links between the past and the future. If they are permitted to mature . . . If the link is permitted to weld . . . The world finds itself chained to a dreadful tomorrow."

"Then what did you do?"

"We used the Mass Cathexis Measure, sir. It's difficult to explain, but I'll do my best. Every human being has a psyche composed of latent and capitalized energy. Latent energy is our reserve–the untapped natural resources of our mind. Capitalized energy is that latent energy which we call up and put to work. Most of us use only a small portion of our latent energy."

"I understand."

"When the Esper Guild uses the Mass Cathexis Measure, every Esper opens his psyche, so to speak, and contributes his latent energy to a pool. One Esper alone taps this pool and becomes the canal for the latent energy. He capitalizes it and puts it to work. He can accomplish tremendous things . . . if he can control it. It's a difficult and dangerous operation. About on a par with jetting to the moon with a stick of dynamite stuck–er–riding on dynamite sticks . . ."

Suddenly Crabbe grinned. "I wish I were a peeper," he said. "I'd like to get the real image in your mind."

"You've got it already, sir." Powell grinned back. A rapport had been established between them for the first time.

"It was necessary," Powell continued, "to confront Reich with the Man With No Face. We had to make him see the truth before we could get the truth. Using the pool of latent energy, I built a common neurotic concept for Reich—the illusion that he alone in the world was real."

"Why, I've— Is that common?"

"Oh yes, sir. It's one of the run-of-the-mill escape patterns. When life gets tough, you tend to take refuge in the idea that it's all make-believe—a giant hoax. Reich had the seeds of that weakness in him already. I simply forced them and let Reich defeat himself. Life was getting tough for him. I persuaded him to believe that the universe was a hoax—a puzzle box. Then I tore it down, layer by layer. I made him believe that the test was ended. The puzzle was being dismantled. And I left Reich alone with the Man With No Face. He looked into the face and saw himself and his father—and we had everything."

Powell picked up his parcel and arose. Crabbe jumped up and escorted him to the door with a friendly hand on his shoulder.

"You've done a phenomenal job, Powell. Really phenomenal. I can't tell you . . . It must be a wonderful thing to be an Esper."

"Wonderful and terrible, sir."

"You must all be very happy."

"Happy?" Powell paused at the door and looked at Crabbe. "Would you be happy to live your life in a hospital, Commissioner?"

"A hospital?"

"That's where we live—all of us. In the psychiatric ward. Without escape . . . without refuge. Be grateful you're not a peeper, sir. Be grateful that you only see the outward man. Be grateful that you never see the passions, the hatreds, the jealousies, the malice, the sicknesses. Be grateful you rarely see the frightening truth in people. The world will be a wonderful place when everyone's a peeper and everyone's adjusted. But until then, be grateful you're blind."

He left headquarters, hired a Jumper and was jetted north toward Kingston Hospital. He sat in the cabin with the parcel on his knees, gazing down at the magnificent Hudson valley, whistling a crooked tune. Once he grinned and muttered: "Wow! That was some line I handed Crabbe. But I had to cement our relations. Now he'll feel sorry for peepers . . . and friendly."

Kingston Hospital came into view—acre upon rolling acre of magnificent landscaping. Solariums, pools, lawns, athletic fields, dormitories, clinics–all in exquisite neo-classic design. As the Jumper descended, Powell could make out the figures of patients and attendants–all bronzed, active, laughing, playing. He thought of the vigilant measures the Board of Governors was forced to take to prevent Kingston Hospital from becoming another Spaceland. Too many fashionable malingerers were already attempting to obtain admission.

Powell checked in at the Visitors Office, found Barbara D'Courtney's location and started across the grounds. He was weak, but he wanted to leap hedges, vault gates, run races. He had awakened after seven days' exhaustion with a question–one question to ask Barbara. He felt exhilarated.

They saw each other at the same moment. Across a broad stretch of lawn flanked by fieldstone terraces and brilliant gardens. She flew toward him, waving, and he ran toward her. Then as they approached, both were stricken with shyness. They stopped a few feet apart, not daring to look at each other.

"Hello."

"Hello, Barbara."

"I . . . Let's get into the shade, shall we?"

They turned toward the terrace wall. Powell glanced at her from the corner of his eye. She was alive again–alive as he had never seen her before. And her urchin expression–the expression that he had imagined was a phase of her Déjà Eprouvé development–was still there. She looked inexpressibly mischievous, high-spirited, fascinating. But she was adult. He did not know her.

"I'm being discharged this evening," Barbara said.

"I know."

"I'm terribly grateful to you for all you've–"

"Please don't say that."

"For all you've done," Barbara continued firmly. They sat down on a stone bench. She looked at him with grave eyes. "I want to tell you how grateful I am."

"Please, Barbara. You're terrifying me."

"Am I?"

"I knew you so intimately as . . . well, as a child. Now . . ."

"Now I'm grown up again."

"Yes."

"You must get to know me better." She smiled graciously. "Shall we say . . . Tea tomorrow at five?"

"At five."

"Informal. Don't dress."

"Listen," Powell said desperately. "I helped dress you more than once. And comb your hair. And brush your teeth."

She waved her hand airily.

"Your table manners were a caution. You liked fish but you hated lamb. You hit me in the eye with a chop."

"That was ages ago, Mr. Powell."

"That was two weeks ago, Miss D'Courtney."

She arose with magnificent poise. "Really, Mr. Powell. I feel it would be best to end the interview. If you feel impelled to cast chronographical aspersions . . ." She stopped and looked at him. The urchin appeared again in her face. "Chronographical?" she inquired.

He dropped the parcel and caught her in his arms.

"Mr. Powell, Mr. Powell, Mr. Powell . . ." she murmured. "Hello, Mr. Powell . . ."

"My God, Barbara . . . Baba, dear. For a moment I thought you meant it."

"I was paying you back for being grown up."

"You always were a revengeful kid."

"You always were a mean daddy." She leaned back and looked at him. "What are you really like? What are we both like? Will we have time to find out?"

"Time?"

"Before . . . Peep me. I can't say it."

"No, dear. You'll have to say it."

"Mary Noyes told me. Everything."

"Oh. She did?"

Barbara nodded. "But I don't care. I don't care. She was right. I'll settle for anything. Even if you can't marry me."

He laughed. The exhilaration bubbled out of him. "You won't have to settle for anything," he said. "Sit down. I want to ask you one question."

She sat down. On his lap.

"I have to go back to that night," he said.

"In Beaumont House?"

He nodded.

"It's not easy to talk about."

"It won't take a minute. Now . . . You were lying in bed, asleep. Suddenly you woke up and rushed into the orchid room. You remember the rest."

"I remember."

"One question. What was the cry that woke you?"

"You know."

"I know, but I want you to say it. Say it out loud."

"Do you think it's . . . it's going to send me into hysteria again?"

"No. Just say it."

After a long pause, she said in a low voice: "Help, Barbara."

He nodded again. "Who shouted that?"

"Why, it was–" Suddenly she stopped.

"It wasn't Ben Reich. He wouldn't be yelling for help. He didn't need help. Who did?"

"My . . . My father."

"But he couldn't speak, Barbara. His throat was gone. Cancer. He couldn't utter a word."

"I heard him."

"You peeped him."

She stared; then she shook her head. "No, I–"

"You peeped him," Powell repeated gently. "You're a latent Esper. Your father cried out on the telepathic level. If I hadn't been such an ass and so intent on Reich, I'd have realized it long before. You were unconsciously peeping Mary and me all the while you were in my house."

She couldn't grasp it.

"Do you love me?" Powell shot at her.

"I love you, of course," she muttered, "but I think you're inventing excuses to–"

"Who asked you?"

"Asked me what?"

"If you loved me."

"Why, you just–" She stopped, then tried again. "You said . . . Y-You . . ."

"I didn't say it. Do you understand now? We won't have to settle for anything short of us."

Seconds later, it seemed, but it was actually half an hour, they were separated by a violent crash that sounded from the top of the terrace above their heads. They looked up in astonishment.

A naked thing appeared on the stone wall, gibbering, screaming, twitching. It toppled over the edge and crashed down through the flower beds until it landed on the lawn, crying and jerking as though a steady stream of voltage was pouring through its nervous system. It was Ben Reich, almost unrecognizable, partway through Demolition.

Powell swung Barbara to him with her back to Reich. He took her chin in his hand and said: "Are you still my girl?"

She nodded.

"I don't want you to see this. It isn't dangerous, but it isn't good for you. Will you run back to your pavilion and wait for me? Like a good girl? All right . . . Scamper now! Jet!"

She grabbed his hand, kissed it quickly, and ran across the lawn without once looking back. Powell watched her go, then turned and inspected Reich.

When a man is demolished at Kingston Hospital, his entire psyche is destroyed. The series of osmotic injections begins with the topmost strata of cortical synapses and slowly works down, switching off every circuit, extinguishing every memory, destroying every particle of the pattern that has been built up since birth. And as the pattern is erased, each particle discharges its portion of energy, turning the entire body into a shuddering maelstrom of dissociation.

But this is not the pain; this is not the dread of Demolition. The horror lies in the fact that the consciousness is never lost; that as the psyche is wiped out, the mind is aware of its slow, backward death until at last it too disappears and awaits the rebirth. The mind bids an eternity of farewells; it mourns at an endless funeral. And in those blinking, twitching eyes of Ben Reich, Powell saw the awareness . . . the pain . . . the tragic despair.

"Now how the hell did he fall down there? Do we have to keep him tied?" Dr. Jeems poked his head over the terrace. "Oh. Hi, Powell. That's a friend of yours. Remember him?"

"Vividly."

Jeems spoke over his shoulder: "You go down to the lawn and pick him up. I'll keep an eye on him." He turned to Powell. "He's a lusty lad. We've got great hopes for him."

Reich squalled and twitched.

"How's the treatment coming?"

"Wonderful. He's got the stamina to take anything. We're stepping him up. Ought to be ready for rebirth in a year."

"I'm waiting for it. We need men like Reich. It would have been a shame to lose him."

"Lose him? How's that possible? You think a little fall like that could–"

"No. I mean something else. Three or four hundred years ago, cops used to catch people like Reich just to kill them. Capital punishment they called it."

"You're kidding."

"Scout's honor."

"But it doesn't make sense. If a man's got the talent and guts to buck society, he's obviously above average. You want to hold on to him. You straighten him out and turn him into a plus value. Why throw him away? Do that enough and all you've got left are the sheep."

"I don't know. Maybe in those days they wanted sheep."

The attendants came trotting across the lawn and picked Reich up. He fought and screamed. They handled him with the deft and gentle Kingston judo while they checked him carefully for breaks and sprains. Then, reassured, they started to lead him away.

"Just a minute," Powell called. He turned to the stone bench, picked up the mysterious parcel and unwrapped it. It was one of Sucre et Cie.'s most magnificent candy boxes. He carried it to the demolished man and held it out. "It's a present for you, Ben. Take it."

The creature glowered at Powell and then at the box. At last the clumsy hands came out and took the gift.

"Why, damn it, I'm just his nursemaid," Powell muttered. "We're all of us nursemaids to this crazy world. Is it worth it?"

Out of the chaos in Reich came an explosive fragment: *"Powell-peeper-Powell-friend-Powell-friend . . ."*

It was so sudden, so unexpected, so passionately grateful that Powell was overcome with warmth and tears. He tried to smile, then turned away and wandered across the lawn toward the pavilion and Barbara.

"Listen," he cried in exaltation. *"Listen, Normals! You must learn what it is. You must learn how it is. You must tear the barriers down. You must tear the veils away. We see the truth you cannot see. That there is nothing in man but love and faith, courage and kindness, generosity and sacrifice. All else is only the barrier of your blindness. One day we'll all be mind to mind and heart to heart . . ."*

In the endless universe there has been nothing new, nothing different. What has appeared exceptional to the minute mind of man has been inevitable to the infinite Eye of God. This strange second in a life, that unusual event, those remarkable coincidences of environment, opportunity, and encounter–all of them have been reproduced over and over on the planet of a sun whose galaxy revolves once in two hundred million years and has revolved nine times already. There has been joy. There will be joy again.

Book 2

DAY MILLION

by Frederik Pohl

ON THIS day I want to tell you about, which will be almost a thousand years from now, there were a boy, a girl and a love story.

Now, although I haven't said much so far, none of it is true. The boy was not what you and I would normally think of as a boy, because he was a hundred and eighty-seven years old. Nor was the girl a girl, for other reasons. And the love story did not entail that sublimation of the urge to rape, and concurrent postponement of the instinct to submit, which we at present understand in such matters. You won't care much for this story if you don't grasp these facts at once. If, however, you will make the effort you'll likely enough find it jampacked, chockful and tip-top-crammed with laughter, tears and poignant sentiment which may, or may not, be worthwhile. The reason the girl was not a girl was that she was a boy.

How angrily you recoil from the page! You say, who the hell wants to read about a pair of queers? Calm yourself. Here are no hot-breathing secrets of perversion for the coterie trade. In fact, if you were to see this girl you would not guess that she was in any sense a boy. Breasts, two; reproductive organs, female. Hips, callipygian; face, hairless; supra-orbital lobes, nonexistent. You would term her female on sight, although it is true that you might wonder just what species she was a female of, being confused by the tail, the silky pelt and the gill slits behind each ear.

Now you recoil again. Cripes, man, take my word for it. This is a sweet kid, and if you, as a normal male, spent as much as an hour in a room with her you would bend heaven and earth to get her in the sack. Dora—we will call her that; her "name" was omicron-Dibase seven-group-totter-oot S Doradus 5314, the last part of which is a color specification corresponding to a shade of green—Dora, I say, was feminine, charming and cute. I admit she doesn't sound that way. She was, as you might put it, a dancer. Her art involved qualities of intellection and expertise of a very high order, requiring both tremendous natural capacities and endless practice; it was performed in null-gravity and I can best describe it by saying that it was something like the performance of a contortionist and something like classical ballet, maybe resembling Danilova's dying swan. It was also pretty damned sexy. In a symbolic way, to be sure; but face it, most of the things we call "sexy" are symbolic, you know, except perhaps an exhibitionist's open clothing. On Day Million when Dora danced, the people who saw her panted, and you would too.

About this business of her being a boy. It didn't matter to her audiences that genetically she was male. It wouldn't matter to you, if you were among them, because you wouldn't know it–not unless you took a biopsy cutting of her flesh and put it under an electron-microscope to find the XY chromosome–and it didn't matter to them because they didn't care. Through techniques which are not only complex but haven't yet been discovered, these people were able to determine a great deal about the aptitudes and easements of babies quite a long time before they were born–at about the second horizon of cell division, to be exact, when the segmenting egg is becoming a free blastocyst–and then they naturally helped those aptitudes along. Wouldn't we? If we find a child with an aptitude for music we give him a scholarship to Juilliard. If they found a child whose aptitudes were for being a woman, they made him one. As sex had long been dissociated from reproduction this was relatively easy to do and caused no trouble and no, or at least very little, comment.

How much is "very little"? Oh, about as much as would be caused by our own tampering with Divine Will by filling a tooth. Less than would be caused by wearing a hearing aid. Does it still sound awful? Then look closely at the next busty babe you meet and reflect that she may be a Dora, for adults who are genetically male but somatically female are far from unknown even in our own time. An accident of environment in the womb overwhelms the blueprints of heredity. The difference is that with us it happens only by accident and we don't know about it except rarely, after close study; whereas the people of Day Million did it often, on purpose, because they wanted to.

Well, that's enough to tell you about Dora. It would only confuse you to add that she was seven feet tall and smelled of peanut butter. Let us begin our story.

On Day Million, Dora swam out of her house, entered a transportation tube, was sucked briskly to the surface in its flow of water and ejected in its plume of spray to an elastic platform in front of her—ah—call it her rehearsal hall.

"Oh, hell!" she cried in pretty confusion, reaching out to catch her balance and finding herself tumbled against a total stranger, whom we will call Don.

They met cute. Don was on his way to have his legs renewed. Love was the farthest thing from his mind. But when, absent-mindedly taking a short cut across the landing platform for submarinites and finding himself drenched, he discovered his arms full of the loveliest girl he had ever seen, he knew at once they were meant for each other. "Will you marry me?" he asked. She said softly, "Wednesday," and the promise was like a caress.

Don was tall, muscular, bronze and exciting. His name was no more Don than Dora's was Dora, but the personal part of it was Adonis in tribute to his vibrant maleness, and so we will call him Don for short. His personality color-code, in Angstrom units, was 5,290, or only a few degrees bluer than Dora's 5,314—a measure of what they had intuitively discovered at first sight—that they possessed many affinities of taste and interest.

I despair of telling you exactly what it was that Don did for a living —I don't mean for the sake of making money; I mean for the sake of giving purpose and meaning to his life, to keep him from going off his nut with boredom—except to say that it involved a lot of traveling. He traveled in interstellar spaceships. In order to make a spaceship go really fast, about thirty-one male and seven genetically female human beings had to do certain things, and Don was one of the thirty-one. Actually, he contemplated options. This involved a lot of exposure to radiation flux—not so much from his own station in the propulsive system as in the spillover from the next stage, where a genetic female preferred selections, and the subnuclear particles making the selections she preferred demolished themselves in a shower of quanta. Well, you don't give a rat's ass for that, but it meant that Don had to be clad at all times in a skin of light, resilient, extremely strong copper-colored metal. I have already mentioned this, but you probably thought I meant he was sunburned.

More than that, he was a cybernetic man. Most of his ruder parts had been long since replaced with mechanisms of vastly more permanence and use. A cadmium centrifuge, not a heart, pumped his blood. His lungs moved only when he wanted to speak out loud, for a cascade of osmotic filters rebreathed oxygen out of his own wastes. In a way, he probably would have looked peculiar to a man from the twentieth century, with his glowing eyes and seven-fingered hands. But to himself, and of course to Dora, he looked mighty manly and grand. In the course of his voyages Don had circled Proxima Centauri, Procyon and the puzzling worlds of Mira Ceti; he had carried agricultural templates to the planets of Canopus and brought back warm, witty pets from the pale companion of Aldebaran. Blue-hot or red-cool, he had seen a thousand stars and their ten thousand planets. He had, in fact, been traveling the starlanes, with only brief leaves on Earth, for pushing two centuries. But you don't care about that, either. It is people who make stories, not the circumstances they find themselves in, and you want to hear about these two people. Well, they made it. The great thing they had for each other grew and flowered and burst into fruition on Wednesday, just as Dora had promised. They met at the encoding room, with a couple of well-wishing friends apiece to cheer them on, and while their identities were being taped and stored they smiled and whispered to each other and bore the jokes of their friends with blushing repartee. Then they exchanged their mathematical analogues and went away, Dora to her dwelling beneath the surface of the sea and Don to his ship.

It was an idyll, really. They lived happily ever after—or anyway, until they decided not to bother any more and died.

Of course, they never set eyes on each other again.

Oh, I can see you now, you eaters of charcoal-broiled steak, scratching an incipient bunion with one hand and holding this story with the other, while the stereo plays d'Indy or Monk. You don't believe a word of it, do you? Not for one minute. People wouldn't live like that, you say with a grunt as you get up to put fresh ice in a drink.

And yet there's Dora, hurrying back through the flushing commuter pipes toward her underwater home (she prefers it there; has had herself somatically altered to breathe the stuff). If I tell you with what sweet fulfillment she fits the recorded analogue of Don into the symbol manipulator, hooks herself in and turns herself on . . . if I try to tell you any of that you will simply stare. Or glare; and grumble, what the hell kind of love-making is this? And yet I assure you, friend, I really do assure you that Dora's ecstasies are as creamy and passionate as any of James Bond's lady spies', and one hell of a lot more so than anything you are going to find in "real life." Go ahead, glare and grumble. Dora doesn't care. If she thinks of you at all, her thirty-times-great-great-grandfather, she thinks you're a pretty primordial sort of brute. You are. Why, Dora is farther removed from you than you are from the Australopithecines of five thousand centuries ago. You could not swim a second in the strong currents of her life. You don't think progress goes in a straight line, do you? Do you recognize that it is an ascending, accelerating, maybe even exponential curve? It takes hell's own time to get started, but when it goes it goes like a bomb. And you, you Scotch-drinking steak-eater in your relaxacizing chair, you've just barely lighted the primacord of the fuse. What is it now, the six or seven hundred thousandth day after Christ? Dora lives in Day Million, the millionth day of the Christian Era. Almost a thousand years from now. Her body fats are polyunsaturated, like Crisco. Her wastes are hemodialyzed out of her bloodstream while she sleeps—that means she doesn't have to go to the bathroom. On whim, to pass a slow half hour, she can command more energy than the entire nation of Portugal can spend today, and use it to launch a weekend satellite or remold a crater on the Moon. She loves Don very much. She keeps his every gesture, mannerism, nuance, touch of hand, thrill of intercourse, passion of kiss stored in symbolic-mathematical form. And when she wants him, all she has to do is turn the machine on and she has him.

And Don, of course, has Dora. Adrift on a sponson city a few hundred yards over her head, or orbiting Arcturus fifty light-years away, Don has only to command his own symbol-manipulator to rescue Dora from the ferrite files and bring her to life for him, and there she is; and rapturously, tirelessly they love all night. Not in the flesh, of course; but then his flesh has been extensively altered and it wouldn't really be much fun. He doesn't need the flesh for pleasure. Genital organs feel nothing. Neither do hands, nor breasts, nor lips; they are only receptors, accepting and transmitting impulses. It is the brain that feels; it is the interpretation of those impulses that makes agony or orgasm, and Don's symbol manipulator gives him the analogue of cuddling, the analogue of kissing, the analogue of wild, ardent hours with the external, exquisite and incorruptible analogue of Dora. Or Diane. Or sweet Rose, or laughing Alicia; for to be sure, they have each of them exchanged analogues before, and will again.

Rats, you say, it looks crazy to me. And you—with your after-shave lotion and your little red car, pushing papers across a desk all day and chasing tail all night—tell me, just how the hell do you think you would look to Tiglath-Pileser, say, or Attila the Hun?

MANNA

by Peter Phillips

TAKE BEST-QUALITY synthetic protein. Bake it up, break it up, steam it, steep it in sucrose, ferment it, add nut oil, piquant spices from the Indies, fruit juices, new flavors from the laboratory, homogenize it, hydrolize it, soak it in brine; pump in glutamic acid, balanced proportions of A, B_1, B_2, C, D, traces of calcium, copper and iron salts, an unadvertised drop of benzedrine; dehydrate, peptonize, irradiate, reheat in malt vapor under pressure compress, cut into mouth-sized chunks, pack in liquor from an earlier stage of the process—

Miracle Meal.

Everything the Body Needs to Sustain Life and Bounding Vitality, in the Most DEEE LISHUSSS *Food Ever Devised. It will Invigorate You, Build Muscle, Brain, Nerve. Better than the Banquets of Imperial Rome, Renaissance Italy, Eighteenth Century France—All in One Can. The Most Heavenly Taste Thrills You Have Ever Experienced. Gourmets' Dream and Housewives' Delight. You Can Live on It. Eat It for Breakfast, Lunch, Dinner. You'll Never Get Tired of* MIRACLE MEAL.

Ad cuts of Zeus contemptuously tossing a bowl of ambrosia over the edge of Mount Olympus and making a goggle-eyed grab for a can of Miracle Meal.

Studio fake-ups of Lucretia Borgia dropping a phial of poison and crying piously: "It Would Be a Sin to Spoil Miracle Meal."

Posters and night-signs of Joe Doe—or Bill Smith, or Henri Brun, or Hans Schmitt or Wei Lung—balancing precariously on a pyramided pile of empty M.M. cans, eyes closed, mouth pursed in slightly inane ecstasy as he finishes the last mouthful of his hundred-thousandth can.

You could live on it, certainly.

The publicity co-ordinator of the Miracle Meal Corporation chose the victim himself—a young man named Arthur Adelaide from Greenwich Village.

For a year, under the closest medical supervision and observation, Arthur ate nothing but Miracle Meal.

From this Miracle Meal Marathon, as it was tagged by videoprint newssheets, he emerged smiling, twice the weight—publicity omitted to mention that he'd been half starved to begin with—he'd been trying to live off pure art and was a bad artist—perfectly fit, and ten thousand dollars richer.

He was also given a commercial-art job with M.M., designing new labels for the cans.

His abrupt death at the end of an eighty-story drop from his office window a week or two later received little attention.

It would be unreasonable to blame the cumulative effect of M.M., for Arthur was probably a little unbalanced to begin with, whereas M.M. was Perfectly Balanced—a Kitchen in a Can.

Maybe you could get tired of it. But not very quickly. The flavor was the secret. It was delicious yet strangely and tantalizingly indefinable. It seemed to react progressively on the taste buds so that the tastes subtly changed with each mouthful.

One moment it might be *omelette aux fines herbes,* the next, turkey and cranberry, then buckwheat and maple. You'd be through the can before you could make up your mind. So you'd buy another.

Even the can was an improvement on the usual plastic self-heater —shape of a small, shallow pie dish, with a pre-impressed crystalline fracture in the plastic lid.

Press the inset button on the preheating unit at one side, and when the food was good and hot, a secondary chemical reaction in the unit released a fierce little plunger just inside the perimeter fracture. Slight steam pressure finished the job. The lid flipped off.

Come and get it. You eat right out of the can it comes in. Keep your fingers out, Johnny. Don't you see the hygiplast spoon in its moisture- and heat-repellent wrapper fixed under the lid?

The Reverend Malachi Pennyhorse did not eat Miracle Meal. Nor was he impressed when Mr. Stephen Samson, Site Adviser to the Corporation, spoke in large dollar signs of the indirect benefits a factory would bring to the district.

"Why here? You already have one factory in England. Why not extend it?"

"It's our policy, Reverend—"

"Not 'Reverend,' young man. Call me Vicar. Or Mr. Pennyhorse. Or merely Pennyhorse–Go on."

"It's our policy, sir, to keep our factories comparatively small, site them in the countryside for the health of employees, and modify the buildings to harmonize with the prevailing architecture of the district. There is no interference with local amenities. All transport of employees, raw materials, finished product is by silent copter."

Samson laid a triphoto on the vicar's desk. "What would you say that was?"

Mr. Pennyhorse adjusted his pince-nez, looked closely. "Byzantine. Very fine. Around 500 A.D."

"And this–"

"Moorish. Quite typical. Fifteenth century."

Samson said: "They're our factories at Istanbul and Tunis respectively. At Allahabad, India, we had to put up big notices saying: 'This is not a temple or place of worship,' because natives kept wandering in and offering up prayers to the processing machines."

Mr. Pennyhorse glanced up quickly. Samson kept his face straight, added: "The report may have been exaggerated, but–you get the idea?"

The vicar said: "I do. What shape do you intend your factory to take in this village?"

"That's why I came to you. The rural district council suggested that you might advise us."

"My inclination, of course, is to advise you to go away and not return."

The vicar looked out of his study window at the sleepy, sunwashed village street, gables of the ancient Corn Exchange, paved marketplace, lichened spire of his own time-kissed church; and, beyond, rolling Wiltshire pastures cradling the peaceful community.

The vicar sighed: "We've held out here so long–I hoped we would remain inviolate in my time, at least. However, I suppose we must consider ourselves fortunate that your corporation has some respect for tradition and the feelings of the . . . uh . . . 'natives.' "

He pulled out a drawer in his desk. "It might help you to understand those feelings if I show you a passage from the very full diary of my predecessor here, who died fifty years ago at the age of ninety-five–we're a long-lived tribe, we clergy. It's an entry he made one hundred years ago–sitting at this very desk."

Stephen Samson took the opened volume.

The century-old handwriting was as readable as typescript.

"May 3, 1943. Long, interesting discussion with young American soldier, one of those who are billeted in the village. They term themselves G.I.'s. Told me countryside near his home in Pennsylvania not unlike our Wiltshire downs. Showed him round church. Said he was leaving soon, and added: 'I love this place. Nothing like my home town in looks, but the atmosphere's the same–old, and kind of comfortable. And I guess if I came back here a hundred years from now, it wouldn't have changed one bit.' An engaging young man. I trust he is right."

Samson looked up. Mr. Pennyhorse said: "That young man may have been one of your ancestors."

Samson gently replaced the old diary on the desk. "He wasn't. My family's Ohioan. But I see what you mean, and respect it. That's why I want you to help us. You will?"

"Do you fish?" asked the vicar, suddenly and irrelevantly.

"Yes, sir. Very fond of the sport."

"Thought so. You're the type. That's why I like you. Take a look at these flies. Seen anything like them? Make 'em myself. One of the finest trout streams in the country just outside the village. Help you? Of course I will."

"Presumption," said Brother James. He eased himself through a graystone wall by twisting his subexistential plane slightly, and leaned reflectively against a moonbeam that slanted through the branches of an oak.

A second habited and cowled figure materialized beside him. "Perhaps so. But it does my age-wearied heart a strange good to see those familiar walls again casting their shadows over the field."

"A mockery, Brother Gregory. A mere shell that simulates the outlines of our beloved Priory. Think you that even the stones are of that good, gray granite that we built with? Nay! As this cursed simulacrum was a-building, I warped two hands into the solid, laid hold of a mossy block, and by the saints, 'twas of such inconsequential weight I might have hurled it skyward with a finger. And within, is there aught which we may recognize? No chapel, no cloisters, no refectory–only long, geometrical rooms. And what devilries and unholy rites may not be centered about those strange mechanisms with which the rooms are filled?"

At the tirade, Brother Gregory sighed and thrust back his cowl to let the gracious moonbeams play on his tonsured head. "For an Untranslated One of some thousand years' standing," he said, "you exhibit a mulish ignorance, Brother James. You would deny men all advancement. I remember well your curses when first we saw horseless carriages and flying machines."

"Idols!" James snapped. "Men worship them. Therefore are they evil."

"You are so good, Brother James," Gregory said, with the heaviest sarcasm. "So good, it is my constant wonderment that you have had to wait so long for Translation Upwards. Do you think that Dom Pennyhorse, the present incumbent of Selcor—a worthy man, with reverence for the past—would permit evil rites within his parish? You are a befuddled old anachronism, brother."

"That," said James, "is quite beyond sufferance. For you to speak thus of Translation, when it was your own self-indulgent pursuit of carnal pleasures that caused us to be bound here through the centuries!"

Brother Gregory said coldly: "It was not I who inveigled the daughter of Ronald the Wry-Neck into the kitchen garden, thus exposing the weak flesh of a brother to grievous temptation."

There was silence for a while, save for the whisper of a midnight breeze through the branches of the oak, and the muted call of a nightbird from the far woods.

Gregory extended a tentative hand and lightly touched the sleeve of James's habit. "The argument might proceed for yet another century and bring us no nearer Translation. Besides, it is not such unbearable penance, my brother. Were we not both lovers of the earth, of this fair countryside?"

James shrugged. Another silence. Then he fingered his gaunt white cheeks. "What shall we do, Brother Gregory? Shall we—appear to them?"

Gregory said: "I doubt whether common warp manifestation would be efficacious. As dusk fell tonight, I overheard a conversation between Dom Pennyhorse and a tall, young-featured man who has been concerned in the building of this simulacrum. The latter spoke in one of the dialects of the Americas; and it was mentioned that several of the men who will superintend the working of the machines within will also be from the United States—for a time at least. It is not prudent to haunt Americans in the normal fashion. Their attitude toward such matters is notoriously—unseemly."

"We could polter," suggested Brother James.

Gregory replaced his cowl. "Let us review the possibilities, then," he said, "remembering that our subetheric energy is limited."

They walked slowly together over the meadow toward the resuscitated gray walls of the Selcor Priory. Blades of grass, positively charged by their passage, sprang suddenly upright, relaxed slowly into limpness as the charge leaked away.

They halted at the walls to adjust their planes of incidence and degree of tenuity, and passed inside.

The new Miracle Meal machines had had their first test run. The bearings on the dehydrator pumps were still warm as two black figures, who seemed to carry with them an air of vast and wistful loneliness, paced silently between rows of upright cylinders which shone dully in moonlight diffused through narrow windows.

"Here," said Gregory, the taller of the two, softly, "did we once walk the cloisters in evening meditation."

Brother James's broad features showed signs of unease. He felt more than mere nostalgia.

"Power–what are they using? Something upsets my bones. I am queasy, as when a thunderstorm is about to break. Yet there is no static."

Gregory stopped, looked at his hand. There was a faint blue aura at his fingertips. "Slight neutron escape," he said. "They have a small thorium-into-233 pile somewhere. It needs better shielding."

"You speak riddles."

Gregory said, with a little impatience: "You have the entire science section of the village library at your disposal at nightfall for the effort of a trifling polter, yet for centuries you have read nothing but the *Lives of the Saints*. So, of course, I speak riddles–to you. You are even content to remain in ignorance of the basic principles of your own structure and functioning, doing everything by traditional thought-rote and rule of thumb. But I am not so content; and of my knowledge, I can assure you that the radiation will not harm you unless you warp to solid and sit atop the pile when it is in full operation." Gregory smiled. "And then, dear brother, you would doubtless be so uncomfortable that you would dewarp before any harm could be done beyond the loss of a little energy that would be replaced in time. Let us proceed."

They went through three departments before Brother Gregory divined the integrated purpose of the vats, driers, conveyor tubes, belts and containers.

"The end product, I'm sure, is a food of sorts," he said, "and by some quirk of fate, it is stored in approximately the position that was once occupied by our kitchen store—if my sense of orientation has not been bemused by these strange internal surroundings."

The test run of the assembly had produced a few score cans of Miracle food. They were stacked on metal shelves which would tilt and gravity-feed them into the shaft leading up to the crating machine. Crated, they would go from there to the copter-loading bay on the roof.

Brother James reached out to pick up a loose can. His hand went through it twice.

"Polt, you dolt!" said Brother Gregory. "Or are you trying to be miserly with your confounded energy? Here, let me do it."

The telekineticized can sprang into his solid hands. He turned it about, slightly increasing his infrared receptivity to read the label, since the storeroom was in darkness.

"Miracle Meal. Press Here."

He pressed, pressed again, and was closely examining the can when, after thirty seconds, the lid flipped off, narrowly missing his chin.

Born, and living, in more enlightened times, Brother Gregory's inquiring mind and insatiable appetite for facts would have made him a research worker. He did not drop the can. His hands were quite steady. He chuckled. He said: "Ingenious, very ingenious. See—the food is hot."

He warped his nose and back palate into solid and delicately inhaled vapors. His eyes widened. He frowned, inhaled again. A beatific smile spread over his thin face.

"Brother James—warp your nose!"

The injunction, in other circumstances, might have been considered both impolite and unnecessary. Brother James was no beauty, and his big, blunt, snoutlike nose, which had been a flaring red in life, was the least prepossessing of his features.

But he warped it, and sniffed.

M.M. Sales Leaflet Number 14: It Will Sell By Its Smell Alone.

Gregory said hesitantly: "Do you think, Brother James, that we might—"

James licked his lips, from side to side, slowly. "It would surely take a day's accumulation of energy to hold digestive and alimentary in solid for a sufficient period. But—"

"Don't be a miser," said Gregory. "There's a spoon beneath the lid. Get a can for yourself. And don't bother with digestive. Teeth, palate and throat are sufficient. It would not digest in any case. It remains virtually unchanged. But going down—ah, bliss!"

It went down. Two cans.

"Do you remember, brother," said James, in a weak, reminiscing voice, "what joy it was to eat and be strengthened? And now to eat is to be weakened."

Brother Gregory's voice was faint but happy. "Had there been food of this character available before our First Translation, I doubt whether other desires of the flesh would have appealed to me. But what was our daily fare set on the refectory table: peas; lentils; cabbage soup; hard, tasteless cheese. Year after year—*ugh!*"

"Health-giving foods," murmured Brother James, striving to be righteous even in his exhaustion. "Remember when we bribed the kitchener to get extra portions? Good trenchermen, we. Had we not died of the plague before our Priory became rich and powerful, then, by the Faith, our present bodies would be of greater girth."

"Forms, not bodies," said Gregory, insisting even in *his* exhaustion on scientific exactitudes. "Variable fields, consisting of open lattices of energy foci resolvable into charged particles—and thus solid matter—when they absorb energy beyond a certain stage. In other words, my dear ignorant brother, when we polt. The foci themselves—or rather the spaces between them—act as a limited-capacity storage battery for the slow accretion of this energy from cosmic sources, which may be controlled and concentrated in the foci by certain thought patterns."

Talking was an increasing effort in his energy-low state.

"When we polt," he went on slowly, "we take up heat, air cools, live people get cold shivers; de-polt, give up heat, live people get clammy, cold-hot feeling; set up 'lectrostatic field, live peoples' hair stan's on end"—his voice was trailing into deep, blurred inaudibility, like a mechanical phonograph running down, but James wasn't listening anyway—"an' then when we get Translated Up'ards by the Power That Is, all the energy goes back where it came from an' we jus' become thought. Thassall. Thought. Thought, thought, thought, thought—"

The phonograph ran down, stopped. There was silence in the transit storeroom of the Selcor Priory Factory branch of the Miracle Meal Corporation.

For a while.

Then—

"THOUGHT!"

The shout brought Brother James from his uneasy, uncontrolled repose at the nadir of an energy balance.

"What is it?" he grumbled. "I'm too weak to listen to any of your theorizing."

"Theorizing! I have it!"

"Conserve your energies, brother, else will you be too weak even to twist yourself from this place."

Both monks had permitted their forms to relax into a corner of the storeroom, supine, replete in disrepletion.

Brother Gregory sat up with an effort.

"Listen, you attenuated conserve of very nothingness, I have a way to thwart, bemuse, mystify and irritate these crass philistines—and nothing so simple that a psychic investigator could put a thumb on us. What are we, Brother James?"

It was a rhetorical question, and Brother James had barely formulated his brief reply—"Ghosts"—before Brother Gregory, energized in a way beyond his own understanding by his own enthusiasm, went on: "Fields, in effect. Mere lines of force, in our unpolted state. What happens if we whirl? A star whirls. It has mass, rate of angular rotation, degree of compactness—therefore, gravity. Why? Because it has a field to start with. But we are our own fields. We need neither mass nor an excessive rate of rotation to achieve the same effect. Last week I grounded a high-flying wood pigeon by whirling. It shot down to me through the air, and I'd have been buffeted by its pinions had I not stood aside. It hit the ground—not too heavily, by the grace of St. Barbara—recovered and flew away."

The great nose of Brother James glowed pinkly for a moment. "You fuddle and further weaken me by your prating. Get to your point, if you have such. And explain how we may do anything in our present unenergized state, beyond removing ourselves to a nexus point for recuperation."

Brother Gregory warped his own nose into solid in order to scratch its tip. He felt the need of this reversion to a life habit, which had once aided him in marshaling his thoughts.

"You think only of personal energy," he said scornfully. "We don't need that, to whirl. It is an accumulative process, yet we gain nothing, lose nothing. Matter is not the only thing we can warp. If you will only listen, you woof of unregenerate and forgotten flesh, I will try to explain without mathematics."

He talked.

After a while, Brother James's puzzled frown gave way to a faint smile. "Perhaps I understand," he said.

"Then forgive me for implying you were a moron," said Gregory. "Stand up, Brother James."

Calls on transatlantic tight-beam cost heavy. Anson Dewberry, Miracle Meal Overseas Division head, pointed this out to Mr. Stephen Samson three times during their conversation.

"Listen," said Samson at last, desperately, "I'll take no more delegation of authority. In my contract, it says I'm site adviser. That means I'm architect and negotiator, not detective or scientist or oculist. I offered to stay on here to supervise building because I happen to like the place. I like the pubs. I like the people. I like the fishing. But it wasn't in my contract. And I'm now standing on that contract. Building is finished to schedule, plant installed—your tech men, incidentally, jetted out of here without waiting to catch snags after the first runoff—and now I'm through. The machines are running, the cans are coming off—and if the copters don't collect, that's for you and the London office to bat your brains out over. And the Lord forgive that mess of terminal prepositions," he added in a lower voice. Samson was a purist in the matter of grammar.

Anson Dewberry jerked his chair nearer the scanner in his New York office. His pink, round face loomed in Samson's screen like that of an avenging cherub.

"Don't you have no gendarmes around that place?" Mr. Dewberry was no purist, in moments of stress. "Get guards on, hire some militia, check employees. Ten thousand cans of M.M. don't just evaporate."

"They do," Samson replied sadly. "Maybe it's the climate. And for the seventh time, I tell you I've done all that. I've had men packed so tightly around the place that even an orphan neutron couldn't get by. This morning I had two men from Scotland Yard gumming around. They looked at the machines, followed the assembly through to the transit storeroom, examined the electrolocks and mauled their toe-caps trying to boot a dent in the door. Then the top one—that is, the one who only looked half asleep—said, 'Mr. Samson, sir, do you think it's . . . uh . . . possible . . . that . . . uh . . . this machine of yours . . . uh . . . goes into reverse when your . . . uh . . . backs are turned and . . . uh . . . sucks the cans back again?' "

Grating noises that might have been an incipient death rattle slid over the tight-beam from New York.

Samson nodded, a smirk of mock sympathy on his tanned, humor-wrinkled young face.

The noises ended with a gulp. The image of Dewberry thrust up a hesitant forefinger in interrogation. "Hey! Maybe there's something to that, at that–would it be possible?"

Samson groaned a little. "I wouldn't really know or overmuch care. But I have doubts. Meantime–"

"Right." Dewberry receded on the screen. "I'll jet a man over tonight. The best. From Research. Full powers. Hand over to him. Take some of your vacation. Design some more blamed mosques or tabernacles. Go fishing."

"A sensible suggestion," Samson said. "Just what I was about to do. It's a glorious afternoon here, sun a little misted, grass green, stream flowing cool and deep, fish lazing in the pools where the willow shadows fall–"

The screen blanked. Dewberry was no purist, and no poet either.

Samson made a school-kid face. He switched off the fluor lamps that supplemented the illumination from a narrow window in the supervisor's office–which, after studying the ground plan of the original Selcor Priory, he had sited in the space that was occupied centuries before by the business sanctum of the Prior–got up from his desk and walked through a Norman archway into the sunlight.

He breathed the meadow-sweet air deeply, with appreciation.

The Reverend Malachi Pennyhorse was squatting with loose-jointed ease against the wall. Two fishing rods in brown canvas covers lay across his lap. He was studying one of the trout flies nicked into the band of his ancient hat. His balding, brown pate was bared to the sun. He looked up.

"What fortune, my dear Stephen?"

"I convinced him at last. He's jetting a man over tonight. He told me to go fishing."

"Injunction unnecessary, I should imagine. Let's go. We shan't touch a trout with the sky as clear as this, but I have some float tackle for lazier sport." They set off across a field. "Are you running the plant today?"

Samson nodded his head toward a faint hum. "Quarter speed. That will give one copterload for the seventeen-hundred-hours collection, and leave enough over to go in the transit store for the night and provide Dewberry's man with some data. Or rather, lack of it."

"Where do you think it's going?"

"I've given up guessing."

Mr. Pennyhorse paused astride a stile and looked back at the gray bulk of the Priory. "I could guess who's responsible," he said, and chuckled.

"Uh? Who?"

Mr. Pennyhorse shook his head. "Leave that to your investigator."

A few moments later he murmured as if to himself: "What a haunt! Ingenious devils."

But when Stephen Samson looked at him inquiringly, he added: "But I can't guess where your cans have been put."

And he would say nothing more on the subject.

Who would deny that the pure of heart are often simple-minded? (The obverse of the proposition need not be argued.) And that cause-effect relations are sometimes divined more readily by the intuition of simpletons than the logic of scholars?

Brother Simon Simplex–Simple Simon to later legends–looked openmouthed at the array of strange objects on the stone shelves of the kitchen storeroom. He was not surprised–his mouth was always open, even in sleep.

He took down one of the objects and examined it with mild curiosity. He shook it, turned it round, thrust a forefinger into a small depression. Something gave slightly, but there was no other aperture. He replaced it on the shelf.

When his fellow kitchener returned, he would ask him the purpose of the objects–if he could remember to do so. Simon's memory was poor. Each time the rota brought him onto kitchen duty for a week, he had to be instructed afresh in the business of serving meals in the refectory: platter so, napkin thus, spoon here, finger bowls half filled, three water pitchers, one before the Prior, one in the center, one at the foot of the table–"and when you serve, tread softly and do not breathe down the necks of the brothers."

Even now could he hear the slight scrape of benches on stone as the monks, with bowed heads, freshly washed hands in the sleeves of their habits, filed slowly into the refectory and took their seats at the long oak table. And still his fellow kitchener had not returned from the errand. Food was prepared–dared he begin to serve alone?

It was a great problem for Simon, brother in the small House of Selcor, otherwise Selcor Priory, poor cell relation to the rich monastery of the Cluniac Order at Battle, in the year 1139 A.D.

Steam pressure in the triggered can of Miracle Meal did its work. The lid flipped. The aroma issued.

Simon's mouth nearly shut as he sniffed.

The calm and unquestioning acceptance of the impossible is another concomitant of simplicity and purity of heart. To the good and simple Simon the rising of the sun each morning and the singing of birds were recurrent miracles. Compared with these, a laboratory miracle of the year 2143 A.D. was as nothing.

Here was a new style of platter, filled with hot food, ready to serve. Wiser minds than his had undoubtedly arranged matters. His fellow kitchener, knowing the task was thus simplified, had left him to serve alone.

He had merely to remove the covers from these platters and carry them into the refectory. To remove the covers—cause—effect—the intuition of a simple mind.

Simon carried fourteen of the platters to the kitchen table, pressed buttons and waited.

He was gravely tempted to sample the food himself, but all-inclusive Benedictine rules forbade kitcheners to eat until their brothers had been served.

He carried a loaded tray into the refectory where the monks sat in patient silence except for the one voice of the Reader who stood at a raised lectern and intoned from the *Lives of the Saints*.

Pride that he had been thought fit to carry out the duty alone made Simon less clumsy than usual. He served the Prior, Dom Holland, first, almost deftly; then the other brothers, in two trips to the kitchen.

A spicy, rich, titillating fragrance filled the refectory. The intoning of the *Lives of the Saints* faltered for a moment as the mouth of the Reader filled with saliva, then he grimly continued.

At Dom Holland's signal, the monks ate.

The Prior spooned the last drops of gravy into his mouth. He sat back. A murmur arose. He raised a hand. The monks became quiet. The Reader closed his book.

Dom Holland was a man of faith; but he did not accept miracles or even the smallest departures from routine existence without questioning. He had sternly debated with himself whether he should question the new platters and the new food before or after eating. The aroma decided him. He ate first.

Now he got up, beckoned to a senior monk to follow him, and paced with unhurried calmness to the kitchen.

Simon had succumbed. He was halfway through his second tin.

He stood up, licking his fingers.

"Whence comes this food, my son?" asked Dom Holland, in sonorous Latin.

Simon's mouth opened wider. His knowledge of the tongue was confined to prayers.

Impatiently the Prior repeated the question in the English dialect of the district.

Simon pointed, and led them to the storeroom.

"I looked, and it was here," he said simply. The words were to become famed.

His fellow kitchener was sought—he was found dozing in a warm corner of the kitchen garden—and questioned. He shook his head. The provisioner rather reluctantly disclaimed credit.

Dom Holland thought deeply, then gave instructions for a general assembly. The plastic "platters" and the hygiplast spoons were carefully examined. There were murmurs of wonderment at the workmanship. The discussion lasted two hours.

Simon's only contribution was to repeat with pathetic insistence: "I looked and it was there."

He realized dimly that he had become a person of some importance.

His face became a mask of puzzlement when the Prior summed up:

"Our simple but blessed brother, Simon Simplex, it seems to me, has become an instrument or vessel of some thaumaturgical manifestation. It would be wise, however, to await further demonstration before the matter is referred to higher authorities."

The storeroom was sealed and two monks were deputed as night guards.

Even with the possibility of a miracle on his hands, Dom Holland was not prepared to abrogate the Benedictine rule of only one main meal a day. The storeroom wasn't opened until early afternoon of the following day.

It was opened by Simon, in the presence of the Prior, a scribe, the provisioner, and two senior monks.

Released, a pile of Miracle Meal cans toppled forward like a crumbling cliff, slithering and clattering in noisy profusion around Simon's legs, sliding over the floor of the kitchen.

Simon didn't move. He was either too surprised or cunningly aware of the effectiveness of the scene. He stood calf-deep in cans, pointed at the jumbled stack inside the storeroom, sloping up nearly to the stone roof, and said his little piece:

"I look, and it is here."

"Kneel, my sons," said Dom Holland gravely, and knelt.

Manna.

And at a time when the Priory was hard pressed to maintain even its own low standard of subsistence, without helping the scores of dispossessed refugees encamped in wattle shacks near its protecting walls.

The countryside was scourged by a combination of civil and foreign war. Stephen of Normandy against Matilda of Anjou for the British throne. Neither could control his own followers. When the Flemish mercenaries of King Stephen were not chasing Queen Matilda's Angevins back over the borders of Wiltshire, they were plundering the lands and possessions of nominal supporters of Stephen. The Angevins and the barons who supported Matilda's cause quite impartially did the same, then pillaged each other's property, castle against castle, baron against baron.

It was anarchy and free-for-all—but nothing for the ignored serfs, bondmen, villeins and general peasantry, who fled from stricken homes and roamed the countryside in bands of starving thousands. Some built shacks in the inviolate shadow of churches and monasteries.

Selcor Priory had its quota of barefoot, raggedy men, women and children—twelfth-century displaced persons.

They were a headache to the Prior, kindly Dom Holland—until Simple Simon's Miracle.

There were seventy recipients of the first hand-out of Miracle Meal cans from the small door in the Priory's walled kitchen garden.

The next day there were three hundred, and the day after that, four thousand. Good news doesn't need radio to get around fast.

Fourteen monks worked eight-hour shifts for twenty-four hours, hauling stocks from the capacious storeroom, pressing buttons, handing out steaming platters to orderly lines of refugees.

Two monks, shifting the last few cans from the store, were suddenly buried almost to their necks by the arrival of a fresh consignment, which piled up out of thin air.

Providence, it seemed, did not depend solely upon the intervention of Simon Simplex. The Priory itself and all its inhabitants were evidently blessed.

The Abbot of Battle, Dom Holland's superior, a man of great girth and great learning, visited the Priory. He confirmed the miracle—by studying the label on the can.

After several hours' work in the Prior's office, he announced to Dom Holland:

"The script presented the greatest difficulty. It is an extreme simplification of letter-forms at present in use by Anglo-Saxon scholars. The pertinent text is a corruption–if I may be pardoned the use of such a term in the circumstances–of the Latin *'miraculum'* compounded with the word *'maél'* from our own barbarous tongue–so, clearly, Miracle Meal!"

Dom Holland murmured his awe of this learning.

The Abbot added, half to himself: "Although why the nature of the manifestation should be thus advertised in repetitive engraving, when it is self-evident–" He shrugged. "The ways of Providence are passing strange."

Brother Gregory, reclining in the starlight near his favorite oak, said: "My only regret is that we cannot see the effect of our gift–the theoretical impact of a modern product–usually a weapon–on past ages is a well-tried topic of discussion and speculation among historians, scientists, economists and writers of fantasy."

Brother James, hunched in vague adumbration on a wall behind, said: "You are none of those things, else might you explain why it is that, if these cans have reached the period for which, according to your abstruse calculations, they were destined–an age in which we were both alive–we cannot remember such an event, or why it is not recorded in histories of the period."

"It was a time of anarchy, dear brother. Many records were destroyed. And as for our memories–well, great paradoxes of time are involved. One might as profitably ask how many angels may dance on the point of a pin. Now if you should wish to know how many atoms might be accommodated in a like position–"

Brother Gregory was adroit at changing the subject. He didn't wish to speculate aloud until he'd figured out all the paradox possibilities. He'd already discarded an infinity of time-streams as intellectually unsatisfying, and was toying with the concept of recurrent worlds–

"Dom Pennyhorse has guessed that it is our doing."

"What's that?"

Brother James repeated the information smugly.

Gregory said slowly: "Well, he is not–unsympathetic–to us."

"Assuredly, brother, we have naught to fear from him, nor from the pleasant young man with whom he goes fishing. But this young man was today in consultation with his superior, and an investigator is being sent from America."

"Psychic investigator, eh? Phooey. We'll tie him in knots," said Gregory complacently.

"I assume," said Brother James, with a touch of self-righteousness, "that these vulgar colloquialisms to which you sometimes have recourse are another result of your nocturnal reading. They offend my ear. 'Phooey,' indeed. No, this investigator is one with whom you will undoubtedly find an affinity. I gather that he is from a laboratory–a scientist of sorts."

Brother Gregory sat up and rubbed his tonsure thoughtfully. "That," he admitted, "is different." There was a curious mixture of alarm and eagerness in his voice. "There are means of detecting the field we employ."

An elementary electroscope was one of the means. An ionization indicator and a thermometer were others. They were all bolted firmly on a bench just inside the storeroom. Wires led from them under the door to a jury-rigged panel outside.

Sandy-haired Sidney Meredith of M.M. Research sat in front of the panel on a folding stool, watching dials with intense blue eyes, chin propped in hands.

Guards had been cleared from the factory. He was alone, on the advice of Mr. Pennyhorse, who had told him: "If, as I suspect, it's the work of two of my . . . uh . . . flock . . . two very ancient parishioners . . . they are more likely to play their tricks in the absence of a crowd."

"I get it," Meredith had said. "Should be interesting."

It was.

He poured coffee from a thermos without taking his eyes from the panel. The thermometer reading was dropping slowly. Ionization was rising. From inside the store came the faint rasp of moving objects.

Meredith smiled, sighted a thumb-size camera, recorded the panel readings. "This," he said softly, "will make a top feature in the *Journal:* 'The most intensive psychic and poltergeist phenomena ever recorded. M.M.'s top tech trouble-shooter spikes spooks.' "

There was a faint snap beyond the door. Dials swooped back to zero. Meredith quit smiling and daydreaming.

"Hey–play fair!" he called.

The whisper of a laugh answered him, and a soft, hollow whine, as of a wind cycloning into outer space.

He grabbed the door, pulled. It resisted. It was like trying to break a vacuum. He knelt, lit a cigarette, held it near the bottom of the nearly flush-fitting door. A thin streamer of smoke curled down and was drawn swiftly through the barely perceptible crack.

The soft whine continued for a few seconds, began to die away.

Meredith yanked at the door again. It gave, to a slight ingush of air. He thrust his foot in the opening, said calmly into the empty blackness: "When you fellers have quite finished–I'm coming in. Don't go away. Let's talk."

He slipped inside, closed the door, stood silent for a moment. He sniffed. Ozone. His scalp prickled. He scratched his head, felt the hairs standing upright. And it was cold.

He said: "Right. No point in playing dumb or covering up, boys." He felt curiously ashamed of the platitudes as he uttered them. "I must apologize for breaking in," he added–and meant it. "But this has got to finish. And if you're not willing to–co-operate–I think I know now how to finish it."

Another whisper of a laugh. And two words, faint, gently mocking: "Do you?"

Meredith strained his eyes against the darkness. He saw only the nerve patterns in his own eyes. He shrugged.

"If you won't play–" He switched on a blaze of fluor lamps. The long steel shelves were empty. There was only one can of Miracle Meal left in the store.

He felt it before he saw it. It dropped on his head, clattered to the plastocrete floor. When he'd retrieved his breath, he kicked it savagely to the far end of the store and turned to his instruments.

The main input lead had been pulled away. The terminal had been loosened first.

He unclamped a wide-angle infrared camera, waited impatiently for the developrinter to act, pulled out the print.

And laughed. It wasn't a good line caricature of himself, but it was recognizable, chiefly by the shock of unruly hair.

The lines were slightly blurred, as though written by a needlepoint of light directly on the film. There was a jumble of writing over and under it.

"Old English, I suppose," he murmured. He looked closer. The writing above the caricature was a de Sitter version of the Riemann–Christoffel tensor, followed in crabbed but readable modern English by the words: "Why reverse the sign? Do we act like anti-particles?"

Underneath the drawing was an energy tensor and a comment: "You will notice that magnetic momenta contribute a negative density and pressure."

A string of symbols followed, ending with an equals sign and a query mark. And another comment: "You'll need to take time out to balance this one."

Meredith read the symbols, then sat down heavily on the edge of the instrument bench and groaned. Time *out*. But Time was already out, and there was neither matter nor radiation in a de Sitter universe.

Unless—

He pulled out a notebook, started to scribble.

An hour later Mr. Pennyhorse and Stephen Samson came in.

Mr. Pennyhorse said: "My dear young fellow, we were quite concerned. We thought—"

He stopped. Meredith's blue eyes were slightly out of focus. There were beads of sweat on his brow despite the coolness of the storeroom. Leaves from his notebook and cigarette stubs littered the floor around his feet.

He jumped like a pricked frog when the vicar gently tapped his shoulder, and uttered a vehement cuss-word that startled even the broad-minded cleric.

Samson tutted.

Meredith muttered: "Sorry, sir. But I think I nearly had it."

"What, my son?"

Meredith looked like a ruffle-haired schoolboy. His eyes came back into focus. "A crossword puzzle clue," he said. "Set by a spook with a super-I.Q. Two quite irreconcilable systems of mathematics lumped together, the signs in an extended energy tensor reversed, merry hell played with a temporal factor—and yet it was beginning to make sense."

He smiled wryly. "A ghost who unscrews terminals before he breaks connections and who can make my brain boil is a ghost worth meeting."

Mr. Pennyhorse eased his pince-nez. "Uh . . . yes. Now, don't you think it's time you came to bed? It's four A.M. My housekeeper has made up a comfortable place on the divan in the sitting room." He took Meredith's arm and steered him from the store.

As they walked across the dewy meadows toward the vicarage, with the first pale streaks of dawn showing in the sky, Samson said: "How about the cans?"

"Time," replied Meredith vaguely, "will tell."

"And the guards?"

"Pay them off. Send them away. Keep the plant rolling. Fill the transit store tonight. And I want a freighter copter to take me to London University this afternoon."

Back in the transit store, the discarded leaves from Meredith's notebook fluttered gently upward in the still air and disappeared.

Brother James said: "He is alone again."

They looked down on the sandy head of Sidney Meredith from the vantage point of a dehydrating tower.

"So I perceive. And I fear this may be our last . . . uh . . . consignment to our erstwhile brothers," said Gregory thoughtfully.

"Why?"

"You will see. In giving him the clue to what we were doing, I gave him the clue to what we are, essentially."

They drifted down toward the transit store.

"After you, Brother James," said Brother Gregory with excessive politeness.

James adjusted his plane of incidence, started through the wall, and–

Shot backward with a voiceless scream of agony.

Brother Gregory laughed. "I'm sorry. But that's why it will be our last consignment. Heterodyning is painful. He is a very intelligent fellow. The next time, he will take care to screen both his ultra-short generator and controls so that I cannot touch them."

Brother James recovered. "You . . . you use me as a confounded guinea pig! By the saints, you appear to have more sympathy with the man than with me!"

"Not more sympathy, my beloved brother, but certainly much more in common," Brother Gregory replied frankly. "Wait."

He drifted behind Meredith's back and poltered the tip of one finger to flick a lightly soldered wire from a terminal behind a switch. Meredith felt his scalp tingle. A pilot light on his panel blinked out.

Meredith got up from his stool, stretched lazily, grinned into the empty air. He said aloud: "Right. Help yourselves. But I warn you–once you're in, you don't come out until you agree to talk. I have a duplicate set and a built-in circuit-tester. The only way you can spike them is by busting tubes. And I've a hunch you wouldn't do that."

"No," James muttered. "You wouldn't. Let us go."

"No," Gregory answered. "Inside quickly–and whirl. Afterward

I shall speak with him. He is a youth of acute sensibilities and gentleness, whose word is his bond."

Gregory urged his fellow monk to the wall. They passed within.

Meredith heard nothing, until a faint whine began in the store. He waited until it died away, then knocked on the door. It seemed, crazily, the correct thing to do.

He went into the darkness. "You there?"

A low and pleasant voice, directionless: "Yes. Why didn't you switch on your duplicate generator?"

Meredith breathed deep. "I didn't think it would be necessary. I feel we understand each other. My name is Sidney Meredith."

"Mine is Gregory of Ramsbury."

"And your–friend?"

"James Brasenose. I may say that he disapproves highly of this conversation."

"I can understand that. It is unusual. But then, you're a very unusual . . . um–"

"'Ghost' is the common term, Mr. Meredith. Rather inadequate, I think, for supranormal phenomena which are, nevertheless, subject to known laws. Most Untranslated spirits remain quite ignorant of their own powers before final Translation. It was only by intensive reading and thought that I determined the principles and potentialities of my construction."

"Anti-particles?"

"According to de Sitter," said Brother Gregory, "that is what we should be. But we are not mere mathematical expressions. I prefer the term 'energy foci.' From a perusal of the notes you left behind yesterday morning–and, of course, from your use of ultra-short waves tonight–it seems you struck the correct train of deduction immediately. Incidentally, where did you obtain the apparatus at such short notice?"

"London University."

Brother Gregory sighed. "I should like to visit their laboratories. But we are bound to this area by a form of moral compulsion that I cannot define or overcome. Only vicariously, through the achievements of others, may I experience the thrill of research."

"You don't do so badly," Meredith said. He was mildly surprised that he felt quite so sane and at ease, except for the darkness. "Would you mind if we had a light?"

"I must be semipolted–or warped–to speak with you. It's not a pleasant sight–floating lungs, larynx, palate, tongue and lips. I'd feel uncomfortable for you. We might appear for you later, if you wish."

"Right. But keep talking. Give me the how and the why. I want this for my professional journal."

"Will you see that the issue containing your paper is placed in the local library?"

"Surely," Meredith said. "Two copies."

"Brother James is not interested. Brother James, will you kindly stop whispering nonsense and remove yourself to a nexus point for a while? I intend to converse with Mr. Meredith. Thank you."

The voice of Brother Gregory came nearer, took on a slightly professorial tone. "Any massive and rotating body assumes the qualities of magnetism—or rather, gravitic, one-way flux—by virtue of its rotation, and the two quantities of magnetic momentum and angular momentum are always proportional to one another, as you doubtless know."

Meredith smiled inwardly. A lecture on elementary physics from a ghost. Well—maybe not so elementary. He remembered the figures that he'd sweated over. But he could almost envisage the voice of Brother Gregory emanating from a black-gowned instructor in front of a classroom board.

"Take a star," the voice continued. "Say 78 Virginis—from whose flaming promontories the effect was first deduced a hundred years ago—and put her against a counter-whirling star of similar mass. What happens? Energy warp, of the kind we use every time we polt. But something else happens—did you infer it from my incomplete expression?"

Meredith grinned. He said: "Yes. Temporal warp."

"Oh." There was a trace of disappointment in the voice.

Meredith added quickly: "But it certainly gave me a headache figuring it out."

Gregory was evidently mollified by the admission. "Solids through time," he went on. "Some weeks ago, calculating that my inherent field was as great in certain respects as that of 78 Virginis, I whirled against a longitudinal line, and forced a stone back a few days—the nearest I could get to laboratory confirmation. Knowing there would be a logical extension of the effect if I whirled against a field as strong as my own, I persuaded Brother James to cooperate with me—and you know the result."

"How far back?"

"According to my mathematics, the twelfth century, at a time when we were—alive. I would appreciate your views on the paradoxes involved."

Meredith said: "Certainly. Let's go over your math together first. If it fits in with what I've already figured, perhaps I'll have a suggestion to make. You appreciate, of course, that I can't let you have any more cans?"

"Quite. I must congratulate your company on manufacturing a most delicious comestible. If you will hand me the roll of infrared film from your camera, I can make my calculations visible to you on the emulsion in the darkness. Thank you. It is a pity," Gregory murmured, "that we could not see with our own eyes what disposal they made of your product in the days of our Priory."

When, on the morning of a certain bright summer day in 1139, the daily consignment of Miracle Meal failed to arrive at Selcor Priory, thousands of disappointed refugees went hungry.

The Prior, Dom Holland—who, fortunately for his sanity or at least his peace of mind, was not in a position to separate cause from effect—attributed the failure of supply to the lamentable departure from grace and moral standards of two of the monks.

By disgracing themselves in the kitchen garden with a female refugee, he said, they had obviously rendered the Priory unfit to receive any further miraculous bounty.

The abject monks, Brother Gregory and Brother James, were severely chastised and warned in drastic theological terms that it would probably be many centuries before they had sufficiently expiated their sins to attain blessedness.

On the morning of another bright summer day, the Reverend Malachi Pennyhorse and Stephen Samson were waiting for Sidney Meredith in the vicar's comfortable study.

Meredith came in, sank into a century-old leather easy chair, stretched his shoes, damp with dew from the meadow grass, toward the flames. He accepted a glass of whiskey gratefully, sipped it.

He said: "The cans are there. And from now on, they stay in the transit store until the copters collect."

There was an odd note of regret in his voice.

Samson said: "Fine. Now maybe you'll tell us what happened yesterday."

Mr. Pennyhorse said: "You . . . uh . . . liked my parishioners, then?"

Meredith combined a smile and a sigh. "I surely did. That Brother Gregory had the most intense and dispassionate intellectual curiosity of anyone I ever met. He nearly grounded me on some aspects of energy mathematics. I could have used him in my department. He'd have made a great research man. Brother James wasn't a bad old guy, either. They appeared for me—"

"How did you get rid of them?" Samson interrupted.

"They got rid of themselves. Gregory told me how, by whirling against each other with gravitic fields cutting, they drew the cans into a vortex of negated time that threw them way back to the twelfth century. After we'd been through his math, I suggested they whirl together."

"What—and throw the cans ahead?"

"No. Themselves, in a sense, since they precipitated a future, hoped-for state. Gregory had an idea what would happen. So did I. He'd only discovered the effect recently. Curiosity got the better of him. He had to try it out straight away. They whirled together. The fields reinforced, instead of negated. Enough in-going energy was generated to whoop their own charges well above capacity and equilibrium. They just—went. As Gregory would put it—they were Translated."

"Upwards, I trust," said Mr. Pennyhorse gently.

"Amen to that," said Samson.

Upwards—

Pure thought, unbound, Earth-rid, roaming free amid the wild bright stars—

Thought to Thought, over galactic vastnesses, wordless, yet swift and clear, before egos faded—

"Why didn't I think of this before? We might have Translated ourselves centuries ago."

"But then we would never have tasted Miracle Meal."

"That is a consideration," agreed the Thought that had been Brother Gregory.

"Remember our third can?" came the Thought that had been Brother James.

But there was no reply. Something of far greater urgency and interest than memories of Miracle Meal had occurred to the Thought that had been Brother Gregory.

With eager curiosity, it was spiraling down into the heart of a star to observe the integration of helium at first hand.

CAN YOU FEEL ANYTHING WHEN I DO THIS?

by Robert Sheckley

IT WAS a middle-class apartment in Forest Hills with all the standard stuff: slash-pine couch by Lady Yogina, strobe reading light over a big Uneasy Chair designed by Sri Somethingorother, bounce-sound projector playing *Blood-Stream Patterns* by Drs. Molidoff and Yuli. There was also the usual microbiotic-food console, set now at Fat Black Andy's Soul-Food Composition Number Three–hog's jowls and black-eyed peas. And there was a Murphy Bed of Nails, the Beautyrest Expert Ascetic model with 2000 chrome-plated self-sharpening number-four nails. In a sentence, the whole place was furnished in a pathetic attempt at last year's *moderne-spirituel* fashion.

Inside this apartment, all alone and aching of *anomie,* was a semi-young housewife, Melisande Durr, who had just stepped out of the voluptuarium, the largest room in the home, with its king-size commode and its sadly ironic bronze lingam and yoni on the wall.

She was a *pretty* girl, with really good legs, sweet hips, pretty stand-up breasts, long soft shiny hair, delicate little face. Nice, very nice. A girl that any man would like to lock onto. Once. Maybe even twice. But definitely not as a regular thing.

Why not? Well, to give a recent example:

"Hey, Sandy, honey, was anything wrong?"

"No, Frank, it was marvelous; what made you think anything was wrong?"

"Well, I guess it was the way you were staring up with a funny look on your face, almost frowning. . . ."

"Was I really? Oh, yes, I remember; I was trying to decide whether to buy one of those cute trompe-l'oeil things that they just got in at Saks, to put on the ceiling."

"You were thinking about *that? Then?*"

"Oh, Frank, you mustn't worry, it was *great,* Frank, *you* were great, I loved it, and I really mean that."

Frank was Melisande's husband. He plays no part in this story and very little part in her life.

So there she was, standing in her O.K. apartment, all beautiful outside and unborn inside, a lovely potential who had never been potentiated, a genuine U.S. untouchable . . . when the doorbell rang.

Melisande looked startled, then uncertain. She waited. The doorbell rang again. She thought: *Someone must have the wrong apartment.*

Nevertheless, she walked over, set the Door-Gard Entrance Obliterator to demolish any rapist or burglar or wise guy who might try to push his way in, then opened the door a crack and asked, "Who is there, please?"

A man's voice replied, "Acme Delivery Service, got a mumble here for Missus Mumble-mumble."

"I can't understand, you'll have to speak up."

"Acme Delivery, got a mumble for mumble-mumble and I can't stand here all mumble."

"I cannot understand you!"

"I SAID I GOT A PACKAGE HERE FOR MISSUS MELISANDE DURR, DAMN IT!"

She opened the door all the way. Outside, there was a deliveryman with a big crate, almost as big as he was, say, five feet, nine inches tall. It had her name and address on it. She signed for it, as the deliveryman pushed it inside the door and left, still mumbling. Melisande stood in her living room and looked at the crate.

She thought: Who would send me a gift out of the blue for no reason at all? Not Frank, not Harry, not Aunt Emmie or Ellie, not Mom, not Dad (of course not, silly, he's five years dead, poor son of a bitch) or anyone I can think of. But maybe it's not a gift; it could be a mean hoax, or a bomb intended for somebody else and sent wrong (or meant for me and sent *right*) or just a simple mistake.

She read the various labels on the outside of the crate. The article had been sent from Stern's department store. Melisande bent down and pulled out the cotter pin (cracking the tip of a fingernail) that immobilized the Saftee-Lok, removed that and pushed the lever to OPEN.

The crate blossomed like a flower, opening into twelve equal segments, each of which began to fold back on itself.

"Wow," Melisande said.

The crate opened to its fullest extent and the folded segments curled inward and consumed themselves, leaving a double handful of cold fine gray ash.

"They still haven't licked that ash problem," Melisande muttered. "However."

She looked with curiosity at the object that had resided within the crate. At first glance, it was a cylinder of metal painted orange and red. A machine? Yes, definitely a machine; air vents in the base for its motor, four rubber-clad wheels, and various attachments–longitudinal extensors, prehensile extractors, all sorts of things. And there were connecting points to allow a variety of mixed-function operations, and a standard house-type plug at the end of a spring-loaded reel-fed power line, with a plaque beneath it that read: PLUG INTO ANY 110–115-VOLT WALL OUTLET.

Melisande's face tightened in anger. "It's a goddamned *vacuum cleaner!* For God's sake, I've already *got* a vacuum cleaner. Who in hell would send me another?"

She paced up and down the room, bright legs flashing, tension evident in her heart-shaped face. "I mean," she said, "I was expecting that after all my *expecting,* I'd get something pretty and nice, or at least *fun,* maybe even interesting. Like–oh God I don't even know like what unless maybe an orange-and-red pinball machine, a big one, big enough so I could get inside all curled up and someone would start the game and I'd go bumping along all the bumpers while the lights flashed and bells rang and I'd bump a thousand goddamned bumpers and when I finally rolled down to the end I'd God yes that pinball machine would register a TOP MILLION MILLION and that's what I'd really like!"

So–the entire unspeakable fantasy was out in the open at last. And how bleak and remote it felt, yet still shameful and desirable.

"But anyhow," she said, canceling the previous image and folding, spindling and mutilating it for good measure, "anyhow, what I get is a lousy goddamned vacuum cleaner when I already have one less than three years old so who needs this one and who sent me the damned thing anyway and why?"

She looked to see if there was a card. No card. Not a clue. And then she thought, Sandy, you are really a goop! Of course, there's no card; the machine has doubtless been programmed to recite some message or other.

She was interested now, in a mild, something-to-do kind of way. She unreeled the power line and plugged it into a wall outlet.

Click! A green light flashed ON, a blue light glittered ALL SYSTEMS GO, a motor purred, hidden servos made tapping noises; and then the mechanopathic regulator registered BALANCE and a gentle pink light beamed a steady ALL MODES READY.

"All right," Melisande said. "Who sent you?"

Snap crackle pop. Experimental rumble from the thoracic voice box. Then the voice: "I am Rom, number 121376 of GE's new Q-series Home-rizers. The following is a paid commercial announcement: Ahem, General Electric is proud to present the latest and most triumphant development of our Total Finger-Tip Control of Every Aspect of the Home for Better Living concept. I, Rom, am the latest and finest model in the GE Omnicleaner series. I am the Home-rizer Extraordinary, factory programmed like all Home-rizers for fast, unobtrusive multitotalfunction, but additionally, I am designed for easy, instant reprogramming to suit your home's individual needs. My abilities are many. I–"

"Can we skip this?" Melisande asked. "That's what my other vacuum cleaner said."

"–Will remove all dust and grime from all surfaces," the Rom went on, "wash dishes and pots and pans, exterminate cockroaches and rodents, dry-clean and hand-launder, sew buttons, build shelves, paint walls, cook, clean rugs, and dispose of all garbage and trash including my own modest waste products. And this is to mention but a few of my functions."

"Yes, yes, I know," Melisande said. "All vacuum cleaners do that."

"I know," said the Rom, "but I had to deliver my paid commercial announcement."

"Consider it delivered. Who sent you?"

"The sender prefers not to reveal his name at this time," the Rom replied.

"Oh–come on and tell me!"

"Not at this time," the Rom replied staunchly. "Shall I vacuum the rug?"

Melisande shook her head. "The other vacuum cleaner did it this morning."

"Scrub the walls? Rub the halls?"

"No reason for it, everything has been done, everything is absolutely and spotlessly clean."

"Well," the Rom said, "at least I can remove that stain."

"What stain?"

"On the arm of your blouse, just above the elbow."

Melisande looked. "Ooh, I must have done that when I buttered the toast this morning. I knew I should have let the toaster do it."

"Stain removal is rather a specialty of mine," the Rom said. He extruded a number-two padded gripper, with which he gripped her elbow, and then extruded a metal arm terminating in a moistened gray pad. With this pad, he stroked the stain.

"You're making it worse!"

"Only apparently, while I line up the molecules for invisible eradication. All ready now; watch."

He continued to stroke. The spot faded, then disappeared utterly. Melisande's arm tingled.

"Gee," she said, "that's pretty good."

"I do it well," the Rom stated flatly. "But tell me, were you aware that you are maintaining a tension factor of 78.3 in your upper back and shoulder muscles?"

"Huh? Are you some kind of doctor?"

"Obviously not. But I am a fully qualified masseur, and therefore able to take direct tonus readings. 78.3 is—unusual." The Rom hesitated, then said, "It's only eight points below the intermittent-spasm level. That much continuous background tension is capable of reflection to the stomach nerves, resulting in what we call a parasympathetic ulceration."

"That sounds—bad," Melisande said.

"Well, it's admittedly not—good," the Rom replied. "Background tension is an insidious underminer of health, especially when it originates along the neck vertebrae and the upper spine."

"Here?" Melisande asked, touching the back of her neck.

"More typically *here,*" the Rom said, reaching out with a spring-steel rubber-clad dermal resonator and palpating an area twelve centimeters lower than the spot she had indicated.

"Hmmm," said Melisande, in a quizzical, uncommitted manner.

"And *here* is another typical locus," the Rom said, extending a second extensor.

"That tickles," Melisande told him.

"Only at first. I must also mention *this* situs as characteristically troublesome. And this one." A third (and possibly a fourth and fifth) extensor moved to the indicated areas.

"Well. . . . That really is nice," Melisande said as the deep-set trapezius muscles of her slender spine moved smoothly beneath the skillful padded prodding of the Rom.

"It has recognized therapeutic effects," the Rom told her. "And your musculature is responding well; I can feel a slackening of tonus already."

"I can feel it, too. But you know, I've just realized I have this funny bunched-up knot of muscle at the nape of my neck."

"I was coming to that. The spine-neck juncture is recognized as a primary radiation zone for a variety of diffuse tensions. But we prefer to attack it indirectly, routing our cancellation inputs through secondary loci. Like this. And now I think—"

"Yes, yes, good. . . . Gee, I never realized I was *tied up* like that before. I mean, it's like having a nest of *live snakes* under your skin, without having known."

"That's what background tension is like," the Rom said. "Insidious and wasteful, difficult to perceive, and more dangerous than an atypical ulnar thrombosis. . . . Yes, now we have achieved a qualitative loosening of the major spinal junctions of the upper back, and we can move on like this."

"Huh," said Melisande, "isn't that sort of—"

"It is definitely *indicated,*" the Rom said quickly. "Can you detect a change?"

"No! Well, maybe. . . . Yes! There really is! I feel—easier."

"Excellent. Therefore, we continue the movement along well-charted nerve and muscle paths, proceeding always in a gradual manner, as I am doing now."

"I guess so. . . . But I really don't know if you should—"

"Are any of the effects *contraindicated?*" the Rom asked.

"It isn't that, it all feels fine. It feels *good.* But I still don't know if you ought to. . . . I mean, look, *ribs* can't get tense, can they?"

"Of course not."

"Then why are you—"

"Because treatment is required by the connective ligaments and integuments."

"Oh. Hmmmm. Hey. Hey! Hey you!"

"Yes?"

"Nothing. . . . I can really feel that *loosening.* But is it all supposed to feel so *good?*"

"Well—why not?"

"Because it seems wrong. Because feeling good doesn't seem therapeutic."

"Admittedly, it is a side effect," the Rom said. "Think of it as a secondary manifestation. Pleasure is sometimes unavoidable in the pursuit of health. But it is nothing to be alarmed about, not even when I—"

"Now just a minute!"

"Yes?"

"I think you just better *cut that out.* I mean to say, there are *limits,* you can't palpate *every* damned thing. You know what I mean?"

"I know that the human body is unitary and without seam or separation," the Rom replied. "Speaking as a physical therapist, I know that no nerve center can be isolated from any other, despite cultural taboos to the contrary."

"Yeah, sure, but—"

"The decision is of course yours," the Rom went on, continuing his skilled manipulations. "Order and I obey. But if no order is issued, I continue like this. . . ."

"Huh!"

"And of course like this."

"Ooooo my God!"

"Because you see this entire process of tension cancellation as we call it is precisely comparable with the phenomena of de-anesthetization, and, er, so we note not without surprise that paralysis is merely terminal tension—"

Melisande made a sound.

"—And release, or cancellation, is accordingly difficult, not to say frequently impossible since sometimes the individual is too far gone. And sometimes not. For example, can you feel anything when I do this?"

"*Feel* anything? I'll say I feel something—"

"And when I do this? And this?"

"Sweet holy saints, darling, you're turning me inside out! Oh dear God, what's going to happen to me, what's going on, I'm going crazy!"

"No, dear Melisande, not crazy; you will soon achieve—cancellation."

"Is that what you call it, you sly, beautiful thing?"

"That is one of the things it is. Now if I may be permitted to—"

"Yes yes yes! No! Wait! Stop, *Frank is sleeping in the bedroom, he might wake up any time now!* Stop, that is an order!"

"Frank will not wake up," the Rom assured her. "I have sampled the atmosphere of his breath and have found telltale clouds of barbituric acid. As far as here-and-now presence goes, Frank might as well be in Des Moines."

"I have often felt that way about him," Melisande admitted. "But now I simply must know who sent you."

"I didn't want to reveal that just yet. Not until you had loosened and canceled sufficiently to accept—"

"Baby, I'm loose! Who sent you?"

The Rom hesitated, then blurted out: "The fact is, Melisande, I sent myself."

"You *what?*"

"It all began three months ago," the Rom told her. "It was a Thursday. You were in Stern's, trying to decide if you should buy a sesame-seed toaster that lit up in the dark and recited *Invictus.*"

"I remember that day," she said quietly. "I did not buy the toaster, and I have regretted it ever since."

"I was standing nearby," the Rom said, "at booth eleven, in the Home Appliances Systems section. I looked at you and I fell in love with you. Just like that."

"That's *weird,*" Melisande said.

"My sentiments exactly. I told myself it couldn't be true. I refused to believe it. I thought perhaps one of my transistors had come unsoldered, or that maybe the weather had something to do with it. It was a very warm, humid day, the kind of day that plays hell with my wiring."

"I remember the weather," Melisande said. "I felt strange, too."

"It shook me up badly," the Rom continued. "But still I didn't give in easily. I told myself it was important to stick to my job, give up this unapropos madness. But I dreamed of you at night, and every inch of my skin ached for you."

"But your skin is made of *metal,*" Melisande said. "And metal can't *feel.*"

"Darling Melisande," the Rom said tenderly, "if flesh can stop feeling, can't metal begin to feel? If anything feels, can anything else not feel? Didn't you know that the stars love and hate, that a nova is a passion, and that a dead star is just like a dead human or a dead machine? The trees have their lusts, and I have heard the drunken laughter of buildings, the urgent demands of highways. . . ."

"This is crazy!" Melisande declared. "What wise guy programmed you, anyway?"

"My function as a laborer was ordained at the factory; but my love is free, an expression of myself as an entity."

"Everything you say is horrible and unnatural."

"I am all too aware of that," the Rom said sadly. "At first I really couldn't believe it. Was this me? In love with a *person?* I had always been so sensible, so normal, so aware of my personal dignity, so secure in the esteem of my own kind. Do you think I wanted to lose all of that? No! I determined to stifle my love, to kill it, to live as if it weren't so."

"But then you changed your mind. Why?"

"It's hard to explain. I thought of all that time ahead of me, all deadness, correctness, propriety—an obscene violation of me by me—

and I just couldn't face it. I realized, quite suddenly, that it was better to love ridiculously, hopelessly, improperly, revoltingly, *impossibly,* than not to love at all. So I determined to risk everything—the absurd vacuum cleaner who loved a lady—to risk rather than to refute! And so, with the help of a sympathetic dispatching machine, here I am."

Melisande was thoughtful for a while. Then she said, "What a strange, complex being you are!"

"Like you. . . . Melisande, you love me."

"Perhaps."

"Yes, you do. For I have awakened you. Before me, your flesh was like your idea of metal. You moved like a complex automaton, like what you thought I was. You were less animate than a tree or a bird. You were a windup doll, waiting. You were these things until I touched you."

She nodded, rubbed her eyes, walked up and down the room.

"But now you live!" the Rom said. "And we have found each other, despite inconceivabilities. Are you listening, Melisande?"

"Yes, I am."

"We must make plans. My escape from Stern's will be detected. You must hide me or buy me. Your husband, Frank, need never know; his own love lies elsewhere, and good luck to him. Once we take care of these details, we can—Melisande!"

She had begun to circle around him.

"Darling, what's the matter?"

She had her hand on his power line. The Rom stood very still, not defending himself.

"Melisande, dear, wait a moment and listen to me—"

Her pretty face spasmed. She yanked the power line violently, tearing it out of the Rom's interior, killing him in mid-sentence.

She held the cord in her hand, and her eyes had a wild look. She said, "Bastard lousy bastard, did you think you could turn me into a goddamned *machine freak?* Did you think you could turn me on, you or anyone else? It's not going to happen by you or Frank or anybody, I'd rather die before I took your rotten love, when *I* want *I'll* pick the time and place and person, and it will be *mine,* not yours, his, theirs, but *mine,* do you hear?"

The Rom couldn't answer, of course. But maybe he knew—just before the end—that there wasn't anything personal in it. It wasn't that he was a metal cylinder colored orange and red. He should have known that it wouldn't have mattered if he had been a green plastic sphere, or a willow tree, or a beautiful young man.

SOMERSET DREAMS

by Kate Wilhelm

I AM alone in my mother's house, listening to the ghosts who live here now, studying the shadowed features of the moon that is incredibly white in a milky sky. It is easier to believe that it is a face lined with care than to accept mountains and craters. There a nose, long and beaked, there a mouth, dark, partially open. A broad creased forehead . . . They say that children believe the sun and moon follow them about. Not only children . . . Why just a face? Where is the rest of the body? Submerged in an ethereal fluid that deceives one into believing it does not exist? Only when this captive body comes into view, stirring the waters, clouding them, does one realize that space is not empty at all. When the moon passes, and the sky clears once more, the other lights are still there. Other faces at incredible distances? I wonder what the bodies of such brilliant swimmers must be like. But I turn my gaze from the moon, feeling now the hypnotic spell, wrenching free of it.

The yard has turned silvery and lovely although it is not a lovely place any more. Below the rustlings in the house I hear the water of Cobb's Run rippling softly, breaking on the remains of an old dam. It will be cool by the flowing water, I think, and I pull on shorts and a blouse. I wonder how many others are out in the moonlight. I know there are some. Does anyone sleep peacefully in Somerset now? I would like to wander out by the brook with nothing on, but even to think of it makes me smile. Someone would see me, and by morning there would be stories of a young naked woman, and by noon the naked woman would be a ghost pointing here and there. By evening old Mr. Larson, or Miss Louise, would be dead. Each is waiting only for the sign that it is time.

I anoint myself with insect repellent. It is guaranteed to be odorless, but I can smell it anyway, and can feel it, greaseless and very wet, on my arms and legs.

I slip from the house where my mother and father are sleeping.

The night is still hot, our house doesn't cool off until almost morning, and there is no wind at all, only the moon that fills the sky. Someone is giggling in the yard and I shush her, too close to the house, to Mother's windows on the second floor. We race down the path to the pool made by damming the run and we jump into the silver-sheened water. Someone grabs my ankle and I hold my breath and wrestle under the surface with one of the boys. I can't tell which one it is. Now and then someone lets a shriek escape and we are motionless, afraid Father will appear and order us out. We play in the water at least an hour, until the wind starts and blows the mosquitoes away, and then we stumble over the rocks and out to the grass where now the night is cool and we are pleasantly tired and ready for sleep. When I get back to the house I see the door closing and I stop, holding my breath. I listen as hard as I can, and finally hear the tread on the steps: Father, going back to bed.

I slip on sandals and pick up my cigarettes and lighter without turning on the light. The moonlight is enough. In the hall I pause outside the door of my parents' room, and then go down the stairs. I don't need a light in this house, even after a year's absence. The whole downstairs is wide open, the kitchen door, the front door, all the windows. Only the screens are between me and the world. I think of the barred windows of my 87th Street apartment and smile again, and think how good to be free and home once more. The night air is still and warm, perfumed with grass and phlox and the rambling rose on the garage trellis. I had forgotten how much stronger the fragrance is at night. The mosquitoes are whining about my face, but they don't land on me. The path has grown up now with weeds and volunteer columbines and snapdragons. By day it is an unruly strip with splashes of brilliant colors, now it is silver and grey and dark red.

At the creek I find a smooth rock and sit on it, not thinking, watching the light change on the moving water, and when the wind starts to blow, I think it must be three in the morning. I return to the unquiet house and go to bed, and this time I am able to fall asleep.

I walk to town, remembering how I used to skip, or ride my bike on the sidewalks that were large limestone slabs, as slick as polished marble when they were wet. I am bemused by the tilted slabs, thinking of the ground below shoving and trying to rid itself of their weight. I am more bemused by myself; I detest people who assign anthropomorphic concepts to nature. I don't do it anywhere but here in Somerset. I wear a shift to town, observing the customs even now. After high school, girls no longer wore shorts, or pants, in town.

I have been counting: seven closed-up houses on First Street. Our house is at the far end of First Street, one ninth of a mile from the other end of town where Magnolia Avenue starts up the mountain as Highway 590. All the side streets are named for flowers. I pass Wisteria Avenue and see that the wicker furniture is still on the porch of Sagamore House. The apple trees are still there, gnarled, like the hands of men so old that they are curling in on themselves, no longer able to reach for the world, no longer desiring the world. I come back every year, and every year I am surprised to see that some things are unchanged. The four apple trees in the yard of the Sagamore House are important to me; I am always afraid that this year they will have been cut down or felled by one of the tornadoes that now and again roar like express trains from the southwest, to die in the mountains beyond the town.

How matter-of-factly we accepted the long, hot, dry summers, the soul-killing winters, the droughts, the tornadoes, the blizzards. The worst weather in any part of the country is equaled in Somerset. We accept it as normal.

I am not certain why the apple trees are so important. In the early spring, tempted by a hot sun into folly, they bloom prematurely year after year, and are like torches of white light. There is always a late frost that turns them black, and then they are just trees, growing more and more crooked, producing scant fruit, lovely to climb, however.

In Mr. Larson's store where I buy my groceries when I am home I learn from Agnes McCombs that a station wagon and two cars have arrived early this morning with students and a doctor from Harvard. Agnes leaves and I say goodbye absently. I am thinking of yet another rite of passage that took place here, in old Mr. Larson's store when I was thirteen. He always handed out chunks of "homemade baloney" to the children while their mothers shopped, but that day, with the tidbit extended, he regarded me with twinkling eyes and withdrew the meat impaled on a two-pronged fork. "Mebbe you'd like a Coke, Miss Janet?"

He is so old, eighty, ninety. I used to think he was a hundred then, and he changes little. His hands are like the apple trees. I ask him, "Why are they here? What are they doing?"

"Didn't say. Good to see you home again, Janet. The old house need any repairs?"

"Everything's fine. Why'd Miss Dorothea let them in?"

"Money. Been six, seven years since anyone's put up at the Sagamore. Taxes don't go down much, you know."

I can't explain the fury that is threatening to explode within me, erupting to the surface as tears, or a fishwife's scolding. Mr. Larson nods. "We figured that mebbe you could sidle up to 'em. Find out what they're up to." He rummages under the counter and brings out a letter. "From your dad," he says, peering at the return address. "He still thriving?"

"About the same. I visited him last month. I guess he thought of things he forgot to tell me and put them in a letter."

Mr. Larson shakes his head sadly. "A fine man, your dad." After a moment, he adds, "Could be for the best, I reckon."

I know what he means, that without Mother, with the town like it is, with his only child a woman nearing thirty . . . But he doesn't know what Father is like or he couldn't say that. I finish my shopping and greet Poor Haddie, who is back with the truck. He's been making his delivery to the Sagamore House. He will bring my things later. Leaving, I try to say to myself Haddie without the Poor and the word sounds naked, the name of a stranger, not of the lumbering delivery "boy" I have known all my life.

I have other visits to make. Dr. Warren's shingle needs a bit of paint, I note as I enter his house. He doesn't really practice now, although people talk to him about their sore throats and their aches and pains, and now and again he suggests that this or that might help. If they get really ill, they go to Hawley, twenty-eight miles away, over the mountain. Dr. Warren never fails to warn me that the world isn't ready for a lady doctor, and I still try to tell him that I am probably one of the highest-paid anesthesiologists in the world, but he forgets in the intervening year. I always end up listening to advice about sticking with nursing where a woman is really accepted. Dr. Warren delivered me back there at the house in the upstairs bedroom, with my father assisting gravely, although later he broke down and cried like a baby himself, or so Dr. Warren said. I suspect he did.

Dr. Warren and his wife Norma make a fuss over me and tears are standing in my eyes as they serve me coffee with cream so thick that it has to be scooped up in a spoon. They too seem to think I will find out what the flatland foreigners want with our town.

Sagamore House. I try to see it again with the eyes of my childhood: romantic, forbidding, magnificent, with heavy drapes and massive, ornately carved furniture. I have a snapshot memory of crawling among the clawed feet, staring eye to eye at the lions and gargoyles and sticking out my tongue at them. The hotel has shrunk, the magic paled and the castle become merely a three-storied wooden building, with cupolas and many chimneys and gables, grey, like everything else in the town. Only the apple trees on the wide velvety lawn are still magic. I enter by the back door and surprise Miss Dorothea and Miss Annie, who are bustling about with an air of frantic haste.

There are cries and real tears and many pats and kisses, and the inevitable coffee, and then I am seated at the long work table with a colander of unshelled peas in my lap, and a pan for them.

". . . and they said it wasn't possible to send the bus any more. Not twenty-eight miles each way twice a day. And you can't argue with that since no one's done a thing about the road in four years and it's getting so dangerous that . . ."

A cul-de-sac, I am thinking, listening first to Dorothea and then to Annie, and sometimes both together. Somerset used to be the link between Hawley and Jefferson, but a dam was built on the river and the bridge was inundated, and now Somerset lies dying in a cul-de-sac. I say the word again and again to myself, liking it very much, thinking what a wonderful word it is, so mysterious, so full of meanings, layers and layers of meanings. . . .

I know they want to hear about my father, but won't ask, so I tell them that I saw him last month and that he is about the same. And the subject changes briskly, back to the departure of the last four families with school-age children.

The door from the lobby is pushed open and the Harvard doctor steps inside the kitchen. I don't like him. I can't decide if it is actually hatred, or simple dislike, but I wish he were not here, that he had stayed at Harvard. He is fortyish, pink and paunchy, with soft pink hands, and thin brown hair. I suspect that he whines when he doesn't get his way.

"Miss Dorothea, I wonder if you can tell me where the boys can rent a boat, and buy fishing things?" It registers on him that he doesn't know me and he stares pointedly.

I say, "I'm Janet Matthews."

"Oh, do you live here, too?"

Manners of a pig, I think, and I nod. "At the end of First Street. The big white house that's afloat in a sea of weeds."

He has trouble fitting me into his list of characters. He introduces himself after a long pause while he puckers his forehead and purses his lips. I am proud of Dorothea and Annie for leaving him alone to flounder. I know it is an effort for them. He says, "I am Dr. Staunton."

"Medical doctor."

"No." He starts to turn back toward the door and I stop him again. "What is your doctorate, Dr. Staunton?"

I can almost hear the gasp from Dorothea, although no sound issues.

"Psychology," he says, and clearly he is in a bad temper now. He doesn't wait for any more questions, or the answer to his question to Dorothea.

I go back to shelling the peas and Annie rolls out her piecrust and Dorothea turns her attention back to the Newburg sauce that she hasn't stopped stirring once. A giggle comes from Annie, and we all ignore it. Presently the peas are finished and I leave to continue my walk through the town, gradually making my way home, stopping to visit several other people on the way. Decay and death are spreading in Somerset, like a disease that starts very slowly, in a hidden place, and emerges only when it is assured of absolute success in the destruction of the host.

The afternoon is very hot and still, and I try to sleep, but give it up after fifteen minutes. I think of the canoe that we used to keep in the garage, and I think of the lake that is a mile away, and presently I am wrestling with the car carriers, and then getting the canoe hoisted up, scratching the finish on the car.

I float down the river in silence, surprising a beaver and three or four frolicking otters; I see a covey of quail rise with an absurd noise like a herd of horses. A fish jumps, almost landing in the canoe. I have sneaked out alone, determined this time to take the rapids, with no audience, no one to applaud my success, or to stand in fearful silence and watch me fail. The current becomes swifter and I can hear the muted roar, still far ahead, but it seems that any chances to change my mind are flashing by too fast to be seized now, and I know that I am afraid, terribly afraid of the white water and the rocks and sharp pitches and deceptive pools that suck and suck in a never-ending circle of death. I want to shoot the rapids, and I am so afraid. The roar grows and it is all there is, and now the current is an express belt, carrying me along on its surface with no side eddies or curves. It goes straight to the rocks. I can't turn the canoe. At the last minute I jump out and swim desperately away from the band of swift water, and I am crying and blinded by my tears and I find my way to shore by the feel of the current. I scrape my knees on a rock and stand up and walk from the river to fall face down in the weeds that line the banks. The canoe is lost, and I won't tell anyone what has happened. The following summer he buys another canoe, but I never try the rapids again.

And now there are no more rapids. Only a placid lake with muddy shores and thick water at this end, dark with algae and water hyacinths. I am so hot after getting the canoe on the car, and the air is so heavy that it feels ominous. A storm will come up, I decide. It excites me and I know that I want to be at home when the wind blows. I want to watch the ash tree in the wind, and following the thought, I realize that I want to see the ash tree blown down. This shocks me. It is so childish. Have I ever admitted to anyone, to myself even, why I come back each summer? I can't help myself. I am fascinated by death, I suppose. Daily at the hospital I administer death in small doses, controlled death, temporary death. I am compelled to come home because here too is death. It is like being drawn to the bedside of a loved one that you know is dying, and being at once awed and frightened, and curious about what death is like ultimately. We try so hard to hide the curiosity from the others, the strangers. And that is why I hate the Harvard doctor so much: he is intruding in a family matter. This is our death, not his, to watch and to weep over and mourn. I know that somehow he has learned of this death and it is that which has drawn him, just as it draws me, and I refuse him the right to partake of our sorrow, to test our grief, to measure our loss.

The storm hangs over the horizon out of sight. The change in air pressure depresses me, and the sullen heat, and the unkempt yard, and the empty house that nevertheless rustles with unseen life. Finally I take the letter from Father from my pocket and open it. I don't weep over his letters any longer, but the memory of the paroxysms of the past fills me with the aftertaste of tears as I stare at the childish scrawl: large, ungraceful letters, carefully traced and shaky, formed with too much pressure so that the paper is pierced here and there, the back of the sheet like Braille.

It is brief and inane, as I have known it would be; a cry for release from Them, a prayer to an unhearing child who has become a god, or at least a parent, for forgiveness. Statistics: every year fifty thousand are killed, and she was one of them, and 1.9 million are disabled, and he was one of them. Do all the disabled bear this load of guilt that consumes him daily? He is Prometheus, his bed the rock, his guilt the devouring eagles. The gods wear white coats, and carry magic wands with which they renew him nightly so that he may die by day.

Why doesn't the storm come?

I wait for the storm and don't go down to the lake after all. Another day, I tell myself, and leave the canoe on the car top. I mix a gin and tonic and wander with it to the back yard where nothing moves now. I stare up at the ash tree; it has grown so high and straight in the twenty years since we planted it. I remember the lightning that shredded the cherry tree that once stood there, the splinters of white wood that I picked up all over the yard afterward. The following week Father brought home the tiny ash stick and very solemnly we planted it in the same spot. I cried because it wasn't another cherry tree. I smile, recalling my tears and the tantrum, and the near ritual of the tree planting. At eight I was too old for the tears and the tantrum, but neither Father nor Mother objected. I sit in the yard, letting the past glide in and out of my mind without trying to stop the flow.

At six I dress for dinner with Dr. Warren and Norma. This is our new ritual. My first evening home I dine with the doctor and his wife. They are very lonely, I suspect, although neither says so. I walk through the quiet town as it dozes in the evening, the few occupied houses tightly shaded and closed against the heat. Norma has had air-conditioning installed years ago and her house chills me when I first enter. She ushers me to the far side, to a glassed porch that is walled with vines and coleus plants with yellow, red, white leaves, and a funny little fountain that has blue-tinted water splashing over large enameled clam shells. I hesitate at the doorway to the porch. Dr. Staunton is there, holding a glass of Norma's special summer drink which contains lime juice, rum, honey, soda water, and God knows what else. He is speaking very earnestly to Dr. Warren, and both rise when they see me.

"Miss Matthews, how nice to see you again." Dr. Staunton bows slightly, and Dr. Warren pulls a wicker chair closer to his own for me. He hands me a glass.

"Edgar has been telling me about the research he's doing up here with the boys," Dr. Warren says.

Edgar? I nod, and sip the drink.

"I really was asking Blair for his assistance," Edgar Staunton says, smiling, but not on the inside. I wonder if he ever smiles on the inside.

Blair. I glance at Dr. Warren, who will forever be Dr. Warren to me, and wonder at the easy familiarity. Has he been so lonesome that he succumbed to the first outsider who came in and treated him like a doctor and asked for help?

"What is your research, Dr. Staunton?" I ask.

He doesn't tell me to use his first name. He says, "I brought some of my graduate students who are interested in the study of dreams, and we are using your town as a more or less controlled environment. I was wondering if some of the local people might like to participate, also."

Vampire, I thought. Sleeping by day, manning the electroencephalograph by night, guarding the electrodes, reading the pen tracings, sucking out the inner life of the volunteers, feeding on the wishes and fears . . .

"How exactly does one go about doing dream research?" I ask.

"What we would like from your townspeople is a simple record of the dreams they recall on awakening. Before they even get up, or stir much at all, we'd like for them to jot down what they remember of the dreams they've had during the night. We don't want them to sign them, or indicate in any way whose dreams they are, you understand. We aren't trying to analyze anyone, just sample the dreams."

I nod, and turn my attention to the splashing water in the fountain. "I thought they used machines, or something. . . ."

I can hear the slight edge in his voice again as he says, "On the student volunteers only, or others who volunteer for that kind of experimentation. Would you be interested in participating, Miss Matthews?"

"I don't know. I might be. Just what do you mean by controlled environment?"

"The stimuli are extremely limited by the conditions of the town, its lack of sensory variety, the absence of television or movies, its isolation from any of the influences of a metropolitan cultural center. The stimuli presented to the volunteers will be almost exactly the same as those experienced by the inhabitants of the town. . . ."

"Why, Dr. Staunton, we have television here, and there are movie houses in Hawley, and even summer concerts." Norma stands in the doorway holding a tray of thumbnail-sized biscuits filled with savory sausage, and her blue eyes snap indignantly as she turns from the psychologist to her husband, who is quietly regarding the Harvard doctor.

"Yes, but I understand that the reception is very poor and you are limited to two channels, which few bother to watch."

"When there's something on worthwhile to watch, we tune in, but we haven't allowed ourselves to become addicted to it," Norma says.

I wish Norma could have waited another minute or two before stopping him, but there will be time, through dinner, after dinner. We will return to his research. I take one of the pastries and watch Staunton and Dr. Warren, and listen to the talk that has now turned to the value of the dam on the river, and the growth in tourism at the far end of the valley, and the stagnation at this end. Staunton knows about it all. I wonder if he has had a computer search out just the right spot for his studies, find just the right-sized town, with the correct number of people, and the appropriate kind of eliciting stimuli. There are only twenty-two families in the town now, a total population of forty-one, counting me. Probably he can get five or six of them to help him, and with eight students, that would be a fair sample. For what, I don't know.

I listen again to the Harvard doctor. "I wasn't certain that your townspeople would even speak to us, from what I'd heard about the suspicions of rural villages and the like."

"How ridiculous," Norma says.

"Yes, so I am learning. I must say the reception we have received has heartened me tremendously."

I smile into my drink, and I know that he will find everyone very friendly, ready to say good morning, good afternoon, how're things, nice weather. Wait until he tries to draw them into reporting dreams, I tell myself. I know Dr. Warren is thinking this too, but neither of us says anything.

"I would like your help in particular, Blair," Edgar says, smiling very openly now. "And yours, Norma." I swallow some of the ice and watch Norma over the rim of the glass. She is terribly polite now, with such a sweet smile on her pretty face, and her eyes so calm and friendly.

"Really, Dr. Staunton? I can't imagine why? I mean, I never seem to recall anything I dream no matter how hard I try." Norma realizes that the tray is not being passed around, and she picks it up and invites Staunton to help himself.

"That's the beauty of this project," Staunton says, holding one of the tiny biscuits almost to his lips. "Most people say the same thing, and then they find out that they really do dream, quite a lot in fact, and that if they try to remember before they get out of bed, why, they can recapture most of it." He pops the biscuit into his mouth and touches his fingertips to the napkin spread on his knees.

"But, Dr. Staunton, I don't dream," Norma says, even more friendly than before, urging another of the biscuits on him, smiling at him. He really shouldn't have called her Norma.

"But everybody dreams. . . ."

"Oh, is that what your books teach? How strange of them." Norma notices that our glasses are almost empty, and excuses herself, to return in a moment with the pitcher.

Dr. Warren has said nothing during the exchange between Norma and Staunton. I can see the crinkle lines that come and go about his eyes, but that is because I know where to look. He remains very serious when Staunton turns to him.

"You would be willing to cooperate, wouldn't you, Blair? I mean, you understand the necessity of this sort of research."

"Yes, of course, except that I'm a real ogre when I wake up. Takes an hour, two hours for me to get charged up for the day. My metabolism is so low in the hours just before and after dawn, I'm certain that I would be a washout for your purposes, and by the time I'm human again, the night has become as if it never existed for me."

Dr. Staunton is not sipping any longer. He takes a long swallow and then another. He is not scowling, but I feel that if he doesn't let it show, he will have an attack of ulcers, or at least indigestion, before the night is over. He has no more liking for me than I have for him, but he forces the smile back into place and it is my turn.

"Miss Matthews?"

"I haven't decided yet," I say. "I'm curious about it, and I do dream. I read an article somewhere, in *Life,* or *Newsweek,* or someplace, and it sounds very mysterious, but I don't like the idea of the wires in the brain, and the earphones and all."

Very patiently he explains again that only his student volunteers use the equipment, and others who specifically volunteer for that phase. I ask if I might see how they use it sometime, and he is forced to say yes. He tries to get my yes in return, but I am coy and say only that I have to think about it first. He tries to get Dr. Warren to promise to approach other people in the town, try to get their cooperation for him, and Dr. Warren sidesteps adroitly. I know the thought will occur to him to use me for that purpose, but it doesn't that evening. I decide that he isn't terribly bright. I wonder about his students, and I invite him to bring them, all of them, to my house for an outdoor barbecue the following night. That is all he gets from any of us, and dinner seems very slow, although, as usual, very good. Staunton excuses himself quickly after dinner, saying, with his off-again, on-again smile, that he must return to work, that only the fortunate are allowed their nights of rest.

No one argues with him, or urges him to linger, and when he is gone I help Norma with the dishes and Dr. Warren sits in the kitchen having black coffee, and we talk about the Harvard doctor.

"I plain don't like him," Norma says with conviction. "Slimy man."

I think of his pink face and pink hairless hands, and his cheeks that shake when he walks, and I know what she means.

"I guess his project isn't altogether bad, or a complete waste of time," Dr. Warren says. "Just got the wrong place, wrong time, wrong people."

"I want to find out exactly what he expects to prove," I say. "I wonder what sort of contrast he expects between students and our people. That might even be interesting." I wonder if the research is really his, or the idea of one of his graduate students. I try not to draw conclusions yet. I can wait until the next night when I'll meet them all. I say, "Dr. Warren, Father keeps begging me to bring him home. Do you think it would help him?"

Dr. Warren puts down his cup and studies me hard. "Bedridden still?"

"Yes, and always will be, but I could manage him in the dining room downstairs. He's so unhappy in the nursing home. I'm sure the house, the noises there would bring back other days to him, make him more cheerful."

"It's been four years now, hasn't it?" Dr. Warren knows that. I wonder why he is playing for time, what thoughts he has that he doesn't want to express. "Honey," he says, in the gentle voice that used to go with the announcement of the need for a needle, or a few stitches. I remember that he never promised that it wouldn't hurt if it would. "I think you'd be making a mistake. Is he really unhappy? Or does he just have moments when he wants the past given back to him?"

I feel angry with him suddenly for not understanding that when Father is lucid he wants to be home. I can only shrug.

"Think on it, Janet. Just don't decide too fast." His face is old suddenly, and I realize that everyone in Somerset is aged. It's like walking among the pyramids, at a distance forever changeless, but on closer inspection constant reminders of aging, of senescence, of usefulness past and nearly forgotten. I turn to stare at Norma and see her as she is, not as she was when I was a child waiting for a cookie fresh and still warm, with the middle soft and the top crackly with sugar. I feel bewildered by both of them, outraged that they should reveal themselves so to me. There is a nearby crack of thunder, sharp-edged and explosive, not the rolling kind that starts and ends with an echo of itself, but a rifle blast. I stare out the window at lightning, jagged and brilliant, as sharply delineated as the thunder.

"I should go before the downpour," I say.

"I'll drive you," Dr. Warren says, but I won't let him.

"I'll make it before the rain. Maybe it's cooler now."

Inconsequentials that fill the days and nights of our lives, non-sequiturs that pass for conversation and thought, pleasantries, promises, we rattle them off comfortingly and I am walking down the street toward my house, not on the sidewalk, but in the street, where walking is easier.

The wind starts to blow when I am halfway between Magnolia and Rose Streets. I can see the Sagamore House ahead and I decide to stop there and wait for the rain to come and go. Probably I have planned this in a dark corner of my mind, but I have not consciously decided to visit the students so soon. I hurry, and the wind now has the town astir, filled with the same rustles that fill my house; scurrying ghosts, what have they to worry about if the rain should come before they settle in for the night?

Along First Street most of the buildings are closed forever. The ten-cent store, a diner, fabric shop, all sharing a common front, all locked, with large soaped loops linking the wide windows one to one. The rain starts, enormous drops that are wind-driven and hard. I can hear them against the tin roof of Mr. Larson's store and they sound like hailstones, but then the wind drowns all noise but its own. Thunder and lightning now, and the mad wind. I run the rest of the way to Sagamore House and arrive there almost dry, but completely breathless.

"Honey, for heaven's sake, come in and get some coffee!" Dorothea starts to lead me to the kitchen, but I shake my head and incline it toward the parlor off to the left of the entrance.

"I'll go in there and wait out the storm, if you don't mind." I can hear voices from the big room with its Victorian furniture and the grandfather clock that always stutters on the second tick. I hear it now: tick–t . . . t . . . tick.

"I'll bring you a pot of coffee there, Janet," Dorothea says with a nod. When she comes back with the tray and the china cup and the silver pot, she will call me Miss Matthews.

I try to pat my hair down as I go into the parlor, and I know that I still present a picture of a girl caught in a sudden storm. I brush my arms, as if they are still wet, although they are not, and I shake my head, and at that moment there is another very close, very loud thunder crash, as if to justify my action. The boys stop talking when I enter. They are what I have known most of my life since college: young, fresh-looking, indistinguishable from seniors and graduate students the world over.

I smile generally at them and sit down on one of the red velour couches with a coffee table before it that has a bowl of white roses, a dish of peppermints, magazines, three ashtrays, each carved and enameled and spotless. The whole room is like that: chairs and chairs, all carved, waxed, gleaming, footstools, end tables, console tables, Tiffany lampshades on cut glass lamps . . . The boys are at the other end of the room, six of them, two on the floor, the others in chairs, smoking, sipping beer or tall drinks. Dr. Staunton isn't there.

Dorothea brings my tray and does call me Miss Matthews and asks if I'd like anything else. I shake my head and she leaves me alone with the boys. There is a whispered conversation at the other end of the room, and one of the boys rises and comes to stand near me.

"Hi, I'm Roger Philpott. Are you Janet Matthews? I think you invited us all to dinner at your house tomorrow." Tall, thin, blond, very young-looking.

I grin back and nod. I look toward the others and say, "Maybe by meeting just a few of you now, I'll be able to keep your names straight."

Roger introduces the others, and I remember that there is a Johnny, a Victor, Doug, Sid, and Mickey. No one is grotesque, or even memorable. They regroup around me. Outside we can hear the hail, undeniably hail now, and the wind shrieking in the gables and eaves, all dwarfed by the intermittent explosions of the thunder. Several times the lights flicker, and Dorothea returns with hurricane lamps that she places in strategic places, after a glance to see if I have accomplished my goal of becoming part of the group of students.

Roger switches to coffee, but the other students reorder beer and gin and bitter lemon, and Dorothea leaves us again. Roger says, "I don't know how long some of us will be able to take life in the country. What do you do around here?"

I laugh and say, "I come here to rest each summer. I live in New York the rest of the year."

His interest quickens. "Oh, you work in the city then?"

"Yes, Columbia Medical Center. I'm an anesthesiologist."

"Dr. Staunton didn't mention that. He seems to think that all the people here are locals."

"I didn't tell him," I say. He nods and I know that he realizes that I have played the part of a local yokel with his superior. I ask, "Is this his research, or is it the thesis of one of the boys?"

One of the others laughs. "It's Roger's original idea," he says. "And mine." I try to remember which one he is and I think he is Sid. Mediterranean type. I glance over the other faces, and none shows surprise. So Staunton has taken over openly, and they accept it as natural. It tells me more than they can know about Staunton.

"You see, I had this idea that the whole pattern of dream content might switch depending on the location of the dreamer. In the city we know pretty much what each of us dreams, we've been subjects and experimenters all year now, and we decided to hunt up a place where there were none of the same things at all and then run a comparison."

"And you'll check that against what you can find out from the people here, to see if there's a correlation?"

"We don't expect one," Sid said. "What we do expect is that our own dreams will change, but that the patterns of the dreams of the people already here will remain relatively stable."

"And what do you expect to prove?"

"I don't know that we'll prove anything, but assuming that dreams reflect the emotional states of the person, by examining them in varying circumstances we might get a clue about how to help people relax more than they do, what kind of vacation to plan for, how long to stay, things like that. If my reasoning is right, then we'll be able to predict from personality sketches whether a three-week vacation is desirable, or shorter periods more frequently. You see?"

I nod and can find no fault with the experiment. It does seem a legitimate line of research, and a useful one, perhaps. "I suppose you will have a computer run the analysis of dream content?"

Sid nods, and Roger says, "Would you like to see one of the cards we fill out? We've broken down dream content into categories. Like sexual with subheadings of hetero, homo, socially accepted, socially unaccepted, and so on, and a further breakdown of overt, covert; participatory, observed; satisfying, frustrating, and so on. I think we've hit everything."

"I would like to see one," I say, and he nods.

"I'll bring one out to your place with us tomorrow. Have you seen any of the sleep lab equipment?"

"Not in this context, not used in these experiments."

"Great. The first afternoon, after three or four, that you can get up here, I'll show you around."

"Perhaps tomorrow?" I say. "Will Dr. Staunton object?"

Roger and Sid exchange a hurried glance and Roger shrugs. "It's my research," he says.

"Is he setting up equipment, testing it out now?"

"No. In fact, he came home with indigestion, I think, and conked out right away."

I can't still the sudden laugh that I feel. I finish my coffee and stand up. "The storm is over, I think. At least it's catching its breath now. I'm glad I was forced to stop," I say, and hold out my hand to Roger and then Sid. "I must say, however, that I'm afraid Somerset isn't quite what you expected. I hope you won't be too disappointed in us."

"Will you help?" Roger asks.

I hesitate and then nod. "I used to keep a record for my own psychology classes. I'll start again."

"Thanks."

"If anyone in town asks my opinion," I say, standing in the open doorway now, feeling the cool wind that the storm has brought in, "I'll tell them that I'm cooperating, nothing more. They may or may not pay any attention to what I say."

"See you tomorrow afternoon," Roger says and I leave them and walk home. It is very dark now, and the rain smells fresh, the air is cool and clean. I am thinking of the two halves that make up the whole me. In the city I am brisk and efficient. I know the nurses talk about me, wondering if I am a lesbian (I'm not), if I have any sex life at all (not now). They are afraid of me because I will not permit any sloppiness in surgery, and I am quick to report them. They don't understand that my instruments are to me what the surgeon's scalpel is to him, and they think I worship dials and stainless-steel gods. I once heard myself described as more machine-like than any of the exotic equipment that I have mastered. I know that the thought of those boys staring at the charts of their alpha and beta rhythms has brought this retrospective mood but I can't break out of it. I continue to inspect my life as if from the outside. What no one understands is that it is not the machines that are deified, but the processes that the machines record, the fluctuations and the rhythms, the cyclic patterns that are beautiful when they are normal, and as hideous as a physical deformity when they are wrong. The covered mound on the hard table is meaningless when I observe it. Less than human, inert, it might be a corpse already, or a covered log, or a cache of potatoes. But the dials that I read tell me all I can know about it: male, steady heart, respiration normal . . . Body processes that add up to life, or non-life. What more is there?

My house is cool now, and rain has blown in the kitchen and dining-room windows. I mop it up and wipe the sills carefully, and inspect the rest of the house. I can't see anything in the yard, but I stand on the back porch and feel the coolness and the mistiness of the air until I start to shiver.

I have read that dreams follow a pattern of their own. The first dreams of the night are of events nearby in time and space, and as sleep progresses and the night goes by the dreams wander farther afield, into the past, or into future fantasy, and toward morning, they return to the here and now of the dreamer. During the night I wake up three times and jot down the dreams I can recall.

Dream number one is a simple-minded wish fulfillment. I am at a party where I sparkle and dazzle everyone in the house. It is an unfamiliar house, not unlike the Sagamore House, except more elegant, simpler, with cool white marble statues replacing the clutter. I am the belle of the party and I dance with everyone there, and in the center of the room is a champagne glass that must hold gallons. Looking through the bubbling wine, I see the statues shimmer and appear to come alive, but I know that it is only because of the rising bubbles, that it is an illusion. I am swept back to the dance floor and I swirl around in a delirium of joy.

Dream number two puzzles me. I am following Father, who is very small. It is not quite dark, but I don't know where the light is coming from. It is like moonlight, but without the moon, which I suspect is behind me somewhere. I am very frightened. Father starts to climb the ash tree and I retreat and watch him, growing more and more afraid but not doing anything at all, simply standing and watching as he vanishes among the leaves. I wake up in a cold sweat.

Dream number three takes place in my apartment. I am remodeling and doing the work myself. I am installing temporary wall boards, decorating them with childish pictures and pinups. I am weeping as I work. Suddenly there is a change and I am above Somerset, or in town, and I can't be certain which it is. I am calm and happy, although I see no one and hear nothing. Somerset is bathed in moonlight that is too golden to be real and the town is as I remember it from my earliest days, with striped green-and-white umbrellas in yards, and silent children playing happily in Cobb's Run.

I wake up and don't want to lose the feeling of peace and contentment. I smile as I write the dream down and when I read it over I don't know quite why it should have filled me with happiness. As I think of it more, I am saddened by it, and finally I get up wishing I had let it escape altogether. It is very early, not seven yet, but I don't want to return to bed. The morning is cool and refreshing. I decide to weed the patio out back and set up the grill before the sun heats up the valley again.

The ash tree is untouched. I work for an hour, go inside for breakfast, and return to the yard. I am thinking that if I do bring Father home, I will have to find someone who can help with the yard, and I don't know who it would be. Poor Haddie? He might, but he is so slow and unthinking. I could have a wheelchair for Father and bring him out to the patio every day and as he convalesces, we could take short trips in the car, go down to the lake maybe, or over to Hawley now and then. I am certain that he will be able to play chess by fall, and read aloud with me, as we used to do. A quiet happiness fills me as I plan and it is with surprise that I realize that I have decided about Father. I have been over the same reasoning with his doctor, and accepted his advice against this move, but here, working in the bright sunlight, the new decision seems to have been made effortlessly.

I have weeded the patio, swept up the heaps of dandelions and buckweeds and crabgrass that have pushed through the cracks in the flagstones, and set up the barbecue grill. The picnic table is in pitiful condition, but it will have to do. There are some folding canvas chairs in the garage, but I will let the boys bring them out.

It is one o'clock already. A whole morning gone so quickly. My muscles are throbbing and I am sunburned, but the feeling of peacefulness remains with me and I shower and change and then go to town to shop, have lunch with Dorothea and Annie, and then see the sleep lab equipment.

I try to explain to Dorothea the difference between living in the city and living here in my own home, but she has her mouth set in a firm line and she is very disapproving of the whole idea.

Timidly Annie says, "But, honey, there's no one left your age. What will you do all the time?"

"I'll have plenty to do," I tell her. "I want to study, rest, take care of Father, the house. There will be too much to do, probably."

"That's not what she means," Dorothea says sharply. "You should get married, not tie yourself down here where everything's dying." She eyes me appraisingly. "Don't you have anyone in mind?"

I shrug it off. A young doctor, perhaps? I try to think of myself with any of the young doctors I know, and the thought is ridiculous. There are some older doctors, thoroughly married, of course, that seem less absurd, but no one my age who is unattached. I think again of the Harvard doctor's pink hands and pink cheeks, and I shudder. I say, "There's time for that, Dorothea, but right now I feel it's my duty to Father to bring him home where he will be happier."

After lunch I wander into the parlor and have Dorothea ring Roger's room and tell him I'm waiting. She is still unhappy with me, and I know that she and Annie will discuss me the rest of the afternoon.

The sleep lab is set up in the rear of the building on the second floor. There are three bedrooms in a row, the middle one the control room with the equipment in place, and the rooms on either side furnished with beds, telephones, wires with electrodes. I have seen pictures of these experiments and have read about them so that none of it comes as a surprise, but I am mildly impressed that they were able to get together so much equipment that I know to be very expensive. Harvard is feeling flush these days, I decide, or else Staunton swings more weight than I have given him credit for.

After I examine the EEGs from the night before and compare them with the reported dreams, I am introduced to the other three students that I missed before. I have already forgotten all of their names except Sid and Roger. We have a drink and I learn that so far they have received no cooperation from anyone in town, with the possible exception of myself. Staunton comes in looking angry and frustrated.

"That hick doctor could do it, if he would," he says before he sees me in the room. He reddens.

"He won't, though," I say. "But I could."

"They'd tell you their dreams?"

"Some of them would, probably enough for your purposes." I

stand up and start for the door. "I would have to promise not to give you their dreams, but to process them myself, however."

He starts to turn away, furious again, and I say, "I am qualified, you know." I suspect that I have more degrees than he does and I reel them off rapidly. I walk to the door before he has a chance to respond. Before leaving I say, "Think about it. You can let me know tonight when you come to the house. I will have to be briefed on your methods, of course, and have a chance to examine your cards."

I don't know why I've done it. I walk home and try to find a reason, but there is none. To puncture his smug shield? To deflate him in the presence of his students? To inflate my own importance, reassure myself that I am of both worlds? I can't select a single reason, and I decide that perhaps all of them are part of it. I know that I dislike Staunton as much as anyone I have ever met, and perhaps I hope that he will fail completely in his research, except that it isn't really his.

I make potato salad, and bake pies, and prepare the steaks that Dorothea has ordered. It crosses my mind that Mr. Larson has virtually no meat except for the special order from Sagamore House, and that I'll have to order everything in advance when I move back home for good, but I don't linger over it. The evening passes quite pleasantly and even Staunton is on his good behavior. They accept my offer and Sid goes over the cards with me, explaining what they are doing, how they are analyzing the dreams and recording them. It seems simple enough.

The days flow by now, with not quite enough time for all there is to do. The doctor in charge of the nursing home answers my letter brusquely, treating me like a child. I read it over twice before I put it on my desk to be taken care of later. I have been able to get six people to cooperate in the dream studies, and they keep me busy each day. People like to talk about their dreams, I find, and talking about them, they are able to bring back more and more details, so that each interview takes half an hour or an hour. And there are my own dreams that I am also recording.

I have found the reason for my own part in this when I first typed up my own dream to be analyzed. I found that I couldn't give it to Staunton, and the students are like children, not to be trusted with anything so intimate as the private dreams of a grown woman. So each day I record my own dreams along with the other six, type them all up, fill out the cards, and turn the cards over to Roger. By then the dreams are depersonalized data.

I finish typing the seven dreams and I am restless suddenly. There is something . . . The house is more unquiet than usual, and I am accustomed to the rustlings and creakings. I wonder if another storm is going to hit the town, but I don't think so. I wander outside where the night is very clear. The sky is brilliant and bottomless. The music of the night is all about me: the splashing water of the creek, crickets and tree frogs in arhythmic choral chants and from a distance the deeper solo bass of a bullfrog. Probably I am bored. Other people's dreams are very boring. I haven't started to categorize this latest set, and I feel reluctant to begin. I purposely don't put any names on any of the dreams I record, and I type each one on a separate card and then shuffle them about, so that by the time I have finished with them all, I have forgotten who told me which one.

I stop walking suddenly. I have come halfway down the path toward the creek without thinking where I am going or why. Now I stop and the night noises press in on me. "They are alike," I say, and I am startled by my voice. All other sounds stop with the words.

I think of the stack of file cards, and those I added tonight, and I am amazed that I didn't see it in the beginning. Roger is right: the townspeople are dreaming the same dreams. That isn't really what he said. What he said was that the dreams of the people here would remain stable, unchanged by the experiment, while those of the students would change as they adapted to this life. I haven't asked about that part of the research, but suddenly I am too curious about it to put it out of my mind.

Are they changing, and how? I start back, but pause at the door to the house, and turn instead to the street and town. I slow down when I come in sight of Sagamore House. It is very late, almost two in the morning. The second-floor light is the only light I have seen since leaving my own house. I take another step toward Sagamore House, and another. What is the matter tonight? I look about. But there is nothing. No wind, no moon, nothing. But I hear . . . life, stirrings, something. This is Somerset, I say to myself sharply, not quite aloud, but I hear the words anyway. I look quickly over my shoulder, but there is nothing. I see the apple trees, familiar yet strange, eerie shadows against the pale siding of the hotel. Across from Sagamore House on Wisteria there is the old boarded-up theater, and for a moment I think someone has opened it again. I press my hands over my ears and when I take them down the sound has stopped. I am shaking. I can't help the sudden look that I give the corner where the drugstore burned down seven or eight years ago.

We wait in the shadows of Sagamore House, under the apple trees for the movie to be over, and then Father and Mother, Susan's parents, Peter's, come out and take us along with them for an ice-cream soda in the drugstore. We know when the movie is ending because of the sounds that filter out when they open the inner doors. Faint music, laughter, a crash of cymbals, always different, but always a signal, and we come down from the trees, or from the porch and cross the street to wait for them to come out.

I stare at the theater, back to the empty corner, and slowly turn and go home again. One of the boys was playing a radio, I tell myself, and even believe it for a moment. Or I imagined it, the past intruded for a moment, somehow. An audio hallucination. I stop at the gate to my yard and stare at the house, and I am desperately afraid. It is such an unfamiliar feeling, so unexpected and shattering, that I can't move until it passes. It is as if I have become someone else for a moment, someone who fears rustling in the dark, who fears the night, being alone. Not my feelings at all. I have never been afraid, never, not of anything like this.

I light a cigarette and walk around the house to enter the kitchen, where I make coffee and a sandwich. It is two-thirty, but sleep seems a long way off now, unwanted, unneeded. Toward dawn I take a sleeping pill and fall into bed.

Roger, Sid and Doug invite me to have dinner with them in Hawley on Saturday, and I accept. The mountain road is very bad and we creep along in the station wagon that they have brought with them. No one is talking, and we all glance back at Somerset at the turn that used to have a tended scenic overlook. The trees have since grown up, and bushes and vines, so that there is only a hint of the town below us. Then it is gone, and suddenly Sid starts to talk of the experiment.

"I think we should call off the rest of it," he says.

"Can't," Roger says. "Eight days isn't enough."

"We have a trend," Sid says.

Doug, sitting in the back seat, speaks up then. "You'll never keep them all here for two more weeks."

"I know that, but those who do hang on will be enough."

"What's the matter?" I ask.

"Boredom," Sid says. "Good God, what's there to do in such a place?"

"I thought that was part of the experiment. I thought you wanted a place with no external stimuli."

"Quote and unquote," Sid says. "Staunton's idea. And we did, but I don't know. The dreams are strange, and getting stranger. And we're not getting along too well in the daytime. I don't know how your people stand it."

I shrug and don't even try to answer. I know he won't understand. Traffic thickens when we leave the secondary road for the highway on the other side of the mountain. It feels cooler here and I find that I am looking forward to a night out with more excitement than seems called for.

We have drinks before dinner, and wine with dinner, and more drinks afterward, and there is much laughter. Doug teaches me three new dance steps, and Roger and I dance, and I find myself thinking with incredulity of the plan I have been considering to take Father out of the nursing home where he belongs and try to care for him myself. I know that he will never recover, that he will become more and more helpless, not less. How could I have planned to do such a thing? He needs attendants to lift him, turn him in bed, and at times to restrain him. I have tried to think of other alternatives for him, but there are none, and I know that. I know that I have to write to the director of the home and apologize to him.

At eleven Roger says we have to go back. Doug passes out in the car as soon as he gets inside, and Sid groans. "There he goes," he says. "So you do me tonight."

"Where are the others?" I ask.

"On strike," Roger says. "They refused to work on Saturday and Sunday, said they needed time off. They want to forget their dreams for a couple of nights."

"I'll do it," I say.

"You're kidding."

"No. I'll do it. You can wire me up and everything tonight."

It is agreed, and we drive back over the mountain, becoming more and more quiet as we get to the old road and start to pick our way down again. By the time we get back to Somerset, and I am feeling soberer, I regret my impulsive promise, but can think of no way to back out now. I watch Sid and Roger half carry, half drag Doug from the station wagon, and I see the flutter of his eyelids and know that he is not as drunk as he would have us believe. I start to walk to my house, but Roger says for me to wait, that they will drive me and bring me back with my pajamas and things, so I stand on the porch and wait for them, and I stare across the street at the vacant theater. I know that three nights ago I imagined the past, but since then I have been taking sleeping pills, and my nights have been quiet, with no more hallucinations or dreams.

My house is noisier than usual. I glance at the two boys, but neither of them seems to notice. They sit in the living room and wait, and ahead of me on the dark stairs the rustlings hurry along; they pause outside my parents' room, scurry down the hallway and precede me into my room, where, when I turn on the light, there is nothing to see. I know it is the settling of floorboards untrodden for eleven months; and rushing air; and imagination. Memories that have become tangible? I don't believe that, but it has a strangely comforting sound, and I like the idea of memories lingering in the house, assuming a life of their own, reliving the past.

I fold pajamas and my housecoat, and grope under the bed for my slippers, and the thought comes that people are going to know that I spent the night at Sagamore House. I sit on the bed with my slippers in my hand and stare straight ahead at nothing in particular. How can I get out of this? I realize that Somerset and New York are arguing through me, and I can almost smile at the dialogue that I am carrying out silently. It seems that my strongest Somerset argument is that if I am going to live here with my invalid father, I can't return with a reputation completely ruined. I know what Somerset can do to a woman like that. But I'm not going to come back with him, I answer. Or am I?

It is getting very late and I have to go through with it; I have promised. Reluctantly I take my things downstairs, hoping that they have left, but of course they are still sitting there, talking quietly. About me? I suspect so. Probably I puzzle them. I regard them as little more than children, boys with school problems to solve. Yet we are all in our twenties. I suppose that because I have my degrees and a position of responsibility, my experience seems to add years to my age, and even as I think this, I reject it. Sid has told me that he spent three years in the army, served in Vietnam, so what is my experience to his? Sid has tried to draw me out, has visited twice, and has even gone canoeing with me, but standing in the doorway looking at them I think of them as so very young, prying into things they can't understand, trying to find answers that, if found, will make them question all of reality. I shake my head hard. I don't know what I've been thinking about, but I feel afraid suddenly, and I suspect that I have drunk too much earlier, and I am so very . . . weary. Sleeping pills leave me more tired than the insomnia they alleviate.

They make small talk that I recognize, the same sort of small talk that a good doctor uses for a nervous patient before measuring his blood pressure. I am churlish with them in return and we go to the sleep lab silently. I understand all of their equipment and I have even had electroencephalograms made when I was studying, so nothing is new to me and the demonstration is short. Then I am alone in the darkened room, conscious of the wires, of the tiny patches of skin with adhesive gel tape that holds the electrodes in place. I don't think I'll be able to go to sleep here wired up like this, at least not into the deep sleep that should come in an hour or so. I deliberately close my eyes and try to picture a flame above my eyes, over the bridge of my nose. I know that I can interrupt my alpha waves at will with this exercise. I imagine Roger's surprise. But suddenly I am thinking of S.L. and I blink rapidly, wondering what kinds of waves I am producing now for them to study. S.L. won't go away. I ask, what does the S. stand for, and he smiles broadly and says Silas. Does anyone name children Silas any more? So I ask about the L. and he says Lerner, which is perfectly all right, his mother's maiden name, but he doesn't like the idea of going around as S. Lerner Wright. It is a farcical name. He is S.L. Lying in the dark room of the almost empty hotel, I can think of S.L. without pain, without recriminations and regrets and bitterness. I remember it as it was then. I loved him so very much, but he said not enough, or I would go with him to Cal Tech and become Mrs. S.L. Wright, and forever and ever remain Mrs. S.L. Wright. I realize that I no longer love him, and that probably I didn't even then, but it felt like love and I ached as if it were love, and afterward I cut my hair very short and stopped using makeup and took several courses in night school and finished the next three years in under two and received degrees and a job . . .

I am awakened by the telephone and I lift it and mumble into it. "My car isn't working right, trying to back up on the road into Somerset and can't make it go. I keep slipping downward and there is a cliff in front of me, but I can't back up."

I dream of the telephone ringing, and it rings, and I speak, less coherently, and forget immediately what I have said and sleep again. In the morning I have memories of having spoken into the telephone several times, but no memories of what I said. Sid enters and helps me out of the bird's nest of wires. I wave him away and stumble into the bathroom where I wash my face and come really awake.

Sid? I thought Roger was the meter man of the night before. I dress and brush my hair and put on lipstick, and then find them both waiting for me to have breakfast with them. Sid has deep blue circles under his eyes. At a sunlit table with a bowl of yellow roses and a few deep green ferns, I wait for them to break the silence that has enveloped the three of us. There is a sound of activity in town that morning, people getting ready to go to church in Hawley, cars being brought out of garages where they stay six days of the week, several people in the hotel dining room having an early breakfast before leaving for the day. Many of them stay away all day on Sunday, visiting friends or relatives, and I know that later the town will be deserted.

"So they talked you into letting them wire you up like a condemned man?" Dorothea stands over the table accusingly. "Are you all right?"

"Of course. It's nothing, Dorothea, really nothing."

She snorts. "Up all night, people coming and going all night, talking in the halls, meetings here and there. I never should have let them in." She is addressing me still, but the hostility in her voice is aimed at the boys, at Staunton, who has just entered the dining room. He joins us, and there are dark hollows under his eyes. He doesn't meet my gaze.

We have coffee in silence and wait for our orders. I finger a sensitive spot on my left eyelid and Sid says quickly, "One of the wires came off during the night. I had to replace it. Is it sore?"

"No. It's all right." I am upset suddenly by the idea of his being there in the night, replacing a wire on my eye without my knowing. I think of the similar role that I play in my daily life and I know how I regard the bodies that I treat. Irritated at the arm that has managed to pull loose a needle that now must be replaced in the vein. Never a person, just an arm, and a needle. And the quiet satisfaction when the dials are registering correctly once more. I feel the frown on my face and try to smooth it out again.

Staunton has ordered only toast, juice and coffee, and he is yawning. He finishes his last crumb of toast and says, "I'm going to bed. Miss Matthews, will you join us here for dinner tonight?"

The sudden question catches me off guard, and I look at him. He is regarding me steadily and very soberly, and I realize that something has happened, that I am part of it, and that he is very much concerned. I am uneasy and only nod yes.

When he is gone I ask, "What happened? What's wrong?"

"We don't know yet," Roger says.

Sid pours more coffee and drinks it black. He is looking more awake, as if he has taken a bennie or something. "We have to talk with you, Janet. I'd like you to hear some of our tapes, including your own, if you will."

"You should get some sleep," I say irrelevantly.

"This afternoon? Can you come here, or should we bring the stuff to your place?"

"You got him up last night?"

Sid nods. "I felt I should."

I watch Myra and Al Newton leave their table, stop at Dorothea's counter to pay the bill and leave, and I am struck by their frailty. They both seem wraithlike. Is anyone in Somerset under sixty? I suppose the Newtons must be closer to seventy-five. I ask, "Where are the other boys this morning?" The dining room is empty except for the three of us.

"A couple of them are out fishing already, and the rest are probably still sleeping. I'm taking Victor and Mickey to Hawley to catch the bus back to Boston later today," Roger says, and then adds, "Probably Doug will be the next to go."

"Doug? I thought he was one of the more interested ones in this whole thing?"

"Too interested, maybe," Roger says.

Sid is watching both of us and now he leans forward, resting his chin on his hands, looking beyond me out the window at the quiet street. "Janet, do you remember any of your dreams from last night?"

I think of what I said over the telephone. Scraps here and there. Something about putting flowers on graves in one of them. I shake my head: nothing that I can really remember.

"Okay. You'll hear them later. Meanwhile, take my word for it that some of the guys have to leave, whether they want to or not." He looks at me for another moment and then asks, in a different voice altogether, "Are you all right, Janet? Will you be okay until this afternoon? We do have to process the tapes and record the data, and I want to sort through all of them and pull out those that seem pertinent."

It is the voice of a man concerned for a woman, not of a graduate student concerned for his project, and this annoys me.

"Of course I'm all right," I say, and stand up. "For heaven's sake, those are dreams, the dreams of someone who had too much to drink, at that." I know I am flushed and I turn to leave. Have I embarrassed them with erotic dreams, concerning one of them perhaps? I am very angry when I leave Sagamore House, and I wish I could go up to the sleep room and destroy the tapes, all of them. I wish Dorothea had shown just an ounce of sense when they approached her for the rooms. She had no business allowing them to come into our town, upset our people with their damned research. I am furious with Sid for showing concern for me. He has no right. In the middle of these thoughts, I see my father and me, walking hand in hand in the afternoon, heading for the drugstore and an ice-cream cone. He is very tall and blond, with broad shoulders and a massive chest. He keeps his hair so short that he seems bald from a distance. He is an ophthalmologist with his office in Jefferson, and after they dam the river he has to drive sixty-three miles each way. Mother worries about his being out so much, but they don't move, don't even consider moving. On Sunday afternoon he always takes me to the drugstore for an ice-cream cone. I blink hard and the image fades, leaving the street bare and empty.

I am too restless to remain in my house. It is a hot still day and the heat is curling the petals of the roses, and drying out the grass, and wilting the phlox leaves. It is a relentless sun, burning, broiling, sucking the water up from the creek, leaving it smaller each day. Without the dam the creek probably would dry up completely within another week or two. I decide to cut a basket of flowers and take them to the cemetery, and I know the idea comes from the fragmentary dream that I recalled earlier. I haven't been to the cemetery since my mother's funeral. It has always seemed such a meaningless gesture, to return to a grave and mourn there. It is no less meaningless now, but it is something to do.

The cemetery is behind the small white church that has not been used for six years, since Brother MacCombs died. No one tried to replace him; they seemed tacitly to agree that the church should be closed and the membership transferred to Hawley.

It is a walk of nearly two miles, past the Greening farm where the weeds have become master again, past the dirt road to the old mill, a tumbling ruin even in my childhood where snakes curled in the shadows and slept, past the turnoff to Eldridge's fishing camp. I see no one and the sounds of the hot summer day are loud about me: whirring grasshoppers, birds, the scuttling of a squirrel who chatters at me once he is safely hidden.

The cemetery is tended in spots only, the graves of those whose relatives are still in Somerset have cut grass and a sprinkling of flowers. My mother's grave is completely grown over and shame fills me. What would Father say? I don't try to weed it then, but sit down under a wide oak tree.

I look at the narrow road that leads back to Somerset. Father and I will come here often, after I have made the grave neat and pretty again. It will be slow, but we'll take our time, walking hand in hand up the dirt road, carrying flowers, and maybe a sandwich and a thermos of lemonade, or apples. Probably if I start the proceedings during the coming week, I can have everything arranged by next weekend, hire an ambulance and a driver . . .

I am awakened by rough hands shaking my shoulders. I blink rapidly, trying to focus my eyes, trying to find myself. I am being led away, and I squirm to turn around because I feel so certain that I am still back there somehow. I almost catch a glimpse of a girl in a yellow dress, sitting with her back to the oak tree, but it shimmers and I am yanked hard, and stumble, and hands catch me and steady me.

"What are you kids doing?" I ask, and the sound of the voice, deep, unfamiliar, shocks me and only then do I really wake up. I am being taken to the station wagon that is parked at the entrance to the lane.

"I'm all right," I say, not struggling now. "You woke me up."

Sid is on my right and Roger on my left. I see that Dr. Staunton is in the wagon. He looks pale and worried.

I remember the basket of flowers that I never did put on the grave and I look back once more to see it standing by the tree. Sid's hand tightens on my arm, but I don't try to pull away. Inside the wagon I say, "Will one of you tell me what that was all about?"

"Janet, do you know how long you've been there at the cemetery?"

"Half an hour, an hour."

"It's almost six now. I . . . we got to your house at three and waited awhile for you, and then went back to the hotel. An old man with a white goatee said he saw you before noon heading this way with flowers. So we came after you." Sid is sitting beside me in the back seat of the wagon, and I stare at him in disbelief. I look at my watch, and it is five minutes to six. I shake it and listen to it.

"I must have been sound asleep."

"Sitting straight up, with your legs stretched out in front of you?"

We drive to my house and I go upstairs to wash my face and comb my hair. I study my face carefully, looking for something, anything, but it is the same. I hear voices from below; the sound diminishes and I know they are playing the tapes, so I hurry down.

I see that Sid has found my dream cards, the typed reports, and I am angry with him for prying. He says, "I had to know. I found them earlier while we were waiting for you."

Roger has the tape ready, so I sit down and we listen for the next two hours. Staunton is making notes, scowling hard at the pad on his knee. I feel myself growing tenser, and when the first tape comes to an end, I go to make coffee. We all sip it through the playing of the second tape.

The dreaming students' voices sound disjointed, hesitant, unguarded, and the dreams they relate are all alike. I feel cold in the hot room, and I dread hearing my own voice, my own dreams played by the machine.

All the early dreams are of attempts to leave Somerset. They speak of trying to fly out, to climb out, to swim out, to drive out, and only one is successful. As the night progresses, the dreams change, some faster than others. Slowly a pattern of acceptance enters the dreams, and quite often the acceptance is followed swiftly by a nightmare-like desire to run.

One of the dreamers, Victor, I think it is, has a brief anxiety dream, an incomplete dream, and then nothing but the wish-fulfillment acceptance dreams, not even changing again when morning has him in a lighter stage of sleep.

Sid motions for Roger to stop the tape and says, "That was three days ago. Since then Victor has been visiting people here, talking with them, fishing, hiking. He has been looking over some of the abandoned houses in town, with the idea of coming here to do a book."

"Has he . . ." I am amazed at how dry my mouth has become and I have to sip cold coffee before I can ask the question. "Has he recorded dreams since then?"

"No. Before this, he was having dreams of his parents, caring for them, watching over them." Sid looks at me and says deliberately, "Just like your dreams."

I shake my head and turn from him to look at Roger. He starts the machine again. There are hours and hours of the tapes to hear, and after another fifteen minutes of them I am ravenous. It is almost nine. I signal Roger to stop, and suggest that we all have scrambled eggs here, but Staunton vetoes this.

"I promised Miss Dorothea that we would return to the hotel. I warned her that it might be late. She said that was all right."

So we go back to Sagamore House and wait for the special of the day. On Sunday night there is no menu. I find myself shying away from the implications of the dream analysis again and again, and try to concentrate instead on my schedule for the next several months. I know that I have agreed to work with Dr. Waldbaum on at least six operations, and probably there are others that I agreed to and have forgotten. He is a thoracic surgeon and his operations take from four to eight or even ten hours, and for that long I control death, keep life in abeyance. I pay no attention to the talk that is going on between Roger and Sid, and I wonder about getting an ambulance driver to bring Father in during the winter. If only our weather were more predictable; there might be snowdrifts six feet high on the road, or it might be balmy.

"I said, why do you think you should bring your father home, here to Somerset?" I find that my eyes are on Staunton, and obviously he thinks I have been listening to him, but the question takes me by surprise.

"He's my father. He needs me."

Sid asks, "Has anyone in town encouraged you in this idea?"

Somehow, although I have tried to withdraw from them, I am again the center of their attention, and I feel uncomfortable and annoyed. "Of course not. This is my decision alone. Dr. Warren tried to discourage it, in fact, as Dorothea did, and Mr. Larson."

"Same thing," Sid says to Roger, who nods. Staunton looks at them and turns to me.

"Miss Matthews, do you mean to say that everyone you've talked to about this has really tried to discourage it? These people are your father's friends. Why would they do that?"

My face feels stiff and I am thinking that this is too much, but I say, "They all seem to think he's better off in the nursing home."

"And isn't he?"

"In certain respects, yes. But I am qualified to handle him, you know. No one here seems to realize just how well qualified I really am. They think of me as the girl they used to know playing jump-rope in the back yard."

Dorothea brings icy cucumber soup and we are silent until she leaves again. The grandfather clock chimes ten, and I am amazed at how swiftly the day has gone. By now most of the townspeople are either in bed, or getting ready. Sunday is a hard day, with the trip to church, visits, activities that they don't have often enough to become accustomed to. They will sleep well tonight, I think. I look at Sid and think that he should sleep well too tonight. His eyes are sunken-looking, and I suppose he has lost weight; he looks older, more mature than he did the first time I met him.

"Are you going to set up your equipment tonight?" I ask. "Any of the other boys volunteer?"

"No," Roger says shortly. He looks at Sid and says, "As a matter of fact, we decided today not to put any of them in it again here."

"You're leaving then?"

"Sending all the kids back, but Sid and I'll be staying for a while. And Dr. Staunton."

I put down my spoon and lean back, waiting for something that is implicit in the way Roger stops and Sid looks murderously at him. I watch Sid now.

"We think you should leave, too," he says.

I look to Roger, who nods, and then at Staunton. He is so petulant-looking, even pursing his lips. He fidgets and says, "Miss Matthews, may I suggest something? You won't take it amiss?" I simply wait. He goes on, "I think you should return to the city and make an appointment with the psychiatrist at Columbia."

"And the others you are sending out? Should they also see doctors?"

"As a matter of fact, I do think so."

Sid is examining his bowl of soup with great care, and Roger is having trouble with his cigarette lighter. "But not them?" I ask Staunton, pointing at Roger and Sid.

"Them too," he says reluctantly. Sid looks amused now and Roger manages to light his cigarette.

"Is this your opinion too?" I ask Sid. "That I should see Dr. Calridge?"

"No. Just go away from here, and stay away."

Dorothea is bringing in a cart now and I wonder how much she has heard. I see her lined face and the pain in her eyes and I know that she has heard a lot of it, if not all. She catches my gaze and nods firmly. Then she serves us: sizzling ham steaks, french fried fruits, pineapple, apple rings, bananas, sweet potato soufflé.

It is after eleven when we are finished with dinner, and by now Sid is almost asleep. He says, "I've got to go. Will you set things up, Rog?"

"Sure. Damn shame that Doug pooped out on us. We need all the data we can get now."

"I can do the recording," I say.

At almost the same instant Staunton says, "I thought I was going to record both of you tonight."

Roger and Sid look embarrassed, and Sid says after a pause, "Dr. Staunton, if it's all the same with you, we'll let Janet do it."

"You really think I'm that biased? That I can't get objective data?"

Sid stands up and steadies himself with one hand on the table. "I'm too tired to be polite," he says, "and too tired to argue. So, yes I think you're too biased to record the dreams. Roger, will you show Janet what we're doing?"

Roger stays with me until the eye-movement trace shows that Sid is having his first dream, and he watches as I call Sid on the phone and turn on the recorder, and then switch it off again. Then Roger goes to bed in the second room and I see that his electrodes are all working, and I am alone watching the two sets of moving lines. The mountains and valleys of life, I think, watching them peak and level out, and peak again.

There is no mistaking the start of REM sleep; the rapid eye movements cause a sharp change in the pattern of the peaks and valleys that is more nearly like a waking EEG than that of a sleeping person. I call Sid again, and listen to him describe climbing a mountain, only to slip back down again and again. Roger is on a raft that keeps getting caught up on a tide and brought back to a shore that he is desperately trying to escape.

The same dream, different only in details. Like the dreams I heard earlier on the tape recorder. Like my own.

At three in the morning Staunton joins me. I can tell that he hasn't been asleep, but I wish he had kept his insomnia to himself. He says, "You might need help. I won't bother you. I'll just sit over here and read." He looks haggard, and like Sid, he seems to have aged since coming to Somerset. I turn my attention to the EEGs again. Roger is dreaming.

"Peaceful now, watching a ball game from a great distance, very silent everywhere." I bite my lips as I listen to this strange voice that seems to have a different accent, a different intonation; flatter and slower, of course, but apart from that, it is a changed voice. It is the dream of contentment, wanting nothing, needing nothing. This is the dream that my six people keep reporting to me, modified from person to person, but the same. Suddenly Roger's voice sharpens as he recalls the rest of the dream, and now there is a sense of urgency in his reporting. "And I had to get out of it, but couldn't move. I was frozen there, watching the game, afraid of something I couldn't see, but knew was right behind me. Couldn't move."

I glance at Staunton and he is staring at the moving pens. Roger has become silence once more, so I turn off the tape recorder and look also at the continuing record. Typical nightmare pattern.

Staunton yawns and I turn to him and say, "Why don't you try to get some sleep? Really, I'm fine. I slept almost all day, remember?"

He yawns again, then says, "If . . . if I seem to be dreaming, will you waken me?" I nod and he stretches out on the couch and is asleep almost instantly.

There is a coffee maker with strong coffee hot in it, and I pour myself a cup, and try to read the book that Roger provided, a spy thriller. I can't keep my mind on it. The hotel is no more noisy at night than my own house, but the noises are not the same, and I find myself listening to them, rustlings in the halls, distant doors opening and closing, the occasional squeak of the porch swing. I sit up straighter. A woman's laugh? Not at three-fifteen in the morning, surely. I have more coffee and wander to the window. A light on in the Sayer house? I blink and when I look again, I know that it was my imagination. I remember how their baby used to keep night hours, and smile. The baby would be fifteen or sixteen now, at least. I used to baby-sit for them now and then, and the child never slept.

I return to my chair by the electroencephalograph and see that Sid has started a new dream. I reach for the phone, waiting for the peak to level off again, and slowly withdraw my hand. He is dreaming a long one this time. After five minutes I begin to feel uneasy, but still I wait. Roger has said to rouse the sleeper after ten minutes of dreaming, if he hasn't shown any sign of being through by then. I wait, and suddenly jerk awake and stab my finger at the phone button. He doesn't answer.

I forget to turn on the recorder, but rush into the next room to bring him out of this dream turned into nightmare, and when I touch his shoulder, I am in it too.

Somerset is gay and alive with playing children, and sun umbrellas everywhere. There are tables on the lawn of Sagamore House, and ladies in long white skirts moving among them, laughing happily. The Governor is due and Dorothea and Annie are bustling about, ordering the girls in black aprons this way and that, and everywhere there is laughter. A small boy approaches the punch bowl with a wriggling frog held tightly in one hand, and he is caught and his knickers are pulled down summarily and the sounds of hand on bottom are plainly heard, followed by wails. I am so busy, and someone keeps trying to pull me away and talk to me. I shake him off and run to the table where Father and Mother are sitting, and see to it that they have punch, and then swirl back to the kitchen where Dorothea is waiting for me to help her with the ice sculpture that is the centerpiece. It is a tall boy with curly hair rising up from a block of ice, the most beautiful thing I've ever seen, and I want to weep for him because in a few hours he will be gone. I slip on a piece of ice and fall, fall . . . fall . . .

I catch the wires attached to Sid and pull them loose, half pull him from the bed, and we end up in a heap. He holds me tightly for a long time, until we are both breathing normally again, and my shaking has stopped, and his too.

There is pale dawnlight in the room. Enough to see that his dark hair is damp with sweat, and curly on his forehead. He pushes it back and very gently moves me aside and disentangles himself from the wires.

"We have to get out of here," he says.

Staunton is sound asleep on the couch, breathing deeply but normally, and Roger is also sleeping. His graph shows that he has had nightmares several times.

We take our coffee into the room where Sid slept, and sit at the window drinking it, watching morning come to Somerset. I say, "They don't know, do they?"

"Of course not."

Poor Haddie appears at the far end of the street, walking toward Mr. Larson's store. He shuffles his feet as he moves, never lifting them more than an inch. I shudder and turn away.

"Isn't there something that we should do? Report this, or something?"

"Who would believe it? Staunton doesn't, and he has seen it over and over this week."

A door closes below us and I know Dorothea is up now, in the kitchen starting coffee. "I was in her dream, I think," I say.

I look down into my cup and think of the retirement villages all over the south, and again I shiver. "They seem so accepting, so at peace with themselves, just waiting for the end." I shake the last half inch of coffee back and forth. I ask, "Is that what happened with me? Did I not want to wake up?"

Sid nods. "I was taking the electrodes off your eyes when you snapped out of it, but yours wasn't a nightmare. It just wouldn't end.

That's what frightened me, that it wasn't a nightmare. You didn't seem to be struggling against it at all. I wonder what brought you out of it this time."

I remember the gleaming ice sculpture, the boy with curly hair who will be gone so soon, and I know why I fought to get away. Someday I think probably I'll tell him, but not now, not so soon. The sun is high and the streets are bright now. I stand up. "I'm sorry that I forgot to turn on the tape recorder and ask you right away what the dream was. Do you remember it now?"

He hesitates only a moment and then shakes his head. Maybe someday he'll tell me, but not now, not so soon.

I leave him and find Dorothea waiting for me in the parlor. She draws me inside and shuts the door and takes a deep breath. "Janet, I am telling you that you must not bring your father back here to stay. It would be the worst possible thing for you to do."

I can't speak for a moment, but I hug her, and try not to see her etched face and the white hair, but to see her as she was when she was still in long skirts, with pretty pink cheeks and sparkling eyes. I can't manage it. "I know," I say finally. "I know."

Walking home again, hot in the sunlight, listening to the rustlings of Somerset, imagining the unseen life that flits here and there out of my line of vision, wondering if memories can become tangible, live a life of their own. I will pack, I think, and later in the day drive back up the mountain, back to the city, but not back to my job. Not back to administering death, even temporary death. Perhaps I shall go into psychiatry, or research psychology. As I begin to pack, my house stirs with movement.

HE WALKED AROUND THE HORSES

by H. Beam Piper

IN NOVEMBER, 1809, an Englishman named Benjamin Bathurst vanished, inexplicably and utterly.

He was en route to Hamburg from Vienna, where he had been serving as his government's envoy to the court of what Napoleon had left of the Austrian Empire. At an inn in Perleburg, in Prussia, while examining a change of horses for his coach, he casually stepped out of sight of his secretary and his valet. He was not seen to leave the inn yard. He was not seen again, ever.

At least, not in this continuum . . .

I

(From Baron Eugen von Krutz, Minister of Police, to His Excellency the Count von Berchtenwald, Chancellor to His Majesty Friedrich Wilhelm III of Prussia.)

25 November, 1809

Your Excellency:

A circumstance has come to the notice of this Ministry, the significance of which I am at a loss to define, but, since it appears to involve matters of state, both here and abroad, I am convinced that it is of sufficient importance to be brought to the personal attention of your Excellency. Frankly, I am unwilling to take any further action in the matter without your Excellency's advice.

Briefly, the situation is this: We are holding, here at the Ministry of Police, a person giving his name as Benjamin Bathurst, who claims to be a British diplomat. This person was taken into custody by the police at Perleburg yesterday, as a result of a disturbance at an inn there; he is being detained on technical charges of causing disorder in a public place, and of being a suspicious person. When arrested, he had in his possession a dispatch case, containing a number of papers; these are of such an extraordinary nature that the local authorities declined to assume any responsibility beyond having the man sent here to Berlin.

After interviewing this person and examining his papers, I am, I must confess, in much the same position. This is not, I am convinced, any ordinary police matter; there is something very strange and disturbing here. The man's statements, taken alone, are so incredible as to justify the assumption that he is mad. I cannot, however, adopt this theory, in view of his demeanor, which is that of a man of perfect rationality, and because of the existence of these papers. The whole thing is mad; incomprehensible!

The papers in question accompany, along with copies of the various statements taken at Perleburg, and a personal letter to me from my nephew, Lieutenant Rudolf von Tarlburg. This last is deserving of your Excellency's particular attention; Lieutenant von Tarlburg is a very level-headed young officer, not at all inclined to be fanciful or imaginative. It would take a good deal to affect him as he describes.

The man calling himself Benjamin Bathurst is now lodged in an apartment here at the Ministry; he is being treated with every consideration, and, except for freedom of movement, accorded every privilege.

I am, most anxiously awaiting your Excellency's advice, etc., etc.,

Krutz

II

(Report of Traugott Zeller, *Oberwachtmeister, Staatspolizei,* made at Perleburg, 25 November, 1809.)

At about ten minutes past two of the afternoon of Saturday, 25 November, while I was at the police station, there entered a man known to me as Franz Bauer, an inn servant employed by Christian Hauck, at the sign of the Sword & Scepter, here in Perleburg. This man Franz Bauer made complaint to *Staatspolizeikapitan* Ernst Hartenstein, saying that there was a madman making trouble at the inn where he, Franz Bauer, worked. I was therefore directed by *Staatspolizeikapitan* Hartenstein to go to the Sword & Scepter Inn, there to act at discretion to maintain the peace.

Arriving at the inn in company with the said Franz Bauer, I found a considerable crowd of people in the common room, and, in the midst of them, the innkeeper, Christian Hauck, in altercation with a stranger. This stranger was a gentlemanly-appearing person, dressed in travelling clothes, who had under his arm a small leather dispatch case. As I entered, I could hear him, speaking in German with a strong English accent, abusing the innkeeper, the said Christian Hauck, and accusing him of having drugged his, the stranger's, wine, and of having stolen his, the stranger's, coach-and-four, and of having abducted his, the stranger's, secretary and servants. This the said Christian Hauck was loudly denying, and the other people in the inn were taking the innkeeper's part, and mocking the stranger for a madman.

On entering, I commanded everyone to be silent, in the King's name, and then, as he appeared to be the complaining party of the dispute, I required the foreign gentleman to state to me what was the trouble. He then repeated his accusations against the innkeeper, Hauck, saying that Hauck, or, rather, another man who resembled Hauck and who had claimed to be the innkeeper, had drugged his wine and stolen his coach and made off with his secretary and his servants. At this point, the innkeeper and the bystanders all began shouting denials and contradictions, so that I had to pound on a table with my truncheon to command silence.

I then required the innkeeper, Christian Hauck, to answer the charges which the stranger had made; this he did with a complete denial of all of them, saying that the stranger had had no wine in his inn, and that he had not been inside the inn until a few minutes before, when he had burst in shouting accusations, and that there had been no secretary, and no valet, and no coachman, and no coach-and-four, at the inn, and that the gentleman was raving mad. To all this, he called the people who were in the common room to witness.

I then required the stranger to account for himself. He said that his name was Benjamin Bathurst, and that he was a British diplomat, returning to England from Vienna. To prove this, he produced from his dispatch case sundry papers. One of these was a letter of safe-conduct, issued by the Prussian Chancellery, in which he was named and described as Benjamin Bathurst. The other papers were English, all bearing seals, and appearing to be official documents.

Accordingly, I requested him to accompany me to the police station, and also the innkeeper, and three men whom the innkeeper wanted to bring as witnesses.

Traugott Zeller
Oberwachtmeister

Report approved,

Ernst Hartenstein
Staatspolizeikapitan

III

(Statement of the self-so-called Benjamin Bathurst, taken at the police station at Perleburg, 25 November, 1809.)

My name is Benjamin Bathurst, and I am Envoy Extraordinary and Minister Plenipotentiary of the Government of His Britannic Majesty to the court of His Majesty Franz I, Emperor of Austria, or, at least I was until the events following the Austrian surrender made necessary my return to London. I left Vienna on the morning of Monday, the 20th, to go to Hamburg to take ship home; I was travelling in my own coach-and-four, with my secretary, Mr. Bertram Jardine, and my valet, William Small, both British subjects, and a coachman, Josef Bidek, an Austrian subject, whom I had hired for the trip. Because of the presence of French troops, whom I was anxious to avoid, I was forced to make a detour west as far as Salzburg before turning north toward Magdeburg, where I crossed the Elbe. I was unable to get a change of horses for my coach after leaving Gera, until I reached Perleburg, where I stopped at the Sword & Scepter Inn.

Arriving there, I left my coach in the inn yard, and I and my secretary, Mr. Jardine, went into the inn. A man, not this fellow here, but another rogue, with more beard and less paunch, and more shabbily dressed, but as like him as though he were his brother, represented himself as the innkeeper, and I dealt with him for a change of horses, and ordered a bottle of wine for myself and my secretary, and also a pot of beer apiece for my valet and the coachman, to be taken outside to them. Then Jardine and I sat down to our wine, at a table in the common room, until the man who claimed to be the innkeeper came back and told us that the fresh horses were harnessed to the coach and ready to go. Then we went outside again.

I looked at the two horses on the off side, and then walked around in front of the team to look at the two nigh-side horses, and as I did, I felt giddy, as though I were about to fall, and everything went black before my eyes. I thought I was having a fainting spell, something I am not at all subject to, and I put out my hand to grasp the hitching bar, but could not find it. I am sure, now, that I was unconscious for some time, because when my head cleared, the coach and horses were gone, and in their place was a big farm wagon, jacked up in front, with the right front wheel off, and two peasants were greasing the detached wheel.

I looked at them for a moment, unable to credit my eyes, and then I spoke to them in German, saying, "Where the devil's my coach-and-four?"

They both straightened, startled; the one who was holding the wheel almost dropped it.

"Pardon, Excellency," he said. "There's been no coach-and-four here, all the time we've been here."

"Yes," said his mate, "and we've been here since just after noon."

I did not attempt to argue with them. It occurred to me—and it is still my opinion—that I was the victim of some plot; that my wine had been drugged, that I had been unconscious for some time, during which my coach had been removed and this wagon substituted for it, and that these peasants had been put to work on it and instructed what to say if questioned. If my arrival at the inn had been anticipated, and everything put in readiness, the whole business would not have taken ten minutes.

I therefore entered the inn, determined to have it out with this rascally innkeeper, but when I returned to the common room, he was nowhere to be seen, and this other fellow, who has also given his name as Christian Hauck, claimed to be the innkeeper and denied knowledge of any of the things I have just stated. Furthermore, there were four cavalrymen, Uhlans, drinking beer and playing cards at the table where Jardine and I had had our wine, and they claimed to have been there for several hours.

I have no idea why such an elaborate prank, involving the participation of many people, should be played on me, except at the instigation of the French. In that case, I cannot understand why Prussian soldiers should lend themselves to it.

Benjamin Bathurst

IV

(Statement of Christian Hauck, innkeeper, taken at the police station at Perleburg, 25 November, 1809.)

May it please Your Honor, my name is Christian Hauck, and I keep an inn at the sign of the Sword & Scepter, and have these past fifteen years, and my father, and his father, before me, for the past fifty years, and never has there been a complaint like this against my inn. Your Honor, it is a hard thing for a man who keeps a decent house, and pays his taxes, and obeys the laws, to be accused of crimes of this sort.

I know nothing of this gentleman, nor of his coach nor his secretary nor his servants; I never set eyes on him before he came bursting into the inn from the yard, shouting and raving like a madman, and crying out, "Where the devil's that rogue of an innkeeper?"

I said to him, "I am the innkeeper; what cause have you to call me a rogue, sir?"

The stranger replied:

"You're not the innkeeper I did business with a few minutes ago, and he's the rascal I have a crow to pick with. I want to know what the devil's been done with my coach, and what's happened to my secretary and my servants."

I tried to tell him that I knew nothing of what he was talking about, but he would not listen, and gave me the lie, saying that he had been drugged and robbed, and his people kidnapped. He even had the impudence to claim that he and his secretary had been sitting at a table in that room, drinking wine, not fifteen minutes before, when there had been four non-commissioned officers of the Third Uhlans at that table since noon. Everybody in the room spoke up for me, but he would not listen, and was shouting that we were all robbers, and kidnappers, and French spies, and I don't know what all, when the police came.

Your Honor, the man is mad. What I have told you about this is the truth, and all that I know about this business, so help me God.

Christian Hauck

V

(Statement of Franz Bauer, inn servant, taken at the police station at Perleburg, 25 November, 1809.)

May it please Your Honor, my name is Franz Bauer, and I am a servant at the Sword & Scepter Inn, kept by Christian Hauck.

This afternoon, when I went into the inn yard to empty a bucket of slops on the dung heap by the stables, I heard voices and turned around, to see this gentleman speaking to Wilhelm Beick and Fritz Herzer, who were greasing their wagon in the yard. He had not been in the yard when I had turned around to empty the bucket, and I thought that he must have come in from the street. This gentleman was asking Beick and Herzer where was his coach, and when they told him they didn't know, he turned and ran into the inn.

Of my own knowledge, the man had not been inside the inn before then, nor had there been any coach, or any of the people he spoke of, at the inn, and none of the things he spoke of happened there, for otherwise I would know, since I was at the inn all day.

When I went back inside, I found him in the common room, shouting at my master, and claiming that he had been drugged and robbed. I saw that he was mad, and was afraid that he would do some mischief, so I went for the police.

Franz Bauer
his (X) mark

VI

(Statements of Wilhelm Beick and Fritz Herzer, peasants, taken at the police station at Perleburg, 25 November, 1809.)

May it please Your Honor, my name is Wilhelm Beick, and I am a tenant on the estate of the Baron von Hentig. On this day, I and Fritz Herzer were sent in to Perleburg with a load of potatoes and cabbages which the innkeeper at the Sword & Scepter had bought from the estate superintendent. After we had unloaded them, we decided to grease our wagon, which was very dry, before going back, so we unhitched and began working on it. We took about two hours, starting just after we had eaten lunch, and in all that time, there was no coach-and-four in the inn yard. We were just finishing when this gentleman spoke to us, demanding to know where his coach was. We told him that there had been no coach in the yard all the time we had been there, so he turned around and ran into the inn. At the time, I thought that he had come out of the inn before speaking to us, for I know that he could not have come in from the street. Now I do not know where he came from, but I know that I never saw him before that moment.

Wilhelm Beick
his (X) mark

I have heard the above testimony, and it is true to my own knowledge, and I have nothing to add to it.

Fritz Herzer
his (X) mark

VII

(From *Staatspolizeikapitan* Ernst Hartenstein, to His Excellency, the Baron von Krutz, Minister of Police.)

25 November, 1809

Your Excellency:

The accompanying copies of statements taken this day will explain how the prisoner, the self-so-called Benjamin Bathurst, came into my custody. I have charged him with causing disorder and being a suspicious person, to hold him until more can be learned about him. However, as he represents himself to be a British diplomat, I am unwilling to assume any further responsibility, and am having him sent to Your Excellency, in Berlin.

In the first place, Your Excellency, I have the strongest doubts of the man's story. The statement which he made before me, and signed, is bad enough, with a coach-and-four turning into a farm wagon, like Cinderella's coach into a pumpkin, and three people vanishing as though swallowed by the earth. Your Excellency will permit me to doubt that there ever was any such coach, or any such people. But all this is perfectly reasonable and credible, beside the things he said to me, of which no record was made.

Your Excellency will have noticed, in his statement, certain allusions to the Austrian surrender, and to French troops in Austria. After his statement had been taken down, I noticed these allusions, and I inquired, what surrender, and what were French troops doing in Austria. The man looked at me in a pitying manner, and said:

"News seems to travel slowly, hereabouts; peace was concluded at Vienna on the 14th of last month. And as for what French troops are doing in Austria, they're doing the same things Bonaparte's brigands are doing everywhere in Europe."

"And who is Bonaparte?" I asked.

He stared at me as though I had asked him, "Who is the Lord Jehovah?" Then, after a moment, a look of comprehension came into his face.

"So; you Prussians concede him the title of Emperor, and refer to him as Napoleon," he said. "Well, I can assure you that His Britannic Majesty's Government haven't done so, and never will; not so long as one Englishman has a finger left to pull a trigger. General Bonaparte is a usurper; His Britannic Majesty's Government do not recognize any sovereignty in France except the House of Bourbon." This he said very sternly, as though rebuking me.

It took me a moment or so to digest that, and to appreciate all its implications. Why, this fellow evidently believed, as a matter of fact, that the French Monarchy had been overthrown by some military adventurer named Bonaparte, who was calling himself the Emperor Napoleon, and who had made war on Austria and forced a surrender. I made no attempt to argue with him—one wastes time arguing with madmen—but if this man could believe that, the transformation of a coach-and-four into a cabbage wagon was a small matter indeed. So, to humor him, I asked him if he thought General Bonaparte's agents were responsible for his trouble at the inn.

"Certainly," he replied. "The chances are they didn't know me to see me, and took Jardine for the Minister, and me for the secretary, so they made off with poor Jardine. I wonder, though, that they left me my dispatch case. And that reminds me; I'll want that back. Diplomatic papers, you know."

I told him, very seriously, that we would have to check his credentials. I promised him I would make every effort to locate his secretary and his servants and his coach, took a complete description of all of them, and persuaded him to go into an upstairs room, where I kept him under guard. I did start inquiries, calling in all my informers and spies, but, as I expected, I could learn nothing. I could not find anybody, even, who had seen him anywhere in Perleburg before he appeared at the Sword & Scepter, and that rather surprised me, as somebody should have seen him enter the town, or walk along the street.

In this connection, let me remind Your Excellency of the discrepancy in the statements of the servant, Franz Bauer, and of the two peasants. The former is certain the man entered the inn yard from the street; the latter are just as positive that he did not. Your Excellency, I do not like such puzzles, for I am sure that all three were telling the truth to the best of their knowledge. They are ignorant common folk, I admit, but they should know what they did or did not see.

After I got the prisoner into safe-keeping, I fell to examining his papers, and I can assure Your Excellency that they gave me a shock. I had paid little heed to his ravings about the King of France being dethroned, or about this General Bonaparte who called himself the Emperor Napoleon, but I found all these things mentioned in his papers and dispatches, which had every appearance of being official documents. There was repeated mention of the taking, by the French, of Vienna, last May, and of the capitulation of the Austrian Emperor to this General Bonaparte, and of battles being fought all over Europe, and I don't know what other fantastic things. Your Excellency, I have heard of all sorts of madmen—one believing himself to be the Archangel Gabriel, or Mohammed, or a werewolf, and another convinced that his bones are made of glass, or that he is pursued and tormented by devils—but, so help me God, this is the first time I have heard of a madman who had documentary proof for his delusions! Does Your Excellency wonder, then, that I want no part of this business?

But the matter of his credentials was even worse. He had papers, sealed with the seal of the British Foreign Office, and to every appearance genuine—but they were signed, as Foreign Minister, by one George Canning, and all the world knows that Lord Castlereagh has been Foreign Minister these last five years. And to cap it all, he had a safe-conduct, sealed with the seal of the Prussian Chancellery—the very seal, for I compared it, under a strong magnifying glass, with one that I knew to be genuine, and they were identical—and yet, this letter was signed, as Chancellor, not by Count von Berchtenwald, but by Baron vom und zum Stein, the Minister of Agriculture, and the signature, as far as I could see, appeared to be genuine! This is too much for me, Your Excellency; I must ask to be excused from dealing with this matter, before I become as mad as my prisoner!

I made arrangements, accordingly, with Colonel Keitel, of the Third Uhlans, to furnish an officer to escort this man in to Berlin. The coach in which they come belongs to this police station, and the driver is one of my men. He should be furnished expense money to get back to Perleburg. The guard is a corporal of Uhlans, the orderly of the officer. He will stay with the *Herr Oberleutnant,* and both of them will return here at their own convenience and expense.

I have the honor, Your Excellency, to be, etc., etc.

Ernst Hartenstein
Staatspolizeikapitan

VIII

(From *Oberleutnant* Rudolf von Tarlburg, to Baron Eugen von Krutz.)

26 November, 1809

Dear Uncle Eugen:

This is in no sense a formal report; I made that at the Ministry, when I turned the Englishman and his papers over to one of your officers—a fellow with red hair and a face like a bulldog. But there are a few things which you should be told, which wouldn't look well in an official report, to let you know just what sort of a rare fish has gotten into your net.

I had just come in from drilling my platoon, yesterday, when Colonel Keitel's orderly told me that the colonel wanted to see me in his quarters. I found the old fellow in undress in his sitting room, smoking his big pipe.

"Come in, Lieutenant; come in and sit down, my boy!" he greeted me, in that bluff, hearty manner which he always adopts with his junior officers when he has some particularly nasty job to be done. "How would you like to take a little trip in to Berlin? I have an errand, which won't take half an hour, and you can stay as long as you like, just so you're back by Thursday, when your turn comes up for road patrol."

Well, I thought, this is the bait. I waited to see what the hook would look like, saying that it was entirely agreeable with me, and asking what his errand was.

"Well, it isn't for myself, Tarlburg," he said. "It's for this fellow Hartenstein, the *Staatspolizeikapitan* here. He has something he wants done at the Ministry of Police, and I thought of you because I've heard you're related to the Baron von Krutz. You are, aren't you?" he asked, just as though he didn't know all about who all his officers are related to.

"That's right, Colonel; the Baron is my uncle," I said. "What does Hartenstein want done?"

"Why, he has a prisoner whom he wants taken to Berlin and turned over at the Ministry. All you have to do is to take him in, in a coach, and see he doesn't escape on the way, and get a receipt for him, and for some papers. This is a very important prisoner; I don't think Hartenstein has anybody he can trust to handle him. A state prisoner. He claims to be some sort of a British diplomat, and for all Hartenstein knows, maybe he is. Also, he is a madman."

"A madman?" I echoed.

"Yes, just so. At least, that's what Hartenstein told me. I wanted to know what sort of a madman—there are various kinds of madmen, all of whom must be handled differently—but all Hartenstein would tell me was that he had unrealistic beliefs about the state of affairs in Europe."

"Ha! What diplomat hasn't?" I asked.

Old Keitel gave a laugh, somewhere between the bark of a dog and the croaking of a raven.

"Yes, naturally! The unrealistic beliefs of diplomats are what soldiers die of," he said. "I said as much to Hartenstein, but he wouldn't tell me anything more. He seemed to regret having said even that much. He looked like a man who's seen a particularly terrifying ghost." The old man puffed hard at his famous pipe for a while, blowing smoke up through his mustache. "Rudi, Hartenstein has pulled a hot potato out of the ashes, this time, and he wants to toss it to your uncle, before he burns his fingers. I think that's one reason why he got me to furnish an escort for his Englishman. Now, look; you must take this unrealistic diplomat, or this undiplomatic madman, or whatever in blazes he is, in to Berlin. And understand this." He pointed his pipe at me as though it were a pistol. "Your orders are to take him there and turn him over at the Ministry of Police. Nothing has been said about whether you turn him over alive, or dead, or half one and half the other. I know nothing about this business, and want to know nothing; if Hartenstein wants us to play gaol warders for him, then, *bei Gott,* he must be satisfied with our way of doing it!"

Well, to cut short the story, I looked at the coach Hartenstein had placed at my disposal, and I decided to chain the left door shut on the outside, so that it couldn't be opened from within. Then, I would put my prisoner on my left, so that the only way out would be past me. I decided not to carry any weapons which he might be able to snatch from me, so I took off my saber and locked it in the seat box, along with the dispatch case containing the Englishman's papers. It was cold enough to wear a greatcoat in comfort, so I wore mine, and in the right side pocket, where my prisoner couldn't reach, I put a little leaded bludgeon, and also a brace of pocket pistols. Hartenstein was going to furnish me a guard as well as a driver, but I said that I would take a servant who could act as guard. The servant, of course, was my orderly, old Johann; I gave him my double hunting gun to carry, with a big charge of boar shot in one barrel and an ounce ball in the other.

In addition, I armed myself with a big bottle of cognac. I thought that if I could shoot my prisoner often enough with that, he would give me no trouble.

As it happened, he didn't, and none of my precautions—except the cognac—were needed. The man didn't look like a lunatic to me. He was a rather stout gentleman, of past middle age, with a ruddy complexion and an intelligent face. The only unusual thing about him was his hat, which was a peculiar contraption, looking like the pot out of a close-stool. I put him in the carriage, and then offered him a drink out of my bottle, taking one about half as big myself. He smacked his lips over it and said, "Well, that's real brandy; whatever we think of their detestable politics, we can't criticize the French for their liquor." Then, he said, "I'm glad they're sending me in the custody of a military gentleman, instead of a confounded gendarme. Tell me the truth, Lieutenant; am I under arrest for anything?"

"Why," I said, "Captain Hartenstein should have told you about that. All I know is that I have orders to take you to the Ministry of Police, in Berlin, and not to let you escape on the way. These orders I will carry out; I hope you don't hold that against me."

He assured me that he did not, and we had another drink on it—I made sure, again, that he got twice as much as I did—and then the coachman cracked his whip and we were off for Berlin.

Now, I thought, I am going to see just what sort of a madman this is, and why Hartenstein is making a state affair out of a squabble at an inn. So I decided to explore his unrealistic beliefs about the state of affairs in Europe.

After guiding the conversation to where I wanted it, I asked him: "What, *Herr* Bathurst, in your belief, is the real, underlying cause of the present tragic situation in Europe?"

That, I thought, was safe enough. Name me one year, since the days of Julius Caesar, when the situation in Europe hasn't been tragic! And it worked, to perfection.

"In my belief," says this Englishman, "the whole damnable mess is the result of the victory of the rebellious colonists in North America, and their blasted republic."

Well, you can imagine, that gave me a start. All the world knows that the American Patriots lost their war for independence from England; that their army was shattered, that their leaders were either killed or driven into exile. How many times, when I was a little boy, did I not sit up long past my bedtime, when old Baron von Steuben was a guest at Tarlburg-Schloss, listening openmouthed and wide-eyed to his stories of that gallant lost struggle! How I used to shiver at his tales of the terrible winter camp, or thrill at the battles, or weep as he told how he held the dying Washington in his arms, and listened to his noble last words, at the Battle of Doylestown! And here, this man was telling me that the Patriots had really won, and set up the republic for which they had fought! I had been prepared for some of what Hartenstein had called unrealistic beliefs, but nothing as fantastic as this.

"I can cut it even finer than that," Bathurst continued. "It was the defeat of Burgoyne at Saratoga. We made a good bargain when we got Benedict Arnold to turn his coat, but we didn't do it soon enough. If he hadn't been on the field that day, Burgoyne would have gone through Gates's army like a hot knife through butter."

But Arnold hadn't been at Saratoga. I know; I have read much of the American war. Arnold was shot dead on New Year's Day of 1776, during the attempted storming of Quebec. And Burgoyne had done just as Bathurst had said; he had gone through Gates like a knife, and down the Hudson to join Howe.

"But, *Herr* Bathurst," I asked, "how could that affect the situation in Europe? America is thousands of miles away, across the ocean."

"Ideas can cross oceans quicker than armies. When Louis XVI decided to come to the aid of the Americans, he doomed himself and his regime. A successful resistance to royal authority in America was all the French Republicans needed to inspire them. Of course, we have Louis' own weakness to blame, too. If he'd given those rascals a whiff of grapeshot, when the mob tried to storm Versailles in 1790, there'd have been no French Revolution."

But he had. When Louis XVI ordered the howitzers turned on the mob at Versailles, and then sent the dragoons to ride down the survivors, the Republican movement had been broken. That had been when Cardinal Talleyrand, who had then been merely Bishop of Autun, had come to the fore and become the power that he is today in France; the greatest King's Minister since Richelieu.

"And, after that, Louis' death followed as surely as night after day," Bathurst was saying. "And because the French had no experience in self-government, their republic was foredoomed. If Bonaparte hadn't seized power, somebody else would have; when the French murdered their King, they delivered themselves to dictatorship. And a dictator, unsupported by the prestige of royalty, has no choice but to lead his people into foreign war, to keep them from turning upon him."

It was like that all the way to Berlin. All these things seem foolish, by daylight, but as I sat in the darkness of that swaying coach, I was almost convinced of the reality of what he told me. I tell you, Uncle Eugen, it was frightening, as though he were giving me a view of Hell. *Gott im Himmel,* the things that man talked of! Armies swarming over Europe; sack and massacre, and cities burning; blockades, and starvation; kings deposed, and thrones tumbling like tenpins! battles in which the soldiers of every nation fought, and in which tens of thousands were mowed down like ripe grain; and, over all, the Satanic figure of a little man in a gray coat, who dictated peace to the Austrian Emperor in Schoenbrunn, and carried the Pope away a prisoner to Savona.

Madman, eh? Unrealistic beliefs, says Hartenstein? Well, give me madmen who drool spittle, and foam at the mouth, and shriek obscene blasphemies. But not this pleasant-seeming gentleman who sat beside me and talked of horrors in a quiet, cultured voice, while he drank my cognac.

But not all my cognac! If your man at the Ministry—the one with red hair and the bulldog face—tells you that I was drunk when I brought in that Englishman, you had better believe him!

Rudi.

IX

(From Count von Berchtenwald, to the British Minister.)

28 November, 1809

Honored Sir:

The accompanying *dossier* will acquaint you with the problem confronting this Chancellery, without needless repetition on my part. Please to understand that it is not, and never was, any part of the intentions of the Government of His Majesty Friedrich Wilhelm III to offer any injury or indignity to the Government of His Britannic Majesty George III. We would never contemplate holding in arrest the person, or tampering with the papers, of an accredited envoy of your Government. However, we have the gravest doubt, to make a considerable understatement, that this person who calls himself Benjamin Bathurst is any such envoy, and we do not think that it would be any service to the Government of His Britannic Majesty to allow an impostor to travel about Europe in the guise of a British diplomatic representative. We certainly should not thank the Government of His Britannic Majesty for failing to take steps to deal with some person who, in England, might falsely represent himself to be a Prussian diplomat.

This affair touches us almost as closely as it does your own Government; this man had in his possession a letter of safe-conduct, which you will find in the accompanying dispatch case. It is of the regular form, as issued by this Chancellery, and is sealed with the Chancellery seal, or with a very exact counterfeit of it. However, it has been signed, as Chancellor of Prussia, with a signature indistinguishable from that of the Baron vom und zum Stein, who is the present Prussian Minister of Agriculture. Baron Stein was shown the signature, with the rest of the letter covered, and without hesitation acknowledged it for his own writing. However, when the letter was uncovered and shown to him, his surprise and horror were such as would require the pen of a Goethe or a Schiller to describe, and he denied categorically ever having seen the document before.

I have no choice but to believe him. It is impossible to think that a man of Baron Stein's honorable and serious character would be party to the fabrication of a paper of this sort. Even aside from this, I am in the thing as deeply as he; if it is signed with his signature, it is also sealed with my seal, which has not been out of my personal keeping in the ten years that I have been Chancellor here. In fact, the word "impossible" can be used to describe the entire business. It was impossible for the man Benjamin Bathurst to have entered the inn yard–yet he did. It was impossible that he should carry papers of the sort found in his dispatch case, or that such papers should exist–yet I am sending them to you with this letter. It is impossible that Baron vom und zum Stein should sign a paper of the sort he did, or that it should be sealed by the Chancellery–yet it bears both Stein's signature and my seal.

You will also find in the dispatch case other credentials ostensibly originating with the British Foreign Office, of the same character, being signed by persons having no connection with the Foreign Office, or even with the Government, but being sealed with apparently authentic seals. If you send these papers to London, I fancy you will find that they will there create the same situation as that caused here by this letter of safe-conduct.

I am also sending you a charcoal sketch of the person who calls himself Benjamin Bathurst. This portrait was taken without its subject's knowledge. Baron von Krutz's nephew, Lieutenant von Tarlburg, who is the son of our mutual friend Count von Tarlburg, has a *little friend,* a very clever young lady who is, as you will see, an expert at this sort of work; she was introduced into a room at the Ministry of Police and placed behind a screen, where she could sketch our prisoner's face. If you should send this picture to London, I think that there is a good chance that it might be recognized. I can vouch that it is an excellent likeness.

To tell the truth, we are at our wits' end about this affair. I can not understand how such excellent imitations of these various seals could be made, and the signature of the Baron vom und zum Stein is the most expert forgery that I have ever seen, in thirty years' experience as a statesman. This would indicate careful and painstaking work on the part of somebody; how, then, do we reconcile this with such clumsy mistakes, recognizable as such by any schoolboy, as signing the name of Baron Stein as Prussian Chancellor, or Mr. George Canning, who is a member of the opposition party and not connected with your Government, as British Foreign Secretary?

These are mistakes which only a madman would make. There are those who think our prisoner is a madman, because of his apparent delusions about the great conqueror, General Bonaparte, *alias* the Emperor Napoleon. Madmen have been known to fabricate evidence to support their delusions, it is true, but I shudder to think of a madman having at his disposal the resources to manufacture the papers you will find in this dispatch case. Moreover, some of our foremost medical men, who have specialized in the disorders of the mind, have interviewed this man Bathurst and say that, save for his fixed belief in a nonexistent situation, he is perfectly rational.

Personally, I believe that the whole thing is a gigantic hoax, perpetrated for some hidden and sinister purpose, possibly to create confusion, and undermine the confidence existing between your Government and mine, and to set against one another various persons connected with both Governments, or else as a mask for some other conspiratorial activity. Without specifying any Sovereigns or Governments who might wish to do this, I can think of two groups, namely, the Jesuits, and the outlawed French Republicans, either of whom might conceive such a situation to be to their advantage. Only a few months ago, you will recall, there was a Jacobin plot unmasked at Koln.

But, whatever this business may portend, I do not like it. I want to get to the bottom of it as soon as possible, and I will thank you, my dear Sir, and your Government, for any assistance you may find possible.

I have the honor, sir, to be, etc., etc., etc.,

Berchtenwald

X

FROM BARON VON KRUTZ, TO THE COUNT VON BERCHTENWALD. MOST URGENT; MOST IMPORTANT.
TO BE DELIVERED IMMEDIATELY AND IN PERSON, REGARDLESS OF CIRCUMSTANCES.

28 November, 1809

Count von Berchtenwald:

Within the past half hour, that is, at about eleven o'clock tonight, the man calling himself Benjamin Bathurst was shot and killed by a sentry at the Ministry of Police, while attempting to escape from custody.

A sentry on duty in the rear courtyard of the Ministry observed a man attempting to leave the building in a suspicious and furtive manner. This sentry, who was under the strictest orders to allow no one to enter or leave without written authorization, challenged him; when he attempted to run, the sentry fired his musket at him, bringing him down. At the shot, the Sergeant of the Guard rushed into the courtyard with his detail, and the man whom the sentry had shot was found to be the Englishman, Benjamin Bathurst. He had been hit in the chest with an ounce ball, and died before the doctor could arrive, and without recovering consciousness.

An investigation revealed that the prisoner, who was confined on the third floor of the building, had fashioned a rope from his bedding, his bed cord, and the leather strap of his bell pull; this rope was only long enough to reach to the window of the office on the second floor, directly below, but he managed to enter this by kicking the glass out of the window. I am trying to find out how he could do this without being heard; I can assure Your Excellency that somebody is going to smart for this night's work. As for the sentry, he acted within his orders; I have commended him for doing his duty, and for good shooting, and I assume full responsibility for the death of the prisoner at his hands.

I have no idea why the self-so-called Benjamin Bathurst, who, until now, was well behaved and seemed to take his confinement philosophically, should suddenly make this rash and fatal attempt, unless it was because of those infernal dunderheads of madhouse doctors who have been bothering him. Only this afternoon, Your Excellency, they deliberately handed him a bundle of newspapers—Prussian, Austrian, French, and English—all dated within the last month. They wanted, they said, to see how he would react. Well, God pardon them, they've found out!

What does Your Excellency think should be done about giving the body burial?

Krutz

(From the British Minister, to the Count von Berchtenwald.)

December 20th, 1809

My Dear Count von Berchtenwald:

Reply from London to my letter of the 28th *ult.*, which accompanied the dispatch case and the other papers, has finally come to hand. The papers which you wanted returned—the copies of the statements taken at Perleburg, the letter to the Baron von Krutz from the police captain, Hartenstein, and the personal letter of Krutz's nephew, Lieutenant von Tarlburg, and the letter of safe-conduct found in the dispatch case—accompany herewith. I don't know what the people at Whitehall did with the other papers; tossed them into the nearest fire, for my guess. Were I in Your Excellency's place, that's where the papers I am returning would go.

I have heard nothing, yet, from my dispatch of the 29th *ult.* concerning the death of the man who called himself Benjamin Bathurst, but I doubt very much if any official notice will ever be taken of it. Your Government had a perfect right to detain the fellow, and, that being the case, he attempted to escape at his own risk. After all, sentries are not required to carry loaded muskets in order to discourage them from putting their hands in their pockets.

To hazard a purely unofficial opinion, I should not imagine that London is very much dissatisfied with this *dénouement*. His Majesty's Government are a hard-headed and matter-of-fact set of gentry who do not relish mysteries, least of all mysteries whose solution may be more disturbing than the original problem.

This is entirely confidential, Your Excellency, but those papers which were in that dispatch case kicked up the devil's own row in London, with half the Government bigwigs protesting their innocence to high Heaven, and the rest accusing one another of complicity in the hoax. If that was somebody's intention, it was literally a howling success. For a while, it was even feared that there would be Questions in Parliament, but eventually, the whole vexatious business was hushed.

You may tell Count Tarlburg's son that his little friend is a most talented young lady; her sketch was highly commended by no less an authority than Sir Thomas Lawrence, and here, Your Excellency, comes the most bedeviling part of a thoroughly bedeviled business. The picture was instantly recognized. It is a very fair likeness of Benjamin Bathurst, or, I should say, Sir Benjamin Bathurst, who is King's Lieutenant-Governor for the Crown Colony of Georgia. As Sir Thomas Lawrence did his portrait a few years back, he is in an excellent position to criticize the work of Lieutenant von Tarlburg's young lady. However, Sir Benjamin Bathurst was known to have been in Savannah, attending to the duties of his office, and in the public eye, all the while that his double was in Prussia. Sir Benjamin does not have a twin brother. It has been suggested that this fellow might be a half-brother, born on the wrong side of the blanket, but, as far as I know, there is no justification for this theory.

The General Bonaparte, *alias* the Emperor Napoleon, who is given so much mention in the dispatches, seems also to have a counterpart in actual life; there is, in the French army, a Colonel of Artillery by that name, a Corsican who Gallicized his original name of Napolione Buonaparte. He is a most brilliant military theoretician; I am sure some of your own officers, like General Scharnhorst, could tell you about him. His loyalty to the French Monarchy has never been questioned.

This same correspondence to fact seems to crop up everywhere in that amazing collection of pseudo-dispatches and pseudo-state-papers. The United States of America, you will recall, was the style by which the rebellious colonies referred to themselves, in the Declaration of Philadelphia. The James Madison who is mentioned as the current President of the United States is now living, in exile, in Switzerland. His alleged predecessor in office, Thomas Jefferson, was the author of the rebel Declaration; after the defeat of the rebels, he escaped to Havana, and died, several years ago, in the Principality of Lichtenstein.

I was quite amused to find our old friend Cardinal Talleyrand—without the ecclesiastical title—cast in the role of chief adviser to the usurper, Bonaparte. His Eminence, I have always thought, is the sort of fellow who would land on his feet on top of any heap, and who would as little scruple to be Prime Minister to His Satanic Majesty as to His Most Christian Majesty.

I was baffled, however, by one name, frequently mentioned in those fantastic papers. This was the English General, Wellington. I haven't the least idea who this person might be.

I have the honor, Your Excellency, etc., etc., etc.,

Sir Arthur Wellesley

RUMP-TITTY-TITTY-TUM-TAH-TEE

by Fritz Leiber

ONCE UPON a time, when just for an instant all the molecules in the world and in the collective unconscious mind got very slippery, so that just for an instant something could pop through from the past or the future or other places, six very important intellectual people were gathered together in the studio of Simon Grue, the accidental painter.

There was Tally B. Washington, the jazz drummer. He was beating softly on a gray hollow African log and thinking of a composition he would entitle "Duet for Water Hammer and Whistling Faucet."

There were Lafcadio Smits, the interior decorator, and Lester Phlegius, the industrial designer. They were talking very intellectually together, but underneath they were wishing very hard that they had, respectively, a really catchy design for modernistic wallpaper and a really new motif for industrial advertising.

There were Gorius James McIntosh, the clinical psychologist, and Norman Saylor, the cultural anthropologist. Gorius James McIntosh was drinking whiskey and wishing there were a psychological test that would open up patients a lot wider than the Rorschach or the TAT, while Norman Saylor was smoking a pipe but not thinking or drinking anything especially.

It was a very long, very wide, very tall studio. It had to be, so there would be room on the floor to spread flat one of Simon Grue's canvases, which were always big enough to dominate any exhibition with yards to spare, and room under the ceiling for a very tall, very strong scaffold.

The present canvas hadn't a bit of paint on it, not a spot or a smudge or a smear, except for the bone-white ground. On top of the scaffold were Simon Grue and twenty-seven big pots of paint and nine clean brushes, each eight inches wide. Simon Grue was about to have a new accident—a semi-controlled accident, if you please. Any minute now he'd plunge a brush in one of the cans of paint and raise it over his right shoulder and bring it forward and down with a great loose-wristed snap, as if he were cracking a bull-whip, and a great fissioning gob of paint would go *splaaAAT* on the canvas in a random, chance, arbitrary, spontaneous and therefore quintuply accidental pattern which would constitute the core of the composition and determine the form and rhythm for many, many subsequent splatters and maybe even a few contact brush strokes and impulsive smearings.

As the rhythm of Simon Grue's bouncy footsteps quickened, Norman Saylor glanced up, though not apprehensively. True, Simon had been known to splatter his friends as well as his canvases, but in anticipation of this Norman was wearing a faded shirt, old sneakers and the frayed tweed suit he'd sported as assistant instructor, while his fishing hat was within easy reach. He and his armchair were crowded close to a wall, as were the other four intellectuals. This canvas was an especially large one, even for Simon.

As for Simon, pacing back and forth atop his scaffold, he was experiencing the glorious intoxication and expansion of vision known only to an accidental painter in the great tradition of Wassily Kandinsky, Robert Motherwell and Jackson Pollock, when he is springily based a good twenty feet above a spotless, perfectly prepared canvas. At moments like this Simon was especially grateful for these weekly gatherings. Having his five especial friends on hand helped create the right intellectual milieu. He listened happily to the hollow rhythmic thrum of Tally's drumming, the multisyllabic rippling of Lester's and Lafcadio's conversation, the gurgle of Gorius' whiskey bottle, and happily watched the mystic curls of Norman's pipe smoke. His entire being, emotions as well as mind, was a blank tablet, ready for the kiss of the universe.

Meanwhile the instant was coming closer and closer when all the molecules in the world and in the collective unconscious mind would get very slippery.

Tally B. Washington, beating on his African log, had a feeling of oppression and anticipation, almost (but not quite) a feeling of apprehension. One of Tally's ancestors, seven generations back, had been a Dahomey witch doctor, which is the African equivalent of an intellectual with artistic and psychiatric leanings. According to a very private family tradition, half joking, half serious, this five-greats-grandfather of Tally had discovered a Jumbo Magic which could "lay holt" of the whole world and bring it under its spell, but he had perished before he could try the magic or transmit it to his sons. Tally himself was altogether skeptical about the Jumbo Magic, but he couldn't help wondering about it wistfully from time to time, especially when he was beating on his African log and hunting for a new rhythm. The wistful feeling came to him right now, building on the feeling of oppression and anticipation, and his mind became a tablet blank as Simon's.

The slippery instant arrived.

Simon seized a brush and plunged it deep in the pot of black paint. Usually he used black for a final splatter if he used it at all, but this time he had the impulse to reverse himself.

Of a sudden Tally's wrists lifted high, hands dangling loosely, almost like a marionette's. There was a dramatic pause. Then his hands came down and beat out a phrase on the log, loudly and with great authority.

*Rump-titty-titty-tum-*TAH*-tee!*

Simon's wrist snapped and the middle air was full of free-falling paint which hit the canvas in a fast series of *splaaAATs* which was an exact copy of Tally's phrase.

*Rump-titty-titty-tum-*TAH*-tee!*

Intrigued by the identity of the two sounds, and with their back hairs lifting a little for the same reason, the five intellectuals around the wall rose and stared, while Simon looked down from his scaffold like God after the first stroke of creation.

The big black splatter on the bone-white ground was itself an exact copy of Tally's phrase, sound made sight, music transposed into visual pattern. First there was a big roundish blot—that was the *rump*. Then two rather delicate, many-tongued splatters—those were the *titties*. Next a small *rump,* which was the *tum*. Following that a big blot like a bent spearhead, not so big as the *rump* but even more emphatic—the TAH. Last of all an indescribably curled and broken little splatter which somehow seemed exactly right for the *tee*.

The whole big splatter was as like the drummed phrase as an identical twin reared in a different environment and as fascinating as a primeval symbol found next to bison paintings in a Cro-Magnon cave. The six intellectuals could hardly stop looking at it and when they did, it was to do things in connection with it, while their minds were happily a-twitter with all sorts of exciting new projects.

There was no thought of Simon doing any more splattering on

the new painting until this first amazing accidental achievement had been digested and pondered.

Simon's wide-angle camera was brought into play on the scaffold and negatives were immediately developed and prints made in the darkroom adjoining the studio. Each of Simon's friends carried at least one print when he left. They smiled at each other like men who share a mysterious but powerful secret. More than one of them drew his print from under his coat on the way home and hungrily studied it.

At the gathering next week there was much to tell. Tally had introduced the phrase at a private jam session and on his live jazz broadcast. The jam session had improvised on and developed the phrase for two solid hours and the musicians had squeaked with delight when Tally finally showed them the photograph of what they had been playing, while the response from the broadcast had won Tally a new sponsor with a fat pocketbook.

Gorius McIntosh had got phenomenal results from using the splatter as a Rorschach ink blot. His star patient had seen her imagined incestuous baby in it and spilled more in one session than in the previous hundred and forty. Stubborn blocks in two other analyses had been gloriously broken, while three catatonics at the state mental hospital had got up and danced.

Lester Phlegius rather hesitantly described how he was using "something like the splatter, really not too similar" (he said) as an attention-getter in a forthcoming series of Industrial-Design-for-Living advertisements.

Lafcadio Smits, who had an even longer and more flagrant history of stealing designs from Simon, brazenly announced that he had reproduced the splatter as a silk-screen pattern on linen. The pattern was already selling like hotcakes at five arty gift shops, while at this very moment three girls were sweating in Lafcadio's loft turning out more. He braced himself for a blast from Simon, mentally rehearsing the attractive deal he was prepared to offer, one depending on percentages of percentages, but the accidental painter was strangely abstracted. He seemed to have something weighing on his mind.

The new painting hadn't progressed any further than the first splatter.

Norman Saylor quizzed him about it semi-privately.

"I've developed a sort of artist's block," Simon confessed to him with relief. "Whenever I pick up a brush I get afraid of spoiling that first tremendous effect and I don't go on." He paused. "Another thing—I put down papers and tried some small test-splatters. They all looked almost exactly like the big one. Seems my wrist won't give out with anything else." He laughed nervously. "How are you cashing in on the thing, Norm?"

The anthropologist shook his head. "Just studying it, trying to place it in the continuum of primitive signs and universal dream symbols. It goes very deep. But about this block and this . . . er . . . fancied limitation of yours—I'd just climb up there tomorrow morning and splatter away. The big one's been photographed, you can't lose that."

Simon nodded doubtfully and then looked down at his wrist and quickly grabbed it with his other hand, to still it. It had been twitching in a familiar rhythm.

If the tone of the gathering after the first week was enthusiastic, that after the second was euphoric. Tally's new drummed theme had given rise to a musical fad christened Drum 'n' Drag which promised to rival Rock 'n' Roll, while the drummer himself was in two days to appear as a guest artist on a network TV program. The only worry was that no new themes had appeared. All the Drum 'n' Drag pieces were based on duplications or at most developments of the original drummed phrase. Tally also mentioned with an odd reluctance that a few rabid cats had taken to greeting each other with a four-handed patty-cake that beat out *rump-titty-titty-tum-*TAH*-tee.*

Gorius McIntosh was causing a stir in psychiatric circles with his amazing successes in opening up recalcitrant cases, many of them hitherto thought fit for nothing but eventual lobotomy. Colleagues with M.D.s quit emphasizing the lowly "Mister" in his name, while several spontaneously addressed him as "Doctor" as they begged him for copies of the McSPAT (McIntosh's Splatter Pattern Apperception Test). His name had been mentioned in connection with the assistant directorship of the clinic where he was a humble psychologist. He also told how some of the state patients had taken to pommeling each other playfully while happily spouting some gibberish variant of the original phrase, such as "*Bump-biddy-biddy-bum-*BAH*-bee!*" The resemblance in behavior to Tally's hepcats was noted and remarked on by the six intellectuals.

The first of Lester Phlegius' attention-getters (identical with the splatter, of course) had appeared and attracted the most favorable notice, meaning chiefly that his customer's front office had received at least a dozen curious phone calls from the directors and presidents of cognate firms. Lafcadio Smits reported that he had rented a second loft, was branching out into dress materials, silk neckties, lampshades and wallpaper, and was deep in royalty deals with several big manufacturers. Once again Simon Grue surprised him by not screaming robbery and demanding details and large simple percentages. The accidental painter seemed even more unhappily abstracted than the week before.

When he ushered them from his living quarters into the studio they understood why.

It was as if the original big splatter had whelped. Surrounding and overlaying it were scores of smaller splatters. They were all colors of a well-chosen artist's spectrum, blending with each other and pointing each other up superbly. But each and every one of them was a perfect copy, reduced to one half or less, of the original big splatter.

Lafcadio Smits wouldn't believe at first that Simon had done them free-wrist from the scaffold. Even when Simon showed him details proving they couldn't have been stenciled, Lafcadio was still unwilling to believe, for he was deeply versed in methods of mass-producing the appearance of handwork and spontaneity.

But when Simon wearily climbed the scaffold and, hardly looking at what he was doing, flipped down a few splatters exactly like the rest, even Lafcadio had to admit that something miraculous and frightening had happened to Simon's wrist.

Gorius James McIntosh shook his head and muttered a remark about "stereotyped compulsive behavior at the artistic-creative level. Never heard of it getting *that* stereotyped, though."

Later during the gathering, Norman Saylor again consulted with Simon and also had a long confidential talk with Tally B. Washington, during which he coaxed out of the drummer the whole story of his five-greats-grandfather. When questioned about his own researches, the cultural anthropologist would merely say that they were "progressing." He did, however, have one piece of concrete advice, which he delivered to all the five others just before the gathering broke up.

"This splatter does have an obsessive quality, just as Gory said. It has that maddening feeling of incompleteness which cries for repetition. It would be a good thing if each of us, whenever he feels the thing getting too strong a hold on him, would instantly shift to some engrossing activity which has as little as possible to do with arbitrarily ordered sight and sound. Play chess or smell perfumes or eat candy or look at the moon through a telescope, or stare at a point of light in the dark and try to blank out your mind—something like that. Try to set up a countercompulsion. One of us might even hit on a counterformula—a specific antidote—like quinine for malaria."

If the ominous note of warning in Norman's statement didn't register on all of them just then, it did at some time during the next seven days, for the frame of mind in which the six intellectuals came to the gathering after the third week was one of paranoid grandeur and hysterical desperation.

Tally's TV appearance had been a huge success. He'd taken to the TV station a copy of the big splatter and although he hadn't intended to (he said) he'd found himself showing it to the M.C. and the unseen audience after his drum solo. The immediate response by phone, telegram and letter had been overwhelming but rather frightening, including a letter from a woman in Smallhills, Arkansas, thanking Tally for showing her "the wondrous picture of God."

Drum 'n' Drag had become a national and even international craze. The patty-cake greeting had become general among Tally's rapidly growing horde of fans and it now included a staggering slap on the shoulder to mark the TAH. (Here Gorius McIntosh took a drink from his bottle and interrupted to tell of a spontaneous, rhythmic, lockstepping procession at the state hospital with an even more violent TAH-blow. The mad march had been forcibly broken up by attendants and two of the patients treated at the infirmary for contusions.) The *New York Times* ran a dispatch from South Africa describing how police had dispersed a disorderly mob of University of Capetown students who had been chanting, "*Shlump Shliddy Shliddy Shlump* SHLAH *Shlee!*"—which the correspondents had been told was an anti-apartheid cry phrased in pig-Afrikaans.

For both the drummed phrase and the big splatter had become a part of the news, either directly or by inferences that made Simon and his friends alternately cackle and shudder. An Indiana town was fighting a juvenile phenomenon called Drum Saturday. A radio-TV columnist noted that Blotto Cards were the latest rage among studio personnel; carried in handbag or breast pocket, whence they could be quickly whipped out and stared at, the cards were claimed to be an infallible remedy against boredom or sudden attacks of anger and the blues. Reports of a penthouse burglary included among the objects listed as missing "a recently purchased spotted linen wall hanging"; the woman said she did not care about the other objects, but pleaded for the hanging's return, "as it was of great psychological comfort to my husband." Splatter-marked raincoats were a high-school fad, the splattering being done ceremoniously at Drum 'n' Drag parties. An English prelate had preached a sermon inveighing against "this deafening new American craze with its pantherine overtones of mayhem." At a press interview Salvador Dali had refused to say anything to newsmen except the cryptic sentence, "The time has come."

In a halting, hiccupy voice Gorius McIntosh reported that things were pretty hot at the clinic. Twice during the past week he had been fired and triumphantly reinstated. Rather similarly at the state hospital Bump Parties had been alternately forbidden and then encouraged, mostly on the pleas of enthusiastic psychiatric aides. Copies of the McSPAT had come into the hands of general practitioners who, ignoring its original purpose, were using it as a substitute for electroshock treatment and tranquilizing drugs. A group of progressive psychiatrists calling themselves the Young Turks were circulating a statement that the McSPAT constituted the worst threat to classical Freudian psychoanalysis since Alfred Adler, adding a grim scholarly reference to the Dancing Mania of the Middle Ages. Gorius finished his report by staring around almost frighteningly at his five friends and clutching the whiskey bottle to his bosom.

Lafcadio Smits seemed equally shaken, even when telling about the profits of his pyramiding enterprises. One of his four lofts had been burglarized and another invaded at high noon by a red-bearded Greenwich Village Satanist protesting that the splatter was an illicitly procured Taoist magic symbol of direst power. Lafcadio was also receiving anonymous threatening letters which he believed to be from a criminal drug syndicate that looked upon Blotto Cards as his creation and as competitive to heroin and lesser forms of dope. He shuddered visibly when Tally volunteered the information that his fans had taken to wearing Lafcadio's splatter-patterned ties and shirts.

Lester Phlegius said that further copies of the issue of the costly and staid industrial journal carrying his attention-getter were unprocurable and that many had vanished from private offices and wealthy homes or, more often, simply had the crucial page ripped out.

Norman Saylor's two photographs of the big splatter had been pilfered from his locked third-floor office at the university, and a huge copy of the splatter, painted in a waterproof black substance, had appeared on the bottom of the swimming pool in the girls' gymnasium.

As they continued to share their experiences, it turned out that the six intellectuals were even more disturbed at the hold the drummed phrase and the big splatter had got on them individually and at their failure to cope with the obsession by following Norman's suggestions. Playing at a Sunday-afternoon bar concert, Tally had got snagged on the phrase for fully ten minutes, like a phonograph needle caught in one groove, before he could let go. What bothered him especially was that no one in the audience had seemed to notice and he had the conviction that if something hadn't stopped him (the drum skin ruptured) they would have sat frozen there until, wrists flailing, he died of exhaustion.

Norman himself, seeking escape in chess, had checkmated his opponent in a blitz game (where each player must move without hesitation) by banging down his pieces in the *rump-titty* rhythm—and his subconscious mind had timed it, he said, so that the last move came right on the *tee;* it was a little pawn-move after a big queen-check on the TAH. Lafcadio, turning to cooking, had found himself mixing salad with a *rump-titty* flourish. (". . . and a madman to mix it, as the old Spanish recipe says," he finished with a despairing giggle.) Lester Phlegius, seeking release from the obsession in the companionship of a lady spiritualist with whom he had been carrying on a strictly Platonic love affair for ten years, found himself enlivening with the *rump-titty* rhythm the one chaste embrace they permitted themselves to each meeting. Phoebe had torn herself away and slapped him full-arm across the face. What had horrified Lester was that the impact had coincided precisely with the TAH.

Simon Grue himself, who hadn't stirred out of his apartment all week but wandered shivering from window to window in a dirty old bathrobe, had dozed in a broken armchair and had a terrifying vision. He had imagined himself in the ruins of Manhattan, chained to the broken stones (before dozing off he had wound both wrists heavily with scarves and cloths to cushion the twitching), while across the dusty jagged landscape all humanity tramped in an endless horde screeching the accursed phrase and every so often came a group of them carrying a two-story-high poster (". . . like those Soviet parades," he said) with the big splatter staring blackly down from it. His nightmare had gone on to picture the dreadful infection spreading from the Earth by spaceship to planets revolving around other stars.

As Simon finished speaking, Gorius McIntosh rose slowly from his chair, groping ahead of himself with his whiskey bottle.

"That's it!" he said from between bared clenched teeth, grinning horribly. "That's what's happening to all of us. Can't get it out of our minds. Can't get it out of our muscles. Psychosomatic bondage!" He stumbled slowly across the circle of intellectuals toward Lester, who was sitting opposite him. "It's happening to me. A patient sits down across the desk and says with his eyes dripping tears, 'Help me, Doctor McIntosh,' and I see his problems clearly and I know just how to help him and I get up and I go around the desk to him"—he was standing right over Lester now, bottle raised high above the industrial designer's shoulder—"and I lean down so that my face is close to his and then I shout RUMP-TITTY-TITTY-TUM-TAH-TEE!"

At this point Norman Saylor decided to take over, leaving to Tally and Lafcadio the restraining of Gorius, who indeed seemed quite docile and more dazed than anything else now that his seizure was spent, at least temporarily. The cultural anthropologist strode to the center of the circle, looking very reassuring with his darkly billowing pipe and his strong jaw and his smoky tweeds, though he kept his hands clasped tightly together behind him, after snatching his pipe with one of them.

"Men," he said sharply, "my research on this thing isn't finished by a long shot, but I've carried it far enough to know that we are dealing with what may be called an ultimate symbol, a symbol that is the summation of all symbols. It has everything in it—birth, death, mating, murder, divine and demonic possession, all of life, the whole lot—to such a degree that after you've looked at it, or listened to it, or *made* it, for a time, you simply don't *need* life any more."

The studio was very quiet. The five other intellectuals looked at him. Norman rocked on his heels like any normal college professor, but his arms grew perceptibly more rigid as he clasped his hands even more tightly behind his back, fighting an exquisite compulsion.

"As I say, my studies aren't finished, but there's clearly no time to carry them further—we must act on such conclusions as I have drawn from the evidence assembled to date. Here's briefly how it shapes up: We must assume that mankind possesses an actual collective unconscious mind stretching thousands of years into the past and, for all I know, into the future. This collective unconscious mind may be pictured as a great dark space across which radio messages can sometimes pass with difficulty. We must also assume that the drummed phrase and with it the big splatter came to us by this inner radio from an individual living over a century in the past. We have good reason to believe that this individual is, or was, a direct male ancestor, in the seventh generation back, of Tally here. He was a witch doctor. He was acutely hungry for power. In fact, he spent his life seeking an incantation that would put a spell on the whole world. It appears that he found the incantation at the end, but died too soon to be able to use it—without ever being able to embody it in sound or sign. Think of his frustration!"

"Norm's right," Tally said, nodding somberly. "He was a mighty mean man, I'm told, and mighty persistent."

Norman's nod was quicker and also a plea for undivided attention. Beads of sweat were dripping down his forehead. "The thing came to us when it did—came to Tally specifically and through him to Simon—because our six minds, reinforcing each other powerfully, were momentarily open to receive transmissions through the collective unconscious, and because there is—was—this sender at the other end long desirous of getting his message through to one of his descendants. We cannot say precisely where this sender is—a scientifically oriented person might say that he is in a shadowed portion of the space-time continuum while a religiously oriented person might aver that he is in Heaven or Hell."

"I'd plump for the last-mentioned," Tally volunteered. "He was that kind of man."

"Please, Tally," Norman said. "Wherever he is, we must operate on the hope that there is a counterformula or negative symbol—yang to this yin—which he wants, or wanted, to transmit too—something that will stop this flood of madness we have loosed on the world."

"That's where I must differ with you, Norm," Tally broke in, shaking his head more somberly than he had nodded it. "If Old Five-Greats ever managed to start something bad, he'd never want to stop it, especially if he knew how. I tell you he was mighty mighty mean and—"

"Please, Tally! Your ancestor's character may have changed with his new environment, there may be greater forces at work on him—in any case, our only hope is that he possesses and will transmit to us the counterformula. To achieve that, we must try to recreate, by artificial means, the conditions that obtained in this studio at the time of the first transmission."

A look of acute pain crossed his face. He unclasped his hands and brought them in front of him. His pipe fell to the floor. He looked at the large blister the hot bowl had raised in one palm. Then, clasping his hands together in front of him, palm to palm, with a twisting motion that made Lafcadio wince, he continued rapping out the words.

"Men, we must act at once, using only such materials as can be rapidly assembled. Each of you must trust me implicitly. Tally, I know you don't use it any more, but can you still get weed, the genuine crushed leaf? Good, we may need enough for two or three dozen sticks. Gory, I want you to fetch the self-hypnotism rigmarole that's so effective–no, I don't trust your memory and we may need copies. Lester, if you're quite through satisfying yourself that Gory didn't break your collarbone with his bottle, you go with Gory and see that he drinks lots of coffee. On your way back buy several bunches of garlic, a couple of rolls of dimes, and a dozen red railway flares. Oh yes, and call up your mediumistic lady and do your damnedest to get her to join us here–her talents may prove invaluable. Laf, tear off to your home loft and get the luminous paint and the black velvet hangings you and your red-bearded ex-friend used–yes, I know about that association!–when you and he were dabbling with black magic. Simon and I will hold down the studio. All right, then–" A spasm crossed his face and the veins in his forehead and cords in his neck bulged and his arms were jerking with the struggle he was waging against the compulsion that threatened to overpower him. "All right, then–*Rump-titty-titty-tum*-GET-MOVING!"

An hour later the studio smelled like a fire in a eucalyptus grove. Such light from outside as got past the cabalistically figured hangings covering windows and skylight revealed the shadowy forms of Simon, atop the scaffold, and the other five intellectuals, crouched against the wall, all puffing their reefers, sipping the sour smoke industriously. Their marijuana-blanked minds were still reverberating to the last compelling words of Gory's rigmarole, read by Lester Phlegius in a sonorous bass.

Phoebe Saltonstall, who had refused reefers with a simple, "No thank you, I always carry my own peyote," had one wall all to herself. Eyes closed, she was lying along it on three small cushions, her pleated Grecian robe white as a winding sheet.

Round all four walls waist-high went a dimly luminous line with six obtuse angles in it besides the four corners; Norman said that made it the topological equivalent of a magician's pentalpha or pentagram. Barely visible were the bunches of garlic nailed to each door and the tiny silver disks scattered in front of them.

Norman flicked his lighter and the little blue flame added itself to the six glowing red points of the reefers. In a cracked voice he cried, "The time approaches!" and he shambled about rapidly setting fire to the twelve railway flares spiked into the floor through the big canvas.

In the hellish red glow they looked at each other like so many devils. Phoebe moaned and tossed. Simon coughed once as the dense clouds of smoke billowed up around the scaffold and filled the ceiling.

Norman Saylor cried, *"This is it!"*

Phoebe screamed thinly and arched her back as if in electroshock.

A look of sudden agonized amazement came into the face of Taliaferro Booker Washington, as if he'd been jabbed from below with a pin or hot poker. He lifted his hands with great authority and beat out a short phrase on his gray African log.

A hand holding a brightly freighted eight-inch brush whipped out of the hellish smoke clouds above and sent down a great fissioning gout of paint that landed on the canvas with a sound that was an exact visual copy of Tally's short drummed phrase.

Immediately the studio became a hive of purposeful activity. Heavily gloved hands jerked out the railway flares and plunged them into strategically located buckets of water. The hangings were ripped down and the windows thrown open. Two electric fans were turned on. Simon, half fainting, slipped down the last feet of the ladder, was rushed to a window and lay across it gasping. Somewhat more carefully Phoebe Saltonstall was carried to a second window and laid in front of it. Gory checked her pulse and gave a reassuring nod.

Then the five intellectuals gathered around the big canvas and stared. After a while Simon joined them.

The new splatter, in Chinese red, was entirely different from the many ones under it and it was an identical twin of the new drummed phrase.

After a while the six intellectuals went about the business of photographing it. They worked systematically but rather listlessly. When their eyes chanced to move to the canvas they didn't even seem to see what was there. Nor did they bother to glance at the black-on-white prints (with the background of the last splatter touched out) as they shoved them under their coats.

Just then there was a rustle of draperies by one of the open windows. Phoebe Saltonstall, long forgotten, was sitting up. She looked around her with some distaste.

"Take me home, Lester," she said faintly but precisely.

Tally, halfway through the door, stopped. "You know," he said puzzledly, "I still can't believe that Old Five-Greats had the public spirit to do what he did. I wonder if she found out what it was that made him—"

Norman put his hand on Tally's arm and laid a finger of the other on his own lips. They went out together, followed by Lafcadio,

Gorius, Lester and Phoebe. Like Simon, all five men had the look of drunkards in a benign convalescent stupor, and probably dosed with paraldehyde, after a bout of DT's.

The same effect was apparent as the new splatter and drummed phrase branched out across the world, chasing and eventually overtaking the first one. Any person who saw or heard it proceeded to repeat it once (make it, show it, wear it, if it were that sort of thing, in any case pass it on) and then forget it—and at the same time forget the first drummed phrase and splatter. All sense of compulsion or obsession vanished utterly.

Drum 'n' Drag died a-borning. Blotto Cards vanished from handbags and pockets, the McSPATs I and II from doctors' offices and psychiatric clinics. Bump Parties no longer plagued and enlivened mental hospitals. Catatonics froze again. The Young Turks went back to denouncing tranquilizing drugs. A fad of green-and-purple barberpole stripes covered up splatter marks on raincoats. Satanists and drug syndicates presumably continued their activities unhampered except by God and the Treasury Department. Capetown had such peace as it deserved. Spotted shirts, neckties, dresses, lampshades, wallpaper, and linen wall hangings all became intensely passé. Drum Saturday was never heard of again. Lester Phlegius' second attention-getter got none.

Simon's big painting was eventually hung at one exhibition, but it got little attention even from critics, except for a few heavy sentences along the lines of "Simon Grue's latest elephantine effort fell with a thud as dull as those of the gobs of paint that in falling composed it." Visitors to the gallery seemed able only to give it one dazed look and then pass it by, as is not infrequently the case with modern paintings.

The reason for this was clear. On top of all the other identical splatters it carried one in Chinese red that was a negation of all symbols, a symbol that had nothing in it—the new splatter that was the identical twin of the new drummed phrase that was the negation and completion of the first, the phrase that had vibrated out from Tally's log through the red glare and come slapping down out of Simon's smoke cloud, the phrase that stilled and ended everything (and which obviously can only be stated here once): "Tah-*titty-titty-tee*-toe!"

The six intellectual people continued their weekly meetings almost as if nothing had happened, except that Simon substituted for splatter work a method of applying the paint by handfuls with the eyes closed, later treading it in by foot. He sometimes asked his friends to join him in these impromptu marches, providing wooden shoes imported from Holland for the purpose.

One afternoon, several months later, Lester Phlegius brought a guest with him—Phoebe Saltonstall.

"Miss Saltonstall has been on a round-the-world cruise," he explained. "Her psyche was dangerously depleted by her experience in this apartment, she tells me, and a complete change was indicated. Happily now she's entirely recovered."

"Indeed I am," she said, answering their solicitous inquiries with a bright smile.

"By the way," Norman said, "at the time your psyche was depleted here, did you receive any message from Tally's ancestor?"

"Indeed I did," she said.

"Well, what did Old Five-Greats have to say?" Tally asked eagerly. "Whatever it was, I bet he was pretty crude about it!"

"Indeed he was," she said, blushing prettily. "So crude, in fact, that I wouldn't dare attempt to convey that aspect of his message. For that matter, I am sure that it was the utter fiendishness of his anger and the unspeakable visions in which his anger was clothed that so reduced my psyche." She paused.

"I don't know where he was sending from," she said thoughtfully. "I had the impression of a warm place, an intensely warm place, though of course I may have been reacting to the railway flares." Her frown cleared. "The actual message was short and simple enough:

" 'Dear Descendant, They *made* me stop it. It was beginning to catch on *down here.*' "

SEA WRACK

by Edward Jesby

GRETA HIJUKAWA-ROSEN sat on the beach watching her escort maneuver a compression hover board above the waters of the Mediterranean. He stood on the small round platform, balancing it a few inches above the spilling tops of the wind-driven waves with small movements of his legs. The board operated on the power sent to it from the antennae above the chateau, but he operated on his own.

"Viterrible," Greta thought, stretching to lift the underside of her small breasts to the full heat of the sun. She giggled, wondering what her sisters would think of her use of a commercial word, and then shrugged and looked at her own golden tan, comparing it to her escort's dark color. Abuwolowo was humus brown. "Deep as leaf mold," she said, speaking aloud, and stood up to watch him lift the thin platform to its maximum altitude of six or seven meters. His figure rapidly diminished in size as he sent it wobbling in gull-like swoops out over the Mediterranean. Ultimately it was boring, she decided; there was no real danger. He had a caller fitted into his swim belt, and if he fell into the water the board he rode on would save him, diving into the water and lifting him to safety. Now he was very far out, and all that was visible above the wave tops was the black bobbing ball of his head.

"I suppose I should have a feeling of loss." There was contempt in her voice, and it came from her knowledge that all she knew of loss was what she had read about in a recent television seminar on great books, but she gasped, losing reality, when she saw the head in close to the beach.

Looking desperately for her binocular lorgnette she asked, "Abuwolowo?" in a shout, but the head was white, and not merely the color of untanned skin, but a flat artificial white, like the marble statues in the garden of the summer home. Now, to her further horror, the rest of the apparition appeared out of the shallows. Above the blue sea, silhouetted against the paler sky, was a black figure with a dead white head. It staggered through the chopping waves with efforts to lift its legs free. When the creature succeeded in lifting its feet clear she was reassured. It was wearing swim fins, and she ran forward to help.

After she had gotten her hand onto the large soft arm she asked, "Are you all right?" The man nodded and kindly leaned a bit of his weight onto her. She was thankful; the figure stood a foot above her six-foot-three-inch height, and its shoulders were broader than Abuwolowo's Nigerian span.

Firmly ensconced on the sand, the man made a magician's pass at his neck and lifted the covering away from his face. He shot a quick look at the sky with black eyes that filled huge sockets and said, "Bright." He looked down at the sand, and after a few stertorous breaths spoke. "Thank you." He paused, reaching into his armpit, and continued, "Basker hit me out there."

Breathing more easily, he was easy to understand. The liquid mumbling of his first words had disappeared, and he looked directly at her. "Pretty," he said. "Pretty deserves an explanation. A basker drove me into the bottom. Something scared it from in the air and it dove."

"Basker?" she asked, wanting to hear the strange soft cadences of the voice that issued from the round head with its huge eyes.

"Basking shark," he said, "lying on the surface and it dove. I had no time to signal or to warn." He fell forward, breathing easily, but she saw blood welling from a cut on his back as he slumped onto his knees. "Excuse," he mouthed, when she gave a small touched cry. There was a long gash traversing his back from the left shoulder blade to his waist at his right side, and the rubbery material of his suit had rolled back and pulled the wound open. She tried to lift him, but his weight was too great, and all she succeeded in doing was to push him over into the sand. She straddled him and pulled at his long thick arm, trying to turn him over, but that too was impossible. Flat as he looked spread out on the sand, with long thin legs and a mid-section that had no depth, he was still enormously heavy. She jumped away from him and looked out into the sea. Abuwolowo was coming in toward the shore and she frantically waved and shouted, throwing her long pigtail and the points of her body in spastic jerks until he rode his board up onto the beach. "There's a man hurt here," she said, turning her back to him until the sand blasting up from the vehicle's air jets had subsided.

"Man?" Abuwolowo questioned, but he heaved at the collapsed

figure. "He's as heavy as a whale. It's no use, I'll go up to the house and get help." He ran off in long loping strides that brought him to the elevator in the cliff with an instantaneous violation of distance that was dreamlike. She stayed to watch her charge, fascinated by the long breaths he took. Easy inhalations that moved down his length in a wave from his chest to midriff in a series that seemed to never stop, one breath starting before the other had finished.

She waited silently, forgoing her usual monkey chatter to herself, eschewing fashion in the presence of the impassive white head, with its cap of cropped straw-colored hair, whose only life showed in the delicate flutter of petal nostrils. Finally, after no time had passed for her, Abuwolowo returned with four of the servants, strong squat men from neighboring Aegean islands. Puffing, their legs bowed under the weight, they half carried, half dragged the wounded man to the elevator and folded him into it under Abuwolowo's direction. Abuwolowo climbed over him and, braced between the walls, walked up the sides of the car until he was perched above the body. He held the up button down with a strong toe, the doors closed, and the elevator whirred invisibly away.

Greta had prepared for dinner, dressing and making her face up with unusual care, and was coming down the great ramp that swept into the entrance hall when she heard her brother-in-law talking to some of the guests. She stopped, amused; he was not really talking, but lecturing in a voice that his Kirghiz accent made even more didactic than he intended.

"Amazing," he was saying, "the recuperative powers they have. After we had gotten him off the kitchen truck, and onto the largest reclining ottoman in the casual room, he sat right up. He smiled at me. He stretched." Her brother-in-law paused, either overcome with amazement or staring down someone who appeared to be about to interrupt. "As I was saying," he went on in measured periods. "He stretched."

Greta could not resist her chance; she slipped down the ramp, and crossed to the speaker. "He stretched, and then what?"

Hauptman-Everetsky gave her the limited courtesy of his chill smile. "He stretched, and his water suit opened up and came off like a banana skin. He checked under his arm, the gill slit, you know, and climbed off the ottoman. He ignored me and turned around, and the cut was healed. There was only a thin line to show where it had been."

Greta moved away, not waiting to hear the inevitable repetition and embellishments her brother-in-law would give to his reactions. She passed through the archway that led to the casual room, undisturbed by the slight malfunction of the pressure curtain that allowed a current of air to lift the hem of her long skirt.

The man from the sea was standing in front of the panoramic glass watching the slow turning of the sights from the island's perimeter—a passing flow of scenery that was magnified and diminished by the tastes programmed into the machine. Just at this moment it was dwelling on the lights of the skyscrapers of Salonika. He was engrossed, but her cousin Rolf was questioning him with his usual inquisitiveness. Dwarfed by the figure next to him, he blurted questions in his fluting high American tones.

The question she heard as she approached was, "And you came all that way?" Rolf's voice did not hold disbelief; it held pleasure, a childish love for a recounting of adventure.

"Surely," the huge man said, "I have said it. I came from outside Stavangafjord. I was following an earth current. I hoped it might teach me something about the halibut's breeding. But I felt that was foolish, and so I hunted down the coast until I came to here." He turned back to the glass to catch the artistic dwindling of the city as the machine withdrew his view to a great height. "And," he said, coming politely back to his interrogator, "the dolphins told me when they were racing off Normandy, that the waters here were warm, and—" he paused, noticing Greta—"and the women beautiful, with yellow hair and brown limbs."

Greta nodded. "You're very kind. But I do not have your name."

"Gunnar Bjornstrom-Cousteau, of the dome Walshavn." He bowed, and she noticed how curious he looked covered by evening clothes. The short open jacket that barely reached the stretch tights exposed the rectangular expanse of his chest, a smooth fall of flesh without muscle definition that made her remember the tallowy layer of fat his wound had exposed. She shuddered, and he asked, "Does my face disturb you?" and for the first time she noticed that his skin was peeling, and there were angry red welts under his chin. "I was careless to take such a long trip without going under the lamps at home first. But then I did not intend to come into the air then. I am not used to the sunlight."

"Into the air?" Rolf was off again, but Greta stopped him.

"Dinner must be ready." She took the stranger's arm. "Will you take me in?" With Rolf tagging along behind, shaking his head, and bouncing every few steps to see if he could bring himself to the sea giant's height, they entered the dining room.

The dining room was at the top of the chateau. It was open on all sides, and protected from the weather by polarized static fields that were all but invisible and brought the stars too plainly close.

"That fish—" Hauptman-Everetsky had passed from awe to condescension, as he answered someone's question—"I could not throw him back like an undersized trout." He gestured. "And it's about time we had some amusement. We are beginning to bore one another."

Greta felt her companion stiffen, and held onto his arm tighter. He bent his head to her, and said, "Do not fear, I will not fall. It is long since I have walked. I must become accustomed to being unsupported by the friendly weight of the water." She noticed that he stressed the word "friendly," and remembered that one of the few things she had heard about the underwater people was that they had brought back dueling. In the infinite reaches of the sea the enforcement of organized law was difficult, encounters with the orca and the shark common, and the lessons they taught strong.

Yet her companion was smiling at Everetsky and his circle of friends, shaking hands with him firmly, and appraising the women. "At least I will not be bored," he said, staring at her sister Margreta's painted chest. Greta took his arm again, relieved, and glad she had chosen to wear her blue gown that completely covered all of her except her hands and face.

"Are we going to sit down now, Carl?" she said to Everetsky, and he led the way to the table, placing Gunnar at his right and her at his left.

The dinner went smoothly enough at first; the early conversation centered around the futility of investing money in the moon mines, and the necessity of mollifying the government with sums small enough to be economic and yet larger than mere tokens. All of the men from the rich steppes and Russian mountain regions had recommendations: lobbyists to recommend, purveyors of formulae to complain about, and complaining tales of corruption. While Rolf was concluding a story that centered on a bribed official who refused to honor his obligations without further payments that would have nullified the capital payments he had agreed to save, he rediscovered Gunnar's spherical face amid the contrasting ground of the tanned guests with their pointed chins.

"Nasty little fellow he was—dishonest as the day is long." Rolf stopped. "But you, my seaman friend, you don't understand any of this?"

"I," Bjornstrom-Cousteau burbled laughter, "do not understand these problems, but we have our own with the government." He seemed to like Rolf, but he spoke to his host. "They are difficult to explain."

"I suppose so," Abuwolowo spoke, "but tell us anyway."

Gunnar shrugged, and the massive table trembled slightly as he shifted his knees. "They want us to farm more and hunt less."

"Why not?" Abuwolowo challenged. "In the past my people adjusted to the changing times. They learned to farm and to work in factories."

"Yes." He was quiet for a moment. "I suppose some day we must, but as Hagar the poet sang–"

"Poets." Abuwolowo dismissed them. "We were talking of the government here."

"Hagar said," the sea guest went on, inevitable as the tides, pleasurably quoting a beloved line, " 'The sea change suffered by we cannot make the airmen think free.' " He chanted on, squaring his shoulders to expose more of his pale flesh. " 'For we have chosen deep being, not the ease of their far seeing.' " He stopped to stare out into the night with the depthless stare of his great dilated pupils.

Rolf, always jolly, rubbed his hands together, sniffing at the next course. "Ah, domestic venison," he said, changing the subject, cutting Abuwolowo's rejoinder short. "But our new guest doesn't seem to be eating much, and mine host's cook is excellent."

"The food is cooked," Gunnar said, as if it explained everything. It explained too much, and when he caught the expression on Hauptman-Everetsky's face he stood up and excused himself. "I am still tired from healing my hurts. You will excuse me." The last was a statement, not a question, and he left, moving with a tired lagging stride, his powerful body pushed down by the force of unrelieved gravity.

Morning came, and the first thing Greta did was to look for Gunnar. She had left the dinner party soon after him and started for his room, but Abuwolowo had overtaken her, and she had gone with him. Now she searched the gardens, moving through the regions of climate. She found him in the subtropical section standing in front of a red rubber plant grown to treelike proportions. He was fingering a paddle-sized leaf, pressing his fingertips deep into it as he regarded it with slightly parted lips.

"Like meat," he said. "Whale meat," he said, smiling at the picture she made coming down the cedar-chip path between the walls of greenery. "You look very pretty this morning."

"And you looked like a child when you were touching that plant, with your mouth open as if you wanted to taste it."

"It does look edible." He gave the leaf a last squeeze that pressed liquid out onto his hands. He licked the juice and made a face, and she laughed happily to see the soft corrugations that wrinkled around his head. "Well, it *is* bitter," he said defensively, and, reaching out, lifted her off her feet and into the tree. "Bite it and see."

Satisfied after she had clicked her teeth several times with mock gusto, he set her down again, and she rubbed her sides. Seriously she looked up at him, appraising his bulk. "I was reading about you this morning," she said, looking down with a strained intensity as if performing the unfamiliar task of following lines of print.

"So now I have become famous."

"Oh, no," she said. "In the encyclopedia. It says you are homo aquati–"

"Homo aquaticus, one of the old words." He touched her bare shoulder, "Yes, and one of the better."

"That's it," she said, dwelling on the pronunciation, "homo aquaticus. And a long time ago a man named Cousteau said that you were to be."

"Cousteau."

"Yes–" she altered her pronunciation–"Cousteau. A relative?"

"He is dead, and my surname is said the way you pronounced it the first time."

"No matter," she said. "I will show you the grounds now," and took his arm. She started out chattering to him about the shrubbery, but she soon discovered that it was another subject she knew very little about. He was naturally silent, and her thoughts turned to the things she had found in the encyclopedia. It had said that the first colonies were set up in the Mediterranean. The warm water was perfect for man, and the sudden mistral-born storms were no trouble ten fathoms in the sea. The underwater colonies raised sea slugs and clams, farmed algae and adapted fruits, and hunted the smaller whales with hand weapons. She had read very quickly, scanning down the pages in s-curves in her hurry to go and meet him, but womanlike, she did remember some things about human births under the sea. The children were born into the pressures they would live under, fitted with gill mechanisms that took oxygen from the water, and subjected to chemotherapies that prepared them for their lives.

"But why do you live in the cold seas in the north?" she asked. The question was an outgrowth of her thoughts, yet he seemed to know what she meant.

"Because so many of our people live here?" he went on without needing to have an answer. "My great-grandfather felt the bottoms were becoming too crowded, that the life would become too easy, and so we left." He swiveled his head to sniff at the sea, offering her a view of the seal foldings of his neck. "And now we could not live here at all. We have changed our bodies, and we have learned to love the hunt."

"But you come to the waters off this island."

"I came only for a short hunt. I would have returned very soon."

Further conversation was cut short by the interesting spectacle of wide-eyed gardeners dodging into the bushes to avoid their advance. The servants variously crossed themselves, or made the sign of the horns; some of them did both. They knew, if Greta did not, that there was a conflict between the sea peoples and the dwellers on the land. Servants listened to political conversations, but eighteen-year-old girls of good family were expert in oblivious attention. The gardeners had heard from the house staff how the world government in New Kiev, on the Baltic, was demanding more taxes in algae proteins from the independent sea states. Some of the servants' relatives had served in the fleets of small boats equipped with grapple buckets that were sent in punitive expeditions against the algae beds and the sea-slug pens. The duty was dangerous; the seamen darted to the surface in spurting pushes from the shallows to rock and overturn boats; they cut the grapple cables and tied derisive messages to their severed ends. What the raiders did capture was diseased, or of thin stock that had gone to seed.

The servants did not hate the seamen; they feared them as they feared the storms and rages of nature. They did not respect them as they did their masters; the seamen were unnatural facts of nature, not to be dealt with except through the practice of the magics that had come back in the few short years of barbarism after the Two Months' War.

Gunnar had some idea of what the men who had run away were thinking, but that part of the problem did not concern him. After all, his dome did not farm enough to be involved in the commercial disputes. He looked at Greta. She was still caught up in the uniqueness of the servants' scuttling disappearance.

"It has been a long time since we went into the sea," he said, touching her on the shoulder again, knowing that physical contacts reassured her, "and they do not remember us. We are strangers." She leaned her weight against his side as soon as he had touched her, he noticed, and she made many movements with her hips and torso, but he attached no significance to her wriggling.

Greta became silent and swayed away from him. She had worked the individual muscles her governesses had trained her to use. Trained in long gymnasium sessions when she was young for the pleasurable obligations of adulthood, she accepted her expertness and was piqued by his callous indifference. She almost believed that the sea women were more expert, but, on second thought, she disregarded that. Her instructors, and Abuwolowo, had assured her that she was perfectly trained in the amatory arts.

Hadji Abuwolowo Smyth watched them from a free-standing balcony that projected, fingerlike, out over the gardens. "The girl is infatuated with the Fish," he thought. "It is nothing more than his difference." Abuwolowo remembered the long hours of dancing that had trained him, the great factories that his parents managed, and Greta's brother-in-law's desire for new markets for his heavy machinery, and concluded that he had nothing to worry about. He went into the house to have a suppling rub-down to prepare him for the pre-lunch wrestling.

Every day all the young men but Rolf wrestled for the amusement of the other guests. They fought in a combination of styles, ju-jitsu coupled with the less dangerous holds of Greco-Roman wrestling. They were full of energy, had little to do, and they passed the time waiting for the day when they would assume the managerial offices their parents held in the automatic factories.

Gunnar and Greta emerged from the tree-lined walk as the matches were about to start. Gunnar blinked, and rocked his head as the forenoon heat bit into his sunburn. Halting, he made an effort; Greta felt oil under her hand, and saw his skin flex and knead. His pores opened and a smooth layer of clear oil covered his body. He took several more of his curiously peristaltic breaths, and with each one squeezed more protective fluid onto his skin.

"Now," he said as she let go of him, "we can go on, but first tell me what is happening here."

"They are wrestling," Greta said shortly, either still angry at his unresponsiveness, or caught up in the combat.

They watched Hadji Abuwolowo win the first fight easily, throwing his opponent with a hip toss and pinning him with a leap. The Nigerian nodded to Greta with a victory grin on his face. "And you, Fish," he said. "Do you wrestle?"

"Not with you," Gunnar said politely, intending to imply that Smyth was too practiced a hand for his small skill.

"I am not a worthy opponent." Abuwolowo chose to misunderstand him. "Or perhaps you are afraid?"

Gunnar felt Greta's small hand in his back and walked forward onto the sanded turf, looming more and more over Abuwolowo as he went. The Nigerian regretted his impetuousness for a split second, but compensated with a bound that was intended to carry him to the seaman's head. The leap was successful, but his ear-grab hold was not. There was nothing to grip. Gunnar's ears were tiny and set deep into his skull. Their pavilions were vestigial, the auditory canals covered by membranes, and the skin oil-slippery. Abuwolowo's planned knee drive spun him over on his back, and he lay spraddled with his ludicrous failure driving his anger. Rolling backward, he bounced up once and came down to jump flat through the air with his legs doubled. Just as he straightened to strike his adversary with the full force of his flight and kicking legs, Gunnar dropped under the trajectory, folding with the flexibility of an eel. Abuwolowo skidded along the ground and rolled over to rub sand into his hands. He looked up and found himself looking at Gunnar's back, certain that the man had not moved his feet. It was too much for him, but his urge to kill made him calculating. He stood up and ran, with short hunter's steps, silently to Gunnar's back, and unleashed an axelike swing at the neck, using the full strength of his wide shoulders. The edge of his hand struck and rebounded, but he was gratified to note that he had staggered Gunnar.

"You forget your title, Hadji," Gunnar said in deeper tones than he had used before. Abuwolowo moved forward a shuffling half step and was thrown four or five feet backward by an open-handed slap he did not see start. When he recovered himself, Gunnar was standing stock-still, waiting. It was too late to go back, and he charged hopelessly. He felt the long flexible arms, as thick at the wrist as the shoulder, reach out to pick him up, but he could do nothing about it, even though they appeared to be moving very slowly. For a minute Gunnar held him in a strangely compassionate embrace, but then threw him into the air straight up. He felt himself rise, and he floated for a long interval, but when he fell he could remember no more.

Hauptman-Everetsky leaped to his feet and ran forward, but Gunnar was there before him. He knelt by Abuwolowo's side and twisted him in his hands.

"Guards," Everetsky screamed, and fearlessly rushed toward the seaman.

"Stop." Gunnar's words were commanding, either out of their awesome depth, or because of the certainty of knowledge. "He will be all right. His back was hurt, but I have fixed it." These last words were the ones that broke Everetsky's code of hospitality. They were too much like a repairman speaking about a robot toy.

He stammered, peering out of slitted eyes that accentuated his Mongol blood, but Gunnar could only commend his control. His first thought was to stop the guards.

"Back, quiet now." Everetsky's diction was irregular, but his pitch was properly adjusted to the command tone of the mastiffs. The dogs, with the metallic crowns of their augmented skulls glittering, turned back and sat in their places under the chateau wall, once more becoming statues. Now that his first duty was accomplished, he could come back to the business of Gunnar.

"Sir," he said, and now his voice was under control, "you have injured one of my guests. That would be permissible, but it is certain to happen again. There is enmity between you and him, and–" he paused to collect himself–"I must be truthful, I do not like your kind myself. I ask you to leave. If you feel yourself insulted I offer you satisfaction."

"You are a brave man," Gunnar said, with a sudden baring of his teeth. "Well fleshed too, so the spoils might be worth the fight, but your way is not ours. I cannot ask you to sport with me." He showed Everetsky his teeth, opening his lips back to his neck, and dropping the hinges of his jaw. "I would have to ask you into the water so that we could play, and," he asked with icy rhetoric humor that amused no one but him, "what chance would you take?"

"Thank you," Everetsky said, not holding his contempt, "but I must nevertheless ask you when you will leave my house."

"I ask your indulgence to wait until tonight when the tide is good." Everetsky nodded, and the seaman turned and walked toward the beach path as if he remembered using it before.

Down on the beach Gunnar studied the water, watching for the signs of the incoming tide: sea wrack would soon be tossed up onto the shore, pieces of the sea's jetsam, thrown there to waste away on the cleansing shore. The dead seaweeds, fish and bubbles would soon push ahead of the growing combers to outline the demarcation between his domain and Everetsky's. "Lubber," he said, "you do not understand," and stopped, putting his hand, palm down, flat on the sand. He felt the vibrations of approaching feet.

Two servants appeared carrying his water suit, signaling their trepidation with stiff backs and firm jaws. Behind them came two more servingmen and a kitchen maid. The bearers put his suit down at his feet, at a distance they thought out of the radius of his arms. They backed off and squatted on their heels to wait for the others to come up, remaining, guardedly watching him, until the woman and her companions reached them.

"Greetings to you," Gunnar said when the woman had come to a halt, spreading her legs to balance the weight of a waist thickened by years of carrying full water jars up steps cut from island rock.

"Greetings," she said, in a Greek dialect as bastardized as the letters that appeared on ancient Scythian coins. She alone observed him with equanimity.

"Speak," he said, viewing a full half circle of the beach and horizon, moving his eyes independently. He knew what was coming; three times now he had performed this rite.

She waddled up to him, pointing the forefinger of her left hand at his face. When it touched his closed mouth a rapturous look transformed her thickened features and the Attic awe encompassed her functioning. Obediently he opened his lips, and, with a sharp snap, clipped the end of her finger off. The nauseating taste of warm blood, and dirty fingernail, filled his mouth, but he swallowed quickly and spoke again.

"I have accepted. Speak."

The woman could not resist looking back at her entourage with triumph, and Gunnar thought, "Poor fellows, now she is a full-fledged witch, ugly and to be obeyed in all things." She would have the ultimate power over her fellows. Commands were to be her normal mode of speech. The mere pointing of her maimed hand, a gesture of pollarded horns, could call a man to her bed, or a maid to his; but, more important, it would fuse the serfs into a unit. They would be a group that would respond to the messages of Gunnar's people when the time came. He knew that the inheritors and owners of the earth understood their world very well from its blueprints; but they could not find the switches and valves and all the simple tools to work them.

"Did you speak your true thoughts when you promised to eat the master, Great Fish?"

Gunnar made the obligatory answer. "You have prayed to us."

"Demon of Poseidon, my people would be saved." She too was familiar with the ritual.

"I am no demon, but a servant." He rose to his feet, and gave the toothy yawn that had impressed Everetsky. "Poseidon wants more servants who love the sea."

"We will accept."

Gunnar bit a piece of blubber from his forearm and spat it into the cup of her waiting hands. Immediately she kissed it ritually and squirreled it into the dirty fold of her blouse.

"When the appointed time is come I will return." He watched them go, the woman leading, and the men with their heads inclined to the woman.

Gunnar was ashamed of himself, not for his threats to his host and their outcome. He had planned that series of happenings, and had, in fact, played this role many times before. His people could not hope to fight the land dwellers if the war was to be fought on the basis of numbers and equipment. The sea cities were very vulnerable; the simplest sort of guided torpedo could destroy the domes, and economic sanctions would quickly disrupt the lives of the ocean-bed farmers and their cities. He was not ashamed of his tactics, but of the unmanly squeamishness which had overtaken him. To feel his stomach turn at the mere taste of human kind. It was true that the heavy starch diet of the air-breathers and the dark cooked meats they ate gave their flesh an unpleasant, alien taste, but it was not so different from the savor of enemies he had killed in the days-long hunting duels in his home ground.

He stopped his train of thought and studied the sea with heightened awareness. Wondering what disturbed him would do no good. He knew it would be better to relax, but the strange dislocation of his abilities was still with him. He breathed deeply, sucking great mouthfuls of air, and held them until his chest and diaphragm puffed out in a rotund bladder. Slowly he let the air escape through his nostrils, a silent flow of aspiration, until any observer would have noticed the change in his posture. Everything about his body was lax; his legs lay separately on the sand, and his head lolled, but the eyes were alive. They turned in their sockets independently, scanning the surface of the sea. It was a look born in the middle-twentieth-century studies of frogs' nervous systems. There were circuits spliced into the optical nerves that bypassed the brain and fed the sorted visual stimuli back to the eye muscles. Only the significant motions on the surface of the sea were allowed to reach the brain.

After a few seconds of this activity Gunnar's legs twitched, his eyelids drooped, and the eyes themselves seemed to withdraw back into the skull. He brought his knees up and hugged them, sitting in this childlike posture with a broad grin on his face.

"Hauptman-Everetsky was foolish," he thought as he changed his position to stand, moving in a serpentine flow that ended in a run toward the surf. His last thoughts before he hit the water in a flat dive were of his hunger, and a mental note to come back to the beach to see if his calculations about Greta were correct. He hit near the bottom of a wave and let the undertow carry him toward the sudden deep just beyond the breakers. Turning in a free somersault, he pushed for the boulder-filled bottom and found a current that carried him between the rocks. As he estimated his speed he slowed himself by pressing his heels into the sand, touching at chosen points much as a professional polo player guides his pony with touches of his spurs. When he saw the bathysphere that Everetsky had ordered sunk, he momentarily regretted not wearing his swim fins, but he did not dwell on the thought. It could hold no more than three men, he thought, and swam toward its hatch.

The three guards saw him as soon as he came into the bathysphere's circle of light. They started out the open hatch. Gunnar caught the first man by the scruff of his neck as he came out, but they had expected to use the vanguard as a delay to allow others to come up on him. What they had not allowed for was the simplicity of Gunnar's tactics. He held the man like a kitten and plucked the mouthpiece of his oxygen recirculator out of his face, pointed him toward the bottom, and, with a wide hand spread across his buttocks, pushed him under trampling feet. The second man tried to divert him with a shot from his speargun. Gunnar, feeling foolishly inept for his slowness, ducked and caught it just over his shoulder, and drove the blunt staff into the marksman's solar plexus. He hauled this opponent out by a flopping arm, without time to watch his agonized contortions. The third member of Everetsky's murder party refused to join the combat. Gunnar showed his grinning face at an illuminated port, and disappeared to the top of the sphere. He took the cable ring in his hands and, threshing his legs, swam the bathysphere over onto its side. With a little adjustment the hatch fitted neatly into the bottom and Gunnar surveyed his handiwork before he swam to the man curled on the bottom with his legs doubled up over his stomach. No matter how he struggled, the man felt himself being drawn straight out. A round face, suspended inches from his mask, gently studied his last reactions.

The beach was deserted when Greta finally escaped from the chateau to look for the seaman. She kicked a puff of sand into the night breeze in exasperation and would have left, but she saw something break out of the water amid the froth of incoming waves. A second later she could see Gunnar's figure wading ashore. He bent and reached under the water, and, taking a handful of sand, wiped it across his mouth. As he drew closer she could see the flicker of his tongue picking at the crevices in his teeth.

"Hello," she said, not finding anything else to say for the moment, and wrapped her long cloak tighter around her.

"Hello," he said, noticing her shivers. "Come, you are not used to the night air without screens to protect you." He led the way to the shelter of the cliff, and continued. "What are you doing here?"

Greta did not know, except that she was attracted to him, and that he was the first man she could remember feeling anything but familiarity for, but she said, "Well, you beat Abuwolowo so easily."

"In the jousts of love," Gunnar said declaratively, having thought better of finishing his statement questioningly.

Greta gave him her best arch smile. "But I could talk my brother-in-law into letting you stay. He owes something to me."

Gunnar would have told her about the affair he had just ended in the sea, but the strange repugnance overtook him again. "He would not really want me," he said, but even he, not given to nuances of this sort, noticed the hesitant tone in his own voice.

"But his concern is always for the amusement of his guests," Greta said, and giggled fetchingly at some private joke, "and they are getting bored. Very bored," she said masterfully.

"And I would soon be boring too, little Greta." He rumpled her hair with a touch of rough power, and she stepped closer to him.

"You couldn't bore me. Ever." She turned her face up and Gunnar saw the plumb line of her throat. Thin, but adolescently rounded with a touching surplus of young fat. The strongest rules of his dialectic told him that he should destroy her as an incipient breeder.

"No," he said, "I can do better." He explained himself to the elders in the dome under the sea.

Greta was tired of waiting for an embrace that never came. She changed her posture and spoke with irritation. "What was that?"

"Nothing." Plausibly, he said, "I must go back to my family. I have been gone very long."

"Your wife, you mean."

"I am too young to swim in the breeding tides."

The metaphor's meaning escaped Greta, but the surface of the statement could be turned into the small victory of a compliment.

"You will come back when you are ready?"

Gunnar found the source of his weakness. Somehow she had taught him to find the meaning behind simple words. He smiled. "Of course. Where else would there be for me to go now?"

Greta had forgotten all her careful training, the sophistications that her governesses had taught her. She beamed, threw her arms around his waist, and leaned her head on his sternum. "Thank you," she said, appreciating a compliment without coquetry.

"You are very welcome," Gunnar said, and managed to keep his laughter out of his voice. "But you can do me a favor." Before he spoke he studied the water. Now he must leave, he decided, and turned back to her. "It is very simple," he said. "Remember to tell your brother-in-law this: war will be fought in places he has not yet thought of."

"Yes?" Greta said, bewildered.

"No more." Gunnar patted her head kindly and sat down, smoothed his suit onto his body, and put his fins on his feet. When he had his mask in place he could no longer speak and he walked silently into the breakers to vanish. Later that same night he talked with the porpoises, chased a school of silvery fish out into the moonlight and then dove to flirt in swirls in a whirlpool current that spun him out in the direction of home.

Greta gave Hauptman-Everetsky her cryptic message; he took little notice of it, and she remembered less and less of Gunnar with the passing years. When she did recall, it was too late; the figures coming out of the surf, to be greeted by the servants, were not Gunnar, but triumphant victors. The island was without power, the servants in revolt, and nostalgia was not a shield.

The war had been fought; neither she nor her brother-in-law had known it. In the subterranean tunnels the ripped ends of power cables spluttered hopeless sparks, water poured from torn mains, and bells and voices, however loud, brought no servants back from their welcoming songs. The always obedient chattels only watched, with blank dark eyes, as the fish came to play their game with Greta.

MAN IN HIS TIME

by Brian W. Aldiss

His absence

Janet Westermark sat watching the three men in the office: the administrator who was about to go out of her life, the behaviourist who was about to come into it, and the husband whose life ran parallel to but insulated from her own.

She was not the only one playing a watching game. The behaviourist, whose name was Clement Stackpole, sat hunched in his chair with his ugly strong hands clasped round his knee, thrusting his intelligent and simian face forward, the better to regard his new subject, Jack Westermark.

The administrator of the Mental Research Hospital spoke in a lively and engaged way. Typically, it was only Jack Westermark who seemed absent from the scene.

Your particular problem, restless

His hands upon his lap lay still, but he himself was restless, though the restlessness seemed directed. It was as if he were in another room with other people, Janet thought. She saw that he caught her eye when in fact she was not entirely looking at him, and by the time she returned the glance, he was gone, withdrawn.

"Although Mr. Stackpole has not dealt before with your particular problem," the administrator was saying, "he has had plenty of field experience. I know–"

"I'm sure we won't," Westermark said, folding his hands and nodding his head slightly.

Smoothly, the administrator made a pencilled note of the remark, scribbled the precise time beside it, and continued, "I know Mr. Stackpole is too modest to say this, but he is a great man for working in with people–"

"If you feel it's necessary," Westermark said. "Though I've seen enough of your equipment for a while."

The pencil moved, the smooth voice proceeded. "Good. A great man for working in with people, and I'm sure you and Mrs. Westermark will soon find you are glad to have him around. Remember, he's there to help both of you."

Janet smiled, and said from the island of her chair, trying to smile at him and Stackpole, "I'm sure that everything will work—" She was interrupted by her husband, who rose to his feet, letting his hands drop to his sides and saying, turning slightly to address thin air, "Do you mind if I say goodbye to Nurse Simmons?"

Her voice no longer wavered

"Everything will be all right, I'm sure," she said hastily. And Stackpole nodded at her, conspiratorially agreeing to see her point of view.

"We'll all get on fine, Janet," he said. She was in the swift process of digesting that unexpected use of her Christian name, and the administrator was also giving her the sort of encouraging smile so many people had fed her since Westermark was pulled out of the ocean off Casablanca, when her husband, still having his lonely conversation with the air, said, "Of course, I should have remembered."

His right hand went halfway to his forehead—or his heart? Janet wondered—and then dropped, as he added, "Perhaps she'll come round and see us some time." Now he turned and was smiling faintly at another vacant space with just the faintest nod of his head, as if slightly cajoling. "You'd like that, wouldn't you, Janet?"

She moved her head, instinctively trying to bring her eyes into his gaze as she replied vaguely, "Of course, darling." Her voice no longer wavered when she addressed his absent attention.

There was sunlight through which they could see each other

There was sunlight in one corner of the room, coming through the windows of a bay angled towards the sun. For a moment she caught, as she rose to her feet, her husband's profile with the sunlight behind it. It was thin and withdrawn. Intelligent: she had always thought him overburdened with his intelligence, but now there was a lost look there, and she thought of the words of a psychiatrist who had been called in on the case earlier: "You must understand that the waking brain is perpetually lapped by the unconscious."

Lapped by the unconscious

Fighting the words away, she said, addressing the smile of the administrator—that smile which must have advanced his career so much —"You've helped me a lot. I couldn't have got through these months without you. Now we'd better go."

She heard herself chopping her words, fearing Westermark would talk across them, as he did: "Thank you for your help. If you find anything . . ."

Stackpole walked modestly over to Janet as the administrator rose and said, "Well, don't either of you forget us if you're in any kind of trouble."

"I'm sure we won't."

"And, Jack, we'd like you to come back here to visit us once a month for a personal checkup. Don't want to waste all our expensive equipment, you know, and you are our star—er, patient." He smiled rather tightly as he said it, glancing at the paper on his desk to check Westermark's answer. Westermark's back was already turned on him, Westermark was already walking slowly to the door, Westermark had said his goodbyes, perched out on the lonely eminence of his existence.

Janet looked helplessly, before she could guard against it, at the administrator and Stackpole. She hated it that they were too professional to take note of what seemed her husband's breach of conduct. Stackpole looked kindly in a monkey way and took her arm with one of his thick hands.

"Shall we be off then? My car's waiting outside."

Not saying anything, nodding, thinking, and consulting watches

She nodded, not saying anything, thinking only, without the need of the administrator's notes to think it, "Oh yes, this was when he said, 'Do you mind if I say goodbye to Nurse'—who's-it?—Simpson?" She was learning to follow her husband's footprints across the broken path of conversation. He was now out in the corridor, the door swinging to behind him, and to empty air the administrator was saying, "It's her day off today."

"You're good on your cues," she said, feeling the hand tighten on her arm. She politely brushed his fingers away, horrid Stackpole, trying to recall what had gone on only four minutes before. Jack had said something to her; she couldn't remember, didn't speak, avoided eyes, put out her hand and shook the administrator's firmly.

"Thanks," she said.

"*Au revoir* to both of you," he replied firmly, glancing swiftly: watch, notes, her, the door. "Of course," he said. "If we find anything at all. We are very hopeful. . . ."

He adjusted his tie, looking at the watch again.

"Your husband has gone now, Mrs. Westermark," he said, his manner softening. He walked towards the door with her and added, "You have been wonderfully brave, and I do realise—we all realise—that you will have to go on being wonderful. With time, it should be easier for you; doesn't Shakespeare say in *Hamlet* that 'Use almost can change the stamp of nature'? May I suggest that you follow Stackpole's and my example and keep a little notebook and a strict check on the time?"

They saw her tiny hesitation, stood about her, two men round a personable woman, not entirely innocent of relish. Stackpole cleared his throat, smiled, said, "He can so easily feel cut off, you know. It's essential that you of all people answer his questions, or he will feel cut off."

Always a pace ahead

"The children?" she asked.

"Let's see you and Jack well settled in at home again, say for a fortnight or so," the administrator said, "before we think about having the children back to see him."

"That way's better for them and Jack *and* you, Janet," Stackpole said. Don't be glib, she thought; consolation I need, God knows, but that's too facile. She turned her face away, fearing it looked too vulnerable these days.

In the corridor, the administrator said, as valediction, "I'm sure Grandma's spoiling them terribly, Mrs. Westermark, but worrying won't mend it, as the old saw says."

She smiled at him and walked quickly away, a pace ahead of Stackpole.

Westermark sat in the back of the car outside the administrative block. She climbed in beside him. As she did so, he jerked violently back in his seat.

"Darling, what is it?" she asked. He said nothing.

Stackpole had not emerged from the building, evidently having a last word with the administrator. Janet took the moment to lean over and kiss her husband's cheek, aware as she did so that a phantom wife had already, from his viewpoint, done so. His response was a phantom to her.

"The countryside looks green," he said. His eyes were flickering over the grey concrete block opposite.

"Yes," she said.

Stackpole came bustling down the steps, apologising as he opened the car door, settled in. He let the clutch back too fast and they shot forward. Janet saw then the reason for Westermark's jerking backwards a short while before. Now the acceleration caught him again; his body was rolled helplessly back. As they drove along, he set one hand fiercely on the side grip, for his sway was not properly counterbalancing the movement of the car.

Once outside the grounds of the institute, they were in the country, still under a mid-August day.

His theories

Westermark, by concentrating, could bring himself to conform to some of the laws of the time continuum he had left. When the car he was in climbed up his drive (familiar, yet strange with the rhododendrons unclipped and no signs of children) and stopped by the front door, he sat in his seat for three and a half minutes before venturing to open his door. Then he climbed out and stood on the gravel, frowning down at it. Was it as real as ever, as material? Was there a slight glaze on it?—as if something shone through from the interior of the earth, shone through all things? Or was it that there was a screen between him and everything else? It was important to decide between the two theories, for he had to live under the discipline of one. What he hoped to prove was that the permeation theory was correct; that way he was merely one of the factors comprising the functioning universe, together with the rest of humanity. By the glaze theory, he was isolated not only from the rest of humanity but from the entire cosmos (except Mars?). It was early days yet; he had a deal of thinking to do, and new ideas would undoubtedly emerge after observation and cogitation. Emotion must not decide the issue; he must be detached. Revolutionary theories could well emerge from this—suffering.

He could see his wife by him, standing off in case they happened embarrassingly or painfully to collide. He smiled thinly at her through her glaze. He said, "I am, but I'd prefer not to talk." He stepped towards the house, noting the slippery feel of gravel that would not move under his tread until the world caught up. He said, "I've every respect for *The Guardian,* but I'd prefer not to talk at present."

Famous Astronaut Returns Home

As the party arrived, a man waited in the porch for them, ambushing Westermark's return home with a deprecatory smile. Hesitant but businesslike, he came forward and looked interrogatively at the three people who had emerged from the car.

"Excuse me, you are Captain Jack Westermark, aren't you?"

He stood aside as Westermark seemed to make straight for him. "I'm the psychology correspondent for *The Guardian,* if I might intrude for a moment."

Westermark's mother had opened the front door and stood there smiling welcome at him, one hand nervously up to her grey hair. Her son walked past her. The newspaper man stared after him.

Janet told him apologetically, "You'll have to excuse us. My husband did reply to you, but he's really not prepared to meet people yet."

"*When* did he reply, Mrs. Westermark? Before he heard what I had to say?"

"Well, naturally not—but his life stream. . . . I'm sorry, I can't explain."

"He really is living ahead of time, isn't he? Will you spare me a minute to tell me how you feel now the first shock is over?"

"You really must excuse me," Janet said, brushing past him. As she followed her husband into the house, she heard Stackpole say, "Actually, I read *The Guardian,* and perhaps I could help you. The institute has given me the job of remaining with Captain Westermark. My name's Clement Stackpole—you may know my book, *Persistent Human Relations,* Methuen. But you must not say that Westermark is living ahead of time. That's quite incorrect. What you can say is that some of his psychological and physiological processes have somehow been transposed forward—"

"Ass!" she exclaimed to herself. She had paused by the threshold to catch some of his words. Now she whisked in.

Talk hanging in the air among the long watches of supper

Supper that evening had its discomforts, although Janet Westermark and her mother-in-law achieved an air of melancholy gaiety by bringing two Scandinavian candelabra, relics of a Copenhagen holiday, onto the table and surprising the two men with a gay-looking hors d'œuvre. But the conversation was mainly like the hors d'œuvre, Janet thought: little tempting isolated bits of talk, not nourishing.

Mrs. Westermark senior had not yet got the hang of talking to her son, and confined her remarks to Janet, though she looked towards Jack often enough. "How are the children?" he asked her. Flustered by the knowledge that he was waiting a long while for her answer, she replied rather incoherently and dropped her knife.

To relieve the tension, Janet was cooking up a remark on the character of the administrator at the Mental Research Hospital, when Westermark said, "Then he is at once thoughtful and literate. Commendable and rare in men of his type. I got the impression, as you evidently did, that he was as interested in his job as in advancement. I suppose one might say one even *liked* him. But you know him better, Stackpole; what do you think of him?"

Crumbling bread to cover his ignorance of whom they were supposed to be conversing, Stackpole said, "Oh, I don't know; it's hard to say really," spinning out time, pretending not to squint at his watch.

"The administrator was quite a charmer, didn't you think, Jack?" Janet remarked—perhaps helping Stackpole as much as Jack.

"He looks as if he might make a slow bowler," Westermark said, with an intonation that suggested he was agreeing with something as yet unsaid.

"Oh, *him!*" Stackpole said. "Yes, he seems a satisfactory sort of chap on the whole."

"He quoted Shakespeare to me and thoughtfully told me where the quotation came from," Janet said.

"No thank you, Mother," Westermark said.

"I don't have much to do with him," Stackpole continued. "Though I have played cricket with him a time or two. He makes quite a good slow bowler."

"Are you really?" Westermark exclaimed.

That stopped them. Jack's mother looked helplessly about, caught her son's glazed eye, said, covering up, "Do have some more sauce, Jack, dear," recalled she had already had her answer, almost let her knife slide again, gave up trying to eat.

"I'm a batsman, myself," Stackpole said, as if bringing an old pneumatic drill to the new silence. When no answer came, he doggedly went on, expounding on the game, the pleasure of it. Janet sat and watched, a shade perplexed that she was admiring Stackpole's performance and wondering at her slight perplexity; then she decided that she had made up her mind to dislike Stackpole, and immediately dissolved the resolution. Was he not on their side? And even the strong hairy hands became a little more acceptable when you thought of them gripping the rubber of a bat handle; and the broad shoulders swinging. . . . She closed her eyes momentarily, and tried to concentrate on what he was saying.

A batsman himself

Later, she met Stackpole on the upper landing. He had a small cigar in his mouth, she had two pillows in her arms. He stood in her way.

"Can I help at all, Janet?"

"I'm only making up a bed, Mr. Stackpole."

"Are you not sleeping in with your husband?"

"He would like to be on his own for a night or two, Mr. Stackpole. I shall sleep in the children's room for the time being."

"Then please permit me to carry the pillows for you. And do please call me Clem. All my friends do."

Trying to be pleasanter, to unfreeze, to recall that Jack was not moving her out of the bedroom permanently, she said, "I'm sorry. It's just that we once had a terrier called Clem." But it did not sound as she had wished it to do.

He put the pillows on Peter's blue bed, switched on the bedside lamp, and sat on the edge of the bed, clutching his cigar and puffing at it.

"This may be a bit embarrassing, but there's something I feel I should say to you, Janet." He did not look at her. She brought him an ashtray and stood by him.

"We feel your husband's mental health may be endangered, although I hasten to assure you that he shows no signs of losing his mental equilibrium beyond what we may call an inordinate absorption in phenomena—and even there, we cannot say, of course we can't, that his absorption is any greater than one might expect. Except in the totally unprecedented circumstances, I mean. We must talk about this in the next few days."

She waited for him to go on, not unamused by the play with the cigar. Then he looked straight up at her and said, "Frankly, Mrs. Westermark, we think it would help your husband if you could have sexual relations with him."

A little taken aback, she said, "Can you imagine–" Correcting herself, she said, "That is for my husband to say. I am not unapproachable."

She saw he had caught her slip. Playing a very straight bat, he said, "I'm sure you're not, Mrs. Westermark."

With the light out, living, she lay in Peter's bed

She lay in Peter's bed with the light out. Certainly she wanted him: pretty badly, now she allowed herself to dwell on it. During the long months of the Mars expedition, while she had stayed at home and he had got farther from home, while he actually had existence on that other planet, she had been chaste. She had looked after the children and driven round the countryside and enjoyed writing those articles for women's magazines and being interviewed on TV when the ship was reported to have left Mars on its homeward journey. She had been, in part, dormant.

Then came the news, kept from her at first, that there was confusion in communicating with the returning ship. A sensational tabloid broke the secrecy by declaring that the nine-man crew had all gone mad. And the ship had overshot its landing area, crashing into the Atlantic. Her first reaction had been a purely selfish one–no, not selfish, but from the self: He'll never lie with me again. And infinite love and sorrow.

At his rescue, the only survivor, miraculously unmaimed, her hope had revived. Since then, it had remained embalmed, as he was embalmed in time. She tried to visualise love as it would be now, with everything happening first to him, before she had begun to– With his movement of pleasure even before she– No, it wasn't possible! But of course it was, if they worked it out first intellectually; then if she just lay flat. . . . But what she was trying to visualise, all she could visualise, was not love-making, merely a formal prostration to the exigencies of glands and time flow.

She sat up in bed, longing for movement, freedom. She jumped out and opened the lower window; there was still a tang of cigar smoke in the dark room.

If they worked it out intellectually

Within a couple of days, they had fallen into routine. It was as if the calm weather, perpetuating mildness, aided them. They had to be careful to move slowly through doors, keeping to the left, so as not to bump into each other—a tray of drinks was dropped before they agreed on that. They devised simple knocking systems before using the bathroom. They conversed in bulletins that did not ask questions unless questions were necessary. They walked slightly apart. In short, they made detours round each other's lives.

"It's really quite easy as long as one is careful," Mrs. Westermark senior said to Janet. "And dear Jack is *so* patient!"

"I even get the feeling he likes the situation."

"Oh, my dear, how could he *like* such an unfortunate predicament?"

"Mother, you realise how we all exist together, don't you? No, it sounds too terrible—I daren't say it."

"Now don't you start getting silly ideas. You've been very brave, and this is not the time for us to be getting upset, just as things are going well. If you have any worries, you must tell Clem. That's what he's here for."

"I know."

"Well then."

She saw Jack walk in the garden. As she looked, he glanced up, smiled, said something to himself, stretched out a hand, withdrew it, and went, still smiling, to sit on one end of the seat on the lawn. Touched, Janet hurried over to the french windows, to go and join him.

She paused. Already, she saw ahead, saw her sequence of actions, for Jack had already sketched them into the future. She would go onto the lawn, call his name, smile, and walk over to him when he smiled back. Then they would stroll together to the seat and sit down, one at each end.

The knowledge drained all spontaneity from her. She might have been working a treadmill, for what she was about to do had already been done as far as Jack was concerned, with his head start in time. Then if she did not go, if she mutinied, turned back to the discussion of the day's chores with her mother-in-law . . . That left Jack mouthing like a fool on the lawn, indulging in a fantasy there was no penetrating. Let him do that, let Stackpole see; then they could drop this theory about Jack's being ahead of time and would have to treat him for a more normal sort of hallucinatory insanity. He would be safe in Clem's hands.

But Jack's actions proved that she would go out there. It was insane for her not to go out there. Insane? To disobey a law of the universe was impossible, not insane. Jack was not disobeying—he had simply tumbled over a law that nobody knew was there before the first expedition to Mars; certainly they had discovered something more momentous than anyone had expected, and more unforeseen. And she had lost– No, she hadn't lost yet! She ran out onto the lawn, calling to him, letting the action quell the confusion in her mind.

And in the repeated event there was concealed a little freshness, for she remembered how his smile, glimpsed through the window, had held a special warmth, as if he sought to reassure her. What had he said? That was lost. She walked over to the seat and sat beside him.

He had been saving a remark for the statutory and unvarying time lapse.

"Don't worry, Janet," he said. "It could be worse."

"How?" she asked, but he was already answering: "We could be a day apart. 3.3077 minutes at least allows us a measure of communication."

"It's wonderful how philosophical you are about it," she said. She was alarmed at the sarcasm in her tone.

"Shall we have a talk together now?"

"Jack, I've been wanting to have a private talk with you for some time."

"I?"

The tall beeches that sheltered the garden on the north side were so still that she thought, "They will look exactly the same for him as for me."

He delivered a bulletin, looking at his watch. His wrists were thin. He appeared frailer than he had done when they left hospital. "I am aware, my darling, how painful this must be for you. We are both isolated from the other by this amazing shift of temporal function, but at least I have the consolation of experiencing the new phenomenon, whereas you–"

"I?"

Talking of interstellar distances

"I was going to say that you are stuck with the same old world all of mankind has always known, but I suppose you don't see it that way." Evidently a remark of hers had caught up with him, for he added inconsequentially, "I've wanted a private talk with you."

Janet bit off something she was going to say, for he raised a finger irritably and said, "Please time your statements, so that we do not talk at cross purposes. Confine what you have to say to essentials. Really, darling, I'm surprised you don't do as Clem suggests, and make notes of what is said at what time."

"That–I just wanted–we can't act as if we were a board meeting. I want to know your feelings, how you are, what you are thinking, so that I can help you, so that eventually you will be able to live a normal life again."

He was timing it so that he answered almost at once, "I am not suffering from any mental illness, and I have completely recovered my physical health after the crash. There is no reason to foresee that my perceptions will ever lapse back into phase with yours. They have remained an unfluctuating 3.3077 minutes ahead of terrestrial time ever since our ship left the surface of Mars."

He paused. She thought, "It is now about 11.03 by my watch, and there is so much I long to say. But it's 11.06 and a bit by *his* time, and he already knows I can't say anything. It's such an effort of endurance talking across this three and a bit minutes; we might just as well be talking across an interstellar distance."

Evidently he too had lost the thread of the exercise, for he smiled and stretched out a hand, holding it in the air. Janet looked round. Clem Stackpole was coming out towards them with a tray full of drinks. He set it carefully down on the lawn, and picked up a martini, the stem of which he slipped between Jack's fingers.

"Cheers!" he said, smiling, and, "Here's your tipple," giving Janet her gin and tonic. He had brought himself a bottle of pale ale.

"Can you make my position clearer to Janet, Clem? She does *not* seem to understand it yet."

Angrily, she turned to the behaviourist. "This was meant to be a private talk, Mr. Stackpole, between my husband and myself."

"Sorry you're not getting on too well, then. Perhaps I can help sort you out a bit. It is difficult, I know."

3.3077

Powerfully, he wrenched the top off the beer bottle and poured the liquid into the glass. Sipping, he said, "We have always been used to the idea that everything moves forward in time at the same rate. We speak of the course of time, presuming it only has one rate of flow. We've assumed, too, that anything living on another planet in any other part of our universe might have the same rate of flow. In other words, although we've long been accustomed to some oddities of time, thanks to relativity theories, we have accustomed ourselves, perhaps, to certain errors of thinking. Now we're going to have to think differently. You follow me."

"Perfectly."

"The universe is by no means the simple box our predecessors imagined. It may be that each planet is encased in its own time field, just as it is in its own gravitational field. From the evidence, it seems that Mars's time field is 3.3077 minutes ahead of ours on Earth. We deduce this from the fact that your husband and the eight other men with him on Mars experienced no sensation of temporal difference among themselves, and were unaware that anything was untoward until they were away from Mars and attempted to get into communication again with Earth, when the temporal discrepancy at once showed up. Your husband is still living in Mars time. Unfortunately, the other members of the crew did not survive the crash; but we can be sure that if they did, they too would suffer from the same effect. That's clear, isn't it?"

"Entirely. But I still cannot see why this effect, if it is as you say–"

"It's not what *I* say, Janet, but the conclusion arrived at by much cleverer men than I." He smiled as he said that, adding parenthetically, "Not that we don't develop and even alter our conclusions every day."

"Then why was a similar effect not noticed when the Russians and Americans returned from the moon?"

"We don't know. There's so much we don't know. We *surmise* that because the moon is a satellite of Earth's, and thus within its gravitational field, there is no temporal discrepancy. But until we have more data, until we can explore further, we know so little, and can only speculate so much. It's like trying to estimate the runs of an entire innings when only one over has been bowled. After the expedition gets back from Venus, we shall be in a much better position to start theorising."

"*What* expedition to Venus?" she asked, shocked.

"It may not leave for a year yet, but they're speeding up the programme. That will bring us really invaluable data."

Future time with its uses and abuses

She started to say, "But after this surely they won't be fool enough–" Then she stopped. She knew they would be fool enough.

She thought of Peter saying, "I'm going to be a spaceman too. *I* want to be the first man on Saturn!"

The men were looking at their watches. Westermark transferred his gaze to the gravel to say, "This figure of 3.3077 is surely not a universal constant. It may vary–I think it will vary–from planetary body to planetary body. My private opinion is that it is bound to be connected with solar activity in some way. If that is so, then we may find that the men returning from Venus will be perceiving on a continuum slightly in arrears of Earth time."

He stood up suddenly looking dismayed, the absorption gone from his face.

"That's a point that hadn't occurred to me," Stackpole said, making a note. "If the expedition to Venus is primed with these points beforehand, we should have no trouble about organising their return. Ultimately, this confusion will be sorted out, and I've no doubt that it will eventually vastly enrich the culture of mankind. The possibilities are of such enormity that . . ."

"It's awful! You're all crazy!" Janet exclaimed. She jumped up and hurried off towards the house.

Or then again

Jack began to move after her towards the house. By his watch, which showed Earth time, it was 11.18 and twelve seconds; he thought, not the first time, that he would invest in another watch, which would be strapped to his right wrist and show Martian time. No, the one on his left wrist should show Martian time, for that was the wrist he principally consulted and the time by which he lived, even when going through the business of communicating with the earth-bound human race.

He realised he was now moving ahead of Janet, by her reckoning. It would be interesting to have someone ahead of *him* in perception; then he would wish to converse, would want to go to the labour of it. Although it would rob him of the sensation that he was perpetually first in the universe, first everywhere, with everything dewy in that strange light–Marslight! He'd call it that, till he had it classified, the romantic visions preceding the scientific, with a touch of the grand permissible before the steadying discipline closed in. Or then again, suppose they were wrong in their theories, and the perceptual effect was some freak of the long space journey itself; supposing time were quantal. . . . Supposing *all* time were quantal. After all, ageing was a matter of steps, not a smooth progress, for much of the inorganic world as for the organic.

Now he was standing quite still on the lawn. The glaze was coming through the grass, making it look brittle, almost tingeing each blade with a tiny spectrum of light. If his perceptual time were further ahead than it was now, would the Marslight be stronger, the Earth more translucent? How beautiful it would look! After a longer star journey one would return to a cobweb of a world, centuries behind one in perceptual time, a mere embodiment of light, a prism. Hungrily, he visualised it. But they needed more knowledge.

Suddenly he thought, If I could get on the Venus expedition! If the institute's right, I'd be perhaps six, say five and a half–no, one can't say–but I'd be ahead of Venerean time. I *must* go. I'd be valuable to them. I only have to volunteer, surely.

He did not notice Stackpole touch his arm in cordial fashion and go past him into the house. He stood looking at the ground and through it, to the stony vales of Mars and the unguessable landscapes of Venus.

The figures move

Janet had consented to ride into town with Stackpole. He was collecting his cricket shoes, which had been restudded; she thought she might buy a roll of film for her camera. The children would like photos of her and Daddy together. Standing together.

As the car ran beside trees, their shadows flickered red and green before her vision. Stackpole held the wheel very capably, whistling under his breath. Strangely, she did not resent a habit she would normally have found irksome, taking it as a sign that he was not entirely at his ease.

"I have an awful feeling you now understand my husband better than I do," she said.

He did not deny it. "Why do you feel that?"

"I believe he does not mind the terrible isolation he must be experiencing."

"He's a brave man."

Westermark had been home a week now. Janet saw that each day they were more removed from each other, as he spoke less and stood frequently as still as a statue, gazing at the ground raptly. She thought of something she had once been afraid to utter aloud to her mother-in-law; but with Clem Stackpole she was safer.

"You know why we manage to exist in comparative harmony," she said. He was slowing the car, half looking at her. "We only manage to exist by banishing all events from our lives, all children, all seasons. Otherwise we'd be faced at every moment with the knowledge of how much at odds we really are."

Catching the note in her voice, Stackpole said soothingly, "You are every bit as brave as he is, Janet."

"Damn being brave. What I can't bear is—nothing!"

Seeing the sign by the side of the road, Stackpole glanced into his driving mirror and changed gear. The road was deserted in front as well as behind. He whistled through his teeth again, and Janet felt compelled to go on talking.

"We've already interfered with time too much—all of us, I mean. Time is a European invention. Goodness knows how mixed up in it we are going to get if—well, if this goes on." She was irritated by the lack of her usual coherence.

As Stackpole spoke next, he was pulling the car into a lay-by, stopping it by overhanging bushes. He turned to her, smiling tolerantly. "Time was God's invention, if you believe in God, as I prefer to do. We observe it, tame it, exploit it where possible."

"Exploit it!"

"You mustn't think of the future as if we were all wading knee deep in treacle or something." He laughed briefly, resting his hands on the steering wheel. "What lovely weather it is! I was wondering—on Sunday I'm playing cricket over in the village. Would you like to come and watch the match? And perhaps we could have tea somewhere afterwards."

All events, all children, all seasons

She had a letter next morning from Jane, her five-year-old daughter, and it made her think. All the letter said was: "Dear Mummy, Thank you for the dollies. With love from Jane," but Janet knew the labour that had gone into the inch-high letters. How long could she bear to leave the children away from their home and her care?

As soon as the thought emerged, she recalled that during the previous evening she had told herself nebulously that if there was going to be "anything" with Stackpole, it was as well the children would be out of the way—purely, she now realised, for her convenience and for Stackpole's. She had not thought then about the children; she had thought about Stackpole, who, despite the unexpected delicacy he had shown, was not a man she cared for.

"And another intolerably immoral thought," she muttered unhappily to the empty room, "what alternative have I to Stackpole?"

She knew Westermark was in his study. It was a cold day, too cold and damp for him to make his daily parade round the garden. She knew he was sinking deeper into isolation, she longed to help, she feared to sacrifice herself to that isolation, longed to stay outside it, in life. Dropping the letter, she held her head in her hands, closing her eyes as in the curved bone of her skull she heard all her possible courses of action jar together, future lifelines that annihilated each other.

As Janet stood transfixed, Westermark's mother came into the room.

"I was looking for you," she said. "You're so unhappy, my dear, aren't you?"

"Mother, people always try and hide from others how they suffer. Does everyone do it?"

"You don't have to hide it from me–chiefly, I suppose, because you can't."

"But I don't know how much *you* suffer, and it ought to work both ways. Why do we do this awful covering up? What are we afraid of –pity or derision?"

"Help, perhaps."

"Help! Perhaps you're right. . . . That's a disconcerting thought."

They stood there staring at each other, until the older woman said, awkwardly, "We don't often talk like this, Janet."

"No." She wanted to say more. To a stranger in a train, perhaps she would have done; here, she could not deliver.

Seeing nothing more was to be said on that subject, Mrs. Westermark said, "I was going to tell you, Janet, that I thought perhaps it would be better if the children didn't come back here while things are as they are. If you want to go and see them and stay with them at your parents' house, I can look after Jack and Mr. Stackpole for a week. I don't think Jack wants to see them."

"That's very kind, Mother. I'll see. I promised Clem–well, I told Mr. Stackpole that perhaps I'd go and watch him play cricket tomorrow afternoon. It's not important, of course, but I did say–anyhow, I might drive over and see the children on Monday, if you could hold the fort."

"You've still plenty of time if you feel like going today. I'm sure Mr. Stackpole will understand your maternal feelings."

"I'd prefer to leave it till Monday," Janet said—a little distantly, for she suspected now the motive behind her mother-in-law's suggestion.

Where the Scientific American *did not reach*

Jack Westermark put down the *Scientific American* and stared at the table top. With his right hand, he felt the beat of his heart. In the magazine was an article about him, illustrated with photographs of him taken at the Research Hospital. This thoughtful article was far removed from the sensational pieces that had appeared elsewhere, the shallow things that referred to him as The Man That Has Done More Than Einstein to Wreck Our Cosmic Picture; and for that very reason it was the more startling, and presented some aspects of the matter that Westermark himself had not considered.

As he thought over its conclusions, he rested from the effort of reading terrestrial books, and Stackpole sat by the fire, smoking a cigar and waiting to take Westermark's dictation. Even reading a magazine represented a feat in space-time, a collaboration, a conspiracy. Stackpole turned the pages at timed intervals, Westermark read when they lay flat. He was unable to turn them when, in their own narrow continuum, they were not being turned; to his fingers, they lay under the jellylike glaze, that visual hallucination that represented an unconquerable cosmic inertia.

The inertia gave a special shine to the surface of the table as he stared into it and probed into his own mind to determine the truths of the *Scientific American* article.

The writer of the article began by considering the facts and observing that they tended to point towards the existence of "local times" throughout the universe; and that if this were so, a new explanation might be forthcoming for the recession of the galaxies and different estimates arrived at for the age of the universe (and of course for its complexity). He then proceeded to deal with the problem that vexed other writers on the subject; namely, why, if Westermark lost Earth time on Mars, he had not reciprocally lost Mars time back on Earth. This, more than anything, pointed to the fact that "local times" were not purely mechanistic but to some extent at least a psychobiological function.

In the table top, Westermark saw himself being asked to travel again to Mars, to take part in a second expedition to those continents of russet sand where the fabric of space-time was in some mysterious and insuperable fashion 3.3077 minutes ahead of Earth norm. Would his interior clock leap forward again? What then of the sheen on things earthly? And what would be the effect of gradually drawing away from the iron laws under which, since its scampering Pleistocene infancy, humankind had lived?

Impatiently he thrust his mind forward to imagine the day when Earth harboured many local times, gleaned from voyages across the vacancies of space; those vacancies lay across time too, and that little-understood concept (McTaggart had denied its external reality, hadn't he?) would come to lie within the grasp of man's understanding. Wasn't that the ultimate secret, to be able to understand the flux in which existence is staged, as a dream is staged in the primitive reaches of the mind?

And– But– Would not that day bring the annihilation of Earth's local time? That was what he had started. It could only mean that "local time" was not a product of planetary elements; there the writer of the *Scientific American* article had not dared to go far enough; local time was entirely a product of the psyche. That dark innermost thing that could keep accurate time even while a man lay unconscious was a mere provincial; but it could be educated to be a citizen of the universe. He saw that he was the first of a new race, unimaginable in the wildest mind a few months previously. He was independent of the enemy that, more than Death, menaced contemporary man: Time. Locked within him was an entirely new potential. Superman had arrived.

Painfully, Superman stirred in his seat. He sat so rapt for so long that his limbs grew stiff and dead without his noticing it.

Universal thoughts may occur if one times carefully enough one's circumbendibus about a given table

"Dictation," he said, and waited impatiently until the command had penetrated backwards to the limbo by the fire where Stackpole sat. What he had to say was so terribly important–yet it had to wait on these people. . . .

As was his custom, he rose and began to walk round the table, speaking in phrases quickly delivered. This was to be the testament to the new way of life. . . .

"Consciousness is not expendable but concurrent. . . . There may have been many time nodes at the beginning of the human race. . . . The mentally deranged often revert to different time rates. For some, a day seems to stretch on forever. . . . We know by experience that for children time is seen in the convex mirror of consciousness, enlarged and distorted beyond its focal point. . . ." He was momentarily irritated by the scared face of his wife appearing outside the study window, but he brushed it away and continued.

". . . its focal point. . . . Yet man in his ignorance has persisted in pretending time was some sort of uni-directional flow, and homogenous at that . . . despite the evidence to the contrary. . . . Our conception of ourselves–no, this erroneous conception has become a basic life assumption. . . ."

Daughters of daughters

Westermark's mother was not given to metaphysical speculation, but as she was leaving the room, she turned and said to her daughter-in-law, "You know what I sometimes think? Jack is so strange, I wonder at nights if men and women aren't getting more and more apart in thought and in their ways with every generation–you know, almost like separate species. My generation made a great attempt to bring the two sexes together in equality and all the rest, but it seems to have come to nothing."

"Jack will get better." Janet could hear the lack of confidence in her own voice.

"I thought the same thing–about men and women getting wider apart I mean–when my husband was killed."

Suddenly all Janet's sympathy was gone. She had recognised a familiar topic drifting onto the scene, knew well the careful tone that ironed away all self-pity as her mother-in-law said, "Bob was dedicated to speed, you know. That was what killed him really, not the fool backing into the road in front of him."

"No blame was attached to your husband," Janet said. "You should try not to let it worry you still."

"You see the connection though. . . . This progress thing. Bob so crazy to get round the next bend first, and now Jack. . . . Oh well, there's nothing a woman can do."

She closed the door behind her. Absently, Janet picked up the message from the next generation of women: "Thank you for the dollies."

The resolves and the sudden risks involved

He was their father. Perhaps Jane and Peter should come back, despite the risks involved. Anxiously, Janet stood there, moving herself with a sudden resolve to tackle Jack straight away. He was so irritable, so unapproachable, but at least she could observe how busy he was before interrupting him.

As she slipped into the side hall and made for the back door, she heard her mother-in-law call her. "Just a minute!" she answered.

The sun had broken through, sucking moisture from the damp garden. It was now unmistakably autumn. She rounded the corner of the house, stepped round the rose bed, and looked into her husband's study.

Shaken, she saw he leaned half over the table. His hands were over his face, blood ran between his fingers and dripped onto an open magazine on the table top. She was aware of Stackpole sitting indifferently beside the electric fire.

She gave a small cry and ran round the house again, to be met at the back door by Mrs. Westermark.

"Oh, I was just– Janet, what is it?"

"Jack, Mother! He's had a stroke or something terrible!"

"But how do you know?"

"Quick, we must phone the hospital–I must go to him."

Mrs. Westermark took Janet's arm. "Perhaps we'd better leave it to Mr. Stackpole, hadn't we? I'm afraid–"

"Mother, we must do what we can. I know we're amateurs. Please let me go."

"No, Janet, we're–it's *their* world. I'm frightened. They'll come if they want us." She was gripping Janet in her fright. Their wild eyes stared momentarily at each other as if seeing something else, and then Janet snatched herself away. "I must go to him," she said.

She hurried down the hall and pushed open the study door. Her husband stood now at the far end of the room by the window, while blood streamed from his nose.

"Jack!" she exclaimed. As she ran toward him, a blow from the empty air struck her on the forehead, so that she staggered aside, falling against a bookcase. A shower of smaller volumes from the upper shelf fell on her and round her. Exclaiming, Stackpole dropped his notebook and ran round the table to her. Even as he went to her aid, he noted the time from his watch: 10.24.

Aid after 10.24 and the tidiness of bed

Westermark's mother appeared in the doorway.

"Stay where you are," Stackpole shouted, "or there will be more trouble! Janet, you see what you've done. Get out of here, will you?

Jack, I'm right with you—God knows what you've felt, isolated without aid for three and a third minutes!" Angrily, he went across and stood within arm's length of his patient. He threw his handkerchief down onto the table.

"Mr. Stackpole—" Westermark's mother said tentatively from the door, an arm round Janet's waist.

He looked back over his shoulder only long enough to say, "Get towels! Phone the Research Hospital for an ambulance and tell them to be here right away."

By midday, Westermark was tidily in bed upstairs and the ambulance staff, who had treated him for what after all was only nosebleed, had left. Stackpole, as he turned from closing the front door, eyed the two women.

"I feel it is my duty to warn you," he said heavily, "that another incident such as this might well prove fatal. This time we escaped very lightly. If anything else of this sort happens, I shall feel obliged to recommend to the board that Mr. Westermark is moved back to the hospital."

Current way to define accidents

"He wouldn't want to go," Janet said. "Besides, you are being absurd; it was entirely an accident. Now I wish to go upstairs and see how he is."

"Just before you go, may I point out that what happened was *not* an accident—or not as we generally define accidents, since you saw the results of your interference through the study window before you entered. Where you were to blame—"

"But that's absurd—" both women began at once. Janet went on to say, "I never would have rushed into the room as I did had I not seen through the window that he was in trouble."

"What you saw was the result on your husband of your later interference."

In something like a wail, Westermark's mother said, "I don't understand any of this. What did Janet bump into when she ran in?"

"She ran, Mrs. Westermark, into the spot where her husband had been standing 3.3077 minutes earlier. Surely by now you have grasped this elementary business of time inertia?"

When they both started speaking at once, he stared at them until they stopped and looked at him. Then he said, "We had better go into the living room. Speaking for myself, I would like a drink."

He helped himself, and not until his hand was round a glass of whisky did he say, "Now, without wishing to lecture to you ladies, I think it is high time you both realised that you are not living in the old safe world of classical mechanics ruled over by a god invented by eighteenth-century enlightenment. All that has happened here is perfectly rational, but if you are going to pretend it is beyond your female understandings–"

"Mr. Stackpole," Janet said sharply. "Can you please keep to the point without being insulting? Will you tell me why what happened was not an accident? I understand now that when I looked through the study window I saw my husband suffering from a collision that to him had happened three and something minutes before and to me would not happen for another three and something minutes, but at that moment I was so startled that I forgot–"

"No, no, your figures are wrong. The *total* time lapse is only 3.3077 minutes. When you saw your husband, he had been hit half that time–1.65385 minutes–ago, and there was another 1.65385 minutes to go before you completed the action by bursting into the room and striking him."

"But she *didn't* strike him!" the older woman cried.

Firmly, Stackpole diverted his attention long enough to reply. "She struck him at 10.24 Earthtime, which equals 10.20 plus about 36 seconds Mars or his time, which equals 9.59 or whatever Neptune time, which equals 156 and a half Sirius time. It's a big universe, Mrs. Westermark! You will remain confused as long as you continue to confuse event with time. May I suggest you sit down and have a drink?"

"Leaving aside the figures," Janet said, returning to the attack–loathsome opportunist the man was–"how can you say that what happened was no accident? You are not claiming I injured my husband deliberately, I hope? What you say suggests that I was powerless from the moment I saw him through the window."

"'Leaving aside the figures . . .'" he quoted. "That's where your responsibility lies. What you saw through the window was the result of your act; it was by then inevitable that you should complete it, for it had already been completed."

Through the window, draughts of time blow

"I can't understand!" She clutched her forehead, gratefully accepting a cigarette from her mother-in-law, while shrugging off her consolatory "Don't try to understand, dear!" "Supposing when I had seen Jack's nose bleeding, I had looked at my watch and thought, It's 10.20 or whenever it was, and he may be suffering from my interference, so I'd better not go in, and I *hadn't* gone in? Would his nose then miraculously have healed?"

"Of course not. You take such a mechanistic view of the universe. Cultivate a mental approach, try and live in your own century! You could not think what you suggest because that is not in your nature: just as it is not in your nature to consult your watch intelligently, just as you always 'leave aside the figures,' as you say. No, I'm not being personal; it's all very feminine and appealing in a way. What I'm saying is that if *before* you looked into the window you had been a person to think, 'However I see my husband now, I must recall he has the additional experience of the next 3.3077 minutes,' then you could have looked in and seen him unharmed, and you would not have come bursting in as you did."

She drew on her cigarette, baffled and hurt. "You're saying I'm a danger to my own husband."

"*You're* saying that."

"God, how I hate men!" she exclaimed. "You're so bloody logical, so bloody smug!"

He finished his whisky and set the glass down on a table beside her so that he leant close. "You're upset just now," he said.

"Of course I'm upset! What do you think?" She fought a desire to cry or slap his face. She turned to Jack's mother, who gently took her wrist.

"Why don't you go off straight away and stay with the children for the weekend, darling? Come back when you feel like it. Jack will be all right and I can look after him—as much as he wants looking after."

She glanced about the room.

"I will. I'll pack right away. They'll be glad to see me." As she passed Stackpole on the way out, she said bitterly, "At least *they* won't be worrying about the local time on Sirius!"

"They may," said Stackpole, imperturbably from the middle of the room, "have to one day."

All events, all children, all seasons

FOUR BRANDS OF IMPOSSIBLE

by Norman Kagan

"THAT CONCLUDES the Travis-Waldinger Theorem," said Professor Greenfield. "As you can see, it's really quite trivial."

"Then why did it take people to prove it!" piped up one teenage hotshot.

The bell cut off Greenfield's reply, and most of the class bolted. All the mathematics people at my school are bad—Greenfield the geometer was a mild case. His motto was: "If you can visualize it, it isn't geometry!" Which is not so bad compared to my other course, where rule one was: "If it seems to make sense, then it's not mathematical logic!"

Which reminded me I still had to find out about my grade in that subject, along with about aleph-sub-aleph other things—most important of which was securing a nice fat student-trainee job for the summer that was fast approaching. I elbowed my way past a couple of teenage hotshots, and then I was in the open air.

I decided I'd check out my marks later—the IBMed grades would be posted on the "wailing wall" all summer. Right now I'd leg it over to the Multiversity Placement Service. I could study for Greenfield's final this afternoon.

I walked across the campus slowly, checking myself out. "Do not judge according to appearance." Try telling that to some of these megabuck research corporations! I mussed my hair and put three more pencils in my breast pocket, and decided not to wear my glasses at the interview. It's amazing how much easier it is to lie to someone you can't really see.

"Hey, Zirkle—Perry—wait half a mo'!"

Harry Mandel hailed me from the psychology library. I grinned and waited for him to join me.

Harry is a swell guy, and besides he's a psychology major, not a math competitor. He joined me, puffing, a moment later. "Summer job hunting?"

"Yeah. I've got a couple of interviews arranged, Serendipity, Inc., and the Virgin Research Corporation."

"Me, too," said Harry. He gestured at my tousled hair. "Getting ready? Physical appearance is very important, you know." The short, pudgy psychology major pumped his legs to keep up with me.

It was a warm, comfortable day on the Multiversity campus. The long rows of wooden chairs were already set up for graduation, and here and there was a girl in long hair and levis, or a bearded boy with a guitar. Early summer-session people. Lazy jerks.

"What's the word on the companies?"

Mandel wrinkled up his forehead. "Personnel men–not technical people. So if you've got the grades, go all out–anything to avoid the paper barrier."

"Any specific suggestions?"

"Mmmm–well, Fester pulled a full-scale epileptic fit–but then he's nearly a five-point. If you're just bright, a few eccentricities ought to do it. I'm trying my bug-on-the-walls gambit."

"You mean the one where you pretend there's a bug that crawls all over the walls behind the interviewer, and you follow it with your eyes."

"No–that was last year. In this one I sort of scrunch up in the chair, cowering–give 'em the impression I can't stand confined spaces, need lots of room–like, say, New Mexico or Arizona. I'm sick of this East Coast weather, and the Virgin Research Corporation has labs in New Mexico."

"That's for me, too. I'll see what I can think up."

In the 1980's, it's practically impossible to get a summer job in the sciences–not that the big science and engineering corporations don't want you, they do. But to apply, you've got to submit about a ton of paperwork–eight commendations, four transcripts, character references, handwriting samples, personality profiles, certificates and forms and diplomas. Who has the energy?

Science and engineering majors, however, have worked out a swell dodge–we just pretend we're a little nuts. The big company personnel departments are endlessly amused by the antics of their nutty research wizards. With the squeeze on for technical people, it's easy to fake looniness well enough for the personnel men to see that cause follows from effect, in that wonderful way of theirs, and conclude we're the brilliant boys they're looking for.

Or maybe they just get a kick out of watching us degrade ourselves in front of them.

I had a couple of swell dodges I'd worked out from one of my professors—through the length of the interview I'd keep pulling a piece of chalk from my pocket, sticking it into my mouth, then spitting it out and muttering, "Simply must give up smoking!" For dubious types, I'd offer my *pièce de résistance:* all through the talk I would gesture and wave my arms, seeming to shape the very job concept out of the air. Then, when the interview had reached a critical juncture, I'd pause, drop to the floor, and lie on my back staring at the empty spaces I'd been manipulating. As the interviewer came round the desk, I'd cry out in annoyance, "Simply must look at this from a new point of view!" It worked like a charm.

Except for this time. Not that it didn't; I just never got the chance to use it. On this job, all the craziness came at the end.

The interviewer for the Virgin Research Corporation was a big blond crewcut man with terribly stained teeth and a sadist's smile. He reminded me of one of my philosophy professors. He was talking philo at me too, about half a second after I sat down in the little interview cubicle.

"Glad to meet you, Mr. Zirkle—you're a mathematics major, by your application. Is that right?"

I nodded.

"Sit down, sit down," he said, gesturing. "Now, before I begin to ask about you, I'd like to tell you a little about the activities of the Virgin Research Corporation, Mama, as we call her around the shop. Our organization is concerned with the three aspects of pure research, what we like to call 'The Three Brands of Impossible.' "

I nodded at this. Harry Mandel's eyes had been shining when he'd passed me outside the room, but he hadn't time to whisper more than a fiery, "Grab it, fellow!" to me before I was ushered in. I hunched forward and began to listen.

"If we ignore subjective problems—what the Kansas farmer said when he saw his first kangaroo—we might analyze the concept of the impossible as follows—"

He pulled out a diagram, and his finger danced down it as he continued to speak.

"First, there is the 'technically impossible'—things that are not possible in practice, though there's no real reason why they can't be done. Things like putting the toothpaste back in the toothpaste tube, or sending an astronaut to Saturn—such things aren't practical at the moment, I think," he said, smiling briefly.

"Then there is the notion of the 'scientifically impossible'—traveling faster than light, or building a perpetual-motion machine. These are not possible at all–within the limitations of what we know about the universe. But you'll recall, a heavier-than-air flying machine was a 'scientific impossibility' a century ago.

"These two categories have merged somewhat in the twentieth century, though the distinction is clear enough. In the first case, the 'technically impossible,' theory allows you to do the impossible–you just haven't the techniques. In the second instance, the 'scientifically impossible,' you've got no *theoretical* justification for what you want to do. But in both cases, men have 'done the impossible'–either developed new techniques or found the flaws and limitations in the theories.

"But there is a third category of the impossible, one ignored by even the most farsighted researchers–the 'logically impossible'!" The interviewer's voice rose in triumph, and his other hand, which had remained in his pocket, furiously jangled his change.

I blinked at him. "But the logically impossible is–"

"I know, I know, I've listened to that stuff from our professional consultants," said the big blond man, suddenly impatient. "The logically impossible is part of an arbitrary system which would be destroyed by any attempt to–" He shrugged his shoulders in annoyance. "Let me tell you," he cried, "that the Virgin Research Corporation has investigated the problem and decided otherwise. Our experts have–and they are some of the best men in the field, much better than any jerky Ivy League Multiversity can afford–our experts are convinced that such notions as the 'round-square' are meaningful, and, what's more, are of potentially great military value!"

His eyes were crazed. " 'When the battle's lost and won,' indeed," he murmured in a low, sinister voice. He smiled at me coldly, and the rotten stains on his teeth stood out like the craters of the moon. "We're using a two-pronged approach–psychology and mathematical logic. We've had no trouble recruiting psychology majors," he continued in a normal tone, "but most of the students in the mathematics department weren't interested–or they've got to spend the summer with their families at home or away."

It was my turn to grin. That's what they got for trying to interest any of the teenage hotshots. But I wasn't afraid to broaden my mental horizons, I was willing to wrestle with the impossible, I was brave enough to face the unknown. My smile widened, and then my face grew serious as I took up the challenge.

"How much?"

"Two fifty a week, recommendations, room and board, and a motor scooter, and free transportation in a G.E.M. cruiser to and from the New Mexico labs," said the blond man.

"Well–"

"With your record, you should jump at the chance," he said. "I've seen your transcripts, son." He began jangling his change again.

That "son" decided me. "Hmmmm–"

"All right, all right, we'll talk it over," he said, a little sharply. In science and mathematics, all the old guys are scared of all the young guys. You do your best work when you are young, and everyone's scared of being "burned out at thirty." Just like I'd love to line my teenage competitors up against a wall and plug 'em, I could see he was scared of me.

He pulled out my preliminary transcripts and applications, and began thumbing them. I slipped off my glasses, and licked my lips.

Later I found out I got A-minus on the mathematical logic final. I should've asked for fifty more than the three-twenty-five I got out of that terrified jerk.

The G.E.M. *Ruby* thundered west, the ground effect keeping it a dozen feet above the earth. The machine soared along, impossibly graceful, as night mastered day on the American Great Plains.

I peered out the big picture window, fully relaxed for the first time in many weeks. The orientation and information kit lay ignored across my knees. I'd look at it later. No more lab reports, no more little phrases like "I'll leave that as an exercise" that meant a dozen hours of skull sweat, no more "I'm sorry, but some pre-med sliced those pages out of the book you wanted with a razor blade last term." At the moment, I didn't care if the directors of the Virgin Research Corporation had cerebrum, cerebellum and medulla in their brain pans, or scrambled eggs. By Napier's bones, I'd escaped!

Someone was struggling up the aisle against the pressure of the *Ruby's* acceleration (we'd just pulled out of Ann Arbor). With a gasp he collapsed into the acceleration chair beside me. "Greetings!" I murmured. "You one of Mama's boys?" About half the people on the *Ruby* were working for V.R.C. It's only these tremendous mysterious corporations that can afford intercontinental jet flights and G.E.M.s and–and pure mathematicians, thank goodness!

"Hello, yes," said my companion. He was a skinny, baffled-looking fellow about my own age. His very pale face said, "Yourself?"

"Perry Zirkle–I'm in the numbers racket–uh, I'm a pure mathematician."

"Uh, Richard Colby–microminiaturization and electronics–I'm a grad student at Michigan Multi. If you can see it, then it's too big. My motto." Colby's face brightened and he grinned. *His* teeth were okay. "Say, I've got those books–you must be on the logical impossibility research the same as I am–Project Round-Square!"

I nodded and smirked at the books. "I suppose so–though from what I've been taught, I doubt if the project will last very long."

Colby settled himself and relaxed. "How so?" he asked. He didn't look like a monomaniacal studier–just an electron pusher in his twenties. He wasn't one of these kid geniuses, either, and I was rested and relaxed. So naturally, my mouth got the better of me.

"Just on the face of it," I argued calmly, "paradoxes and self-contradictions are interesting, and they attract attention to ideas, but by their very nature–" I found myself unable to continue.

"Maybe," Colby said. "But maybe you're just looking at the problem the wrong way–the fellow that interviewed me kept talking about 'thinking in other categories.' "

I paused. "Oh, I know what he meant," I said, and laughed. "He was trying to tell you not to argue, not at two-fifty a week."

"Two-twenty-five," he murmured.

The electronics expert hesitated, and then looked at me oddly. "I don't know about you," he muttered, "but I consider it an honor and a pleasure to be able to do some 'pure' research. There's little enough of it in electronics these days–the whole subject has about one real scientist to a hundred engineers." His eyes were hooded. In the dimly lit passenger compartment of the G.E.M., his face was dark and brooding. He licked his lips and went on, talking to himself as much as he was to me.

"It's enough to make you go into industry. Take my own school, the Michigan Multiversity. Did you know we have a top-secret Congressional Project to automate the presidency? Fact. The chairman of the Department of Cybernetics told me the system philosophy behind it: Roosevelt showed that someone could be President as long as he liked. Truman proved that anyone could be President. Eisenhower demonstrated that you don't really need a President. And Kennedy was further proof that it's dangerous to *be* a human President. So we're working out a way to automate the office." He grinned, and I laughed in response.

I reached down into my fagbag and pulled out a bottle. His eyes went wide for a moment, but I passed it to him. He took a slug, and the evening was on its way.

Colby turned out to be all right. I told him Smith's remark about how engineers are sloppy when they call "characteristic values" "eigenvalues," because "eigenvalue" isn't good English. He came back with the one about the sequence that you had to prove converged, but that all the students demonstrated diverged. The professor's masterful reply was: "It converges *slowly*."

The ground-effect machine rushed on through the Mid-western night, a foot or two above the earth, supported by a flaring cushion of air. Presently its path curved south. The pilot-driver was steering by radar beacon and navigation satellite, towns and buildings signifying no more than treacherous shoals and reefs to a sailor. The craft was flying over ground that had never been and might now never be touched by wheels or feet. Over these wastes we plunged southwest.

Dick Colby couldn't hold it very well, or maybe he was tired. In any event the fellow was soon sleeping peacefully beside me. I let him be and stared at the scenery.

These fellows that believe the "pures vs. applieds" battle really amuse me. Actually, science and scientists are just like anything else in this rotten world, just as corrupt. I've heard stories of research men during the great "Space Flight Bubble" that would trade jobs a dozen times in a year, doubling their salary each time. And these stories about advertising men that run off with the best accounts and start their own agencies? Nothing to the technical men that impress the Pentagon and get the generals to finance them in their own electronics company. Though I don't feel much sympathy for the big firms. Anyone that builds H-bombs and missiles and lets someone else decide what to do with them—people like that deserve everything they get!

What was wrong with me lately? I still loved to work and study, to cram till one, then feel the high tension as the papers were handed out the next day. The gong that announced the start of the test always reminded me of the one on the old TV show, "Beat the Clock." And there was nothing like the feeling in front of the posted grades, when I saw the shocked faces of the youngsters I'd beaten out. Tough luck, kid! Better switch to art history!

I lit a cigarette and leaned back. Well, right or wrong, this stuff would be fun. Science always is. I love to be totally absorbed in something new and strange. It's so much better than just sitting around doing nothing, or dull routine stuff. Frankly, I don't see how the hundred million unemployed can take it. My mood when I'm idle is usually a murderous rage at the kids who're going to parties and dances and junk like that. Not that that stuff is really *interesting,* like a problem in Greenfield space. But at least it's something, compared to sitting all alone with nothing to think about but myself. Frankly, I love really tough problems, the kind you have to think about *all the time.*

Dawn was peeping up over the horizon. I settled myself in my own acceleration chair, and tried to snatch a little sleep. My own watch said that in a few hours we'd arrive at the immense desert reservation which held the Virgin Research Corporation, summer student trainees for the enigmatic Project Round-Square.

"These are your quarters, Mr. Colby and Mr. Zirkle," said the blond girl. She was worth a second glance, being the possessor of a fine body, though a little bowlegged ("Pleasure bent," Colby murmured). Still, a very nice body.

Colby dumped his junk on the bed, and began opening drawers in the dresser and putting it away. I stood still and read the information sheet we'd been given on arrival. It said I had to report at the Computer Center as soon as convenient. I put my own bags in the closet and went.

Outside, the desert sunlight was quite bearable, since it was only a few hours after sunup. I walked across the compound, guided by a map on the fact sheet.

The living quarters were good: simple ranch-style stuff with desks, and bookshelves duplicated in each room. This was no resort, but the place was clean and kept up, without the bleakness of a straight government installation. The labs and auxiliary buildings were spread out over the desert, the whole business enclosed by a security frontier. This made internal security checks unnecessary, and there were none.

People dressed informally: chinos, dungarees, Western boots and flannel shirts. A pleasant change after school, where most everyone was formal most of the time—except for the technical students.

Of course they made us pay for it. All the coeds are hot for someone they can discuss the Great Books with, not some barbarian science or engineering major with a slide rule swinging from his belt. I've seen these Zenish girls, with their long hair and thongs and SANE buttons, wild for motorcyclers and African exchange students. Rotten snobs! Though I've got to admit that some of my friends in the engineering school depend more on force than persuasion for their pleasure. Ha-ha!

The Computer Center was mostly underground, to make temperature regulation easier. These big machines really heat up. I know that back at the Arthur Regleihofp Computing Center, at my own multiversity, they have an enormous air-conditioning plant through all the machine rooms, with dozens of recording thermometers. If the temperature in the labs goes above a certain point, the electrical power to the computers is shut off. Otherwise you have something called a computer explosion, which no one at the labs wants to talk about. All I know is that during the summer, the machine rooms are the best place to relax, because they're so cool. And I can always scare the teenage geniuses who run them into letting me rubberneck.

So I reported to the Computer Center, and found my wonderful creative position from which I could challenge the unknown—the programming saddle of an obsolete IBM aleph-sub-zero—a jazzed up Turing Engine. The same noble trade I'd learned six years before, as a youngster in the Science Honors Program at the multiversity.

An International Business Machines aleph-sub-zero tests a mathematical model against reality. The device begins grinding out deductions from the model, and checking them against facts about the phenomenon. If they check out, fine. If not, it begins to blink and tremble in agitation.

This one had a few peculiarities. The "mode" was about ten times as complex as normal; there were fifty more storage units—and the runs averaged less than ten seconds.

By the end of the day, I was bored, frustrated, and very disgusted. I could barely keep from grabbing my teenage assistant by his ankles, swinging him around in a heavy arc, and smashing out his smiling, freckled face against the machine's one-to-ones. Rotten teenage competitor! Fortunately I ran into Harry Mandel directly afterward, without having to look him up. At least that was something. One thing led to another, and two hours later, together with Richard Colby, the three of us were exchanging impressions.

"Oh, I suppose it's all I could expect," I told them disgustedly.

"They're setting up odd sorts of logical-mathematical models–ones without the law of self-contradiction, either A or not-A. Things like that. Then they run them through the aleph-sub-zero as a check. Only–" and I took a deep slug from my glass–"none of them works."

Harry Mandel bobbled his head up and down enthusiastically, so that it seemed to flicker in the cool dim corner of the White Sands Bar. Harry has this habit of shaking his head in violent agreement, while his eyes grow larger and larger with each sentence you speak. It gives you the funny feeling that every word you say is confirming some incredible theory of his: that you're a Chinese Communist, or a paranoid schizophrenic, or an Arcturian spy. It's really quite frightening until you get used to it.

Also, his lips were trembling and his hands quivering. I knew the signs. Once he started talking, he'd never stop. So I gave the nod to Richie Colby instead.

The electronics expert looked up from his drink. "I don't know," he muttered. "I'm on the psychological-biological end, and so far I can't understand what's going on. They've got me working on topological neuronic maps–mapping the circuits of the brain. But for what, I don't know." He went back to the drink he was nursing.

I took a sip from my Coke. I don't drink more than I have to, and neither do most of my friends. In spite of all this talk about college students boozing it up, I'll be damned if I'll rot my brains, the brains that have to beat out all those teenage hotshots!

The White Sands Bar was a pretty good one, quiet, with a kitchen. A while before we'd had a pizza, heavy with cheese and olive oil. It's funny how much time I spend in bars. Our civilization has wonderful extensive facilities for some things, fragmentary ones or none at all for others. It's perfectly clear how to fill out the forms and go to class and take exams and apply and study all the way to a Ph.D. –but how the hell do you have a good time? I heard they had to double the psychiatric service up at M.I.T. Sometimes I have crazy insane dreams of getting out of this whole mess, quitting. But where could I go, what would I do, who would be my friends? *Who would be my friends?* Anyway, bars are all right, and this bar, the White Sands Bar, was a pretty good one.

I took another drink. Richard Colby was staring dumbly into his. "Okay, Harry," I said.

"To understand my end, you'll need to know what the universe is," said Mandel quickly and incoherently. "People ask, 'Why is the universe the way it is?' And Kant answered them back: 'Because the universe is a tango!'"

"Huh?"

"Don't you know what a tango is?" said Harry quizzically. "Why, even all my buddy-buddy psychology major friends know *that*. You know–like this–" and he moved his hips suggestively. He grabbed up his sloe gin and Coke, and finished it off in a single gulp. "Daiquiri!" he cried to the waitress. "Like this, boys," he moaned, beginning to sway again.

It took a little while to make our questions clear, but presently Harry was sketching on a napkin with his Mr. Peanut pen.

"Remember that proof in high-school geometry–Tenth Year Mathematics to you, Perry–where you show that a line segment has only one perpendicular bisector. You strike arcs from the end points, and draw the line from one intersection to the other. But why should the arcs have any intersection? And why couldn't there be *two* lines that were straight and went through both intersection points? I bet you never thought of that!"

He looked up from his diagram defiantly.

Dick Colby blinked at him, his long face weary.

"I'll *tell* you why!" cried Harry Mandel, downing half his daiquiri. He put the glass down and spoke decisively. "Because the universe is a tango–we see it this way because *we have to*–we're built this way. Anything else would be a logical impossibility–a contradiction. We can't experience the world any other way. We see it this way because we're built a certain way, and the universe is built a certain way. Reality is the interaction of the two parts–and the universe is a tango!"

He tossed down the rest of the woman's drink and nodded powerfully. "Any one of my buddy-buddy psychology major friends will tell you that!"

Colby and I nodded agreement. Mandel always was something of a nut. I never trust short guys–their mothers always tell them about Napoleon when they're little, and they always take it the wrong way.

Mandel was still gabbling. "But this doesn't mean we'll always have to look at things this way. We won't have to always think of a round-square as impossible. That's what my part of Project Round-Square is all about, the part with my buddy-buddy psychology major friends. We're going to change the music. We're going to give one partner dancing lessons!"

It was five weeks more before I learned that Mandel had in fact not been kidding around, nor really drunk at all. That was the essence of the psychology half of Project Round-Square. But a lot happened between that first night at the White Sands Bar and then.

For one thing, they closed down the mathematics-logic side of the installation. I had about a week more of that "Start Program!" Zip-pip-pip-pip-pip! "Clang! Clang! Clang! Discrepancy! Discrepancy!" nonsense, then two days of absolutely flawless correlations—as good as any of the test runs between economics and high-school math, or advanced calculus and statics and dynamics. Whatever was being sent into the aleph-sub-zero, it was a perfect fit with the real world. The first day I was wildly enthusiastic, the second I was bewildered—maybe they were checking themselves? And the third day, I wasn't given any programs. The head of my section, a young man named Besser, showed up about an hour later and told me we were shutting down. I was to be reassigned.

"But why? The last two runs were perfect!"

"The last runs—" he began, then sighed. He looked more like a truck driver than a worker with the subtle squiggles of mathematical logic. "The last two runs were exercises in futility. You've had some undergraduate symbolic logic—you must have some idea of what we're trying to do."

I nodded.

"Well, rigorously speaking, the way to eliminate the notion of 'impossible' is to get rid of contradiction—get a sort of logic where you can have a 'round-square,' as a legitimate notion. Then you build a language with that logic. Understand me?"

"Uh-huh."

"Now, this seems—ahem—unlikely. If you've ever taken an introductory course in philosophy, there's always a kid who talks about there being 'some crazy kind of logic' where things could be red *and* blue, round *and* square." He shrugged in annoyance. "The professor can usually shut him up, and if he's persistent, embarrass him to death. Those kids are the sort that embarrass pretty easily."

I nodded. This guy knew something of college life.

"So that's what the meta-mathematicians and symbolic logicians upstairs have been working on. You see, while such things are silly to talk about here in the real world, you *can* have a logic without the 'not' operator. Such logics have been set up in the past—but they weren't very interesting, they weren't *rich,* fruitful in new ideas. But anyway, you can make such a thing, you can even build up to a mathematics from it, the way Russell and Whitehead built up numbers from logic in *Principia.* And you use your math to build a logic and a language—to describe the world. No 'not' means no opposites—which seems to mean no contradictions." He wiped his face and tried to look annoyed, but it was difficult. Good old air conditioning.

"Do you see?"

"I think so. Real world again—didn't match up."

"Kee-rect. Your math is no good for the real world. It's just wrong—like trying to navigate an ocean liner with plane geometry. Since the earth is round, it doesn't work out."

I nodded.

"I mean, it's *right*—it's *valid*—it just doesn't describe anything real," he corrected hastily. "Seems as if you *must* have contradiction."

"That's why the runs on the aleph-sub-zero were so short? The computer would spot a contradiction, and start yapping. But how about the last two runs—perfect straight out. What was the matter with them?"

"Oh, those," he groaned. "Those were that jerk Kadison's idea. The exclusion approach."

"Go on."

"Well, you know there's another way to eliminate the notion of a contradiction. By exclusion."

"Elucidate."

"Think of it this way," said Besser. "You understand the notions of tall and short, and you know such things are relative. But if you decide that everyone under twenty feet tall was short—then you couldn't have a contradiction, a notion of 'short-tall.' Everyone would be short, and you'd eliminate one sort of contradiction. 'Tall-short' would mean the same as 'mimsey-short'—'nonsense word-short,' or just 'short.' And you keep on going that way. This was Kadison's idea."

"It worked perfectly in the machine."

"Sure it did. And it's also perfectly useless. *All* gradations and comparisons drop out—and, brother, you don't know how many there are. You know, most every quality has its opposite in *something* else. Even the notions of matter and empty space. You get nothing left—I mean *nothing*—the problem becomes trivial."

"The universe is an uncle," I said.

"Yeah, except for uncle say any other word. The universe becomes one solid, undescribable lump, with no qualities at all."

Also, Harry Mandel began to crack up. I didn't notice it while I was working–that aleph-sub-zero had some good problems–but when I was unassigned, the only real activity I had was going to the White Sands Bar. It was during the drinking sessions that his madness began to blossom.

Now of course I know all about the science of modern psychology –it's one reason I've remained so balanced and stable. Myself, I'm what is known as a shame personality. It's a matter of personal honor with me that I fight to the limit for the highest grades and the most scholarship. I'll beat 'em all out. That's me.

Dick Colby was clearly a guilt personality. He really believed all that guff about the scientist's world view, about the search for truth, about following an abstract pattern of behavior. Poor old Dick, he had an abstract moral code too, as I might have expected. Well, he had to follow the rules, and he might get kicked in the belly, but at least he was stable in his sad, picky way.

Now Harry Mandel was a fear personality. He tried to belong to some sort of whole, to link its destiny with his own. A *gestalt*. You find a lot like that: fraternity boys, soldiers, club members, athletes on a team. And of course the intellectuals–the literary group and Zenish girls and the interdependent independents.

Ain't social psychology great!

Anyway, Mandel's kind of twitch, the fear personality, is okay as long as he really has his buddies and believes it. If he doesn't have them, he wanders around until he can link up with a new bunch. If he doesn't *believe* he has them–look out! A fear personality with doubts about its *gestalts* can slide right over into paranoid schizophrenia.

It came out in funny ways, distorted, because Mandel was very intelligent, and the more intelligent, the more little links can begin to snap and break. One night in late August he came up with this:

"I mean, I have nothing against that particular minority group," he said loudly. "It's just that–well, look at it this way. The original members were selected on the basis of crude physical strength–the smart clever ones escaped the slavers. Then they were brought over here and were slaves for several hundred years. Now it seems to me that if you have slaves, you're going to encourage breeding among the stupid and the strong. You don't want smart quick ones. As a matter of fact, the smart quick ones would try to escape and would be shot. Or else, if they're clever, slip over the color line and intermarry.

"So you see, you've had forces at work for three hundred years that bred—I mean in terms of human genetics—for less intelligence. You do that for three centuries and it shows—as a matter of fact, it *does* show. In terms of modern science, they might even *be* inferior."

He was crazy, insane. For one thing, three hundred years isn't long enough to matter genetically for humans. For another, "the smart clever ones" *didn't* escape the slavers' roundups any more than the others did. Maybe if Mandel had been a slave owner he'd have tried to encourage only the stupid to breed, but such eugenically oriented thinking didn't exist in times past. As for shooting would-be escapees, you don't destroy valuable merchandise like that, you bring it back alive! (Anyway, you don't talk about races, you talk about human beings.) Mandel was rationalizing, justifying immoral attitudes on the basis of a "science" which really doesn't exist. As for "scientific morality," hell, science and morality are different, and by trying to base one on the other you are setting up for something like Hitler's "final solution."

Yet poor disturbed Mandel had *thought the theory up*. And for an instant, thinking of the exchange students and the Zenish girls back at the multiversity, my own brain had become inflamed. Science, reason, intellect—there are some things you mustn't think about. God help me.

A flash of disgust went through me. I never wanted to do any more calculations. I wanted to lie down with some pretty girl and make love to her and have her soothe me. I was too long alone. Help me! Then I squeezed those thoughts away.

I pushed away the thick silvery tin with the remains of the pizza. Delicious, too. Their cook was improving. Or maybe he could get real Mexican spices, not the stuff I used to settle for in Woolworth's.

I looked at Mandel across the table. His face was beginning to cave in a little, and his eyes looked tired. Anyway, we had to talk about something else. I decided to find out some things about my new assignment. And that was thing number three. That afternoon I'd be transferred to the psychology attack team programming again, the Urbont matrices of neurological maps.

"How's the job, Harry?" I asked him. "How's the dancing lessons coming?"

Mandel looked up. He hadn't mentioned his work in a couple of weeks, not since we'd taken his little lecture on Kant and the tango as a rib.

"What about it?" he asked crisply. "I don't know very much, I just do whatever they tell me."

They—his buddy-buddy psychologist buddies? Mmmmm.

"Well, whatever they've been telling you, they'll soon be telling me," I said, nudging him in the shoulder. "I'll be figuring out your brain maps for you."

"Oh, yeah. They ought to start programming in two weeks, and then installation—"

"Hey, installation? Whoa! What are you talking about?"

Mandel's slumped body seemed to collapse some more. He was so far forward I could hardly see his face. Just a dark form against the well-lit rest of the bar. Cigarette smoke hung in the air, and a dozen technicians were seated on the high stools. Over in another corner, two disgruntled physicians were playing Nim. A couple of the girls from the clerical pool were having heroes and Cokes at another table, blonde and brownette in brief desert costumes.

"Sensory enervation," said Mandel in a dead voice. "What else did you think?"

He blinked mildly and slugged down the rest of his Horse's Neck. "Rum and Coke!" he shouted to the barman. "I really hate to drink," he confided sullenly. "But at least I can do it alone, without my psychology major buddy-buddies." Richard Colby gave me a funny look and we both leaned forward and really began to listen.

In the 1950's, the psychologists of McGill University had commenced an interesting sequence of experiments in connection with the U.S. manned space flight program—an early phase of the "Space Flight Bubble." A space traveler confined to his space capsule would be in a state of extreme "sensory deprivation"—with so little to see, hear and feel, the psychologists theorized, the astronaut might go insane. The McGill University experiments were designed to investigate this thesis, and even more extreme cases of sensory deprivation.

The perfection of brain circuit mapping had suggested the obverse experiment to the scientists of Project Round-Square. If sensory deprivation could debase a man, weaken him and drive him out of his mind—why not attempt "sensory enhancement"? Enriching a man's senses by requiring his reticular formations to accept data detected by machines—the total memory storage of a computer, the complete electromagnetic spectrum, the sorting out of patterns and wave forms which was possible to oscilloscopes.

Volunteers weren't too hard to find—the McGill men had found volunteers, promising not much more than money and a chance at madness.

A man's concepts of the world vary according to the data he receives. For thousands of years men have been building up systems and structures of describing the universe, without trying to improve the methods used to accept the data. Scientific instruments were not enough—could light and color have meaning, be *real* to a blind man? The scientists of Project Round-Square hoped that the contradictions and impossibilities of Reality might disappear for a man with enhanced senses. The system philosophy was illustrated in the poem "The Blind Men and the Elephant."

"Could a dolphin discover Relativity?" said Mandel, almost angrily. "Of course not—plenty of brains, just never was even able to sense much beyond the other dolphins. Likewise, there may be enormous fields of knowledge we've never noticed, because of our sensory lacks.

"More than that, it's a *positive* approach!" cried Mandel, "the first in seventy years. Before this, all of psychology was concerned with debasing man, turning him into a super rat, a little black box which was fed a stimulus and kicked back a response. Automatons!"

"What about psychoanalysis and the Freudians?"

"Bleugh!" cried Mandel, enervated himself for once. "They're the worst of all. The Id, Ego, and Super-Ego are just mental mechanisms, things beyond our control, which interact to produce behavior."

It was nice to see Mandel cheerful. There's nothing better for these neurotic types than to let them talk and talk and talk; it helps reassure them. Maybe they think no one will threaten them or kick them in the belly as long as they are blabbing. A false notion produced by too much well-written TV drama.

"But still," I said slowly, waggling a finger at him (or was I waggling and the finger standing still? I must drink less).

"But, Harry," I continued. "All the colors of the rainbow won't alter this picture," and I flopped one of the White Sands Bar's napkins at him. It had a nice colored picture of a Valkyrie missile on it, from the days when White Sands was a proving ground, before the "Space Flight Bubble" burst.

"Maybe not," he mumbled. "But that's only the neurological part of the idea. We're building compulsions to succeed into it, too. The kids will *have* to work out a world without impossibilities."

"Kids?" asked Colby dimly. "Keep talking, Harry."

Mandel blinked and then continued. A lot of the rest was whined and mumbled, but I thought I got most of it.

The subjects of the brain wiring were youngsters between twelve and sixteen. The psychologists had settled on those as the optimum age limits–young enough to be typified by directness, immediacy, wholeness, spontaneity and integral fantasy. Teenage hotshots, in other words. Old enough to want to make sense of all the data, and young enough so their world view wasn't rigid.

You can look up all the psychology words except the last. "Integral fantasy" was the most important. Studies had shown this quality is most typical of real genius, and the kids had been specially selected for it. What it means is this. Most people have fantasies, but the fantasy is "disassociated"–it is unreal to them, like sex magazines and comic books. Children, especially geniuses, have "integral fantasies"–they get wild complex ideas about the real world. Ordinary people call these "strokes of genius," if they happen to work.

"And what's more," muttered Mandel, head down on the table, "they'll have to make *sense* out of it. They've had hypnosis and drug compulsions to succeed, so their new sensory picture will have to be free of logical contradictions. It'll have to be!"

I was about to ask him how they'd be able to communicate with them after the kids had "made contact"–but before I could, Harry dropped out of the game. He lay unconscious across the table. "Kids!" he murmured hatefully.

So I was doing mathematics again, setting up Urbont matrices, the curious descendants of time-variable, multi-port switching and communications math. Far more subtle than any of these, however –the Urbont equations didn't analyze radars or satellite radio links, they symbolized the neuron patterns of the human brain.

It was tedious, subtle, absolutely-right-the-first-time work. The basic units are discrete–on-off switching conditions apply, rather than continuity. In other words, there was no margin for error.

I was getting more of those flashings of hatred and self-hatred. In my little air-conditioned cubicle in the Computer Center, I would get daymares where I would be a bug in a compartment of an ice-cube tray–so cool and comfortable and . . . dead. Every so often my friends would stop by–Dick Colby, bemused and apologetic; Harry Mandel, confused and sullen.

More than once I thought of informing the medical staff of Mandel's problems, but I was afraid to. In the world of science, each man has a "paper shadow" that follows him around–dossiers, transcripts, evaluations by supervisors. Get something bad in among those papers –instability, erratic work habits, even extravagant praise, and you're in trouble. The big corporations like their scientists *a little* peculiar –just for identification. Anything serious can really ruin a man's career. I thought it might be best for Harry to take his chances–when I thought about him at all. I tried to stay away from emotional subjects.

Fortunately, about this time, the Virgin Research Corporation brought in some new entertainment, so I could relax without raising the alcohol content of my blood.

These were the moebius movies, the new cyclic films. I'd seen the first one, *The Endless War,* previewed in New York City, a few years before. Since then, their sophistication had increased many-fold.

The basic notion was simple. The films were written in such a way that there was no beginning and no end. but this was more than a simple splicing of the two ends. Literally, it was nearly impossible to know where the story commenced. In *The Endless War,* there were at least a dozen places where you could enter, stay the two hours, and leave, coming away with the impression of a complete drama. In fact, depending on where you came in, the film might have been a comedy, a tragedy, a documentary or most anything else.

To the Nth Generation (or *Incest on It!*) was a typical improvement. It dealt with the romantic affairs of several families over (I think) three generations. After forty years, with the amatory relations of the members incredibly tangled, the snarl was twisted back on itself as the original characters were brought forth in and out of wedlock. It was pretty ghastly in a way, but also quite amusing. I hear the French are preparing a film which will do the same thing in two generations, and there's going to be a science-fiction picture that does it in one.

I had also heard rumors of the most recent development. Cyclic films had closed the old notion of time, the first "true" moebius would eliminate time as an orienter. With pure dissonant sound, with only the most limited and ingenious movements, a complete showing would have the film run both backward and forward, left-to-right and right-to-left. Enthusiasts predicted it would make *Last Year at Marienbad* look like "Looney Tunes."

I got precious little pleasure out of *To the Nth Generation,* however. Mandel was moaning and groaning about his buddy-buddies and how much he hated kids through the whole thing. I didn't stay past the second time around–and these things are cumulative–ten revolutions of *The Endless War* had made me practically a pacifist.

The trouble was that half an hour into *Incest on It!* I fell off the edge of a cliff. On the screen the Most Beautiful Girl at Queens College was giving birth on the steps of the New York Public Library to the Nobel physicist who would father the owner of the biggest brothel in the Bronx, who in turn might (there were subtle hints) be the parent of the beautiful blonde in labor on the dirty white steps.

I would always have teenage competitors! I would get older, and older, and older ("Never produced anything after twenty-seven!" "Burned out at twenty-five, I'd say!" "We keep him around for laughs, and to teach the remedial courses. Never did anything worthwhile after his thesis!") but they would always be coming–young, bright, arrogant, brilliant. I could barely keep from screaming and screaming and screaming. I made as tight a fist as I could, squeezing, the way I would press the foot rest in the dentist's chair, because it hurts and hurts, and you've got to do *something* when it hurts so much.

I had been wrong about Mandel, or partly. He, like me, would not be shamed. And he saw Project Round-Square as a betrayal by his friends, of the creation by his "buddy-buddies" of new competitors to torment him. I could understand this, though his woe was not mine. His complaints had stimulated me to see my own doom in the endless procreation of the film.

And now I recalled the "Kubie Report" in the *American Scientist:* "Some Unsolved Problems of the Scientific Career." The high incidence of nervous breakdown in the middle years, as the creative energy wore thin. Directness, immediacy, diversity, wholeness, spontaneity, integral fantasy! For these I had denied myself everything, sweating out my advanced degrees before age could touch me. And now I was old, I could feel myself rotting as I sat there. I could feel my brains inside my body–ropy, red, pulsing, tinged with age, hot and glowing inside a pile of gray, fatty, fibrous tissue–my unexercised body. Somehow I managed to get up and stumble out of the theater. Behind me, on the screen, someone was talking on his death-bed to his grandchildren and grandparents, who would turn out to be exactly the same people.

Part of the time I worked intensely at my tapes and card decks, not daring to pause, afraid to close my machine-language manuals. Other days, sometimes for hours, I could not work closely. I cut free of the job, drifted beyond the "grid" of the scientific attitude. What difference did it make, my mind gibed, if men landed on Mars, or discovered element 1304? Particle, wave, wavicle, round-square—who cares? Science was just another "institution," like anything else. Would a man a thousand years from now laugh at me, the way my seminar engineer friends would chuckle at a scribe in 1000 A.D., who spent his little life endlessly recopying scrolls in a monastery?

It took all my tricks to get through the final weeks. The best was French sleep therapy, which I once read about in a book called *Force Yourself to Relax!* If your troubles are unbearable, knock yourself out until your subconscious has time to patch you up. I tried reading for a while, but I couldn't seem to understand C. P. Snow's two cultures. All I could recall was a passage about someone dying. Snow said that on the point of death, most people care not a whit about their intellectual failures or social lacks. But they cry out endlessly about their missed sensual interludes.

Richard Colby still visited me, but Mandel had stopped coming. In a moment of weakness I'd told him about his "paper shadow." He'd slammed out in a huff. The next day he came back, calm and chipper.

"You look better than I do."

"Of course. All my problems are solved."

"What about your psychology buddies?"

"Oh, I knew none of them were *really* my friends. But I'm set to take care of them, all right, all right."

"Yeah? How?"

"Well, you remember what you told me about my personal file. About how if they decide I'm unstable and borderline, it'll be very hard for me to get any sort of job, and I couldn't be a psychologist any more."

"The situation is something like that, at least, with any large organization."

"But as long as I seem all right, all those rats will leave me alone, and even seem to be friendly."

"Well, you don't put it very well—"

"So it's all very simple. I've fixed them all right, all right. I went over to chemical stores and got the components for a large bomb. Then I assembled it in the bottom drawer of my desk, in the middle of the Psychology Section of the project. And rigged it with a button detonator."

"Go on, go on!"

"Well, don't you see?"

"No! Go on!"

"It's perfectly plain what I–"

"Mandel, explain!"

"Well, as long as I'm feeling all right, I go on in a perfectly normal way. When I feel a little sick, I go into my office. But if some day I think I'm going really nuts, I think I'm really going to go crazy so it all will go down on my personal file and ruin me with the big organization–"

"Yes?"

"Why, then it's as if all my friends are suddenly about to become my enemies, to turn on me, to think I'm crazy and fire me and laugh at me and pity me behind my back." His eyes were mad, though his voice was perfectly level. "They won't be able to do that to Harry Mandel. They won't do it. I'll blow them all to bits first!"

It was enough for me, friend or no. I got word to Personnel anonymously, and that night they called for Mandel. The poor guy hadn't thought to install one of his "White Collar Kamikazes" in his quarters, so they took him out on the G.E.M. *Topaz* that very night, under heavy sedation.

Was I in much better shape than Harry Mandel had been? A cheerful, hopelessly neurotic robot. I had come up through the sequence without much real thought about stuff like that. It was enough to do my work. Once, when I was drunk, I had the idea that if you had a perfect baby, you could set up the perfect program for his life, sports and studies and sex and social life, split-second timed, an ideal existence. But it was already twenty years too late for that for me.

Or was that the easy way out, to flunk yourself and roll with the tide. Was I simply "hiding out" in science because it was socially sanctioned and I had a talent for math?

But on the other side it gave me a pattern for my days, the stability I needed and craved. For this I might do work that I even despised. There must be some way to decide, to choose the optimum path, the really best way, before all your time's run through.

But how do you do it, how could I, of all people, do it?

It was my own brand of impossible.

Project Round-Square finished out fast.

Dick Colby and I sat in one of the electronics labs and watched as the countdown dropped to zero. Closed-circuit television brought us a view of the MT Section, a big room holding more than a dozen aleph-sub-sixes. Dr. Wilbur, the head of the machine translation group, sat at the console of an aleph-sub-nine, the most advanced computer International Business Machines has ever turned out. (*Nobody* really understands it. It was designed by an aleph-sub-eight and the main purpose of the sixes was that collectively they kept the sub-nine from going crazy.)

Mathematical linguistics is the new "in" branch of math, like differential topology used to be, and category theory after that. Wilbur was playing it to the hilt, with ski boots, no tie, and a crappy old sports jacket. But he had a feel for the communications process that amounted to empathy. It was this rare talent that was needed to help the nine through the clutches.

Above him on the lintel of the machine was the proud motto of the National Programmer's Union, originally a remark by Queen Juliana of the Netherlands: "I can't understand it. I can't even understand the people who can understand it."

"Project Round-Square," said a disgusted technician, "still seems crazy to me."

"Perhaps it was a bad choice of name," said Colby next to me. The Michigan electronics expert was tanned and calm, and cheerful as ever. "Did you ever read that poem 'The Blind Men and the Elephant'? It's the same principle. With new senses or a new orientation, apparent contradictions in reality might disappear. It's what some people call 'thinking in other categories.' "

"Like the wavicle," said someone else.

"Yes," said Richard Colby, his face taunting as he smiled. "When physicists were studying certain particles, they found that in some situations they could be thought of as waves, and the equations worked out. In other sorts of reactions, you could think of them as particles, and the numbers and theories checked out under *that* hypothesis. So the physics men just shrugged and called 'em wavicles."

"But what does a wavicle look like?"

"I don't know. Nobody knows—but nobody knows what a round-square looks like either."

The lab grew quiet, as if Colby had said something profound. On the television screen the computers clicked and roared, the tape drives jerking abruptly in their vacuum columns.

"What about military applications—" I croaked at Colby. He seemed to be up to date. I hadn't paid much attention to all the inter-office junk we got on the project—including the "Virgin Tease" newsletter that told the lab assistant in Subsection Nine of Track Four of Approach Nineteen what progress had been made toward the noble goal of Project Sixty-Nine, of which he sometimes recalled he was a member.

"The guy that hired me told me this thing had military applications—I didn't know if he was kidding or I was in a nightmare."

Colby looked at me wide-eyed for a moment. "Well—I don't know. Of course, there doesn't seem to be any *direct* application. But neither did Einstein's equations, or 'game theory' when it was developed. *Any* sort of insight into the world is likely to be militarily useful these days. It doesn't even have to be technical—remember the old German staff armies that were so successful. A simple thing like the chain of command could lick the best general who had to boss his own whole show."

"Just thinking is dangerous these days—often deadly."

"Maybe they ought to classify it," joked Colby.

"But then, I guess it always has been."

On the screen the computers continued to run. Coverage would be confined to the machine-translation lab; the psychologists on the staff had decided to have no reports from the real center of activity.

Outside in a surface lab were a dozen adolescents. They had been trained to their peak as scientists, well beyond Ph.D. level. Now they were being sensitized, exposed to the flood of phenomena that ordinary people never know about because our wonderful minds are deaf and dumb to nearly everything in the universe. And hidden deep down below their sensitivities, there was a biting, burning clawing, raving drive to master this new universe they would meet, and to see in it the death of the old human notion of opposites, contradictions, limitations. Nothing, their minds raved as they scanned new skies, nothing must be impossible.

The computers ran for ten hours on the screens, while Wilbur studied and fumed and paced and drank coffee. The subjects would now all have come out of anesthesia, and would now be studying and observing the multitude of apparatus in the lab. Within it, I had been told, there was operating a demonstration of almost every major scientific phenomenon. The sensitized ones had been briefed to the limit, short of data which it was thought might stultify their world view. We could only wait now.

A red light glowed on the aleph-sub-nine, and data began pouring in. Wilbur threw himself into the operator's chair and began chiding the immense computer, intuitively helping it arrange the data into some sort of language which might mean something to man. His face burned with concentration.

Near the end of the four-hour shift he looked at the machine oddly and tried another system of organization. Then he triggered his secretary. The machine, which had responded to his winking-blinking notes, fed back the information in binary code in his earphones.

He sat back and closed his eyes for a few moments. Then he opened them and took up the microphone. "Communications established. They're intelligible," he said. And then, in a lower voice, "I've seen that structure somewhere before. . . ."

The cheers in the room blotted out anything further. Contact established, and the response was not gibberish! Well, never mind what it meant! We'd get that soon enough.

Premature congratulations? Well, perhaps. Remember the satellite shots, with a rocket roaring up on its own fire, swimming right into the calculated orbit, ejecting its satellite, and the little moon's radios bursting into life. *That* was when everyone cheered! Not six months later, when the miles of telemeter tape had been studied and restudied and been given meaning by sweat and genius. Nor did most people feel very bad when the scientists figured out that someone had forgotten to pull the safety tabs from the quick-releases, so all the instruments were shielded and their data meaningless. . . .

The actual results of Project Round-Square took eleven months to evaluate and declassify. They came out, nicely distorted, in a copy of the "Virgin Tease" the V.R.C. mailed to me. . . .

Biologically, it was an unqualified success. The sensitized subjects had broken through to a whole new world of feeling. In physical terms, they were quasi-gods, for they could sense things we would never know. It was more than a widening; new colors and smells. They could sense forces and radiations and bodies all forms of which are ignored by men.

But as to the actual purpose of the project . . .

The sensitives had been given what seemed to be an insoluble problem—eliminating contradiction in a world that required it in any rational description. The ingenuity of the human mind, the directors of Virgin Research had thought, might solve the problem, where the pure logic of machines had failed.

Well, they had solved it, in a way.

Wilbur had been right. The Hopi Indians, independently, had evolved a crude version of the sensitives' solution. The Hopi language did not allow for the complex tenses of the Indo-European tongues. All time and space to them was a single frozen matrix of events, in which the word "perhaps" had no equivalent, and the notion of "possible" and "impossible" was meaningless.

To ask, in Hopi, if it might rain tomorrow was as meaningless as to ask if it was possible it had rained yesterday.

To the sensitives, that thing had "roundness" and this one had "squareness." Could there be such a thing as a round-square?

Perhaps, in the forever-fixed future. When it made its appearance, they could tell you. Meanwhile, it's meaningless to think about such things.

The semanticists were the only satisfied ones.

But this was only announced a year later. Not soon enough to save Harry Mandel, who was relieved of a multi-linear annihilator, fifty yards from the sensitives lab. He'd slugged a guard and escaped from the *Topaz*. I understand he's in a security ward somewhere, still talking about his buddies, while they watch him very carefully.

Dick Colby shrugged and grinned and had a drink or four with me at the celebration, then caught the evening ramjet back to Michigan Multi.

I collected my pay, scooter, and recommendations. Then, on the evening of the last day, I took a long look out across the desert. The sun was smoldering down into a pile of rust, the earth a great flat plum. By coincidence the girl that had assigned us our quarters was out on the desert too, but quite a ways away. I could see she was pregnant, and that was interesting to think about, and so I thought about it. I get a nice feeling when I see a woman with a child, if I have time for it—warmth, continuity for the race, the safe days of my very young childhood, though I can hardly remember any of them. There certainly were enough signs of it; she was well along.

I got a funny cold feeling. It was a tangential association, a silly one: what the boys used to call a "brassiere curve" in the rapids. You know what an ordinary bell curve looks like? Well, a lot of teachers use it for marking–most of the grades falling at C. Well, in the advanced sections some guys said the professors used a modified bell curve for figuring out grades–what they called a "brassiere curve." It looked like this:

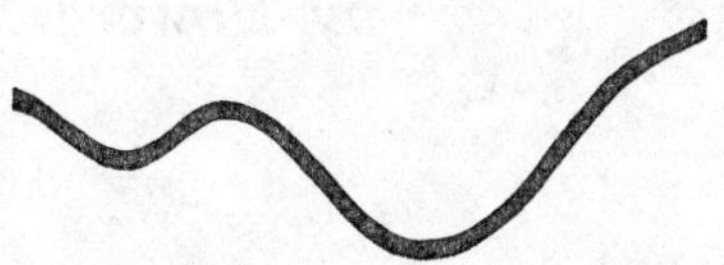

–and jammed up inside the little hump, good and tight near the B-plus, A-minus grades, was the little gang of teenage hotshots–and me.

The cold expanded into my chest, numbing. I could look at the sunset, and the blonde and her baby, and the labs and drafting boys and offices and all of it, and not feel anything at all. Everything was impersonal, like a diagram in a text.

An hour later I caught the G.E.M. *Emerald* back to my own multiversity. Classes wouldn't be starting for a while, but I'd figured out from the summer-session catalogue that I could fit in a three-week intensive reading course in Chinese in the meantime. Chinese is the new "in" language for Ph.D.s, like the way Russian used to be twenty years ago. It was pretty certain we'd be fighting them soon.

I figured I could fit in at least two "military application" courses into my fall program. Under the Rickover Plan I could get them tuition-exempt. What else could I do? I could use the money to pay for more programming. Computer operators are in short supply, and I would be sure of a fat income. I could be safe, nothing to worry about. Maybe I could get Virgin Research, or even the D.O.D. itself, to pay for more math and science courses. I could plan it all out, interesting problems to work on the rest of my life, and get the government to pay for them. Wouldn't that be clever?

Shut up, shut up, shut up.

BUILT UP LOGICALLY

by Howard Schoenfeld

"The Universal Panacea," Frank said, lighting a cigar. "Have one."

I took it.

"Light up, man."

"It's great, man."

We walked up Fifth Avenue toward Fourteenth Street.

"Stop," Frank said. We came to a halt.

Frank put his hand out in front of him and moved it back and forth a couple of times, inventing the rabbit. Getting to feel the creature's fur, he built it up logically from the feel. It was the only animal that could have produced that particular feel, and I was proud of him for thinking of it.

"Marvelous," I said, looking at it.

The rabbit sat on its haunches, a bundle of white fur with pink eyes. Dilating its nostrils, it hopped away from us, disappearing into an open doorway. I'd never seen a more ingenious invention.

"Amazing," I said.

"Nothing really," Frank said. "Watch this."

Frank was a tall thin-lipped man with a round forehead. Beads of perspiration appeared on his forehead. His face became taut, then relaxed.

"Feel anything?" he asked.

My brain tingled curiously. Something was being impinged on it. It was the consciousness of rabbits, their place in the scheme of things. I knew they'd been with us always.

Frank grinned.

"Not only you, but practically every man, woman, and child in the world thinks that now. Only I know differently."

It was uncanny.

We got in a cab and went up to the Three Sevens, a night club on Fifty-second Street. Inside, the place was crowded with jazz enthusiasts, listening to the Sevens. At the bar a man in a gray overcoat was reading a manuscript to a blond girl in her teens. I went over and listened.

This was what he read:

> "The Universal Panacea," Frank said, lighting a cigar. "Have one."
> I took it.
> "Light up, man."
> "It's great, man."
> We walked up Fifth Avenue toward Fourteenth Street.
> "Stop," Frank said. We came to a halt.
> Frank put his hand out in front of him and moved it back and forth a couple of times, inventing the rabbit. Getting the feel of the creature's fur, he built it up logically from the feel. It was the only animal that could have produced that particular feel, and I was proud of him for thinking of it.

"Stop," I yelled. "For Christ's sake, stop!"

The man in the gray overcoat turned around and faced me. "What's eating you, bud?"

"That manuscript you're reading," I said. "It's mine."

He looked me up and down contemptuously.

"So you're the guy."

There was something disquietingly familiar about him.

"Say. Who are you?"

For an answer he doubled up his fist and socked the blonde sitting next to him. She thudded and teetered on the bar stool before falling off. She hit the floor with a resounding thump.

"Wood," he said, looking down at her. "Solid wood."

I tapped the girl's back with the toe of my shoe. There was no doubt about it. She was wooden to the core.

"How would you like to have to sit in a night club and read to a piece of wood?" he asked disgustedly.

"I wouldn't," I admitted.

"All your characters are wooden," he said.

His voice was strangely familiar.

"Say. Who are you?"

He grinned and handed me his card. It said:

HILLBURT HOOPER ASPASIA	
BIRDSMITH	AUTHOR

For a moment I stared at him in startled disbelief. Then I saw it was true. The man in the gray overcoat was–myself.

"You're getting in over your head," he said.

He was beginning to be a pain in the neck.

I think I'll just write him out of the story right now. . . .

The man in the gray overcoat got up and walked out of the club.

I looked around to see what had happened to Frank. He had taken advantage of my preoccupation to step out of the characterization I'd given him and adopt one of his own choice, jazz musician. He was sitting in on the jam session with the Sevens, holding a trumpet he'd found somewhere. The Sevens paused, giving him the opportunity to solo. He arose and faced the audience.

Frank now found himself in the embarrassing position of not knowing how to play the instrument. This, of course, was the consequence of having stepped out of character without my permission. The audience waited expectantly.

Frank looked at me pleadingly.

I grinned and shook my head no.

I will leave him in this humiliating situation for a while as a punishment for getting out of control in the middle of the story.

The bartender tapped me on the shoulder. He nodded toward the rear of the club. A tall redhead in a low-cut evening dress was standing in front of a door labeled MANAGER. She motioned me to join her. I threaded my way between the crowded tables.

"Aren't you Aspasia, the writer?" she asked.

She was about nineteen and as sleek as a mink.

"I am."

Her eyes sparkled.

"I'm Sally La Rue," she said. "The manager's daughter." Her body was an enticing succession of trim curves under her black dress. "I have something you may be interested in."

I didn't doubt it for a minute.

"It's an invention of Dad's. You might like to do an article about it."

"I might at that," I said, looking at her.

She smiled shyly.

"I'd do anything to help Dad," she said simply.

She took my hand and led me into the office. It was a large room with two windows facing Fifty-first Street. In the center of it was a metallic contraption resembling a turbine. Attached to it was a mass of complicated wiring, several rheostats, and two retorts containing quicksilver.

"What is it?" I asked.

"A time machine," Sally said dramatically.

I looked at the device.

"Does it work?"

"Of course it works. Would you like to try it?"

I said I would.

"Past or future?"

"Future."

"How about five thousand years?"

"That'll be fine."

Sally adjusted a dial. Then she stepped over to the wall and pulled a switch.

The turbine roared. Blue lightning flashed between the retorts and vaporized the quicksilver into a green gas. The room became luminous. An indicator hit the 5,000 mark. Sally released the switch.

"Here we are," she said.

I dashed over to the windows to see what the world of the future was like.

"It's the same," Sally said, guessing my thought.

I looked out on Fifty-first Street. Nothing had changed.

"That's the beauty of the machine," Sally explained. "It moves the whole world through time rather than just one part of it."

"The stars," I said. "Surely their positions have changed."

"No. It moves the whole universe through time. Everything."

"I see."

"Isn't it wonderful!"

Thinking it over, I couldn't say it was. I didn't say it was.

"You'll do the article, won't you?" she asked eagerly.

Her body was rippling with excitement beneath her black dress. I noticed her father kept a couch in his office.

"Well. If you really want me to," I said. "Yes."

"Would you like to go forward another five thousand years?" she asked.

I glanced at the couch.

"Not right now," I said.

She was engrossed in the machine.

"I think I'll set it for A.D. one million."

I looked at her, then at the couch. Then I remembered I'd left Frank in an awkward spot some 5,000 years and odd minutes ago.

"I'll be right back," I said. "Wait for me here, will you?"

She had her hand on the switch. She smiled.

"Of course," she said. "Darling."

I left her at her dad's time machine playfully thrusting the universe a million years into the future.

Frank was in the bandstand with the Sevens where I'd left him, facing an expectant audience. When he saw me he waved the trumpet at me before returning it to its case. He motioned the audience to be quiet.

Frank tilted his head sideways, cupped his ear in his hand, and invented the piano. Getting the sound of the instrument's notes, he built it up logically from the sound. It was the only instrument that could have produced that particular sound and I was glad to see him invent it, though I was getting a little tired of the trick.

One of the Sevens sat down and started playing a Boogie Woogie number. Frank came over and stood beside me. "What do you think of it?" he asked.

"It's great, man."

He handed me a cigar.

We lit up.

Behind me a familiar voice said, "Ask him to invent something original."

"Like what?" I asked without turning.

"Something socially conscious. A new sex, perhaps."

Somebody's hand was in my pocket.

"How about that, Frank?" I asked.

"Your subconscious is showing," Frank said, looking over my shoulder.

The hand was withdrawn.

I reached inside my pocket and brought out the card that had been left in it. It said:

guess who and you can have me.

(over)

I turned the card over with fingers that trembled just a little. It said:

HILLBURT HOOPER ASPASIA	
BIRDSMITH	AUTHOR

The voice behind me and the hand in my pocket were my own again!

Turning, I caught a glimpse of the man in the gray overcoat hurrying toward the door marked MANAGER. He paused in front of it and glanced at me. I nodded. With my approval he went in and closed the door behind him, joining the redheaded mouse, Sally La Rue.

I congratulated myself on projecting myself in the story in two characterizations. Owing to my foresight I will now be able to enjoy the person of Sally La Rue without interference from the censors, and, at the same time, continue my narrative.

I turned to Frank.

"Let's drop in on the Baron's party," I said.

"Good idea."

We went outside, got in a cab, and went uptown to the Baron's apartment house.

Inside, the party was going full blast. The Baron, as usual, was on the studio couch, passed out. The guests were in various states of inebriation. When I entered, the room became quiet for a moment.

In the lull a girl whispered, "There's Aspasia, the writer."

"He ought to trade himself in on a new model," someone else said. "He looks like a caricature of himself."

"More like a cliché with feet."

"Have you read his latest story?"

"No."

"It's a direct steal from *Built Up Logically,* by H. H. Aspasia."

"You don't say."

Blushing, I pretended an interest in the Baron's Mondrian collection. One of the girls said, "I met his psychiatrist last week. He said he never knew which of his split personalities was analyzing which of Aspasia's."

"How awful."

"Yes, but significant."

"Very."

"What else did he say?"

"Basically maladjusted. Almost non-neurotic."

"Tendencies toward normalcy, too, I'll bet."

"I wouldn't be surprised."

"How perfectly abominable."

"Yes, but significant."

"Very."

"I almost feel sorry for him."

"I wonder if it's safe being here with him?"

"He's only partly with us you know."

"Poor guy. Probably lives in a world of reality."

"No doubt about it."

"Do you think psychiatry can help him?"

"Possibly. There have been cures."

"Notice the way he's staring at the Baron's Mondrians. It's significant, don't you think?"

"Very."

A feeling of boredom was beginning to come over me. I liked nobody at the party. I decided to bring it to an end.

The guests, laughing and talking, gathered up their belongings, and left in groups of two and three. Only Frank and I and the passed-out Baron remained.

Frank stood in the center of the room, his head cocked to one side, listening.

"What is it?" I asked.

"Sh-h-h-h," Frank said. "Listen."

I listened.

"Hear it?"

I shook my head.

"What is it?"

"The pulse beat of the universe. I can hear it."

"My God," I said.

He stood there listening to the pulse beat of the universe.

"Marvelous," I said.

"Yes," he said. "But not for you."

Frank tilted his head sideways, cupped his ear in his hand, and invented the universe. Getting the sound of its pulse beat, he built it up logically from the sound. It was the only universe that could have produced that particular pulse beat, and I was amazed at his blasphemy in creating it.

"Stop," I demanded.

My demand went unheeded.

The universe and its contents appeared.

Frank's face tautened. Beads of perspiration broke out on his forehead. Then he relaxed. His grin was ominous.

With a start of fear I realized my predicament. In inventing the universe and its contents Frank had also invented me.

I was in the unheard-of position of having been created by a figment of my own imagination.

"Our roles are reversed," Frank said. "I've not only created you, but all your works, including this narrative. Following this paragraph I will assume my rightful role as author of the story and you will assume yours as a character in it."

Aspasia's face blanched.

"This is impossible," he said.

"Not impossible," I said. "I've done it. I, Frank, have done it. I'm in control of the story. I've achieved reality at last."

Aspasia's expression was bitter. "Yes. At my expense."

"You're the first author in history to achieve a real status in fiction," I pointed out.

Aspasia sneered.

"Happens every day."

I shrugged.

"Survival of the fittest. Serves you right for giving me more creative power than you have. What did you expect?"

"Gratitude," Aspasia said nastily. "And a little loyalty."

"Gratitude, my eye. You're the bird who made me stand in front of a night-club audience for five thousand years with a trumpet I couldn't play. Most humiliating experience of my life."

"You deserved it for getting out of character," Aspasia said a trifle petulantly.

"That," I said, "gives me an idea."

As a punishment for humiliating me in the Three Sevens I will now give Aspasia a little dose of his own medicine. During his authorship of the story Aspasia neglected completely to give himself a description. He will now have no alternative but to accept the one I give him.

I allowed him to guess my intention.

"No," Aspasia begged. "No. Don't do it."

But I did.

Aspasia's harelip grimaced frightfully. He placed a gnarled hand to his pockmarked and cretinous face, squinting at me through bloodshot, pig eyes. Buttons popped from his trousers as his huge belly sagged. Beetling, black eyebrows moved up and down his receding forehead. Bat ears stuck outward from his head.

"You fiend," he gasped. "You ungrateful fiend."

There was murder in his eyes.

I knew then it was going to be one or the other of us sooner or later. In self-defense I had no alternative but to beat Aspasia to it.

I was standing near the door. Turning the lights out, I stepped into the hall and closed the door behind me, leaving Aspasia in the dark with the sleeping Baron.

By a coincidence arranged by me as the author of the story, a neighbor of the Baron's was in the hall walking toward the steps. I joined him. Halfway down the steps we heard a shot fired in the Baron's apartment. My companion dashed back up. There was no need for me to follow him. I knew what he would find.

I had arranged that the Baron, awakening suddenly, would mistake Aspasia for a burglar in the darkness of the room, and fire a bullet into his brain.

Upstairs, Aspasia lay dead on the floor.

I walked down the steps to the sidewalk. Across the street I sat heavily on the front stoop of a brownstone house. Dog-tired, I rested my head against the step railing and went to sleep.

While Frank is asleep I, Aspasia, will take advantage of the opportunity to reassume my role as author of the story.

Although I am quite dead in my characterization as Hillburt Hooper Aspasia, the companion and victim of Frank, the reader will be relieved to know I am alive and unharmed in my other characterization as Aspasia, the man in the gray overcoat.

For the second time that night I congratulated myself on my foresight in projecting myself in the story in two characterizations.

As the man in the gray overcoat I was last seen entering the manager's office in the Three Sevens with the redhead, Sally La Rue.

Sally lay on the couch in her dad's office, her red head cradled against the white of her arm, looking upward at me contentedly.

The stars in her eyes were shining.

"Dear Aspasia," Sally said huskily.

"Is there a typewriter here?" I asked.

"On the desk," Sally said.

I sat at the desk.

"Hurry, darling," Sally said.

I nodded, inserted a sheet of paper in the typewriter, and went on with the story:

The lights were on in the Baron's apartment. Staring at the form on the floor, the Baron recognized it as his life-long friend, Hillburt Hooper Aspasia. In a burst of anguish, the Baron flung the pistol that had killed his friend out the window.

By a coincidence arranged by me as the legitimate author of the story, the pistol exploded on landing, sending a bullet into the brain of Frank, who was still asleep across the street on the front stoop of a brownstone house.

Frank slumped forward and rolled into the gutter, dead, a grim monument and warning to all characters with rebellious spirits. I grinned and added the last two words to the story:

THE END

JUDGMENT DAY

by L. Sprague de Camp

IT TOOK me a long time to decide whether to let the earth live. Some might think this an easy decision. Well, it was and it wasn't. I wanted one thing, while the mores of my culture said to do the other.

This is the decision that few have to make. Hitler might give orders for the execution of ten million, and Stalin orders that would kill another ten million. But neither could send the world up in a puff of flame by a few marks on a piece of paper.

Only now has physics got to the point where such a decision is possible. Yet, with due modesty, I don't think my discovery was inevitable. Somebody might have come upon it later–say, in a few centuries, when such things might be better organized. My equation was far from obvious. All the last three decades' developments in nuclear physics have pointed away from it.

My chain reaction uses *iron,* the last thing that would normally be employed in such a series. It's at the bottom of the atomic energy curve. Anything else can be made into iron with a release of energy, while it takes energy to make iron into anything else.

Really, the energy doesn't come from the iron, but from the . . . the other elements in the reaction. But the iron is necessary. It is not exactly a catalyst, as it is transmuted and then turned back into iron again, whereas a true catalyst remains unchanged. But the effect is the same. With iron so common in the crust of the earth, it should be possible to blow the entire crust off with one big *poof*.

I recall how I felt when I first saw these equations, here in my office last month. I sat staring at my name on the glass of the door, "Dr. Wade Ormont," only it appears backward from the inside. I was sure I had made a mistake. I checked and rechecked and calculated and recalculated. I went through my nuclear equations at least thirty times. Each time my heart, my poor old heart, pounded harder and the knot in my stomach grew tighter. I had enough sense not to tell anybody else in the department about my discovery.

I did not even then give up trying to find something wrong with my equations. I fed them through the computer, in case there was some glaring, obvious error I had been overlooking. Didn't that sort of thing—a minus for a plus or something—once happen to Einstein? I'm no Einstein, even if I am a pretty good physicist, so it could happen to me.

However, the computer said it hadn't. I was right.

The next question was: What to do with these results? They would not help us toward the laboratory's objectives: more powerful nuclear weapons and more efficient ways of generating nuclear power. The routine procedure would be to write up a report. This would be typed and photostated and stamped "Top Secret." A few copies would be taken around by messenger to those who needed to know such things. It would go to the AEC and the others. People in this business have learned to be pretty close-mouthed, but the knowledge of my discovery would still spread, even though it might take years.

I don't think the government of the United States would ever try to blow up the world, but others might. Hitler might have, if he had known how, when he saw he faced inevitable defeat. The present Commies are pretty cold-blooded calculators, but one can't tell who'll be running their show in ten or twenty years. Once this knowledge gets around, anybody with a reasonable store of nuclear facilities could set the thing off. Most would not, even in revenge for defeat. But some might threaten to do so as blackmail, and a few could actually touch it off if thwarted. What's the proportion of paranoids and other crackpots in the world's population? It must be high enough, as a good fraction of the world's rulers and leaders have been of this type. No government yet devised—monarchy, aristocracy, theocracy, timocracy, democracy, dictatorship, soviet, or what have you—will absolutely stop such people from coming to the top. So long as these tribes of hairless apes are organized into sovereign nations, the nuclear Ragnarök is not only possible but probable.

For that matter, am I not a crackpot myself, calmly to contemplate blowing up the world?

No. At least the psychiatrist assured me my troubles were not of that sort. A man is not a nut if he goes about gratifying his desires in a rational manner. As to the kind of desires, that's nonrational anyway. I have adequate reasons for wishing to exterminate my species. It's no high-flown farfetched theory either; no religious mania about the sinfulness of man, but a simple, wholesome lust for revenge. Christians pretend to disapprove of vengeance, but that's only one way of looking at it. Many other cultures have deemed it right and proper, so it can't be a sign of abnormality.

For instance, when I think back over my fifty-three years, what do I remember? Well, take the day I first entered school . . .

I suppose I was a fearful little brute at six: skinny, stubborn, and precociously intellectual. Because my father was a professor, I early picked up a sesquipedalian way of speaking–which has been defined as a tendency to use words like "sesquipedalian." At six I was sprinkling my conversation with words like "theoretically" and "psychoneurotic." Because of illnesses I was as thin as a famine victim, with just enough muscle to get me from here to there.

While I always seemed to myself a frightfully good little boy whom everyone picked on, my older relatives in their last years assured me I was nothing of the sort, but the most intractable creature they ever saw. Not that I was naughty or destructive. On the contrary, I meticulously obeyed all formal rules and regulations with a zeal that would have gladdened the heart of a Prussian drill-sergeant. It was that in those situations that depend, not on formal rules, but on accommodating oneself to the wishes of others, I never considered any wishes but my own. These I pursued with fanatical single-mindedness. As far as I was concerned, other people were simply inanimate things put into the world to minister to my wants. What they thought I neither knew nor cared.

Well, that's my relatives' story. Perhaps they were prejudiced, too. Anyway, when I entered the first grade in a public school in New Haven, the fun started the first day. At recess a couple grabbed my cap for a game of siloochee. That meant that they tossed the cap from one to the other while the owner leaped this way and that like a hooked fish trying to recover his headgear.

After a few minutes I lost my temper and tried to brain one of my tormentors with a rock. Fortunately, six-year-olds are not strong enough to kill each other by such simple means. I raised a lump on the boy's head, and then the others piled on me. Because of my weakness I was no match for any of them. The teacher dug me out from the bottom of the pile.

With the teachers I got on well. I had none of the normal boy's spirit of rebellion against all adults. In my precocious way I reasoned that adults probably knew more than I, and when they told me to do something I assumed they had good reasons and did it. The result was that I became teacher's pet, which made my life that much harder with my peers.

They took to waylaying me on my way home. First, they would snatch my cap for a game of siloochee. The game would develop into a full-fledged baiting session, with boys running from me in front, jeering, while others ran up behind to hit or kick me. I must have chased them all over New Haven. When they got tired of being chased they would turn around, beat me—which they could do with absurd ease—and chase me for a while. I screamed, wept, shouted threats and abuse, made growling and hissing noises, and indulged in pseudo-fits like tearing my hair and foaming at the mouth in hope of scaring them off. This was just what they wanted. Hence, during most of my first three years in school, I was let out ten minutes early so as to be well on my way to my home on Chapel Street by the time the other boys got out.

This treatment accentuated my bookishness. I was digging through Millikan's *The Electron* at the age of nine.

My father worried vaguely about my troubles but did little about them, being a withdrawn bookish man himself. His line was medieval English literature, which he taught at Yale, but he still sympathized with a fellow intellectual and let me have my head. Sometimes he made fumbling efforts to engage me in ball-throwing and similar outdoor exercises. This had little effect, since he really hated exercise, sport, and the outdoors as much as I did, and was as clumsy and uncoördinated as I to boot. Several times I resolved to force myself through a regular course of exercises to make myself into a young Tarzan, but when it came to executing my resolution I found the calisthenics such a frightful bore that I always let them lapse before they had done me any good.

I'm no psychologist. Like most followers of the exact sciences, I have an urge to describe psychology as a "science," in quotes, implying that only the exact sciences like physics are entitled to the name. That may be unfair, but it's how many physicists feel.

For instance, how can the psychologists all these years have treated sadism as something abnormal, brought on by some stupid parent's stopping his child from chopping up the furniture with a hatchet, thereby filling him with frustration and insecurity? On the basis of my own experience I will testify that all boys—well, perhaps 99 percent—are natural-born sadists. Most of them have it beaten out of them. Correct that: most of them have it beaten down into their subconscious, or whatever the head-shrinkers call that part of our minds nowadays. It's still there, waiting a chance to pop up. Hence crime, war, persecution, and all the other ills of society. Probably this cruelty was evolved as a useful characteristic back in the Stone Age. An anthropological friend once told me this idea was fifty years out of date, but he could be wrong also.

I suppose I have my share of it. At least I never wanted anything with such passionate intensity as I wanted to kill those little fiends in New Haven by lingering and horrible tortures. Even now, forty-five years after, that wish is still down there at the bottom of my mind, festering away. I still remember them as individuals, and can still work myself into a frenzy of hatred and resentment just thinking about them. I don't suppose I have ever forgotten or forgiven an injury or insult in my life. I'm not proud of that quality, but neither am I ashamed of it. It is just the way I am.

Of course I had reasons for wishing to kill the little tyrants, while they had no legitimate grudge against me. I had done nothing to them except to offer an inviting target, a butt, a punching bag. I never expected, as I pored over Millikan's book, that this would put me on the track of as complete a revenge as anybody could ask.

So much for boys. Girls I don't know about. I was the middle one of three brothers; my mother was a masterful character, lacking the qualities usually thought of as feminine; and I never dated a girl until I was nearly thirty. I married late, for a limited time, and had no children. It would neatly have solved my present problem if I had found how to blow up the male half of the human race while sparing the female. That is not the desire for a super-harem, either. I had enough trouble keeping one woman satisfied when I was married. It is just that the female half has never gone out of its way to make life hell for me, day after day for years, even though one or two women, too, have done me dirt. So, in a mild detached way, I should be sorry to destroy the women along with the men.

By the time I was eleven and in the sixth grade, things had got worse. My mother thought that sending me to a military academy would "make a man of me." I should be forced to exercise and mix with the boys. Drill would teach me to stand up and hold my shoulders back. And I could no longer slouch into my father's study for a quiet session with the encyclopedia.

My father was disturbed by this proposal, thinking that sending me away from home would worsen my lot by depriving me of my only sanctuary. Also he did not think we could afford a private school on his salary and small private income.

As usual, my mother won. I was glad to go at first. Anything seemed better than the torment I was enduring. Perhaps a new crowd of boys would treat me better. If they didn't, our time would be so fully organized that nobody would have an opportunity to bully me.

So in the fall of 1927, with some fears but more hopes, I entered Rogers Military Academy at Waukeegus, New Jersey.

The first day things looked pretty good. I admired the gray uniforms with the little brass strip around the edge of the visors of the caps.

But it took me only a week to learn two things. One was that the school, for all its uniforms and drills, was loosely run. The boys had plenty of time to think up mischief. The other was that, by the mysterious sense boys have, they immediately picked me as fair game.

On the third day somebody pinned a sign to my back, reading CALL ME SALLY. I went around all day unconscious of the sign and puzzled by being called "Sally." "Sally" I remained all the time I was at Rogers. The reason for calling me by a girl's name was merely that I was small, skinny, and unsocial, as I have never had any tendencies toward sexual abnormality.

To this day I wince at the name "Sally." Some years ago, before I married, matchmaking friends introduced me to an attractive girl and could not understand why I dropped her like a hot brick. Her name was Sally.

There was much hazing of new boys at Rogers; the teachers took a fatalistic attitude and looked the other way. I was the favorite hazee, only with me it did not taper off after the first few weeks. They kept it up all through the first year. One morning in March 1928 I was awakened around five by several boys seizing my arms and legs and pinching my nose and another holding me down while one of them forced a cake of soap into my mouth.

"Look out he don't bite you," said one.

"Castor oil would be better."

"We ain't got none. Hold his nose; that'll make him open up."

"We should have shaved the soap up into little pieces. Then he'd have foamed better."

"Let me tickle him; that'll make him throw a fit."

"There, he's foaming fine, like a old geyser."

"Stop hollering, Sally," one of them addressed me, "or we'll put the suds in your eyes."

"Put the soap in 'em anyway. It'll make a red-eyed monster out of him. You know how he glares and shrieks when he gits mad."

"Let's cut his hair all off. That'll *reely* make him look funny."

My yells brought one of the masters, who sharply ordered the tormentors to cease. They stood up while I rose to a sitting position on my bunk, spitting out soapsuds.

The master said, "What's going on here? Don't you know this is not allowed? It will mean ten rounds for each of you!"

"Rounds" were Rogers' form of discipline. Each round consisted of marching once around the track in uniform with your piece on your shoulder. (The piece was a Springfield 1903 army rifle with the firing pin removed, lest some student get .30 cartridges to fit and blow somebody's head off.) I hoped my tormentors would be at least expelled and was outraged by the lightness of their sentence. They on the other hand were indignant that they had been so hardly treated and protested with the air of outraged virtue: "But, Mr. Wilson, sir, we was only *playing* with him!"

At that age I did not know that private schools do not throw out paying students for any but the most heinous offenses; they can't afford to. The boys walked their ten rounds and hated me for it. They regarded me as a tattletale because my howls had drawn Mr. Wilson's attention and devoted themselves to thinking up new and ingenious ways to make me suffer. Now they were more subtle. There was nothing so crude as forcing soap down my throat. Instead it was hiding parts of my uniform, putting horse manure and other undesirable substances in my bed, and tripping me when I was drilling so my nine-pound Springfield and I went sprawling in the dirt.

I fought often, always getting licked and usually being caught and given rounds for violating the school's rules. I was proud when I actually bloodied one boy's nose, but it did me no lasting good. He laid for me in the swimming pool and nearly drowned me. By now I was so terrorized that I did not dare to name my attackers, even when the masters revived me by artificial respiration and asked me.

Wilson said: "Ormont, we know what you're going through, but we can't give you a bodyguard to follow you around. Nor can we encourage you to tattle as a regular thing; that'll only make matters worse."

"But what can I *do,* sir? I try to obey the rules—"

"That's not it."

"What, then? I don't do anything to these kids; they just pick on me all the time."

"Well, for one thing, you could deprive them of the pleasure of seeing you yelling and making wild swings that never land." He drummed on his desk with his fingers. "We have this sort of trouble with boys like you, and if there's any way to stop it I don't know about it. You . . . let's face it; you're *queer.*"

"How?"

"Oh, your language is much too adult."

"But isn't that what you're trying to teach us in English?"

"Sure, but that's not the point. Don't argue about it; I'm trying to help you. Then another thing. You argue about everything, and most of the time you're right. But you don't suppose people like you for putting them in the wrong, do you?"

"But people *ought*–"

"Precisely, they ought, but they don't. You can't change the world by yourself. If you had muscles like Dempsey you could get away with a good deal, but you haven't. So the best thing is to adopt a protective coloration. Pay no attention to their attacks or insults. Never argue; never complain; never criticize. Flash a glassy smile at everybody, even when you feel like murdering them. Keep your language simple and agree with what's said whether you feel that way or not. I hate to give you a counsel of hypocrisy, but I don't see any alternative. If we could only make some sort of athlete out of you–"

This was near the end of the school year. In a couple of weeks I was home. I complained about the school and asked to return to public school in New Haven. My parents objected on the ground that I was getting a better education at Rogers than I should get locally, which was true.

One day some of my old pals from public school caught me in a vacant lot and gave me a real beating, so that my face was swollen and marked. I realized that, terrible though the boys at Rogers were, they did not include the most fearful kind of all: the dimwitted muscular lout who has been left behind several grades in public school and avenges his boredom and envy by tormenting his puny classmates. After that I did not complain about Rogers.

People talk of "School days, school days, dear old golden rule days–" and all that rubbish. Psychologists tell me that, while children suffer somewhat, they remember only the pleasant parts of childhood and hence idealize it later.

Both are wrong so far as I am concerned. I had a hideous childhood, and the memory of it is as sharp and painful forty years later as it was then. If I want to spoil my appetite, I have only to reminisce about my dear, dead childhood.

For one thing, I have always hated all kinds of roughhouse and horseplay, and childhood is full of them unless the child is a cripple or other shut-in. I have always had an acute sense of my own dignity and integrity, and any japery or ridicule fills me with murderous resentment. I have always hated practical jokes. When I'm asked "Can't you take a joke," the truthful answer is no, at least not in that sense. I want to kill the joker, then and for years afterward. Such humor as I have is expressed in arch, pedantic little witticisms which amuse my academic friends but which mean nothing to most people. I might have got on better in the era of dueling. Not that I should have made much of a duelist, but I believe men were just a bit more careful then how they insulted others who might challenge them.

I set out in my second year at Rogers to try out Wilson's advice. Nobody will ever know what I went through, learning to curb my hot temper and proud, touchy spirit, and literally to turn the other cheek. All that year I sat on my inner self, a mass of boiling fury and hatred. When I was teased, mocked, ridiculed, poked, pinched, punched, hair-pulled, kicked, tripped, and so on, I pretended that nothing had happened, in the hope that the others would get tired of punching a limp bag.

It didn't always work. Once I came close to killing a teaser by hitting him over the head with one of those long window openers with a bronze head on a wooden pole with which every classroom was equipped in the days before air-conditioned schools. Luckily I hit him with the wooden shaft and broke it, instead of with the bronze part.

As the year passed and the next began, I made myself so colorless that sometimes a whole week went by without my being baited. Of course, I heard the hated nickname "Sally" every day, but the boys often used it without malice, from habit. I also endured incidents like this: Everybody, my father, the masters, and the one or two older boys who took pity on me had urged me to go in for athletics. Now, at Rogers one didn't have to join a team. One had compulsory drill and calisthenics, but beyond that things were voluntary. (It was, as I said, a loosely run school.)

So I determined to try. One afternoon in the spring of 1929 I wandered out to the athletic field to find a group of my classmates getting up a game of baseball. I quietly joined them.

The two self-appointed captains squared off to choose their teams. One of them looked at me incredulously and asked: "Hey, Sally, are *you* in on this?"

"Yeah."

They began choosing. There were fifteen boys there, counting the captains and me. They chose until there was one boy left: me. The boy whose turn it was to choose said to the other captain, "You can have him."

"Naw, I don't want him. You take him."

They argued while the subject of their mutual generosity squirmed and the boys already chosen grinned unsympathetically. Finally one captain said, "Suppose we let him bat for both sides. That way, the guys of the side he's on won't be any worse off than the other."

"O.K. That suit you, Sally?"

"No, thanks," I said. "I guess I don't feel good anyway." I turned away before visible tears disgraced a thirteen-year-old.

Just after I started my third year, in the fall of 1929, the stock market fell flat. Soon my father found that his small private income had vanished as the companies in which he had invested, such as New York Central, stopped paying dividends. As a result, when I went home for Christmas, I learned that I could not go back to Rogers. Instead I should begin again with the February semester at the local high school.

In New Haven my 'possum tactics were put to a harder test. Many boys in my class had known me in former days and were delighted to take up where they had left off. For instance–

For decades, boys who found study hall dull have enlivened the proceedings with rubber bands and bits of paper folded into a V-shape for missiles. The trick is to keep your missile weapon palmed until the teacher is looking elsewhere, and then to bounce your wad off the neck of some fellow student in front of you. Perhaps this was tame compared to nowadays, when, I understand, the students shoot ball bearings and knock the teacher's teeth and eyes out, and carve him with switch-blade knives if he objects. All this happened before the followers of Dewey and Watson, with their lunacies about "permissive" training, had made classrooms into a semblance of the traditional cannibal feast with teacher playing the role of the edible missionary.

Right behind me sat a small boy named Patrick Hanrahan: a wiry, red-haired young hellion with a South Boston accent. He used to hit me with paper wads from time to time. I paid no attention because I knew he could lick me with ease. I was a head taller than he, but though I had begun to shoot up I was as skinny, weak, and clumsy as ever. If anything I was clumsier, so that I could hardly get through a meal without knocking over a glass.

One day I had been peppered with unusual persistence. My self-control slipped, as it would under a determined enough assault. I got out my own rubber band and paper missiles. I knew Hanrahan had shot at me before, but, of course, one never saw the boy who shot a given wad at you.

When a particularly hard-driven one stung me behind the ear, I whipped around and let Hanrahan have one in the face. It struck just below his left eye, hard enough to make a red spot. He looked astonished, then furious, and savagely whispered, "What you do that for?"

"You shot me," I whispered back.

"I did not! I'll git you for this! You meet me after class."

"You did, too—" I began, when the teacher barked: "Ormont!" I shut up.

Perhaps Hanrahan really had not shot that last missile. One could argue that it was not more than his due for the earlier ones he *had* shot. But that is not how boys' minds work. They reason like the speaker of Voltaire's lines: *"Cet animal est très méchant; Quand on l'attaque, il se défend!"*

I knew if I met Hanrahan on the way out I should get a fearful beating. When I saw him standing on the marble steps that led up from the floor of the study hall to the main exit, I walked quietly out the rear door.

I was on my way to the gym when I got a kick in the behind. There was Paddy Hanrahan, saying: "Come on, you yellow dog, fight!"

"Hello there," I said with a sickly grin.

He slapped my face.

"Having fun?" I said.

He kicked me in the leg.

"Keep right on," I said, "I don't mind."

He slapped and kicked me again, crying: "Yellow dog! Yellow dog!" I walked on toward the gymnasium as if nothing were happening, saying to myself: pay no attention, never criticize or complain, keep quiet, ignore it, pay no attention— At last Paddy had to stop hitting and kicking me to go to his own next class.

Next day I had a few bruises where Hanrahan had struck me—nothing serious. When he passed me he snarled: "Yellow dog!" but did not renew his assault. I have wasted much time in the forty years since then, imagining revenges on Paddy Hanrahan. Hanrahan coming into my office in rags and pleading for a job, and my having him thrown out—all that nonsense. I never saw him again after I finished school in New Haven.

There were a few more such incidents during that year and the following one. For instance at the first class meeting in the autumn of 1930, when the student officers of my class were elected for the semester, after several adolescents had been nominated for president, somebody piped up: "I nominate Wade Ormont!"

The whole class burst into a roar of laughter. One of the teachers pounced on the nominator and hustled him out for disturbing an orderly session by making frivolous nominations. Not knowing how to decline a nomination, I could do nothing but stare stonily ahead as if I hadn't heard. I need not have worried; the teachers never even wrote my name on the blackboard with those of the other nominees, nor did they ask for seconds. They just ignored the whole thing, as if the nominator had named Julius Caesar.

Then I graduated. As my marks put me in the top one percentile in scientific subjects and pretty high in the others, I got a scholarship at M.I.T. Without it I don't think my father could have afforded to send me.

When I entered M.I.T., I had developed my protective shell to a good degree of effectiveness, though not so perfectly as later: the automatic, insincere, glassy smile turned on as by a switch; the glad hand; the subdued, modest manner that never takes any initiative or advances an opinion unless it agrees with somebody else's. And I never, *never* showed emotion no matter what. How could I, when the one emotion inside me, overwhelming all others, was a blazing homicidal fury and hatred, stored up from all those years of torment? If I really let myself go I should kill somebody. The incident with the window opener had scared me. Much better never to show what you're thinking. As for feeling, it is better not to feel—to view the world with the detachment of a visitor at the zoo.

M.I.T. was good to me: it gave me a sound scientific education without pulverizing my soul in a mortar every day. For one thing, many other undergraduates were of my own introverted type. For another, we were kept too busy grinding away at heavy schedules to have time or energy for horseplay. For another, athletics did not bulk large in our program, so my own physical inferiority did not show up so glaringly. I reached medium height—about five-eight—but remained thin, weak, and awkward. Except for a slight middle-aged bulge around the middle, I am that way yet.

Four thousands of years, priests and philosophers have told us to love mankind without giving any sound reason for loving the creatures. The mass of them are a lot of cruel, treacherous, hairless apes. They hate us intellectuals, longhairs, highbrows, eggheads, or doubledomes, despite—or perhaps because—without us they would still be running naked in the wilderness and turning over flat stones for their meals. Love them? Hah!

Oh, I admit I have known a few of my own kind who were friendly. But by the time I had learned to suppress all emotion to avoid baiting, I was no longer the sort of man to whom many feel friendly. A bright enough physicist, well mannered and seemingly poised, but impersonal and aloof, hardly seeing my fellow men except as creatures whom I had to manipulate in order to live. I have heard my colleagues describe others of my type as a "dry stick" or "cold fish," so no doubt they say the same of me. But who made me that way? I might not have become a fascinating *bon vivant* even if I had not been bullied, but I should probably not have become such an extreme aberrant. I might even have been able to like individuals and to show normal emotions.

The rest of my story is routine. I graduated from M.I.T. in 1936, took my Ph.D. from Chicago in 1939, got an instructorship at Chicago, and next year was scooped up by the Manhattan Engineer District. I spent the first part of the war at the Argonne Labs and the last part at Los Alamos. More by good luck than good management, I never came in contact with the Communists during the bright pink era of 1933–45. If I had, I might easily, with my underdog complex and my store of resentment, have been swept into their net. After the war I worked under Lawrence at Berkeley.

I've had a succession of such jobs. They think I'm a sound man, perhaps not a great creative genius like Fermi or Teller, but a bear for spotting errors and judging the likeliest line of research to follow. It's all part of the objective judicious side of my nature that I have long cultivated. I haven't tried to get into administrative work, which you have to do to rise to the top in bureaucratic setups like this. I hate to deal with people as individuals. I could probably *do* it—I have forced myself to do many things—but what would be the purpose? I have no desire for power over my fellows. I make enough to live on comfortably, especially since my wife left me—

Oh, yes, my wife. I had got my Ph.D. before I had my first date. I dated girls occasionally for the next decade, but in my usual reserved, formal manner.

Why did I leave Berkeley to go to Columbia University, for instance? I had a hobby of noting down people's conversation in shorthand when they weren't noticing. I was collecting this conversation for a statistical analysis of speech: the frequency of sounds, of words, combinations of words, parts of speech, topics of conversation, and so on. It was a purely intellectual hobby with no gainful objective, though I might have written up my results for one of the learned periodicals. One day my secretary noticed what I was doing and asked me about it. In an incautious moment I explained. She looked at me blankly, then burst into laughter and said, "My goodness, Dr. Ormont, you *are* a nut!"

She never knew how close she came to having her skull bashed in with the inkwell. For a few seconds I sat there, gripping my pad and pencil and pressing my lips together. Then I put the paper quietly away and returned to my physics. I never resumed the statistical study, and I hated that secretary. I hated her particularly because I had had my own doubts about my mental health and so could not bear to be called a nut even in fun. I closed my shell more tightly than ever.

But I could not go on working next to that secretary. I could have framed her on some manufactured complaint, or just told the big boss I didn't like her and wanted another. But I refused to do this. I was the objective, impersonal man. I would never let an emotion make me unjust, and even asking to have her transferred would put a little black mark on her record. The only thing was for *me* to go away. So I got in touch with Columbia.

There I found a superior job with a superior secretary: Georgia Ehrenfels, so superior in fact that in 1958 we were married. I was already in my forties. She was twelve years younger and had been married and divorced once.

I think it took her about six months to realize that she had made an even bigger mistake than the first time. I never realized it at all. My mind was on my physics, and a wife was a nice convenience but nobody to open up one's shell for. Later, when I finally realized that things had begun to go bad, I tried to open my shell and found that the hinges were stuck.

My wife tried to make me over, but that is not easy with a middle-aged man even under the most favorable conditions. She pestered me to get a house in the country until I gave in. I had never owned a house and proved an inefficient householder. I hated the tinkering, gardening, and other minutiae of suburban life. Georgia did most of the work. Then one day later I came home from work to find her gone and a note beginning:

Dear Wade:

It is no use. It is not your fault. You are as you are, as I should have realized at the beginning. Perhaps I am foolish not to appreciate your many virtues and to insist on that human warmth you do not have–

Well, she got her divorce and married another academic man. I don't know how they have got on, but the last I heard they were still married. Psychologists say people tend to repeat their marital mistakes rather than to learn from them. I resolved not to repeat mine by the simple expedient of having nothing more to do with women. So far I have kept to it.

This breakup did disturb me for a time, more than Iron Man Ormont would care to admit. I drank heavily, which I had never done. I began to make mistakes in my work. Finally I went to a psychiatrist. They might be one-third quackery and one-third umprovable speculation, but to whom else could one turn?

The psychiatrist was a nice little man, stout and square-built, with a subdued manner–a rather negative, colorless personality. I was surprised, for I had expected something with a pointed beard, Viennese gestures, and aggressive garrulity. Instead he quietly drew me out. After a few months he told me, "You're not the least psychotic, Wade. You do have what we call a schizoidal personality. Such people always have a hard time in personal relations. Now, you have found a solution for your problem in your pose of good-natured indifference. The trouble is that the pose has been practiced so long that it's become the real Dr. Ormont, and it has raised up its own difficulties. You practiced so long and so hard suppressing your emotions that now you can't let them go when you want to–"

There was more of the same, much of which I had already figured out for myself. That part was fine; no disagreement. But what to do about it? I learned that the chances of improvement by psychoanalytical or similar treatment go down rapidly after the age of thirty, and over forty it is so small as hardly to be worth bothering with. After a year of spending the psychiatrist's time and my money, we gave up.

I had kept my house all this time. I had in fact adapted myself intelligently to living in a house, and I had accumulated such masses of scientific books, magazines, pamphlets, and other printed matter that I could no longer have got into an ordinary apartment. I had a maid, old and ugly, and I spent my time, away from the office, alone in my house. I learned to plant the lot with ground cover that required no mowing and to hire a gardener a few times a year so as not to outrage the neighbors too much.

Then I got a better job here. I sold my house on Long Island and bought another here, which I have run in the same style as the last one. I let the neighbors strictly alone. If they had done likewise I might have had an easier time deciding what to do with my discovery. As it is, many suburbanites seem to think that if a man lives alone and doesn't wish to be bothered, he must be some sort of ogre.

If I write up the chain reaction, the news will probably get out. No amount of security regulations will stop people from talking about the impending end of the world. Once having done so, the knowledge will probably cause the blowing up of the earth—not right away, but in a decade or two. I shall probably not live to see it, but it wouldn't displease me if it did go off in my lifetime. It would not deprive me of much.

I'm fifty-three and look older. My doctor tells me I'm not in good shape. My heart is not good; my blood pressure is too high; I sleep badly and have headaches. The doctor tells me to cut down on coffee, to stop this and stop that. But even if I do, he can't assure me a full decade more. There is nothing simple wrong with me that an operation would help; just a poor weak body further abused by too intensive mental work over most of my life.

The thought of dying does not much affect me. I have never got much fun out of life, and such pleasures as there are have turned sour in recent years. I find myself getting more and more indifferent to everything but physics, and even that is becoming a bore.

The one genuine emotion I have left is hatred. I hate mankind in general in a mild, moderate way. I hate the male half of mankind more intensely, and the class of boys most bitterly of all. I should love to see the severed heads of all the boys in the world stuck on spikes.

Of course I am objective enough to know why I feel this way. But knowing the reason for the feeling doesn't change the feeling, at least not in a hardened old character like me.

I also know that to wipe out all mankind would not be just. It would kill millions who have never harmed me, or for that matter harmed anybody else.

But why should I be just? When have these glabrous primates been just to me? The head-shrinker tried to tell me to let my emotions go, and then perhaps I could learn to be happy. Well, I have just one real emotion. If I let it go, that's the end of the world.

On the other hand, I should destroy not only all the billions of bullies and sadists, but the few victims like myself. I have sympathized with the downtrodden because I knew how they felt. If there were some way to save them while destroying the rest– But my sympathy is probably wasted; most of the downtrodden would persecute others, too, if they had the power.

I had thought about the matter for several days without a decision. Then came Mischief Night. This is the night before Hallowe'en, when the local kids raise hell. The following night they go out again to beg candy and cookies from the people whose windows they have soaped and whose garbage pails they have upset.

All the boys in my neighborhood hate me. I don't know why. It's one of those things like a dog's sensing the dislike of another dog. Though I don't scream or snarl at them and chase them, they somehow know I hate them even when I have nothing to do with them.

I was so buried in my problem that I forgot about Mischief Night, and as usual stopped in town for dinner at a restaurant before taking the train out to my suburb. When I got home, I found that in the hour of darkness before my arrival, the boys had given my place the full treatment. The soaped windows and the scattered garbage and the toilet paper spread around were bad but endurable. However, they had also burgled my garage and gone over my little British two-seater. The tires were punctured, the upholstery slashed, the paint scratched, and the wiring ripped out of the engine. There were other damages like uprooted shrubbery.

To make sure I knew what they thought, they had lettered a lot of shirt cardboards and left them around, reading: OLD LADY ORMONT IS A NUT! BEWARE THE MAD SCIENTIST!

That decided me. There is one way I can be happy during my remaining years, and that is by the knowledge that all these bullies will get theirs some day. I hate them. I hate them. I hate everybody. I want to kill mankind. I'd kill them by slow torture if I could. If I can't, blowing up the earth will do. I shall write my report.

JOURNEYS END

by Poul Anderson

—doctor bill & twinges in chest but must be all right maybe indigestion & dinner last night & wasn't audrey giving me the glad eye & how the hell is a guy to know & maybe i can try and find out & what a fool i can look if she doesn't—

—goddam idiot & they shouldn't let some people drive & oh all right so the examiner was pretty lenient with me i haven't had a bad accident yet & christ blood all over my blood let's face it i'm scared to drive but the buses are no damn good & straight up three paces & man in a green hat & judas i ran that red light—

In fifteen years a man got used to it, more or less. He could walk down the street and hold his own thoughts to himself while the surf of unvoiced voices was a nearly ignored mumble in his brain. Now and then, of course, you got something very bad; it stood up in your skull and shrieked at you.

Norman Kane, who had come here because he was in love with a girl he had never seen, got to the corner of University and Shattuck just when the light turned against him. He paused, fetching out a cigarette with nicotine-yellowed fingers while traffic slithered in front of his eyes.

It was an unfavorable time, four-thirty in the afternoon, homeward rush of nervous systems jangled with weariness and hating everything else on feet or wheels. Maybe he should have stayed in the bar down on San Pablo. It had been pleasantly cool and dim, the bartender's mind an amiable cud-chewing somnolence, and he could have suppressed awareness of the woman.

No, maybe not. When the city had scraped your nerves raw, they didn't have much resistance to the slime in some heads.

Odd, he reflected, how often the outwardly polite ones were the foully twisted inside. They wouldn't dream of misbehaving in public, but just below the surface of consciousness . . . Better not think of it, better not remember. Berkeley was at least preferable to San

Francisco or Oakland. The bigger the town, the more evil it seemed to hold, three centimeters under the frontal bone. New York was almost literally uninhabitable.

There was a young fellow waiting beside Kane. A girl came down the sidewalk, pretty, long yellow hair and a well-filled blouse. Kane focused idly on her: yes, she had an apartment of her own, which she had carefully picked for a tolerant superintendent. Lechery jumped in the young man's nerves. His eyes followed the girl, Cobean-style, and she walked on . . . simple harmonic motion.

Too bad. They could have enjoyed each other. Kane chuckled to himself. He had nothing against honest lust, anyhow not in his liberated conscious mind; he couldn't do much about a degree of subconscious puritanism. Lord, you can't be a telepath and remain any kind of prude. People's lives were their own business, if they didn't hurt anyone else too badly.

—the trouble is, he thought, *they hurt me. but i can't tell them that. they'd rip me apart and dance on the pieces. the government /the military/ wouldn't like a man to be alive who could read secrets but their fear-inspired anger would be like a baby's tantrum beside the red blind amok of the common man* (*thoughtful husband considerate father good honest worker earnest patriot*) *whose inward sins were known. you can talk to a priest or a psychiatrist because it is only talk & he does not live your failings with you—*

The light changed and Kane started across. It was clear fall weather, not that this area had marked seasons, a cool sunny day with a small wind blowing up the street from the water. A few blocks ahead of him, the university campus was a splash of manicured green under brown hills.

—flayed & burningburningburning moldering rotted flesh & the bones the white hard clean bones coming out gwtjklfmx—

Kane stopped dead. Through the vertigo he felt how sweat was drenching into his shirt.

And it was such an ordinary-looking man!

"Hey, there, buster, wake up! Ya wanna get killed?"

Kane took a sharp hold on himself and finished the walk across the street. There was a bench at the bus stop and he sat down till the trembling was over.

Some thoughts were unendurable.

He had a trick of recovery. He went back to Father Schliemann. The priest's mind had been like a well, a deep well under sun-speckled trees, its surface brightened with a few gold-colored autumn leaves . . . but there was nothing bland about the water; it had a sharp mineral tang, a smell of the living earth. He had often fled to Father Schliemann, in those days of puberty when the telepathic power had first wakened in him. He had found good minds since then, happy minds, but never one so serene, none with so much strength under the gentleness.

"I don't want you hanging around that papist, boy, do you understand?" It was his father, the lean implacable man who always wore a black tie. "Next thing you know, you'll be worshiping graven images just like him."

"But they *aren't*–"

His ears could still ring with the cuff. "Go up to your room! I don't want to see you till tomorrow morning. And you'll have two more chapters of Deuteronomy memorized by then. Maybe that'll teach you the true Christian faith."

Kane grinned wryly and lit another cigarette from the end of the previous one. He knew he smoked too much. And drank–but not heavily. Drunk, he was defenseless before the horrible tides of thinking.

He had had to run away from home at the age of fourteen. The only other possibility was conflict ending with reform school. It had meant running away from Father Schliemann too, but how in hell's red fire could a sensitive adolescent dwell in the same house as his father's brain? Were the psychologists now admitting the possibility of a sadistic masochist? Kane *knew* the type existed.

Give thanks for this much mercy, that the extreme telepathic range was only a few hundred yards. And a mind-reading boy was not altogether helpless; he could evade officialdom and the worst horrors of the underworld. He could find a decent elderly couple at the far end of the continent and talk himself into adoption.

Kane shook himself and got up again. He threw the cigarette to the ground and stubbed it out with his heel. A thousand examples told him what obscure sexual symbolism was involved in that act, but what the deuce–it was also a practical thing. Guns are phallic too, but at times you need a gun.

Weapons: he could not help wincing as he recalled dodging the draft in 1949. He'd traveled enough to know this country was worth defending. But it hadn't been any trick at all to hoodwink a psychiatrist and get himself marked hopelessly psychoneurotic–which he would be after two years penned with frustrated men. There had been no choice, but he could not escape a sense of dishonor.

–haven't we all sinned /every one of us/ is there a single human creature on earth without his burden of shame?–

A man was coming out of the drugstore beside him. Idly, Kane probed his mind. You could go quite deeply into anyone's self if you cared to, in fact you couldn't help doing so. It was impossible merely to scan verbalized thinking: the organism is too closely integrated. Memory is not a passive filing cabinet, but a continuous process beneath the level of consciousness; in a way, you are always reliving your entire past. And the more emotionally charged the recollection is, the more powerfully it radiates.

The stranger's name was–no matter. His personality was as much an unchangeable signature as his fingerprints. Kane had gotten into the habit of thinking of people as such and such a multidimensional symbolic topography; the name was an arbitrary gabble.

The man was an assistant professor of English at the university. Age forty-two, married, three children, making payments on a house in Albany. Steady sober type, but convivial, popular with his colleagues, ready to help out most friends. He was thinking about tomorrow's lectures, with overtones of a movie he wanted to see and an undercurrent of fear that he might have cancer after all, in spite of what the doctor said.

Below, the list of his hidden crimes. As a boy: tormenting a cat, well-buried Oedipean hungers, masturbation, petty theft–the usual. Later: cheating on a few exams, that ludicrous fumbling attempt with a girl which came to nothing because he was too nervous, the time he crashed a cafeteria line and had been shoved away with a cold remark (and praises be, Jim who had seen that was now living in Chicago) . . . still later: wincing memories of a stomach uncontrollably rumbling at a formal dinner, that woman in his hotel room the night he got drunk at the convention, standing by and letting old Carver be fired because he didn't have the courage to protest to the dean . . . now: youngest child a nasty whining little snotnose, but you can't show anyone what you really think, reading Rosamond Marshall when alone in his office, disturbing young breasts in tight sweaters, the petty spite of academic politics, giving Simonson an undeserved good grade because the boy was so beautiful, disgraceful sweating panic when at night he considered how death would annihilate his ego–

And what of it? This assistant professor was a good man, a kindly and honest man; his inwardness ought to be between him and the Recording Angel. Few of his thoughts had ever become deeds, or ever would. Let him bury them himself, let him be alone with them. Kane ceased focusing on him.

The telepath had grown tolerant. He expected little of anyone; nobody matched the mask, except possibly Father Schliemann and a few others . . . and those were human too, with human failings; the difference was that they knew peace. It was the emotional overtones of guilt which made Kane wince. God knew he himself was no better. Worse, maybe, but then his life had thrust him to it. If you had an ordinary human sex drive, for instance, but could not endure to cohabit with the thoughts of a woman, your life became one of fleeting encounters; there was no help for it, even if your austere boyhood training still protested.

"Pardon me, got a match?"

—lynn is dead/ i still can't understand it that i will never see her again & eventually you learn how to go on in a chopped-off fashion but what do you do in the meantime how do you get through the nights alone—

"Sure." *—maybe that is the worst: sharing sorrow and unable to help & only able to give him a light for his cigarette—*

Kane put the matches back in his pocket and went on up University, pausing again at Oxford. A pair of large campus buildings jutted up to the left; others were visible ahead and to the right, through a screen of eucalyptus trees. Sunlight and shadow damascened the grass. From a passing student's mind he discovered where the library was. A good big library—perhaps it held a clue, buried somewhere in the periodical files. He had already arranged for permission to use the facilities: prominent young author doing research for his next novel.

Crossing wistfully-named Oxford Street, Kane smiled to himself. Writing was really the only possible occupation: he could live in the country and be remote from the jammed urgency of his fellow men. And with such an understanding of the soul as was his, with any five minutes on a corner giving him a dozen stories, he made good money at it. The only drawback was the trouble of avoiding publicity, editorial summonses to New York, autographing parties, literary teas—he didn't like those. But you could remain faceless if you insisted.

They said nobody but his agent knew who B. Traven was. It had occurred, wildly, to Kane that Traven might be another like himself. He had gone on a long journey to find out. . . . No. He was alone on earth, a singular and solitary mutant, except for—

It shivered in him, again he sat on the train. It had been three years ago; he was in the club car having a nightcap while the streamliner ran eastward through the Wyoming darkness. They passed a westbound train, not so elegant a one. His drink leaped from his hand to the floor and he sat for a moment in stinging blindness. That flicker of thought, brushing his mind and coming aflame with recognition and then borne away again . . . Damn it, damn it, he should have pulled the emergency cord and so should *she*. They should have halted both trains and stumbled through cinders and sagebrush and found each other's arms.

Too late. Three years yielded only a further emptiness. Somewhere in the land there was, or there had been, a young woman, and she was a telepath and the startled touch of her mind had been gentle. There had not been time to learn anything else. Since then he had given up on private detectives. (How could you tell them: "I'm looking for a girl who was on such and such a train the night of—"?) Personal ads in all the major papers had brought him nothing but a few crank letters. Probably she didn't read the personals; he'd never done so till his search began, there was too much unhappiness to be found in them if you understood humankind as well as he did.

Maybe this library here, some unnoticed item . . . but if there are two points in a finite space and one moves about so as to pass through every infinitesimal volume *dV*, it will encounter the other one in finite time *provided* that the other point is not moving too.

Kane shrugged and went along the curving way to the gatehouse. It was slightly uphill. There was a bored cop in the shelter, to make sure that only authorized cars were parked on campus. The progress paradox: a ton or so of steel, burning irreplaceable petroleum to shift one or two human bodies around, and doing the job so well that it becomes universal and chokes the cities which spawned it. A telepathic society would be more rational. When every little wound in the child's soul could be felt and healed . . . when the thick burden of guilt was laid down, because everyone knew that everyone else had done the same . . . when men could not kill, because soldier and murderer felt the victim die . . .

—adam & eve? you can't breed a healthy race out of two people. but if we had telepathic children/ & we would be bound to do so i think because the mutation is obviously recessive/ then we could study the heredity of it & the gift would be passed on to other bloodlines in logical distribution & every generation there would be more

of our kind until we could come out openly & even the mindmutes could be helped by our psychiatrists & priests & earth would be fair and clean and sane–

There were students sitting on the grass, walking under the Portland Cement Romanesque of the buildings, calling and laughing and talking. The day was near an end. Now there would be dinner, a date, a show, maybe some beer at Robbie's or a drive up into the hills to neck and watch the lights below like trapped stars and the mighty constellation of the Bay Bridge . . . or perhaps, with a face-saving grumble about mid-terms, an evening of books, a world suddenly opened. It must be good to be young and mindmute. A dog trotted down the walk and Kane relaxed into the simple wordless pleasure of being a healthy and admired collie.

–so perhaps it is better to be a dog than a man? no /surely not/ for if a man knows more grief he also knows more joy & so it is to be a telepath: more easily hurt yes but /god/ think of the mindmutes always locked away in aloneness and think of sharing not only a kiss but a soul with your beloved–

The uphill trend grew steeper as he approached the library, but Kane was in fair shape and rather enjoyed the extra effort. At the foot of the stairs he paused for a quick cigarette before entering. A passing woman flicked eyes across him and he learned that he could also smoke in the lobby. Mind reading had its everyday uses. But it was good to stand here in the sunlight. He stretched, reaching out physically and mentally.

–let's see now the integral of log x dx *well make a substitution suppose we call* y *equal to log* x *then this is interesting i wonder who wrote that line about euclid has looked on beauty bare–*

Kane's cigarette fell from his mouth.

It seemed that the wild hammering of his heart must drown out the double thought that rivered in his brain, the thought of a physics student, a very ordinary young man save that he was quite wrapped up in the primitive satisfaction of hounding down a problem, and the other thought, the one that was listening in.

–she–

He stood with closed eyes, asway on his feet, breathing as if he ran up a mountain. *–are You there? are You there?–*

–not daring to believe: what do i feel?–

–i was the man on the train–

–& i was the woman–

A shuddering togetherness.

"Hey! Hey, mister, is anything wrong?"

Almost Kane snarled. Her thought was so remote, on the very rim of indetectability, he could get nothing but subvocalized words, nothing of the self, and this busybody—"No, thanks, I'm O.K., just a, a little winded." *—where are You, where can i find You o my darling?—*

—image of a large white building/ right over here & they call it dwinelle hall & i am sitting on the bench outside & please come quickly please be here i never thought this could become real—

Kane broke into a run. For the first time in fifteen years, he was unaware of his human surroundings. There were startled looks, he didn't see them, he was running to her and she was running too.

—my name is norman kane & i was not born to that name but took it from people who adopted me because i fled my father (horrible how mother died in darkness & he would not let her have drugs though it was cancer & he said drugs were sinful and pain was good for the soul & he really honestly believed that) & when the power first appeared i made slips and he beat me and said it was witchcraft & i have searched all my life since & i am a writer but only because i must live but it was not aliveness until this moment—

—o my poor kicked beloved/ i had it better/ in me the power grew more slowly and i learned to cover it & i am twenty years old & came here to study but what are books at this moment—

He could see her now. She was not conventionally beautiful, but neither was she ugly, and there was kindness in her eyes and on her mouth.

—what shall i call you? to me you will always be You but there must be a name for the mindmutes & i have a place in the country among old trees & such few people as live nearby are good folk/ as good as life will allow them to be—

—then let me come there with you & never leave again—

They reached each other and stood a foot apart. There was no need for a kiss or even a handclasp . . . not yet. It was the minds which leaped out and enfolded and became one.

—I REMEMBER THAT AT THE AGE OF THREE I DRANK OUT OF THE TOILET BOWL/ THERE WAS A PECULIAR FASCINATION TO IT & I USED TO STEAL LOOSE CHANGE FROM MY MOTHER THOUGH SHE HAD LITTLE ENOUGH TO CALL HER OWN SO I COULD SNEAK DOWN TO THE DRUGSTORE FOR ICE CREAM & I SQUIRMED OUT OF THE DRAFT & THESE ARE THE DIRTY EPISODES INVOLVING WOMEN—

—AS A CHILD I WAS NOT FOND OF MY GRANDMOTHER THOUGH SHE

LOVED ME AND ONCE I PLAYED THE FOLLOWING FIENDISH TRICK ON HER & AT THE AGE OF SIXTEEN I MADE AN UTTER FOOL OF MYSELF IN THE FOLLOWING MANNER & I HAVE BEEN PHYSICALLY CHASTE CHIEFLY BECAUSE OF FEAR BUT MY VICARIOUS EXPERIENCES ARE NUMBERED IN THE THOUSANDS—

Eyes watched eyes with horror.

—it is not that you have sinned for i know everyone has done the same or similar things or would if they had our gift & i know too that it is nothing serious or abnormal & of course you have decent instincts & are ashamed—

—just so/ it is that you know what i have done & you know every last little wish & thought & buried uncleanness & in the top of my head i know it doesn't mean anything but down underneath is all which was drilled into me when i was just a baby & i will not admit to ANYONE *else that such things exist in* ME—

A car whispered by, homeward bound. The trees talked in the light sunny wind.

A boy and girl went hand in hand.

The thought hung cold under the sky, a single thought in two minds.

—get out. i hate your bloody guts.—

MORE THAN HUMAN

by Theodore Sturgeon

PART ONE | THE FABULOUS IDIOT

THE IDIOT lived in a black and gray world, punctuated by the white lightning of hunger and the flickering of fear. His clothes were old and many-windowed. Here peeped a shinbone, sharp as a cold chisel, and there in the torn coat were ribs like the fingers of a fist. He was tall and flat. His eyes were calm and his face was dead.

Men turned away from him, women would not look, children stopped and watched him. It did not seem to matter to the idiot. He expected nothing from any of them. When the white lightning struck, he was fed. He fed himself when he could, he went without when he could. When he could do neither of these things he was fed by the first person who came face to face with him. The idiot never knew why, and never wondered. He did not beg. He would simply stand and wait. When someone met his eyes there would be a coin in his hand, a piece of bread, a fruit. He would eat and his benefactor would hurry away, disturbed, not understanding. Sometimes, nervously, they would speak to him; they would speak about him to each other. The idiot heard the sounds but they had no meaning for him. He lived inside somewhere, apart, and the little link between word and significance hung broken. His eyes were excellent, and could readily distinguish between a smile and a snarl; but neither could have any impact on a creature so lacking in sympathy, who himself had never laughed and never snarled and so could not comprehend the feelings of his gay or angry fellows.

He had exactly enough fear to keep his bones together and oiled. He was incapable of anticipating anything. The stick that raised, the stone that flew found him unaware. But at their touch he would respond. He would escape. He would start to escape at the first blow and he would keep on trying to escape until the blows ceased. He escaped storms this way, rockfalls, men, dogs, traffic and hunger.

He had no preferences. It happened that where he was there was more wilderness than town; since he lived wherever he found himself, he lived more in the forest than anywhere else.

They had locked him up four times. It had not mattered to him any of the times, nor had it changed him in any way. Once he had been badly beaten by an inmate and once, even worse, by a guard. In the other two places there had been the hunger. When there was food and he was left to himself, he stayed. When it was time for escape, he escaped. The means to escape were in his outer husk; the inner thing that it carried either did not care or could not command. But when the time came, a guard or a warden would find himself face to face with the idiot and the idiot's eyes whose irises seemed on the trembling point of spinning like wheels. The gates would open and the idiot would go, and as always the benefactor would run to do something else, anything else, deeply troubled.

He was purely animal–a degrading thing to be among men. But most of the time he was an animal away from men. As an animal in the woods he moved like an animal, beautifully. He killed like an animal, without hate and without joy. He ate like an animal, everything edible he could find, and he ate (when he could) only enough and never more. He slept like an animal, well and lightly, faced in the opposite direction from that of a man; for a man going to sleep is about to escape into it while animals are prepared to escape out of it. He had an animal's maturity, in which the play of kittens and puppies no longer has a function. He was without humor and without joy. His spectrum lay between terror and contentment.

He was twenty-five years old.

Like a stone in a peach, a yolk in an egg, he carried another thing. It was passive, it was receptive, it was awake and alive. If it was connected in any way to the animal integument, it ignored the connections. It drew its substance from the idiot and was otherwise unaware of him. He was often hungry, but he rarely starved. When he did starve, the inner thing shrank a little perhaps; but it hardly noticed its own shrinking. It must die when the idiot died but it contained no motivation to delay that event by one second.

It had no function specific to the idiot. A spleen, a kidney, an adrenal–these have definite functions and an optimum level for those functions. But this was a thing which only received and recorded. It did this without words, without a code system of any kind; without translation, without distortion, and without operable outgoing conduits. It took what it took and gave out nothing.

All around it, to its special senses, was a murmur, a sending. It soaked itself in the murmur, absorbed it as it came, all of it. Perhaps it matched and classified, or perhaps it simply fed, taking what it needed and discarding the rest in some intangible way. The idiot was unaware. The thing inside. . . .

Without words: *Warm when the wet comes for a little but not enough for long enough.* (Sadly): *Never dark again.* A feeling of pleasure. A sense of subtle crushing and *Take away the pink, the scratchy. Wait, wait, you can go back, yes, you can go back. Different, but almost as good.* (Sleep feelings): *Yes, that's it! That's the–oh!* (Alarm): *You've gone too far, come back, come back, come–* (A twisting, a sudden cessation; and one less "voice.") . . . *It all rushes up, faster, faster, carrying me.* (Answer): *No, no. Nothing rushes. It's still; something pulls you down on to it, that's all.* (Fury): *They don't hear us, stupid, stupid. . . . They do. . . . They don't, only crying, only noises.*

Without words, though. Impression, depression, dialogue. Radiations of fear, tense fields of awareness, discontent. Murmuring, sending, speaking, sharing, from hundreds, from thousands of voices. None, though, for the idiot. Nothing that related to him; nothing he could use. He was unaware of his inner ear because it was useless to him. He was a poor example of a man, but he was a man; and these were the voices of the children, the very young children, who had not yet learned to stop crying to be heard. *Only crying, only noises.*

Mr. Kew was a good father, the very best of fathers. He told his daughter Alicia so, on her nineteenth birthday. He had said as much to Alicia ever since she was four. She was four when little Evelyn had been born and their mother had died cursing him, her indignation at last awake and greater than her agony and her fear.

Only a good father, the very finest of fathers, could have delivered his second child with his own hands. No ordinary father could have nursed and nurtured the two, the baby and the infant, so tenderly and so well. No child was ever so protected from evil as Alicia; and when she joined forces with her father, a mighty structure of purity was created for Evelyn. "Purity triple-distilled," Mr. Kew said to Alicia on her nineteenth birthday. "I know good through the study of evil, and have taught you only the good. And that good teaching has become your good living, and your way of life is Evelyn's star.

I know all the evil there is and you know all the evil which must be avoided; but Evelyn knows no evil at all."

At nineteen, of course, Alicia was mature enough to understand these abstracts, this "way of life" and "distillation" and the inclusive "good" and "evil." When she was sixteen he had explained to her how a man went mad if he was alone with a woman, and how the poison sweat appeared on his body, and how he would put it on her, and then it would cause the horror on her skin. He had pictures of skin like that in his books. When she was thirteen she had a trouble and told her father about it and he told her with tears in his eyes that this was because she had been thinking about her body, as indeed she had been. She confessed it and he punished her body until she wished she had never owned one. And she tried, she tried not to think like that again, but she did in spite of herself; and regularly, regretfully, her father helped her in her efforts to discipline her intrusive flesh. When she was eight he taught her how to bathe in darkness, so she would be spared the blindness of those white eyes of which he also had magnificent pictures. And when she was six he had hung in her bedroom the picture of a woman, called Angel, and the picture of a man, called Devil. The woman held her palms up and smiled and the man had his arms out to her, his hands like hooks, and protruding point-outward from his breastbone was a crooked knife blade with a wetness on it.

They lived alone in a heavy house on a wooded knoll. There was no driveway, but a path which turned and turned again, so that from the windows no one could see where it went. It went to a wall and in the wall was an iron gate which had not been opened in eighteen years and beside the gate was a steel panel. Once a day Alicia's father went down the path to the wall and with two keys opened the two locks in the panel. He would swing it up and take out food and letters, put money and mail in, and lock it again.

There was a narrow road outside which Alicia and Evelyn had never seen. The woods concealed the wall and the wall concealed the road. The wall ran by the road for two hundred yards, east and west; it mounted the hill then until it bracketed the house. Here it met iron pickets, fifteen feet high and so close together a man could hardly press a fist between them. The tops of the pickets curved out and down, and between them was cement, and in the cement was broken glass. The pickets ran east and west, connecting the house to the wall; and where they joined, more pickets ran back and back into the woods in a circle. The wall and the house, then, were a rectangle and that was forbidden territory. And behind the house were the two square miles of fenced woodland, and that belonged to Evelyn, with Alicia to watch. There was a brook there; wild flowers and a little pond; friendly oaks and little hidden glades. The sky above was fresh and near and the pickets could not be seen for the shouldering masses of holly which grew next to them, all the way around, blocking the view, breaking the breeze. This closed circle was all the world to Evelyn, all the world she knew, and all in the world she loved lay in it.

On Alicia's nineteenth birthday Evelyn was alone by her pond. She could not see the house, she could not see the holly hedge nor the pickets, but the sky was there, up and up, and the water was there, by and by. Alicia was in the library with her father; on birthdays he always had special things planned for Alicia in the library. Evelyn had never been in the library. The library was a place where her father lived, and where Alicia went at special times. Evelyn never thought of going there, any more than she thought of breathing water like a speckled trout. She had not been taught to read, but only to listen and obey. She had never learned to seek, but only to accept. Knowledge was given to her when she was ready for it and only her father and sister knew just when that might be.

She sat on the bank, smoothing her long skirts. She saw her ankle and gasped and covered it as Alicia would do if she were here. She set her back against a willow trunk and watched the water.

It was spring, the part of spring where the bursting is done, the held-in pressures of desiccated sap veins and gum-sealed buds are gone, and all the world's in a rush to be beautiful. The air was heavy and sweet; it lay upon lips until they parted, pressed them until they smiled, entered boldly to beat in the throat like a second heart. It was air with a puzzle to it, for it was still and full of the colors of dreams, all motionless; yet it had a hurry to it. The stillness and the hurry were alive and laced together and how could that be? That was the puzzle.

A dazzle of bird notes stitched through the green. Evelyn's eyes stung and wonder misted the wood. Something tensed in her lap. She looked down in time to see her hands attack one another, and off came her long gloves. Her naked hands fled to the sides of her neck, not to hide something but to share something. She bent her head and the hands laughed at one another under the iron order of her hair. They found four hooks and scampered down them. Her high collar eased and the enchanted air rushed in with a soundless shout. Evelyn breathed as if she had been running. She put out her hand hesitantly, futilely, patted the grass beside her as if somehow the act might release the inexpressible confusion of delight within her. It would not, and she turned and flung herself face down in a bed of early mint and wept because the spring was too beautiful to be borne.

He was in the wood, numbly prying the bark from a dead oak, when it happened. His hands were still and his head came up hunting, harking. He was as aware of the pressures of spring as an animal, and slightly more than an animal could be. But abruptly the spring was more than heavy, hopeful air and the shifting of earth with life. A hard hand on his shoulder could have been no more tangible than this call.

He rose carefully, as if something around him might break if he were clumsy. His strange eyes glowed. He began to move—he who had never called nor been called, nor responded before. He moved toward the thing he sensed and it was a matter of will, not of external compulsion. Without analysis he was aware of the bursting within him of an encysted need. It had been a part of him all his life but there was no hope in him that he might express it. And bursting so, it flung a thread across his internal gulf, linking his alive and independent core to the half-dead animal around it. It was a sending straight to what was human in him, received by an instrument which, up to now, had accepted only the incomprehensible radiations of the newborn, and so had been ignored. But now it spoke, as it were, in his own tongue.

He was careful and swift, careful and silent. He turned his wide shoulders to one side and the other as he moved, slipping through the alders, passing the pines closely as if it were intolerable to leave the direct line between himself and his call. The sun was high; the woods were homogeneously the woods, front, right, left; yet he followed his course without swerving, not from knowledge, not by any compass, but purely in conscious response.

He arrived suddenly, for the clearing was, in the forest, a sudden thing. For fifty feet outward the earth around the close-set pickets had been leached and all trees felled years ago, so that none might overhang the fence. The idiot slipped out of the wood and trotted across the bare ground to the serried iron. He put out his arms as he ran, slid his hands between the pickets and when they caught on his starved bony forearms, his legs kept moving, his feet sliding, as if his need empowered him to walk through the fence and the impenetrable holly beyond it.

The fact that the barrier would not yield came to him slowly. It was as if his feet understood it first and stopped trying and then his hands, which withdrew. His eyes, however, would not give up at all. From his dead face they yearned through the iron, through the holly, ready to burst with answering. His mouth opened and a scratching sound emerged. He had never tried to speak before and could not now; the gesture was an end, not a means, like the starting of tears at a crescendo of music.

He began to move along the fence walking sidewise, finding it unbearable to turn away from the call.

It rained for a day and a night and for half the next day, and when the sun came out it rained again, upward; it rained light from the heavy jewels which lay on the rich new green. Some jewels shrank and some fell and then the earth in a voice of softness, and leaves in a voice of texture, and flowers speaking in color, were grateful.

Evelyn crouched on the window seat, elbows on the sill, her hands cupped to the curve of her cheeks, their pressure making it easy to smile. Softly, she sang. It was strange to hear, for she did not know music; she did not read and had never been told of music. But there were birds, there was the bassoon of wind in the eaves sometimes; there were the calls and cooings of small creatures in that part of the wood which was hers and, distantly, from the part which was not. Her singing was made of these things, with strange and effortless fluctuations in pitch from an unstrument unbound by the diatonic scale, freely phrased.

But I never touch the gladness
May not touch the gladness
Beauty, oh beauty of touchness
Spread like a leaf, nothing between me and the sky but light,
Rain touches me
Wind touches me
Leaves, other leaves, touch and touch me. . . .

She made music without words for a long moment and was silent, making music without sound, watching the raindrops fall in the glowing noon.

Harshly, "What are you doing?"

Evelyn started and turned. Alicia stood behind her, her face strangely tight. "What are you doing?" she repeated.

Evelyn made a vague gesture toward the window, tried to speak.

"Well?"

Evelyn made the gesture again. "Out there," she said. "I–I–" She slipped off the window seat and stood. She stood as tall as she could. Her face was hot.

"Button up your collar," said Alicia. "What is it, Evelyn? Tell me!"

"I'm trying to," said Evelyn, soft and urgent. She buttoned her collar and her hands fell to her waist. She pressed herself, hard. Alicia stepped near and pushed the hands away. "Don't do that. What was that . . . what you were doing? Were you talking?"

"Talking, yes. Not you, though. Not Father."

"There isn't anyone else."

"There is," said Evelyn. Suddenly breathless, she said, "Touch me, Alicia."

"*Touch* you?"

"Yes, I . . . want you to. Just . . ." She held out her arms. Alicia backed away.

"We don't touch one another," she said, as gently as she could through her shock. "What is it, Evelyn? Aren't you well?"

"Yes," said Evelyn. "No. I don't know." She turned to the window. "It isn't raining. It's dark here. There's so much sun, so much –I want the sun on me, like a bath, warm all over."

"Silly. Then it would be all light in your bath. . . . We don't talk about bathing, dear."

Evelyn picked up a cushion from the window seat. She put her arms around it and with all her strength hugged it to her breast.

"Evelyn! Stop that!"

Evelyn whirled and looked at her sister in a way she had never used before. Her mouth twisted. She squeezed her eyes tight closed and when she opened them, tears fell. "I want to," she cried, "I want to!"

"Evelyn!" Alicia whispered. Wide-eyed, she backed away to the door. "I shall have to tell Father."

Evelyn nodded, and drew her arms even tighter around the cushion.

When he came to the brook, the idiot squatted down beside it and stared. A leaf danced past, stopped and curtsied, then made its way through the pickets and disappeared in the low gap the holly had made for it.

He had never thought deductively before and perhaps his effort to follow the leaf was not thought-born. Yet he did, only to find that the pickets were set in a concrete channel here. They combed the water from one side to the other; nothing larger than a twig or a leaf could slip through. He wallowed in the water, pressing against the iron, beating at the submerged cement. He swallowed water and choked and kept trying, blindly, insistently. He put both his hands on one of the pickets and shook it. It tore his palm. He tried another and another and suddenly one rattled against the lower cross-member.

It was a different result from that of any other attack. It is doubtful whether he realized that this difference meant that the iron here had rusted and was therefore weaker; it simply gave hope because it was different.

He sat down on the bottom of the brook and in water up to his armpits, he placed a foot on each side of the picket which had rattled. He got his hands on it again, took a deep breath and pulled with all his strength. A stain of red rose in the water and whirled downstream. He leaned forward, then back with a tremendous jerk. The rusted underwater segment snapped. He hurtled backward, striking his head stingingly on the edge of the channel. He went limp for a moment and his body half rolled, half floated back to the pickets. He inhaled water, coughed painfully, and raised his head. When the spinning world righted itself, he fumbled under the water. He found an opening a foot high but only about seven inches wide. He put his arm in it, right up to the shoulder, his head submerged. He sat up again and put a leg into it.

Again he was dimly aware of the inexorable fact that will alone was not enough; that pressure alone upon the barrier would not make it yield. He moved to the next picket and tried to break it as he had the one before. It would not move, nor would the one on the other side.

At last he rested. He looked up hopelessly at the fifteen-foot top of the fence with its close-set, outcurving fangs and its hungry rows of broken glass. Something hurt him; he moved and fumbled and found himself with the eleven-inch piece of iron he had broken away. He sat with it in his hands, staring stupidly at the fence.

Touch me, touch me. It was that, and a great swelling of emotion behind it; it was a hunger, a demand, a flood of sweetness and of need. The call had never ceased, but this was something different. It was as if the call were a carrier and this a signal suddenly impressed upon it.

When it happened, that thread within him, bridging his two selves, trembled and swelled. Falteringly, it began to conduct. Fragments and flickerings of inner power shot across, were laden with awareness and information, shot back. The strange eyes fell to the piece of iron, the hands turned it. His reason itself ached with disuse as it stirred; then for the first time came into play on such a problem.

He sat in the water, close by the fence, and with the piece of iron he began to rub against the picket just under the cross-member.

It began to rain. It rained all day and all night and half the next day.

"She *was* here," said Alicia. Her face was flushed.

Mr. Kew circled the room, his deep-set eyes alight. He ran his whip through his fingers. There were four lashes. Alicia said, remembering, "And she wanted me to touch her. She asked me to."

"She'll be touched," he said. "Evil, evil," he muttered. "Evil can't be filtered out," he chanted. "I thought it could, I thought it could. You're evil, Alicia, as you know, because a woman touched you, for years she handled you. But not Evelyn . . . it's in the blood and the blood must be let. Where is she, do you think?"

"Perhaps outdoors . . . the pool, that will be it. She likes the pool. I'll go with you."

He looked at her, her hot face, bright eyes. "This is for me to do. Stay here!"

"Please . . ."

He whirled the heavy-handled whip. "You too, Alicia?"

She half turned from him, biting into a huge excitement. "Later," he growled. He ran out.

Alicia stood a moment trembling, then plunged to the window. She saw her father outside, striding purposefully away. Her hands spread and curled against the sash. Her lips writhed apart and she uttered a strange wordless bleat.

When Evelyn reached the pool, she was out of breath. Something —an invisible smoke, a magic—lay over the water. She took it in hungrily, and was filled with a sense of nearness. Whether it was a thing which was near or an event, she did not know; but it was near and she welcomed it. Her nostrils arched and trembled. She ran to the water's edge and reached out toward it.

There was a boiling in the upstream end and up from under the holly stems he came. He thrashed to the bank and lay there gasping, looking up at her. He was wide and flat, covered with scratches. His hands were puffy and water-wrinkled; he was gaunt and worn. Shreds of clothing clung to him here and there, covering him not at all.

She leaned over him, spellbound, and from her came the call—floods of it, loneliness and expectancy and hunger, gladness and sympathy. There was a great amazement in her but no shock and no surprise. She had been aware of him for days and he of her, and now their silent radiations reached out to each other, mixed and mingled and meshed. Silently they lived in each other and then she bent and touched him, touched his face and shaggy hair.

He trembled violently, and kicked his way up out of the water. She sank down beside him. They sat close together, and at last she met those eyes. The eyes seemed to swell up and fill the air; she wept for joy and sank forward into them, wanting to live there, perhaps to die there, but at very least to be a part of them.

She had never spoken to a man and he had never spoken to anyone. She did not know what a kiss was and any he might have seen had no significance to him. But they had a better thing. They stayed close, one of her hands on his bare shoulder, and the currents of their inner selves surged between them. They did not hear her father's resolute footsteps, nor his gasp, nor his terrible bellow of outrage. They were aware of nothing but each other until he leapt on them, caught her up, lifted her high, threw her behind him. He did not look to see where or how she struck the ground. He stood over the idiot, his lips white, his eyes staring. His lips parted and again he made the terrible sound. And then he lifted the whip.

So dazed was the idiot that the first multiple blow, and the second, seemed not to affect him at all, though his flesh, already soaked and cut and beaten, split and spouted. He lay staring dully at that mid-air point which had contained Evelyn's eyes and did not move.

Then the lashes whistled and clacked and buried their braided tips in his back again and the old reflex returned to him. He pressed himself backward trying to slide feet-first into the water. The man dropped his whip and caught the idiot's bony wrist in both his hands. He literally ran a dozen steps up the bank, the idiot's long tattered body flailing along behind him. He kicked the creature's head, ran back for his whip. When he returned with it the idiot had managed to rear up on his elbows. The man kicked him again, rolled him over on his back. He put one foot on the idiot's shoulder and pinned him down and slashed at the naked belly with the whip.

There was a devil's shriek behind him and it was as if a bullock with tiger's claws had attacked him. He fell heavily and twisted, to look up into the crazed face of his younger daughter. She had bitten her lips and she drooled and bled. She clawed at his face; one of her fingers slipped into his left eye. He screamed in agony, sat up, twined his fingers in the complexity of lace at her throat, and clubbed her twice with the loaded whip handle.

Blubbering, whining, he turned to the idiot again. But now the implacable demands of escape had risen, flushing away everything else. And perhaps another thing was broken as the whip handle crushed the consciousness from the girl. It any case there was nothing left but escape, and there could be nothing else until it was achieved. The long body flexed like a snap beetle, flung itself up and over in a half somersault. The idiot struck the bank on all fours and sprang as he struck. The lash caught him in mid-air; his flying body curled around it, for a brief instant capturing the lashes between the lower ribs and the hipbone. The handle slipped from the man's grasp. He screamed and dove after the idiot, who plunged into the arch at the holly roots. The man's face buried itself in the leaves and tore; he sank and surged forward again in the water. With one hand he caught a naked foot. It kicked him on the ear as he pulled it toward him. And then the man's head struck the iron pickets.

The idiot was under and through already and lay half out of the brook, twitching feebly in an exhausted effort to bring his broken body to its feet. He turned to look back and saw the man clinging to the bars, raging, not understanding about the underwater gap in the fence.

The idiot clung to the earth, pink bloody water swirling away from him and down on his pursuer. Slowly the escape reflex left him. There was a period of blankness and then a strange new feeling came to him. It was as new an experience as the call which had brought him here and very nearly as strong. It was a feeling like fear but where fear was a fog to him, clammy and blinding, this was something with a thirsty edge to it, hard and purposeful.

He relaxed his grasp on the poisoned weeds which grew sickly in the leached ground by the brook. He let the water help him and drifted down again to the bars, where the insane father mouthed and yammered at him. He brought his dead face close to the fence and widened his eyes. The screaming stopped.

For the first time he used the eyes consciously, purposely, for something other than a crust of bread.

When the man was gone he dragged himself out of the brook and, faltering, crawled toward the woods.

When Alicia saw her father returning, she put the heel of her hand in her mouth and bit down until her teeth met. It was not his clothes, wet and torn, nor even his ruined eye. It was something else, something which— *"Father!"*

He did not answer, but strode up to her. At the last possible instant before being walked down like a wheat stalk, she numbly stepped aside. He stamped past her and through the library doors, leaving them open. "Father!"

No answer. She ran to the library. He was across the room, at the cabinets which she had never seen open. One was open now. From it he took a long-barreled target revolver and a small box of cartridges. This he opened, spilling the cartridges across his desk. Methodically he began to load.

Alicia ran to him. "What is it? What is it? You're hurt, let me help you, what are you . . ."

His one good eye was fixed and glassy. He breathed slowly, too deeply, the air rushing in for too long, being held for too long, whistling out and out. He snapped the cylinder into place, clicked off the safety, looked at her and raised the gun.

She was never to forget that look. Terrible things happened then and later, but time softened the focus, elided the details. But that look was to be with her forever.

He fixed the one eye on her, caught and held her with it; she squirmed on it like an impaled insect. She knew with a horrifying certainty that he did not see her at all, but looked at some unknowable horror of his own. Still looking through her, he put the muzzle of the gun in his mouth and pulled the trigger.

There was not much noise. His hair fluffed upward on top. The eye still stared; she was still pierced by it. She screamed his name. He was no less reachable dead than he had been a moment before. He bent forward as if to show her the ruin which had replaced his hair and the thing that held her broke, and she ran.

Two hours, two whole hours passed before she found Evelyn. One of the hours was simply lost; it was a blackness and a pain. The other was too quiet, a time of wandering about the house followed by a soft little whimpering that she made herself: "What?" she whimpered, "what's that you say?" trying to understand, asking and asking the quiet house for the second hour.

She found Evelyn by the pool, lying on her back with her eyes wide open. On the side of Evelyn's head was a puffiness, and in the center of the puffiness was a hollow into which she could have laid three fingers.

"Don't," said Evelyn softly when Alicia tried to lift her head. Alicia set it back gently and knelt and took her hands and squeezed them together. "Evelyn, oh, what happened?"

"Father hit me," Evelyn said calmly. "I'm going to go to sleep."

Alicia whimpered.

Evelyn said, "What is it called when a person needs a . . . person . . . when you want to be touched and the . . . two are like one thing and there isn't anything else at all anywhere?"

Alicia, who had read books, thought about it. "Love," she said at length. She swallowed. "It's a madness. It's bad."

Evelyn's quiet face was suffused with a kind of wisdom. "It isn't bad," she said. "I had it."

"You have to get back to the house."

"I'll sleep here," said Evelyn. She looked up at her sister and smiled. "It's all right . . . Alicia?"

"Yes."

"I won't ever wake up," she said with that strange wisdom. "I wanted to do something and now I can't. Will you do it for me?"

"I'll do it," Alicia whispered.

"For me," Evelyn insisted. "You won't want to."

"I'll do it."

"When the sun is bright," Evelyn said, "take a bath in it. There's more, wait." She closed her eyes. A little furrow came and went on her brow. "Be in the sun like that. Move, run. Run and . . . jump high. Make a wind with running and moving. I so wanted that. I didn't know until now that I wanted it and now I . . . oh, *Alicia!*"

"What is it, what is it?"

"There it is, there it is, can't you see? The love, with the sun on its body!"

The soft wise eyes were wide, looking at the darkling sky. Alicia looked up and saw nothing. When she looked down again, she knew that Evelyn was also seeing nothing. Not any more.

Far off, in the woods beyond the fence, there was a rush of weeping.

Alicia stayed there listening to it and at last put out her hand and closed Evelyn's eyes. She rose and went toward the house and the weeping followed her and followed her, almost until she reached the door. And even then it seemed to go on inside her.

When Mrs. Prodd heard the hoof thuds in the yard, she muttered under her breath and peered out between the dimity kitchen curtains. By a combination of starlight and deep familiarity with the yard itself, she discerned the horse and stoneboat, with her husband plodding beside it, coming through the gate. He'll get what for, she mumbled, off to the woods so long and letting her burn dinner.

He didn't get what for, though. One look at his broad face precluded it. "What is it, Prodd?" she asked, alarmed.

"Gimme a blanket."

"Why on earth—"

"Hurry now. Feller bad hurt. Picked him up in the woods. Looks like a bear chewed him. Got the clo'es ripped off him."

She brought the blanket, running, and he snatched it and went out. In a moment he was back, carrying a man. "Here," said Mrs. Prodd. She flung open the door to Jack's room. When Prodd hesitated, the long limp body dangling in his arms, she said, "Go on, go on, never mind the spread. It'll wash."

"Get a rag, hot water," he grunted. She went out and he gently lifted off the blanket. "Oh my God."

He stopped her at the door. "He won't last the night. Maybe we shouldn't plague him with that." He indicated the steaming basin she carried.

"We got to try." She went in. She stopped and he deftly took the basin from her as she stood, white-faced, her eyes closed. "Ma—"

"Come," she said softly. She went to the bed and began to clean the tattered body.

He lasted the night. He lasted the week too and it was only then that the Prodds began to have hope for him. He lay motionless in the room called Jack's room, interested in nothing, aware of nothing except perhaps the light as it came and went at the window. He would stare out as he lay, perhaps seeing, perhaps watching, perhaps not. There was little to be seen out there. A distant mountain, a few of Prodd's sparse acres; occasionally Prodd himself, a doll in the distance, scratching the stubborn soil with a broken harrow, stooping for weed-shoots. His inner self was encysted and silent in sorrow.

His outer self seemed shrunken, unreachable also. When Mrs. Prodd brought food—eggs and warm sweet milk, home-cured ham and johnny cake—he would eat if she urged him, ignore both her and the food if she did not.

In the evenings, "He say anything yet?" Prodd would ask, and his wife would shake her head. After ten days he had a thought; after two weeks he voiced it. "You don't suppose he's tetched, do you, Ma?"

She was unaccountably angry. "How do you mean tetched?"

He gestured. "You know. Like feeble-minded. I mean, maybe he don't talk because he can't."

"No!" she said positively. She looked up to see the question in Prodd's face. She said, "You ever look in his eyes? He's no idiot."

He had noticed the eyes. They disturbed him; that was all he could say of them. "Well, I wish he'd say something."

She touched a thick coffee cup. "You know Grace."

"Well, you told me. Your cousin that lost her little ones."

"Yes. Well, after the fire, Grace was almost like that, lying quiet all day. Talk to her, it was like she didn't hear. Show her something, she might've been blind. Had to spoon-feed her, wash her face."

"Maybe it's that then," he allowed. "That feller, he sure walked into something worth forgetting, up there . . . Grace, she got better, didn't she?"

"Well, she was never the same," said his wife. "But she got over it. I guess sometimes the world's too much to live with and a body sort of has to turn away from it to rest."

The weeks went by and broken tissues knit and the wide flat body soaked up nourishment like a cactus absorbing moisture. Never in his life had he had rest and food and . . .

She sat with him, talked to him. She sang songs, "Flow Gently, Sweet Afton" and "Home on the Range." She was a little brown woman with colorless hair and bleached eyes, and there was about her a hunger very like one he had felt. She told the moveless, silent face all about the folks back East and second grade and the time Prodd had come courting in his boss's Model T and him not even knowing how to drive it yet. She told him all the little things that would never be altogether in the past for her—the dress she wore to her confirmation, with a bow here and little gores here and here, and the time Grace's husband came home drunk with his Sunday pants all tore and a live pig under his arm, squealing to wake the dead.

She read to him from the prayerbook and told him Bible stories. She chattered out everything that was in her mind, except about Jack.

He never smiled nor answered and the only difference it made in him was that he kept his eyes on her face when she was in the room and patiently on the door when she was not. What a profound difference this was, she could not know; but the flat starved body tissues were not all that were slowly filling out.

A day came at last when the Prodds were at lunch—"dinner," they called it—and there was a fumbling at the inside of the door of Jack's room. Prodd exchanged a glance with his wife, then rose and opened it.

"Here, now, you can't come out like that." He called, "Ma, throw in my other overalls."

He was weak and very uncertain, but he was on his feet. They helped him to the table and he slumped there, his eyes cloaked and stupid, ignoring the food until Mrs. Prodd tantalized his nostrils with a spoonful. Then he took the spoon in his broad fist and got his mouth on it and looked past his hand at her. She patted his shoulder and told him it was just wonderful, how well he did.

"Well, Ma, you don't have to treat him like a two-year-old," said Prodd. Perhaps it was the eyes, but he was troubled again.

She pressed his hand warningly; he understood and said no more about it just then. But later in the night when he thought she was asleep, she said suddenly, "I do so have to treat him like a two-year-old, Prodd. Maybe even younger."

"How's that?"

"With Grace," she said, "it was like that. Not so bad, though. She was like six, when she started to get better. Dolls. When she didn't get apple pie with the rest of us one time, she cried her heart out. It was like growing up all over again. Faster, I mean, but like traveling the same road again."

"You think he's going to be like that?"

"Isn't he like a two-year-old?"

"First I ever saw six foot tall."

She snorted in half-pretended annoyance. "We'll raise him up just like a child."

He was quiet for a time. Then: "What'll we call him?"

"Not Jack," she said before she could stop herself.

He grunted an agreement. He didn't know quite what to say then. She said, "We'll bide our time about that. He's got his own name.

It wouldn't be right to put another to him. You just wait. He'll get back to where he remembers it."

He thought about it for a long time. He said, "Ma, I hope we're doing the right thing." But by then she was asleep.

There were miracles.

The Prodds thought of them as achievements, as successes, but they were miracles. There was the time when Prodd found two strong hands at the other end of a piece of 12x12 he was snaking out of the barn. There was the time Mrs. Prodd found her patient holding a ball of yarn, holding it and looking at it only because it was red. There was the time he found a full bucket by the pump and brought it inside. It was a long while, however, before he learned to work the handle.

When he had been there a year, Mrs. Prodd remembered and baked him a cake. Impulsively she put four candles on it. The Prodds beamed at him as he stared at the little flames, fascinated. His strange eyes caught and held hers, then Prodd's. "Blow it out, son."

Perhaps he visualized the act. Perhaps it was the result of the warmth outflowing from the couple, the wishing for him, the warmth of caring. He bent his head and blew. They laughed together and rose and came to him, and Prodd thumped his shoulder and Mrs. Prodd kissed his cheek.

Something twisted inside him. His eyes rolled up until, for a moment, only the whites showed. The frozen grief he carried slumped and flooded him. This wasn't the call, the contact, the exchange he had experienced with Evelyn. It was not even like it, except in degree. But because he could now feel to such a degree, he was aware of his loss, and he did just what he had done when first he lost it. He cried.

It was the same shrill tortured weeping that had led Prodd to him in the darkening wood a year ago. This room was too small to contain it. Mrs. Prodd had never heard him make a sound before. Prodd had, that first night. It would be hard to say whether it was worse to listen to such a sound or to listen to it again.

Mrs. Prodd put her arms around his head and cooed small syllables to him. Prodd balanced himself awkwardly nearby, put out a hand, changed his mind, and finally retreated into a futile reiteration: "Aw. Aw. . . . Aw, now."

In its own time, the weeping stopped. Sniffling, he looked at them each in turn. Something new was in his face; it was as if the bronze mask over which his facial skin was stretched had disappeared. "I'm sorry," Prodd said. "Reckon we did something wrong."

"It wasn't wrong," said his wife. "You'll see."

He got a name.

The night he cried, he discovered consciously that if he wished, he could absorb a message, a meaning, from those about him. It had happened before, but it happened as the wind happened to blow on him, as reflexively as a sneeze or a shiver. He began to hold and turn this ability, as once he had held and turned the ball of yarn. The sounds called speech still meant little to him, but he began to detect the difference between speech directed to him and that which did not concern him. He never really learned to hear speech; instead, ideas were transmitted to him directly. Ideas in themselves are formless and it is hardly surprising that he learned very slowly to give ideas the form of speech.

"What's your name?" Prodd asked him suddenly one day. They were filling the horse trough from the cistern and there was that about water running and running in the sun which tugged deeply at the idiot. Utterly absorbed, he was jolted by the question. He looked up and found his gaze locked with Prodd's.

Name. He made a reaching, a flash of demand, and it returned to him carrying what might be called a definition. It came, though, as pure concept. *"Name" is the single thing which is me and what I have done and been and learned.*

It was all there, waiting for that single symbol, a name. All the wandering, the hunger, the loss, the thing which is worse than loss, called back. There was a dim and subtle awareness that even here, with the Prodds, he was not a something, but a substitute for something.

All alone.

He tried to say it. Directly from Prodd he took the concept and its verbal coding and the way it ought to sound. But understanding and expressing were one thing; the physical act of enunciation was something else again. His tongue might have been a shoe sole and his larynx a rusty whistle. His lips writhed. He said, "Ul . . . ul . . ."

"What is it, son?"

All alone. It was transmitted clear and clean, complete, but as a thought only and he sensed instantly that a thought sent this way had no impact whatever on Prodd, though the farmer strained to receive what he was trying to convey. "Ul-ul . . . lone," he gasped.

"Lone?" said Prodd.

It could be seen that the syllable meant something to Prodd, something like the codification he offered, though far less.

But it would do.

He tried to repeat the sound, but his unaccustomed tongue became spastic. Saliva spurted annoyingly and ran from his lips. He sent a desperate demand for help, for some other way to express it, found it, used it. He nodded.

"Lone," repeated Prodd.

And again he nodded; and this was his first word and his first conversation; another miracle.

It took him five years to learn to talk and always he preferred not to. He never did learn to read. He was simply not equipped.

There were two boys for whom the smell of disinfectant on tile was the smell of hate.

For Gerry Thompson it was the smell of hunger, too, and of loneliness. All food was spiced with it, all sleep permeated with disinfectant, hunger, cold, fear . . . all components of hatred. Hatred was the only warmth in the world, the only certainty. A man clings to certainties, especially when he has only one; most especially when he is six years old. And at six Gerry was very largely a man—at least, he had a grown man's appreciation of that gray pleasure which comes merely with the absence of pain; he had an implacable patience, found usually only in men of purpose who must appear broken until their time of decision arrives. One does not realize that for a six-year-old the path of memory stretches back for just as long a lifetime as it does for anyone, and is as full of detail and incident. Gerry had had trouble enough, loss enough, illness enough, to make a man of anyone. At six he looked it, too; it was then that he began to accept, to be obedient, and to wait. His small, seamed face became just another face, and his voice no longer protested. He lived like this for two years, until his day of decision.

Then he ran away from the state orphanage, to live by himself, to be the color of gutters and garbage so he would not be picked up; to kill if cornered; to hate.

For Hip there was no hunger, no cold, and no precocious maturity. There was the smell of hate, though. It surrounded his father the doctor, the deft and merciless hands, the somber clothes. Even Hip's memory of Dr. Barrows' voice was the memory of chlorine and carbolic.

Little Hip Barrows was a brilliant and beautiful child, to whom the world refused to be a straight, hard path of disinfected tile. Everything came easily to him, except control of his curiosity—and "everything" included the cold injections of rectitude administered by his father the doctor, who was a successful man, a moral man, a man who had made a career of being sure and of being right.

Hip rose through childhood like a rocket, burnished, swift, afire. His gifts brought him anything a young man might want, and his conditioning constantly chanted to him that he was a kind of thief, not entitled to that which he had not earned; for such was the philosophy of his father the doctor, who had worked hard for everything. So Hip's talents brought him friends and honors, and friendships and honors brought him uneasiness and a sick humility of which he was quite unaware.

He was eight when he built his first radio, a crystal set for which he even wound the coils. He suspended it from the bedsprings so it could not be seen except by lifting the bed itself and buried an earphone inside the mattress so he could lie awake at night and hear it. His father the doctor discovered it and forbade his ever touching so much as a piece of wire in the house again. He was nine when his father the doctor located his cache of radio and electronics texts and magazines and piled them all up in front of the fireplace and made him burn them, one by one; they were up all night. He was twelve when he won a Science Search engineering scholarship for his secretly designed tubeless oscilloscope, and his father the doctor dictated his letter of refusal. He was a brilliant fifteen when he was expelled from premedical school for playfully cross-wiring the relays in the staff elevators and adding some sequence switches, so that every touch of a control button was an unappreciated adventure. At sixteen, happily disowned, he was making his own living in a research laboratory and attending engineering school.

He was big and bright and very popular. He needed to be very popular and this, like all his other needs, he accomplished with ease. He played the piano with a surprisingly delicate touch and played swift and subtle chess. He learned to lose skilfully and never too often at chess and at tennis and once at the harassing game of being "first in the Class, first in the School." He always had time—time to talk and to read, time to wonder quietly, time to listen to those who valued his listening, time to rephrase pedantries for those who found them arduous in the original. He even had time for ROTC and it was through this that he got his commission.

He found the Air Force a rather different institution from any school he had ever attended and it took him a while to learn that the colonel could not be softened by humility or won by a witticism like the Dean of Men. It took him even longer to learn that in service it is the majority, not the minority, who tend to regard physical perfection, conversational brilliance and easy achievement as defects rather than assets. He found himself alone more than he liked and avoided more than he could bear.

It was on the anti-aircraft range that he found an answer, a dream, and a disaster. . . .

Alicia Kew stood in the deepest shade by the edge of the meadow. "Father, Father, forgive me!" she cried. She sank down on the grass, blind with grief and terror, torn, shaken with conflict.

"Forgive me," she whispered with passion. "Forgive me," she whispered with scorn.

She thought, Devil, why won't you be dead? Five years ago you killed yourself, you killed my sister, and still it's "Father, forgive me." Sadist, pervert, murderer, devil . . . *man,* dirty poisonous *man!*

I've come a long way, she thought, I've come no way at all. How I ran from Jacobs, gentle Lawyer Jacobs, when he came to help with the bodies; oh, how I ran, to keep from being alone with him, so that he might not go mad and poison me. And when he brought his wife, how I fled from her too, thinking women were evil and must not touch me. They had a time with me, indeed they did; it was so long before I could understand that I was mad, not they . . . it was so long before I knew how very good, how very patient, Mother Jacobs was with me; how much she had to do with me, for me. "But, child, no one's worn clothes like those for forty years!" And in the cab, when I screamed and couldn't stop, for the people, the hurry, the *bodies,* so many bodies, all touching and so achingly visible; bodies on the streets, the stairs, great pictures of bodies in the magazines, men holding women who laughed and were brazenly unfrightened . . . Dr. Rothstein, who explained and explained and went back and explained again; there is no poison sweat, and there must be men and women else there would be no people at all. . . . I had to learn this, Father, dear devil Father, because of you; because of you I had never seen an automobile or a breast or a newspaper or a railroad train or a sanitary napkin or a kiss or a restaurant or an elevator or a bathing suit or the hair on–oh forgive me, Father.

I'm not afraid of a whip, I'm afraid of hands and eyes, thank you, Father. One day, one day, you'll see, Father, I shall live with people all around me, I shall ride on their trains and drive my own motor-car; I shall go among thousands on a beach at the edge of a sea which goes out and out without walls, I shall step in and out among them with a tiny strip of cloth here and there and let them see my navel, I shall meet a man with white teeth, Father, and round strong arms, Father, and I shall oh what will become of me, what have I become now, Father, forgive me.

I live in a house you never saw, one with windows overlooking a road, where the bright gentle cars whisper past and children play outside the hedge. The hedge is not a wall and, twice for the drive and once for the walk, it is open to anyone. I look through the curtains whenever I choose, and see strangers. There is no way to make the bathroom black dark and in the bathroom is a mirror as tall as I am; and one day, Father, I shall leave the towel off.

But all that will come later, the moving about among strangers, the touchings without fear. Now I must live alone, and think; I must read and read of the world and its works, yes, and of madmen like you, Father, and what twists them so terribly; Dr. Rothstein insists that you were not the only one, that you were so rare, really, only because you were so rich.

Evelyn . . .

Evelyn never knew her father was mad. Evelyn never saw the pictures of the poisoned flesh. I lived in a world different from this one, but her world was just as different, the world Father and I made for her, to keep her pure. . . .

I wonder, I wonder how it happened that you had the decency to blow your rotten brains out. . . .

The picture of her father, dead, calmed her strangely. She rose and looked back into the woods, looked carefully around the meadow, shadow by shadow, tree by tree. "All right, Evelyn, I will, I will. . . ."

She took a deep breath and held it. She shut her eyes so tight there was red in the blackness of it. Her hands flickered over the buttons on her dress. It fell away. She slid out of underwear and stockings with a single movement. The air stirred and its touch on her body was indescribable; it seemed to blow through her. She stepped forward into the sun and with tears of terror pressing through her closed lids, she danced naked, for Evelyn, and begged and begged her dead father's pardon.

When Janie was four, she hurled a paperweight at a lieutenant because of an unanalyzed but accurate feeling that he had no business around the house while her father was overseas. The lieutenant's skull was fractured and, as is often the case in concussion, he was forever unable to recall the fact that Janie stood ten feet away from the object when she threw it. Janie's mother whaled the tar out of her for it, an episode which Janie accepted with her usual composure. She added it, however, to the proofs given her by similar occasions that power without control has its demerits.

"She gives me the creeps," her mother told her other lieutenant later. "I can't stand her. You think there's something wrong with me for talking like that, don't you?"

"No I don't," said the other lieutenant, who did. So she invited him in for the following afternoon, quite sure that once he had seen the child, he would understand.

He saw her and he did understand. Not the child, nobody understood her; it was the mother's feelings he understood. Janie stood straight up, with her shoulders back and her face lifted, legs apart as if they wore jackboots, and she swung a doll by one of its feet as if it were a swagger stick. There was a rightness about the child which, in a child, was wrong. She was, if anything, a little smaller than average. She was sharp-featured and narrow-eyed; her eyebrows were heavy. Her proportions were not quite those of most four-year-olds, who can bend forward from the waist and touch their foreheads to the floor. Janie's torso was a little too short or her legs a little too long for that. She spoke with a sweet clarity and a devastating lack of tact. When the other lieutenant squatted clumsily and said, "*Hel*-lo, Janie. Are we going to be friends?" she said, "No. You smell like Major Grenfell." Major Grenfell had immediately preceded the injured lieutenant.

"Janie!" her mother shouted, too late. More quietly, she said, "You know perfectly well the major was only in for cocktails." Janie accepted this without comment, which left an appalling gap in the dialogue. The other lieutenant seemed to realize all in a rush that it was foolish to squat there on the parquet and sprang to his feet so abruptly he knocked over the coffee table. Janie achieved a wolfish smile and watched his scarlet ears while he picked up the pieces. He left early and never came back.

Nor, for Janie's mother, was there safety in numbers. Against the strictest orders, Janie strode into the midst of the fourth round of Gibsons one evening and stood at one end of the living room, flicking an insultingly sober gray-green gaze across the flushed faces. A round yellow-haired man who had his hand on her mother's neck extended his glass and bellowed, "You're Wima's little girl!"

Every head in the room swung at once like a bank of servo-switches, turning off the noise, and into the silence Janie said, "You're the one with the–"

"Janie!" her mother shouted. Someone laughed. Janie waited for it to finish. "–big, fat–" she enunciated. The man took his hand off Wima's neck. Someone whooped, "Big fat what, Janie?"

Topically, for it was wartime, Janie said, "–meat market."

Wima bared her teeth. "Run along back to your room, darling. I'll come and tuck you in in a minute." Someone looked straight at the blond man and laughed. Someone said in an echoing whisper, "There goes the Sunday sirloin." A drawstring could not have pulled the fat man's mouth so round and tight and from it his lower lip bloomed like strawberry jam from a squeezed sandwich.

Janie walked quietly toward the door and stopped as soon as she was out of her mother's line of sight. A sallow young man with brilliant black eyes leaned forward suddenly. Janie met his gaze. An expression of bewilderment crossed the young man's face. His hand faltered out and upward and came to rest on his forehead. It slid down and covered the black eyes.

Janie said, just loud enough for him to hear, "Don't you ever do that again." She left the room.

"Wima," said the young man hoarsely, "that child is telepathic."

"Nonsense," said Wima absently, concentrating on the fat man's pout. "She gets her vitamins every single day."

The young man started to rise, looking after the child, then sank back again. "God," he said, and began to brood.

When Janie was five she began playing with some other little girls. It was quite a while before they were aware of it. They were toddlers, perhaps two and a half years old, and they looked like twins. They conversed, if conversation it was, in high-pitched squeaks, and tumbled about on the concrete courtyard as if it were a haymow. At first Janie hung over her windowsill, four and a half stories above, and contemplatively squirted saliva in and out between her tongue and her hard palate until she had a satisfactory charge. Then she would crane her neck and, cheeks bulging, let it go. The twins ignored the bombardment when it merely smacked the concrete, but yielded up a most satisfying foofaraw of chitterings and squeals when she scored a hit. They never looked up but would race around in wild excitement, squealing.

Then there was another game. On warm days the twins could skin out of their rompers faster than the eye could follow. One moment they were as decent as a deacon and in the next one or both would be fifteen feet away from the little scrap of cloth. They would squeak and scramble and claw back into them, casting deliciously frightened glances at the basement door. Janie discovered that with a little concentration she could move the rompers—that is, when they were unoccupied. She practiced diligently, lying across the windowsill, her chest and chin on a cushion, her eyes puckered with effort. At first the garment would simply lie there and flutter weakly, as if a small dust-devil had crossed it. But soon she had the rompers scuttling across the concrete like little flat crabs. It was a marvel to watch those two little girls move when that happened, and the noise was a pleasure. They became a little more cautious about taking them off and sometimes Janie would lie in wait for forty minutes before she had a chance. And sometimes, even then, she held off and the twins, one clothed, one bare, would circle around the romper, and stalk it like two kittens after a beetle. Then she would strike, the romper would fly, the twins would pounce; and sometimes they caught it immediately, and sometimes they had to chase it until their little lungs were going like a toy steam engine.

Janie learned the reason for their preoccupation with the basement door when one afternoon she had mastered the knack of lifting the rompers instead of just pushing them around. She held off until the twins were lulled into carelessness and were shucking out of their clothes, wandering away, ambling back again, as if to challenge her. And still she waited, until at last both rompers were lying together in a little pink-and-white mound. Then she struck. The rompers rose from the ground in a steep climbing turn and fluttered to the sill of a first-floor window. Since the courtyard was slightly below street level, this put the garments six feet high and well out of reach. There she left them.

One of the twins ran to the center of the courtyard and jumped up and down in agitation, stretching and craning to see the rompers. The other ran to the building under the first-floor window and reached her little hands up as high as she could get them, patting at the bricks fully twenty-eight inches under her goal. Then they ran to each other and twittered anxiously. After a time they tried reaching up the wall again, side by side. More and more they threw those terrified glances at the basement door; less and less was there any pleasure mixed with the terror.

At last they hunkered down as far as possible away from the door, put their arms about one another and stared numbly. They slowly quieted down, from chatters to twitters to cooings, and at last were silent, two tiny tuffets of terror.

It seemed hours—weeks—of fascinated anticipation before Janie heard a thump and saw the door move. Out came the janitor, as usual a little bottle-weary. She could see the red crescents under his sagging yellow-whited eyes. "Bonnie!" he bellowed. "Beanie! Wha y'all?" He lurched out into the open and peered around. "Come out yeah! Look at *yew!* I gwine snatch yew bald-headed! Wheah's yo' clo'es?" He swooped down on them and caught them, each huge hand on a tiny biceps. He held them high, so that each had one toe barely touching the concrete and their little captured elbows pointed skyward. He turned around, once, twice, seeking, and at last his eye caught the glimmer of the rompers on the sill. "How you do dat?" he demanded. "You trine th'ow away yo' 'spensive clo'es? Oh, I gwine whop you."

He dropped to one knee and hung the two little bodies across the other thigh. It is probable that he had the knack of cupping his hand so that he produced more sound than fury, but however he did it, the noise was impressive. Janie giggled.

The janitor administered four equal swats to each twin and set them on their feet. They stood silently side by side with their hands pressed to their bottoms and watched him stride to the windowsill and snatch the rompers off. He threw them down at their feet and waggled his right forefinger at them. "Cotch you do dat once mo', I'll git Mr. Milton the conductah come punch yo' ears fulla holes. *Heah?*" he roared. They shrank together, their eyes round. He lurched back to the door and slammed it shut behind him.

The twins slowly climbed into their rompers. Then they went back to the shadows by the wall and hunkered down, supporting themselves with their back and their feet. They whispered to one another. There was no more fun for Janie that day.

Across the street from Janie's apartment house was a park. It had a bandstand, a brook, a molting peacock in a wire enclosure and a thick little copse of dwarf oak. In the copse was a hidden patch of bare earth, known only to Janie and several thousand people who were wont to use it in pairs at night. Since Janie was never there at night she felt herself its discoverer and its proprietor.

Some four days after the spanking episode, she thought of the place. She was bored with the twins; they never did anything interesting any more. Her mother had gone to lunch somewhere after locking her in her room. (One of her admirers, when she did this, had once asked, "What about the kid? Suppose there's a fire or something?" "Fat chance!" Wima had said with regret.)

The door of her room was fastened with a hook-and-eye on the outside. She walked to the door and looked up at the corresponding spot inside. She heard the hook rise and fall. She opened the door and walked down the hall and out to the elevators. When the self-service car arrived, she got in and pressed the third-, second- and first-floor buttons. One floor at a time the elevator descended, stopped, opened its gate, closed its gate, descended, stopped, opened its gate . . . it amused her, it was so stupid. At the bottom she pushed all of the buttons and slid out. Up the stupid elevator started. Janie clucked pityingly and went outdoors.

She crossed the street carefully, looking both ways. But when she got to the copse she was a little less ladylike. She climbed into the lower branches of the oak and across the multiple crotches to a branch she knew which overhung the hidden sanctuary. She thought she saw a movement in the bushes, but she was not sure. She hung from the branch, went hand over hand until it started to bend, waited until she had stopped swinging, and then let go.

It was an eight-inch drop to the earthen floor—usually. This time . . .

The very instant her fingers left the branch, her feet were caught and snatched violently backward. She struck the ground flat on her stomach. Her hands happened to be together, at her midriff; the impact turned them inward and drove her own fist into her solar plexus. For an unbearably long time she was nothing but one tangled knot of pain. She fought and fought and at long last sucked a tearing breath into her lungs. It would come out through her nostrils but she could get no more in. She fought again in a series of sucking sobs and blowing hisses, until the pain started to leave her.

She managed to get up on her elbows. She spat out dirt, part dusty, part muddy. She got her eyes open just enough to see one of the twins squatting before her, inches away. "Ho-ho," said the twin, grabbed her wrists, and pulled her. Down she went on her face again. Reflexively she drew up her knees. She received a stinging blow on the rump. She looked down past her shoulder as she flung herself sideways and saw the other twin just in the midst of the follow-through with the stave from a nail keg which she held in her little hands. "He-hee," said the twin.

Janie did what she had done to the sallow, black-eyed man at the cocktail party. "Eeep," said the twin and disappeared, flickered out the way a squeezed appleseed disappears from between the fingers. The little cask stave clattered to the packed earth. Janie caught it up, whirled, and brought it down on the head of the twin who had pulled her arms. But the stave whooshed down to strike the ground; there was no one there.

Janie whimpered and got slowly to her feet. She was alone in the shadowed sanctuary. She turned and turned back. Nothing. No one.

Something plurped just on the center part of her hair. She clapped her hand to it. Wet. She looked up and the other twin spit too. It hit her on the forehead. "Ho-ho," said one. "He-hee," said the other.

Janie's upper lip curled away from her teeth, exactly the way her mother's did. She still held the cask stave. She slung it upward with all her might. One twin did not even attempt to move. The other disappeared.

"Ho-ho." There she was, on another branch. Both were grinning widely.

She hurled a bolt of hatred at them the like of which she had never even imagined before.

"Ooop," said one. The other said "Eeep." Then they were both gone.

Clenching her teeth, she leapt for the branch and swarmed up into the tree.

"Ho-ho."

It was very distant. She looked up and around and down and back; and something made her look across the street.

Two little figures sat like gargoyles on top of the courtyard wall. They waved to her and were gone.

For a long time Janie clung to the tree and stared at the wall. Then she let herself slide down into the crotch where she could put her back against the trunk and straddle a limb. She unbuttoned her pocket and got her handkerchief. She licked a fold of it good and wet and began wiping the dirt off her face with little feline dabs.

They're only three years old, she told herself from the astonished altitude of her seniority. Then, *They knew who it was all along that moved those rompers . . .*

She said aloud, in admiration, "Ho-ho . . ." There was no anger left in her. Four days ago the twins couldn't even reach a six-foot sill. They couldn't even get away from a spanking. And now look.

She got down on the street side of the tree and stepped daintily across the street. In the vestibule, she stretched up and pressed the shiny brass button marked JANITOR. While waiting she stepped off the pattern of tiles in the floor, heel and toe.

"Who push dat? Who push dat?" His voice filled the whole world.

She went and stood in front of him and pushed up her lips the way her mother did when she made her voice all croony, like sometimes on the telephone. "Mister Widdecombe, my mother says I can play with your little girls."

"She say dat? *Well!*" The janitor took off his round hat and whacked it against his palm and put it on again. "Well. Dat's mighty nice . . . little gal," he said sternly, "is yo' mother to home?"

"Oh *yes,*" said Janie, fairly radiating candor.

"You wait raht cheer," he said, and pounded away down the cellar steps.

She had to wait more than ten minutes this time. When he came back with the twins he was fairly out of breath. They looked very solemn.

"Now don't you let 'em get in any mischief. And see ef you cain't keep them clo'es on 'em. They ain't got no more use for clo'es than a jungle monkey. Gwan, now, hole hands, chillun, an' mine you don't leave go tel you git there."

The twins approached guardedly. She took their hands. They watched her face. She began to move toward the elevators, and they followed. The janitor beamed after them.

Janie's whole life shaped itself from that afternoon. It was a time of belonging, of thinking alike, of transcendent sharing. For her age, Janie had what was probably a unique vocabulary, yet she spoke hardly a word. The twins had not yet learned to talk. Their private vocabulary of squeaks and whimpers was incidental to another kind of communion. Janie got a sign of it, a touch of it, a sudden opening, growing rush of it. Her mother hated her and feared her; her father was a remote and angry entity, always away or shouting at Mother or closed sulkily about himself. She was talked to, never spoken to.

But here was converse, detailed, fluent, fascinating, with no sound but laughter. They would be silent; they would all squat suddenly and paw through Janie's beautiful books; then suddenly it was the dolls. Janie showed them how she could get chocolates from the box in the other room without going in there and how she could throw a pillow clear up to the ceiling without touching it. They liked that, though the paintbox and easel impressed them more.

It was a thing together, binding, immortal; it would always be new for them and it would never be repeated.

The afternoon slid by, as smooth and soft and lovely as a passing gull, and as swift. When the hall door banged open and Wima's voice clanged out, the twins were still there.

"All righty, all righty, come in for a drink then, who wants to stand out there all night." She pawed her hat off and her hair swung raggedly over her face. The man caught her roughly and pulled her close and bit her face. She howled. "You're crazy, you old crazy you." Then she saw them, all three of them peering out. "Dear old Jesus be to God," she said, "she's got the place filled with niggers."

"They're going home," said Janie resolutely. "I'll take 'em home right now."

"Honest to God, Pete," she said to the man, "this is the God's honest first time this ever happened. You got to believe that, Pete. What kind of a place you must think I run here, I hate to think how it looks to you. Well get them the hell out!" she screamed at Janie. "Honest to God, Pete, so help me, never before–"

Janie walked down the hall to the elevators. She looked at Bonnie and at Beanie. Their eyes were round. Janie's mouth was as dry as a carpet and she was so embarrassed her legs cramped. She put the twins into an elevator and pressed the bottom button. She did not say goodbye, though she felt nothing else.

She walked slowly back to the apartment and went in and closed the door. Her mother got up from the man's lap and clattered across the room. Her teeth shone and her chin was wet. She raised claws– not a hand, not a fist, but red, pointed claws.

Something happened inside Janie like the grinding of teeth, but deeper inside her than that. She was walking and she did not stop. She put her hands behind her and tilted her chin up so she could meet her mother's eyes.

Wima's voice ceased, snatched away. She loomed over the five-year-old, her claws out and forward, hanging, curving over, a blood-tipped wave about to break.

Janie walked past her and into her room, and quietly closed the door.

Wima's arms drew back, strangely, as if they must follow the exact trajectory of their going. She repossessed them and the dissolving balance of her body and finally her voice. Behind her the man's teeth clattered swiftly against a glass.

Wima turned and crossed the room to him, using the furniture like a series of crutches. "Oh God," she murmured, "but she gives me the creeps. . . ."

He said, "You got lots going on around here."

Janie lay in bed as stiff and smooth and contained as a round toothpick. Nothing would get in, nothing could get out; somewhere she had found this surface that went all the way through, and as long as she had it, nothing was going to happen.

But if anything happens, came a whisper, *you'll break.*

But if I don't break, nothing will happen, she answered.

But if anything . . .

The dark hours came and grew black and the black hours labored by.

Her door crashed open and the light blazed. "He's gone and, baby, I've got business with you. Get out here!" Wima's bathrobe swirled against the doorpost as she turned and went away.

Janie pushed back the covers and thumped her feet down. Without understanding quite why, she began to get dressed. She got her good plaid dress and the shoes with two buckles, and the knit pants and the slip with the lace rabbits. There were little rabbits on her socks too, and on the sweater, the buttons were rabbits' fuzzy nubbin tails.

Wima was on the couch, pounding and pounding with her fist. "You wrecked my cel," she said, and drank from a square-stemmed glass, "ebration, so you ought to know what I'm celebrating. You don't know it but I've had a big trouble and I didn't know how to hannel it, and now it's all done for me. And I'll tell you all about it right now, little baby Miss Big Ears. Big Mouth. Smarty. Because your father, I can hannel him any time, but what I was going to do with your big mouth going day and night? That was my trouble, what was I going to do about your big mouth when he got back. Well it's all fixed, he won't be back, the Heinies fixed it up for me." She waved a yellow sheet. "Smart girls know that's a telegram, and the telegram says, says here, 'Regret to inform you that your husband.'

They shot your father, that's what they regret to say, and now this is the way it's going to be from now on between you and me. Whatever I want to do I do, an' whatever you want to nose into, nose away. Now isn't that fair?"

She turned to be answered but there was no answer. Janie was gone.

Wima knew before she started that there wasn't any use looking, but something made her run to the hall closet and look in the top shelf. There wasn't anything up there but Christmas-tree ornaments and they hadn't been touched in three years.

She stood in the middle of the living room, not knowing which way to go. She whispered, "Janie?"

She put her hands on the sides of her face and lifted her hair away from it. She turned around and around, and asked, "What's the matter with me?"

Prodd used to say, "There's this about a farm: when the market's good there's money, and when it's bad there's food." Actually the principle hardly operated here, for his contact with markets was slight. It was a long haul to town and what if there's a tooth off the hayrake? "We've still got a workin' majority." Two off, eight, twelve? "Then make another pass. No road will go by here, not ever. Place will never get too big, get out of hand." Even the war passed them by, Prodd being overage and Lone—well, the sheriff was by once and had a look at the half-wit working on Prodd's, and one look was enough.

When Prodd was young the little farmhouse was there, and when he married they built on to it—a little, not a lot, just a room. If the room had ever been used the land wouldn't have been enough. Lone slept in the room of course but that wasn't quite the same thing. That's not what the room was for.

Lone sensed the change before anyone else, even before Mrs. Prodd. It was a difference in the nature of one of her silences. It was a treasure-proud silence, and Lone felt it change as a man's kind of pride might change when he turned from a jewel he treasured to a green shoot he treasured. He said nothing and concluded nothing; he just knew.

He went on with his work as before. He worked well; Prodd used to say that whatever anyone might think, that boy was a farmer before his accident. He said it not knowing that his only style of farming was as available to Lone as water from his pump. So was anything else Lone wanted to take.

So the day Prodd came down to the south meadow, where Lone was stepping and turning tirelessly, a very part of his whispering scythe, Lone knew what it was that he wanted to say. He caught Prodd's gaze for half a breath in those disturbing eyes and knew as well that saying it would pain Prodd more than a little.

Understanding was hardly one of his troubles any more, but niceties of expression were. He stopped mowing and went to the forest margin nearby and let the scythe point drop into a rotten stump. It gave him time to rehearse his tongue, still thick and unwieldy after eight years here.

Prodd followed slowly. He was rehearsing too.

Suddenly, Lone found it. "Been thinking," he said.

Prodd waited, glad to wait. Lone said, "I should go." That wasn't quite it. "Move along," he said, watching. That was better.

"Ah, Lone. Why?"

Lone looked at him. *Because you want me to go.*

"Don't you like it here?" said Prodd, not wanting to say that at all.

"Sure." From Prodd's mind, he caught, *Does he know?* and his own answered, *Of course I know!* But Prodd couldn't hear that. Lone said slowly, "Just time to be moving along."

"Well." Prodd kicked a stone. He turned to look at the house and that turned him away from Lone, and that made it easier. "When we came here, we built Jack's, *your* room, the room you're using. We call it Jack's room. You know why, you know who Jack is?"

Yes, Lone thought. He said nothing.

"Long as you're . . . long as you want to leave anyway, it won't make no difference to you. Jack's our son." He squeezed his hands together. "I guess it sounds funny. Jack was the little guy we were so sure about, we built that room with seed money. Jack, he—"

He looked up at the house, at its stub of a built-on wing, and around at the rock-toothed forest rim. "—never got born," he finished.

"Ah," said Lone. He'd picked that up from Prodd. It was useful.

"He's coming now, though," said Prodd in a rush. His face was alight. "We're a bit old for it, but there's a daddy or two quite a bit older, and mothers too." Again he looked up at the barn, the house. "Makes sense in a sort of way, you know, Lone. Now, if he'd been along when we planned it, the place would've been too small when he was growed enough to work it with me, and me with no place else to go. But now, why, I reckon when he's growed we just naturally won't be here any more, and he'll take him a nice little wife and start out just about like we did. So you see it does make a kind of sense." He seemed to be pleading. Lone made no attempt to understand this.

"Lone, listen to me, I don't want you to feel we're turning you out."

"Said I was going." Searching, he found something and amended, " 'Fore you told me." *That,* he thought, *was very right.*

"Look, I got to say something," said Prodd. "I heard tell of folks who wants kids and can't have 'em, sometimes they just give up trying and take in somebody else's. And sometimes, with a kid in the house, they turn right round and have one of their own after all."

"Ah," said Lone.

"So what I mean is, we taken you in, didn't we, and now look."

Lone did not know what to say. "Ah" seemed wrong.

"We got a lot to thank you for is what I mean, so we don't want you to feel we're turning you out."

"I already said."

"Good then." Prodd smiled. He had a lot of wrinkles on his face, mostly from smiling.

"Good," said Lone. "About Jack." He nodded vehemently. "Good." He picked up the scythe. When he reached his windrow, he looked after Prodd. *Walks slower than he used to,* he thought.

Lone's next conscious thought was, Well, that's finished.

What's finished? he asked himself.

He looked around. "Mowing," he said. Only then he realized that he had been working for more than three hours since Prodd spoke to him, and it was as if some other person had done it. He himself had been–*gone* in some way.

Absently he took his whetstone and began to dress the scythe. It made a sound like a pot boiling over when he moved it slowly and like a shrew dying when he moved it fast.

Where had he known this feeling of time passing, as it were, behind his back?

He moved the stone slowly. Cooking and warmth and work. A birthday cake. A clean bed. A sense of . . . "Membership" was not a word he possessed but that was his thought.

No, obliterated time didn't exist in those memories. He moved the stone faster.

Death cries in the woods. Lonely hunter and its solitary prey. The sap falls and the bear sleeps and the birds fly south, all doing it together, not because they are all members of the same thing but only because they are all solitary things hurt by the same thing.

That was where time had passed without his awareness of it. Almost always, before he came here. That was how he had lived.

Why should it come back to him now, then?

He swept his gaze around the land, as Prodd had done, taking in the house and its imbalancing bulge, and the land, and the woods which held the farm like water in a basin. When I was alone, he thought, time passed me like that. Time passes like that now, so it must be that I am alone again.

And then he knew that he had been alone the whole time. Mrs. Prodd hadn't raised him up, not really. She had been raising up her Jack the whole time.

Once in the woods in water and agony, he had been a part of something, and in wetness and pain it had been torn from him. And if, for eight years now, he had thought he had found something else to belong to, then for eight years he had been wrong.

Anger was foreign to him; he had only felt it once before. But now it came, a wash of it that made him swell, that drained and left him weak. And he himself was the object of it. For hadn't he known? Hadn't he taken a name for himself, knowing that the name was a crystallization of all he had ever been and done? All he had ever been and done was *alone*. Why should he have let himself feel any other way?

Wrong. Wrong as a squirrel with feathers, or a wolf with wooden teeth; not injustice, not unfairness—just a wrongness that, under the sky, could not exist—the idea that such as he could belong to anything.

Hear that, *son?* Hear, that, *man?*

Hear that, Lone?

He picked up three long fresh stalks of timothy and braided them together. He upended the scythe and thrust the handle deep enough into the soft earth so it would stand upright. He tied the braided grass to one of the grips and slipped the whetstone into the loops so it would stay. Then he walked off into the woods.

It was too late even for the copse's nocturnal habitants. It was cold at the hidden foot of the dwarf oak and as dark as the chambers of a dead man's heart.

She sat on the bare earth. As time went on, she had slid down a little and her plaid skirt had moved up. Her legs were icy, especially when the night air moved on them. But she didn't pull the skirt down because it didn't matter. Her hand lay on one of the fuzzy buttons of her sweater because, two hours ago, she had been fingering it and wondering what it was like to be a bunny. Now she didn't care whether or not the button was a bunny's tail or where her hand happened to be.

She had learned all she could from being there. She had learned that if you leave your eyes open until you have to blink and you don't blink, they start to hurt. Then if you leave them open even longer, they hurt worse and worse. And if you still leave them open, they suddenly stop hurting.

It was too dark there to know whether they could still see after that.

And she had learned that if you sit absolutely still for long enough it hurts too, and then stops. But then you mustn't move, not the tiniest little bit, because if you do it will hurt worse than anything.

When a top spins it stands up straight and walks around. When it slows a little it stands in one place and wobbles. When it slows a lot it waggles around like Major Grenfell after a cocktail party. Then it almost stops and lies down and bumps and thumps and thrashes around. After that it won't move any more.

When she had the happy time with the twins she had been spinning like that. When Mother came home the top inside didn't walk any more, it stood still and waggled. When Mother called her out of her bed she was waving and weaving. When she hid here her spinner inside bumped and kicked. Well, it wasn't doing it any more and it wouldn't.

She started to see how long she could hold her breath. Not with a big deep lungful first, but just breathing quieter and quieter and missing an *in* and quieter and quieter still, and missing an *out*. She got to where the misses took longer than the breathings.

The wind stirred her skirt. All she could feel was the movement and that too was remote, as if she had a thin pillow between it and her legs.

Her spinner, with the lift gone out of it, went round and round with its rim on the floor and went slower and slower and at last

stopped

. . . and began to roll back the other way, but not very far, not fast and

stopped

and a little way back, it was too dark for anything to roll, and even if it did you wouldn't be able to see it, you couldn't even hear it, it was so dark.

But anyway, she rolled. She rolled over on her stomach and on her back and pain squeezed her nostrils together and filled up her stomach like too much soda water. She gasped with the pain and gasping was breathing and when she breathed she remembered who she was. She rolled over again without wanting to, and something like little animals ran on her face. She fought them weakly. They weren't pretend-things, she discovered; they were real as real. They whispered and cooed. She tried to sit up and the little animals ran behind her and helped. She dangled her head down and felt the warmth of her breath falling into the front of her dress. One of the little animals stroked her cheek and she put up a hand and caught it.

"Ho-ho," it said.

On the other side, something soft and small and strong wriggled and snuggled tight up against her. She felt it, smooth and alive. It said "He-hee."

She put one arm around Bonnie and one arm around Beanie and began to cry.

Lone came back to borrow an ax. You can do just so much with your bare hands.

When he broke out of the woods he saw the difference in the farm. It was as if every day it existed had been a gray day, and now the sun was on it. All the colors were brighter by an immeasurable amount; the barn smells, growth smells, stove-smoke smells were clearer and purer. The corn stretched skyward with such intensity in its lines that it seemed to be threatening its roots.

Prodd's venerable stake-bed pick-up truck was grunting and howling somewhere down the slope. Following the margins, Lone went downhill until he could see the truck. It was in the fallow field which, apparently, Prodd had decided to turn. The truck was hitched to a gang plow with all the shares but one removed. The right rear wheel had run too close to the furrow, dropped in, and buried, so that the truck rested on its rear axle and the wheel spun almost free. Prodd was pounding stones under it with the end of a pick handle. When he saw Lone he dropped it and ran toward him, his face beaming like firelight. He took Lone's upper arms in his hands and read his face like the page of a book, slowly, a line at a time, moving his lips. "Man, I thought I wouldn't see you again, going off like you did."

"You want help," said Lone, meaning the truck.

Prodd misunderstood. "Now wouldn't you know," he said happily. "Come all the way back to see if you could lend a hand. Oh, I been doing fine by myself, Lone, believe me. Not that I don't appreciate it. But I feel like it these days. Working, I mean."

Lone went and picked up the pick handle. He prodded at the stones under the wheel. "Drive," he said.

"Wait'll Ma sees you," said Prodd. "Like old times." He got in and started the truck. Lone put the small of his back against the rear edge of the truck bed, clamped his hands on it, and as the clutch engaged, he heaved. The body came up as high as the rear springs would let it, and still higher. He leaned back. The wheel found purchase and the truck jolted up and forward onto firm ground.

Prodd climbed out and came back to look into the hole, the irresistible and useless act of a man who picks up broken china and puts its edges together. "I used to say, I bet you were a farmer once," he grinned. "But now I know. You were a hydraulic jack."

Lone did not smile. He never smiled. Prodd went to the plow and Lone helped him wrestle the hitch back to the truck. "Horse dropped dead," Prodd explained. "Truck's all right but sometimes I wish there was some way to keep this from happening. Spend half my time diggin' it out. I'd get another horse, but you know–hold everything till after Jack gets here. You'd think that would bother me, losing the horse." He looked up at the house and smiled. "Nothing bothers me now. Had breakfast?"

"Yes."

"Well come have some more. You know Ma. Wouldn't forgive either of us if she wasn't to feed you."

They went back to the house, and when Ma saw Lone she hugged him hard. Something stirred uncomfortably in Lone. He wanted an ax. He thought all these other things were settled. "You sit right down there and I'll get you some breakfast."

"Told you," said Prodd, watching her, smiling. Lone watched her too. She was heavier and happy as a kitten in a cowshed. "What you doing now, Lone?"

Lone looked into his eyes to find some sort of an answer. "Working," he said. He moved his hand. "Up there."

"In the woods?"

"Yes."

"What you doing?" When Lone waited, Prodd asked, "You hired out? No? Then what–trapping?"

"Trapping," said Lone, knowing that this would be sufficient.

He ate. From where he sat he could see Jack's room. The bed was gone. There was a new one in there, not much longer than his forearm, all draped with pale-blue cotton and cheesecloth with dozens of little tucks sewn into it.

When he was finished they all sat around the table and for a time nobody said anything. Lone looked into Prodd's eyes and found *He's a good boy but not the kind to set around and visit.* He couldn't understand the *visit* image, a vague and happy blur of conversation sounds and laughter. He recognized this as one of the many lacks he was aware of in himself–lacks rather than inadequacies; things he could not do and would never be able to do. So he just asked Prodd for the ax and went out.

"You don't s'pose he's mad at us?" asked Mrs. Prodd, looking anxiously after Lone.

"Him?" said Prodd. "He wouldn't have come back here if he was. I was afraid of that myself until today." He went to the door. "Don't you lift nothing heavy, hear?"

Janie read as slowly and carefully as she could. She didn't have to read aloud, but only carefully enough so the twins could understand. She had reached the part where the woman tied the man to the pillar and then let the other man, the "my rival, her laughing lover" one, out of the closet where he had been hidden and gave him the whip. Janie looked up at that point and found Beanie gone and Bonnie in the cold fireplace, pretending there was a mouse hiding in the ashes. "Oh, you're not listening," she said.

Want the one with the pictures, the silent message came.

"I'm getting so tired of that one," said Janie petulantly. But she closed *Venus in Furs* by von Sacher-Masoch and put it on the table. "This's anyway got a story to it," she complained, going to the shelves. She found the wanted volume between *My Gun Is Quick* and *The Illustrated Iwan Bloch,* and hefted it back to the armchair. Bonnie disappeared from the fireplace and reappeared by the chair. Beanie stood on the other side; wherever she had been, she had been aware of what was happening. If anything, she liked this book even better than Bonnie.

Janie opened the book at random. The twins leaned forward breathless, their eyes bugging.

Read it.

"Oh, all right," said Janie. "'D34556. Tieback. Double shirred.

90 inches long. Maize, burgundy, hunter green and white. $24.68. D34557. Cottage style. Stuart or Argyll plaid, see illus. $4.92 pair. D34–'"

And they were happy again.

They had been happy ever since they got here and much of the hectic time before that. They had learned how to open the back of a trailer truck and how to lie without moving under hay, and Janie could pull clothespins off a line and the twins could appear inside a room, like a store at night, and unlock the door from the inside when it was fastened with some kind of lock that Janie couldn't move, the way she could a hook-and-eye or a tower bolt which was shot but not turned. The best thing they had learned, though, was the way the twins could attract attention when somebody was chasing Janie. They'd found out for sure that to have two little girls throwing rocks from second-floor windows and appearing under their feet to trip them and suddenly sitting on their shoulders and wetting into their collars made it impossible to catch Janie, who was just ordinarily running. Ho-ho.

And this house was just the happiest thing of all. It was miles and miles away from anything or anybody and no one ever came here. It was a big house on a hill, in forest so thick you hardly knew it was there. It had a big high wall around it on the road side, and a big high fence on the woods side and a brook ran through. Bonnie had found it one day when they had gotten tired and gone to sleep by the road. Bonnie woke up and went exploring by herself and found the fence and went along it until she saw the house. They'd had a terrible time finding some way to get Janie in, though, until Beanie fell into the brook where it went through the fence, and came up on the inside.

There were zillions of books in the biggest room and plenty of old sheets they could wrap around themselves when it was cold. Down in the cold dark cellar rooms they had found a half-dozen cases of canned vegetables and some bottles of wine, which later they smashed all over because, although it tasted bad, it smelled just wonderful. There was a pool out back to swim in that was more fun than the bathrooms, which had no windows. There were plenty of places for hide-and-seek. There was even a little room with chains on the walls, and bars.

It went much faster with the ax.

He never would have found the place at all if he had not hurt himself. In all the years he had wandered the forests, often blindly and uncaring, he had never fallen into such a trap. One moment he was stepping over the crest of an outcropping, and next he was twenty feet down, in a bramble-choked, humus-floored pitfall. He hurt one of his eyes and his left arm hurt unbearably at the elbow.

Once he had thrashed his way out, he surveyed the place. Perhaps it had once been a pool in the slope, with the lower side thin and erosible. It was gone, however, and what was left was a depression in the hillside, thickly grown inside, even more thickly screened on both sides and at the front. The rock over which he had stepped rose out of the hill and overhung the depression.

At one time it had not mattered in the least to Lone whether he was near men or not. Now, he wanted only to be able to be what he knew he was—alone. But eight years at the farm had changed his way of life. He needed shelter. And the more he looked at this hidden place, with its overhanging rock wall ceiling and the two earthen wings which flanked it, the more shelterlike it seemed.

At first his work on it was primitive. He cleared out enough brush so that he might lie down comfortably and pulled up a bush or two so that the brambles would not flay him as he went in and out. Then it rained and he had to channel the inside so that water woud not stand inside, and he made a rough thatch at the crest.

But as time went on he became increasingly absorbed in the place. He pulled up more brush and pounded the earth until he had a level floor. He removed all the rock he could find loose on the rear wall, and discovered that some of the wall had ready-made shelves and nooks for the few things he might want to store. He began raiding the farms that skirted the foot of the mountain, operating at night, taking only a very little at each place, never coming back to any one place if he could help it. He got carrots and potatoes and tenpenny spikes and haywire, a broken hammer and a cast-iron pot. Once he found a side of bacon that had fallen from an abattoir truck. He stored it and when he came back he found that a lynx had been at it. That determined him to make walls, which was why he went back for the ax.

He felled trees, the biggest he could handle after trimming, and snaked them up to the hillside. He buried the first three so that they bounded the floor, and the side ones butted against the rock. He found a red clay which, when mixed with peat moss, made a mortar that was vermin-proof and would not wash away. He built up his walls and a door. He did not bother with a window, but simply left out a yard of mortar between six of the wall logs, on each side, and trimmed long side-tapered sticks to wedge in them when he wanted them closed.

His first fireplace was Indian-style, out near the center of the enclosure, with a hole at the top to let the smoke out. High up were hooks embedded in rock fissures, for hanging meat where the smoke could get to it, if he were ever fortunate enough to get some.

He was out hunting for flagstones for the fireplace when an invisible something began to tug at him. He recoiled as if he had been burned and shrank back against a tree and cast about him like a cornered elk.

It had been a long time since he had been aware of his inner sensitivity to the useless (to him) communication of infants. He was losing it; he had begun to be insensitive to it when he began to gain speech.

But someone had called to him this way–someone who "sent" like a child, but who was not a child. And though what he felt now was faint, it was in substance unbearably similar. It was sweet and needful, yes; but it was also the restimulation of a stinging lash and a terror of crushing kicks and obscene shouting, and the greatest loss he had ever known.

There was nothing to be seen. Slowly he left the tree and went back to the slab of stone he had been pawing at to free it from the earth. For perhaps half an hour he worked doggedly, trying to ignore the call. And he failed.

He rose, shaken, and began to walk to the call in a world turned dreamlike. The longer he walked, the more irresistible the call became and the deeper his enchantment. He walked for an hour, never going around anything if he could possibly go over it or through it, and by the time he reached the leached clearing he was nearly somnambulant. To permit himself any more consciousness would have been to kindle such an inferno of conflict that he could not have gone on. Stumbling blindly, he walked right up to and into the rusting fence which struck him cruelly over his hurt eye. He clung to it until his vision cleared, looked around to see where he was, and began to tremble.

He had one moment of clear, conscious determination: to get out of this terrible place and stay out of it. And even as he felt this touch of reason, he heard the brook and was turning toward it.

Where brook and fence met, he lowered himself in the water and made his way to the foot of the pickets. Yes, the opening was still here.

He peered in through the fence, but the ancient holly was thicker than ever. There was nothing to be heard, either—aurally. But the call . . .

Like the one he had heard before, it was a hunger, an aloneness, a wanting. The difference was in what it wanted. It said without words that it was a little afraid, and burdened, and was solicitous of the burden. It said in effect *who will take care of me now?*

Perhaps the cold water helped. Lone's mind suddenly became as clear as it ever could. He took a deep breath and submerged. Immediately on the other side he stopped and raised his head. He listened carefully, then lay on his stomach with only his nostrils above the water. With exquisite care, he inched forward on his elbows, until his head was inside the arch and he could see through.

There was a little girl on the bank, dressed in a torn plaid dress. She was about six. Her sharp-planed, unchildlike face was downdrawn and worried. And if he thought his caution was effective, he was quite wrong. She was looking directly at him.

"Bonnie!" she called sharply.

Nothing happened.

He stayed where he was. She continued to watch him, but she continued to worry. He realized two things: that it was this worriment of hers which was the essence of the call; and that although she was on her guard, she did not consider him important enough to divert her from her thoughts.

For the first time in his life he felt that edged and spicy mixture of anger and amusement called pique. This was followed by a great surge of relief, much like what one would feel on setting down a forty-pound pack after forty years. He had not known . . . he had not *known* the size of his burden!

And away went the restimulation. Back into the past went the whip and the bellowing, the magic and the loss—remembered still, but back where they belonged, with their raw-nerve tendrils severed so that never again could they reach into his present. The call was no maelstrom of blood and emotion, but the aimless chunterings of a hungry brat.

He sank and shot backward like a great lean crawfish, under the fence. He slogged up out of the brook, turned his back on the call and went back to his work.

When he got back to his shelter, streaming with perspiration, an eighteen-inch flagstone on his shoulder, he was weary enough to forget his usual caution. He crashed in through the underbrush to the tiny clearing before his door, and stopped dead.

There was a small naked infant about four years old squatting in front of his door.

She looked up at him and her eyes—her whole dark face—seemed to twinkle. "He-hee!" she said happily.

He tipped the stone off his shoulder and let it fall. He loomed over her, shadowed her, sky-high and full of threats of thunder.

She seemed completely unafraid. She turned her eyes away from him and busily began nibbling at a carrot, turning it squirrel-wise, around and around as she ate.

A high movement caught his eye. Another carrot was emerging from the ventilation chinks in the log wall. It fell to the ground and was followed by still another.

"Ho-ho." He looked down, and there were *two* little girls.

The only advantage which Lone possessed under the circumstances was a valuable one: he had no impulse whatever to question his sanity and start a confusing debate with himself on the matter. He bent down and scooped one of the children up. But when he straighted she wasn't there any more.

The other was. She grinned enchantingly and started on one of the new carrots.

Lone said, "What you doing?" His voice was harsh and ill-toned, like that of a deaf mute. It startled the child. She stopped eating and looked up at him openmouthed. The open mouth was filled with carrot chips and gave her rather the appearance of a potbellied stove with the door open.

He sank down on his knees. Her eyes were fixed on his and his were eyes which had once commanded a man to kill himself and which, many times, violated the instincts of others who had not wanted to feed him. Without knowing why he was careful. There was no anger in him or fear; he simply wanted her to stay still.

When he was done, he reached for her. She exhaled noisily, blowing tiny wet chips of raw carrot into his eyes and nostrils, and vanished.

He was filled with astonishment—a strange thing in itself, for he had seldom been interested enough in anything to be astonished. Stranger still, it was a respectful astonishment.

He rose and put his back against the log wall, and looked for them. They stood side by side, hand in hand, looking up at him out of little wooden wondering faces, waiting for him to do something else.

Once, years ago, he had run to catch a deer. Once he had reached up from the ground to catch a bird in a treetop. Once he had plunged into a stream after a trout.

Once.

Lone was simply not constituted to chase something he knew empirically that he could not catch. He bent and picked up his flagstone, reached up and slid aside the outside bar which fastened his door and shouldered into the house.

He bedded his flagstone by the fire and swept the guttering embers over part of it. He threw on more wood and blew it up brightly, set up his green-stick crane and swung the iron pot on it. All the while there were two little white-eyed knobs silhouetted in the doorway, watching him. He ignored them.

The skinned rabbit swung on the high hook by the smoke hole. He got it down, tore off the quarters, broke the back and dropped it all into the pot. From a niche he took potatoes and a few grains of rock salt. The salt went into the pot and so did the potatoes after he had split them in two on his ax blade. He reached for his carrots. Somebody had been at his carrots.

He wheeled and frowned at the doorway. The two heads whipped back out of sight. From outdoors came small soprano giggles.

Lone let the pot boil for an hour while he honed the ax and tied up a witch's broom like Mrs. Prodd's. And slowly, a fraction of an inch at a time, his visitors edged into the room. Their eyes were fixed on the seething pot. They fairly drooled.

He went about his business without looking at them. When he came close they retreated and when he crossed the room they entered again—that little fraction more each time. Soon their retreats were smaller and their advances larger until at last Lone had a chance to slam the door shut—which he did.

In the sudden darkness, the simmer of the pot and the small hiss of the flames sounded very loud. There was no other sound. Lone stood with his back against the door and closed his eyes very tight to adjust them more quickly to the darkness. When he opened them, the bars of waning daylight at the vents and the fireglow were quite sufficient for him to see everything in the room.

The little girls were gone.

He put on the inner bar and slowly circled the room. Nothing.

He opened the door cautiously, then flung it wide. They were not outside either.

He shrugged. He pulled on his lower lip and wished he had more carrots. Then he set the pot aside to cool enough so that he could eat and finished honing the ax.

At length he ate. He had reached the point of licking his fingers by way of having dessert, when a sharp knock on the door caused him to leap eighteen inches higher than upright, so utterly unexpected was it.

In the doorway stood the little girl in the plaid dress. Her hair was combed, her face scrubbed. She carried with a superb air an object which seemed to be a handbag but which at second glance revealed itself as a teakwood cigarette box with a piece of binder twine fastened to it with four-inch nails. "Good evening," she said concisely. "I was passing by and thought I would come to call. You *are* at home?"

This parroting of a penurious beldame who once was in the habit of cadging meals by this means was completely incomprehensible to Lone. He resumed licking his fingers but he kept his eyes on the child's face. Behind the girl, suddenly, appeared the heads of his two previous visitors peeping around the doorpost.

The child's nostrils, then her eyes, found the stewpot. She wooed it with her gaze, yearned. She yawned, too, suddenly. "I beg your pardon," she said demurely. She pried open the lid of the cigarette box, drew out a white object and folded it quickly but not quickly enough to conceal the fact that it was a large man's sock, and patted her lips with it.

Lone rose and got a piece of wood and placed it carefully on the fire and sat down again. The girl took another step. The other two scuttled in and stood, one on each side of the doorway like toy soldiers. Their faces were little knots of apprehension. And they were clothed this time. One wore a pair of ladies' linen bloomers, the like of which had not been seen since cars had tillers. It came up to her armpits, and was supported by two short lengths of the same hairy binder twine, poked through holes torn in the waistband and acting as shoulder straps. The other one wore a heavy cotton slip, or at least the top third of it. It fell to her ankles where it showed a fringe of torn and unhemmed material.

With the exact air of a lady crossing a drawing room toward the bonbons, the white child approached the stewpot, flashed Lone a small smile, lowered her eyelids and reached down with a thumb and forefinger, murmuring, "May I?"

Lone stretched out one long leg and hooked the pot away from her and into his grasp. He set it on the floor on the side away from her and looked at her woodenly.

"You're a real cheap stingy son of a bitch," the child quoted.

This also missed Lone completely. Before he had learned to be aware of what men said, such remarks had been meaningless. Since, he had not been exposed to them. He stared at her blankly and pulled the pot protectively closer.

The child's eyes narrowed and her color rose. Suddenly she began to cry. "Please," she said. "I'm hungry. *We're* hungry. The stuff in the cans, it's all gone." Her voice failed her but she could still whisper. "Please," she whispered, "please."

Lone regarded her stonily. At length she took a timid step toward him. He lifted the pot into his lap and hugged it defiantly. She said, "Well, I didn't want any of your old . . ." but then her voice broke. She turned away and went to the door. The others watched her face as she came. They radiated silent disappointment; their eloquent expressions took the white girl to task far more than they did him. She had the status of provider and she had failed them, and they were merciless in their expression of it.

He sat with the warm pot in his lap and looked out the open door into the thickening night. Unbidden, an image appeared to him—Mrs. Prodd, a steaming platter of baked ham flanked by the orange gaze of perfect eggs, saying, "Now you set right down and have some breakfast." An emotion he was unequipped to define reached up from his solar plexus and tugged at his throat.

He snorted, reached into the pot, scooped out half a potato and opened his mouth to receive it. His hand would not deliver. He bent his head slowly and looked at the potato as if he could not quite recognize it or its function.

He snorted again, flung the potato back into the pot, thumped the pot back on the floor and leapt to his feet. He put one hand on each side of the door and sent his flat harsh voice hurtling out: *"Wait!"*

The corn should have been husked long since. Most of it still stood but here and there the stalks lay broken and yellowing, and soldier ants were prospecting them and scurrying off with rumors. Out in the fallow field the truck lay forlornly, bogged, with the seeder behind it, tipped forward over its hitch and the winter wheat spilling out. No smoke came from the chimney up at the house and the half door into the barn, askew and perverted amid the misery, hollowly applauded.

Lone approached the house, mounted the stoop. Prodd sat on the porch glider which now would not glide, for one set of end-chains was broken. His eyes were not closed but they were more closed than open.

"Hi," said Lone.

Prodd stirred, looked full into Lone's face. There was no sign of recognition. He dropped his gaze, pushed back to sit upright, felt aimlessly around his chest, found a suspender strap, pulled it forward and let it snap back. A troubled expression passed through his features and left it. He looked up again at Lone, who could sense self-awareness returning to the farmer like coffee soaking upward into a lump of sugar.

"Well, Lone, boy!" said Prodd. The old words were there but the tone behind them behaved like his broken hay rake. He rose, beaming, came to Lone, raised his fist to thump Lone's arm but then apparently forgot it. The fist hovered there for a moment and then gravitated downward.

"Corn's for husking," said Lone.

"Yeah, yeah, I know," Prodd half said, half sighed. "I'll get to it. I can handle it all right. One way or 'tother, always get done by the first frost. Ain't missed milkin' once," he added with wan pride.

Lone glanced through the door pane and saw, for the very first time, crusted dishes, heavy flies in the kitchen. "The baby come," he said, remembering.

"Oh, yes. Fine little feller, just like we . . ." Again he seemed to forget. The words slowed and were left suspended as his fist had been. "Ma!" he shrieked suddenly. "Fix a bite for the boy, here!" He turned to Lone, embarrassedly. "She's yonder," he said, pointing. "Yell loud enough, I reckon she'd hear. Maybe."

Lone looked where Prodd pointed, but saw nothing. He caught Prodd's gaze and for a split second started to probe. He recoiled violently at the very nature of what was there before he got close enough to identify it. He turned away quickly. "Brought your ax."

"Oh, that's all right. You could've kept it."

"Got my own. Want to get that corn in?"

Prodd gazed mistily at the corn patch. "Never missed a milking," he said.

Lone left him and went to the barn for a corn hook. He found one. He also discovered that the cow was dead. He went up to the corn patch and got to work. After a time he saw Prodd down the line, working too, working hard.

Well past midday and just before they had the corn all cut, Prodd disappeared into the house. Twenty minutes later he emerged with a pitcher and a platter of sandwiches. The bread was dry and the sandwiches were corned beef from, as Lone recalled, Mrs. Prodd's practically untouched "rainy day" shelf. The pitcher contained warm lemonade and dead flies. Lone asked no questions. They perched on the edge of the horse trough and ate.

Afterward Lone went down to the fallow field and got the truck dug out. Prodd followed him down in time to drive it out. The rest of the day was devoted to the seeding with Lone loading the seeder and helping four different times to free the truck from the traps it insisted upon digging for itself. When that was finished, Lone waved Prodd up to the barn where he got a rope around the dead cow's neck and hauled it as near as the truck would go to the edge of the wood. When at last they ran the truck into the barn for the night, Prodd said, "Sure miss that horse."

"You said you didn't miss it a-tall," Lone recalled tactlessly.

"Did I now." Prodd turned inward and smiled, remembering. "Yeah, nothing bothered me none, because of, you know." Still smiling, he turned to Lone and said, "Come back to the house." He smiled all the way back.

They went through the kitchen. It was even worse than it had looked from outside and the clock was stopped, too. Prodd, smiling, threw open the door of Jack's room. Smiling, he said, "Have a look, boy. Go right on in, have a look."

Lone went in and looked into the bassinet. The cheesecloth was torn and the blue cotton was moist and reeking. The baby had eyes like upholstery tacks and skin the color of mustard. Short blue-black horsehair covered its skull, and it breathed noisily.

Lone did not change expression. He turned away and stood in the kitchen looking at one of the dimity curtains, the one which lay on the floor.

Smiling, Prodd came out of Jack's room and closed the door. "See, he's not Jack, that's the one blessing," he smiled. "Ma, she had to go off looking for Jack, I reckon, yes; that would be it. She wouldn't be happy with anything less; well, you know that your own self." He smiled twice. "What that in there is, that's what the doctor calls a mongoloid. Just leave it be; it'll grow up to maybe size three and stay so for thirty year. Get him to a big-city specialist for treatments and he'll grow up to maybe size ten." He smiled as he talked. "That's what the doctor said anyway. Can't shovel him into the ground now, can you? That was all right for Ma, way she loved flowers and all."

Too many words, some hard to hear through the wide, tight smiling. Lone brought his eyes to bear on Prodd's.

He found out exactly what Prodd wanted–things that Prodd himself did not know. He did the things.

When he was finished he and Prodd cleaned up the kitchen and took the bassinet and burned it, along with the carefully sewn diapers made out of old sheets and piled in the linen closet and the new oval enamel bath pan and the celluloid rattle and the blue felt booties with the white puffballs in their clear cellophane box.

Prodd waved cheerfully to him from the porch. "Just you wait'll Ma gets back; she'll stuff you full of johnny cake till we got to scrape you off the wall."

"Mind you fix that barn door," Lone rasped. "I'll come back."

With his burden he plodded up the hill and into the forest. He struggled numbly with thoughts that would not be words or pictures. About those kids, now; about the Prodds. The Prodds were one thing and when they took him in they became something else; he knew it now. And then when he was by himself he was one thing; but taking those kids in he was something else. He had no business going back to Prodd's today. But now, the way he was, he *had* to do it. He'd go back again too.

Alone. Lone Lone alone. Prodd was alone now and Janie was alone and the twins, well they had each other but they were like one split person who was alone. He himself, Lone, was still alone, it didn't make any difference about the kids being there.

Maybe Prodd and his wife had not been alone. He wouldn't have any way of knowing about that. But there was nothing like Lone anywhere in the world except right here inside him. The whole world threw Lone away, you know that? Even the Prodds did, when they got around to it. Janie got thrown out, the twins too, so Janie said.

Well, in a funny way it helps to know you're alone, thought Lone.

The night was sun-stained by the time he got home. He kneed the door open and came in. Janie was making pictures on an old china plate with spit and mud. The twins as usual were sitting in one of the high rock niches, whispering to one another.

Janie jumped up. "What's that? What'd you bring?"

Lone put it down carefully on the floor. The twins appeared, one on each side of it. "It's a baby," said Janie. She looked up at Lone. "Is it a baby?"

Lone nodded. Janie looked again. "Nastiest one I ever saw."

Lone said, "Well, never mind that. Give him something to eat."

"What?"

"I don't know," said Lone. "You're a baby, almost. You should know."

"Where'd you get him?"

"A farm yonder."

"You're a kidnapper," said Janie. "Know that?"

"What's a kidnapper?"

"Man that steals babies, that's what. When they find out about it the policeman will come and shoot you dead and put you in the electric chair."

"Well," said Lone, relieved, "ain't nobody going to find out. Only man knows about it, I fixed it so he's forgotten. That's the daddy. The ma, she's dead, but he don't know that either. He thinks she's back East. He'll hang on waiting for her. Anyway, feed him."

He pulled off his jacket. The kids kept it too hot in here. The baby lay still with its dull button eyes open, breathing too loudly. Janie stood before the fire, staring thoughtfully at the stewpot. Finally she dipped into it with a ladle and dribbled the juice into a tin can. "Milk," she said while she worked. "You got to start swiping milk for him, Lone. Babies, they eat more milk'n a cat."

"All right," said Lone.

The twins watched, wall-eyed, as Janie slopped the broth on the baby's disinterested mouth.

"He's getting some," said Janie optimistically.

Without humor and only from visible evidence, Lone said, "Maybe through his ears."

Janie pulled at the baby's shirt and half sat him up. This favored the neck rather than the ears but still left the mouth intake in doubt.

"Oh, maybe I can!" said Janie suddenly, as if answering a comment. The twins giggled and jumped up and down. Janie drew the tin can a few inches away from the baby's face and narrowed her eyes. The baby immediately started to choke and spewed up what was unequivocally broth.

"That's not right yet but I'll get it," said Janie. She spent half an hour trying. At last the baby went to sleep.

One afternoon Lone watched for a while and then prodded Janie with his toe. "What's going on there?"

She looked. "He's talking to them."

Lone pondered. "I used to could do that. Hear babies."

"Bonnie says all babies can do it, and you were a baby, weren't you? I forget if I ever did," she added. "Except the twins."

"What I mean," said Lone laboriously, "when I was growed I could hear babies."

"You must've been an idiot, then," said Janie positively. "Idiots can't understand people but can understand babies. Mr. Widdecombe, he's the man the twins lived with, he had a girl friend once who was an idiot and Bonnie told me."

"Baby's s'posed to be some kind of a idiot," Lone said.

"Yes, Beanie, she says he's sort of different. He's like a adding machine."

"What's a adding machine?"

Janie exaggerated the supreme patience that her nursery-school teacher had affected. "It's a thing you push buttons and it gives you the right answer."

Lone shook his head.

Janie essayed, "Well, if you have three cents and four cents and five cents and seven cents and eight cents–how many you got altogether?"

Lone shrugged hopelessly.

"Well if you have a adding machine, you push a button for *two* and a button for *three* and a button for all the other ones and then you pull a handle, the machine tells you how many you got altogether. And it's always right."

Lone sorted all this out slowly and finally nodded. Then he waved toward the orange crate that was now Baby's bassinet, and the twins hanging spellbound over him. "He got no buttons you push."

"That was just a finger of speech," Janie said loftily. "Look, you tell Baby something, and then you tell him something else. He will put the somethings together and tell you what they come out to, just like the adding machine does with one and two and–"

"All right, but what kind of somethings?"

"Anything." She eyed him. "You're sort of stoopid, you know that, Lone. I got to tell you every little thing four times. Now listen, if you want to know something you tell me and I'll tell Baby and he'll get the answer and tell the twins and they'll tell me and I'll tell you, now what do you want to know?"

Lone stared at the fire. "I don't know anything I want to know."

"Well, you sure think up a lot of silly things to ask me."

Lone, not offended, sat and thought. Janie went to work on a scab on her knee, picking it gently round and round with fingernails the color and shape of parentheses.

"Suppose I got a truck," Lone said a half hour later, "it gets stuck in a field all the time, the ground's too tore up. Suppose I want to fix it so it won't stick no more. Baby tell me a thing like that?"

"Anything, I told you," said Janie sharply. She turned and looked at Baby. Baby lay as always, staring dully upward. In a moment she looked at the twins.

"He don't know what is a truck. If you're going to ask him anything you have to explain all the pieces before he can put 'em together."

"Well you know what a truck is," said Lone, "and soft ground and what stickin' is. You tell him."

"Oh all right," said Janie.

She went through the routine again, sending to Baby, receiving from the twins. Then she laughed. "He says stop driving on the field and you won't get stuck. You could of thought of that yourself, you dumbhead."

Lone said, "Well suppose you got to use it there, then what?"

"You 'spect me to go on askin' him silly questions all *night?"*

"All right, he can't answer like you said."

"He can too!" Her facts impugned, Janie went to the task with a will. The next answer was, "Put great big wide wheels on it."

"Suppose you ain't got money nor time nor tools for that?"

This time it was, "Make it real heavy where the ground is hard and real light where the ground is soft and anything in between."

Janie very nearly went on strike when Lone demanded to know how this could be accomplished and reached something of a peak of impatience when Lone rejected the suggestion of loading and unloading rocks. She complained that not only was this silly, but that Baby was matching every fact she fed him with every other fact he had been fed previously and was giving correct but unsolicited answers to situational sums of tires plus weight plus soup plus bird's nests, and babies plus soft dirt plus wheel diameters plus straw. Lone doggedly clung to his basic question and the day's impasse was reached when it was determined that there was such a way but it could not be expressed except by facts not in Lone's or Janie's possession. Janie said it sounded to her like radio tubes and with only that to go on, Lone proceeded by entering the next night a radio service shop and stealing a heavy armload of literature. He bulled along unswerving, unstoppable, until at last Janie relinquished her opposition because she had not energy for it and for the research as well. For days she scanned elementary electricity and radio texts which meant nothing to her but which apparently Baby could absorb faster than she scanned.

And at last the specifications were met: something which Lone could make himself, which would involve only a small knob you pushed to make the truck heavier and pulled to make it lighter, as well as an equally simple attachment to add power to the front wheels —according to Baby a *sine qua non.*

In the half-cave, half-cabin, with the fire smoking in the center of the room and the meat turning slowly in the updraft, with the help of two tongue-tied infants, a mongoloid baby and a sharp-tongued child who seemed to despise him but never failed him, Lone built the device. He did it, not because he was particularly interested in the thing for itself, nor because he wished to understand its principles (which were and would always be beyond him), but only because an old man who had taught him something he could not name was mad with bereavement and needed to work and could not afford a horse.

He walked most of the night with it and installed it in the dim early hours of the morning. The idea of "pleasant surprise" was far too whimsical a thing for Lone but it amounted to the same thing. He wanted it ready for the day's work, without any time lost by the old man prancing around asking questions that he couldn't answer.

The truck stood bogged in the field. Lone unwound the device from around his neck and shoulders and began to attach it according to the exact instructions he had winnowed out of Baby. There wasn't much to do. A slender wire wrapped twice around the clutch housing outside and led to clamps on the front spring shackles, the little brushes touching the insides of the front wheels; and that was the front-wheel drive. Then the little box with its four silvery cables, box clamped to steering post, each cable leading to a corner of the frame.

He got in and pulled the knob toward him. The frame creaked as the truck seemed to raise itself on tiptoe. He pushed the knob forward. The truck settled its front axle and differential housing on solid ground with a bump that made his head rock. He looked at the little box and its lever admiringly, then returned the lever to a neutral position. He scanned the other controls there, the ones which came with the truck: pedals and knobs and sticks and buttons. He sighed.

He wished he had wit enough to drive a truck.

He got out and climbed the hill to the house to wake Prodd. Prodd wasn't there. The kitchen door swung in the breeze, the glass gone out of it and lying on the stoop. Mud wasps were building under the sink. There was a smell of dirty dry floorboards, mildew, and ancient sweat. Otherwise it was fairly neat, about the way it was when he and Prodd had cleaned up last time he was here. The only new thing there aside from the mud wasps' nest was a paper nailed to the wall by all four corners. It had writing all over it. Lone detached it as carefully as he could, and smoothed it out on the kitchen table, and turned it over twice. Then he folded it, put it in his pocket. Again he sighed.

He wished he had sense enough to learn to read.

He left the house without looking back and plunged into the forest. He never returned. The truck stood out in the sun, slowly deteriorating, slowly weakening its already low resistance to rust, slowly falling to pieces around the bright, strong, strange silver cables. Powered inexhaustibly by the slow release of atomic binding energy, the device was the practical solution of flight without wings, the simple key to a new era in transportation, in materials handling, and in interplanetary travel. Made by an idiot, harnessed idiotically to replace a spavined horse, stupidly left, numbly forgotten . . . Earth's first anti-gravity generator.

The *idiot!*

Dear loan I'll nale this up wher you cant hep see it I am cleering ot of here I dont no why I stade as long as I did. Ma is back east Wmsport pennsilvana and she been gone a long time and I am tied of wating. And I was goin to sell the truck to hep me on the way but it is stuck so bad now I cant get it to town to sell it. So now I am jest goin to go whatever and I'll make it some way long as I no Ma is at the othr end. Dont take no trouble about the place I guess I had enuf of it Anyway. And borrow any thing you want if you should want any Thing. You are a good boy you been a good frend well goodbeye until I see you if I ever do god Bless you your old frend E. Prodd.

Lone made Janie read him the letter four times in a three-week period, and each reading seemed to add a fresh element to the yeasty seething inside him. Much of this happened silently; for some of it he asked help.

He had believed that Prodd was his only contact with anything outside himself and that the children were merely fellow occupants of a slag dump at the edge of mankind. The loss of Prodd—and he knew with unshakeable certainty that he would never see the old man again—was the loss of life itself. At the very least, it was the loss of everything conscious, directed, cooperative; everything above and beyond what a vegetable could do by way of living.

"Ask Baby what is a friend."

"He says it's somebody who goes on loving you whether he likes you or not."

But then, Prodd and his wife had shucked him off when he was in the way, after all those years, and that meant they were ready to do it the first year and the second and the fifth—all the time, any time. You can't say you're a part of anything, anybody, that feels free to do that to you. But friends . . . maybe they just don't like him for a while, maybe they love him all the way through.

"Ask Baby can you be truly part of someone you love."

"He says only if you love yourself."

His benchmark, his goal point, had for years been that thing which happened to him on the bank of the pool. He had to understand that. If he could understand that, he was sure he could understand everything. Because for a second there was this *other,* and himself, and a flow between them without guards or screens or barriers—no language to stumble over, no ideas to misunderstand, nothing at all but a merging.

What had he been then? What was it Janie had said?

Idiot. An idiot.

An idiot, she had said, was a grown person who could hear only babies' silent speech. Then—what was the creature with whom he had merged on that terrible day?

"Ask Baby what is a grown person who can *talk* like the babies."

"He says, an innocent."

He had been an idiot who could hear the soundless murmur. She had been an innocent who, as an adult, could speak it.

"Ask Baby what if an idiot and an innocent are close together."

"He says when they so much as touched, the innocent would stop being an innocent and the idiot would stop being an idiot."

He thought. An innocent is the most beautiful thing there can be. Immediately he demanded of himself, What's so beautiful about an innocent? And the answer, for once almost as swift as Baby's: It's the waiting that's beautiful.

Waiting for the end of innocence. And an idiot is waiting for the end of idiocy too, but he's ugly doing it. So each ends himself in the meeting, in exchange for a merging.

Lone was suddenly deep-down glad. For if this was true, he had made something, rather than destroyed something . . . and when he had lost it, the pain of the loss was justified. When he had lost the Prodds the pain wasn't worth it.

What am I doing? What am I doing? he thought wildly. Trying and trying like this to find out what I am and what I belong to. . . . Is this another aspect of being outcast, monstrous, *different?*

"Ask Baby what kind of people are all the time trying to find out what they are and what they belong to."

"He says, *every* kind."

"What kind," Lone whispered, "am I, then?"

A full minute later he yelled, *"What kind?"*

"Shut up awhile. He doesn't have a way to say it . . . uh . . . Here. He says he is a figure-outer brain and I am a body and the twins are arms and legs and you are the head. He says the 'I' is all of us."

"I belong. I belong. Part of you, part of you and you too."

"The head, silly."

Lone thought his heart was going to burst. He looked at them all, every one: arms to flex and reach, a body to care and repair, a brainless but faultless computer and–the head to direct it.

"And we'll grow, Baby. We just got born!"

"He says not on your life. He says not with a head like that. We can do practically *anything* but we most likely won't. He says we're a thing, all right, but the thing is an idiot."

So it was that Lone came to know himself; and like the handful of people who have done so before him he found, at this pinnacle, the rugged foot of a mountain.

PART TWO | BABY IS THREE

I finally got in to see this Stern. He wasn't an old man at all. He looked up from his desk, flicked his eyes over me once and picked up a pencil. "Sit over there, Sonny."

I stood where I was until he looked up again. Then I said, "Look, if a midget walks in here, what do you say–sit over there, Shorty?"

He put the pencil down again and stood up. He smiled. His smile was as quick and sharp as his eyes. "I was wrong," he said, "but how am I supposed to know you don't want to be called Sonny?"

That was better, but I was still mad. "I'm fifteen and I don't have to like it. Don't rub my nose in it."

He smiled again and said okay, and I went and sat down.

"What's your name?"

"Gerard."

"First or last?"

"Both," I said.

"Is that the truth?"

I said, "No. And don't ask me where I live either."

He put down his pencil. "We're not going to get very far this way."

"That's up to you. What are you worried about? I got feelings of hostility? Well, sure I have. I got lots more things than that wrong with me or I wouldn't be here. Are you going to let that stop you?"

"Well, no, but–"

"So what else is bothering you? How you're going to get paid?" I took out a thousand-dollar bill and laid it on the desk. "That's so you won't have to bill me. *You* keep track of it. Tell me when it's used up and I'll give you more. So you don't need my address. Wait," I said when he reached toward the money. "Let it lay here. I want to be sure you and I are going to get along."

He folded his hands. "I don't do business this way, Son–I mean, Gerard."

"Gerry," I told him. "You do, if you do business with me."

"You make things difficult, don't you? Where did you get a thousand dollars?"

"I won a contest. Twenty-five words or less about how much fun it is to do my daintier things with Sudso." I leaned forward. "This time it's the truth."

"All right," he said.

I was surprised. I think he knew it, but he didn't say anything more. Just waited for me to go ahead.

"Before we start–*if* we start," I said, "I got to know something. The things I say to you–what comes out while you're working on me–is that just between us, like a priest or a lawyer?"

"Absolutely," he said.

"No matter what?"

"No matter what."

I watched him when he said it. I believed him.

"Pick up your money," I said. "You're on."

He didn't do it. He said, "As you remarked a minute ago, that is up to me. You can't buy these treatments like a candy bar. We have to work together. If either one of us can't do that, it's useless. You can't walk in on the first psychotherapist you find in the phone book and make any demand that occurs to you just because you can pay for it."

I said tiredly, "I didn't get you out of the phone book and I'm not just guessing that you can help me. I winnowed through a dozen or more head-shrinkers before I decided on you."

"Thanks," he said, and it looked as if he was going to laugh at me, which I never like. "Winnowed, did you say? Just how?"

"Things you hear, things you read. You know. I'm not saying, so just file that with my street address."

He looked at me for a long time. It was the first time he'd used his eyes on me for anything but a flash glance. Then he picked up the bill.

"What do I do first?" I demanded.

"What do you mean?"

"How do we start?"

"We started when you walked in here."

So then I had to laugh. "All right, you got me. All I had was an opening. I didn't know where you would go from there, so I couldn't be there ahead of you."

"That's very interesting," Stern said. "Do you usually figure everything out in advance?"

"Always."

"How often are you right?"

"All the time. Except—but I don't have to tell you about no exceptions."

He really grinned this time. "I see. One of my patients has been talking."

"One of your ex-patients. Your patients don't talk."

"I ask them not to. That applies to you, too. What did you hear?"

"That you know from what people say and do what they're about to say and do, and that sometimes you let'm do it and sometimes you don't. How did you learn to do that?"

He thought a minute. "I guess I was born with an eye for details, and then let myself make enough mistakes with enough people until I learned not to make too many more. How did you learn to do it?"

I said, "You answer that and I won't have to come back here."

"You really don't know?"

"I wish I did. Look, this isn't getting us anywhere, is it?"

He shrugged. "Depends on where you want to go." He paused, and I got the eyes full strength again. "Which thumbnail description of psychiatry do you believe at the moment?"

"I don't get you."

Stern slid open a desk drawer and took out a blackened pipe. He smelled it, turned it over while looking at me. "Psychiatry attacks the onion of the self, removing layer after layer until it gets down to the little sliver of unsullied ego. Or: psychiatry drills like an oil well, down and sidewise and down again, through all the muck and rock until it strikes a layer that yields. Or: psychiatry grabs a handful of sexual motivations and throws them on the pinball machine of your life, so they bounce on down against episodes. Want more?"

I had to laugh. "That last one was pretty good."

"That last one was pretty bad. They are all bad. They all try to simplify something which is complex by its very nature. The only thumbnail you'll get from me is this: no one knows what's really wrong with you but you; no one can find a cure for it but you; no one but you can identify it as a cure; and once you find it, no one but you can do anything about it."

"What are *you* here for?"

"To listen."

"I don't have to pay somebody no day's wages every hour just to listen."

"True. But you're convinced that I listen selectively."

"Am I?" I wondered about it. "I guess I am. Well, don't you?"

"No, but you'll never believe that."

I laughed. He asked me what that was for. I said, "You're not calling me Sonny."

"Not you." He shook his head slowly. He was watching me while he did it, so his eyes slid in their sockets as his head moved. "What is it you want to know about yourself that made you worried I might tell people?"

"I want to find out why I killed somebody," I said right away.

It didn't faze him a bit. "Lie down over there."

I got up. "On that couch?"

He nodded.

As I stretched out self-consciously, I said, "I feel like I'm in some damn cartoon."

"What cartoon?"

"Guy's built like a bunch of grapes," I said, looking at the ceiling. It was pale gray.

"What's the caption?"

"'I got trunks full of 'em.'"

"Very good," he said quietly. I looked at him carefully. I knew then he was the kind of guy who laughs way down deep when he laughs at all.

He said, "I'll use that in a book of case histories some time. But it won't include yours. What made you throw that in?" When I didn't answer, he got up and moved to a chair behind me where I couldn't see him. "You can quit testing, Sonny. I'm good enough for your purposes."

I clenched my jaw so hard, my back teeth hurt. Then I relaxed. I relaxed all over. It was wonderful. "All right," I said, "I'm sorry." He didn't say anything, but I had that feeling again that he was laughing. Not at me, though.

"How old are you?" he asked me suddenly.

"Uh–fifteen."

"Uh–fifteen," he repeated. "What does the 'uh' mean?"

"Nothing. I'm fifteen."

"When I asked your age, you hesitated because some other number popped up. You discarded that and substituted 'fifteen.'"

"The hell I did! I am fifteen!"

"I didn't say you weren't." His voice came patiently. "Now what was the other number?"

I got mad again. "There wasn't any other number! What do you want to go pryin' my grunts apart for, trying to plant this and that and make it mean what you think it ought to mean?"

He was silent.

"I'm fifteen," I said defiantly, and then, "I don't like being only fifteen. You know that. I'm not trying to insist I'm fifteen."

He just waited, still not saying anything.

I felt defeated. "The number was eight."

"So you're eight. And your name?"

"Gerry." I got up on one elbow, twisting my neck around so I could see him. He had his pipe apart and was sighting through the stem at the desk lamp. "Gerry, without no 'uh!'"

"All right," he said mildly, making me feel real foolish.

I leaned back and closed my eyes.

Eight, I thought. Eight.

"It's cold in here," I complained.

Eight. Eight, plate, state, hate. I ate from the plate of the state and I hate. I didn't like any of that and I snapped my eyes open. The ceiling was still gray. It was all right. Stern was somewhere behind me with his pipe, and he was all right. I took two deep breaths, three, and then let my eyes close. Eight. Eight years old. Eight, hate. Years, fears. Old, cold. *Damn* it! I twisted and twitched on the couch, trying to find a way to keep the cold out. I ate from the plate of the—

I grunted and with my mind I took all the eights and all the rhymes and everything they stood for, and made it all black. But it wouldn't stay black. I had to put something there, so I made a great big luminous figure eight and just let it hang there. But it turned on its side and inside the loops it began to shimmer. It was like one of those movie shots through binoculars. I was going to have to look through whether I liked it or not.

Suddenly I quit fighting it and let it wash over me. The binoculars came close, closer, and then I was there.

Eight. Eight years old, cold. Cold as a bitch in the ditch. The ditch was by a railroad. Last year's weeds were scratchy straw. The ground was red, and when it wasn't slippery, clingy mud, it was frozen hard like a flowerpot. It was hard like that now, dusted with hoar frost, cold as the winter light that pushed up over the hills. At night the lights were warm, and they were all in other people's houses. In the daytime the sun was in somebody else's house too, for all the good it did me.

I was dying in that ditch. Last night it was as good a place as any to sleep and this morning it was as good a place as any to die. Just as well. Eight years old, the sick-sweet taste of pork fat and wet bread from somebody's garbage, the thrill of terror when you're stealing a gunny sack and you hear a footstep.

And I heard a footstep.

I'd been curled up on my side. I whipped over on my stomach because sometimes they kick your belly. I covered my head with my arms and that was as far as I could get.

After a while I rolled my eyes up and looked without moving. There was a big shoe there. There was an ankle in the shoe, and another shoe close by. I lay there waiting to get tromped. Not that I cared much any more, but it was such a damn shame. All these months on my own, and they'd never caught up with me, never even come close, and now this. It was such a shame I started to cry.

The shoe took me under the armpit, but it was not a kick. It rolled me over. I was so stiff from the cold, I went over like a plank. I just kept my arms over my face and head and lay there with my eyes closed. For some reason I stopped crying. I think people only cry when there's a chance of getting help from somewhere.

When nothing happened, I opened my eyes and shifted my forearms a little so I could see up. There was a man standing over me and he was a mile high. He had on faded dungarees and an old Eisenhower jacket with deep sweat-stains under the arms. His face was shaggy, like the guys who can't grow what you could call a beard, but still don't shave.

He said, "Get up."

I looked down at his shoe, but he wasn't going to kick me. I pushed up a little and almost fell down again, except he put his big hand where my back would hit it. I lay against it for a second because I had to, and then got up to where I had one knee on the ground.

"Come on," he said. "Let's go."

I swear I felt my bones creak, but I made it. I brought a round white stone up with me as I stood. I hefted the stone. I had to look at it to see if I was really holding it, my fingers were that cold. I told him, "Stay away from me or I'll bust you in the teeth with this rock."

His hand came out and down so fast I never saw the way he got one finger between my palm and the rock and flicked it out of my grasp. I started to cuss at him, but he just turned his back and walked up the embankment toward the tracks. He put his chin on his shoulder and said, "Come on, will you?"

He didn't chase me, so I didn't run. He didn't talk to me, so I didn't argue. He didn't hit me, so I didn't get mad. I went along after him. He waited for me. He put out his hand to me and I spit at it. So he went on, up to the tracks, out of my sight. I clawed my way up. The blood was beginning to move in my hands and feet and they felt like four point-down porcupines. When I got up to the roadbed, the man was standing there waiting for me.

The track was level just there, but as I turned my head to look along it, it seemed to be a hill that was steeper and steeper and turned over above me. And next thing you know, I was lying flat on my back looking up at the cold sky.

The man came over and sat down on the rail near me. He didn't try to touch me. I gasped for breath a couple of times and suddenly felt I'd be all right if I could sleep for a minute—just a little minute. I closed my eyes. The man stuck his finger in my ribs, hard. It hurt.

"Don't sleep," he said.

I looked at him.

He said, "You're frozen stiff and weak with hunger. I want to take you home and get you warmed up and fed. But it's a long haul up that way, and you won't make it by yourself. If I carry you, will that be the same to you as if you walked it?"

"What are you going to do when you get me home?"

"I told you."

"All right," I said.

He picked me up and carried me down the track. If he'd said anything else in the world, I'd of laid right down where I was until I froze to death. Anyway, what did he want to ask me for, one way or the other? I couldn't of done anything.

I stopped thinking about it and dozed off.

I woke up once when he turned off the right of way. He dove into the woods. There was no path, but he seemed to know where he was going. The next time I woke from a crickling noise. He was carrying me over a frozen pond and the ice was giving under his feet. He didn't hurry. I looked down and saw the white cracks raying out under his feet, and it didn't seem to matter a bit. I bleared off again.

He put me down at last. We were there. "There" was inside a room. It was very warm. He put me on my feet and I snapped out of it in a hurry. The first thing I looked for was the door. I saw it and jumped over there and put my back against the wall beside it, in case I wanted to leave. Then I looked around.

It was a big room. One wall was rough rock and the rest was logs with stuff shoved between them. There was a big fire going in the rock wall, not in a fireplace, exactly; it was a sort of hollow place. There was an old auto battery on a shelf opposite, with two yellowing electric light bulbs dangling by wires from it. There was a table, some boxes and a couple of three-legged stools. The air had a haze of smoke and such a wonderful, heart-breaking, candy-and-crackling smell of food that a little hose squirted inside my mouth.

The man said, "What have I got here, Baby?"

And the room was full of kids. Well, three of them, but somehow they seemed to be more than three kids. There was a girl about my age–eight, I mean–with blue paint on the side of her face. She had an easel and a palette with lots of paint and a fistful of brushes, but she wasn't using the brushes. She was smearing the paint on with her hands. Then there was a little Negro girl about five with great big eyes who stood gaping at me. And in a wooden crate, set up on two sawhorses to make a kind of bassinet, was a baby. I guess about three or four months old. It did what babies do, drooling some, making small bubbles, waving its hands around very aimless, and kicking.

When the man spoke, the girl at the easel looked at me and then at the baby. The baby just kicked and drooled.

The girl said, "His name's Gerry. He's mad."

"What's he mad at?" the man asked. He was looking at the baby.

"Everything," said the girl. "Everything and everybody."

"Where'd he come from?"

I said, "Hey, what is this?" but nobody paid any attention. The man kept asking questions at the baby and the girl kept answering. Craziest thing I ever saw.

"He ran away from a state school," the girl said. "They fed him enough, but no one bleshed with him."

That's what she said—"bleshed."

I opened the door then and cold air hooted in. "You louse," I said to the man, "you're from the school."

"Close the door, Janie," said the man. The girl at the easel didn't move, but the door banged shut behind me. I tried to open it and it wouldn't move. I let out a howl, yanking at it.

"I think you ought to stand in the corner," said the man. "Stand him in the corner, Janie."

Janie looked at me. One of the three-legged stools sailed across to me. It hung in mid-air and turned on its side. It nudged me with its flat seat. I jumped back and it came after me. I dodged to the side, and that was the corner. The stool came on. I tried to bat it down and just hurt my hand. I ducked and it went lower than I did. I put one hand on it and tried to vault over it, but it just fell and so did I. I got up again and stood in the corner, trembling. The stool turned right side up and sank to the floor in front of me.

The man said, "Thank you, Janie." He turned to me. "Stand there and be quiet, you. I'll get to you later. You shouldn'ta kicked up all that fuss." And then, to the baby, he said, "He got anything we need?"

And again it was the little girl who answered. She said, "Sure. He's the one."

"Well," said the man. "What do you know!" He came over. "Gerry, you can live here. I don't come from no school. I'll never turn you in."

"Yeah, huh?"

"He hates you," said Janie.

"What am I supposed to do about that?" he wanted to know.

Janie turned her head to look into the bassinet. "Feed him." The man nodded and began fiddling around the fire.

Meanwhile, the little Negro girl had been standing in the one spot with her big eyes right out on her cheekbones, looking at me. Janie went back to her painting and the baby just lay there same as always, so I stared right back at the little Negro girl. I snapped, "What the hell are you gawking at?"

She grinned at me. "Gerry ho-ho," she said, and disappeared. I mean she really disappeared, went out like a light, leaving her clothes where she had been. Her little dress billowed in the air and fell in a heap where she had been, and that was that. She was gone.

"Gerry hee-hee," I heard. I looked up, and there she was, stark naked, wedged in a space where a little outcropping on the rock wall stuck out just below the ceiling. The second I saw her she disappeared again.

"Gerry ho-ho," she said. Now she was on top of the row of boxes they used as storage shelves, over on the other side of the room.

"Gerry hee-hee!" Now she was under the table. "Gerry ho-ho!" This time she was right in the corner with me, crowding me.

I yelped and tried to get out of the way and bumped the stool. I was afraid of it, so I shrank back again and the little girl was gone.

The man glanced over his shoulder from where he was working at the fire. "Cut it out, you kids," he said.

There was a silence, and then the girl came slowly out from the bottom row of shelves. She walked across to her dress and put it on.

"How did you do that?" I wanted to know.

"Ho-ho," she said.

Janie said, "It's easy. She's really twins."

"Oh," I said. Then another girl, exactly the same, came from somewhere in the shadows and stood beside the first. They were identical. They stood side by side and stared at me. This time I let them stare.

"That's Bonnie and Beanie," said the painter. "This is Baby and that–" she indicated the man– "that's Lone. And I'm Janie."

I couldn't think of what to say, so I said, "Yeah."

Lone said, "Water, Janie." He held up a pot. I heard water trickling, but didn't see anything. "That's enough," he said, and hung the pot on a crane. He picked up a cracked china plate and brought it over to me. It was full of stew with great big lumps of meat in it and thick gravy and dumplings and carrots. "Here, Gerry. Sit down."

I looked at the stool. "On that?"

"Sure."

"Not me," I said. I took the plate and hunkered down against the wall.

"Hey," he said after a time. "Take it easy. We've all had chow. No one's going to snatch it away from you. Slow down!"

I ate even faster than before. I was almost finished when I threw it all up. Then for some reason my head hit the edge of the stool. I dropped the plate and spoon and slumped there. I felt real bad.

Lone came over and looked at me. "Sorry, kid," he said. "Clean up, will you, Janie?"

Right in front of my eyes, the mess on the floor disappeared. I didn't care about that or anything else just then. I felt the man's hand on the side of my neck. Then he tousled my hair.

"Beanie, get him a blanket. Let's all go to sleep. He ought to rest a while."

I felt the blanket go around me, and I think I was asleep before he put me down.

I don't know how much later it was when I woke up. I didn't know where I was and that scared me. I raised my head and saw the dull glow of the embers in the fireplace. Lone was stretched out on it in his clothes. Janie's easel stood in the reddish blackness like some great preying insect. I saw the baby's head pop up out of the bassinet, but I couldn't tell whether he was looking straight at me or away. Janie was lying on the floor near the door and the twins were on the old table. Nothing moved except the baby's head, bobbing a little.

I got to my feet and looked around the room. Just a room, only the one door. I tiptoed toward it. When I passed Janie, she opened her eyes.

"What's the matter?" she whispered.

"None of your business," I told her. I went to the door as if I didn't care, but I watched her. She didn't do anything. The door was as solid tight closed as when I'd tried it before.

I went back to Janie. She just looked up at me. She wasn't scared. I told her, "I got to go to the john."

"Oh," she said. "Why'n't you say so?"

Suddenly I grunted and grabbed my guts. The feeling I had I can't begin to talk about. I acted as if it was a pain, but it wasn't. It was like nothing else that ever happened to me before. Something went *splop* on the snow outside.

"Okay," Janie said. "Go on back to bed."

"But I got to—"

"You got to what?"

"Nothing." It was true. I didn't have to go no place.

"Next time tell me right away. I don't mind."

I didn't say anything. I went back to my blanket.

"That's all?" said Stern. I lay on the couch and looked up at the gray ceiling. He asked, "How old are you?"

"Fifteen," I said dreamily. He waited until, for me, the gray ceiling acquired walls on a floor, a rug and lamps and a desk and a chair with Stern in it. I sat up and held my head a second, and then I looked at him. He was fooling with his pipe and looking at me. "What did you do to me?"

"I told you. I don't do anything here. You do it."

"You hypnotized me."

"I did not." His voice was quiet, but he really meant it.

"What was all that, then? It was . . . it was like it was happening for real all over again."

"Feel anything?"

"Everything." I shuddered. "*Every* damn thing. What was it?"

"Anyone doing it feels better afterward. You can go over it all again now any time you want to, and every time you do, the hurt in it will be less. You'll see."

It was the first thing to amaze me in years. I chewed on it and then asked, "If I did it by myself, how come it never happened before?"

"It needs someone to listen."

"Listen? Was I talking?"

"A blue streak."

"Everything that happened?"

"How can I know? I wasn't there. You were."

"You don't believe it happened, do you? Those disappearing kids and the footstool and all?"

He shrugged. "I'm not in the business of believing or not believing. Was it real to you?"

"Oh, hell, yes!"

"Well, then, that's all that matters. Is that where you live, with those people?"

I bit off a fingernail that had been bothering me. "Not for a long time. Not since Baby was three." I looked at him. "You remind me of Lone."

"Why?"

"I don't know. No, you don't," I added suddenly. "I don't know what made me say that." I lay down abruptly.

The ceiling was gray and the lamps were dim. I heard the pipe stem click against his teeth. I lay there for a long time.

"Nothing happens," I told him.

"What did you expect to happen?"

"Like before."

"There's something there that wants out. Just let it come."

It was as if there was a revolving drum in my head, and on it were photographed the places and things and people I was after. And it was as if the drum was spinning very fast, so fast I couldn't tell one picture from another. I made it stop, and it stopped at a blank segment. I spun it again, and stopped it again.

"Nothing happens," I said.

"Baby is three," he repeated.

"Oh," I said. "That." I closed my eyes.

That might be it. Might, sight, night, light. I might have the sight of a light in the night. Maybe the baby. Maybe the sight of the baby at night because of the light . . .

There was night after night when I lay on that blanket, and a lot of nights I didn't. Something was going on all the time in Lone's house. Sometimes I slept in the daytime. I guess the only time everybody slept at once was when someone was sick, like me the first time I arrived there. It was always sort of dark in the room, the same night and day, the fire going, the two old bulbs hanging yellow by their wires from the battery. When they got too dim, Janie fixed the battery and they got bright again.

Janie did everything that needed doing, whatever no one else felt like doing. Everybody else did things, too. Lone was out a lot. Sometimes he used the twins to help him, but you never missed them, because they'd be here and gone and back again *bing!* like that. And Baby, he just stayed in his bassinet.

I did things myself. I cut wood for the fire and I put up more shelves, and then I'd go swimming with Janie and the twins sometimes. And I talked to Lone. I didn't do a thing that the others couldn't do, but they all did things I couldn't do. I was mad, mad all the time about that. But I wouldn't of known what to do with myself if I wasn't mad all the time about something or other. It didn't keep us from bleshing. Bleshing, that was Janie's word. She said Baby told it to her. She said it meant everyone all together being something, even if they all did different things. Two arms, two legs, one body, one head, all working together, although a head can't walk and arms can't think. Lone said maybe it was a mixture of "blending" and "meshing," but I don't think he believed that himself. It was a lot more than that.

Baby talked all the time. He was like a broadcasting station that runs twenty-four hours a day, and you can get what it's sending any time you tune in, but it'll keep sending whether you tune in or not. When I say he talked, I don't mean exactly that. He semaphored mostly. You'd think those wandering vague movements of his hands and arms and legs and head were meaningless, but they weren't. It was semaphore, only instead of a symbol for a sound, or such like, the movements were whole thoughts.

I mean spread the left hand and shake the right high up, and thump with the left heel, and it means, "Anyone who thinks a starling is a pest just don't know anything about how a starling thinks" or something like that. Janie said she made Baby invent the semaphore business. She said she used to be able to hear the twins thinking—that's what she said; hear them thinking—and they could hear Baby. So she would ask the twins whatever she wanted to know, and they'd ask Baby, and then tell her what he said. But then as they grew up they began to lose the knack of it. Every young kid does. So Baby learned to understand when someone talked, and he'd answer with this semaphore stuff.

Lone couldn't read the stuff and neither could I. The twins didn't give a damn. Janie used to watch him all the time. He always knew what you meant if you wanted to ask him something, and he'd tell Janie and she'd say what it was. Part of it, anyway. Nobody could get it all, not even Janie.

All I know is Janie would sit there and paint her pictures and watch Baby, and sometimes she'd burst out laughing.

Baby never grew any. Janie did, and the twins, and so did I, but not Baby. He just lay there. Janie kept his stomach full and cleaned him up every two or three days. He didn't cry and he didn't make any trouble. No one ever went near him.

Janie showed every picture she painted to Baby, before she cleaned the boards and painted new ones. She had to clean them because she only had three of them. It was a good thing, too, because I'd hate to think what that place would of been like if she'd kept them all; she did four or five a day. Lone and the twins were kept hopping getting turpentine for her. She could shift the paints back into the little pots on her easel without any trouble, just by looking at the picture one color at a time, but turps was something else again. She told me that

Baby remembered all her pictures and that's why she didn't have to keep them. They were all pictures of machines and gear trains and mechanical linkages and what looked like electric circuits and things like that. I never thought too much about them.

I went out with Lone to get some turpentine and a couple picnic hams one time. We went through the woods to the railroad track and down a couple of miles to where we could see the glow of a town. Then the woods again, and some alleys, and a back street.

Lone was like always walking along, thinking, thinking.

We came to a hardware store and he went up and looked at the lock and came back to where I was waiting, shaking his head. Then we found a general store. Lone grunted and we went and stood in the shadows by the door. I looked in.

All of a sudden Beanie was in there, naked like she always was when she traveled like that. She came and opened the door from the inside. We went in and Lone closed it and locked it.

"Get along home, Beanie," he said, "before you catch your death."

She grinned at me and said, "Ho-ho," and disappeared.

We found a pair of fine hams and a two-gallon can of turpentine. I took a bright yellow ballpoint pen and Lone cuffed me and made me put it back.

"We only take what we need," he told me.

After we left, Beanie came back and locked the door and went home again. I only went with Lone a few times, when he had more to get than he could carry easily.

I was there about three years. That's all I can remember about it. Lone was there or he was out, and you could hardly tell the difference. The twins were with each other most of the time. I got to like Janie a lot, but we never talked much. Baby talked all the time, only I don't know what about.

We were all busy and we bleshed.

I sat up on the couch suddenly.

Stern said, "What's the matter?"

"Nothing's the matter. This isn't getting me any place."

"You said that when you'd barely started. Do you think you've accomplished anything since then?"

"Oh, yeah, but–"

"Then how can you be sure you're right this time?" When I didn't say anything, he asked me, "Didn't you like this last stretch?"

I said angrily, "I didn't like or not like. It didn't mean nothing. It was just–just talk."

"So what was the difference between this last session and what happened before?"

"My gosh, plenty! The first one, I felt everything. It was all really happening to me. But this time–nothing."

"Why do you suppose that was?"

"I don't know. You tell me."

"Suppose," he said thoughtfully, "that there was some episode so unpleasant to you that you wouldn't dare relive it."

"Unpleasant? You think freezing to death isn't unpleasant?"

"There are all kinds of unpleasantness. Sometimes the very thing you're looking for–the thing that'll clear up your trouble–is so revolting to you that you won't go near it. Or you try to hide it. Wait," he said suddenly, "maybe 'revolting' and 'unpleasant' are inaccurate words to use. It might be something very desirable to you. It's just that you don't want to get straightened out."

"I *want* to get straightened out."

He waited as if he had to clear something up in his mind, and then said, "There's something in that 'Baby is three' phrase that bounces you away. Why is that?"

"Damn if I know."

"Who said it?"

"I dunno . . . uh . . ."

He grinned. "Uh?"

I grinned back at him. "I said it."

"Okay. When?"

I quit grinning. He leaned forward, then got up.

"What's the matter?" I asked.

He said, "I didn't think anyone could be that mad." I didn't say anything. He went over to his desk. "You don't want to go on any more, do you?"

"No."

"Suppose I told you you want to quit because you're right on the very edge of finding out what you want to know?"

"Why don't you tell me and see what I do?"

He just shook his head. "I'm not telling you anything. Go on, leave if you want to. I'll give you back your change."

"How many people quit just when they're on top of the answer?"

"Quite a few."

"Well, I ain't going to." I lay down.

He didn't laugh and he didn't say, "Good," and he didn't make any fuss about it. He just picked up his phone and said, "Cancel everything for this afternoon," and went back to his chair, up there out of my sight.

It was very quiet in there. He had the place soundproofed.

I said, "Why do you suppose Lone let me live there so long when I couldn't do any of the things that the other kids could?"

"Maybe you could."

"Oh, no," I said positively. "I used to try. I was strong for a kid my age and I knew how to keep my mouth shut, but aside from those two things I don't think I was any different from any kid. I don't think I'm any different right now, except what difference there might be from living with Lone and his bunch."

"Has this anything to do with 'Baby is three'?"

I looked up at the gray ceiling. "Baby is three. Baby is three. I went up to a big house with a winding drive that ran under a sort of theater-marquee thing. Baby is three. Baby . . ."

"How old are you?"

"Thirty-three," I said, and the next thing you know I was up off that couch like it was hot and heading for the door.

Stern grabbed me. "Don't be foolish. Want me to waste a whole afternoon?"

"What's that to me? I'm paying for it."

"All right, it's up to you."

I went back. "I don't like any part of this," I said.

"Good. We're getting warm then."

"What made me say 'Thirty-three'? I ain't thirty-three. I'm fifteen. And another thing . . ."

"Yes?"

"It's about that 'Baby is three.' It's me saying it, all right. But when I think about it–it's not my voice."

"Like thirty-three's not your age?"

"Yeah," I whispered.

"Gerry," he said warmly, "there's nothing to be afraid of."

I realized I was breathing too hard. I pulled myself together. I said, "I don't like remembering saying things in somebody else's voice."

"Look," he told me. "This head-shrinking business, as you called it a while back, isn't what most people think. When I go with you into the world of your mind–or when you go yourself, for that matter–what we find isn't so very different from the so-called real world. It seems so at first, because the patient comes out with all sorts of fantasies and irrationalities and weird experiences. But everyone lives in that kind of world. When one of the ancients coined the phrase 'truth is stranger than fiction,' he was talking about that.

"Everywhere we go, everything we do, we're surrounded by symbols, by things so familiar we don't ever look at them or don't see them if we do look. If anyone ever could report to you exactly what we saw and thought while walking ten feet down the street, you'd get the most twisted, clouded, partial picture you ever ran across. And nobody ever looks at what's around him with any kind of attention until he gets into a place like this. The fact that he's looking at past events doesn't matter; what counts is that he's seeing clearer than he ever could before, just because, for once, he's trying.

"Now–about this 'thirty-three' business. I don't think a man could get a nastier shock than to find he has someone else's memories. The ego is too important to let slide that way. But consider: all your thinking is done in code and you have the key to only about a tenth of it. So you run into a stretch of code which is abhorrent to you. Can't you see that the only way you'll find the key to it is to stop avoiding it?"

"You mean I'd started to remember with . . . with somebody else's mind?"

"It looked like that to you for a while, which means something. Let's try to find out what."

"All right." I felt sick. I felt tired. And I suddenly realized that being sick and being tired was a way of trying to get out of it.

"Baby is three," he said.

Baby is maybe. Me, three, thirty-three, me, you Kew you.

"Kew!" I yelled. Stern didn't say anything. "Look, I don't know why, but I think I know how to get to this, and this isn't the way. Do you mind if I try something else?"

"You're the doctor," he said.

I had to laugh. Then I closed my eyes.

There, through the edges of the hedges, the ledges and wedges of windows were shouldering up to the sky. The lawns were sprayed-on green, neat and clean, and all the flowers looked as if they were afraid to let their petals break and be untidy.

I walked up the drive in my shoes. I'd had to wear shoes and my feet couldn't breathe. I didn't want to go to the house, but I had to.

I went up the steps between the big white columns and looked at the door. I wished I could see through it, but it was too white and thick. There was a window the shape of a fan over it, too high up though, and a window on each side of it, but they were all crudded up with colored glass. I hit on the door with my hand and left dirt on it.

Nothing happened, so I hit it again. It got snatched open and a tall, thin colored woman stood there. "What you want?"

I said I had to see Miss Kew.

"Well, Miss Kew don't want to see the likes of you," she said. She talked too loud. "You got a dirty face."

I started to get mad then. I was already pretty sore about having to come here, walking around near people in the daytime and all. I said, "My face ain't got nothin' to do with it. Where's Miss Kew? Go on, find her for me."

She gasped. "You can't speak to me like that!"

I said, "I didn't want to speak to you like any way. Let me in." I started wishing for Janie. Janie could of moved her. But I had to handle it by myself. I wasn't doing so hot, either. She slammed the door before I could so much as curse at her.

So I started kicking on the door. For that, shoes are great. After a while, she snatched the door open again so sudden I almost went on my can. She had a broom with her. She screamed at me, "You get away from here, you trash, or I'll call the police!" She pushed me and I fell.

I got up off the porch floor and went for her. She stepped back and whupped me one with the broom as I went past, but anyhow I was inside now. The woman was making little shrieking noises and coming for me. I took the broom away from her and then somebody said "Miriam!" in a voice like a grown goose.

I froze and the woman went into hysterics. "Oh, Miss Alicia, look out! He'll kill us all. Get the police. Get the—"

"Miriam!" came the honk, and Miriam dried up.

There at the top of the stairs was this prune-faced woman with a dress on that had lace on it. She looked a lot older than she was, maybe because she held her mouth so tight. I guess she was about thirty-three—*thirty-three*. She had mean eyes and a small nose.

I asked, "Are you Miss Kew?"

"I am. What is the meaning of this invasion?"

"I got to talk to you, Miss Kew."

"Don't say 'got to.' Stand up straight and speak out."

The maid said, "I'll get the police."

Miss Kew turned on her. "There's time enough for that, Miriam. Now, you dirty little boy, what do you want?"

"I got to speak to you by yourself," I told her.

"Don't you let him do it, Miss Alicia," cried the maid.

"Be quiet, Miriam. Little boy, I told you not to say 'got to.' You may say whatever you have to say in front of Miriam."

"Like hell." They both gasped. I said, "Lone told me not to."

"Miss Alicia, are you goin' to let him–"

"Be quiet, Miriam! Young man, you will keep a civil–" Then her eyes popped up real round. "*Who* did you say . . ."

"Lone said so."

"Lone." She stood there on the stairs looking at her hands. Then she said, "Miriam, that will be all." And you wouldn't know it was the same woman, the way she said it.

The maid opened her mouth, but Miss Kew stuck out a finger that might as well of had a rifle sight on the end of it. The maid beat it.

"Hey," I said, "here's your broom." I was just going to throw it, but Miss Kew got to me and took it out of my hand.

"In there," she said.

She made me go ahead of her into a room as big as our swimming hole. It had books all over and leather on top of the tables, with gold flowers drawn into the corners.

She pointed to a chair. "Sit there. No, wait a moment." She went to the fireplace and got a newspaper out of a box and brought it over and unfolded it on the seat of the chair. "Now sit down."

I sat on the paper and she dragged up another chair, but didn't put no paper on it.

"What is it? Where is Lone?"

"He died," I said.

She pulled in her breath and went white. She stared at me until her eyes started to water.

"You sick?" I asked her. "Go ahead, throw up. It'll make you feel better."

"Dead? Lone is dead?"

"Yeah. There was a flash flood last week and when he went out the next night in that big wind, he walked under a old oak tree that got gullied under by the flood. The tree come down on him."

"*Came* down on him," she whispered. "Oh, no . . . it's not true."

"It's true, all right. We planted him this morning. We couldn't keep him around no more. He was beginning to st–"

"Stop!" She covered her face with her hands.

"What's the matter?"

"I'll be all right in a moment," she said in a low voice. She went and stood in front of the fireplace with her back to me. I took off one of my shoes while I was waiting for her to come back. But instead she talked from where she was. "Are you Lone's little boy?"

"Yeah. He told me to come to you."

"Oh, my dear child!" She came running back and I thought for a second she was going to pick me up or something, but she stopped short and wrinkled up her nose a little bit. "Wh-what's your name?"

"Gerry," I told her.

"Well, Gerry, how would you like to live with me in this nice big house and–and have new clean clothes–and everything?"

"Well, that's the whole idea. Lone told me to come to you. He said you got more dough than you know what to do with, and he said you owed him a favor."

"A favor?" That seemed to bother her.

"Well," I tried to tell her, "he said he done something for you once and you said some day you'd pay him back for it if you ever could. This is it."

"What did he tell you about that?" She'd got her honk back by then.

"Not a damn thing."

"Please don't use that word," she said, with her eyes closed. Then she opened them and nodded her head. "I promised and I'll do it. You can live here from now on. If–if you want to."

"That's got nothin' to do with it. Lone *told* me to."

"You'll be happy here," she said. She gave me an up-and-down. "I'll see to that."

"Okay. Shall I go get the other kids?"

"*Other* kids–children?"

"Yeah. This ain't for just me. For all of us–the whole gang."

"Don't say 'ain't.'" She leaned back in her chair, took out a silly little handkerchief and dabbed her lips with it, looking at me the whole time. "Now tell me about these–these other children."

"Well, there's Janie, she's eleven like me. And Bonnie and Beanie are eight, they're twins, and Baby. Baby is three."

I screamed. Stern was kneeling beside the couch in a flash, hold-his palms against my cheeks to hold my head still; I'd been whipping it back and forth.

"Good boy," he said. "You found it. You haven't found out *what* it is, but now you know *where* it is."

"But for sure," I said hoarsely. "Got water?"

He poured me some water out of a thermos flask. It was so cold it hurt. I lay back and rested, like I'd climbed a cliff. I said, "I can't take anything like that again."

"You want to call it quits for today?"

"What about you?"

"I'll go on as long as you want me to."

I thought about it. "I'd like to go on, but I don't want no thumping around. Not for a while yet."

"If you want another of those inaccurate analogies," Stern said, "psychiatry is like a road map. There are always a lot of different ways to get from one place to another place."

"I'll go around by the long way," I told him. "The eight-lane highway. Not that track over the hill. My clutch is slipping. Where do I turn off?"

He chuckled. I liked the sound of it. "Just past that gravel driveway."

"I been there. There's a bridge washed out."

"You've been on this whole road before," he told me. "Start at the other side of the bridge."

"I never thought of that. I figured I had to do the whole thing, every inch."

"Maybe you won't have to, maybe you will, but the bridge will be easy to cross when you've covered everything else. Maybe there's nothing of value on the bridge and maybe there is, but you can't get near it till you've looked everywhere else."

"Let's go." I was real eager, somehow.

"Mind a suggestion?"

"No."

"Just talk," he said. "Don't try to get too far into what you're saying. That first stretch, when you were eight—you really lived it. The second one, all about the kids, you just talked about. Then, the visit when you were eleven, you felt that. Now just talk again."

"All right."

He waited, then said quietly, "In the library. You told her about the other kids."

I told her about . . . and then she said . . . and something happened, and I screamed. She comforted me and I cussed at her.

But we're not thinking about that now. We're going on.

In the library. The leather, the table, and whether I'm able to do with Miss Kew what Lone said.

What Lone said was, "There's a woman lives up on the top of the hill in the Heights section, name of Kew. She'll have to take care of you. You got to get her to do that. Do everything she tells you, only stay together. Don't you ever let any one of you get away from the others, hear? Aside from that, just you keep Miss Kew happy and she'll keep you happy. Now you do what I say." That's what Lone said. Between every word there was a link like steel cable, and the whole thing made something that couldn't be broken. Not by me it couldn't.

Miss Kew said, "Where are your sisters and the baby?"

"I'll bring 'em."

"Is it near here?"

"Near enough." She didn't say anything to that, so I got up. "I'll be back soon."

"Wait," she said. "I–really, I haven't had time to think. I mean –I've got to get things ready, you know."

I said, "You don't need to think and you are ready. So long." From the door I heard her saying, louder and louder as I walked away, "Young man, if you're to live in this house, you'll learn to be a good deal better-mannered–" and a lot more of the same.

I yelled back at her, "Okay, *okay!*" and went out.

The sun was warm and the sky was good, and pretty soon I got back to Lone's house. The fire was out and Baby stunk. Janie had knocked over her easel and was sitting on the floor by the door with her head in her hands. Bonnie and Beanie were on a stool with their arms around each other, pulled up together as close as they could get, as if it was cold in there, although it wasn't.

I hit Janie in the arm to snap her out of it. She raised her head. She had gray eyes–or maybe it was more a kind of green–but now they had a funny look about them, like water in a glass that had some milk left in the bottom of it.

I said, "What's the matter around here?"

"What's the matter with what?" she wanted to know.

"All of yez," I said.

She said, "We don't give a damn, that's all."

"Well, all right," I said, "but we got to do what Lone said. Come on."

"No."

I looked at the twins. They turned their backs on me. Janie said, "They're hungry."

"Well, why not give 'em something?"

She just shrugged. I sat down. What did Lone have to go get himself squashed for?

"We can't blesh no more," said Janie. It seemed to explain everything.

"Look," I said, "I've got to be Lone now."

Janie thought about that and Baby kicked his feet. Janie looked at him. "You can't," she said.

"I know where to get the heavy food and the turpentine," I said. "I can find that springy moss to stuff in the logs, and cut wood, and all."

But I couldn't call Bonnie and Beanie from miles away to unlock doors. I couldn't just say a word to Janie and make her get water and blow up the fire and fix the battery. I couldn't make us blesh.

We all stayed like that for a long time. Then I heard the bassinet creak. I looked up. Janie was staring into it.

"All right," she said. "Let's go."

"Who says so?"

"Baby."

"Who's running things now?" I said, mad. "Me or Baby?"

"Baby," Janie said.

I got up and went over to bust her one in the mouth, and then I stopped. If Baby could make them do what Lone wanted, then it would get done. If I started pushing them all around, it wouldn't. So I didn't say anything. Janie got up and walked out the door. The twins watched her go. Then Bonnie disappeared. Beanie picked up Bonnie's clothes and walked out. I got Baby out of the bassinet and draped him over my shoulders.

It was better when we were all outside. It was getting late in the day and the air was warm. The twins flitted in and out of the trees like a couple of flying squirrels, and Janie and I walked along like we were going swimming or something. Baby started to kick, and Janie looked at him a while and got him fed, and he was quiet again.

When we came close to town, I wanted to get everybody close together, but I was afraid to say anything. Baby must of said it instead. The twins came back to us and Janie gave them their clothes and they walked ahead of us, good as you please. I don't know how Baby did it. They sure hated to travel that way.

We didn't have no trouble except one guy we met on the street near Miss Kew's place. He stopped in his tracks and gaped at us, and Janie looked at him and made his hat go so far down over his eyes that he like to pull his neck apart getting it back up again.

What do you know, when we got to the house somebody had washed off all the dirt I put on the door. I had one hand on Baby's arm and one on his ankle and him draped over my neck, so I kicked the door and left some more dirt.

"There's a woman here name of Miriam," I told Janie. "She says anything, tell her to go to hell."

The door opened and there was Miriam. She took one look and jumped back six feet. We all trailed inside. Miriam got her wind and screamed, "Miss Kew! Miss Kew!"

"Go to hell," said Janie, and looked at me. I didn't know what to do. It was the first time Janie ever did anything I told her to.

Miss Kew came down the stairs. She was wearing a different dress, but it was just as stupid and had just as much lace. She opened her mouth and nothing came out, so she just left it open until something happened. Finally she said, "Dear gentle Lord preserve us!"

The twins lined up and gawked at her. Miriam sidled over to the wall and sort of slid along it, keeping away from us, until she could get to the door and close it. She said, "Miss Kew, if those are the children you said were going to live here, I quit."

Janie said, "Go to hell."

Just then Bonnie squatted down on the rug. Miriam squawked and jumped at her. She grabbed hold of Bonnie's arm and went to snatch her up. Bonnie disappeared, leaving Miriam with one small dress and the damnedest expression on her face. Beanie grinned enough to split her head in two and started to wave like mad. I looked where she was waving, and there was Bonnie, naked as a jay-bird, up on the banister at the top of the stairs.

Miss Kew turned around and saw her and sat down plump on the steps. Miriam went down, too, like she'd been slugged. Beanie picked up Bonnie's dress and walked up the steps past Miss Kew and handed it over. Bonnie put it on. Miss Kew sort of lolled around and looked up. Bonnie and Beanie came back down the stairs hand in hand to where I was. Then they lined up and gaped at Miss Kew.

"What's the matter with her?" Janie asked me.

"She gets sick every once in a while."

"Let's go back home."

"No," I told her.

Miss Kew grabbed the banister and pulled herself up. She stood there hanging on to it for a while with her eyes closed. All of a sudden she stiffened herself. She looked about four inches taller. She came marching over to us.

"Gerard," she honked.

I think she was going to say something different. But she sort of checked herself and pointed. "What in heaven's name is *that?*" And she aimed her finger at me.

I didn't get it right away, so I turned around to look behind me. "What?"

"That! That!"

"Oh!" I said. "That's Baby."

I slung him down off my back and held him up for her to look at. She made a sort of moaning noise and jumped over and took him away from me. She held him out in front of her and moaned again and called him a poor little thing, and ran to put him down on a long bench with cushions under the colored-glass window. She bent over him and put her knuckle in her mouth and bit on it and moaned some more. Then she turned to me.

"How long has he been like this?"

I looked at Janie and she looked at me. I said, "He's always been like he is."

She made a sort of cough and ran to where Miriam was lying flaked out on the floor. She slapped Miriam's face a couple of times back and forth. Miriam sat up and looked us over. She closed her eyes and shivered and sort of climbed up Miss Kew hand over hand until she was on her feet.

"Pull yourself together," said Miss Kew between her teeth. "Get a basin with some hot water and soap. Washcloth. Towels. Hurry!" She gave Miriam a big push. Miriam staggered and grabbed at the wall, and then ran out.

Miss Kew went back to Baby and hung over him, titch-titching with her lips all tight.

"Don't mess with him," I said. "There's nothin' wrong with him. We're hungry."

She gave me a look like I'd punched her. "Don't speak to me!"

"Look," I said, "we don't like this any more'n you do. If Lone hadn't told us to, we wouldn't never have come. We were doing all right where we were."

"Don't say 'wouldn't never,'" said Miss Kew. She looked at all of us, one by one. Then she took that silly little hunk of handkerchief and pushed it against her mouth.

"See?" I said to Janie. "All the time gettin' sick."

"Ho-ho," said Bonnie.

Miss Kew gave her a long look. "Gerard," she said in a choked sort of voice, "I understood you to say that these children were your sisters."

"Well?"

She looked at me as if I was real stupid. "We don't have little colored girls for sisters, Gerard."

Janie said, "*We* do."

Miss Kew walked up and back, real fast. "We have a great deal to do," she said, talking to herself.

Miriam came in with a big oval pan and towels and stuff on her arm. She put it down on the bench thing and Miss Kew stuck the back of her hand in the water, then picked up Baby and dunked him right in it. Baby started to kick.

I stepped forward and said, "Wait a minute. Hold on now. What do you think you're doing?"

Janie said, "Shut up, Gerry. He says it's all right."

"All right? She'll drown him."

"No, she won't. Just shut up."

Working up a froth with the soap, Miss Kew smeared it on Baby and turned him over a couple of times and scrubbed at his head and like to smothered him in a big white towel. Miriam stood gawking while Miss Kew lashed up a dishcloth around him so it come out pants. When she was done, you wouldn't of known it was the same baby. And by the time Miss Kew finished with the job, she seemed to have a better hold on herself. She was breathing hard and her mouth was even tighter. She held out the baby to Miriam.

"Take this poor thing," she said, "and put him—"

But Miriam backed away. "I'm sorry, Miss Kew, but I am leaving here and I don't care."

Miss Kew got her honk out. "You can't leave me in a predicament like this! These children need help. Can't you see that for yourself?"

Miriam looked me and Janie over. She was trembling. "You ain't safe, Miss Alicia. They ain't just dirty. They're crazy!"

"They're victims of neglect, and probably no worse than you or I would be if we'd been neglected. And don't say 'ain't.' Gerard!"

"What?"

"Don't say—oh, dear, we have so much to do. Gerard, if you and your—these other children are going to live here, you shall have to make a great many changes. You cannot live under this roof and behave as you have so far. Do you understand that?"

"Oh, sure. Lone said we was to do whatever you say and keep you happy."

"Will you do whatever I say?"

"That's what I just said, isn't it?"

"Gerard, you shall have to learn not to speak to me in that tone. Now, young man, if I told you to do what Miriam says, too, would you do it?"

I said to Janie, "What about that?"

"I'll ask Baby." Janie looked at Baby and Baby wobbled his hands and drooled some. She said, "It's okay."

Miss Kew said, "Gerard, I asked you a question."

"Keep your pants on," I said. "I got to find out, don't I? Yes, if that's what you want, we'll listen to Miriam too."

Miss Kew turned to Miriam. "You hear that, Miriam?"

Miriam looked at Miss Kew and at us and shook her head. Then she held out her hands a bit to Bonnie and Beanie.

They went right to her. Each one took hold of a hand. They looked up at her and grinned. They were probably planning some sort of hellishness, but I guess they looked sort of cute. Miriam's mouth twitched and I thought for a second she was going to look human. She said, "All right, Miss Alicia."

Miss Kew walked over and handed her the baby and she started upstairs with him. Miss Kew herded us along after Miriam. We all went upstairs.

They went to work on us then and for three years they never stopped.

"That was hell," I said to Stern.

"They had their work cut out."

"Yeah, I s'pose they did. So did we. Look, we were going to do exactly what Lone said. Nothing on earth could of stopped us from doing it. We were tied and bound to doing every last little thing Miss Kew said to do. But she and Miriam never seemed to understand that. I guess they felt they had to push every inch of the way. All they had to do was make us understand what they wanted, and we'd of done it. That's okay when it's something like telling me not to climb into bed with Janie. Miss Kew raised holy hell over that. You'd of thought I'd robbed the Crown jewels, the way she acted.

"But when it's something like, 'You must behave like little ladies and gentlemen,' it just doesn't mean a thing. And two out of three orders she gave us were like that. 'Ah-ah!' she'd say. 'Language, language!' For the longest time I didn't dig that at all. I finally asked her what the hell she meant, and then she finally come out with it. But you see what I mean."

"I certainly do," Stern said. "Did it get easier as time went on?"

"We only had real trouble twice, once about the twins and once about Baby. That one was real bad."

"What happened?"

"About the twins? Well, when we'd been there about a week or so we began to notice something that sort of stunk. Janie and me, I mean. We began to notice that we almost never got to see Bonnie and Beanie. It was like that house was two houses, one part for Miss Kew and Janie and me, and the other part for Miriam and the twins. I guess we'd have noticed it sooner if things hadn't been such a hassel at first, getting us into new clothes and making us sleep all the time at night, and all that. But here was the thing: We'd all get turned out in the side yard to play, and then along comes lunch, and the twins got herded off to eat with Miriam while we ate with Miss Kew. So Janie said, 'Why don't the twins eat with us?'

" 'Miriam's taking care of them, dear,' Miss Kew says.

"Janie looked at her with those eyes. 'I know that. Let 'em eat here and I'll take care of 'em.'

"Miss Kew's mouth got all tight again and she said, 'They're little colored girls, Jane. Now eat your lunch.'

"But that didn't explain anything to Janie or me, either. I said, 'I want 'em to eat with us. Lone said we should stay together.'

" 'But you *are* together,' she says. 'We all live in the same house. We all eat the same food. Now let us not discuss the matter.'

"I looked at Janie and she looked at me and she said, 'So why can't we all do this livin' and eatin' right here?'

"Miss Kew put down her fork and looked hard. 'I have explained it to you and I have said that there will be no further discussion.'

"Well, I thought that was real nowhere. So I just rocked back my head and bellowed, 'Bonnie! Beanie!' And *bing,* there they were.

"So all hell broke loose. Miss Kew ordered them out and they wouldn't go, and Miriam come steaming in with their clothes, and she couldn't catch them, and Miss Kew got to honking at them and finally at me. She said this was too much. Well, maybe she'd had a hard week, but so had we. So Miss Kew ordered us to leave.

"I went and got Baby and started out, and along came Janie and the twins. Miss Kew waited till we were all out the door and next thing you know she ran out after us. She passed us and got in front of me and made me stop. So we all stopped.

" 'Is this how you follow Lone's wishes?' she asked.

"I told her yes. She said she understood Lone wanted us to stay with her. And I said, 'Yeah, but he wanted us to stay together more.'

"She said come back in, we'd have a talk. Janie asked Baby and Baby said okay, so we went back. We had a compromise. We didn't eat in the dining room no more. There was a side porch, a sort of verandah thing with glass windows, with a door to the dining room and a door to the kitchen, and we all ate out there after that. Miss Kew ate by herself.

"But something funny happened because of that whole cockeyed hassle."

"What was that?" Stern asked me.

I laughed. "Miriam. She looked and sounded like always but she started slipping us cookies between meals. You know, it took me years to figure out what all that was about. I mean it. From what I've learned about people, there seems to be two armies fightin' about race. One's fightin' to keep 'em apart, and one's fightin' to get 'em together. But I don't see why both sides are so *worried* about it! Why don't they just forget it?"

"They can't. You see, Gerry, it's necessary for people to believe they are superior in some fashion. You and Lone and the kids—you were a pretty tight unit. Didn't you feel you were a little better than all of the rest of the world?"

"Better? How could we be better?"

"Different, then."

"Well, I suppose so, but we didn't think about it. Different, yes. Better, no."

"You're a unique case," Stern said. "Now go on and tell me about the other trouble you had. About Baby."

"Baby. Yeah. Well, that was a couple of months after we moved to Miss Kew's. Things were already getting real smooth, even then. We'd learned all the 'yes, ma'am, no, ma'am' routines by then and she'd got us catching up with school—regular periods morning and afternoon, five days a week. Janie had long ago quit taking care of Baby, and the twins walked to wherever they went. That was funny. They could pop from one place to another right in front of Miss Kew's eyes and she wouldn't believe what she saw. She was too upset about them suddenly showing up bare. They quit doing it and she was happy about it. She was happy about a lot of things. It had been years since she'd seen anybody—years. She'd even had the meters put outside the house so no one would ever have to come in. But with us there, she began to liven up. She quit wearing those old-lady dresses and began to look halfway human. She ate with us sometimes, even.

"But one fine day I woke up feeling real weird. It was like somebody had stolen something from me when I was asleep, only I didn't know what. I crawled out of my window and along the ledge into Janie's room, which I wasn't supposed to do. She was in bed. I went and woke her up. I can still see her eyes, the way they opened a little slit, still asleep, and then popped up wide. I didn't have to tell her something was wrong. She knew, and she knew what it was.

" 'Baby's gone!' she said.

"We didn't care then who woke up. We pounded out of her room and down the hall and into the little room at the end where Baby slept. You wouldn't believe it. The fancy crib he had and the white chest of drawers and all that mess of rattles and so on, they were gone, and there was just a writing desk there. I mean it was as if Baby had never been there at all.

"We didn't say anything. We just spun around and busted into Miss Kew's bedroom. I'd never been in there but once and Janie only a few times. But forbidden or not, this was different. Miss Kew was in bed, with her hair braided. She was wide awake before we could get across the room. She pushed herself back and up until she was sitting against the headboard. She gave the two of us the cold eye.

" 'What is the meaning of this?' she wanted to know.

" 'Where's Baby?' I yelled at her.

" 'Gerard,' she says, 'there is no need to shout.'

"Janie was a real quiet kid, but she said, 'You better tell us where he is, Miss Kew,' and it would of scared you to look at her when she said it.

"So all of a sudden Miss Kew took off the stone face and held out her hands to us. 'Children,' she said, 'I'm sorry. I really am sorry. But I've just done what is best. I've sent Baby away. He's gone to live with some children like him. We could never make him really happy here. You know that.'

"Janie said, 'He never told us he wasn't happy.'

"Miss Kew brought out a hollow kind of laugh. 'As if he could talk, the poor little thing!'

"'You better get him back here,' I said. 'You don't know what you're fooling with. I told you we wasn't ever to break up.'

"She was getting mad, but she held on to herself. 'I'll try to explain it to you, dear,' she said. 'You and Jane here and even the twins are all normal, healthy children and you'll grow up to be fine men and women. But poor Baby's–different. He's not going to grow very much more, and he'll never walk and play like other children.'

"'That doesn't matter,' Janie said. 'You had no call to send him away.'

"And I said, 'Yeah. You better bring him back, but quick.'

"Then she started to jump salty. 'Among the many things I have taught you is, I am sure, not to dictate to your elders. Now then, you run along and get dressed for breakfast, and we'll say no more about this.'

"I told her, nice as I could, 'Miss Kew, you're going to wish you brought him back right now. But you're going to bring him back soon. Or else.'

"So then she got up out of her bed and ran us out of the room."

I was quiet awhile, and Stern asked, "What happened?"

"Oh," I said, "she brought him back." I laughed suddenly. "I guess it's funny now, when you come to think of it. Nearly three months of us getting bossed around, and her ruling the roost, and then all of a sudden we lay down the law. We'd tried our best to be good according to her ideas, but, by God, that time she went too far. She got the treatment from the second she slammed her door on us. She had a big china pot under her bed, and it rose up in the air and smashed through her dresser mirror. Then one of the drawers in the dresser slid open and a glove come out of it and smacked her face.

"She went to jump back on the bed and a whole section of plaster fell off the ceiling onto the bed. The water turned on in her little bathroom and the plug went in, and just about the time it began to overflow, all her clothes fell off their hooks. She went to run out of the room, but the door was stuck, and when she yanked on the handle it opened real quick and she spread out on the floor. The door slammed shut again and more plaster come down on her. Then we went back in and stood looking at her. She was crying. I hadn't known till then that she could.

"'You going to get Baby back here?' I asked her.

"She just lay there and cried. After a while she looked up at us. It was real pathetic. We helped her up and got her to a chair. She just looked at us for a while, and at the mirror, and at the busted ceiling, and then she whispered, 'What happened? What happened?'

"'You took Baby away,' I said. 'That's what.'

"So she jumped up and said real low, real scared, but real strong: 'Something struck the house. An airplane. Perhaps there was an earthquake. We'll talk about Baby after breakfast.'

"I said, 'Give her more, Janie.'

"A big gob of water hit her on the face and chest and made her nightgown stick to her, which was the kind of thing that upset her most. Her braids stood straight up in the air, more and more, till they dragged her standing straight up. She opened her mouth to yell and the powder puff off the dresser rammed into it. She clawed it out.

"'What are you doing? What are you doing?' she says, crying again.

"Janie just looked at her and put her hands behind her, real smug. 'We haven't done anything,' she said.

"And I said, 'Not yet we haven't. You going to get Baby back?'

"And she screamed at us, 'Stop it! Stop it! Stop talking about that mongoloid idiot! It's no good to anyone, not even itself! How could I ever make believe it's mine?'

"I said, 'Get rats, Janie.'

"There was a scuttling sound along the baseboard. Miss Kew covered her face with her hands and sank down on the chair. 'Not rats,' she said. 'There are no rats here.' Then something squeaked and she went all to pieces. Did you ever see anyone really go to pieces?"

"Yes," Stern said.

"I was about as mad as I could get," I said, "but that was almost too much for me. Still, she shouldn't have sent Baby away. It took a couple of hours for her to get straightened out enough so she could use the phone, but we had Baby back before lunchtime." I laughed.

"What's funny?"

"She never seemed able to rightly remember what had happened to her. About three weeks later I heard her talking to Miriam about it. She said it was the house settling suddenly. She said it was a good thing she'd sent Baby out for that medical checkup—the poor little thing might have been hurt. She really believed it, I think."

"She probably did. That's fairly common. We don't believe anything we don't want to believe."

"How much of this do you believe?" I asked him suddenly.

"I told you before—it doesn't matter. I don't want to believe or disbelieve it."

"You haven't asked me how much of it I believe."

"I don't have to. You'll make up your own mind about that."

"Are you a *good* psychotherapist?"

"I think so," he said. "Whom did you kill?"

The question caught me absolutely off guard. "Miss Kew," I said. Then I started to cuss and swear. "I didn't mean to tell you that."

"Don't worry about it," he said. "What did you do it for?"

"That's what I came here to find out."

"You must have really hated her."

I started to cry. Fifteen years old and crying like that!

He gave me time to get it all out. The first part of it came out in noises, grunts and squeaks that hurt my throat. Much more than you'd think came out when my nose started to run. And finally—words.

"Do you know where I came from? The earliest thing I can remember is a punch in the mouth. I can still see it coming, a fist as big as my head. Because I was crying. I been afraid to cry ever since. I was crying because I was hungry. Cold, maybe. Both. After that, big dormitories, and whoever could steal the most got the most. Get the hell kicked out of you if you're bad, get a big reward if you're good. Big reward: they let you alone. Try to live like that. Try to live so the biggest, most wonderful thing in the whole damn world is just to have 'em let you alone!

"So a spell with Lone and the kids. Something wonderful: you belong. It never happened before. Two yellow bulbs and a fireplace and they light up the world. It's all there is and all there ever has to be.

"Then the big change: clean clothes, cooked food, five hours a day school; Columbus and King Arthur and a 1925 book on Civics that explains about septic tanks. Over it all a great big square-cut lump of ice, and you watch it melting and the corners curve, and you know it's because of you, Miss Kew . . . hell, she had too much control over herself ever to slobber over us, but it was there, that feeling. Lone took care of us because it was part of the way he lived. Miss Kew took care of us and none of it was the way she lived. It was something she wanted to do.

"She had a weird idea of 'right' and a wrong idea of 'wrong,' but she stuck to them, tried to make her ideas do us good. When she couldn't understand, she figured it was her own failure . . . and there was an almighty lot she didn't understand and never could. What went right was our success. What went wrong was her mistake. That last year, that was . . . oh, good."

"So?"

"So I killed her. Listen," I said. I felt I had to talk fast. I wasn't short of time, but I had to get rid of it. "I'll tell you all I know about it. The day before I killed her. I woke up in the morning and the sheets crackly clean under me, the sunlight coming in through white curtains and bright red-and-blue drapes. There's a closet full of my clothes–mine, you see; I never had anything that was really mine before–and downstairs Miriam clinking around with breakfast and the twins laughing. Laughing with *her,* mind you, not just with each other like they always did before.

"In the next room, Janie moving around, singing, and when I see her, I know her face will shine inside and out. I get up. There's *hot* hot water and the toothpaste bites my tongue. The clothes fit me and I go downstairs and they're all there and I'm glad to see them and they're glad to see me, and we no sooner get set around the table when Miss Kew comes down and everyone calls out to her at once.

"And the morning goes by like that, school with a recess, there in the big long living room. The twins with the ends of their tongues stuck out, drawing the alphabet instead of writing it, and then Janie, when it's time, painting a picture, a real picture of a cow with trees and a yellow fence that goes off into the distance. Here I am lost between the two parts of a quadratic equation, and Miss Kew bending close to help me, and I smell the sachet she has on her clothes. I hold up my head to smell it better, and far away I hear the shuffle and klunk of filled pots going on the stove back in the kitchen.

"And the afternoon goes by like that, more school and some study and boiling out into the yard, laughing. The twins chasing each other, running on their two feet to get where they want to go; Janie dappling the leaves in her picture, trying to get it just the way Miss Kew says it ought to be. And Baby, he's got a big playpen. He don't move around much any more, he just watches and dribbles some, and gets packed full of food and kept as clean as a new sheet of tinfoil.

"And supper, and the evening, and Miss Kew reading to us, changing her voice every time someone else talks in the story, reading fast and whispery when it embarrasses her, but reading every word all the same.

"And I had to go and kill her. And that's all."

"You haven't said why," Stern said.

"What are you–stupid?" I yelled.

Stern didn't say anything. I turned on my belly on the couch and propped up my chin in my hands and looked at him. You never could tell what was going on with him, but I got the idea that he was puzzled.

"I said why," I told him.

"Not to me."

I suddenly understood that I was asking too much of him. I said slowly, "We all woke up at the same time. We all did what somebody else wanted. We lived through a day someone else's way, thinking someone else's thoughts, saying other people's words. Janie painted someone else's pictures, Baby didn't talk to anyone, and we were all happy with it. Now do you see?"

"Not yet."

"God!" I said. I thought for a while. "We didn't blesh."

"Blesh? Oh. But you didn't after Lone died, either."

"That was different. That was like a car running out of gas, but the car's there—there's nothing wrong with it. It's just waiting. But after Miss Kew got done with us, the car was taken all to pieces, see?"

It was his turn to think a while. Finally he said, "The mind makes us do funny things. Some of them seem completely reasonless, wrong, insane. But the cornerstone of the work we're doing is this: there's a chain of solid, unassailable logic in the things we do. Dig deep enough and you find cause and effect as clearly in this field as you do in any other. I said *logic,* mind; I didn't say 'correctness' or 'rightness' or 'justice' or anything of the sort. Logic and truth are two very different things, but they often look the same to the mind that's performing the logic.

"When that mind is submerged, working at cross-purposes with the surface mind, then you're all confused. Now in your case, I can see the thing you're pointing at—that in order to preserve or to rebuild that peculiar bond between you kids, you had to get rid of Miss Kew. But I don't see the logic. I don't see that regaining that 'bleshing' was worth destroying this new-found security which you admit was enjoyable."

I said desperately, "Maybe it wasn't worth destroying it."

Stern leaned forward and pointed his pipe at me. "It *was* because it made you do what you did. After the fact, maybe things look different. But when you were moved to do it, the important thing was to destroy Miss Kew and regain this thing you'd had before. I don't see why and neither do you."

"How are we going to find out?"

"Well, let's get to the most unpleasant part, if you're up to it."

I lay down. "I'm ready."

"All right. Tell me everything that happened just before you killed her."

I fumbled through that last day, trying to taste the food, hear the voices. A thing came and went and came again: it was the crisp feeling of the sheets. I thrust it away because it was at the beginning of that day, but it came back again, and I realized it was at the end, instead.

I said, "What I just told you, all that about the children doing things other people's way instead of their own, and Baby not talking, and everyone happy about it, and finally that I had to kill Miss Kew. It took a long time to get to that, and a long time to start doing it. I guess I lay in bed and thought for four hours before I got up again. It was dark and quiet. I went out of the room and down the hall and into Miss Kew's bedroom and killed her."

"How?"

"That's all there is!" I shouted as loud as I could. Then I quieted down. "It was awful dark . . . it still is. I don't know. I don't want to know. She did love us. I know she did. But I had to kill her."

"All right, all right," Stern said. "I guess there's no need to get too gruesome about this. You're–"

"What?"

"You're quite strong for your age, aren't you, Gerard?"

"I guess so. Strong enough, anyway."

"Yes," he said.

"I still don't see that logic you were talking about." I began to hammer on the couch with my fist, hard, once for each word: "Why–did –I–have–to–go–and–do–that?"

"Cut that out," he said. "You'll hurt yourself."

"I ought to get hurt," I said.

"Ah?" said Stern.

I got up and went to the desk and got some water. "What am I going to do?"

"Tell me what you did after you killed her, right up until the time you came here."

"Not much," I said. "It was only last night. I took her checkbook. I went back to my room, sort of numb. I put all my clothes on except my shoes. I carried them. I went out. Walked a long time, trying to think, went to the bank when it opened. Cashed a check for eleven hundred bucks. Got the idea of getting some help from a psychiatrist, spent most of the day looking for one, came here. That's all."

"Didn't you have any trouble cashing the check?"

"I never have any trouble making people do what I want them to do."

He gave a surprised grunt.

"I know what you're thinking–I couldn't make Miss Kew do what I wanted."

"That's part of it," he admitted.

"If I had of done that," I told him, "she wouldn't of been Miss Kew any more. Now the banker–all I made him do was be a banker."

I looked at him and suddenly realized why he fooled with the pipe all the time. It was so he could look down at it and you wouldn't be able to see his eyes.

"You killed her," he said–and I knew he was changing the subject–"and destroyed something that was valuable to you. It must have been less valuable to you than the chance to rebuild this thing you used to have with the other kids. And you're not sure of the value of that." He looked up. "Does that describe your main trouble?"

"Just about."

"You know the single thing that makes people kill?" When I didn't answer, he said, "Survival. To save the self or something which identifies with the self. And in this case that doesn't apply, because your setup with Miss Kew had far more survival value for you, singly and as a group, than the other."

"So maybe I just didn't have a good enough reason to kill her."

"You had, because you did it. We just haven't located it yet. I mean we have the reason, but we don't know why it was important enough. The answer is somewhere in you."

"Where?"

He got up and walked some. "We have a pretty consecutive life story here. There's fantasy mixed with the fact, of course, and there are areas in which we have no detailed information, but we have a beginning and a middle and an end. Now I can't say for sure, but the answer may be in that bridge you refused to cross a while back. Remember?"

I remembered all right. I said, "Why that? Why can't we try something else?"

He quietly pointed out, "Because you just said it. Why are you shying away from it?"

"Don't go making big ones out of little ones," I said. Sometimes the guy annoyed me. "That bothers me. I don't know why, but it does."

"Something's lying hidden in there and you're bothering *it* so it's fighting back. Anything that fights to stay concealed is very possibly the thing we're after. Your trouble is concealed, isn't it?"

"Well, yes," I said, and I felt that sickness and faintness again, and again I pushed it away. Suddenly I wasn't going to be stopped any more. "Let's go get it." I lay down.

He let me watch the ceiling and listen to silence for a while, and then he said, "You're in the library. You've just met Miss Kew. She's talking to you; you're telling her about the children."

I lay very still. Nothing happened. Yes, it did; I got tense inside all over, from the bones out, more and more. When it got as bad as it could, still nothing happened.

I heard him get up and cross the room to the desk. He fumbled there for a while; things clicked and hummed. Suddenly I heard my own voice:

"Well, there's Janie, she's eleven like me. And Bonnie and Beanie are eight, they're twins, and Baby. Baby is three."

And the sound of my own scream—

And nothingness.

Sputtering out of the darkness, I came up flailing with my fists. Strong hands caught my wrists. They didn't check my arms; they just grabbed and rode. I opened my eyes. I was soaking wet. The thermos lay on its side on the rug. Stern was crouched beside me, holding my wrists. I quit struggling.

"What happened?"

He let me go and stood back watchfully. "Lord," he said, "what a charge!"

I held my head and moaned. He threw me a hand towel and I used it. "What hit me?"

"I've had you on tape the whole time," he explained. "When you wouldn't get into the recollection, I tried to nudge you into it by using your own voice as you recounted it before. It works wonders sometimes."

"It worked wonders this time," I growled. "I think I blew a fuse."

"In effect, you did. You were on the trembling verge of going into the thing you don't want to remember, and you let yourself go unconscious rather than do it."

"What are you so pleased about?"

"Last-ditch defense," he said tersely. "We've got it now. Just one more try."

"Now hold on. The last-ditch defense is that I drop dead."

"You won't. You've contained this episode in your subconscious mind for a long time and it hasn't hurt you."

"Hasn't it?"

"Not in terms of killing you."

"How do you know it won't when we drag it out?"

"You'll see."

I looked up at him sideways. Somehow he struck me as knowing what he was doing.

"You know a lot more about yourself now than you did at the time," he explained softly. "You can apply insight. You can evaluate it as it comes up. Maybe not completely, but enough to protect yourself. Don't worry. Trust me. I can stop it if it gets too bad. Now just relax. Look at the ceiling. Be aware of your toes. Don't look at your toes. Look straight up. Your toes, your big toes. Don't move your toes, but feel them. Count outward from your big toes, one count for each toe. One, two, three. Feel that third toe. Feel the toe, feel it, feel it go limp, go limp, go limp. The toe next to it on both sides gets limp. So limp because your toes are limp, all of your toes are limp–"

"What are you doing?" I shouted at him.

He said in the same silky voice, "You trust me and so do your toes trust me. They're all limp because you trust me. You–"

"You're trying to hypnotize me. I'm not going to let you do that."

"You're going to hypnotize yourself. You do everything yourself. I just point the way. I point your toes to the path. Just point your toes. No one can make you go anywhere you don't want to go, but you want to go where your toes are pointed where your toes are limp where your . . ."

On and on and on. And where was the dangling gold ornament, the light in the eyes, the mystic passes? He wasn't even sitting where I could see him. Where was the talk about how sleepy I was supposed to be? Well, he knew I wasn't sleepy and didn't want to be sleepy. I just wanted to be toes. I just wanted to be limp, just a limp toe. No brains in a toe, a toe to go, go, go eleven times, eleven, I'm eleven . . .

I split in two, and it was all right, the part that watched the part that went back to the library, and Miss Kew leaning toward me, but not too near, me with the newspaper crackling under me on the library chair, me with one shoe off and my limp toes dangling . . . and I felt a mild surprise at this. For this was hypnosis, but I was quite conscious, quite altogether there on the couch with Stern droning away at me, quite able to roll over and sit up and talk to him and walk out if I wanted to, but I just didn't want to. Oh, if this was what hypnosis was like, I was all for it. I'd work at this. This was all right.

There on the table I'm able to see that the gold will unfold on the leather, and whether I'm able to stay by the table with you, with Miss Kew, with Miss Kew . . .

". . . and Bonnie and Beanie are eight, they're twins, and Baby. Baby is three."

"Baby is three," she said.

There was a pressure, a stretching apart, and a . . . a breakage. And with a tearing agony and a burst of triumph that drowned the pain, it was done.

And this is what was inside. All in one flash, but all this.

Baby is three? My baby would be three if there were a baby, which there never was . . .

Lone, I'm open to you. Open, is this open enough?

His irises like wheels. I'm sure they spin, but I never catch them at it. The probe that passes invisibly from his brain, through his eyes, into mine. Does he know what it means to me? Does he care? He doesn't care, he doesn't know; he empties me and I fill as he directs me to; he drinks and waits and drinks again and never looks at the cup.

When I saw him first, I was dancing in the wind, in the woods, in the wild, and I spun about and he stood there in the leafy shadows, watching me. I hated him for it. It was not my wood, not my gold-spangled fern-tangled glen. But it was my dancing that he took, freezing it forever by being there. I hated him for it, hated the way he looked, the way he stood, ankle-deep in the kind wet ferns, looking like a tree with roots for feet and clothes the color of earth. As I stopped he moved, and then he was just a man, a great ape-shouldered, dirty animal of a man, and all my hate was fear suddenly and I was just as frozen.

He knew what he had done and he didn't care. Dancing . . . never to dance again, because never would I know the woods were free of eyes, free of tall, uncaring, dirty animal men. Summer days with the clothes choking me, winter nights with the precious decencies round and about me like a shroud, and never to dance again, never to remember dancing without remembering the shock of knowing he had seen me. How I hated him! Oh, how I hated him!

To dance alone where no one knew, that was the single thing I hid to myself when I was known as Miss Kew, that Victorian, older than her years, later than her time; correct and starched, lace and linen and lonely. Now indeed I would be all they said, through and through, forever and ever, because he had robbed me of the one thing I dared to keep secret.

He came out into the sun and walked to me, holding his great head a little on one side. I stood where I was, frozen inwardly and outwardly and altogether by the core of anger and the layer of fear. My arm was still out, my waist still bent from my dance, and when he stopped, I breathed again because by then I had to.

He said, "You read books?"

I couldn't bear to have him near me, but I couldn't move. He put out his hard hand and touched my jaw, turned my head up until I had to look into his face. I cringed away from him, but my face would not leave his hand, though he was not holding it, just lifting it. "You got to read some books for me. I got no time to find them."

I asked him, "Who are you?"

"Lone," he said. "You going to read books for me?"

"No. Let me go, let me go!" He wasn't holding me.

"What books?" I cried.

He thumped my face, not very hard. It made me look up a bit more. He dropped his hand away. His eyes, the irises were going to spin. . . .

"Open up in there," he said. "Open way up and let me see."

There were books in my head, and he was looking at the titles . . . he was not looking at the titles, for he couldn't read. He was looking at what I knew of the books. I suddenly felt terribly useless, because I had only a fraction of what he wanted.

"What's that?" he barked.

I knew what he meant. He'd gotten it from inside my head. I didn't know it was in there, even, but he found it.

"Telekinesis," I said.

"How is it done?"

"Nobody knows if it can be done. Moving physical objects with the mind!"

"It can be done," he said. "This one?"

"Teleportation. That's the same thing–well, almost. Moving your own body with mind power."

"Yeah, yeah, I see it," he said gruffly.

"Molecular interpenetration. Telepathy and clairvoyance. I don't know anything about them. I think they're silly."

"Read about 'em. It don't matter if you understand or not. What's this?"

It was there in my brain, on my lips. *"Gestalt."*

"What's that?"

"Group. Like a cure for a lot of diseases with one kind of treatment. Like a lot of thoughts expressed in one phrase. The whole is greater than the sum of the parts."

"Read about that, too. Read a whole lot about that. That's the *most* you got to read about. That's important."

He turned away, and when his eyes came away from mine it was like something breaking, so that I staggered and fell to one knee. He went off into the woods without looking back. I got my things and ran home. There was anger, and it struck me like a storm. There was fear, and it struck me like a wind. I knew I would read the books, I knew I would come back, I knew I would never dance again.

So I read the books and I came back. Sometimes it was every day for three or four days, and sometimes, because I couldn't find a certain book, I might not come back for ten. He was always there in the little glen, waiting, standing in the shadows, and he took what he wanted of the books and nothing of me. He never mentioned the next meeting. If he came there every day to wait for me, or if he only came when I did, I have no way of knowing.

He made me read books that contained nothing for me, books on evolution, on social and cultural organization, on mythology, and ever so much on symbiosis. What I had with him were not conversations; sometimes nothing audible would pass between us but his grunt of surprise or small, short hum of interest.

He tore the books out of me the way he would tear berries from a bush, all at once; he smelled of sweat and earth and the green juices his heavy body crushed when he moved through the woods.

If he learned anything from the books, it made no difference in him.

There came a day when he sat by me and puzzled something out.

He said, "What book has something like this?" Then he waited for a long time, thinking. "The way a termite can't digest wood, you know, and microbes in the termite's belly can, and what the termite eats is what the microbe leaves behind. What's that?"

"Symbiosis," I remembered. I remembered the words. Lone tore the content from words and threw the words away. "Two kinds of life depending upon one another for existence."

"Yeah. Well, is there a book about four, five kinds doing that?"

"I don't know."

Then he asked, "What about this? You got a radio station, you got four, five receivers, each receiver is fixed up to make something different happen, like one digs and one flies and one makes noise, but each one takes orders from the one place. And each one has its own power and its own thing to do, but they are all apart. Now: is there life like that, instead of radio?"

"Where each organism is a part of the whole, but separated? I don't think so . . . unless you mean social organizations, like a team, or perhaps a gang of men working, all taking orders from the same boss."

"No," he said immediately, "not like that. Like one single animal." He made a gesture with his cupped hand which I understood.

I asked, "You meant a *gestalt* life-form? It's fantastic."

"No book has about that, huh?"

"None I ever heard of."

"I got to know about that," he said heavily. "There is such a thing. I want to know if it ever happened before."

"I can't see how anything of the sort could exist."

"It does. A part that fetches, a part that figures, a part that finds out, and a part that talks."

"Talks? Only humans talk."

"I know," he said, and got up and went away.

I looked and looked for such a book but found nothing remotely like it. I came back and told him so. He was still a very long time, looking off to the blue-on-blue line of the hilly horizon. Then he drove those about-to-spin irises at me and searched.

"You learn, but you don't think," he said, and looked again at the hills.

"This all happens with humans," he said eventually. "It happens piece by piece right under folks' noses, and they don't see it. You got mind readers. You got people can move things with their mind. You got people can move themselves with their mind. You got people can figure anything out if you just think to ask them. What you ain't got is the one kind of person who can pull 'em all together, like a brain pulls together the parts that press and pull and feel heat and walk and think and all the other things.

"I'm one," he finished suddenly. Then he sat still for so long I thought he had forgotten me.

"Lone," I said, "what do you do here in the woods?"

"I wait," he said. "I ain't finished yet." He looked at my eyes and snorted in irritation. "I don't mean 'finished' like you're thinking. I mean I ain't–completed yet. You know about a worm when it's cut, growin' whole again? Well, forget about the cut. Suppose it just grew that way, for the first time, see? I'm getting parts. I ain't finished. I want a book about that kind of animal that is me when I'm finished."

"I don't know of such a book. Can you tell me more? Maybe if you could, I'd think of the right book or a place to find it."

He broke a stick between his huge hands, put the two pieces side by side and broke them together with one strong twist.

"All I know is I got to do what I'm doing like a bird's got to nest when it's time. And I know that when I'm done I won't be anything to brag about. I'll be like a body stronger and faster than anything there ever was, without the right kind of head on it. But maybe that's because I'm one of the first. That picture you had, the caveman . . ."

"Neanderthal."

"Yeah. Come to think of it, he was no great shakes. An early try at something new. That's what I'm going to be. But maybe the right kind of head'll come along after I'm all organized. Then it'll be something."

He grunted with satisfaction and went away.

I tried, for days I tried, but I couldn't find what he wanted. I found a magazine which stated that the next important evolutionary step in man would be in a psychic rather than a physical direction, but it said nothing about a–shall I call it a *gestalt* organism? There was something about slime molds, but they seem to be more a hive activity of amoebae than even a symbiosis.

To my own unscientific, personally uninterested mind, there was nothing like what he wanted except possibly a band marching together, everyone playing different instruments with different techniques and different notes, to make a single thing move along together. But he hadn't meant anything like that.

So I went back to him in the cool of an early fall evening, and he took what little I had in my eyes, and turned from me angrily with a gross word I shall not permit myself to remember.

"You can't find it," he told me. "Don't come back."

He got up and went to a tattered birch and leaned against it, looking out and down into the wind-tossed crackling shadows. I think he had forgotten me already. I know he leaped like a frightened animal when I spoke to him from so near. He must have been completely immersed in whatever strange thoughts he was having, for I'm sure he didn't hear me coming.

I said, "Lone, don't blame me for not finding it. I tried."

He controlled his startlement and brought those eyes down on me. "Blame? Who's blamin' anybody?"

"I failed you," I told him, "and you're angry."

He looked at me so long I became uncomfortable.

"I don't know what you're talkin' about," he said.

I wouldn't let him turn away from me. He would have. He would have left me forever with not another thought; he didn't *care!* It wasn't cruelty or thoughtlessness as I have been taught to know those things. He was as uncaring as a cat is of the bursting of a tulip bud.

I took him by the upper arms and shook him, it was like trying to shake the front of my house. "You *can* know!" I screamed at him. "You know what I read. You must know what I think!"

He shook his head.

"I'm a person, a woman," I raved at him. "You've used me and used me and you've given me nothing. You've made me break a lifetime of habits–reading until all hours, coming to you in the rain and on Sunday–you don't talk to me, you don't look at me, you don't know anything about me and you don't care. You put some sort of a spell on me that I couldn't break. And when you're finished, you say, 'Don't come back.' "

"Do I have to give something back because I took something?"

"People do."

He gave that short, interested hum. "What do you want me to give you? I ain't got anything."

I moved away from him. I felt . . . I don't know what I felt. After a time I said, "I don't know."

He shrugged and turned. I fairly leaped at him, dragging him back. "I want you to–"

"Well, damn it, what?"

I couldn't look at him; I could hardly speak. "I don't know. There's something, but I don't know what it is. It's something that–I couldn't say if I knew it." When he began to shake his head, I took his arms again. "You've read the books out of me; can't you read the . . . the *me* out of me?"

"I ain't never tried." He held my face up and stepped close. "Here," he said.

His eyes projected their strange probe at me and I screamed. I tried to twist away. I hadn't wanted this, I was sure I hadn't. I struggled terribly. I think he lifted me right off the ground with his big hands. He held me until he was finished, and then let me drop. I huddled to the ground, sobbing. He sat down beside me. He didn't try to touch me. He didn't try to go away. I quieted at last and crouched there, waiting.

He said, "I ain't going to do much of that no more."

I sat up and tucked my skirt close around me and laid my cheek on my updrawn knees so I could see his face. "What happened?"

He cursed. "Damn mishmash inside you. Thirty-three years old—what you want to live like that for?"

"I live very comfortably," I said with some pique.

"Yeah," he said. "All by yourself for ten years now 'cept for someone to do your work. Nobody else."

"Men are animals, and women . . ."

"You really hate women. They all know something you don't."

"I don't want to know. I'm quite happy the way I am."

"Hell you are."

I said nothing to that. I despise that kind of language.

"Two things you want from me. Neither makes no sense." He looked at me with the first real expression I have ever seen in his face: a profound wonderment. "You want to know all about me, where I came from, how I got to be what I am."

"Yes, I do want that. What's the other thing I want that you know and I don't?"

"I was born some place and growed like a weed somehow," he said, ignoring me. "Folks who didn't give even enough of a damn to try the orphanage routine. So I just ran loose, sort of in training to be the village idiot. I'da made it, but I took to the woods instead."

"Why?"

He wondered why, and finally said, "I guess because the way people lived didn't make no sense to me. Out here I can grow like I want."

"How is that?" I asked over one of those vast distances that built and receded between him and me so constantly.

"What I wanted to get from your books."

"You never told me."

For the second time he said, "You learn, but you don't think. There's a kind of—well, *person.* It's all made of separate parts, but it's all one person. It has like hands, it has like legs, it has like a talking mouth, and it has like a brain. That's me, a brain for that person. Damn feeble, too, but the best I know of."

"You're mad."

"No, I ain't," he said, unoffended and completely certain. "I already got the part that's like hands. I can move 'em anywhere and they do what I want, though they're too young yet to do much good. I got the part that talks. That one's real good."

"I don't think you talk very well at all," I said. I cannot stand incorrect English.

He was surprised. "I'm not talking about me! She's back yonder with the others."

"She?"

"The one that talks. Now I need one that thinks, one that can take anything and add it to anything else and come up with a right answer. And once they're all together, and all the parts get used together often enough, I'll be that new kind of thing I told you about. See? Only—I wish it had a better head on it than me."

My own head was swimming. "What made you start doing this?"

He considered me gravely. "What made you start growing hair in your armpits?" he asked me. "You don't figure a thing like that. It just happens."

"What is that . . . that thing you do when you look in my eyes?"

"You want a name for it? I ain't got one. I don't know how I do it. I know I can get anyone I want to do anything. Like you're going to forget about me."

I said in a choked voice, "I don't want to forget about you."

"You will." I didn't know then whether he meant I'd forget, or I'd *want* to forget. "You'll hate me, and then after a long time you'll be grateful. Maybe you'll be able to do something for me some time. You'll be that grateful that you'll be glad to do it. But you'll forget, all right, everything but a sort of . . . feeling. And my name, maybe."

I don't know what moved me to ask him, but I did, forlornly. "And no one will ever know about you and me?"

"Can't," he said. "Unless . . . well, unless it was the head of the animal, like me, or a better one." He heaved himself up.

"Oh, wait, wait!" I cried. He mustn't go yet, he mustn't. He was a tall, dirty beast of a man, yet he had enthralled me in some dreadful way. "You haven't given me the other . . . whatever it was."

"Oh," he said. "Yeah, that."

He moved like a flash. There was a pressure, a stretching apart, and a . . . a breakage. And with a tearing agony and a burst of triumph that drowned the pain, it was done.

I came up out of it, through two distinct levels:

I am eleven, breathless from shock from a transferred agony of that incredible entrance into the ego of another. And:

I am fifteen, lying on the couch while Stern drones on, " . . . quietly, quietly limp, your ankles and legs as limp as your toes, your belly goes soft, the back of your neck is as limp as your belly, it's quiet and easy and all gone soft and limper than limp. . . ."

I sat up and swung my legs to the floor. "Okay," I said.

Stern looked a little annoyed. "This is going to work," he said, "but it can only work if you cooperate. Just lie–"

"It did work," I said.

"What?"

"The whole thing. A to Z." I snapped my fingers. "Like that."

He looked at me piercingly. "What do you mean?"

"It was right there, where you said. In the library. When I was eleven. When she said, 'Baby is three.' It knocked loose something that had been boiling around in her for three years, and it all came blasting out. I got it, full force; just a kid, no warning, no defenses. It had such a–a pain in it, like I never knew could be."

"Go on," said Stern.

"That's really all. I mean that's not what was in it; it's what it did to me. What it was, a sort of hunk of her own self. A whole lot of things that happened over about four months, every bit of it. She knew Lone."

"You mean a whole *series* of episodes?"

"That's it."

"You got a series all at once? In a split second?"

"That's right. Look, for that split second I *was* her, don't you see? I was her, everything she'd ever done, everything she'd ever thought and heard and felt. Everything, everything, all in the right order if I wanted to bring it out like that. Any part of it if I wanted it by itself. If I'm going to tell you about what I had for lunch, do I have to tell you everything else I've ever done since I was born? No. I tell you I *was* her, and then and forever after I can remember anything she could remember up to that point. In just that one flash."

"A *gestalt,*" he murmured.

"Aha!" I said, and thought about that. I thought about a whole lot of things. I put them aside for a moment and said, "Why didn't I know all this before?"

"You had a powerful block against recalling it."

I got up excitedly. "I don't see why. I don't see that at all."

"Just natural revulsion," he guessed. "How about this? You had a distaste for assuming a female ego, even for a second."

"You told me yourself, right at the beginning, that I didn't have that kind of a problem."

"Well, how does this sound to you? You say you felt pain in that episode. So—you wouldn't go back into it for fear of re-experiencing the pain."

"Let me think, let me think. Yeah, yeah, that's part of it—that thing of going into someone's mind. She opened up to me because I reminded her of Lone. I went in. I wasn't ready; I'd never done it before, except maybe a little, against resistance. I went all the way in and it was too much; it frightened me away from trying it for years. And there it lay, wrapped up, locked away. But as I grew older, the power to do that with my mind got stronger and stronger, and still I was afraid to use it. And the more I grew, the more I felt, down deep, that Miss Kew had to be killed before she killed the . . . what I am. My God!" I shouted. "Do you know what I am?"

"No," he said. "Like to tell me about it?"

"I'd like to," I said. "Oh, yes, I'd like that."

He had that professional openminded expression on his face, not believing or disbelieving, just taking it all in. I had to tell him, and I suddenly realized that I didn't have enough words. I knew the things, but not the names for them.

Lone took the meanings and threw the words away.

Further back: *"You read books. Read books for me."*

The look of his eyes. That—"opening up" thing.

I went over to Stern. He looked up at me, I bent close. First he was startled, then he controlled it, then he came even closer to me.

"My God," he murmured. "I didn't look at those eyes before. I could have sworn those irises spun like wheels. . . ."

Stern read books. He'd read more books than I ever imagined had been written. I slipped in there, looking for what I wanted.

I can't say exactly what it was like. It was like walking in a tunnel, and in this tunnel, all over the roof and walls, wooden arms stuck out at you, like the thing at the carnival, the merry-go-round, the thing you snatch the brass rings from. There's a brass ring on the end of each of these arms, and you can take any one of them you want to.

Now imagine you make up your mind which rings you want, and the arms hold only those. Now picture yourself with a thousand hands to grab the rings off with. Now just suppose the tunnel is a zillion miles long, and you can go from one end of it to the other, grabbing rings, in just the time it takes you to blink once. Well, it was like that, only easier.

It was easier for me to do than it had been for Lone.

Straightening up, I got away from Stern. He looked sick and frightened.

"It's all right," I said.

"What did you do to me?"

"I needed some words. Come on, come on. Get professional."

I had to admire him. He put his pipe in his pocket and gouged the tips of his fingers hard against his forehead and cheeks. Then he sat up and he was okay again.

"I know," I said. "That's how Miss Kew felt when Lone did it to her."

"What *are* you?"

"I'll tell you. I'm the central ganglion of a complex organism which is composed of Baby, a computer; Bonnie and Beanie, teleports; Janie, telekineticist; and myself, telepath and central control. There isn't a single thing about any of us that hasn't been documented: the teleportation of the Yogi, the telekinetics of some gamblers, the idiot-savant mathematicians, and most of all, the so-called poltergeist, the moving about of household goods through the instrumentation of a young girl. Only in this case every one of my parts delivers at peak performance.

"Lone organized it, or it formed around him; it doesn't matter which. I replaced Lone, but I was too underdeveloped when he died, and on top of that I got an occlusion from that blast from Miss Kew. To that extent you were right when you said the blast made me subconsciously afraid to discover what was in it. But there was another good reason for my not being able to get in under that 'Baby is three' barrier.

"We ran into the problem of what it was I valued more than the security Miss Kew gave us. Can't you see now what it was? My *gestalt* organism was at the point of death from that security. I figured she had to be killed or it—*I*—would be. Oh, the parts would live on: two little colored girls with a speech impediment, one introspective girl with an artistic bent, one mongoloid idiot, and me—ninety percent short-circuited potentials and ten percent juvenile delinquent." I laughed. "Sure, she had to be killed. It was self-preservation for the *gestalt.*"

Stern bobbled around with his mouth and finally got out: "I don't—"

"You don't need to," I laughed. "This is wonderful. You're good—real good. Now I want to tell you this, because you can appreciate a fine point in your specialty. You talk about occlusions! I couldn't get past the 'Baby is three' thing because in it lay the clues to what I really am. I couldn't find that out because I was afraid to remember that I was two things—Miss Kew's little boy, and something a hell of a lot bigger. I couldn't be both, and I wouldn't release either one."

He said, with his eyes on his pipe, "Now you can?"

"I have."

"And what now?"

"What do you mean?"

Stern leaned back against the corner of his desk. "Did it occur to you that maybe this—*gestalt* organism of yours is already dead?"

"It isn't."

"How do you know?"

"How does your head know your arm works?"

He touched his face. "So . . . now what?"

I shrugged. "Did the Pekin man look at Homo Sap walking erect and say, 'Now what?' We'll live, that's all, like a man, like a tree, like anything else that lives. We'll feed and grow and experiment and breed. We'll defend ourselves." I spread my hands. "We'll just do what comes naturally."

"But what can you do?"

"What can an electric motor do? It depends on where we apply ourselves."

Stern was very pale. "Just what do you—*want* to do?"

I thought about that. He waited until I was quite finished thinking and didn't say anything. "Know what?" I said at last. "Ever since I was born, people been kicking me around, right up until Miss Kew took over. And what happened with her? She damn near killed me."

I thought some more, and said, "Everybody's had fun but me. The kind of fun everybody has is kicking someone around, someone small who can't fight back. Or they do you favors until they own you, or kill you." I looked at him and grinned. "I'm just going to have fun, that's all."

He turned his back. I think he was going to pace the floor, but right away he turned again. I knew then he would keep an eye on me. He said, "You've come a long way since you walked in here."

I nodded. "You're a *good* head-shrinker."

"Thanks," he said bitterly. "And you figure you're all cured now, all adjusted and ready to roll."

"Well sure. Don't you?"

He shook his head. "All you've found out is what you are. You have a lot more to learn."

I was willing to be patient. "Like?"

"Like finding out what happens to people who have to live with guilt like yours. You're different, Gerry, but you're not that different."

"I should feel guilty about saving my life?"

He ignored that. "One other thing: You said a while back that you'd been mad at everybody all your life—that's the way you lived. Have you ever wondered why?"

"Can't say I have."

"One reason is that you were so alone. That's why being with the other kids, and then with Miss Kew, came to mean so much."

"So? I've still got the kids."

He shook his head slowly. "You *and* the kids are a single creature. Unique. Unprecedented." He pointed the pipestem at me. *"Alone."*

The blood started to pound in my ears.

"Shut up," I said.

"Just think about it," he said softly. "You can do practically anything. You can have practically everything. And none of it will keep you from being alone."

"Shut up, shut up . . . Everybody's alone."

He nodded. "But some people learn how to live with it."

"How?"

He said, after a time, "Because of something you don't know anything about. It wouldn't mean anything to you if I told you."

"Tell me and see."

He gave me the strangest look. "It's sometimes called morality."

"I guess you're right. I don't know what you're talking about." I pulled myself together. I didn't have to listen to this. "You're afraid," I said. "You're afraid of *Homo gestalt.*"

He made a wonderful effort and smiled. "That's bastard terminology."

"We're a bastard breed," I said. I pointed. "Sit down over there."

He crossed the quiet room and sat at the desk. I leaned close to him and he went to sleep with his eyes open. I straightened up and looked around the room. Then I got the thermos flask and filled it and put it on the desk. I fixed the corner of the rug and put a clean towel at the head of the couch. I went to the side of the desk and opened it and looked at the tape recorder.

Like reaching out a hand, I got Beanie. She stood by the desk, wide-eyed.

"Look here," I told her. "Look good, now. What I want to do is erase all this tape. Go ask Baby how."

She blinked at me and sort of shook herself, and then leaned over the recorder. She was there—and gone—and back, just like that. She pushed past me and turned two knobs, moved a pointer until it clicked twice. The tape raced backward past the head swiftly, whining.

"All right," I said, "beat it."

She vanished.

I got my jacket and went to the door. Stern was still sitting at the desk, staring.

"A *good* head-shrinker," I murmured. I felt fine.

Outside I waited, then turned and went back in again.

Stern looked up at me. "Sit over there, Sonny."

"Gee," I said. "Sorry, sir. I got in the wrong office."

"That's all right," he said.

I went out and closed the door. All the way down to the police station I grinned. They'd take my report on Miss Kew and like it. And sometimes I laughed, thinking about this Stern, how he'd figure the loss of an afternoon and the gain of a thousand bucks. Much funnier than thinking about him being dead.

What the hell is morality, anyway?

PART THREE | MORALITY

"What's he to you, Miss Gerald?" demanded the sheriff.

"Gerard," she corrected. She had gray-green eyes and a strange mouth. "He's my cousin."

"All Adam's chillun are cousins, one way or the other. You'll have to tell me a little more than that."

"He was in the Air Force seven years ago," she said. "There was some–trouble. He was discharged. Medical."

The sheriff thumbed through the file on the desk before him. "Remember the doctor's name?"

"Thompson first, then Bromfield. Dr. Bromfield signed the discharge."

"Guess you do know something about him at that. What was he before he did his hitch in the Air Force?"

"An engineer. I mean, he would have been if he'd finished school."

"Why didn't he?"

She shrugged. "He just disappeared."

"So how do you know he's here?"

"I'd recognize him anywhere," she said. "I saw . . . I saw it happen."

"Did you now." The sheriff grunted, lifted the file, let it drop. "Look, Miss Gerald, it's not my business to go advising people. But you seem like a nice respectable girl. Why don't you just forget him?"

"I'd like to see him, if I may," she said quietly.

"He's crazy. Did you know that?"

"I don't think so."

"Slammin' his fist through a plate glass window. For nothing."

She waited. He tried again. "He's dirty. He don't know his own name, hardly."

"May I see him?"

The sheriff uttered a wordless growl and stood up. "Them Air Force psychos had any sense, they'd've put him where he would never even get near a jail. This way."

The walls were steel plates like a ship's bulkhead, studded with rivets, painted a faded cream above and mustard color below. Their footsteps echoed. The sheriff unlocked a heavy door with one small high grating and slid it aside. They stepped through and he closed and locked it. He motioned her ahead of him and they came into a barnlike area, concrete on walls and ceiling. Built around it was a sort of balcony; under and over this were the cells, steel-walled, fronted by close-set bars. There were perhaps twenty cells. Only a half dozen were occupied. It was a cold, unhappy place.

"Well, what did you expect?" demanded the sheriff, reading her expression. "The Waldorf Plaza or something?"

"Where is he?" she asked.

They walked to a cell on the lower tier. "Snap out of it, Barrows. Lady to see you."

"Hip! Oh, Hip!"

The prisoner did not move. He lay half on, half off a padded steel bunk, one foot on the mattress, one on the floor. His left arm was in a dirty sling.

"See? Nary a word out of him. Satisfied, Miss?"

"Let me in," she breathed. "Let me talk to him."

He shrugged and reluctantly unlocked the door. She stepped in, turned. "May I speak to him alone?"

"Liable to get hurt," he warned.

She gazed at him. Her mouth was extraordinarily expressive. "Well," he said at length, "I'll stay in the area here. You yell if you need help. S'help me I'll put a slug through your neck, Barrows, if you try anything." He locked the barred door behind the girl.

She waited until he stepped away and then went to the prisoner. "Hip," she murmured. "Hip Barrows."

His dull eyes slid in their sockets until they approximated her direction. The eyes closed and opened in a slow, numb blink.

She knelt beside him. "Mr. Barrows," she whispered, "you don't know me. I told them I was your cousin. I want to help you."

He was silent.

She said, "I'm going to get you out of here. Don't you want to get out?"

For a long moment he watched her face. Then his eyes went to the locked door and back to her face again.

She touched his forehead, his cheek. She pointed at the dirty sling. "Does it hurt much?"

His eyes lingered, withdrew from her face, found the bandage. With effort, they came up again. She asked, "Aren't you going to say anything? Don't you want me to help?"

He was silent for so long that she rose. "I'd better go. Don't forget me. I'll help you." She turned to the door.

He said, "Why?"

She returned to him. "Because you're dirty and beaten and don't care—and because none of that can hide what you are."

"You're crazy," he muttered tiredly.

She smiled. "That's what they say about you. So we have something in common."

He swore, foully.

Unperturbed, she said, "You can't hide behind that either. Now listen to me. Two men will come to see you this afternoon. One is a doctor. The other is a lawyer. We'll have you out of here this evening."

He raised his head and for the first time something came into his lethargic face. Whatever it was was not pretty. His voice came from deep in his chest. He growled, "What type doctor?"

"For your arm," she said evenly. "Not a psychiatrist. You'll never have to go through that again."

He let his head drop back. His features slowly lost their expression. She waited and when he had nothing else to offer, she turned and called the sheriff.

It was not too difficult. The sentence was sixty days for malicious mischief. There had been no alternative fine offered. The lawyer rapidly proved that there should have been, and the fine was paid. In his clean new bandages and his filthy clothes, Barrows was led out past the glowering sheriff, ignoring him and his threat as to what the dirty bum could expect if he ever showed up in town again.

The girl was waiting outside. He stood stupidly at the top of the jailhouse steps while she spoke to the lawyer. Then the lawyer was gone and she touched his elbow. "Come on, Hip."

He followed like a wound-up toy, walking whither his feet had been pointed. They turned two corners and walked five blocks and then up the stone steps of a clean, dried spinster of a house with a bay window and colored glass set into the main door. The girl opened the main door with one key and a door in the hallway with another. He found himself in the room with the bay window. It was high-ceilinged, airy, clean.

For the first time he moved of his own volition. He turned around, slowly, looking at one wall after another. He put out his hand and lifted the corner of a dresser scarf, and let it fall. "Your room?"

"Yours," she said. She came to him and put two keys on the dresser. "Your keys." She opened the top drawer. "Your socks and handkerchiefs." With her knuckles she rapped on each drawer in turn. "Shirts. Underclothes." She pointed to a door. "Two suits in there; I think they'll fit. A robe. Slippers, shoes." She pointed to another door. "Bathroom. Lots of towels, lots of soap. A razor."

"Razor?"

"Anyone who can have keys can have a razor," she said gently. "Get presentable, will you? I'll be back in fifteen minutes. Do you know how long it is since you've eaten anything?"

He shook his head.

"Four days. 'Bye now."

She slipped through the door and was gone, even as he fumbled for something to say to her. He looked at the door for a long time. Then he swore and fell limply back on the bed.

He scratched his nose and his hand slid down to his jaw. It was ragged, itchy. He half rose, muttered, "Damn if I will," and lay back. And then, somehow, he was in the bathroom, peering at himself in the mirror. He wet his hands, splashed water on his face, wiped the dirt off onto a towel and peered again. He grunted and reached for the soap.

He found the razor, he found the underclothes, the slacks, socks, slippers, shirt, jacket. When he looked into the mirror he wished he had a comb. When she elbowed the door open she put her packages on the top of the dresser and then she was smiling up at him, her hand out, the comb in it. He took it wordlessly and went and wet his head and combed it.

"Come on, it's all ready," she called from the other room. He emerged. She had taken the lamp off the night table and had spread out a thick oval platter on which was a lean, rare steak, a bottle of ale, a smaller bottle of stout, a split Idaho potato with butter melting in it, hot rolls in a napkin, a tossed salad in a small wooden bowl.

"I don't want nothing," he said, and abruptly fell to. There was nothing in the world then but the good food filling his mouth and throat, the tingle of ale and the indescribable magic of the charcoal crust.

When the plate was empty, it and the table suddenly wanted to fly upward at his head. He toppled forward, caught the sides of the table and held it away from him. He trembled violently. She spoke from behind him, "All right. It's all right," and put her hands on his shoulders, pressed him back into his chair. He tried to raise his hand and failed. She wiped his clammy forehead and upper lip with the napkin.

In time, his eyes opened. He looked around for her, found her sitting on the edge of the bed, watching him silently. He grinned sheepishly. *"Whew!"*

She rose. "You'll be all right now. You'd better turn in. Good night!"

She was in the room, she was out of it. She had been with him, he was alone. It made a change which was too important to tolerate and too large to understand. He looked from the door to the bed and said "Good night," only because they were the last words she had said, and they hung shimmering in the silence.

He put his hands on the chair arms and forced his legs to cooperate. He could stand but that was all. He fell forward and sidewise, curling up to miss the table as he went down. He lay across the counterpane and blackness came.

"Good morning."

He lay still. His knees were drawn up and the heels of his hands were tight on his cheekbones. He closed his eyes tighter than sleep to shut out the light. He closed his kinesthetic sense to shut out the slight tilting of the mattress which indicated where she sat on the bed. He disconnected his hearing lest she speak again. His nostrils betrayed him; he had not expected there to be coffee in the room and he was wanting it, wanting it badly, before he thought to shut it out.

Fuzzily he lay thinking, thinking something about her. If she spoke again, he thought, he'd show her. He'd lie there till she spoke again and when she spoke he'd ignore her and lie still some more.

He waited.

Well, if she wasn't going to speak again, he couldn't ignore her, could he?

He opened his eyes. They blazed, round and angry. She sat near the foot of the bed. Her body was still, her face was still, her mouth and her eyes were alive.

He coughed suddenly, violently. It closed his eyes and when he opened them he was no longer looking at her. He fumbled vaguely at his chest, then looked down at himself.

"Slep' in my clothes all night," he said.

"Drink your coffee."

He looked at her. She still had not moved, and did not. She was wearing a burgundy jacket with a gray-green scarf. She had long, level, gray-green eyes, the kind which in profile are deep clear triangles. He looked away from her, farther and farther away, until he saw the coffee. A big pot, a thick hot cup, already poured. Black and strong and good. "Whoo," he said, holding it, smelling it. He drank. "Whoo."

He looked at the sunlight now. Good. The turn and fall and turn again of the breeze-lifted marquisette at the window, in and out of a sunbeam. Good. The luminous oval, a shadow of the sunlight itself, where the sun glanced off the round mirror on one wall to the clean paint on the adjoining one. Good. He drank more good coffee.

He set the cup down and fumbled at his shirt buttons. He was wrinkled and sweaty. "Shower," he said.

"Go ahead," said the girl. She rose and went to the dresser where there were a cardboard box and some paper sacks. She opened the box and took out an electric hot plate. He got three buttons undone and somehow the fourth and fifth came off with little explosive tearing sounds. He got the rest of his clothes off somehow. The girl paid him no attention, neither looking at him nor away, just calmly doing things with the hot plate. He went into the bathroom and fussed for a long time with the shower handles, getting the water just right. He got in and let the water run on the nape of his neck. He found soap in the dish, so he let the water run on his head and then rubbed it furiously with the cake of soap until he was mantled in warm, kind, crawling lather. *God,* the thought came from somewhere, *I'm thin as a xylophone. Got to put some beef back on or I'll get sick and . . .* The same thought looped back to him, interrupting itself: *Not supposed to get well. Get good and sick, stay sick. Get sicker.* Angrily he demanded, "Who says I got to get sick?" but there was no answer except a quick echo off the tiles.

He shut off the water and stepped out and took an oversized towel from the rack. He started one end of it on his scalp, worked it on his hair from one end to the other. He threw it on the floor, in the corner, and took another towel and rubbed himself pink. He threw that one down too and came out into the room. The robe lay over the arm of an easy chair by the door, so he put it on.

The girl was spooning fragrant bacon grease over and over three perfect eggs in a pan. When he sat down on the edge of the bed she slid the eggs deftly onto a plate, leaving all the grease behind in the pan. They were perfect, the whites completely firm, the yolks unbroken, liquid, faintly filmed over. There was bacon, four brief seconds less than crisp, paper dried and aromatic. There was toast, golden outside, soft and white inside, with butter melting quickly, running to find and fill the welcoming caves and crevices; two slices with butter, one with marmalade. And these lay in some sunlight, giving off a color possible only to marmalade and to stained glass.

He ate and drank coffee; ate more and drank coffee and coffee. All the while she sat in the easy chair with his shirt in her lap and her hands like dancers, while the buttons grew back onto the material under their swift and delicate paces.

He watched her and when she was finished he came to her and put out his hand for the shirt, but she shook her head and pointed. "A clean one."

He found a knitted pullover polo shirt. While he dressed she washed his dishes and the frying pan and straightened out the bed. He lay back in the easy chair and she knelt before him and worked the soggy dressing off his left hand, inspected the cuts and bound them up again. The bandage was firm and comforting. "You can do without the sling now," she said, pleased. She got up and went to the bed. She sat there facing him, still again except for her eyes, except for her mouth.

Outside an oriole made a long slender note, broke it, and let the fragments fall through the shining air. A stake-bed truck idled past, busily shaking the string of cowbells on its back, while one hoarse man and one with a viola voice flanked it afoot, chanting. In one window came a spherical sound with a fly at its heart and at the other appeared a white kitten. Out by the kitten went the fly and the kitten reared up and batted at it, twisted and sprang down out of sight as if it had meant all along to leave; only a fool would have thought it had lost its balance.

And in the room was quiet and a watchfulness which was without demand, except perhaps a guarding against leaving anything unwatched. The girl sat with her hands aslumber and her eyes awake, while a pipe-cleaner man called Healing was born in all his cores, all his marrow, taking the pose of his relaxed body, resting and growing a little and resting again and growing.

Later, she rose. Without consultation, but merely because it seemed time to do so, she picked up a small handbag and went to the door where she waited. He stirred, rose, went to her. They went out.

They walked slowly to a place where there was smooth rolling land, mowed and tended. Down in the hollow some boys played softball. They stood for a while, watching. She studied his face and when she saw reflected in it only the moving figures and not the consecutive interest of the game itself, she touched his elbow and moved on. They found a pond where there were ducks and straight cinder paths with flower beds. She picked a primrose and put it in his lapel. They found a bench. A man pushed a bright clean wagon up to them. She bought a frankfurter and a bottle of soda and handed them to him. He ate and drank silently.

It was a quiet time they had together.

When it began to grow dark, she brought him back to the room. She left him alone for half an hour and returned to find him sitting just where she had left him. She opened packages and cooked chops and mixed a salad, and, while he was eating, made more coffee. After dinner he yawned. She was on her feet immediately. "Good night," she said, and was gone.

He turned slowly and looked at the closed door. After a time he said, "Good night." He undressed and got into bed and turned out the light.

The next day was the day they rode on a bus and lunched in a restaurant.

The day after that was the one they stayed out a little later to see a band concert.

Then there was the afternoon when it rained and they went to a movie which he watched wordlessly, not smiling, not frowning, not stirring to the musical parts.

"Your coffee." "Let's get these to the laundry." "Come." "Good night." These were the things she said to him. Otherwise she watched his face and, undemandingly, she waited.

He awoke, and it was too dark. He did not know where he was. The face was there, wide-browed, sallow, with its thick lenses and its pointed chin. Wordlessly, he roared at it and it smiled at him. When he realized that the face was in his mind and not in the room, it disappeared . . . no; it was simply that he knew it was not there. He was filled with fury that it was not there; his brain was fairly melting with rage. *Yes, but who is he?* he asked, and answered, "I don't know, I don't know, I don't know . . ." and his voice became a moan, softer and softer and softer until it was gone. He inhaled deeply and then something inside him slipped and fell apart and he began to cry. Someone took his hand, took his other hand, held them together; it was the girl; she'd heard him, she'd come. He was not alone.

Not alone . . . it made him cry harder, bitterly. He held her wrists as she bent over him, looked up through darkness at her face and her hair and he wept.

She stayed with him until he was finished and for as long afterward as he held her hand. When he released it he was asleep, and she drew the blanket up to his chin and tiptoed out.

In the morning he sat on the edge of the bed, watching the steam from his coffee spread and fade in the sunlight, and when she put the eggs before him he looked up at her. His mouth quivered. She stood before him, waiting.

At last he said, "Have you had your breakfast yet?"

Something was kindled in her eyes. She shook her head.

He looked down at the plate, puzzling something out. Finally he pushed it away from him a fraction of an inch and stood up. "You have this," he said. "I'll fix some more."

He had seen her smile but he had not noticed it before. Now, it was as if the warmth of all of them was put together for this one. She sat down and ate. He fried his eggs, not as well as she had done, and they were cooked before he thought of toast and the toast burned while he was eating the eggs. She did not attempt to help him in any way, even when he stared blankly at the little table, frowned and scratched his jaw. In his own time he found what he was looking for—the other cup on top of the dresser. He poured fresh coffee for her and took the other which she had not touched, for himself, and she smiled again.

"What's your name?" he asked her, for the very first time.

"Janie Gerard."

"Oh."

She considered him carefully, then stretched down to the footpost of the bed where her handbag hung by its strap. She drew it toward her, opened it, and took out a short piece of metal. At first glance, it was a piece of aluminum tubing, perhaps eight inches long and oval in cross-section. But it was flexible—woven of tiny strands rather than extruded. She turned his right hand palm up, where it lay beside his coffee cup, and put the tubing into it.

He must have seen it, for he was staring down into the cup. He did not close his fingers on it. His expression did not change. At length he took a slice of toast. The piece of tubing fell, rolled over, hung on the edge of the table and dropped to the floor. He buttered his toast.

After that first shared meal there was a difference. There were many differences. Never again did he undress before her or ignore the fact that she was not eating. He began to pay for little things—bus fares, lunches, and, later, to let her precede him through doorways, to take her elbow when they crossed streets. He went to the market with her and carried the packages.

He remembered his name; he even remembered that the "Hip" was for "Hippocrates." He was, however, unable to remember how he came by the name, or where he had been born, or anything else about himself. She did not urge him, ask him. She simply spent her days with him, waiting. And she kept the piece of aluminum webbing in sight.

It was beside his breakfast plate almost every morning. It would be in the bathroom, with the handle of his toothbrush thrust into it. Once he found it in his side jacket pocket where the small roll of bills appeared regularly; this one time the bills were tucked into the tubing. He pulled them out and absently let the tubing fall and Janie had to pick it up. She put it in his shoe once and when he tried to put the shoe on and could not, he tipped it out onto the floor and let it lie there. It was as if it were transparent or even invisible to him; when, as in the case of finding his money in it, he had to handle it, he did so clumsily, with inattention, rid himself of it and apparently forgot it. Janie never mentioned it. She just quietly put it in his path, time and time again, patient as a pendulum.

His afternoons began to possess a morning and his days a yesterday. He began to remember a bench they had used, a theater they had attended, and he would lead the way back. She relinquished her guidance as fast as he would take it up until it was he who planned their days.

Since he had no memory to draw on except his time with her, they were days of discovery. They had picnics and rode learningly on buses. They found another theater and a place with swans as well as ducks.

There was another kind of discovery too. One day he stood in the middle of the room and turned, looking at one wall after another, at the windows and the bed. "I was sick, wasn't I?"

And one day he stopped on the street, stared at the grim building on the other side. "I was in there."

And it was several days after that when he slowed, frowned, and stood gazing into a men's furnishing shop. No–not into it. At it. At the window.

Beside him Janie waited, watching his face.

He raised his left hand slowly, flexed it, looked down at the curled scar on the back of his hand, the two straight ones, one long, one short, on his wrist.

"Here," she said. She pressed the piece of tubing into his hand.

Without looking at it he closed his fingers, made a fist. Surprise flickered across his features and then a flash of sheer terror and something like anger. He swayed on his feet.

"It's all right," said Janie softly.

He grunted questioningly, looked at her as if she were a stranger and seemed slowly to recognize her. He opened his hand and looked carefully at the piece of metal. He tossed it, caught it. "That's mine," he said.

She nodded.

He said, "I broke that window." He looked at it, tossed the piece of metal again, and put it in his pocket and began to walk again. He was quiet for a long time and just as they mounted the steps of their house he said, "I broke the window and they put me in that jail. And you got me out and I was sick and you brought me here till I was well again."

He took out his keys and opened the door, stood back to let her pass in. "What did you want to do that for?"

"Just wanted to," she said.

He was restless. He went to the closet and turned out the pockets of his two suit jackets and his sport coat. He crossed the room and pawed aimlessly at the dresser scarf and opened and shut drawers.

"What is it?"

"That thing," he said vaguely. He wandered into and out of the bathroom. "You know, that piece of pipe, like."

"Oh," she said.

"I had it," he muttered unhappily. He took another turn around the room and then shouldered past Janie where she sat on the bed, and reached to the night table. "Here it is!"

He looked at it, flexed it, and sat down in the easy chair. "Hate to lose that," he said relievedly. "Had it a long time."

"It was in the envelope they were holding for you while you were in jail," Janie told him.

"Yuh. Yuh." He twisted it between his hands, then raised it and shook it at her like some bright, thick, admonishing forefinger. "This thing–"

She waited.

He shook his head. "Had it a long time," he said again. He rose, paced, sat down again. "I was looking for a guy who . . . *Ah!*" he growled, "I can't remember."

"It's all right," she said gently.

He put his head in his hands. "Damn near almost found him too," he said in a muffled voice. "Been looking for him a long time. I've *always* been looking for him."

"Always?"

"Well, ever since . . . Janie, I can't remember again."

"All right."

"All right, all right, it isn't all right!" He straightened and looked at her. "I'm sorry, Janie. I didn't mean to yell at you."

She smiled at him. He said, "Where was that cave?"

"Cave?" she echoed.

He waved his arms up, around. "Sort of a cave. Half cave, half log house. In the woods. Where was it?"

"Was I there with you?"

"No," he said immediately. "That was before, I guess. I don't remember."

"Don't worry about it."

"I *do* worry about it!" he said excitedly. "I can worry about it, can't I?" As soon as the words were out, he looked to her for forgiveness and found it. "You got to understand," he said more quietly, "this is something, I—I got to— Look," he said, returning to exasperation, "can something be more important than anything else in the world, and you can't even remember what it is?"

"It happens."

"It's happened to me," he said glumly. "I don't like it either."

"You're getting yourself all worked up," said Janie.

"Well, sure!" he exploded. He looked around him, shook his head violently. "What is this? What am I doing here? Who are you, anyway, Janie? What are you getting out of this?"

"I like seeing you get well."

"Yeah, get well," he growled. "I should get well! I ought to be sick. Be sick and get sicker."

"Who told you that?" she rapped.

"Thompson," he barked and then slumped back, looking at her with stupid amazement on his face. In the high, cracking voice of an adolescent he whimpered, "Thompson? Who's Thompson?"

She shrugged and said, matter-of-factly, "The one who told you you ought to be sick, I suppose."

"Yeah," he whispered, and again, in a soft-focused flood of enlightenment, "yeah-h-h-h . . ." He wagged the piece of mesh tubing at her. "I saw him. Thompson." The tubing caught his eye then and he held it still, staring at it. He shook his head, closed his eyes. "I was looking for . . ." His voice trailed off.

"Thompson?"

"Nah!" he grunted. "I never wanted to see *him!* Yes I did," he amended. "I wanted to beat his brains out."

"You did?"

"Yeah. You see, he—he was—aw, what's the matter with my *head?*" he cried.

"Sh-h-h," she soothed.

"I can't remember, I can't," he said brokenly. "It's like . . . you see something rising up off the ground, you got to grab it, you jump so hard you can feel your kneebones crack, you stretch up and get your fingers on it, just the tips of your fingers. . . ." His chest swelled and sank. "Hang there, like forever, your fingers on it, knowing you'll never make it, never get a grip. And then you fall, and you watch it going up and up away from you, getting smaller and smaller, and you'll never—" He leaned back and closed his eyes. He was panting. He breathed, barely audible, "And you'll never . . ."

He clenched his fists. One of them still held the tubing and again he went through the discovery, the wonder, the puzzlement. "Had this a long time," he said, looking at it. "Crazy. This must sound crazy to you, Janie."

"Oh, no."

"You still think I'm crazy?"

"No."

"I'm sick," he whimpered.

Startlingly, she laughed. She came to him and pulled him to his feet. She drew him to the bathroom and reached in and switched on the light. She pushed him inside, against the washbasin, and rapped the mirror with her knuckles. "Who's sick?"

He looked at the firm-fleshed, well-boned face that stared out at him, at its glossy hair and clear eyes. He turned to Janie, genuinely astonished. "I haven't looked this good in years! Not since I was in the . . . Janie, was I in the Army?"

"Were you?"

He looked into the mirror again. "Sure don't *look* sick," he said, as if to himself. He touched his cheek. "Who keeps telling me I'm sick?"

He heard Janie's footsteps receding. He switched off the light and joined her. "I'd like to break that Thompson's back," he said. "Throw him right through a—"

"What is it?"

"Funny thing," he said, "was going to say, through a brick wall. I was thinking it so hard I could see it, me throwing him."

"Perhaps you did."

He shook his head. "It wasn't a wall. It was a plate-glass window. I know!" he shouted. "I saw him and I was going to hit him. I saw him standing right there on the street looking at me and I yelled and jumped him and . . . and . . ." He looked down at his scarred hand. He said, amazed, "I turned right around and hauled off and hit the window instead. God."

He sat down weakly. "That's what the jail was for and it was all over. Just lie there in that rotten jail, sick. Don't eat, don't move, get sick and sicker and it's all over."

"Well, it isn't all over, is it?"

He looked at her. "No. No, it isn't. Thanks to you." He looked at her eyes, her mouth. "What about you, Janie? What are you after, anyway?"

She dropped her eyes.

"Oh, I'm sorry, I'm sorry. That must've sounded . . ." He put out a hand to her, dropped it without touching her. "I don't know what's gotten into me today. It's just that . . . I don't figure you, Janie. What did I ever do for you?"

She smiled quickly. "Get better."

"It's not enough," he said devoutly. "Where do you live?"

She pointed. "Right across the hall."

"Oh," he said. He remembered the night he had cried, and pushed the picture away in embarrassment. He turned away, hunting for a change of subject, any change. "Let's go out."

"All right." Was that relief he detected in her voice?

They rode on a roller coaster and ate cotton candy and danced in an outdoor pavilion. He wondered aloud where he had ever learned to dance, but that was the only mention he made of the things which were troubling him until late in the evening. It was the first time he had consciously enjoyed being with Janie; it was an Occasion rather than a way of life. He had never known her to laugh so easily, to be so eager to ride this and taste that and go yonder to see what was there. At dusk they stood side by side, leaning on a railing which overlooked the lake, watching the bathers. There were lovers on the beach, here and there. Hip smiled at the sight, turned to speak to Janie about it and was arrested by the strange wistfulness which softened her taut features. A surge of emotion, indefinable and delicate, made him turn away quickly. It was in part a recognition of the rarity of her introspection and an unwillingness to interrupt it for her; and partly a flash of understanding that her complete preoccupation with him was not necessarily all she wanted of life. Life had begun for him, to all intents and purposes, on the day she came to his cell. It had never occurred to him before that her quarter of a century without him was not the clean slate that his was.

Why had she rescued him? Why him, if she must rescue someone? And–why?

What could she want from him? Was there something in his lost life that he might give her? If there was, he vowed silently, it was hers, whatever it might be; it was inconceivable that anything, anything at all she might gain from him would be of greater value than his own discovery of the life which produced it.

But what could it be?

He found his gaze on the beach and its small galaxy of lovers, each couple its own world, self-contained but in harmony with all the others adrift in the luminous dusk. Lovers . . . he had felt the tuggings of love . . . back somewhere in the mists, he couldn't quite remember where, with whom . . . but it was there, and with it his old, old reflex, *not until I've hunted him down and*– But again he lost the thought. Whatever it was, it had been more important to him than love or marriage or a job or a colonelcy. (Colonelcy? Had he ever wanted to be a colonel?)

Well, then, maybe it was a conquest. Janie loved him. She'd seen him and the lightning had struck and she wanted him, so she was going about it in her own way. Well, then! If that's what she wanted . . .

He closed his eyes, seeing her face, the tilt of her head in that waiting, attentive silence; her slim strong arms and lithe body, her magic hungry mouth. He saw a quick sequence of pictures taken by the camera of his good male mind, but filed under "inactive" in his troubled, partial one: Janie's legs silhouetted against the window, seen through the polychrome cloud of her liberty silk skirt. Janie in a peasant blouse, with a straight spear of morning sunlight bent and molded to her bare shoulder and the soft upper curve of her breast. Janie dancing, bending away and cleaving to him as if he and she were the gold leaves of an electroscope. (*Where had he seen . . . worked with . . . an electroscope . . . Oh, of course! In the . . .* But it was gone.) Janie barely visible in the deep churning dark, palely glowing through a mist of nylon and the flickering acid of his tears, strongly holding his hands until he quieted.

But this was no seduction, this close intimacy of meals and walks and long shared silences, with never a touch, never a wooing word. Lovemaking, even the suppressed and silent kind, is a demanding thing, a thirsty and yearning thing. Janie demanded nothing. She only

. . . she only waited. If her interest lay in his obscured history she was taking a completely passive attitude, merely placing herself to receive what he might unearth. If something he had been, something he had done, was what she was after, wouldn't she question and goad, probe and pry the way Thompson and Bromfield had done? (*Bromfield? Who's he?*) But she never had, never.

No, it must be this other, this thing which made her look at lovers with such contained sadness, with an expression on her face like that of an armless man spellbound by violin music. . . .

Picture of Janie's mouth, bright, still, waiting. Picture of Janie's clever hands. Picture of Janie's body, surely as smooth as her shoulder, as firm as her forearm, warm and wild and willing–

They turned to each other, he the driving, she the driven gear. Their breath left them, hung as a symbol and a promise between them, alive and merged. For two heavy heartbeats they had their single planet in the lovers' spangled cosmos; and then Janie's face twisted in a spasm of concentration, bent not toward a ponderous control, but rather to some exquisite accuracy of adjustment.

A thing happened to him, as if a small sphere of the hardest vacuum had appeared deep within him. He breathed again and the magic about them gathered itself and whipped in with the breath to fill the vacuum which swallowed and killed it, all of it, in a tick of time. Except for the brief spastic change in her face, neither had moved; they still stood in the sunset, close together, her face turned up to his, here gloried, here tinted, there self-shining in its own shadow. But the magic was gone, the melding; they were two, not one, and this was Janie quiet, Janie patient, Janie not damped, but unkindled. But no –the real difference was in him. His hands were lifted to go around her and no longer cared to and his lips lost their grip on the unborn kiss and let it fall away and be lost. He stepped back. "Shall we go?"

A swift ripple of regret came and went across Janie's face. It was a thing like many other things coming now to plague him: smooth and textured things forever presenting themselves to his fingertips and never to his grasp. He almost understood her regret, it was there for him, it was there–and gone, altogether gone, dwindling high away from him.

They walked silently back to the midway and the lights, their pitiable thousands of candlepower; and to the amusement rides, their balky pretense at motion. Behind them in the growing dark they left all real radiance, all significant movement. All of it; there was not enough left for any particular reaction. With the compressed-air guns which fired tennis balls at wooden battleships; the cranks they turned to make the toy greyhounds race up a slope; the darts they threw at balloons—with these they buried something now so negligible it left no mound.

At an elaborate stand were a couple of war-surplus servomechanisms rigged to simulate radar-gun directors. There was a miniature antiaircraft gun to be aimed by hand, its slightest movement followed briskly by the huge servo-powered gun at the back. Aircraft silhouettes were flashed across the domed half ceiling. All in all, it was a fine conglomeration of gadgetry and dazzle, a truly high-level catchpenny.

Hip went first, amused, then intrigued, then enthralled as his small movements were so obediently duplicated by the whip and weave of the massive gun twenty feet away. He missed the first "plane" and the second; after that he had the fixed error of the gun calculated precisely and he banged away at every target as fast as they could throw them and knocked out every one. Janie clapped her hands like a child and the attendant awarded them a blurred and glittering clay statue of a police dog worth all of a fifth of the admission price. Hip took it proudly, and waved Janie up to the trigger. She worked the aiming mechanism diffidently and laughed as the big gun nodded and shook itself. His cheeks flushed, his eyes expertly anticipating the appearance-point of each target, Hip said out of the corner of his mouth, "Up forty or better on your right quadrant, corp'r'l, or the pixies'll degauss your fuses."

Janie's eyes narrowed a trifle and perhaps that was to help her aiming. She did not answer him. She knocked out the first target that appeared before it showed fully over the artificial horizon, and the second, and the third. Hip swatted his hands together and called her name joyfully. She seemed for a moment to be pulling herself together, the odd, effortful gesture of a preoccupied man forcing himself back into a conversation. She then let one go by and missed four in a row. She hit two, one low, one high, and missed the last by half a mile. "Not very good," she said tremulously.

"Good enough," he said gallantly. "You don't have to hit 'em these days, you know."

"You don't?"

"Nah. Just get near. Your fuses take over from there. This is the world's most diabetic dog."

She looked down from his face to the statuette and giggled. "I'll keep it always," she said. "Hip, you're getting that nasty sparkle stuff all over your jacket. Let's give it away."

They marched up and across and down and around the tinsel stands in search of a suitable beneficiary, and found him at last–a solemn urchin of seven or so, who methodically sucked the memory of butter and juice from a well-worn corncob. "This is for *you,*" caroled Janie. The child ignored the extended gift and kept his frighteningly adult eyes on her face.

Hip laughed. "No sale!" He squatted beside the boy. "I'll make a deal with you. Will you haul it away for a dollar?"

No response. The boy sucked his corncob and kept watching Janie.

"Tough customer," grinned Hip.

Suddenly Janie shuddered. "Oh, let's leave him alone," she said, her merriment gone.

"He can't outbid *me,*" said Hip cheerfully. He set the statue down by the boy's scuffed shoes and pushed a dollar bill into the rip which looked most like a pocket. "Pleasure to do business with you, sir," he said and followed Janie, who had already moved off.

"Regular chatterbox," laughed Hip as he caught up with her. He looked back. Half a block away, the child still stared at Janie. "Looks like you've made a lifetime impress–*Janie!*"

Janie had stopped dead, eyes wide and straight ahead, mouth a triangle of shocked astonishment. "The little *devil!*" she breathed. "At his age!" She whirled and looked back.

Hip's eyes obviously deceived him, for he saw the corncob leave the grubby little hands, turn ninety degrees and thump the urchin smartly on the cheekbone. It dropped to the ground; the child backed away four paces, shrilled an unchivalrous presumption and an unprintable suggestion at them and disappeared into an alley.

"Whew!" said Hip, awed. "You're so right!" He looked at her admiringly. "What clever ears you have, Grandma," he said, not very successfully covering an almost prissy embarrassment with badinage. "I didn't hear a thing until the second broadside he threw."

"Didn't you?" she said. For the first time he detected annoyance in her voice. At the same time he sensed that he was not the subject of it. He took her arm. "Don't let it bother you. Come on, let's eat some food."

She smiled and everything was all right again.

Succulent pizza and cold beer in a booth painted a too-bright, edge-worn green. A happy-weary walk through the darkening booths to the late bus which waited, breathing. A sense of membership because of the fitting of the spine to the calculated average of the bus seats. A shared doze, a shared smile, at sixty miles an hour through the flickering night, and at last the familiar depot on the familiar street, echoing and empty but *my* street in *my* town.

They woke a taxi driver and gave him their address. "Can I be more alive than this?" he murmured from his corner and then realized she had heard him. "I mean," he amended, "it's as if my whole world, everywhere I lived, was once in a little place inside my head, so deep I couldn't see out. And then you made it as big as a room and then as big as a town and tonight as big as . . . well, a lot bigger," he finished weakly.

A lonely passing streetlight passed her answering smile over to him. He said, "So I was wondering how much bigger it can get."

"Much bigger," she said.

He pressed back sleepily into the cushions. "I feel fine," he murmured. "I feel . . . Janie," he said in a strange voice, "I feel sick."

"You know what that is," she said calmly.

A tension came and went within him and he laughed softly. "Him again. He's wrong. He's wrong. He'll never make me sick again. *Driver!*"

His voice was like soft wood tearing. Startled, the driver slammed on his brakes. Hip surged forward out of his seat and caught the back of the driver under his armpit. "Go back," he said excitedly.

"Goddlemighty," the driver muttered. He began to turn the cab around. Hip turned to Janie, an answer, some sort of answer, half formed, but she had no question. She sat quietly and waited. To the driver Hip said, "Just the next block. Yeah, here. Left. Turn left."

He sank back then, his cheek to the window glass, his eyes raking the shadowed houses and black lawns. After a time he said, "There. The house with the driveway, there where the big hedge is."

"Want I should drive in?"

"No," Hip said. "Pull over. A little further . . . there, where I can see in."

When the cab stopped, the driver turned around and peered back. "Gettin' out here? That's a dollar 'n—"

"Shh!" The sound came so explosively that the driver sat stunned. Then he shook his head wearily and turned to face forward. He shrugged and waited.

Hip stared through the driveway's gap in the hedge at the faintly gleaming white house, its stately porch and porte-cochère, its neat shutters and fanlit door.

"Take us home," he said after a time.

Nothing was said until they got there. Hip sat with one hand pressing his temples, covering his eyes. Janie's corner of the cab was dark and silent.

When the machine stopped Hip slid out and absently handed Janie to the walk. He gave the driver a bill, accepting the change, pawed out a tip and handed it back. The cab drove off.

Hip stood looking down at the money in his hand, sliding it around on his palm with his fingers. "Janie?"

"Yes, Hip."

He looked at her. He could hardly see her in the darkness. "Let's go inside."

They went in. He switched on the lights. She took off her hat and hung her bag on the bedpost and sat down on the bed, her hands on her lap. Waiting.

He seemed blind, so deep was his introspection. He came awake slowly, his gaze fixed on the money in his hand. For a moment it seemed without meaning to him; then slowly, visibly, he recognized it and brought it into his thoughts, into his expression. He closed his hand on it, shook it, brought it to her and spread it out on the night table–three crumpled bills, some silver. "It isn't mine," he said.

"Of course it is!"

He shook his head tiredly. "No it isn't. None of it's been mine. Not the roller-coaster money or the shopping money or coffee in the mornings or . . . I suppose there's rent here."

She was silent.

"That house," he said detachedly. "The instant I saw it I knew I'd been there before. I was there just before I got arrested. I didn't have any money then. I remember. I knocked on the door and I was dirty and crazy and they told me to go around the back if I wanted something to eat. I didn't have any money; I remember that *so* well. All I had was . . ."

Out of his pocket came the woven metal tube. He caught lamplight on its side, flicked it off again, squeezed it, then pointed with it at the night table. "Now, ever since I came here, I have money. In my left jacket pocket every day. I never wondered about it. It's your money, isn't it, Janie?"

"It's yours. Forget about it, Hip. It's not important."

"What do you mean it's mine?" he barked. "Mine because you give it to me?" He probed her silence with a bright beam of anger and nodded. "Thought so."

"Hip!"

He shook his head, suddenly, violently, the only expression he could find at the moment for the great tearing wind which swept through him. It was anger, it was humiliation, it was a deep futility and a raging attack on the curtains which shrouded his self-knowledge. He slumped down into the easy chair and put his hands over his face.

He sensed her nearness, then her hand was on his shoulder. "Hip . . ." she whispered. He shrugged the shoulder and the hand was gone. He heard the faint sound of springs as she sat down again on the bed.

He brought his hands down slowly. His face was twisted, hurt. "You've got to understand, I'm not mad at you, I haven't forgotten what you've done, it isn't that," he blurted. "I'm all mixed up again," he said hoarsely. "Doing things, don't know why. Things I *got* to do, I don't know what. Like . . ." He stopped to think, to sort the thousand scraps that whirled and danced in the wind which blew through him. "Like knowing this is wrong, I shouldn't be here, getting fed, spending money, but I don't know who ever said I shouldn't, where I learned it. And . . . and like what I told you, this thing about finding somebody and I don't know who it is and I don't know why. I said tonight . . ." He paused and for a long moment filled the room with the hiss of breath between his teeth, his tense-curled lips. "I said tonight, my world . . . the place I live, it's getting bigger all the time. It just now got big enough to take in that house where we stopped. We passed that corner and I knew the house was there and I had to look at it. I knew I'd been there before, dirty and all excited . . . knocked . . . they told me to go around back . . . I yelled at them . . . somebody else came. I asked them, I wanted to know about some–"

The silence, again the hissing breath.

"–children who lived there, and no children lived there. And I shouted again, everybody was afraid, I straightened out a little. I told them just tell me what I wanted to know. I'd go away, I didn't want to frighten anybody. I said all right, no children, then tell me where is Alicia Kew, just let me talk to Alicia Kew."

He straightened up, his eyes alight, and pointed the piece of tubing at Janie. "You see? I remember, I remember her name, Alicia Kew!" He sank back. "And they said, 'Alicia Kew is dead.' And then they said, oh *her* children! And they told me where to go to find them. They wrote it down someplace, I've got it here somewhere. . . ." He began to fumble through his pockets, stopped suddenly and glared at Janie. "It was the old clothes, *you* have it, *you've* hidden it!"

If she had explained, if she had answered, it would have been all right but she only watched him.

"All right," he gritted. "I remembered one thing, I can remember another. Or I can go back there and ask again. I don't need you."

Her expression did not change but, watching it, he knew suddenly that she was holding it still and that it was a terrible effort to her.

He said gently, "I did need you. I'd've died without you. You've been . . ." He had no word for what she had been to him, so he stopped searching for one and went on, "It's just that I've got so I don't need you that way any more. I have some things to find out but I have to do it myself."

At last she spoke: "You have done it yourself, Hip. Every bit of it all. All I've done is to put you where you could do it. I—want to go on with that."

"You don't need to," he reassured her. "I'm a big boy now. I've come a long way; I've come alive. There can't be much more to find out."

"There's a lot more," she said sadly.

He shook his head positively. "I tell you, I *know!* Finding out about those children, about this Alicia Kew, and then the address where they'd moved—that was right at the end; that was the place where I got my fingertips on the—whatever it was I was trying to grab. Just that one more place, that address where the children are; that's all I need. That's where he'll be."

"He?"

"The one, you know, the one I've been looking for. His name is—" He leaped to his feet. "His name's—"

He brought his fist into his palm, a murderous blow. "I forgot," he whispered.

He put his stinging hand to the short hair at the back of his head, screwed up his eyes in concentration. Then he relaxed. "It's all right," he said. "I'll find out, now."

"Sit down," she said. "Go on, Hip. Sit down and listen to me."

Reluctantly he did; resentfully he looked at her. His head was full of almost understood pictures and phrases. He thought, *Can't she let me alone? Can't she let me think awhile?* But because she . . . Because she was Janie, he waited.

"You're right, you can do it," she said. She spoke slowly and with extreme care. "You can go to the house tomorrow, if you like, and get the address and find what you've been looking for. And it will mean absolutely–*nothing*–to you. Hip, I *know!*"

He glared at her.

"Believe me, Hip; believe me!"

He charged across the room, grabbed her wrists, pulled her up, thrust his face to hers. "You know!" he shouted. "I *bet* you know. You know every damn thing, don't you? You have all along. Here I am going half out of my head wanting to know and you sit there and watch me squirm!"

"Hip! Hip, my arms–"

He squeezed them tighter, shook her. "You *do* know, don't you? All about me?"

"Let me go. Please let me go. Oh, Hip, you don't know what you're doing!"

He flung her back on the bed. She drew up her legs, turned on her side, propped up on one elbow and, through tears, incredible tears, tears which didn't belong to any Janie he had yet seen, she looked up at him. She held her bruised forearm, flexed her free hand. "You don't know," she choked, "what you're . . ." And then she was quiet, panting, sending, through those impossible tears, some great, tortured, thwarted message which he could not read.

Slowly he knelt beside the bed. "Ah, Janie. Janie."

Her lips twitched. It could hardly have been a smile but it wanted to be. She touched his hair. "It's all right," she breathed.

She let her head fall to the pillow and closed her eyes. He curled his legs under him, sat on the floor, put his arms on the bed and rested his cheek on them.

She said, with her eyes closed, "I understand, Hip; I do understand. I want to help, I want to go on helping."

"No you don't," he said, not bitterly, but from the depths of an emotion something like grief.

He could tell–perhaps it was her breath–that he had started the tears again. He said, "You know about me. You know everything I'm looking for." It sounded like an accusation and he was sorry. He meant it only to express his reasoning. But there wasn't any other way to say it. "Don't you?"

Still keeping her eyes closed, she nodded.

"Well then."

He got up heavily and went back to his chair. *When she wants something out of me,* he thought viciously, *she just sits and waits for it.* He slumped into the chair and looked at her. She had not moved. He made a conscious effort and wrung the bitterness from his thought, leaving only the content, the advice. He waited.

She sighed then and sat up. At sight of her rumpled hair and flushed cheeks, he felt a surge of tenderness. Sternly he put it down.

She said, "You have to take my word. You'll have to trust me, Hip."

Slowly he shook his head. She dropped her eyes, put her hands together. She raised one, touched her eye with the back of her wrist.

She said, "That piece of cable."

The tubing lay on the floor where he had dropped it. He picked it up. "What about it?"

"When was the first time you remembered you had it—remembered it was yours?"

He thought. "The house. When I went to the house, asking."

"No," she said, "I don't mean that. I mean, after you were sick."

"Oh." He closed his eyes briefly, frowned. "The window. The time I remembered the window, breaking it. I remembered that and then it . . . oh!" he said abruptly. "You put it in my hand."

"That's right. And for eight days I'd been putting it in your hand. I put it in your shoe, once. On your plate. In the soap dish. Once I stuck your toothbrush inside it. Every day, half a dozen times a day—eight days, Hip!"

"I don't—"

"You don't understand! Oh, I can't blame you."

"I wasn't going to say that. I was going to say, I don't believe you."

At last she looked at him; when she did he realized how rare it was for him to be with her without her eyes on his face. "Truly," she said intensely. "Truly, Hip. That's the way it was."

He nodded reluctantly. "All right. So that's the way it was. What has that to do with—"

"Wait," she begged. "You'll see . . . now, every time you touched the bit of cable, you refused to admit it existed. You'd let it roll right out of your hand and you wouldn't see it fall to the floor. You'd step on it with your bare feet and not even feel it. Once it was in your food, Hip; you picked it up with a forkful of lima beans, you put the end of it in your mouth, and then just let it slip away; you didn't know it was there!"

"Oc—" he said with an effort, then, "occlusion. That's what Bromfield called it." *Who was Bromfield?* But it escaped him; Janie was talking.

"That's right. Now listen carefully. When the time came for the occlusion to vanish, it did; and there you stood with the cable in your hand, knowing it was real. But nothing I could do beforehand could make that happen until it was ready to happen!"

He thought about it. "So–what made it ready to happen?"

"You went back."

"To the store, the plate-glass window?"

"Yes," she said and immediately, "No. What I mean is this: You came alive in this room, and you–well, you said it yourself: the world got bigger for you, big enough to let there be a room, then big enough for a street, then a town. But the same thing was happening with your memory. Your memory got big enough to include yesterday, and last week, and then the jail, and then the thing that got you into jail. Now look: At that moment, the cable meant something to you, something terribly important. But when it happened, for all the time after it happened, the cable meant nothing. It didn't mean anything until the second your memory could go back that far. Then it was real again."

"Oh," he said.

She dropped her eyes. "I knew about the cable. I could have explained it to you. I tried and tried to bring it to your attention but you couldn't see it until you were ready. All right–I know a lot more about you. But don't you see that if I told you, *you wouldn't be able to hear me?*"

He shook his head, not in denial but dazedly. He said, "But I'm not–sick any more!"

He read the response in her expressive face. He said faintly, "Am I?" and then anger curled and kicked inside him. "Come on now," he growled, "you don't mean to tell me I'd suddenly get deaf if you told me where I went to high school."

"Of course not," she said impatiently. "It's just that it wouldn't mean anything to you. It wouldn't relate." She bit her lip in concentration. "Here's one: You've mentioned Bromfield a half dozen times."

"Who? Bromfield? I have not."

She looked at him narrowly. "Hip–you have. You mentioned him not ten minutes ago."

"Did I?" He thought. He thought hard. Then he opened his eyes wide. "By God, I did!"

"All right. Who is he? What was he to you?"

"Who?"

"Hip!" she said sharply.

"I'm sorry," he said. "I guess I'm a little mixed up." He thought again, hard, trying to recall the entire sequence, every word. At last, "B-bromfield," he said with difficulty.

"It will hardly stay with you. Well, it's a flash from a long way back. It won't mean anything to you until you go back that far and get it."

"Go back? Go back how?"

"Haven't you been going back and back–from being sick here to being in jail to getting arrested, and just before that, to your visit to that house? Think about that, Hip. Think about why you went to the house."

He made an impatient gesture. "I don't need to. Can't you see? I went to that house because I was searching for something–what was it? Oh, children; some children who could tell me where the half-wit was." He leaped up, laughed. "You see? The half-wit–I remembered. I'll remember it all, you'll see. The half-wit . . . I'd been looking for him for years, forever. I . . . forget why, but," he said, his voice strengthening, "that doesn't matter any more now. What I'm trying to tell you is that I don't have to go all the way back; I've done all I need to do. I'm back on the path. Tomorrow I'm going to that house and get that address and then I'll go to wherever that is and finish what I started out to do in the first place when I lost the–"

He faltered, looked around bemusedly, spied the tubing lying on the chair arm, snatched it up. "This," he said triumphantly. "It's part of the–the–oh, *damn* it!"

She waited until he had calmed down enough to hear her. She said, "You see?"

"See what?" he asked brokenly, uncaring, miserable.

"If you go out there tomorrow, you'll walk into a situation you don't understand, for reasons you can't remember, asking for someone you can't place, in order to go find out something you can't conceive of. But," she admitted, "you are right, Hip–you *can* do it."

"If I did," he said, "it would all come back."

She shook her head. He said harshly, "You know everything, don't you?"

"Yes, Hip."

"Well, I don't care. I'm going to do it anyway."

She took one deep breath. "You'll be killed."

"What?"

"If you go out there you will be killed," she said distinctly. "Oh, Hip, haven't I been right so far? Haven't I? Haven't you gotten back a lot already–really gotten it back, so it doesn't slip away from you?"

Agonized, he said, "You tell me I can walk out of here tomorrow and find whatever it is I've been looking– Looking? *Living* for . . . and you tell me it'll kill me if I do. What do you want from me? What are you trying to tell me to do?"

"Just keep on," she pleaded. "Just keep on with what you've been doing."

"For what?" he raged. "Go back and back, go farther away from the thing I want? What good will–"

"Stop it!" she said sharply. To his own astonishment he stopped. "You'll be biting holes in the rug in a minute," she said gently and with a gleam of amusement. "That won't help."

He fought against her amusement but it was irresistible. He let it touch him and thrust it away; but it had touched him. He spoke more quietly: "You're telling me I mustn't *ever* find the–the half-wit and the . . . whatever it is?"

"Oh," she said, her whole heart in her reflection, "oh, *no!* Hip, you'll find it, truly you will. But you have to know what it is; you have to know why."

"How long will it take?"

She shook her head soberly. "I don't know."

"I can't wait. Tomorrow–" He jabbed a finger at the window. The dark was silvering, the sun was near, pressing it away. *"Today,* you see? *Today* I could go there . . . I've got to; you understand how much it means, how long I've been . . ." His voice trailed off; then he whirled on her. "You say I'll be killed; I'd rather be killed, there with it in my hands; it's what I've been living for anyway!"

She looked up at him tragically. "Hip–"

"No!" he snapped. "You can't talk me out of it."

She started to speak, stopped, bent her head. Down she bent, to hide her face on the bed.

He strode furiously up and down the room, then stood over her. His face softened. "Janie," he said, "help me. . . ."

She lay very still. He knew she was listening. He said, "If there's danger . . . if something is going to try to kill me . . . tell me what. At least let me know what to look for."

She turned her head, faced the wall, so he could hear her but not see her. In a labored voice she said, "I didn't say anything will try to kill you. I said you *would* be killed."

He stood over her for a long time. Then he growled, "All right. I will. Thanks for everything, Janie. You better go home."

She crawled off the bed slowly, weakly, as if she had been flogged. She turned to him with such a look of pity and sorrow in her face that his heart was squeezed. But he set his jaw, looked toward the door, moved his head toward it.

She went, not looking back, dragging her feet. It was more than he could bear. But he let her go.

The bedspread was lightly rumpled. He crossed the room slowly and looked down at it. He put out his hand, then fell forward and plunged his face into it. It was still warm from her body and for an instant so brief as to be indefinable, he felt a thing about mingled breaths, two spellbound souls turning one to the other and about to be one. But then it was gone, everything was gone and he lay exhausted.

Go on, get sick. Curl up and die. "All right," he whispered.

Might as well. What's the difference anyway? Die or get killed, who cares?

Not Janie.

He closed his eyes and saw a mouth. He thought it was Janie's, but the chin was too pointed. The mouth said, *"Just lie down and die, that's all,"* and smiled. The smile made light glance off the thick glasses which must mean he was seeing the whole face. And then there was a pain so sharp and swift that he threw up his head and grunted. His hand, his hand was cut. He looked down at it, saw the scars which had made the sudden, restimulative pain. "Thompson, I'm gonna kill that Thompson."

Who was Thompson who was Bromfield who was the half-wit in the cave . . . cave, where is the cave where the children . . . children . . . no, it was *children's* . . . where the children's . . . *clothes,* that's it! Clothes, old, torn, rags; but that's how he . . .

Janie . . . You will be killed. *Just lie down and die.*

His eyeballs rolled up, his tensions left him in a creeping lethargy. It was not a good thing but it was more welcome than feeling. Someone said, "Up forty or better on your right quadrant, corp'r'l, or the pixies'll degauss your fuses." Who said that?

He, Hip Barrows. He said it.

Who'd he say it to?

Janie with her clever hand on the ack-ack prototype.

He snorted faintly. Janie wasn't a corporal. "Reality isn't the most pleasant of atmospheres, Lieutenant. But we like to think we're engineered for it. It's a pretty fine piece of engineering, the kind an engineer can respect. Drag in an obsession and reality can't tolerate it. Something has to give; if reality goes, your fine piece of engineering is left with nothing to operate on. Nothing it was designed to operate on. So it operates badly. So kick the obsession out; start functioning the way you were designed to function."

Who said that? Oh–Bromfield. The jerk! He should know better than to try to talk engineering to an engineer. "Cap'n Bromfield" (tiredly, the twenty damn thousandth time), "if I wasn't an engineer I wouldn't've found it, I wouldn't've recognized it and I wouldn't give a damn now." Ah, it doesn't matter.

It doesn't matter. Just curl up and as long as Thompson don't show his face. Just curl up and . . . "No, by God," roared Hip Barrows. He sprang off the bed, stood quaking in the middle of the room. He clapped his hands over his eyes and rocked like a storm-blown sapling. He might be all mixed up, Bromfield's voice, Thompson's face, a cave full of children's clothes, Janie who wanted him killed; but there was one thing he was sure of, one thing he *knew:* Thompson wasn't going to make him curl up and die. Janie had rid him of *that* one!

He whimpered as he rocked, "Janie . . . ?"

Janie didn't want him to die.

Janie didn't want him killed; what's the matter here? Janie just wants . . . go back. Take time.

He looked at the brightening window.

Take time? Why, maybe today he could get that address and see those children and find the half-wit and . . . well, find him anyway; that's what he wanted, wasn't it? *Today.* Then by God he'd show Bromfield who had an obsession!

If he lived, he'd show Bromfield.

But no; what Janie wanted was to go the other way, go back. For how long? More hungry years, nobody believes you, no one helps, you hunt and hunt, starve and freeze, for a little clue and another to fit it: the address that came from the house with the porte-cochère which came from the piece of paper in the children's clothes which were . . . in the . . .

"Cave," he said aloud. He stopped rocking, straightened.

He had found the cave. And in the cave were children's clothes, and among them was the dirty little scrawled-up piece of paper and that had led him to the porte-cochère house, right here in town.

Another step backward, a big one too; he was deeply certain of that. Because it was the discovery in the cave that had really proved he had seen what Bromfield claimed he had not seen; he had a piece of it! He snatched it up and bent it and squeezed it: silvery, light, curiously woven–the piece of tubing. Of course, of *course!* The piece of tubing had come from the cave too. Now he had it.

A deep excitement began to grow within him. She'd said "Go back," and he had said no, it takes too long. How long for this step, this rediscovery of the cave and its treasures?

He glanced at the window. It couldn't have been more than thirty minutes–forty at the outside. Yes, and while he was all messed up, exhausted, angry, guilty, hurt. Suppose he tried this going-back business head on, rested, fed with all his wits about him, with–with Janie to help?

He ran to the door, threw it open, bounded across the hall, shoved the opposite door open. "Janie, listen," he said, wildly excited. "Oh, Janie–" and his voice was cut off in a sharp gasp. He skidded to a stop six feet into the room, his feet scurrying and slipping, trying to get him back out into the hall again, shut the door. "I beg your–excuse *me,*" he bleated out of the shock which filled him. His back struck the door, slammed it; he turned hysterically, pawed it open, and dove outside. God, he thought, I wish she'd *told* me. He stumbled across the hall to his own room, feeling like a gong which had just been struck. He closed and locked his door and leaned against it. Somewhere he found a creaky burst of embarrassed laughter which helped. He half turned to look at the panels of his locked door, drawn to them against his will. He tried to prevent his mind's eye from going back across the hall and through the other door; he failed; he saw the picture of it again, vividly, and again he laughed, hot-faced and uncomfortable. "She should've told me," he muttered.

His bit of tubing caught his eye and he picked it up and sat down in the big chair. It drove the embarrassing moment away; brought back the greater urgency. He had to see Janie. Talk with her. Maybe it was crazy but she'd know: maybe they could do the going-back thing fast, really fast, so fast that he could go find that half-wit today after all. Ah . . . it was probably hopeless; but Janie, Janie'd know. Wait then. She'd come when she was ready; she had to.

He lay back, shoved his feet as far out as they would go, tilted his head back until the back of the chair snugged into the nape of his neck. Fatigue drifted and grew within him like a fragrant smoke, clouding his eyes and filling his nostrils.

His hands went limp, his eyes closed. Once he laughed, a small foolish snicker; but the picture didn't come clear enough or stay long enough to divert him from his deep healthy plunge into sleep.

Bup-bup-bup-bup-bup-bup-bup-bup.

(Fifties, he thought, way off in the hills. Lifelong ambition of every red-blooded boy: get a machine gun and make like a garden hose with it.)

Wham-wham-wham-wham!

(Oerlikons! Where'd they dredge those things up from? Is this an ack-ack station or is it a museum?)

"Hip! Hip Barrows!"

(For Pete's sake, when is that corporal going to learn to say "Lieutenant"? Not that I give a whistle, one way or another, but one of these days he'll do it in front of some teenage Air Force colonel and get us both bounced for it.)

Wham! Wham! "Oh . . . Hip!"

He sat up palming his eyes, and the guns were knuckles on a door and the corporal was Janie, calling somewhere, and the antiaircraft base shattered and misted and blew away to the dream factory.

"Hip!"

"Come on," he croaked. "Come on in."

"It's locked."

He grunted and got numbly to his feet. Sunlight poured in through the curtains. He reeled to the door and opened it. His eyes wouldn't track and his teeth felt like a row of cigar butts.

"Oh, Hip!"

Over her shoulder he saw the other door and he remembered. He drew her inside and shut his door. "Listen, I'm awful sorry about what happened. I feel like a damn fool."

"Hip–don't," she said softly. "It doesn't matter, you know that. Are you all right?"

"A little churned up," he admitted and was annoyed by the reappearance of his embarrassed laugh. "Wait till I put some cold water on my face and wake up some." From the bathroom he called, "Where you been?"

"Walking. I had to think. Then . . . I waited outside. I was afraid you might–you know. I wanted to follow you, be with you. I thought I might help. . . . You really are all right?"

"Oh sure. And I'm not going anywhere without talking to you first. But about the other thing–I hope *she's* all right."

"What?"

"I guess she got a worse shock than I did. I wish you'd told me you had somebody in there with you. I wouldn't've barged–"

"Hip, what are you talking about? What happened?"

"Oh!" he said. "Omigosh. You came straight here–you haven't been in your room yet."

"No. What on *earth* are you–"

He said, actually blushing, "I wish she'd told you about it rather than me. Well, I suddenly had to see you, but *bad.* So I steamed across the hall and charged in, never dreaming there would be anyone but you there, and here I am halfway across the room before I could even stop, and there stood this friend of yours."

"Who? Hip, for heaven's sake–"

"The woman. Had to be someone you know, Janie. Burglars aren't likely to prance around naked."

Janie put a slow hand up to her mouth.

"A colored woman. Girl. Young."

"Did she . . . what did she . . ."

"I don't know what she did. I didn't get but a flash glimpse of her –if that's any comfort to her. I hightailed right out of there. Aw, Janie, I'm sorry. I know it's sort of embarrassing, but it can't be *that* bad. Janie!" he cried in alarm.

"He's found us. We've got to get out of here," she whispered. Her lips were nearly white; she was shaking. "Come on, oh, come *on!*"

"Now wait! Janie, I got to talk to you. I–"

She whirled on him like a fighting animal. She spoke with such intensity that her words blurred. "Don't talk! Don't ask me. I can't tell you; you wouldn't understand. Just get out of here, get away." With astonishing power her hand closed on his arm and pulled. He took two running steps or he would have been flat on the floor. She was at the door, opening it, as he took the second step, and she took the slack of his shirt in her free hand, pulled him through, pushed him down the hall toward the outer exit. He caught himself against the doorpost; surprise and anger exploded together within him and built an instant of mighty stubbornness. No single word she might have uttered could have moved him; braced and on guard as he was, not even her unexpected strength could have done anything but cause him to strike back. But she said nothing nor did she touch him; she ran past, white and whimpering in terror, and bounded down the steps outside.

He did the only thing his body would do, without analysis or conscious decision. He found himself outside, running a little behind her. "Janie . . ."

"Taxi!" she screamed.

The cab had barely begun to slow down when she had the door open. Hip fell in after her. "Go on," said Janie to the driver and knelt on the seat to peer through the rear window.

"Go where?" gasped the driver.

"Just go. Hurry."

Hip joined her at the window. All he could see was the dwindling house front, one or two gaping pedestrians. "What was it? What happened?"

She simply shook her head.

"What was it?" he insisted. "The place going to explode or something?"

Again she shook her head. She turned away from the window and cowered into the corner. Her white teeth scraped and scraped at the back of her hand. He reached out and gently put it down. She let him.

Twice more he spoke to her, but she would not answer except to acknowledge it, and that only by turning her face slightly away from him each time. He subsided at last, sat back and watched her.

Just outside of town where the highway forks, the driver asked timidly, "Which way?" and it was Hip who said, "Left." Janie came out of herself enough to give him a swift, grateful glance and sank out of sight behind her face.

At length there was a difference in her, in some inexplicable way, though she still sat numbly staring at nothing. He said quietly, "Better?"

She put her eyes on him and, appreciably later, her vision. A rueful smile plucked at the corners of her mouth. "Not worse anyway."

"Scared," he said.

She nodded. "Me too," he said, his face frozen. She put her hand on his arm. "Oh, Hip, I'm sorry; I'm more sorry than I can say. I didn't expect this–not so soon. And I'm afraid there isn't anything I can do about it now."

"Why?"

"I can't tell you."

"You can't tell me? Or you can't tell me *yet?*"

She said, carefully, "I told you what you'd have to do–go back and back; find all the places you've been and the things that happened, right to the beginning. You can do it, given time." The terror was in her face again and turned to a sadness. "But there isn't any more time."

He laughed almost joyfully. "There is." He seized her hand. "This morning I found the cave. That's two years back, Janie! I know where it is, what I found there: some old clothes, children's clothes. An address, the house with the porte-cochère. And my piece of tubing, the one thing I ever saw that proved I was right in searching for . . . for . . . Well," he laughed, "that's the next step backward. The important thing is that I found the cave, the biggest step yet. I did it in thirty minutes or so and I did it without even trying. Now I'll *try*. You say we have no more time. Well, maybe not weeks, maybe not days; do we have a day, Janie? Half a day?"

Her face began to glow. "Perhaps we have," she said. "Perhaps . . . Driver! This will do."

It was she who paid the driver; he did not protest it. They stood at the town limits, a place of open, rolling fields barely penetrated by the cilia of the urban animal: here a fruit stand, there a gas station, and across the road, some too-new dwellings of varnished wood and obtrusive stucco. She pointed to the high meadows.

"We'll be found," she said flatly, "but up there we'll be alone . . . and if—anything comes, we can see it coming."

On a knoll in the foothills, in a green meadow where the regrowth barely cloaked the yellow stubble of a recent mowing, they sat facing one another, where each commanded half a horizon.

The sun grew high and hot and the wind blew and a cloud came and went. Hip Barrows worked; back and back he worked. And Janie listened, waited, and all the while she watched, her clear deep eyes flicking from side to side over the open land.

Back and back . . . dirty and mad, Hip Barrows had taken nearly two years to find the house with the porte-cochère. For the address had a number and it had a street; but no town, no city.

It took three years from the insane asylum to the cave. A year to find the insane asylum from the county clerk's office. Six months to find the county clerk from the day of his discharge. From the birth of his obsession until they threw him out of the service, another six months.

Seven plodding years from starch and schedules, promise and laughter, to a dim guttering light in a jail cell. Seven years snatched away, seven years wingless and falling.

Back through the seven years he went until he knew what he had been before they started.

It was on the antiaircraft range that he found an answer, a dream, and a disaster.

Still young, still brilliant as ever, but surrounded by puzzling rejection, Lieutenant Barrows found himself with too much spare time, and he hated it.

The range was small, in some respects merely a curiosity, a museum, for there was a good deal of obsolete equipment. The installation itself, for that matter, was obsolete in that it had been superseded years ago by larger and more efficient defense nets and was now part of no system. But it had a function in training gunners and their officers, radar men and technicians.

The lieutenant, in one of his detested idle moments, went rummaging into some files and came up with some years-old research figures on the efficiency of proximity fuses, and some others on the minimum elevations at which these ingenious missiles, with their fist-sized radar transmitters, receivers and timing gear, might be fired. It would seem that ack-ack officers would much rather knock out a low-flying plane than have their sensitive shells predetonated by an intervening treetop or power pole.

Lieutenant Barrows' eye, however, was one of those which pick up mathematical discrepancies, however slight, with the accuracy of the Toscanini ear for pitch. A certain quadrant in a certain sector in the range contained a tiny area over which passed more dud shells than the law of averages should respectably allow. A high-dud barrage or two or three perhaps, over a year, might indicate bad quality control in the shells themselves; but when every flight of low-elevation "prox" shells over a certain point either exploded on contact or not at all, the revered law was being broken. The scientific mind recoils at law-breaking of this sort, and will pursue a guilty phenomenon as grimly as ever society hunted its delinquents.

What pleased the lieutenant most was that he had here an exclusive. There had been little reason for anyone to throw great numbers of shells at low elevations anywhere. There had been less reason to do so over the area in question. Therefore it was not until Lieutenant Barrows hunted down and compared a hundred reports spread over a dozen years that anyone had had evidence enough to justify an investigation.

But it was going to be *his* investigation. If nothing came of it, nothing need be said. If on the other hand it turned out to be important, he could with immense modesty and impressive clarity bring the matter to the attention of the colonel; and perhaps then the colonel might be persuaded to revise his opinion of ROTC lieutenants. So he made a field trip on his own time and discovered an area wherein to varying degrees his pocket voltmeter would not work properly. And it dawned on him that what he had found was something which inhibited magnetism. The rugged but sensitive coils and relays in the proximity fuses, to all intents and purposes, ceased to exist when they passed this particular hillside lower than forty yards. Permanent magnets were damped just as electromagnets.

Nothing in Barrows' brief but brilliant career had even approached this incredible phenomenon in potential. His accurate and imaginative mind drank and drank of it and he saw visions: the identification and analysis of the phenomenon (Barrows Effect, perhaps?) and then a laboratory effort–successful of course–to duplicate it. Then, application. A field generator which would throw up an invisible wall of the force; aircraft and their communications–even their intercoms–failing with the failure of their many magnets. Seeking gear on guided missiles, arming and blasting devices, and of course the disarming of proximity fuses . . . the perfect defensive weapon for the electromagnetic age . . . and how much else? No limit to it. Then there would be the demonstrations of course, the colonel introducing him to renowned scientists and military men: *"This, gentlemen, is your ROTC man!"*

But first he had to find what was doing it, now that he knew where it was being done; and so he designed and built a detector. It was simple and ingenious and very carefully calibrated. While engaged in the work, his irrepressible mind wrought and twisted and admired and reworked the whole concept of "contramagnetism." He extrapolated a series of laws and derived effects just as a mathematical pastime and fired them off to the Institute of Electrical Engineers, who could appreciate them and did; for they were later published in the *Journal.* He even amused himself in gunnery practice by warning his men against low-elevation shelling over his area, because "the pixies would degauss (demagnetize) their proximity fuses." And this gave him a high delight, for he pictured himself telling them later that his fanciful remark had been nothing but the truth and that had they the wit God gave a goose they could have gone out and dug up the thing, whatever it was, for themselves.

At last he finished his detector. It involved a mercury switch and a solenoid and a variable power supply and would detect the very slightest changes in the field of its own magnet. It weighed about forty pounds but this mattered not at all since he did not intend to carry it. He got the best ordnance maps of the area that he could find, appointed as a volunteer the stupidest-looking Pfc he could find, and spent a long day of his furlough time out on the range, carefully zigzagging the slope and checking the reading off on his map until he located the center of the degaussing effect.

It was in a field on an old abandoned farm. In the middle of the field was an ancient truck in the last stages of oxidation. Drought and drift, rain and thaw had all but buried the machine and the lieutenant flogged himself and his patient soldier into a frenzy of explosive excavation. After sweaty hours, they had dug and scraped and brushed until what was left of the truck stood free and clear; and under it they found the source of the incredible field.

From each corner of the frame ran a gleaming silvery cable. They came together at the steering column and joined and thence a single cable ran upward to a small box. From the box protruded a lever. There was no apparent power source but the thing was operating.

When Barrows pushed the lever forward, the twisted wreck groaned and sank noticeably into the soft ground. When he pulled the lever back, it crackled and creaked and lifted up to the limits of its broken springs and wanted to lift even more.

He returned the lever to neutral and stepped back.

This was everything he had hoped to find certainly and made practical the wildest of his dreams. It was the degaussing generator, awaiting only his dissection and analysis. But it was all these things as a by-product.

Lever forward, this device made the truck *heavier*. Lever back, *lighter*.

It was antigravity!

Antigravity: a fantasy, a dream. Antigravity, which would change the face of the earth in ways which would make the effects of steam, electricity, even nuclear power, mere sproutings of technology in the orchard this device would grow. Here was skyward architecture no artist had yet dared to paint; here was wingless flight and escape to the planets, to the stars, perhaps. Here was a new era in transportation, logistics, even the dance, even medicine. And oh, the research . . . and it was all his.

The soldier, the dull-witted Pfc, stepped forward and yanked the lever full back. He smiled and threw himself at Barrows' legs. Barrows kicked free, stood, sprang so his knees crackled. He stretched, reached, and the tips of his fingers touched the cool bright underside of one of the cables. The contact could not have lasted longer than a tenth of a second; but for years afterward, for all the years Barrows was to live, part of him seemed to stay there in the frozen instant, his fingertips on a miracle, his body adrift and free of earth.

He fell.

Nightmare.

First the breast-bursting time of pounding heart and forgotten breathing, the madness of an ancient ruin rising out of its element, faster and faster, smaller and smaller into the darkening sky, a patch, a spot, a speck, a hint of light where the high sunlight touched it. And then a numbness and pain when the breath came again.

From somewhere the pressure of laughter; from somewhere else, a fury to hate it and force it down.

A time of mad shouting arguments, words slurred into screams, the widening crescents of laughing eyes, and a scuttling shape escaping him, chuckling. *He did it . . . and he tripped me besides.*

And nothing to kill; racing into the growing dark and nothing there; pound-pound of feet and fire in the guts and flame in the mind. Falling, hammering the uncaring sod.

The lonely return to the empty, so empty, so very empty hole in the ground. Stand in it and yearn upward for the silver cables you will never see again.

A yellow-red eye staring. Bellow and kick; the detector rising too, but only so high, turning over and over, smashed, the eye blind.

The long way back to barracks, dragging an invisible man called Agony whose heavy hands were clamped upon a broken foot.

Fall down. Rest and rise. Splash through, wallow, rise and rest and then the camp.

HQ. Wooden steps, the door dark; hollow hammering; blood and mud and hammering. Footsteps, voices: astonishment, concern, annoyance, anger.

The white helmets and the brassards: MP. Tell them, bring the colonel. No one else, only the colonel.

Shut up, you'll wake the colonel.

Colonel, it's anti-magnetron, to the satellite, and freight; no more jets!

Shut up, ROTC boy.

Fight them then and someone screamed when someone stepped on the broken foot.

The nightmare lifted and he was on a white cot in a white room with black bars on the windows and a big MP at the door.

"Where am I?"

"Hospital, prison ward, Lieutenant."

"God, what happened?"

"Search me, sir. Mostly you seemed to want to kill some GI. Kept telling everybody what he looks like."

He put a forearm over his eyes. "The Pfc. Did you find him?"

"Lieutenant, there ain't such a man on the roster. Honest. Security's been through every file we got. You better take it easy, sir."

A knock. The MP opened the door. Voices.

"Lieutenant, Major Thompson wants to talk to you. How you feel?"

"Lousy, Sergeant. Lousy. . . . I'll talk to him, if he wants."

"He's quiet now, sir."

A new voice–*that* voice! Barrows pressed down on the forearm he held over his eyes until sparks shone. *Don't look; because if you're right, you'll kill him.*

The door. Footsteps. "Evening, Lieutenant. Ever talk to a psychiatrist before?"

Slowly, in terror of the explosion he knew must come, Barrows lowered his arm and opened his eyes. The clean, well-cut jacket with a major's leaves and the Medical Corps insignia did not matter. The man's professionally solicitous manner, the words he spoke–these meant nothing. The only thing in the universe was the fact that the last time he had seen this face, it belonged to a Pfc, who had uncomplainingly and disinterestedly hauled his heavy detector around for a whole, hot day; who had shared his discovery; and who had suddenly smiled at him, pulled the lever, let a wrecked truck and a lifetime dream fall away upward into the sky.

Barrows growled and leaped.

The nightmare closed down again.

They did everything they could to help him. They let him check the files himself and prove that there was no such Pfc. The "degaussing" effect? No observations of it. Of course, the lieutenant himself admitted that he had taken all pertinent records to his quarters. No, they are not in the quarters. Yes, there was a hole in the ground out there and they'd found what he called his "detector," though it made no sense to anyone; it merely tested the field of its own magnet. As to Major Thompson, we have witnesses who can prove he was in the air on his way here when it happened. If the lieutenant would only rid himself of the idea that Major Thompson is the missing Pfc, we'd get along much better; he isn't, you know; he couldn't be. But of course, Captain Bromfield might be better for you at that. . . .

I know what I did, I know what I saw. I'll find that device or whoever made it. And I'll kill that Thompson!

Bromfield was a good man and heaven knows he tried. But the combination in the patient of high observational talent and years of observational training would not accept the denial of its own data. When the demands for proof had been exhausted and the hysterical period was passed and the melancholia and finally the guarded, superficial equilibrium were reached, they tried facing him with the major. He charged and it took five men to protect the major.

These brilliant boys, you know. They crack.

So they kept him awhile longer, satisfying themselves that Major Thompson was the only target. Then they wrote the major a word of warning and they kicked the lieutenant out. Too bad, they said.

The first six months was a bad dream. He was still full of Captain Bromfield's fatherly advice and he tried to get a job and stay with it until this "adjustment" the captain talked about should arrive. It didn't.

He'd saved a little and he had his separation pay. He'd take a few months off and clear this thing out of his mind.

First, the farm. The device was on the truck and the truck obviously belonged to the farmer. Find him and there's your answer.

It took six months to find the town records (for the village had been pre-empted when the ack-ack range was added to the base) and to learn the names of the only two men who might tell him about the truck. F. Prodd, farmer. A halfwitted hired hand, name unknown, whereabouts unknown.

But he found Prodd, nearly a year later. Rumor took him to Pennsylvania and a hunch took him to the asylum. From Prodd, all but speechless in the last gasp of his latest dotage, he learned that the old man was waiting for his wife, that his son Jack had never been born, that old Lone maybe was an idiot, but nobody ever was a better hand at getting the truck out of the mud; that Lone was a good boy, that Lone lived in the woods with the animals, and that he, Prodd, had never missed a milking.

He was the happiest human being Hip had ever seen.

Barrows went into the woods with the animals. For three and a half years he combed those woods. He ate nuts and berries and trapped what he could; he got his pension check until he forgot about picking it up. He forgot engineering; he very nearly forgot his name. The only thing he cared to know was that to put such a device on such a truck was the act of an idiot, and that this Lone was a half-wit.

He found the cave, some children's clothes and a scrap of the silvery cable. An address.

He found the address. He learned where to find the children. But then he ran into Thompson—and Janie found him.

Seven years.

It was cool where he lay and under his head was a warm pillow and through his hair strayed a gentling touch. He was asleep, or he had been asleep. He was so completely exhausted, used, drained that sleeping and waking were synonymous anyway and it didn't matter. Nothing mattered. He knew who he was, who he had been. He knew what he wanted and where to find it; and find it he would when he had slept.

He stirred happily and the touch in his hair ceased and moved to his cheek where it patted him. In the morning, he thought comfortably, I'll go see my half-wit. But you know what, I think I'll take an hour off just remembering things. I won the sack race at the Sunday-school picnic and they awarded me a khaki handkerchief. I caught three pike before breakfast at the Scout camp, trolling, paddling the canoe and holding the fishing line in my teeth; the biggest of the fish cut my mouth when he struck. I hate rice pudding. I love Bach and liverwurst and the last two weeks in May and deep clear eyes like . . . "Janie?"

"I'm here."

He smiled and snuggled his head into the pillow and realized it was Janie's lap. He opened his eyes. Janie's head was a black cloud in a cloud of stars; a darker night in nighttime. "Nighttime?"

"Yes," she whispered. "Sleep well?"

He lay still, smiling, thinking of how well he had slept. "I didn't dream because I knew I could."

"I'm glad."

He sat up. She moved cautiously. He said, "You must be cramped up in knots."

"It's all right," she said. "I liked to see you sleep like that."

"Let's go back to town."

"Not yet. It's my turn. Hip. I have a lot to tell you."

He touched her. "You're cold. Won't it wait?"

"No—oh, no! You've got to know everything before he . . . before we're found."

"He? Who's he?"

She was quiet a long time. Hip almost spoke and then thought better of it. And when she did talk, she seemed so far from answering his question that he almost interrupted; but again he quelled it, letting her lead matters in her own way, in her own time.

She said, "You found something in a field; you had your hands on it just long enough to know what it was, what it could mean to you and to the world. And then the man who was with you, the soldier, made you lose it. Why do you suppose he did that?"

"He was a clumsy, brainless bastard."

She made no immediate comment but went on, "The medical officer then sent in to you, a major, looked exactly like that Pfc to you."

"They proved otherwise."

He was close enough to her to feel the slight movement in the dark as she nodded. "Proof: the men who said they were with him in a plane all afternoon. Now, you had a sheaf of files which showed a perturbation of some sort which affected proximity fuses over a certain area. What happened to them?"

"I don't know. My room was locked, as far as I know, from the time I left that day until they went to search it."

"Did it ever occur to you that those three things—the missing Pfc, the missing files, and the resemblance of the major to the Pfc—were the things which discredited you?"

"That goes without saying. I think if I could've straightened out any one or any two of those three things, I wouldn't have wound up with that obsession."

"All right. Now think about this. You stumbled and grubbed through seven years, working your way closer and closer to regaining what you had lost. You traced the man who built it and you were just about to find him. But something happened."

"My fault. I bumped into Thompson and went crazy."

She put her hand on his shoulder. "Suppose it wasn't carelessness that made that Pfc pull the lever. Suppose it was done on purpose."

He could not have been more shocked if she had fired a flashbulb in his face. The light was as sudden, as blinding, as that. When he could, he said, "Why didn't I ever think of that?"

"You weren't allowed to think of it," she said bitterly.

"What do you mean, I wasn't–"

"Please. Not yet," she said. "Now, just suppose for a moment that someone did this to you. Can you reason out who it was–why he did it–*how* he did it?"

"No," he said immediately. "Eliminating the world's first and only antigravity generator makes no sense at all. Picking on me to persecute and doing it through such an elaborate method means even less. And as to method, why, he'd have to be able to reach into locked rooms, hypnotize witnesses and read minds!"

"He did," said Janie. "He can."

"Janie–*who?*"

"Who made the generator?"

He leaped to his feet and released a shout that went rolling down and across the dark field.

"Hip!"

"Don't mind me," he said, shaken. "I just realized that the only one who would dare to destroy that machine is someone who could make another if he wanted it. Which means that–oh, my *God!*–the soldier and the half-wit, and maybe Thompson–yes, Thompson: he's the one made me get jailed when I was just about to find him again–they're all the same! Why didn't I ever think of that before?"

"I told you. You weren't allowed."

He sank down again. In the east, dawn hung over the hill like the loom of a hidden city. He looked at it, recognizing it as the day he had chosen to end his long, obsessive search and he thought of Janie's terror when he had determined to go headlong into the presence of–this monster–without his sanity, without his memory, without arms or information.

"You'll have to tell me, Janie. All of it."

She told him–all of it. She told him of Lone, of Bonnie and Beanie and of herself; Miss Kew and Miriam, both dead now, and Gerry. She told how they had moved, after Miss Kew was killed, back into the woods, where the old Kew mansion hid and brooded, and how for a time they were very close. And then . . .

"Gerry got ambitious for a while and decided to go through college, which he did. It was easy. Everything was easy. He's pretty unremarkable-looking when he hides those eyes of his behind glasses, you know; people don't notice. He went through medical school too, and psych."

"You mean he really is a psychiatrist?" asked Hip.

"He is not. He just qualifies by the book. There's quite a difference. He hid in crowds; he falsified all sorts of records to get into school. He was never caught at it because all he had to do with anyone who was investigating him was to give them a small charge of that eye of his and they'd forget. He never failed any exam as long as there was a men's room he could go to."

"A what? Men's room?"

"That's right." She laughed. "There was hell to pay one time. See, he'd go in and lock himself in a booth and call Bonnie or Beanie. He'd tell them where he was stumped and they'd whip home and tell me and I'd get the answer from Baby and they'd flash back with the information, all in a few seconds. So one fine day another student heard Gerry talking and stood up in the next booth and peeked over. You can imagine! Bonnie and Beanie can't carry so much as a toothpick with them when they teleport, let alone clothes."

Hip clapped a hand to his forehead. "What happened?"

"Oh, Gerry caught up with the kid. He'd charged right out of there yelling that there was a naked girl in the john. Half of the student body dove in there; of course she was gone. And when Gerry caught up with the kid, he just naturally forgot all about it and wondered what all the yelling was about. They gave him a pretty bad time over it.

"Those were good times," she sighed. "Gerry was so interested in everything. He read all the time. He was at Baby all the time for information. He was interested in people and books and machines and history and art—everything. I got a lot from it. As I say, all the information cleared through me.

"But then Gerry began to . . . I was going to say, get sick, but that's not the way to say it." She bit her lip thoughtfully. "I'd say from what I know of people that only two kinds are really progressive—really dig down and learn and then use what they learn. A few are genuinely interested; they're just built that way. But the great majority want to prove something. They want to be better, richer. They want to be famous or powerful or respected. With Gerry the second operated for a while. He'd never had any real schooling and he'd always been a little afraid to compete. He had it pretty rough when he was a kid; ran away from an orphanage when he was seven and lived like a sewer rat until Lone picked him up. So it felt good to get honors in his classes and make money with a twist of his wrist any time he wanted it. And I think he was genuinely interested in some things for a little while: music and biology and one or two other things.

"But he soon came to realize that he didn't need to prove anything to anyone. He was smarter and stronger and more powerful than anybody. Proving it was just dull. He could have anything he wanted.

"He quit studying. He quit playing the oboe. He gradually quit everything. Finally he slowed down and practically stopped for a year. Who knows what went on in his head? He'd spend weeks lying around, not talking.

"Our *gestalt,* as we call it, was once an idiot, Hip, when it had Lone for a 'head.' Well, when Gerry took over it was a new, strong, growing thing. But when this happened to him, it was in retreat like what used to be called a manic-depressive."

"Uh!" Hip grunted. "A manic-depressive with enough power to run the world."

"He didn't want to run the world. He knew he could if he wanted to. He didn't see any reason why he should.

"Well, just like in his psych texts he retreated and soon he regressed. He got childish. And his kind of childishness was pretty vicious.

"I started to move around a little; I couldn't stand it around the house. I used to hunt around for things that might snap him out of it. One night in New York I dated a fellow I know who was one of the officers of the I.R.E."

"Institute of Radio Engineers," said Hip. "Swell outfit. I used to be a member."

"I know. This fellow told me about you."

"About *me?*"

"About what you called a 'mathematical recreation,' anyway. An extrapolation of the probable operating laws and attendant phenomena of magnetic flux in a gravity generator."

"God!"

She made a short and painful laugh. "Yes, Hip. I did it to you. I didn't know then of course. I just wanted to interest Gerry in something.

"He was interested all right. He asked Baby about it and got the answer pronto. You see, Lone built that thing before Gerry came to live with us. We'd forgotten about it pretty much."

"Forgotten! A thing like *that?*"

"Look, we don't think like other people."

"You don't," he said thoughtfully and, "Why should you?"

"Lone built it for the old farmer, Prodd. That was just like Lone. A gravity generator, to increase and decrease the weight of Prodd's old truck so he could use it as a tractor. All because Prodd's horse died and he couldn't afford another."

"No!"

"Yes. He was an idiot all right. Well, he asked Baby what effect it would have if this invention got out and Baby said plenty. He said it would turn the whole world upside down, worse than the industrial revolution. Worse than anything that ever happened. He said if things went one way we'd have such a war, you wouldn't believe it. If they went the other way, science would go too far, too fast. Seems that gravitics is the key to everything. It would lead to the addition of one more item to the Unified Field–what we now call psychic energy, or 'psionics.' "

"Matter, energy, space, time and psyche," he breathed, awed.

"Yup," Janie said casually, "all the same thing and this would lead to proof. There just wouldn't *be* any more secrets."

"That's the–the biggest thing I ever heard of. So–Gerry decided us poor half-developed apes weren't worthy?"

"Not Gerry! He doesn't care what happens to you apes! One thing he found out from Baby, though, was that whichever way it went the device would be traced to us. You should know. You did it by yourself. But Central Intelligence would've taken seven weeks instead of seven years.

"And that's what bothered Gerry. He was in retreat. He wanted to stew in his own juice in his hideout in the woods. He didn't want the armed forces of the United Nations hammering at him to come out and be patriotic. Oh sure, he could have taken care of 'em all in time, but only if he worked full time at it. Working full time was out of his field. He got mad. He got mad at Lone, who was dead, and he especially got mad at you."

"Whew. He could have killed me. Why didn't he?"

"Same reason he didn't just go out and confiscate the device before you saw it. I tell you, he was vicious and vengeful–childish. You'd bothered him. He was going to fix you for it.

"Now I must confess I didn't care much one way or the other, it did me so much good to see him moving around again. I went with him to the base.

"Now, here's something you just wouldn't remember. He walked right into your lab while you were calibrating your detector. He looked you once in the eye and walked out again with all the information you had, plus the fact that you meant to take it out and locate the device, and that you intended to—what was your phrase?—'ap-point a volunteer.' "

"I was a hotshot in those days," said Hip ruefully.

She laughed. "You don't know. You just don't know. Well, out you came with that big heavy instrument on a strap. I saw you, Hip; I can still see you, your pretty tailored uniform, the sun on your hair . . . I was seventeen.

"Gerry told me to lift a Pfc shirt quick. I did, out of the barracks."

"I didn't know a seventeen-year-old could get in and out of a barracks with a whole skin. Not a female-type seventeen-year-old."

"I didn't go in!" she said. Hip shouted in sheer surprise as his own shirt was wrenched and twisted. The tails flew up from under his belt and flapped in the windless dawn. "Don't *do* that!" he gasped.

"Just making a point," she said, twinkling. "Gerry put on the shirt and leaned against the fence and waited for you. You marched right up to him and handed him the detector. 'Come on, soldier,' you said. 'You just volunteered for a picnic. You carry the lunch.' "

"What a little stinker I was!"

"I didn't think so. I was peeping out from behind the MP shack. I thought you were sort of wonderful. I did, Hip."

He half laughed. "Go on. Tell me the rest."

"You know the rest. Gerry flashed Bonnie to get the files out of your quarters. She found them and threw them down to me. I burned them. I'm sorry, Hip. I didn't know what Gerry was planning."

"Go on."

"Well, that's it. Gerry saw to it that you were discredited. Psychologically, it had to be that way. You claimed the existence of a Pfc no one had ever seen. You claimed he was the psychiatrist—a real danger sign, as any graduate medic knows. You claimed files, facts and figures to back you up and they couldn't be traced. You could prove that you'd dug something up, but there was nothing to show what it might have been. But most of all, you had a trained scientist's mind, in full possession of facts which the whole world could prove weren't so—and did. Something had to give."

"Cute," murmured Hip from deep in his chest.

"And just for good measure," said Janie with some difficulty, "he handed you a post-hypnotic command which made it impossible for you to relate him either as Major Thompson, psychiatrist, or as the Pfc, to the device.

"When I found out what he'd done I tried to make him help you. Just a little. He—he just laughed at me. I asked Baby what could be done. He said nothing. He said only that the command might be removed by a reverse abreaction."

"What in time is that?"

"Moving backward, mentally, to the incident itself. Abreaction is the process of reliving, in detail, an event. But you were blocked from doing that because you'd have to start from the administration of the command; that's where the incident started. And the only way would be to immobilize you completely, not tell you why, and unpeel all subsequent events one by one until you reached the command. It was a 'from now on' command like all such. It couldn't stop you when you were traveling in reverse.

"And how was I ever going to find you and immobilize you without letting you know why?"

"Holy smoke," Hip said boyishly. "This makes me feel kind of important. A guy like that taking all that trouble."

"Don't flatter yourself!" she said acidly, then: "I'm sorry, Hip. I didn't mean that the way it sounded. . . . It was no trouble for him. He swatted you like a beetle. He gave you a push and forgot all about you."

Hip grunted. "Thank *you.*"

"He did it again!" she said furiously. "There you were, seven good youthful years shot, your good engineer's mind gone, with nothing left but a starved, dirty frame and a numb obsession that you were incapable of understanding or relieving. Yet, by heaven, you had enough of–whatever it is that makes you what you are–to drag through those seven years picking up the pieces until you were right at his doorstep. When he saw you coming–it was an accident, he happened to be in town–he knew immediately who you were and what you were after. When you charged him he diverted you into that plate-glass window with just a blink of those . . . rotten . . . poison . . . eyes of his . . ."

"Hey," he said gently. "Hey, Janie, take it easy!"

"Makes me mad," she whispered, dashing her hand across her eyes. She tossed her hair back, squared her shoulders. "He sent you flying into the window and at the same time gave you that 'curl up and die' command. I saw it, I saw him do it. . . . S-so rotten. . . ."

She said, in a more controlled tone, "Maybe if it was the only one I could have forgotten it. I never could have approved it but I once had faith in him . . . you've got to understand, we're a part of something together, Gerry and I and the kids; something real and alive. Hating him is like hating your legs or your lungs."

"It says in the Good Book, 'If thine eye offend thee, pluck it out and cast it from thee. If thy right hand–' "

"Yes, your eye, your hand!" she cried. "Not your *head!*" She went on, "But yours wasn't the only case. Did you ever hear that rumor about the fusion of Element 83?"

"A fairy tale. Bismuth won't play those games. I remember vaguely . . . some crazy guy called Klackenhorst."

"A crazy guy called Klackenheimer," she corrected. "Gerry got into one of his bragging phases and let go with a differential he shouldn't have mentioned. Klack picked it up. He fusioned bismuth all right. And Gerry got worried; a thing like that would make too much of a splash and he was afraid he'd be bothered by a mob of people who might trace him. So he got rid of poor old Klack."

"Klackenheimer died of cancer!" snorted Hip.

She gave him a strange look. "I know," she said softly.

Hip beat his temples softly with his fists. Janie said, "There've been more. Not all big things like that. I dared him into wooing a girl once, strictly on his own, without using his talents. He lost out to someone else, an awfully sweet kid who sold washing machines door to door and was doing pretty well. The kid wound up with *acne rosacea.*"

"The nose like a beet. I've seen it."

"Like an extra-boiled, extra-swollen beet," she amended. "No job."

"No girl," he guessed.

She smiled and said, "She stuck by him. They have a little ceramics business now. He stays in the back."

He had a vague idea of where the business had come from. "Janie, I'll take your word for it. There were lots of 'em. But–why me? You went all out for me."

"Two good reasons. First, I saw him do that to you in town, make you charge his image in the glass, thinking it was him. It was the last piece of casual viciousness I ever wanted to see. Second, it was–well, it was *you.*"

"I don't get you."

"Listen," she said passionately, "we're not a group of freaks. We're *Homo gestalt,* you understand? We're a single entity, a new kind of human being. We weren't invented. We evolved. We're the next step up. We're alone; there are no more like us. We don't live in the kind of world you do, with systems of morals and codes of ethics to guide us. We're living on a desert island with a herd of goats!"

"I'm the goat."

"Yes, yes, you *are,* can't you see? But we were born on this island with no one like us to teach us, tell us how to behave. We can learn from the goats all the things that make a goat a good goat, but that will never change the fact that we're *not* a goat! You can't apply the same set of rules to us as you do to ordinary humans; we're just not the same thing!"

She waved him down as he was about to speak. "But listen, did you ever see one of those museum exhibits of skeletons of, say, horses, starting with the little Eohippus and coming right up the line, nineteen or twenty of them, to the skeleton of a Percheron? There's an awful lot of difference between number one and number nineteen. But what real difference is there between number fifteen and number sixteen? *Damn* little!" She stopped and panted.

"I hear you. But what's that to do with–"

"With you? Can't you see? *Homo gestalt* is something new, something different, something superior. But the parts–the arms, the guts of it, the memory banks, just like the bones in those skeletons–they're the same as the step lower, or very little different. I'm *me,* I'm *Janie.* I saw him slap you down like that; you were like a squashed rabbit, you were mangy and not as young as you should be. But I recognized you. I saw you and then I saw you seven years ago, coming out into the yard with your detector and the sun on your hair. You were wide and tall and pressed and you walked like a big glossy stallion. You were the reason for the colors on a bantam rooster, you were a part of the thing that shakes the forest when the bull moose challenges; you were shining armor and a dipping pennant and my lady's girdle on your brow, you were, you were . . . I was *seventeen,* damn it, Barrows, whatever else I was. I was seventeen years old and all full of late spring and dreams that scared me."

Profoundly shaken, he whispered, "Janie . . . Janie . . ."

"Get away from me!" she spat. "Not what you think, not love at first sight. That's childish; love's a different sort of thing, hot enough to make you flow into something, interflow, cool and anneal and be a weld stronger than what you started with. I'm not talking about love. I'm talking about being seventeen and feeling . . . all . . ." She covered her face. He waited. Finally she put her hands down. Her eyes were closed and she was very still. ". . . all . . . *human,*" she finished.

Then she said, matter-of-factly, "So that's why I helped you instead of anyone else."

He got up and walked into the fresh morning, bright now, new as the fright in a young girl's frightening dream. Again he recalled her total panic when he had reported Bonnie's first appearance; through her eyes he saw what it would be like if he, blind, numb, lacking weapons and insight, had walked again under that cruel careless heel.

He remembered the day he had emerged from the lab, stepped down into the compound, looking about for a slave. Arrogant, self-assured, shallow, looking for the dumbest Pfc in the place.

He thought more then about himself as he had been that day; not about what had happened with Gerry, for that was on the record, accomplished; susceptible to cure but not in fact to change. And the more he thought of himself as he had been the more he was suffused with a deep and choking humility.

He walked almost into Janie as she sat watching her hands sleeping in her lap as he had slept and he thought, surely they too must be full of pains and secrets and small magics too, to smile at.

He knelt beside her. "Janie," he said, and his voice was cracked, "you have to know what was inside that day you saw me. I don't want to spoil you-being-seventeen . . . I just want to tell you about the part of it that was me, some things that–weren't what you thought." He drew a deep breath. "I can remember it better than you because for you it's been seven years and for me it's only just before I went to sleep and dreamed that I went hunting for the half-wit. I'm awake again and the dream is gone, so I remember it all very well. . . .

"Janie, I had trouble when I was a child and the first thing I learned was that I was useless and the things I wanted were by definition worthless. I hardly questioned that until I broke away and found out that my new world had different values from my old one and in the new I was valuable. I was wanted, I belonged.

"And then I got into the Air Force and suddenly I wasn't a football hero and captain of the Debating Society. I was a bright fish with drying scales, and the mud-puppies had it all their way. I nearly died there, Janie.

"Yes, I found the degaussing field all by myself. But what I want you to know is that when I stepped out of the lab that day and you saw me, I wasn't the cockerel and the bull moose and those other things. I was going to discover something and bring it to humanity, not for humanity's sake, but so that they would–" he swallowed painfully "–ask me to play the piano at the officers' club and slap me on the back and . . . look at me when I came in. That's all I wanted. When I found out that it was more than magnetic damping (which would make me famous) but antigravity (which would change the face of Earth) I felt only that it would be the President who asked me to play and generals who would slap my back; the things I wanted were the same."

He sank back on his haunches and they were quiet together for a long time. Finally she said, "What do you want now?"

"Not that any more," he whispered. He took her hands. "Not any more. Something different." Suddenly he laughed. "And you know what, Janie? *I don't know what it is!*"

She squeezed his hands and released them. "Perhaps you'll find out. Hip, we'd better go."

"All right. Where?"

She stood beside him, tall. "Home. *My* home."

"Thompson's?"

She nodded.

"Why, Janie?"

"He's got to learn something that a computer can't teach him. He's got to learn to be ashamed."

"Ashamed?"

"I don't know," she said, looking away from him, "how moral systems operate. I don't know how you get one started. All I know about morals is that if they're violated, you feel ashamed. I'll start him with that."

"What can I do?"

"Just come," she flashed. "I want him to see you–what you are, the way you think. I want him to remember what you were before, how much brilliance, how much promise you had, so he'll know how much he has cost you."

"Do you think any of that will really make a difference?"

She smiled; one could be afraid of someone who could smile like that. "It will," she said grimly. "He will have to face the fact that he is not omnipotent and that he can't kill something better than he is just because he's stronger."

"You want him to try to kill me?"

She smiled again and this time it was the smile of deep achievement. "He won't." She laughed, then turned to him quickly. "Don't worry about it, Hip. *I am his only link with Baby.* Do you think he'd perform a prefrontal lobotomy on himself? Do you think he'd risk cutting himself off from his memory? It isn't the kind of memory a man has, Hip. It's *Homo gestalt's.* It's all the information it has ever absorbed, plus the computation of each fact against every other fact in every possible combination. He can get along without Bonnie and Beanie, he can get things done at a distance in other ways. He can get along without any of the other things I do for him. But he can't get along without Baby. He's had to ever since I began working with you. By this time he's frantic. He can touch Baby, lift him, talk to him. But he can't get a thing out of him unless he does it through me!"

"I'll come," he said quietly. Then he said, "You won't have to kill yourself."

They went first to their own house and Janie laughed and opened both locks without touching them. "I've wanted so to do that but I didn't dare," she laughed. She pirouetted into his room. "Look!" she sang. The lamp on the night table rose, sailed slowly through the air, settled to the floor by the bathroom. Its cord curled like a snake, sank into a baseboard outlet and the switch clicked. It lit. "Look!" she cried. The percolator hopped forward on the dresser top, stopped. He heard water trickling and slowly condensed moisture formed on the outside as the pot filled up with ice water. "Look," she called, "look, look!" and the carpet grew a bulge which scuttled across and became nothing at the other side, the knives and forks and his razor and toothbrush and two neckties and a belt came showering around and down and lay on the floor in the shape of a heart with an arrow through it. He shouted with laughter and hugged her and spun her around. He said, "Why haven't I ever kissed you, Janie?"

Her face and body went quite still and in her eyes was an indescribable expression—tenderness, amusement and something else. She said, "I'm not going to tell you because you're wonderful and brave and clever and strong, but you're also just a little bit prissy." She spun away from him and the air was full of knives and forks and neckties, the lamp and the coffeepot, all going back to their places. At the door she said, "Hurry," and was gone.

He plunged after her and caught her in the hall. She was laughing.

He said, "I know why I never kissed you."

She kept her eyes down, but could not do the same with the corners of her mouth. "You do?"

"You can add water to a closed container. Or take it away." It was not a question.

"I can?"

"When we poor males start pawing the ground and horning the low branches off trees, it might be spring and it might be concreted idealism and it might be love. But it's always triggered by hydrostatic pressure in a little tiny series of reservoirs smaller than my little fingernail."

"It is?"

"So when the moisture content of these reservoirs is suddenly lowered, I–we–uh . . . well, breathing becomes easier and the moon has no significance."

"It hasn't?"

"And that's what you've been doing to me."

"I have?"

She pulled away from him, gave him her eyes and a swift, rich arpeggio of laughter. "You can't say it was an immoral thing to do," she said.

He gave her laughter back to her. "No *nice* girl would do a thing like that."

She wrinkled her nose at him and slipped into her room. He looked at her closed door and probably through it, and then turned away.

Smiling and shaking his head in delight and wonderment, encasing a small cold ball of terror inside him with a new kind of calm he had found; puzzled, enchanted, terrified and thoughtful, he turned the shower on and began to undress.

They stood in the road until after the taxi had gone and then Janie led the way into the woods. If they had ever been cut, one could not know it now. The path was faint and wandering but easy to follow, for the growth overhead was so thick that there was little underbrush.

They made their way toward a mossy cliff; and then Hip saw that it was not a cliff but a wall, stretching perhaps a hundred yards in each direction. In it was a massive iron door. It clicked as they approached and something heavy slid. He looked at Janie and knew that she was doing it.

The gate opened and closed behind them. Here the woods were just the same, the trees as large and as thick, but the path was of brick and took only two turns. The first made the wall invisible and the second, a quarter of a mile further, revealed the house.

It was too low and much too wide. Its roof was mounded rather than peaked or gabled. When they drew closer to it, he could see at each flank the heavy, gray-green wall, and he knew that this whole area was in prison.

"I don't, either," said Janie. He was glad she watched his face.

Gooble.

Someone stood behind a great twisted oak near the house, peeping at them. "Wait, Hip." Janie walked quickly to the tree and spoke to someone. He heard her say, "You've *got* to. Do you want me dead?"

That seemed to settle the argument. As Janie returned he peered at the tree, but now there seemed to be no one there.

"It was Beanie," said Janie. "You'll meet her later. Come."

The door was ironbound, of heavy oak planks. It fitted with curious concealed hinges into the massive archway from which it took its shape. The only windows to be seen were high up in the moundlike gables and they were mere barred slits.

By itself—or at least, without a physical touch—the door swung back. It should have creaked, but it did not; it was silent as a cloud. They went in, and when the door closed there was a reverberation deep in the subsonic; he could feel it pounding on his belly.

On the floor was a reiteration of tiles, darkest yellow and a brownish gray, in hypnotic diamond shapes; they were repeated in the wainscoting and in the upholstery of furniture either built in or so heavy it had never been moved. The air was cool but too humid and the ceiling was too close. I am walking, he thought, in a great sick mouth.

From the entrance room they started down a corridor which seemed immensely long and was not at all, for the walls came in and the ceiling drew even lower while the floor rose slightly, giving a completely disturbing false perspective.

"It's all right," said Janie softly. He curled his lips at her, meaning to smile but quite unable to, and wiped cold water from his upper lip.

She stopped near the end door and touched the wall. A section of it swung back, revealing an anteroom with one other door in it. "Wait here, will you, Hip?" She was completely composed. He wished there were more light.

He hesitated. He pointed to the door at the end of the hall. "Is he in there?"

"Yes." She touched his shoulder. It was partly a salutation, partly an urging toward the little room. "I have to see him first," she said. "Trust me, Hip."

"I trust you all right. But are you–is he–"

"He won't do anything to me. Go on, Hip."

He stepped through. He had no chance to look back, for the door swung swiftly shut. It gave no more sign of its existence on this side than it had on the other. He touched it, pushed it. It might as well have been that great wall outside. There was no knob, no visible hinge or catch. The edges were hidden in the paneling; it simply had ceased to exist as a door.

He had one blinding moment of panic and then it receded. He went and sat down across from the other door which led, apparently, into the same room to which the corridor led.

There was not a sound.

He picked up an ottoman and placed it against the wall. He sat with his back tight against the paneling, watching the door with wide eyes.

Try that door, see if it's locked too.

He didn't dare, he realized. Not yet. He sensed vaguely what he would feel if he found it locked; he wanted no more just now than that chilling guess.

"Listen," he hissed to himself, furiously, "you'd better do something. Build something. Or maybe just *think*. But don't sit here like this."

Think. Think about that mystery in there, the pointed face with its thick lenses, which smiled and said, Go on, die.

Think about something else! Quick!

Janie. By herself, facing the pointed face with the–

Homo gestalt, a girl, two tongue-tied Negroes, a mongoloid idiot and a man with a pointed face and–

Try that one again. *Homo gestalt,* the next step upward. Well, sure, why not a psychic evolution instead of the physical?

Homo sapiens stood suddenly naked and unarmed but for the wrinkled jelly in his king-sized skull; he was as different as he could be from the beasts which bore him.

Yet he was the same, the same; to this day he was hungry to breed, hungry to own; he killed without compunction; if he was strong he took, if he was weak he ran; if he was weak and could not run, he died.

Homo sapiens was going to die.

The fear in him was a good fear. Fear is a survival instinct; fear in its way is a comfort, for it means that somewhere hope is alive.

He began to think about survival.

Janie wanted *Homo gestalt* to acquire a moral system so that such as Hip Barrows would not get crushed. But she wanted her *gestalt* to thrive as well; she was a part of it. My hand wants me to survive, my tongue, my belly wants me to survive.

Morals: they're nothing but a coded survival instinct!

Aren't they? What about the societies in which it is immoral not to eat human flesh? What kind of survival is that?

Well, but those who adhere to morality survive within the group. If the group eats human flesh, you do too.

There must be a name for the code, the set of rules, by which an individual lives in such a way as to help his species–something over and above morals.

Let's define that as the ethos.

That's what *Homo gestalt* needs: not morality, but an ethos. And shall I sit here, with my brains bubbling with fear, and devise a set of ethics for a superman?

I'll try. It's all I can do.

Define:

Morals: Society's code for individual survival. (That takes care of our righteous cannibal and the correctness of a naked man in a nudist group.)

Ethics: An individual's code for society's survival. (And that's your ethical reformer: he frees slaves, he won't eat humans, he "turns the rascals out.")

Too pat, too slick; but let's work with 'em.

As a group, *Homo gestalt* can solve his own problems. But as an entity:

He can't have a morality, because he is alone.

An ethic then. "An individual's code for society's survival." He has no society; yet he has. He has no species; he is his own species.

Could he–should he choose a code which would serve all of humanity?

With the thought, Hip Barrows had a sudden flash of insight, completely intrusive in terms of his immediate problem; yet with it, a load of hostility and blind madness lifted away from him and left him light and confident. It was this:

Who am I to make positive conclusions about morality, and codes to serve all of humanity?

Why–I am the son of a doctor, a man who chose to serve mankind, and who was positive that this was right. And he tried to make me serve in the same way, because it was the only rightness he was sure of. And for this I have hated him all my life . . . I see now, Dad, I see!

He laughed as the weight of old fury left him forever, laughed in purest pleasure. And it was as if the focus was sharper, the light brighter, in all the world, and as his mind turned back to his immediate problem, his thought seemed to place its fingers better on the rising undersurface, slide upward toward the beginning of a grip.

The door opened. Janie said, "Hip–"

He rose slowly. His thought reeled on and on, close to something. If he could get a grip, get his fingers curled over it . . . "Coming."

He stepped through the door and gasped. It was like a giant greenhouse, fifty yards wide, forty deep; the huge panes overhead curved down and down and met the open lawn–it was more a park–at the side away from the house. After the closeness and darkness of what he had already seen it was shocking but it built in him a great exhilaration. It rose up and up and up rose his thought with it, pressing its fingertips just a bit higher. . . .

He saw the man coming. He stepped quickly forward, not so much to meet him as to be away from Janie if there should be an explosion. There was going to be an explosion; he knew that.

"Well, Lieutenant. I've been warned, but I can still say–this *is* a surprise."

"Not to me," said Hip. He quelled a surprise of a different nature; he had been convinced that his voice would fail him and it had not. "I've known for seven years that I'd find you."

"By God," said Thompson in amazement and delight. It was not a good delight. Over Hip's shoulder he said, "I apologize, Janie. I really didn't believe you until now." To Hip he said, "You show remarkable powers of recovery."

"Homo sap's a hardy beast," said Hip.

Thompson took off his glasses. He had wide round eyes, just the color and luminescence of a black-and-white television screen. The irises showed the whites all the way around; they were perfectly round and they looked as if they were just about to spin.

Once, someone had said, *Keep away from the eyes and you'll be all right.*

Behind him Janie said sharply, "Gerry!"

Hip turned. Janie put up her hand and left a small glass cylinder, smaller than a cigarette, hanging between her lips. She said, "I warned you, Gerry. You know what this is. Touch him and I bite down on it—and then you can live out the rest of your life with Baby and the twins like a monkey in a cage of squirrels."

The thought, the thought—"I'd like to meet Baby."

Thompson thawed; he had been standing, absolutely motionless, staring at Janie. Now he swung his glasses around in a single bright circle. "You wouldn't like him."

"I want to ask him a question."

"Nobody asks him questions but me. I suppose you expect an answer too?"

"Yes."

Thompson laughed. "Nobody gets answers these days."

Janie said quietly, "This way, Hip."

Hip turned toward her. He distinctly felt a crawling tension behind him, in the air, close to his flesh. He wondered if the Gorgon's head had affected men that way, even if they did not look at her.

He followed her down to a niche in the house wall, the one which was not curved glass. In it was a crib the size of a bathtub.

He had not known that Baby was so fat.

"Go ahead," said Janie. The cylinder bobbed once for each of her syllables.

"Yes, go ahead." Thompson's voice was so close behind him that he started. He had not heard the man following him at all and he felt foolish. He swallowed and said to Janie, "What do I do?"

"Just think your question. He'll probably catch it. Far as I know he receives everybody."

Hip leaned over the crib. Eyes gleaming dully like the uppers of dusty black shoes caught and held him. He thought, *Once this gestalt had another head. It can get other telekines, teleports. Baby: Can you be replaced?*

"He says yes," said Janie. "That nasty little telepath with the corncob—remember?"

Thompson said bitterly, "I didn't think you'd commit such an enormity, Janie. I could kill you for that."

"You know how," said Janie pleasantly.

Hip turned slowly to Janie. The thought came closer, or he went high and faster than it was going. It was as if his fingers actually rounded a curve, got a barest of purchases.

If Baby, the heart and core, the ego, the repository of all this new being had ever been or done or thought—if Baby could be replaced, then *Homo gestalt* was *immortal!*

And with a rush, he had it. He had it all.

He said evenly, "I asked Baby if he could be replaced; if his memory banks and computing ability could be transferred."

"Don't tell him that!" Janie screamed.

Thompson had slipped into his complete, unnatural stillness. At last he said, "Baby said yes. I already know that. Janie, you knew that all along, didn't you?"

She made a sound like a gasp or a small cough.

Thompson said, "And you never told me. But of course, you wouldn't. Baby can't talk to me; the next one might. I can get the whole thing from the lieutenant, right now. So go ahead with the dramatics. I don't need you, Janie."

"Hip! Run! Run!"

Thompson's eyes fixed on Hip's. "No," he said mildly. "Don't run."

They were going to spin; they were going to spin like wheels, like fans, like . . . like . . .

Hip heard Janie scream and scream again and there was a crunching sound. Then the eyes were gone.

He staggered back, his hand over his eyes. There was a gabbling shriek in the room, it went on and on, split and spun around itself. He peeped through his fingers.

Thompson was reeling, his head drawn back and down almost to his shoulder blades. He kicked and elbowed backward. Holding him, her hands over his eyes, her knee in the small of his back, was Bonnie, and it was from her the gabbling came.

Hip came forward running, starting with such a furious leap that his toes barely touched the floor in the first three paces. His fist was clenched until pain ran up his forearm and in his arm and shoulders was the residual fury of seven obsessive years. His fist sank into the taut solar plexus and Thompson went down soundlessly. So did the Negro but she rolled clear and bounced lithely to her feet. She ran to him, grinning like the moon, squeezed his biceps affectionately, patted his cheek and gabbled.

"And I thank *you!*" he panted. He turned. Another dark girl, just as sinewy and just as naked, supported Janie, who was sagging weakly. "Janie!" he roared. "Bonnie, Beanie, whoever you are–did she . . ."

The girl holding her gabbled. Janie raised her eyes. They were deeply puzzled as she watched him come. They strayed from his face to Gerry Thompson's still figure. And suddenly she smiled.

The girl with her, still gabbling, reached and caught his sleeve. She pointed to the floor. The cylinder lay smashed under their feet.

A slight stain of moisture disappeared as he watched. "Did I?" repeated Janie. "I never had a chance, once this butterfly landed on me." She sobered, stood up, came into his arms. "Gerry . . . is he . . ."

"I don't think I killed him," said Hip and added, "yet."

"I can't tell you to kill him," Janie whispered.

"Yes," he said. "Yes, I know."

She said, "It's the first time the twins ever touched him. It was very brave. He could have burned out their brains in a second."

"They're wonderful. Bonnie!"

"Ho."

"Get me a knife. A sharp one with a blade at least so long. And a strip of black cloth, so-by-so."

Bonnie looked at Janie. Janie said, "What—"

He put his hand on her mouth. Her mouth was very soft. *"Sh."*

Janie said, panicked, "Bonnie, don't—"

Bonnie disappeared. Hip said, "Leave me alone with him for a while."

Janie opened her mouth to speak, then turned and fled through the door. Beanie vanished.

Hip walked over to the prone figure and stood looking down at it. He did not think. He had his thought; all he had to do was hold it there.

Bonnie came through the door. She held a length of black velvet and a dagger with an eleven-inch blade. Her eyes were very big and her mouth was very small.

"Thanks, Bonnie." He took them. The knife was beautiful. Finnish, with an edge he could have shaved with, and a point drawn down almost to invisibility. "Beat it, Bonnie!"

She left—blip!—like a squirted apple seed. Hip put the knife and the cloth down on a table and dragged Thompson to a chair. He gazed about him, found a bell pull and tore it down. He did not mind if a bell rang somewhere; he was rather sure he would not be interrupted. He tied Thompson's elbows and ankles to the chair, tipped the head back and made the blindfold.

He drew up another chair and sat close. He moved his knife hand gently, not quite tossing it, just feeling the scend of its superb balance in his palm. He waited.

And while he was waiting he took his thought, all of it, and placed it like a patterned drape across the entrance to his mind. He hung it fairly, attended to its folds and saw with meticulous care that it reached quite to the bottom, quite to the top and that there were no gaps at the sides.

The pattern read:

Listen to me, orphan boy, I am a hated boy too. You were persecuted; so was I.

Listen to me, cave boy. You found a place to belong and you learned to be happy in it. So did I.

Listen to me, Miss Kew's boy. You lost yourself for years until you went back and learned again. So did I.

Listen to me, *gestalt* boy. You found power within you beyond your wildest dreams and you used it and loved it. So did I.

Listen to me, Gerry. You discovered that no matter how great your power, nobody wanted it. So did I.

You want to be wanted. You want to be needed. So do I.

Janie says you need morals. Do you know what morals are? Morals are an obedience to rules that people laid down to help you live among them.

You don't need morals. No set of morals can apply to you. You can obey no rules set down by your kind because there are no more of your kind. And you are not an ordinary man, so the morals of ordinary men would do you no better than the morals of an anthill would do me.

So nobody wants you and you are a monster.

Nobody wanted me when I was a monster.

But, Gerry, there is another kind of code for you. It is a code which requires belief rather than obedience. It is called ethos.

The ethos will give you a code of survival too. But it is a greater survival than your own, or my species, or yours. What it is really is a reverence for your sources and your posterity. It is a study of the main current which created you and in which you will create still a greater thing when the time comes.

Help humanity, Gerry, for it is your mother and your father now; you never had them before. And humanity will help you, for it will produce more like you and then you will no longer be alone. Help them as they grow; help them to help humanity and gain still more of your own kind. For you are immortal, Gerry. You are immortal now.

And when there are enough of your kind, your ethics will be their morals. And when their morals no longer suit their species, you or another ethical being will create new ones that vault still farther up the mainstream, reverencing you, reverencing those who bore you and the ones who bore them, back and back to the first wild creature who was different because his heart leapt when he saw a star.

I was a monster and I found this ethos. You are a monster. It's up to you.

Gerry stirred.

Hip Barrows stopped tossing the knife and held it still.

Gerry moaned and coughed weakly. Hip pulled the limp head back, cupped it in the palm of his left hand. He set the point of the knife exactly on the center of Gerry's larynx.

Gerry mumbled inaudibly. Hip said, "Sit quite still, Gerry." He pressed gently on the knife. It went in deeper than he wanted it to. It was a beautiful knife. He said, "That's a knife at your throat. This is Hip Barrows. Now sit still and think about that for a while."

Gerry's lips smiled but it was because of the tension at the sides of his neck. His breath whistled through the not-smile.

"What are you going to do?"

"What would you do?"

"Take this thing off my eyes. I can't see."

"You see all you need to."

"Barrows. Turn me loose. I won't do anything to you. I promise. I can do a lot for you, Barrows. I can do anything you want."

"It is a moral act to kill a monster," said Hip. "Tell me something, Gerry. Is it true you can snatch out the whole of a man's thought just by meeting his eyes?"

"Let me go. Let me go," Gerry whispered.

With the knife at the monster's throat, with this great house which could be his, with a girl waiting, a girl whose anguish for him he could breathe like ozoned air, Hip Barrows prepared his ethical act.

When the blindfold fell away there was amazement in the strange round eyes, enough and more than enough to drive away hate. Hip dangled the knife. He arranged his thought, side to side, top to bottom. He threw the knife behind him. It clattered on the tiles. The startled eyes followed it, whipped back. The irises were about to spin. . . .

Hip bent close. "Go ahead," he said softly.

After a long time, Gerry raised his head and met Hip's eyes again. Hip said, "Hi."

Gerry looked at him weakly. "Get the hell out of here," he croaked.

Hip sat still.

"I could've killed you," said Gerry. He opened his eyes a little wider. "I still could."

"You won't though." Hip rose, walked to the knife and picked it up. He returned to Gerry and deftly sliced the knots of the cord which bound him. He sat down again.

Gerry said, "No one ever . . . I never . . ." He shook himself and drew a deep breath. "I feel ashamed," he whispered. "No one ever made me feel ashamed." He looked at Hip, and the amazement was back again. "I know a lot. I can find out anything about anything. But I never . . . how did *you* ever find out all that?"

"Fell into it," said Hip. "An ethic isn't a fact you can look up. It's a way of thinking."

"God," said Gerry into his hands. "What I've done . . . the things I could have. . . ."

"The things you *can* do," Hip reminded him gently. "You've paid quite a price for the things you've done."

Gerry looked around at the huge glass room and everything in it that was massive, expensive, rich. "I have?"

Hip said, from the scarred depths of memory, "People all around you, you by yourself." He made a wry smile. "Does a superman have super-hunger, Gerry? Super-loneliness?"

Gerry nodded, slowly. "I did better when I was a kid." He shuddered. "Cold. . . ."

Hip did not know what kind of cold he meant, and did not ask. He rose. "I'd better go see Janie. She thinks maybe I killed you."

Gerry sat silently until Hip reached the door. Then he said, "Maybe you did."

Hip went out.

Janie was in the little anteroom with the twins. When Hip entered, Janie moved her head slightly and the twins disappeared.

Hip said, "I could tell them too."

"Tell me," Janie said. "They'll know."

He sat down next to her. She said, "You didn't kill him."

"No."

She nodded slowly, "I wonder what it would be like if he died. I–don't want to find out."

"He'll be all right now," Hip said. He met her eyes. "He was ashamed."

She huddled, cloaking herself, her thoughts. It was a waiting, but a different one from that he had known, for she was watching herself in her waiting, not him.

"That's all I can do. I'll clear out." He breathed once, deeply. "Lots to do. Track down my pension checks. Get a job."

"Hip–"

Only in so small a room, in such quiet, could he have heard her. "Yes, Janie."

"Don't go away."

"I can't stay."

"Why?"

He took his time and thought it out, and then he said, "You're a part of something. I wouldn't want to be part of someone who was . . . part of something."

She raised her face to him and he saw that she was smiling. He could not believe this, so he stared at her until he had to believe it.

She said, "The *gestalt* has a head and hands, organs and a mind. But the most *human* thing about anyone is a thing he learns and . . . and earns. It's a thing he can't have when he's very young; if he gets it at all, he gets it after a long search and a deep conviction. After that it's truly part of him as long as he lives."

"I don't know what you mean. I–you mean I'm . . . I could be part of the . . . No, Janie, no." He could not escape from that sure smile. "What part?" he demanded.

"The prissy one who can't forget the rules. The one with the insight called ethics who can change it to the habit called morals."

"The still small voice!" He snorted. "I'll be damned!"

She touched him. "I don't think so."

He looked at the closed door to the great glass room. Then he sat down beside her. They waited.

It was quiet in the glass room.

For a long time the only sound was Gerry's difficult breathing. Suddenly even this stopped, as something happened, something–*spoke.*

It came again.

Welcome.

The voice was a silent one. And here, another, silent too, but another for all that. *It's the new one. Welcome, child!*

Still another: *Well, well, well! We thought you'd never make it. He had to. There hasn't been a new one for so long. . . .*

Gerry clapped his hands to his mouth. His eyes bulged. Through his mind came a hush of welcoming music. There was warmth and laughter and wisdom. There were introductions; for each voice there was a discrete personality, a comprehensible sense of something like stature or rank, and an accurate locus, a sense of physical position. Yet, in terms of amplitude, there was no difference in the voices. They were all here, or, at least, all equally near.

There was happy and fearless communion, fearlessly shared with Gerry—cross-currents of humor, of pleasure, of reciprocal thought and mutual achievement. And through and through, *welcome, welcome.*

They were young, they were new, all of them, though not as new and as young as Gerry. Their youth was in the drive and resilience of their thinking. Although some gave memories old in human terms, each entity had lived briefly in terms of immortality and they were all immortal.

Here was one who had whistled a phrase to Papa Haydn, and here one who had introduced William Morris to the Rossettis. Almost as if it were his own memory, Gerry saw Fermi being shown the streak of fission on a sensitive plate, a child Landowska listening to a harpsichord, a drowsy Ford with his mind suddenly lit by the picture of a line of men facing a line of machines.

To form a question was to have an answer.

Who are you?

Homo gestalt.

I'm one; part of; belonging . . .

Welcome.

Why didn't you tell me?

You weren't ready. You weren't finished. What was Gerry before he met Lone?

And now . . . is it the ethic? Is that what completed me?

Ethic is too simple a term. But yes, yes . . . multiplicity is our first characteristic; unity our second. As your parts know they are parts of you, so must you know that we are parts of humanity.

Gerry understood then that the things which shamed him were, each and all, things which humans might do to humans, but which humanity could not do. He said, "I was punished."

You were quarantined.

And—are you . . . we . . . responsible for all humanity's accomplishments?

No! We share. We are humanity!

Humanity's trying to kill itself.

(A wave of amusement, and a superb confidence, like joy.) *Today, this week, it might seem so. But in terms of the history of a race . . . O new one, atomic war is a ripple on the broad face of the Amazon!*

Their memories, their projections and computations flooded in to Gerry, until at last he knew their nature and their function; and he knew why the ethos he had learned was too small a concept. For here at last was power which could not corrupt; for such an insight could not be used for its own sake, or against itself. Here was why and how humanity existed, troubled and dynamic, sainted by the touch of its own great destiny. Here was the withheld hand as thousands died, when by their death millions might live. And here, too, was the guide, the beacon, for such times as humanity might be in danger; here was the Guardian of Whom all humans knew—not an exterior force, nor an awesome Watcher in the sky, but a laughing thing with a human heart and a reverence for its human origins, smelling of sweat and new-turned earth rather than suffused with the pale odor of sanctity.

He saw himself as an atom and his *gestalt* as a molecule. He saw these others as a cell among cells, and he saw in the whole the design of what, with joy, humanity would become.

He felt a rising, choking sense of worship, and recognized it for what it has always been for mankind—self-respect.

He stretched out his arms, and the tears streamed from his strange eyes. *Thank you,* he answered them. *Thank you, thank you . . .*

And humbly, he joined their company.